# LADY OF STARFIRE

## LADY OF DARKNESS

### BOOK FIVE

## MELISSA K. ROEHRICH

# ALSO BY MELISSA K. ROEHRICH

## LADY OF DARKNESS SERIES

*Lady of Darkness*

*Lady of Shadows*

*Lady of Ashes*

*Lady of Embers*

*The Reaper* (A Lady of Darkness Novella)

*Lady of Starfire*

## THE LEGACY SERIES

*Rain of Shadows and Endings*- Coming August 2023

Lady of Starfire - 1st Edition

ISBN:

979-8-9852991-8-2 *(paperback)*

979-8-9852991-9-9 *(alternate cover paperback)*

978-1-960923-90-5 *(hardcover)*

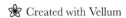 Created with Vellum

# A COUPLE THINGS

TRIGGER WARNINGS

Your mental health matters. This book contains descriptive violence and references to SA. For a full list of possible triggers, please visit my website at https://www.melissakroehrich.com under Book Extras.

PLAYLIST

Music is powerful. When I write I have music blasting in my earbuds, and many asked for a playlist. I adore when books come with playlists that follow along with the story. You feel everything more. It immerses you more. It brings everything to life. If you find this to be true for you too, here you go! Enjoy!

Spotify Link:

If you don't have Spotify, the full Playlist can also be found on my website: https://www.melissakroehrich.com under Book Extras!

*For Clara Grace and Scarlett Mae—*
*the beauty from the damn ashes, baby girls*

# A Lady of Darkness Reference Guide

Having a little trouble remembering all the people, gods, and who fits where?
With this quick and easy reference guide, you'll have all the information
you need at your fingertips.

## THE TWO BIG ONES

**Scarlett Sutara Aditya:**
Scar-let Soo-tar-uh Ah-deet-yah
Our heroine, Death's Maiden,
Queen of the Fae Courts

**Sorin Aditya:** Sore-in Ah-deet-yah
Your new book boyfriend,
Prince of the Fire Court,
King of the Fae Courts,
formerly known as Ryker Renwell

## BAYLORIN CHARACTERS

**Callan Solgard:** Cal-in Soul-guard
King of Windonelle

**Cassius Redding:** Cas-ee-us Red-ing
A member of the Assassin Fellowship,
Scarlett's Guardian,
Hand to Queen Scarlett

**Nuri Halloway:** Noor-ee Hal-o-way
Death's Shadow, Night Child

**Juliette:** Jewel-ee-et
Death Incarnate, Witch, Oracle

**Mikale Lairwood:** Mi-kay-l Lār-wood
Dirty bastard, False King of Windonelle,
Maraan Lord

~~Veda Lairwood~~: Vā-duh Lār-wood
Mikale's sister, Conniving bitch

**Tava Tyndell:** Tā-vah Tin-del
Daughter of Lord Tyndell,
Princess of Rydeon

**Drake Tyndell:** Dr-ache Tin-del
Son of Lord Tyndell,
King of Rydeon

**Lord Balam Tyndell:** Lord Bay-lum Tin-del
Leads the Windonelle armies, Maraan Lord

**Alaric:** Ah-lār-ick
Assassin Lord, Maraan Prince

~~Sloan~~: Sl-own
One of Prince Callan's personal guards

~~Finn~~: Fin
One of Prince Callan's personal guards

## PLACES

**Baylorin:** Bay-lore-in
**Rydeon:** Ride-ee-on
**Solembra:** Soul-em-bruh
**Xylon Forest:** Zy-lon For-est
**Jonaraja Forest:** Jon-uh-raj-uh Fore-est
**Avonleya:** Av-on-lay-uh
**Aelyndee:** Ā-lin-dee
**Tykese River:** Tie-key-s Riv-er

**Windonelle:** Win-dun-el
**Toreall:** Tore-ee-all
**Threlarion:** Thruh-lair-ee-on
**Dresden Forest:** Drez-den For-est
**Shira Forest:** Sheer-uh For-est
**Maara:** Mar-uh
**Edria Sea:** Ed-ree-uh See
**Siofra:** See-ō-fruh

# A Lady of Darkness Reference Guide

## FAE CHARACTERS

**Talwyn Semiria:** Tal-win Si-meer-ee-uh
Former Fae Queen of the Eastern Courts

**Eliné Semiria:** Ell-ee-nay Si-meer-ee-uh
Former Queen of the Western Courts

**Henna Semiria:** Hen-uh Si-meer-ee-uh
Former Queen of the Eastern Courts

## FIRE COURT

**Cyrus:** Sigh-russ
Second-in-Command of the Fire Court

**Rayner:** Rā-nir
Third-in-Command of the Fire Court
The Reaper

**Eliza:** Ee-lie-za
General of the Fire Court

**Beatrix:** Bee-a-trix
Fire Court Healer

## WATER COURT

**Briar Drayce:** Br-eye-er Dr-ace
Prince of the Water Court

**Sawyer Drayce:** Soy-ur Dr-ace
Second-in-Command of the Water Court

**Neve:** Neh-vā
Third-in-Command of the Water Court

**Nakoa:** Nuh-kō-ah
Commander of Water Court armies

## EARTH COURT

**Azrael Luan:** Az-ree-ehl Lou-on
Prince of the Earth Court

## WIND COURT

**Ashtine:** Ash-tin
Princess of the Wind Court

## OTHER CHARCTERS OF NOTE

**Deimas:** Day-i-mas
Former King of Mortal Lands

**Esmeray:** Ez-mer-ā
Former Queen of Mortal Lands

**Hazel Hecate:** Hay-zl Heh-ka-tay
High Witch

**Rosalyn:** Roz-uh-lyn
Former Night Child Contessa

**Stellan Renatus:** Stel-on Ren-ah-tus
Shifter Alpha

**Arianna Renatus:** Are-ee-on-uh Ren-ah-tus
Shifter Beta

**Auberon:** Aw-bur-on
Rosalyn's Second, Night Child

**Tarek:** Tār-ik
Talwyn's twin flame, Fae

**Mordecai:** Moor-di-keye
Chief Seraph Commander

**Arantxa:** Uh-ran-tix-uh
Hazel's Second-in-Command

# A Lady of Darkness Reference Guide

## THE GODS

**Anala:** Ah-nall-ah
Goddess of Sun/Day/Fire

**Saylah:** Say-luh
Goddess of Shadows/Night

**Celeste:** Sell-esst
Goddess of the Moon/Sky

**Sefarina:** Sef-uh-ree-nuh
Goddess of Wind

**Silas:** Sigh-lus
God of Earth/Land/Forests

**Anahita:** Ah-nuh-hee-tuh
God of Sea/Water/Ice

**Reselda:** Ruh-zel-duh
Goddess of Healing/Health

**Falein:** Fae-leen
Goddess of Wisdom/Cleverness

**Arius:** Ar-ee-us
God of Death/Darkness

**Serafina:** Sair-uh-fee-nuh
Goddess of Dreams/Stars

**Temural:** Tem-oor-all
God of the Wild/Untamed/Adventure

**Sargon:** Sar-gone
God of War/Protection/Courage

**Achaz:** A-kaz
God of Beginnings

**Taika:** Tah-kuh
Sister Goddess of Witchcraft/Sorcery

**Zinta:** Zin-tuh
Sister Goddess of Witchcraft/Sorcery

## THE SPIRIT ANIMALS

**Amaré:** Ah-mār-ā
Phoenix, Bonded to Sorin

**Shirina:** Shi-ree-nuh
Panther, Bonded to Scarlett

**Maliq:** Mal-eek
Wolf, Bonded to Talwyn

**Nasima:** Naw-seem-uh
Silver Hawk, bonded to Ashtine

**Rinji:** Rin-gee
Red Stag, bonded to Azrael

**Abrax:** Uh-brax
Water horse, bonded to Briar

**Celene:** Suh-leen
White Fox

**Paja:** Paw-juh
Golden Owl, previously bonded to Eliné

**Ejder:** Edge-der
Dragon

**Kilo:** Kee-low
White Python

**Altaria:** All-tar-ee-uh
Black eagle

**Ranvir:** Ran-ver
Dragon

???

???

???

# A Lady of Darkness Reference Guide

## AVONLEYA CHARACTERS

**Cethin Sutara:** See-thin Soo-tar-uh
King of Avonleya, Son of the Goddess
Saylah, Scarlett's brother

**Kailia Sutara:** Kī-lee-uh Soo-tar-uh
Queen of Avonleya

**Razik Greybane:** Raz-ick Grā-bān
Hand-to-the-Avonleyan King, Cethin's
Guardian, Cassius's Cousin

**Tybalt Greybane:** Ti-balt Grā-bān
Commander of the Avonleyan Armies,
Cassius' Father

**Niara:** Nee-ar-uh
Healer

**Hale Coventry:** Hāl Cuv-in-tree
King of Toreall

~~**Tethys Sutara**~~: Teth-us Soo-tar-uh
Former King of Avonleya, Scarlett and
Cethin's father

## PLACES

**Avonleya:** Av-on-lay-uh
**Elshira:** El-sheer-uh

**Aimonway:** Am-on-way

Chateau
Solembra
Fiera Moutains
Fire Court
Tana River
Aelyndee
To avonleya <---
Windonelle
Rebel Camp
Edria Sea
Baylorin
Water Court
Anahita's Springs
Southern Islands

Wind Court
Shira Cliffs
Dresden Forest
Tykese River
Eternal
Toreall
Witch Kingdoms
Oakenwell
Earth Court
Northern Villa
River Front Estate
Night Children
Shifters

OLWEN
MOUNTAINS

RUN

SHIRA FOREST

SUTARA FAMILY
COUNTRY ESTATE

AVONLEYA

Razik's Cave

Avonleya Castle

Greybane Estate

Hale's Estate

# Nightmist Mountains

Aimonway

# THE FAE QUEEN OF THE WESTERN COURTS

### *Nearly Twenty-One Years Ago*

"That will be all, Prince Drayce," the Fae Queen of the Western Courts said to the Water Prince.

The Water Prince eyed the cloaked stranger carefully before his icy blue eyes went back to his queen. "You are sure about this, your Majesty? I do not mind accompanying you."

Eliné reached out, squeezing his fingers gently. "We will be fine, Prince. No need to worry yourself…or Sorin."

The implication was clear. Do not tell the Fire Prince that she was visiting the Underwater Prison with an unknown visitor. Briar nodded, and the Fae Queen turned, descending a set of stairs. The cloaked figure walked beside her, her footfalls as silent as her own.

When they had descended several levels beneath the sea, the stranger pulled her hood back. Silver eyes settled on the Fae Queen. A circlet of stars was on the female's brow, shadows drifting around them as if they were in the night sky itself.

"You are beloved," the female said.

"I am close with all the Fae Royalty," Eliné answered. "But they have become increasingly protective of me after Esmeray killed Henna."

"Paja reported you took care of Esmeray for her betrayal."

Eliné hid her wince at what she'd had to do to her own sister. "I did. No one else knows."

"Good."

They were nearing their destination when Eliné dared to speak again. "Why now, my Lady?"

The female turned to look at her once more, silver hair slipping free of the cloak and falling over her shoulder. It reached nearly to her waist. "I have brought much upon this world, Eliné," she replied. "You know this. My son has unknowingly done the same. Our time here has come to an end. It must. This world does not deserve to burn. I will make the necessary sacrifices to ensure it does not."

"And Tethys?" Eliné asked softly, pausing at the top of a set of stairs that would lead them to the prisoner they had come to see. She hadn't been to this part of the prison in centuries.

"He made sacrifices of his own to see this through," the female answered, her tone faltering the smallest amount when she spoke of her husband.

Eliné nodded, wanting to comfort the one she served, but she knew the gesture would be unwelcome. She knew the female better than most. She had been serving her for centuries. "Have more come?"

"More have come. Some never left. They have found a way to hide, even from me. Achaz's doing, I am sure." She smoothed a hand along her cloak before she said, "Enough of this."

She moved ahead of Eliné, and the Fae Queen scrambled to catch up to her sovereign. It had been nearly nine centuries since she had seen the female, but it had been half that many since she and her sister, Henna, had come to ask for aid from the being they were about to see.

The sconces along the wall across from the cell flickered when they reached the base of the stairs. The female behind the bars was already on her feet. Lank black hair framed a gaunt face, but vibrant violet eyes glittered as she stared back at them. She wore a beige shift, and her bare feet were covered with dirt and grime.

"Gehenna," her sovereign greeted tersely.

"Saylah," the prisoner purred. "Goddess of the night and shadows." She moved forward, eyes falling to the goddess's torso before they moved back up to her face. A serpentine smile formed that had Eliné remembering exactly why she did not visit the Sorceress unless absolutely necessary. "You have finally come to bargain."

"Or I have finally come to kill you," Saylah said, taking a single step forward.

"Not when I still have something you need," Gehenna replied, beginning to pace in her cell. She stopped suddenly, spinning back to face them. "What are you going to give me, Saylah, daughter of the traitorous ones?"

"Perhaps I will let you keep your life when this is over," Saylah said coldly.

"Considering you cannot kill me without every part of the spell required to do so, I will take my chances. I want something else." Again the Sorceress's eyes flicked down to Saylah's belly.

Eliné stood back, letting Saylah deal with the Sorceress. She and her sisters had followed the goddess here long before the Everlasting War had found its way to this world. The people here did not realize the Great War fought in their lands was just another battle in something much bigger than their little world.

The beings of these lands did not have a name for their world, but the other realms called it Halaya. Saylah had fled here when Achaz began hunting for her and her brother, Temural, god of the wild and untamed, only to find the world inhabited by Legacy and Fae alike, among other beings. Finding Fae and mortals here was not unusual, but finding Legacy here had taken them all by surprise. There had been a treaty in place among the gods long before Saylah had been born that no more Legacy would be created.

Apparently none of the gods had followed their own decrees. That hadn't surprised the Fae sisters at all.

"You will benefit from finding the lock as much as I will, Gehenna," Saylah said sharply. "Without it we are both trapped here. Achaz cannot come for you."

Gehenna stepped up to the bars, her long fingers wrapping around them, and she bit back the hiss of discomfort at the shirastone. It wouldn't affect her like nightstone would, but it would not feel pleasant by any means. "I gave it to Moranna to play with."

3

"You are lying," Saylah hissed.

Gehenna tipped her head back, laughing at the stone ceiling. "I am not."

Saylah stepped closer, shadows coiling around her fingers. No one else may be able to access their magic this deep in the prison, but she was a goddess. The only one in this world. The Sorceress might have been strong enough to access her power at one point in time had her gifts not been stripped from her. As for blood magic, she would need blood to access that power. Her cell was spelled to keep her from accessing her own blood, and no one came close enough to the bars to give her any opportunity to take what didn't belong to her.

"Why would you give it to her?" Saylah asked.

"To keep it from you, of course," Gehenna said, her laughter stopping abruptly. "I told you that you would regret locking me in here."

"She is dead."

"I felt the world shudder when she died," Gehenna replied, stepping back from the bars.

"By giving it to her you doomed us both, you impudent fool," Saylah snarled, unclasping her cloak. She held it out to Eliné when she removed it from her shoulders, not bothering to look at the only remaining Fae Queen.

The goddess stood in a gown as black as the night she'd arrived in. The sleeves and bodice were lace, and she was pushed the sleeves up as shadows seeped from her skin. Her eyes were glowing brightly, like stars in the darkness, and she was hovering above the ground on a cloud of black mist.

Gehenna took one step back. Eliné could see the slight tremor in her limbs, but the deity lifted her chin, violet eyes filled with hatred. "You cannot kill me, Saylah. I am protected by him. I am his most favored."

"You were a means to an end," the goddess sneered.

"Now who is telling lies?" Gehenna snapped.

A wicked smirk curled on Saylah's lips, and Eliné stepped back, pressing her back to the wall. She was loyal to the goddess, but all the gods and goddesses had irrational tempers. They were fickle beings, and she had seen what could happen when they were denied.

The entire Everlasting War was because a god could not have what he so desperately coveted.

"I may not be able to kill you, Gehenna, but I can make you wish for the After," Saylah said far too calmly. "Tell me where the lock is hidden."

"I do not know," Gehenna said, panic seeping into her tone.

"Do not test me," Saylah said, a shadowy mist covering the entire dust-covered floor now. "I have sacrificed much to come to you. You do not wish to be on the receiving end of my wrath this night, daughter of Zinta."

"I do not know where it rests," Gehenna said, having backed up as far as she could go in her cell. "I do not know where she hid it."

"But you know how to find it," Saylah countered. "You would not have given it to her without some way of retrieving it."

"I do not have my spell book. You fools took it from me when you put me in here. I cannot give you what you seek," Gehenna spat. "And even if I could, only one born of the gods and Chaos who holds Fae elements can find it."

"There is no such being," Saylah snapped, her shadows rising around her, filtering between the bars of the cell.

"I know," Gehenna shrieked, fingers clawing at the wall behind her. "That is why I gave the lock to Moranna. She was trying to create such a being."

"You were both fools."

"But yours can do it!" Gehenna wailed as a shadow wrapped around her ankle. "One of yours can do it if you are willing to pay the cost."

"Explain yourself," the goddess demanded, her shadows pausing.

Eliné listened as Gehenna told Saylah what would be required to find the lock. What the cost would be to maintain the balance of such a feat of magic. What trades would need to be made to ensure this world and its inhabitants lived. What sacrifices would be required to unlock the gateway that would allow them to leave, to keep Achaz's wrath from this realm.

And as they left the chamber that housed the Sorceress, Saylah's hand pressed to her belly. The goddess of night and shadows said nothing until they were several halls and two levels away from Gehenna. She stopped then, stepping into a darkened alcove.

"My Lady?" Eliné asked, tentatively following her into the secluded space.

The goddess had one palm pressed to the wall, as though she were trying to steady herself. Her head was down, her breathing rapid, bordering on hyperventilating. When she lifted her gaze to the Fae Queen's, tears glimmered in her silver eyes.

"You will need to prepare her," Saylah said. "I cannot be away from the gateway long enough to do so."

Eliné swallowed thickly, nodding her head. "Of course, my Lady. Tell me what you require."

Saylah's gaze darted to the side, fixating on the stone of the Underwater Prison. She was quiet for several minutes before she met her eyes once more. "Love her, Eliné. Love her in the way I wish to and cannot, but make sure she is prepared to fulfill her destiny."

# PART ONE
## THE LOST

# CHAPTER 1
# SORIN

When Sorin Aditya woke he knew without opening his eyes that she was not in his bed, but he stretched a hand out anyway, feeling the cold space where his wife should have been. He didn't know how long he'd been sleeping since he'd given her the last of his fire. Far longer than what used to be required of him, that he was sure of.

He hadn't felt her get out of the bed. He hadn't heard her slip from their bedchamber in the castle in Avonleya. His senses were as muted as they had been when he'd been in the mortal lands for three years.

He also had no way of finding her.

He could not feel her.

He could not speak to her down a bond they had once shared.

He cracked his eyes open, lifting his arm to stare at his left hand. The black Mark that had once swirled around the back of his hand and down his fingers was gone, not a trace of it left.

In fact, all of his Marks were gone. Every last one.

A mortal could not bear Fae Marks.

A mortal could not be a Source.

A mortal did not have enhanced sight or smell or hearing.

He sighed, throwing back the wool blankets and setting his feet on

9

the ornate rug. Resting his elbows on his knees, his head fell into his hands, and his fingers dug into his ebony hair. He didn't know where Scarlett was, but a part of him was glad she was not here to see him like this. He had made sure the last thing she had felt from him was love and warmth and everything she was to him. He had kept himself together so she could fall apart. Wiping her tears away, he had been the strength she needed him to be. He couldn't be her Source anymore, but he could be that for her.

This felt as though he were back in the mortal lands before she had taken the wards down that prevented beings from accessing their magic. At least when he had been stuck there he had known his power was asleep just beneath the surface. He had known that the moment he stepped over the border into the Fire Court, his flames would be at his fingertips.

He would never hold fire in his palm again.

That reality was driven home when a breeze came through the open window and goosebumps erupted across his skin. They were on the brink of summer, and he was fucking *cold*.

Muttering a curse, he stood and made his way to the large dressing room. Surveying his options, he swiped a hand down his face. He still wore the loose pants he'd worn to bed, but he needed something warmer than the short-sleeve options for his upper half. The only long-sleeved items he owned were ornate jackets for special occasions. He had brought a few of them from the Fire Court. He never wore long-sleeve tunics. With fire in his veins, he didn't need them. He was always warm. Borrowing something from Briar or Sawyer was his next best option, he supposed. He lifted a hand to send the Water Court Second a message before remembering he couldn't do that either.

He cursed again, swiping a hand across the top of the dresser, knocking everything atop it to the ground. Random weapons thudded as they landed on the floor. Smaller items clanged when they hit the opposite wall, rolling beneath clothing and shoes. He braced his hands on the dresser, his head hanging down as he tried to get control of himself. This was worth it. An adjustment period was to be expected, but giving up his magic was a cost he would pay over and over again if it meant being able to stay with Scarlett.

But how did one learn to live without a piece of themselves? How did one get used to a life without something that had been a part of them since they had entered this world?

Taking a deep breath, Sorin pushed off the dresser and padded barefoot through the princess's suite. He made his way down the halls until he came to Briar's rooms. The prince wasn't here, having gone to trade himself for Princess Ashtine, but he hadn't taken the time to pack his belongings either.

Sorin found a long-sleeved tunic hanging in the Water Prince's dressing room, and he pulled the dark blue garment on as he made his way back to his rooms. He'd have to go into Aimonway today and get some warmer clothing. Even with the heavier fabric of the tunic he'd found, he was still chilled. He glanced down at his bare feet. Socks would probably help. At least then he wouldn't feel the cold marble beneath his feet.

When he got back to his rooms, he put some logs in the hearth and got a fire going. It was a feat that took far longer than it should have, but it had been over a year since he'd had to do so without his fire magic. When the logs were finally crackling steadily, he stood, holding his hands above the flickering flames and letting them warm his palms. This was worse than the mortal lands. At least there, his fire had still been in his veins. Now he was just…empty. Void and cold.

He shoved his hands into his pockets, casting a glance out the windows. The sun was high in the sky. It had to be close to midday by now. Which was fine. The Avonleyans preferred the night. Their daily schedule started mid-morning rather than at sunrise. Many of the shops Sorin needed to visit wouldn't be open until this afternoon, but by the gods, he'd slept over half a day.

And where the hell was Scarlett?

He changed into proper pants, slipping on his boots and buckling a few weapons into place. He was making his way out to the main sitting area to look for his wife and possibly find some food when a knock came at the door. Pulling it open, he found Cethin Sutara on the other side.

The King of Avonleya looked like he had been up all night and morning. He had clearly been running his hands through his shoulder-length silver hair repeatedly, and his black tunic and pants were wrinkled. Sorin was fairly certain they were the same clothing he'd been wearing yesterday, but the look on his face told him everything he needed to know.

"What did she do?" Sorin said with a sigh.

"May I come in?" Cethin asked instead, a hand going through his hair again.

"Where are Kailia and Razik?"

"Razik is with Eliza, and Kailia has her own matters to tend to," Cethin answered, his voice strained with an emotion Sorin wasn't quite sure what to do with. He was used to Scarlett's antics. Her brother clearly was not.

He tensed a little at the mention of Razik being with Eliza. He still hadn't decided how he felt about Eliza being Razik's Source. Not that there was anything he could do about it now. Once that Mark was given, there was no undoing it. What that meant for her and Razik, he didn't know. They could never be separated. Not if Razik wanted to be able to refill his magic reserves faster than letting them refill naturally. But he was Cethin's Hand-to-the-King, not to mention his Guardian, and Eliza was now the most powerful Fire Fae. If she wanted, she could claim the royal seat of the Fire Court and rule. She wouldn't, of course. The general had no desire to rule, but if someone else tried to take it and her hand was forced...

Sorin sighed again, stepping aside to let Cethin in. He had a thousand things to be worrying about. The situation between Eliza and Razik was just one of them. He was used to juggling multiple responsibilities, solving problems, and taking care of those entrusted to him. The stress of doing so was nothing new to him, but he had never been good about dealing with his own issues. There was a reason he would find himself in the chateau every once in a while to get away from it all and have a good night with a bottle of liquor.

He hadn't needed to do that since Scarlett though.

Sorin moved back in front of the hearth, getting as close to the heat as he dared. Cethin was standing near the sofa. He seemed to be debating whether or not he should sit. The king ultimately decided against it, instead getting into a stance that made him look like he was preparing for a fight. His feet were planted a little apart, his shoulders thrown back and arms loose at his sides.

"I assure you, I know her better than you do, Cethin," Sorin finally said, folding his arms across his chest. "Whatever you are about to tell me will not surprise me. She is known to be rather dramatic at times."

Cethin pushed out a harsh breath, his hands clenching and unclenching at his sides. "She sent me a message in the night. To meet her in one of the dens. She was there. Playing the piano."

Sorin nodded slowly. "She does that when she is processing emotions. Last night was difficult for us."

"She told me. That she had taken the last of your power from you. That the cost of bringing you back from the After had been completed," Cethin went on. His hands raked through his hair again. "Then she told me she refused to accept this fate."

"If anyone will find a way to defy the Fates, it will be her," Sorin replied, a slight smile tugging at his lips. "Is she in the library? Searching through ancient tombs? Did she find old forgotten catacombs she has fallen asleep in?"

Cethin blinked at him, slowly shaking his head. "I do not know where she is. Kailia has been searching during her hunts, but she has seen no sign of her."

Sorin's arms dropped to his sides. "What exactly are you saying, Cethin? That you let my wife disappear?"

"She... Fuck. I do not know how she did it. She created a Mark and stepped into a pool of darkness. She hasn't come back yet. We cannot create Marks, Sorin. Not blood Marks like that. She should not have been able to do that."

"And you do not know where she went?" Sorin repeated, memories of the last time she had disappeared flooding up. When Alaric had been holding her prisoner in Baylorin. When it had taken them weeks to get to her.

When she hadn't been the same as when she'd left.

"Kailia has been searching—"

"You said that already."

Cethin tried to hide his grimace. He brought a hand up as if to rake it through his hair again before he rubbed the back of his neck instead. "I have...an idea of where she likely went."

"Spit it out, Sutara," Sorin snapped, any measure of respect and decorum between the two kings gone. This was not two rulers discussing policy. This was brother-in-laws discussing where the fuck his wife and Cethin's sister had gone to.

"She went to Saylah."

Sorin lurched forward a step. "Why do you think that?"

"She kept saying that she makes her own fate," Cethin said, his gaze fixing on the flickering hearth. "I begged her not to go. I begged her to wait until I could come and get you, but she…" Cethin sank down onto the sofa. "I have seen her broken, Sorin. I have seen her hopeless and broken in her dreams. I have seen her angry with you. With me. With the world. I have never seen her like that."

"You do not know her, Cethin," Sorin retorted. "I know you wish you did, but you do not know her. You lured her here, threw a bunch of family history at her, placed demands upon her, and then expected what? That she would fall in line and follow the plans you have? Plans that you have not entirely shared with us, I might add."

Cethin was quiet for a long moment, hands clasped loosely in front of him. There was a thread of defeat in his tone when he said, "I thought she would burn the world down when you nearly died, and maybe she would have, but this was not that. She was in all black. She was eerily calm. She did not even sound like herself. Her shadows… My darkness is different. It writhes and kills and strains against my control at all times." His eyes slid to Sorin. Silver irises that matched Scarlett's. "My darkness does not sing to me like hers does."

"Her darkness loves her, and she has learned to love it in return."

"She will not burn the world to nothing, Sorin. The way she moved? How she spoke? What I *felt* emanating from her? She will bring the beings who seek to use her to their knees, and then she will take whatever she wants."

But Sorin got caught on the words 'seek to use her.'

"Who?" he demanded, his tone going as cold as he felt. "Who wants to use her? And for what purpose?"

"We cannot go to the Shira Forest of our own volition, but she did," Cethin replied as if the statement answered the question. "Saylah will not like this."

Sorin could hear the dread in his voice, and he didn't know how to react to it.

"Saylah is her mother," he said. "She has not seen her since she was five. One would think she would be happy to see her. Why do you sound anxious about this meeting? Frankly, it is one that should have happened as soon as we arrived here."

"She is a goddess," Cethin said, dragging a hand down his face this time. "She is a goddess first and a mother second. She is not used to being disobeyed. She has her own plans, her own ends to meet, and Scarlett going there before she is summoned is not part of those plans."

"I think you better start explaining these plans of hers that involve my wife," Sorin said, his tone going dark and steely.

"I do not know them all. She confides in no one. Not since the last Fae Queen died."

"Talwyn lives."

"She is not one of the original queens. Saylah does not care for the daughter of Henna."

"But you know some of Saylah's plans?" Sorin pushed.

"I know that the fate of not only my own kingdom but this entire realm depends on Scarlett," Cethin answered.

"Why? Why would she place that kind of burden on Scarlett without preparing her for any of it?"

"It is my understanding that Eliné was to prepare her for her destiny. Why do you think she was raised in the Black Syndicate? Eliné knew exactly what she was doing when she had her trained to take life. Whether or not she knew the master she was entrusted to was a Maraan, I do not know. Saylah has never divulged that information to me," Cethin said.

"She was a godsdamn *child*," Sorin seethed. He knew if he'd still had his magic there would be embers in his vision and flames winding around his arms. "In the life of a Fae, of an Avonleyan—fuck, in the life of a *god*—she is still a child."

"You think I do not know that?" Cethin snapped, getting back to his feet. "I am older than you are, Fae King."

"And yet you could not solve the problems of your own kingdom without placing the burden on someone who has scarcely lived," Sorin spat in derision. "She has sacrificed more than you ever will."

Darkness exploded out of Cethin, stinging cuts welling with blood instantly where it touched Sorin's skin. He brought up an arm to protect his face. There was nothing he could do except stand there and allow the magic to have its way. It was not as if he could shield against it.

But there was a shield surrounding him. One of ashes and smoke.

Sorin lowered his arm a fraction to find Rayner at his side, his hands raised and ashes pouring out of them. His role of personal guard had been ingrained in him in the Southern Islands. He'd been employed by Sorin's father off and on before Sorin was born and even a few times when Sorin was a child. That was before Rayner had gone back to seek his revenge. It was how Sorin had known of him to seek him out when he was having issues with a thief in the Fire Court. Rayner's jaw was tense as he worked to shield against Cethin's magic.

"What the fuck is going on?" Rayner gritted out.

"We are having a disagreement."

"No shit," the Ash Rider muttered.

"How did you know to come here?" Sorin asked.

"Scarlett sent me a fire message in the night."

Sorin jerked his head in his direction. "What?"

"She said she was going to see someone and wasn't sure when she'd be back, but she asked that I watch out for you as you adjust to being without your magic."

Sorin blinked, reaching to rub at his eyes. The smoke and ashes swirling around him were causing his eyes to water and itch. Now he'd made it worse by rubbing them, and they burned.

"But I was on my way to speak with you anyway," Rayner continued. Then his voice dropped so low Sorin could only catch bits and pieces of what he was saying without his Fae hearing. "I…following Queen…like you… We need…discuss…hunts in the night."

"When Cethin is gone," Sorin gritted out, raising his hand to swipe it down his face again before stopping himself at the last second.

Where the fuck was Scarlett?

It was another few seconds before he saw the tension ease on Rayner's face. Cethin was clearly getting himself under control, and a moment later, Rayner lowered the shield. Smoke still swirled lightly around them though.

"What the fuck was that?" Sorin demanded.

"I apologize," Cethin said tightly.

"I do not want your apology. I want an explanation, and your sister will demand one when she learns of this."

"You speak as if you know any of what I have done for my kingdom, for this realm," Cethin retorted, his back straightening. Darkness flowed from him again, pooling around his feet, but he kept control of it this time. "You think I did not try to fix this myself? You think I wanted this all placed on her shoulders? Do not speak of the sacrifices I have made when you know nothing of them. When you know nothing of the guilt I carry because I added to her responsibilities. When my choices put the people I love in danger daily. When my choices put my own kingdom in danger daily."

Sorin stared back at him. "What does that mean?"

"It means if I could take her place, I would, Sorin," Cethin said, his shoulders dropping a fraction. "I would trade places with her in a heartbeat."

"That does not answer my question. We have been here for weeks. You have had every opportunity to tell us these things. Furthermore, *my* people are here, and you are just now speaking of a danger to your kingdom? We were under the impression we were safe here," Sorin said, taking a few steps towards the Avonleyan King. Rayner moved with him, staying at his side, his shield of smoke still swirling.

"I did not wish to add to the weight she already carries," Cethin said. "Defeating the Maraans and finding the lock will fix everything. It did not seem necessary to add to her burden."

"You mean you did not wish for her to know of your mistakes."

Cethin's lips pressed to a thin line, his gaze darting back to the fire for a moment before he nodded sharply. "Perhaps that was part of it. But I must also continue to protect my people and the ones I love. My Inner Court has kept these secrets for years. It is second nature to us."

Sorin could understand that to an extent. There were plenty of things his Inner Court had kept from their people, taking care of business without ever needing to worry or involve them. Allowing his people to simply live their lives and let him take care of their safety was one of his greatest missions in life. But this was clearly bigger, and the moment it had involved Scarlett, it had involved him and their Courts by default.

The darkness suddenly thickened around them, tendrils of

shadows reaching for him. Rayner's shield swirled faster, ashes drifting among it again, but the shadows brushed them aside.

"Get control of it," Rayner growled at Cethin.

But even before Cethin said, "That is not me," Sorin already knew.

He could tell by the way the shadows slowly coiled around him, stroked down his cheek, drifted through his hair.

His eyes widened as the shadows swirled and converged until a figure stepped from them. The shadows clung to her, white embers flitting through silver hair. She was all in black, just as Cethin had said she'd been, but she was barefoot. Her crown floated above her head, and her silver eyes were glowing. Shirina, the black panther that was the spirit animal of Saylah, was at her side, and Sorin suddenly wondered how that worked. How had the animal bonded with Scarlett when Saylah had been in this world this entire time?

But perhaps even more perplexing was the phoenix at her shoulder. Amaré, the spirit animal of Anala, goddess of day, sun, and fire. The spirit animal that had been bonded to him when he had been the Fire Prince. They had not seen much of the spirit animals since coming to Avonleya. Cethin had said they were resting, preparing for war like the rest of them, but Sorin had assumed this would be another cost of coming back from the After. He assumed his bond with the phoenix would be another sacrifice he would be forced to make. But the bird cooed softly, nipping affectionately at Scarlett's ear before taking flight. He naturally lifted his arm as he had done thousands of times in the past, the phoenix's taloned feet clamping lightly around his forearm. He swallowed thickly, unable to say anything around the lump in his throat.

"Prince," Scarlett said, her voice a sensual purr that skittered along his flesh, making him shiver for an entirely different reason than the cold he'd woken up to. Now he was suddenly too warm as he met her gaze. Before him stood Death's Maiden.

No.

Before him stood a queen.

The Queen of the Fae Courts even though she was not Fae.

Not just the Western Courts. Not since she had stripped Talwyn of her crown.

But even 'queen' did not do her justice. Not with the way she held herself. Not with the look in her eyes. Not with her shadows and fire and ice worshipping her as they moved around her.

She looked every bit a goddess. Sorin had never seen one. But if he had, he imagined one would look exactly as his wife did in this moment.

Then her eyes slid to her brother. Her features sharpened, her eyes hardening, and her voice was that of death itself when she said, "I met our mother."

# CHAPTER 2
# SCARLETT

Cethin did not say anything to her in response, wisely remaining silent. She watched his eyes move over her, taking in the shadows, the crown, the spirit animals. She smiled—a sharp, wicked thing—when the hoot of an owl broke through the tense silence. Both males turned to the window as a golden owl soared through, landing in the place Amaré had vacated.

Paja. The spirit animal of Falein, goddess of wisdom and cleverness. The spirit animal who had once been bonded to Eliné.

Sorin cleared his throat, Amaré moving to his shoulder. "Love… I do not know what to ask here. Are you still bonded to Shirina? And what is Paja doing here? I have not seen him since before Queen Henna was killed…"

He trailed off when Scarlett shrugged lightly, not wanting to disturb the owl. She was still watching her brother. His lips were pressed into a tight line as he continued to watch her, and when he still did not speak, she moved to the alcohol cart, pouring herself a measure of liquor. Shirina sat where they'd appeared, her tail switching as she tracked the males.

She had taken her second sip from the glass when Cethin finally said, "You met Saylah."

"I did."

"And?"

"And what?" she asked, her head tilting as she swirled the ice in her glass.

"Scarlett," he gritted out, frustration ringing in his voice. His hands clenched into fists at his side, but his tone had her straightening.

Her eyes narrowed, and she set the glass down with a sharp thud on the cart, liquid sloshing over the top. Paja gave a disgruntled hoot, flying to the window ledge. "You do not get to be *annoyed* with me, Cethin Sutara."

"What did Saylah say?" he asked, trying and failing to adjust his tone.

"What are you afraid I learned, brother?" she countered, and she saw the uncertainty flicker across his features.

"Did she grant what you requested?"

"Requested?" she sneered. "I *requested* nothing."

Sorin stepped between them, Rayner moving closer too. Amaré had flown to perch atop a nearby chair. "Scarlett, my love, I need to know what has happened since you left."

Her features softened when she looked at Sorin again.

· Her husband.

Her king.

Her Source.

Her twin flame.

It did not matter to her if he could no longer bear those Marks. He did not need black swirls on his left hand to be her twin flame. To be her everything.

"I am sorry I was not here when you woke," she said, her tone the complete opposite of how she'd spoken to her brother.

She watched relief wash over him, probably at the realization she wasn't likely to become violent in the near future. He closed the distance between them, taking her face between his hands and brushing a thumb along her cheekbone. "You met your mother?"

"I did," she whispered.

"And?" he prompted gently, holding her gaze.

"I gave her an ultimatum."

Sorin blinked. "You gave a goddess an ultimatum?"

She reached up, wrapping her fingers around his wrists and

tugging them from her face. "She will find a way to restore your magic, or I will give her to Alaric."

"What?" Cethin blurted. "You threatened a goddess?"

"No," she said coldly. "I named a price for my services."

"Scarlett—"

But a knock on the main door of her suite interrupted him. Her eyes flicked to the sound when a male voice called out, "Scarlett?"

Tybalt Greybane. The Commander of Avonleya's forces, the son of Sargon, and Cassius's father.

"Come in," she called.

Tybalt stepped in, pausing mid-step. His gaze darted from the various spirit animals to the shadows that still swirled loosely around her. She had reached over and picked up her glass, taking another sip of alcohol.

"I am sorry to interrupt," Tybalt finally said, glancing at Cethin before focusing on her once more. "I was hoping you would know where to find Cassius. I have been trying to find him, to check on him after everything that has happened."

Scarlett set her liquor back down, reaching up to undo the buttons on her cloak. Her hands were immediately knocked aside, and Sorin made quick work of them before pulling the cloak from her shoulders as she said, "He was still sleeping on the sofa when I went down to the den last night."

"He was not here when I woke," Sorin supplied, moving to drape the cloak over a chair.

"I went to his rooms, but he did not answer," Tybalt said, standing with his hands clasped behind his back. "I did enter, but he was not there."

"He did not go to his own rooms," Scarlett said. "He would have gone to Cyrus's rooms."

"I thought that too, but there was no response when I knocked on his rooms either."

"He is there," Scarlett said. "I need to bathe, and then I will go to him. He will not want to speak to anyone for a while. Not even me." She turned to Sorin and Rayner. "After I have spent some time with him, we can discuss getting Cyrus back. Cassius not taking a Source is going to change our plans."

"But he will take a Source," Sorin said.

"When we have returned with Cyrus, if that is still their choice, then yes, he will," Scarlett replied, beginning to make her way to the bedchamber.

"That is not the course of action we previously discussed," Cethin said.

Scarlett shrugged. "Plans change."

"So, what, Scarlett? You go speak to Saylah and now everything has changed? The weeks of planning and strategizing mean nothing because you have unilaterally decided to change the plans? Despite the fact that these plans affect more than just you?" her brother snapped, taking a step towards her. Sorin and Rayner both tensed, but neither of them needed to do anything. Shirina stood, a low snarl issuing from the feline.

Scarlett stilled, turning back to face him. Her shadows coiled tighter around her arms and torso when she saw the inky darkness beginning to pool at his feet. "You are right, Cethin. I will let *Cassius* decide if and when he shall take a Source. Seeing as this affects him the most."

"This is about more than Cassius, and you know it."

"I do not care," she snarled, sparks echoing her footsteps when she moved closer to Cethin. "He wants Cyrus. There is no one else he will accept. I will not force him to take someone else. Enough sacrifices have been made for mistakes that are not ours. I will not require him to make another. My safety and wellbeing will not require him to forfeit his own happiness, even if he would willingly do just that."

"He needs to take one so you can draw from him," Cethin insisted. "You cannot find the lock without being at your most powerful."

Ah. There it was.

Her lips slowly curled up in a knowing smirk. "Tell me, dear brother," she said, Cethin stilling at the faux sweetness of her voice. "If this lock is so important, why don't *you* go look for it?" He stared back at her, mouth pressing into that thin line again. She took a single step forward. "Why haven't you come on any of these missions to the continent? Why are you so content to be one of those kings who lets others fight for their kingdoms and their people while he sits safely behind his walls? Or should I say Wards?"

"You know that is not the case," he said, his tone low and dangerous.

"I do now. No thanks to you."

"What did you learn, Scarlett?" Sorin asked carefully.

She kept her stare fixed on Cethin when she said, "My brother has not joined any of the missions because he cannot. He cannot leave these lands. If he crosses the Wards, they all fall and leave his entire kingdom defenseless. He is trapped here until I find the lock. I am, as I am for my mother, a means to an end."

"No," Cethin said, lurching forward a step. "No. You are not that, Scarlett."

"Then why hide it from me?" she demanded, orange embers flickering in her vision.

"Because I did not want this exact situation to occur," he said bitterly. "I did not want you to think I only came for you because I needed you to free me."

"You need me to free you. Saylah needs me to free her. This world needs me to free it," Scarlett sneered. "You all need freedom, and yet *I* am the one who has been required to make sacrifice after sacrifice to ensure you receive it. *I* am the one who is being asked to give up her freedom for everyone else to have theirs." She huffed out a harsh laugh. "I suppose *asked* is not the proper word, is it? It is simply assumed I will fulfill what everyone demands of me."

"I know, Starfire," Cethin said gently as she felt a hand settle on the small of her back. She looked up to find Sorin at her side. His touch still calmed her, and a small part of her felt a surge of relief. It wasn't like it had been when their twin flame bond had been in place and Anointed, but it was still something.

Sorin kept his muted amber eyes fixed on her when he said, "I think everyone needs to leave now. I need to speak with my wife. Alone."

"I am sorry, Sorin," Cethin said, and Scarlett believed he truly was judging by the remorse ringing in his tone. "This cannot wait."

"It can. It will," Sorin replied, his own tone leaving no room for argument.

Another knock sounded on the door interrupting whatever argument was about to ensue. Tybalt moved to answer it, and Azrael Luan, Prince of the Earth Court, came in. He held a small mirror in his hand. He didn't spare anyone else any attention, his earthy brown eyes meeting hers. His black hair was tied up on top of his head, and she knew before he spoke what he was going to say.

"Sawyer made contact. They are meeting with Alaric at sundown to make the exchange for Princess Ashtine."

Scarlett's eyes fell closed. She stretched her neck from side-to-side and rolled her shoulders as she processed this new information. She couldn't go. She needed to save her power for when they went to exchange Talwyn for Cyrus and Neve. Cassius couldn't go. He wasn't in any state to go anywhere, let alone on a rescue mission. Sorin couldn't go because he was powerless.

She reopened her eyes, meeting Azrael's gaze once more. "You are prepared to go?"

He nodded. "I can go and bring Ashtine and Sawyer back here once the exchange is done."

"You cannot go alone. You and Sawyer will not be enough. Alaric proved that last time." Her attention went to her Ash Rider. "Can you go as well, Rayner?"

"As you wish, your Majesty," he said, with a small nod.

"Stop calling me that," she chided at him. Her gaze flicked to Cethin. "Can Razik go? Two able to Travel would be ideal. He seemed able to handle Alaric, aside from leaving two of our company behind."

"You know why the mortal kings need to be protected, Scarlett," Cethin returned, no longer able to keep the irritation from his tone. "Not that you cared when you took Drake back to the continent."

"They get a choice about their fate, Cethin," she retorted. "They get a choice. Cassius gets a choice. *I* get a choice."

Cethin ran his hands through his hair, and a small part of her felt bad for her brother. He was trying to do what was best for his kingdom and his own family. She understood that. He had his own burdens he was trying to balance. She did not blame him for this mess. Well, maybe a little, but not entirely. He was as trapped as she was. Maybe his position had been forced upon him as well. Had he had any choice in whether or not to take the throne when their father died? Did he wish this was not his burden? Not his fate? Perhaps, but either way, they were both fighting for their own freedoms and that of their family and people. He was doing what he felt was right for Avonleya. She was doing what she felt was right for...the realm, she supposed.

Because apparently the entirety of the realm was her responsibility now.

And as she had spoken with Saylah under the stars, she'd realized she might not have a choice in what she needed to do, but she'd give others the choice whenever she could. Drake. Tava. Cassius. Everyone deserved to make their own fate. It was why she'd taken Drake and Tava across the Edria. It was why she would stop pushing Cassius about a Source. It was why she'd gone to Saylah in the first place. She was done letting someone else dictate her path. She was done finding keys and locks unless it suited her own needs. She had her own ends to meet, and right now, her greatest priorities were Ashtine, Cyrus, and Neve.

"I can ask Razik if he will go," Cethin finally said. "That choice will be his."

"You so readily give him choices?" Scarlett scoffed, her brow arching.

"You try telling him what to do," Cethin muttered. He turned to Tybalt. "He was going to check on Eliza. Niara thought she would be able to clear her this morning."

Eliza.

She still wasn't over the shock of her friend becoming Razik's Source. She would find time to talk to her about that soon, but the female could take care of herself. She knew Eliza had spoken the truth when she'd said no one had forced her into this. Nobody could force the fire general to do anything.

Apparently Cethin felt the same way about the dragon shifter.

That would be an incredibly interesting dynamic when she really thought about it.

Later. One thing at a time. Cassius. Cyrus. Ashtine.

But first a bath and food. In that order.

She turned back to Azrael. "Plan it, Prince. We can meet in a few hours to discuss things before you go."

Azrael nodded once, Rayner falling into step beside him as he turned to leave the room. It wasn't lost on her that she had just asked the Earth Prince of all people to take the lead on a mission for her. Two months ago, she would have laughed until she cried at the mere suggestion of entrusting Azrael with such a task.

The door clicked shut, and her attention shifted back to Cethin. "Anything else? Or can I bathe now?"

Cethin sent her a dry look. "Can we have dinner tonight? To discuss what you learned during your time with Saylah?"

"No," she replied, moving towards her bedchamber. "Tomorrow, Cethin," she added over her shoulder. "Just...give me a day to... Just give me a day. Please."

Cethin nodded once, remorse shining in his silver gaze. "Please remember I likely do not know everything she shared with you. Give me a chance to defend myself before you hold something against me."

She gave him a tight nod of her own before she disappeared into her bedchamber. A soft flash of light told her Shirina had disappeared, but Paja would stay and so would Amaré.

Because the spirit animals answered to her now.

"I am a goddess," Saylah said sharply.

"And I am your salvation or your destruction," Scarlett replied. "It appears I am your god now."

"Calling yourself a god does not make you one."

Scarlett shrugged. "Just as calling oneself a mother does not make you one, I suppose."

"Careful, Child," Saylah cautioned.

"No," Scarlett snarled. "You do not get to call me child when you have placed the fate of this world in my hands."

"Do you think I wanted to do that? Do you think I learned of you growing in *my womb and my first thought was to give you a responsibility no one should have to bear, let alone a girl who has scarcely lived?"*

*"You are a goddess!" Scarlett cried. "You could have done any number of things. Anything would have been better than this!"*

*Saylah shook her head, the stars of her crown shimmering in the moonlight filtering through the trees of Shira Forest. Shirina continued to pace back and forth between them, and Amaré ruffled his feathers in agitation at Scarlett's shoulder. "I had no other options, Starfire."*

*"You had no other options?" Scarlett repeated, her voice scarcely a whisper. Then louder she said, "You had no other options but to place the fate of the world on a babe not yet born?"*

*"You are correct."*

*"That is your response to telling me you sacrificed me to save yourself?" Scarlett said in disbelief.*

*"To save this realm," Saylah corrected.*

*"Oh, fuck all the way off," Scarlett snapped.*

*"Were you taught nothing of respect for the gods?" Saylah demanded, her lip curling into a sneer.*

*"Respect for the gods? Which ones in particular? The one who birthed me then abandoned me? The ones who never answered my calls or prayers? Or the gods who have abandoned this world?"*

*"Not by choice," Saylah countered. "They cannot come here. They can do nothing. You stated yourself moments ago that Achaz and Arius cannot come here."*

*"But one was already here. One was already here and could have done something. Instead, she did nothing but hide in a forest." She took another step towards her mother. "But you will do this, Saylah. You will find a way to fix all of this. You will find a way to restore Sorin his power. That is the price of my sacrifice."*

*Saylah blinked at her. Her features were sharp and impassive. Eliné had never looked at her like that. Eliné had always looked at her with love and adoration. Saylah looked at her like...*

*Like she was a means to an end that was being uncooperative.*

*The goddess turned on her heel, the night seeming to part around her. "Come with me."*

"Love?"

Scarlett looked up from the chaise she was sitting on out on their balcony, wrapped in a blanket despite the temperatures getting warmer in the later weeks of spring. She found herself wondering what Solembra looked like in the spring. She'd only seen it at the tail-end of fall and into winter. What did it look like when new life was blooming? What was the Tana River like in the heat of summer? What would the view look like from the chateau windows?

She pulled the blanket back to allow Sorin to settle down with her, and she started when his skin touched her own.

Cold. Even through his clothing she could feel his cool skin.

She was used to his constantly warm touch from the fire in his veins. She hadn't processed the long-sleeve tunic and wool socks he was wearing until now, and she wordlessly passed some of the blanket over to him. He pulled her into his side, pressing a kiss to her temple.

"It will take time, but we will adjust to this," he murmured.

She nodded against his shoulder, swallowing down the emotions clawing at her. This would be fixed. This wasn't forever.

Clearing her throat, she said, "I just need a moment to breathe before I seek out Cassius."

"I know," Sorin replied, winding a tendril of her wet hair around his finger. She could dry it, but he always did that for her. Doing it herself just made all of this more…real.

Too real.

"I had food sent up for you," he said softly.

"Thank you."

"Scarlett."

She tilted her head to look up at him. His eyes may not be as bright, but the love that shone in them was still the same. She reached up, skimming her fingertips along his jaw. "Before we talk about every-thing, can you kiss me?"

The hand playing with her hair moved to her nape, tugging her lips to his. "You never need to ask twice for that, my love."

And Scarlett let herself drown in the taste of him. His tongue moved against hers as his fingers slipped up into her hair, fisting gently, and she shifted, sliding her hand up the bottom of his tunic, fingers gliding over the indents of his torso.

She pulled back first, her breathing ragged. "I am fixing this, Sorin," she rasped.

"And if it cannot be fixed, I do not care, Scarlett. This—a you and me—this is all I need. I will be content. We will figure the rest out as we go." He brushed his lips against hers once more before he stood, tugging her up with him. "Come. Eat and tell me what you learned."

What she'd learned.

She'd learned so much and not nearly enough. She also knew Saylah still hadn't told her everything, especially when it came to Cethin and how exactly he'd become bound to the Wards.

Sorin tossed her a pear, and she took a bite as he began preparing a plate for her. "I am listening," he prompted, selecting some cheese cubes and placing them on the plate.

"I don't know where to start," she said around her mouthful of fruit.

Sorin nodded in understanding of what she was asking of him. Give her somewhere to start. "Why is Paja here?"

"Did you know him?"

"Yes. He was bonded to Eliné. But like I said, I have not seen him since before Henna was killed. That is not to say he did not come to Eliné during that time, but…" He trailed off as he held a plate out to her.

She took it from him, moving to sit at the table in their suite's dining room while he began fixing his own plate of food. "Paja is here because I asked him to come here."

Sorin glanced up briefly from the roast meat sandwich he was preparing. "Are you bonded to him?"

"No?"

He stilled, setting down the utensils in his hands and planting his palms on the tabletop. "This is something you would know, Scarlett."

She sighed, throwing herself back in her chair, and Sorin arched a brow at the action. "I sort of control the spirit animals now." Sorin blinked slowly. When he didn't speak, she added, "I told Saylah if she was going to keep hiding in Shira Forest instead of coming to our aid, the least she could do would be to give me control over the spirit animals."

"You said that. To a goddess."

She debated internally for a moment before saying, "Among other things."

"What of those bonded to them?"

"I do not control them like *that*," she said, picking up her sandwich. "I guess it is more so that instead of residing with Saylah when they are not needed, they reside with me."

"Then where are the rest of them now? Cethin said they have been resting," Sorin said, resuming preparing his own plate.

"Some are still in Shira Forest. Cethin was right. They were resting, but beyond that, I do not know. I learned much, but Saylah still has her secrets," she said bitterly.

"And she let you take control of the spirit animals?"

Scarlett scoffed. *Let her.* But she said, "More or less."

"Scarlett…" he said, dragging out her name in a way that said he knew there was more to this.

She tossed her sandwich back onto her plate. "This was not some joyous reunion, Sorin," she said, her irritation rising.

He had moved to the space beside her, and he reached over, gripping her fingers in his hand. "I am not implying that it was, Love." He jerked his chin at her food. "Eat. You are cranky."

She made a face. "I am not."

"You are," he said, sitting back and picking up his own sandwich. "Rightfully so with no sleep and so much to tend to," he added. "But cranky nevertheless."

"I'll show you cranky," she muttered under her breath.

"What was that?" he asked, arching a brow again.

"Nothing," she mumbled, shoving a piece of cheese into her mouth.

They ate in silence for the next several minutes before Sorin said carefully, "Am I safe to speak again?"

"Yes," she sighed, admittedly feeling slightly better with some food in her belly.

"Are you still bonded to Shirina? In the way that I was bonded to Amaré?"

"You are still bonded to Amaré, Sorin," she answered, reaching for her water glass.

"I should not be."

"Why?"

"Because the spirit animals bond to the most powerful. I am no longer that."

"You are still technically the Fire Prince," Scarlett countered, taking a drink.

"I am not."

"Oh? Did you abdicate the position in the hours I was gone?"

"No, but—"

"Was there a challenge for the position that I am unaware of?"

"Stop being a smartass."

Scarlett smirked at him. "Then, from my understanding of Fae politics, you are still the Fire Prince, and you will remain so, Sorin. Saylah will figure out a way to restore your magic."

"And if she cannot?"

"She does not have that option."

Sorin sat back, wiping his mouth with his napkin, before he turned his full attention on her. "What did you do, Scarlett?"

"I already told you. I gave her an ultimatum."

"You will give her to Alaric."

"Mhmm," she hummed, spearing a piece of melon on her fork.

"To what end, Scarlett? You will truly give him the thing this entire war has been about?"

"This war has not been about Saylah," Scarlett said. "Why do you think that?"

"Because everything we have learned says they want what was being guarded in Shira Forest. What the spirit animals were guarding."

"They were not guarding Saylah," she answered, taking another drink of water.

"Then what were they guarding, Scarlett?" he sighed, clearly growing impatient.

"A mirror gate."

"A mirror gate?" he repeated. "Why? When there are at least two on our own continent?"

"Because the one in Shira Forest is not just a mirror gate. It is *the* mirror gate. A doorway between the stars to other worlds," she said. "And the lock? It is not the lock to the Wards as we have been told. It is the lock to the gateway into this realm."

# CHAPTER 3
# ELIZA

The Fire General stood staring out the window of her room, her arms wrapped tightly around herself. Niara, Cethin's most skilled Healer, had finally cleared her today. It probably helped that she'd been exhausted and sleeping for most of the last two days.

Two days.

It had been two days since a small unit had gone to collect Princess Ashtine and ended up leaving Cyrus and Neve there. Early yesterday morning, Scarlett had taken Briar, Sawyer, and the Tyndells to the Water Court. Sawyer had left his mirror that had been blessed by Anahita, goddess of the sea and water, with Azrael. He would let them know when the exchange was done so that someone could Travel back to the continent and bring Ashtine here.

Eliza rotated her arm to look at the Source Mark that now adorned her skin. She'd seen the dragon shifter once since he had drawn from her before leaving for that mission. She'd woken tangled up with Razik, her head on his chest, the morning after he'd given her the Source Mark. She'd gone to sleep in his tunic and her own loose-fitting pants.

And she'd woken up without the pants.

Razik was so godsdamn *hot* with all that dragon fire in his veins.

She'd obviously gotten uncomfortable in her sleep, but for the love of Anala. Waking up without pants on next to *him*?

Razik had grunted in annoyance when she'd not-so-accidentally elbowed him in the ribs as she'd extracted herself from his hold, immediately missing said dragon fire. She'd shoved her legs into the pants she'd found in a heap on the floor, looking up to find Razik smirking back at her.

"You said we would never have to speak of it again," she'd grumbled. She had been swimming in his tunic that was several sizes too large for her. She wasn't tiny, but she was fit from decades of intense training. His faded grey tunic had hung down to her knees, and the sleeves fell over her hands. She'd bunched her fingers around the fabric. It was a nervous habit from childhood she'd never been able to completely overcome.

Razik had arched a brow. "Did I say anything?"

She'd scowled back at him. "Can you do whatever it is you need to do to fill your reserves so I can go back to my rooms?"

"How is your wound?" he'd asked instead.

She'd wanted to retort that it was not his concern, but she knew he'd spit some bullshit about it becoming his concern when she became his Source. So instead, she'd let out a long-suffering sigh before pulling back the collar of his tunic to let him see that the bandage was still in place and not bleeding through.

"Are you hungry?" he'd asked, seemingly satisfied with the state of her wound.

She'd turned away when he'd climbed out of bed. She'd seen enough of his bare chest and torso in the last twelve hours. Had felt it beneath her fingers. Had slept on it. Had wanted more than that in the initial minutes after he'd given her the Mark. But she knew it hadn't all been the Source Bond.

"*Mai dragocen.*"

The name had preceded a soft touch on her shoulder, and when she'd turned to face him, she'd let out another breath of relief to find he'd pulled a tunic on. Without another word, she'd held out her right arm to him, tugging the sleeve up. She'd watched him slice across the Mark and then his palm with a dagger. Then she'd forced herself to stay completely still when their power coiled and merged as he drew her flames into his dragon fire. She'd made herself hold his sapphire gaze the entire time, her teeth clenched tight. And when it was done, she'd left his rooms without a backward glance. He hadn't sought her out when he'd returned, and she was glad. She'd slept for the most part, other than that meeting with Sorin and Scarlett when they'd asked her to be Cassius's Source.

And the meeting before that where she'd sat and listened to everything that had happened when they'd gone to the Southern Islands. When Razik had Traveled so many of her family across the Edria Sea. When he'd *negotiated* with the Maraan Prince and left Cyrus there. When that meeting had ended, she'd tried to stay up and strategize with Sorin and the other Fae over what to do, not only about Cyrus but Ashtine and the Tyndells too. She'd fallen asleep though, still drained and adjusting to having someone draw power from her. No one had known then that she had become Razik's Source. They'd all assumed she was still recovering from the shirastone stab wound, and she had been. That just hadn't been the entire story.

Eliza heard the main door of her rooms open a moment before a quick knock sounded on the door of her bedchamber. She didn't need to ask who it was. She already knew.

"Just because I am your Source now does not mean you can simply come into my rooms uninvited," she said tersely when the hinges of the door creaked.

"I assumed you would not let me in if I asked, considering you are avoiding me." The low timbre of his voice made her feel things she didn't want to feel, and she slipped her hands into her sleeves.

"What do you want?"

"That is a loaded question, Milady. You may want to rephrase it."

She finally turned to face him, finding him leaning against her doorjamb in that infuriatingly casual way of his. His brown hair brushed his cheekbones, and he was in his usual black attire.

With a glare, she asked, "Why did you seek me out at this particular moment in time?"

His lips twitched, the only sign that he found her agitation amusing. "Niara said your wound is completely healed."

"That does not explain what you are doing here."

"You have slept a lot these past few days."

"I was instructed to rest."

"Because you have proven you follow instruction so well," he retorted dryly.

"I follow instruction when it suits my needs."

Razik's eyes flashed, his pupils shifting to vertical slits for a fraction of a second before he got his power back under control. He cleared his throat, and her head tilted at the mannerism.

"I am going over to my father's estate. I thought you might want to go with me," he said.

"Why would you think that?"

"I thought you might want to get out of the castle after being cooped up for so long."

"I do, but not with you."

"I think there is something we need to discuss, and it would be better done at the estate rather than in a castle full of busybodies," he countered.

"Unless you need to refill your power reserves, which can be done right here, there is nothing else we need to say to each other," Eliza said, turning away from him and facing the window again.

"Wrong," came a low growl in her ear. How could he move so silently that she hadn't even heard him? She was Fae. She should have been able to hear him no matter how quietly he moved. She didn't get a chance to reply when an arm slipped around her waist, and she felt herself being pulled through the air as he Traveled them.

Her bare feet landed on a soft rug, and she found herself in another bedroom. This one was smaller than his rooms at the castle, but it was definitely his. The same earthy colors accented the space. He spun her in his arms, forcing her to tilt her head up to look into his face.

She glared at him. "You cannot simply haul me to wherever you desire me to be."

"Part of becoming my Source was agreeing to trust me," he retorted, his voice low and tinged with anger. "When you avoid me, that is not trusting me. When you refuse to tell me you are upset with me, I cannot trust you."

He released her, and she took a step back from him, folding her arms across her chest. "This Mark on my arm does not mean I immediately trust you."

"No, but it does mean you actively try," he countered. "It does mean that you do not hide in your rooms when you are upset with me. I do not play such games."

"I am not playing games," Eliza bristled. Her finger came up, poking him hard in the chest. "I became your Source so you could better protect my family when you took them to the Southern Islands. Instead, you bartered with Alaric and left one of mine across the fucking sea." Razik opened his mouth to say something, but she wasn't done. "Furthermore, I owe you *nothing*. I volunteered to be your Source. I chose it, and everything that comes with it. You do not get to tell me how I navigate that."

"My negotiations were not personal, Eliza," Razik said, watching her closely. "Those were political moves that needed to be made. I was there on behalf of my king and my kingdom. Negotiations are no place for emotions and feelings."

"Then I guess that's the difference between us," she replied, lowering her hand. "My becoming your Source was entirely personal. It had everything to do with feelings and emotions and nothing to do with *you*."

"You are the leader of your Court's armies, Eliza. I know you understand the reasoning behind how I proceeded with negotiations."

"Of course I understand it. It does not mean I have to like it, and it does not mean I cannot be upset about it. Cyrus is across the sea, being held prisoner, enduring only the gods know what, and I can do nothing. The rest of my family are facing their own crises right now, so you are the only one left for me to irrationally rage at until I can plunge my sword through a seraph or Maraan."

Her breathing had escalated during that verbal tirade, and she knew her cheeks were tinged with red in her anger.

"You are delightfully vicious," was Razik's only reply, that slight smirk returning.

"Why are you smiling? This is not funny," she ground out.

"I am smiling because I was wrong."

"About what?"

He strode past her, pulling the door open and gesturing her through. "You do trust me, *mai dragocen*."

She snorted. "How in the realms do you figure that?"

"You would only allow yourself to— how did you phrase it? Irrationally rage? You would only allow yourself to appear irrational with someone you trust implicitly. That is a vulnerability that you do not give to others."

"Shut up," she muttered, stalking through the doorway.

She found herself in a decent-sized sitting room, but Razik brushed past her, striding to a door on the other side of the room. He disappeared through it, leaving the door open, and Eliza huffed in irritation before she followed him because what else was she going to do? Stand here and stare at the wall? She'd never admit it to him, but it did feel damn good to be out of the castle. She'd love to get into the city and walk around a bit.

When she stepped through the next doorway, she froze. He had told her he had a study here with books, but she had not expected to find a small library. The walls of this room were lined with floor-to-ceiling bookshelves, all packed full. This room was bigger than his bedchamber had been, and he had disappeared somewhere inside. Off to the right was a fireplace with a group of armchairs arranged in front of it, and beyond the chairs was another door. If this was a study, where was his desk?

She had taken a few steps further into the room when the door near the hearth opened, and Commander Tybalt came striding into the room. Eliza stilled again, unsure if she was supposed to be here. They had always stayed in the guest wing of the Greybane manor. She had never been in the private wing.

The Commander smiled warmly at her. He looked nearly identical to Cassius, only his hair was cropped short. Deep brown eyes met her own. "General," he greeted. "What a pleasant surprise."

"Commander," she replied with a small bow. "Razik came to pick up a few things and allowed me to join him."

"Did he now?" Tybalt asked, and she forced herself not to squirm at the way he was studying her.

She cleared her throat. "Yes. He is in here…somewhere."

"Upstairs, I am sure," Tybalt replied, a knowing smile filling his face.

"Upstairs?"

Tybalt chuckled lightly, gesturing toward the back of the room and indicating for her to follow him. "How are you feeling?"

"Better, thank you. Niara cleared me this morning."

"That is good news," the Commander said, leading her through the room. They rounded a corner and, sure enough, there was a spiraling iron staircase that led up through an opening in the ceiling. The stairs were cold on her bare feet, but she was curious just how many books were up there yet. She started climbing, the Commander's boots sounding behind her.

"Is this your study then?"

Tybalt huffed another chuckle. "No, General. This is all Razik's. I never understood why he needed to keep every book he could ever get his hands on, but he would spend days holed up in here when he was a child. I finally had it renovated, letting him design it however he wished."

For the briefest of moments, she wondered about his childhood and why his uncle had raised him instead of his parents, but she quickly shoved the thought from her mind. She didn't care about anything that involved him. When she found herself on the second floor, she blinked against the brightness. The lower level had been dark and lit by various sconces and candles, but this level had one solid wall of windows letting in the daylight. The Nightmist Mountains rose up on the horizon, and she didn't know where to look first— at the stunning view or the additional bookcases everywhere.

"The upper level of his study spans the entirety of his space— his bedchamber, sitting room, and lower level," Tybalt explained from behind her.

This was...

There weren't words for what this was.

"How does he know where everything is?" Her voice was soft and hushed, as if she would disturb something sacred up here.

"I have no idea," Tybalt answered. "But he does."

Then something else occurred to her.

"Can I ask you something?" she asked, turning to face the Commander.

"Of course," he replied, another one of those warm smiles filling his face.

"Do you know what *mai dragocen* means?"

Tybalt's eyes went wide, and he blinked a few times before he said, "Where did you hear that term?"

Suddenly feeling like she had revealed something she shouldn't have, she shook her head in dismissal, turning back to the windows. "Just a phrase I heard in passing. I am not familiar with the Avonleyan language and was curious as to the meaning."

"That term is not Avonleyan," Tybalt replied.

She knew that. Razik had told her it was a language not found in this world. But he'd also told her he wouldn't tell her what it meant until she told him what the Mark over her heart meant. Which was something she would never discuss with him. But Tybalt clearly knew what it meant, and she couldn't decide if his reaction to the term was good or bad.

Eliza shrugged indifferently. "Like I said, I heard it in passing and was curious."

Tybalt hummed some sort of acknowledgment that told her he didn't believe her in the slightest.

Razik appeared then, three books held in one of his large hands. He looked back and forth between her and Tybalt once, not appearing surprised to find them here, but he faltered at the look Tybalt gave him. The male was always emotionless and apathetic, except when Tybalt was around. When he was with his uncle, there was a respect he offered no one else, not even Cethin.

"Magdalena told me you were here," Tybalt said. "I wanted to check in with you."

How had Magdalena known they were here? They had Traveled directly into Razik's rooms.

"Now is not the time," Razik answered, passing one of the books to her.

"You are going to need to make some time, Razik."

Eliza tried to focus on the book he had given her, feeling rather awkward at being here for this conversation. She flipped open the cover and then gave another frustrated sigh. The book was in Avon-leyan. Another book she couldn't read. If he seriously thought she was going to spend more time with him so he could read this to her, she needed to reevaluate his intelligence.

He reached over without looking at her and flipped a few of the pages while he continued to speak with his uncle. "Tonight perhaps."

"Normally that would be acceptable except that we have received news from the Water Court."

Eliza had been studying the page he had turned to, realizing this was a lesson book. He had given her a book that would allow her to begin learning to read the Avonleyan language. But the mention of the Water Court blessedly distracted her from the warm feeling that was growing in her chest.

"Sawyer made contact?" she asked.

Tybalt glanced at her, nodding. "Prince Azrael just informed the Royals. They are planning to send a unit in a few hours. Scarlett has asked if you would be willing to Travel with the unit again," he answered, returning his attention to Razik.

Razik rolled his eyes. "Again? Can the Earth Prince not Travel them?"

"He is going as well. They would prefer two Travelers go for peace of mind. Until Cassius's Source situation is figured out, Scarlett cannot go, nor can he," Tybalt answered. He glanced at Eliza again. "Additionally, as you have acquired a new Source, you would be the strongest member of the unit. You know our kingdom's best interests are aligned with theirs."

"I will go, but I need more than a few hours."

"And Eliza?" Tybalt asked, gaze flicking to her once more.

"Will go with me."

"I will not," Eliza sputtered.

Razik turned to face her fully, his brows rising. "No?"

"No."

"My apologies then, Milady. I thought since Niara had cleared you, you would be ready to go on a mission; but if you do not feel up to the task yet, I understand."

She wanted to punch the male in the throat.

Razik smirked at her, as if he knew exactly what she was feeling, and Tybalt was looking back and forth between the two as though he was trying to work something out.

Something she didn't want anyone to figure out. Ever.

"Either way, I will need to refill my magic before I go," Razik said, turning back to Tybalt. "But when I return, we can have that check in you wish for."

"Razik—" Tybalt started.

"Either you want me to go on this mission, in which case I need to prepare, or you want to have this conversation, in which case I need to return my Source to the castle before we do," Razik interrupted.

Return her? As if she were a possession?

As soon as they were alone, he was going to learn all about her rage—rational and irrational.

Tybalt's features hardened, a muscle feathering in his jaw as he stared back at his adopted son. "As soon as you return, Razik," he finally relented.

Razik nodded as he moved to place a hand on her lower back, gently guiding her deeper into the study. "You have my word."

Tybalt watched them for a moment longer before he moved back to the spiral staircase. She glanced over her shoulder to find his gaze still lingering on them. Waiting until she could no longer hear his boots on the steps, she said, "He seems worried about you."

"A decent father worries about his children," Razik replied, not looking at her. He still held the other two books in his other hand.

He had a point there, she supposed. The male she'd known to be her father had only worried about her power, not her. Tybalt reminded her of how Sorin's father had been. A parent who actually cared for the well-being of their child for no other reason than that they loved them. Razik clearly loathed his father, but at least he'd had Tybalt growing up.

"If you need to speak with him, I can wait here while you do so," Eliza said, eyes dropping back to the book she still held open in her hands.

"As I said, I will speak with him when I return," Razik replied. "But you may remain here as long as you wish. I can let Magdalena know to have food delivered to you while I am gone."

She nearly tripped over her own feet. "What?"

"You said you were not going with me."

"By the gods," she muttered, snapping the book shut.

They stepped through an archway, and Eliza found the desk she had been wondering about. It was large, papers and books neatly arranged atop it. Two chairs sat before it, and along the opposite wall was an overstuffed sofa in front of a hearth. The windows continued behind the desk, the other two walls containing more books. His hand fell from her back, and he moved to the desk, beginning to rummage through drawers while she just…stood there.

"Why did you bring me here, Razik?" she finally asked after a full minute of silence between them.

"I told you. I thought you would want to get out of the castle," he answered, shutting a drawer and grabbing a small satchel. "But since you are here, I can refill my reserves before I leave."

She pressed her tongue to her cheek because godsdamnit. Of course she wanted to go on this mission, but that meant she was going to have to admit her brash reaction to him earlier.

He tossed the satchel onto the desk, pulling a dagger from his belt as he made his way back to her. She narrowed her eyes at him when he took the book and placed it on a chair before taking her wrist and pushing the sleeve of her tunic up. "Something to say, *mai dragocen?*"

That damn name again.

Her gaze darted to the windows when she said begrudgingly, "I will go on this mission with you."

"I know."

Her eyes snapped back to his at the same time he slid the blade across the Mark on her forearm. There was no smirk or vindictive look on his face. He just held her stare while he placed his cut palm onto the Mark.

She tried—gods, did she try—to hold in the gasp at their power merging again, but it escaped her lips anyway. His sapphire gaze dropped to her mouth at the same time she heard a light thump.

The dagger hitting the floor.

His arm looped around her waist, tugging her into his chest as her flames fed his dragon fire. She knew she shouldn't do it, but she breathed deep, taking in his smoke and spice scent. She should stay behind simply because they shouldn't be spending any more time together than necessary, but she also knew she would go anyway.

He knew it too.

"It will be a fast mission," he said, his voice a low rumble in her ear, as though he knew the inner conflict she was having. "We will be back within a day."

"I am not worried about being gone for an extended period of time."

"No. You are worried about spending an extended period of time with me," he replied. There was nothing accusing in his tone. Just a blunt statement of fact that she couldn't argue against.

"I will not apologize for that."

"I am not asking you to," he said. His hand slipped from her arm, and he brought it up to cup her cheek. She expected to feel the warmth of his blood on her face, but his palm had already healed.

"Then what are you asking?"

He searched her eyes for something he would never find there before he leaned in a little closer. His breath danced across her lips when he said, "I am asking you to please learn to read the Avonleyan language so I no longer have to hear you whine about it."

Her hands came up, shoving him hard. "Take me back to the castle," she demanded, stomping over to the book in the chair.

He held a hand out to her with exaggerated flair. "As you wish, Milady."

She flipped him off before she placed her fingers in his waiting palm, his deep chuckle skittering along her bones and heating her skin as he tugged her through the air.

# CHAPTER 4
# TALWYN

T he sound of the door at the top of the stairs opening drew Talwyn Semiria from her thoughts. They kept her in her own area of the dungeons in Avonleya. No other prisoners were in here, and as far she knew, there was only the cell she was currently sitting in. There were no windows. She hadn't seen the sky since Scarlett's brother had escorted her to this cell. She was given three meals, though, so she was able to gather the time of day based on the food given to her. There was a small pallet of straw nearby that she tried to sleep on, but she found sleeping sitting up against the wall easier.

She'd eaten her midday meal a short time ago, which meant the person coming down the stairs was not a sentry with food. She was getting a visitor. She assumed it was Azrael. He was the only one that ever came to see her, although his visits were usually after the evening meal. Something must be happening if he was coming to see her now.

She'd been down here a few days now. She didn't really care. She was stuck waiting no matter where she was being housed. Her fate was out of her hands. She was just waiting for Scarlett to come and finish the job she'd started. But why hadn't she yet?

She hadn't healed from any of the injuries the queen had inflicted upon her, but she had been permitted to clean up at one point. She suspected that was Azrael's doing. They'd removed the nightstone shackles on her wrists while she'd scrubbed down with a rag and luke-warm water, but her ankle shackles had remained in place, which is why no healing had happened. The shirastone shackles they used in the Fae courts kept magic-wielders from accessing their gifts, but nightstone was different. It was as though the stone drained her magic itself and kept it empty. She couldn't access her wind or earth magic, and she couldn't shift into her wolf form. As for her ability to shift energy, she hadn't touched that magic since that day in the throne room. That day she thought she'd killed Sorin.

She could feel her power slowly trickling out of her, though, and she knew that if they ever removed the shackles, her power would remain empty until she could refill her reserves with sleep and food over time. It reminded her of Alaric's power when he would latch it on to her and drain her magic. She moved a bit, hissing at the burn when the shackles were jarred slightly. Her skin was raw where they touched, and the wounds that encircled her wrists and ankles only got deeper when she moved too much.

As she expected, the Earth Prince stepped into view a moment later. The sentry that had escorted him nodded before leaving him alone with her. This had been a fight for him the first few times, but after that, the sentry left without a word. The Avonleyan King must have given approval for Az to speak with her alone.

Azrael lowered to the stone floor like he did every time he came down here. One knee was bent, his arm resting atop it while he leaned back on his other hand. He wore brown pants and a sleeveless black tunic. Fae Marks swirled along his deeply tanned arms. Earthy brown eyes dragged over her, his features tightening when he saw her wrists before he met her gaze. "I will speak with Scarlett about the shackles."

Talwyn nodded once in acknowledgement before she said, "You are early today." Her voice was hoarse and raspy. That happened when you didn't speak for hours on end.

"We are going to get Ashtine in a few hours," he said. She lurched forward, cursing at the nightstone. Az scowled at her. "Sit back. You will injure yourself further."

"You are bringing Ashtine back here? To Avonleya?" Talwyn asked, ignoring his command.

"That is the plan, yes."

"Who is going to retrieve her? Briar?"

Azrael hesitated, a mannerism she had come to learn meant he was debating whether he could share this information with her. And that? That hurt more than the damn nightstone encircling her wrists and ankles. He had once been her Second. She had once been able to confide anything to him, and he had been able to do the same for her. He had been her closest confidant, closer than Ashtine, and the fact that she could not be that for him anymore made her chest ache.

"In a way, Briar will be there, yes," he finally answered.

She wanted to ask what that meant, but knew it would be pointless. If he could tell her more, he would have already.

"Is she safe right now?"

"No, but she will be soon." He shifted closer to the cell bars. "We leave this evening, but I do not know how long I will be gone. If all goes well, we will be back tomorrow. If it does not..." She nodded in understanding of what he was telling her as she carefully settled back against the wall. "I will make sure someone comes down to check on you while I am gone."

"They bring me three meals a day," she said dryly.

"Outside of that."

"I do not need anyone to waste their time on me," she retorted.

"Is that what you think I do every day? Every time I come down here?" Az demanded.

*Yes.*

"No," she replied, knowing that was what he wanted her to say.

Az tsked at her. "Do not lie to me, Talwyn. We are well past that."

"Why do you?" she asked. She had meant to say it sharp and cold, but it came out soft and desperate.

"Why do I what?"

"You know what I am asking." She was staring at the floor, scrubbing at a spot of dried blood with her bare toe.

"Yes, but I want you to say it out loud so you can hear how ridiculous you sound," Azrael chided.

She looked up from the grimy floor to glare at him. "Why do you bother coming to see me every day?"

"Because someday you will not be behind these bars, Talwyn. And on that day, I want you to know that you are not alone, even if you think you deserve to be."

"Scarlett will not let me out of here. And if she does, it will only be to kill me."

"Scarlett will not be the one to let you out," Azrael agreed, getting to his feet.

He was leaving already? He always stayed with her for at least an hour, sometimes longer. She may be questioning why he came to see her every day, but that didn't mean she didn't like it. She sure as shit didn't deserve it, but his visits were keeping her sane. She needed them, and deep down, she knew that was part of the reason he came to her every day.

"On the day you find yourself on the other side of these bars, I think you will discover you have never truly been alone. Not like you believe you are."

She slowly got to her feet, moving carefully so that the shackles didn't dig further into her skin. Her joints cracked as she uncoiled from the ground. The chains had enough give to let her move to a waste bucket and to get the food they brought to her.

"Spend your time preparing, Talwyn," Azrael said.

"Preparing for what?"

"For how you wish to live on the other side of these bars."

"You speak as if I have a future. Perhaps you should be the one preparing."

"I am."

Her lips pursed at what he was insinuating. "You will let me know how things went when you return?"

"I will report on Ashtine's wellbeing," he agreed.

The silence went on for the next several seconds before Azrael turned and began making his way to the stairs.

"Az," Talwyn called out, stumbling forward a step.

He paused, looking back at her over his shoulder expectantly.

"Thank you. For coming to see me every day." Azrael blinked at her. His only show of surprise. "Can you do something for me?"

"I can try," he said with a nod for her to make her request as he turned to face her fully once more.

"In case you are wrong and I do not get to leave this cell, can you tell Ashtine thank you as well?"

"For?"

"For choosing me and asking nothing in return. Tell her…" Her voice caught in her throat, and it was at that moment she realized her face was wet. "Tell her I will find a way to repay her. Even if I must do so from the After."

Azrael took a step back towards her. His hand moved as if he were going to reach for her before he dropped it again. "I will tell her."

Talwyn pressed her lips together, feeling another tear fall. She'd wipe them away, but did not wish to move her wrists again. After being numb for so long, a part of her marveled at the fact that she was feeling anything at all.

"All is not lost, Talwyn," Azrael said. And the way he spoke to her —a softness to his voice she rarely heard from him—it made the ache in her chest throb. Another feeling.

"You are wrong," she whispered. "I had everything, and I lost it all. I cannot get it back."

Azrael's head tilted to the side. "No, you cannot." She huffed a humorless laugh at his bluntness. "But you can decide how to do things differently if you are granted the possibility of doing so."

"I do not know what that looks like."

The corner of his lips tilted the smallest amount. Her mouth nearly fell open at his almost smile.

"Then I suppose the possibilities are endless."

With that, he turned away from her again, and when he made it to the steps, he did not look back. She continued to stare at the stairwell long after she heard the door open and close at the top of the stairs.

Seeing as she was already standing, she took care of her needs and filled the tin cup with water from a pitcher they brought her with her meals before carefully lowering herself back to the floor. She held the cup between her palms, staring down at the still water within.

What if Azrael was right? What if she did find herself free on the other side of these bars? What if she was given that chance, despite not deserving it? What if she wasn't alone? What if she'd just refused to let anyone get close enough to let her see that?

*Spend your time preparing, Talwyn.*

For so long her dreams and plans had revolved around revenge against the very kingdom she was now imprisoned in. She did not know how to dream about anything else.

But she had at one point in time.

Once upon a time she had dreamed of things other than vengeance. Back when being a queen had been the dream. When Eliné had been alive. When she hadn't been at odds with Sorin.

She had lost everything, just like she'd said to Azrael. And while she regretted losing all the *good* in her life—her Courts, Azrael's loyalty, her people's trust— she did not regret losing the things weighing her down. That unyielding need for revenge. The sham of a relationship Tarek had convinced her she had. The bitterness over Sorin. She had lost those things, too.

Ever since she had found herself in cells in Baylorin, she had been thinking about what she would have done differently. How she had brought all this upon herself. How she deserved to be held behind bars, to be stripped of her throne, to meet death at the hand of Scarlett Aditya. It didn't seem to matter what she did anymore. She fucked it up or made things worse in the end. She hadn't thought of anything else because what was the godsdamn point? What was the point when there was nothing left to believe in?

*Spend your time preparing, Talwyn.*

But what if Azrael was right?

That question scared her more than the idea of death.

Nothing would look the same if she was given a mercy she was unworthy of. Nothing would be the same. She did not know how she would find her way in that new world. A world without millions looking to her to lead them. A world without shouldering expectations placed on her since she had entered this world. A world without the need for revenge.

She would carry the weight of her failures, yes, but what would it look like to just…live? To be able to be there for Ashtine, not as her queen but as her friend, as she should have done from the very beginning. To be able to enjoy the rain when it fell. To be able to see the beauty in the mountains and the waves of the sea instead of constantly worrying about the kingdom beyond them. To work beside the people she had once ruled over, to live beside them, to be one of them. To not be as alone as she felt.

What would it look like to dare to dream again?

*Spend your time preparing, Talwyn.*

And for the first time since that throne room, instead of thinking about what she would do differently if she could go back in time, she started planning what she would do if she was given the chance to atone in some way other than death.

# CHAPTER 5
## CALLAN

C allan Solgard rushed down the halls of the castle following the directions he had written on a piece of parchment. He had overheard Commander Greybane telling Magdalena that Razik would be going to the continent to get Sawyer and Princess Ashtine after Prince Briar gave himself over to Alaric in exchange for the female he loved. But this exchange did not involve just Briar and Ashtine. It also involved the Tyndell siblings in exchange for the twin babes growing in Princess Ashtine's belly, and if Razik was going, Eliza was likely going.

He'd heard about that, too. That Eliza had become Razik's Source. From what he'd gathered over the last several weeks being among the Fae and Avonleyans, having a Source was rare and coveted. But it was also necessary for an Avonleyan to refill their power reserves quickly. This was part of the reason King Deimas and Queen Esmeray had separated the Fae from the Avonleyans all those years ago.

Except that the Avonleyans claimed *they* had put the Wards up to protect their kingdom and had to cut themselves off from the Fae as part of the cost.

To be honest, Callan wasn't sure what to believe anymore. The history he'd been taught during all his lessons was turning out to be wrong, or at the very least, not entirely accurate. But none of that was what had him rushing to catch the fire general before she left. He wanted to go back to his own continent.

He wanted to find Tava and keep her from her father, Lord Balam Tyndell, a Maraan Lord. The male wasn't even her real father. No, she and her brother were the last remaining descendants of Dalton and Octavia Middell, the last king and queen of Rydeon. Drake was the rightful heir to the throne, and Tava was the kingdom's princess.

And Scarlett had let them go back. Had taken Tava and Drake back herself when she'd Traveled Prince Briar across the Edria Sea.

Callan came to a stop outside a door and double checked the notes on the parchment to make sure he had the right rooms before he rapped on the wood. A set of guards had stopped him at one point, but as soon as he'd told them his name, they'd let him pass. He hadn't questioned why. Just thanked the gods for giving him this small bit of fortune as he'd raced along the corridors.

The door swung open, and Callan found himself face-to-face with the Hand-to-the-Avonleyan King. Razik looked him up and down once, his signature bored annoyance on his face, before he stepped aside without a word to let him enter. Knowing Eliza was his Source explained why he was likely here, but it was still somewhat surprising to find him in her actual rooms. There had always been such animosity between them.

Callan could hear noises coming from the adjoining bedchamber, and he turned to Razik. "Is she going with you?"

The male cocked his head to the side, his bright sapphire eyes unnerving in the way they studied him. "She is."

"Good," Callan replied, moving to the doorway. Before he stepped through, Eliza met him at the threshold, a pack in her hands. Her brows flew up when she nearly ran into him.

"Callan? What are you doing here?" she asked, recovering quickly from her surprise and brushing past him. She threw the pack at Razik with force, the male catching it with a faint smirk, before she turned back to give Callan her full attention.

"I want to go with you," Callan said, planting his feet. He was prepared to argue with the general until she relented. Not the smartest plan, but the only one he could come up with in such a short amount of time.

"You want to go with us to get Princess Ashtine?" she asked in confusion.

"No. I want you to take me with you to our continent, and if I cannot convince Tava to return with me, I will stay there."

Eliza's eyes widened in disbelief. "Callan," she sighed, her hands coming to her hips as she stared at him. "You cannot simply return to the continent. Not after everything we've gone through to keep you alive."

"Drake did," Callan argued. "Tava did. Briar did. They all went back to the continent even though it jeopardizes their lives."

"Lord Tyndell will not allow harm to come to Drake or Tava," Eliza said. "And Briar went back to protect the female he loves and his *children*. Did you even think about Eva when you came up with this idiotic idea?"

"Of course I did," Callan snapped.

"Really? You did? So, what is the plan then, Callan? Are you dragging her back to her death with you?"

"I spoke with Magdalena and Lynnea—"

"Magdalena is employed by the Greybanes. She is not a nursemaid. And Lynnea is scarcely past her first bleed. You cannot be serious," Eliza interrupted.

"Eva is safer here," Callan said.

"As are you," Eliza countered.

"But Tava is not safer there!" he cried.

Eliza clicked her tongue at him, crossing her arms. "So this is a repeat of Scarlett, then?"

"This is nothing like Scarlett," Callan snarled.

A brow arched. "No? You are not racing off after the woman you think you love to— Do what exactly? Protect her? How do you plan to do that against Maraans?"

"I saved your ass from a Witch, didn't I? I believe I even killed more seraphs than *you* did that day."

Eliza stilled, her arms falling to her sides. The look she sent him made him want to take a step back from the female, but he forced himself to stand there and hold her stare. "You think that because you fought and survived in *one* battle, you are ready to face them on your own? You were fighting with powerful Fae at your side, not to mention the Avonleyans with us that day. Yes, you saved my life, but battles are not about keeping score. We have each other's backs because we fight for the same cause, not to use it against one another in an argument."

"I am sorry, Eliza," he started. "I did not mean that—"

"Have you spoken to Scarlett about this?" she cut in.

"No," he ground out from between his teeth. "She did not speak to me before taking Tava back across the sea. According to her, going to trade herself for a babe was Tava's choice. This is mine."

"And by agreeing to it, I will take the fall," Eliza retorted. "I am the one who will be reprimanded for allowing you to go."

"For *allowing* me?" Callan repeated. "I am a king. No one *allows* me to do a godsdamn thing. If you refuse, I will find another way."

A huff of amusement sounded, and Callan turned. He'd forgotten Razik was here, which was a feat in and of itself.

"Scarlett is the only one who can let you out of these Wards, *your Majesty*," Razik drawled. "So it would appear you will indeed need the princess's approval."

"She is a queen," Eliza snapped at him.

Razik shrugged. "She is not *my* queen. She is my kingdom's princess."

Eliza muttered something under her breath that Callan could not hear, but the corner of Razik's mouth tilted up at whatever he heard.

"If Tava can be allowed to make her own choices, I should be given the same courtesy," Callan said.

"It is not me you need to convince," Razik replied. "But I agree nonetheless."

"You do?" Callan and Eliza said at the same time.

"You left Cyrus and Neve across the sea to keep the mortal kings safe," Eliza said, rounding on the male. "Now you are suddenly fine with Callan giving himself over to them?"

"I was not going to use them in negotiations without their say in how they went," Razik said. "They are, in fact, royalty. Just as Cethin and Scarlett are. If they choose that path themselves, that is their right, just as it was Drake and Tava's."

"You do not get a say in this matter," Eliza snapped at him. "This isn't politicking. This is *personal*, which you have already stated to me you do not factor into your decision-making." The male arched a brow at her, his arms folding across his chest, but he didn't say another word. She turned back to Callan. "I know you care for her, Callan. I see that. I know it is different than Scarlett, but you cannot just go back there and give yourself over."

"I am not giving myself over," Callan interjected. "I am going to get Tava. It would be expected. She is my betrothed."

"I think the ruse is up," Eliza muttered, her hands fisting in the sleeves of her tunic.

"It is not a ruse. Not any longer."

"Does Scarlett know this?"

"I do not know. However, I doubt the knowledge would have changed her actions," he answered bitterly.

"True," Eliza agreed. "But you put your entire kingdom in jeopardy by doing this."

"Only if I am caught," Callan argued.

Eliza huffed a humorless laugh. "And if you are? Who will save you, Callan?"

"Who will save Drake and Tava?"

"Lord Tyndell will not let anything happen to them," Eliza repeated. "For whatever reason, he has protected them for the last two decades. I can only imagine he will continue to do the same."

"To use them!" Callan said, his desperation rising. "If no one else will go aid them, then I will."

"And your kingdom?"

"Will stand with them," Callan said instantly.

"You are not on the throne right now, Callan. You have no forces to command. I do not understand why you do not get this."

Before he knew what he was doing, Callan was advancing on Eliza.

"No!" Eliza cried out, flames flying from her palm, but not at him. At Razik.

Callan hadn't registered the snarl that had come from the male. He looked over at him to find his eyes shifted to vertical pupils and the faint outline of scales creeping along his flesh, but he had stilled, shielding against her flames. Eliza was tense, her eyes darting between him and Razik. Callan immediately took a step back from the fire general, but the rage he felt was still flooding through him. He couldn't even call it rage. It was desperation at this point. He took a deep breath, trying to calm everything he was feeling and push it down.

"Explain to me," he said through gritted teeth, "why when it is Sorin going for Scarlett or Briar going for Ashtine, no one says a word. All plans are paused, and everything is dropped to accommodate them. But when I wish to do the same for someone that *no one* is going after, it is up to someone else as to whether or not I am *allowed* to go."

"I am sorry, Callan," Eliza said, pity filling her grey eyes as she watched him.

"Do you say that because you feel sorry for me, or because you will not do a godsdamn thing to help me?" Callan sneered.

"You need to speak to Scarlett about this."

"And if I can convince her?"

"I think you will be hard pressed to do so, but if she agrees, I will not be the one to stand in your way."

Callan stood and watched the children run around the Coventry Estate. There wasn't much time. He had worked out a plan to catch Scarlett off guard. He would show up ready to leave. That wouldn't give her much of a chance to debate things with him. He would go and get Tava because he couldn't just sit around here, behind these Wards, and do *nothing* while she was risking her life. What kind of king would that make him? What kind of king did it make him that he ran at all?

But that plan also meant he needed to say goodbye to Eva.

He'd spoken with Lynnea again, and he had just come from speaking with Hale. The Toreall King had sworn to watch over her as if she were his own sister when Callan had explained what had happened and where he was going.

"When it comes to it, Toreall will stand with you," Hale had said.

"Know that when we are all back on our thrones, we have an alliance."

Callan wasn't sure when the last time was that the three mortal kingdoms had been so united, but knowing that at the end of all of this, that alliance would stand? It made this even more imperative because that alliance would only stand if Drake was also back on the throne. If the Maraans retained even one mortal throne, the alliance of two kingdoms would not be enough, especially with Rydeon separating Windonelle and Toreall.

Of course, nothing would be enough if the Fae Courts fell.

"Hi, King Callan."

Callan looked down to find Tula looking at him, a wooden sword in her hand.

"Hello, Tula. Do you know where Eva is?"

Tula nodded her head, blond curls bouncing with the movement. Her baby blue eyes were studying him, and he wasn't sure how a child so small made him want to squirm under her scrutiny.

"Do you know where Rayner is?" she asked.

"I do not."

"Oh."

She continued to study him, and Callan found himself shuffling his feet awkwardly. "Can you take me to Eva?"

"Sure!" she exclaimed, her eyes brightening. She reached up and grabbed his hand, tugging him along behind her. She had sheathed the sword in a small sword belt she had buckled around her little waist.

"Your necklace is very pretty," Callan said.

Tula looked up at him again, her smile wide as she reached up with her free hand, fingering the adornment. "Thank you. Scarlett and Sorin made it for me, but Rayner made it extra special."

"Oh?"

She nodded her head, her face going serious. "So he can always come to me if I need help. Like on the ship with the bad flying men."

Callan had heard that Rayner had been particularly savage that day. There were rumors that he had pulled out organs with his bare hands. He hadn't realized that had been because of Tula.

"He said he has to leave for a little while," she said. Her tone had faltered, but there was a look of determination on her little face, as though she were willing herself not to cry.

"He will be back soon," Callan said reassuringly.

"Do you know where he is going?"

"To get Princess Ashtine. She needs his help," Callan answered.

Tula didn't say anything else, appearing to get lost in thought about what he had said. He didn't have time to contemplate that though when she pointed across the gardens to where Eva was playing with a jump rope and a couple of other children.

"Thank you, Tula," he said, releasing her hand.

"You're welcome," she sang in that way that little girls do.

Eva saw him when he was halfway to her, dropping the jump rope handle she held and racing towards him. He caught her as she leapt up into her arms.

"I thought I would not see you until dinner," his sister said when he lowered her back to the ground.

He crouched down to look into her face. Taking her hands in his, he said, "Something has happened, and I am going to be gone for a bit."

A frown formed on Eva's mouth as she processed what he said. He reached up to tuck a strand of light brown hair behind her ear, brushing a small blue and yellow insect from her shoulder as he did so. "Where are you going?" she asked.

"Lady Tava needs my help."

"Is she all right?"

"For now," he replied, squeezing her fingers in his. "But King Hale and Lynnea will look after you while I am gone."

"How long will you be gone?"

He could see the tears welling in her eyes, and it had him second-guessing himself. "Hopefully only a day or two, but I cannot say for sure."

"But you will come back for me?" she asked, a tear slipping free.

"Of course, Eva," he said, tugging her into his arms. "I will come back for you." He ran a hand down her hair, feeling her tears soaking into his tunic. "Part of being a king is making hard choices," he murmured. "When our friends need help, we must help them, and part of being a princess is being brave." He pulled her back so he could see her face. He swiped his thumbs across her cheeks. "Can you be brave for me again, Eva?"

She nodded as more tears slid down her face. "But what if… What if you do not come back? Who will take care of me, Cal? I do not wish to live with King Hale."

"Scarlett will make sure you are taken care of, Eva," Callan said, pulling her back into his chest. He knew she would. Even if she was furious with him for doing this, Scarlett would watch over her. "I promise you will not be forgotten. You will be taken care of, but Tava and I will come back for you."

"Are you going to marry Lady Tava?" she asked, her voice muffled against his shoulder.

"Yes, Eva," he replied, running his hand down her hair again. "Yes, I am. And when this is all over, the three of us are going to live happily ever after. Just like in the stories Mother used to read to you."

"Tava still reads them to me," Eva whispered.

He closed his eyes at her words, sighing into her hair as he stood, bringing her up with him. "Do you want to stay here with your friends?" She shook her head against his shoulder. "Where would you like to go?"

"Home."

"I can take you back to the estate—"

"Home," she interrupted. "I wish to go *home*, Callan."

"I know, Eva," he said thickly. "Soon. I promise we will go home soon. This will all be over soon."

And in one way or another, it would be. Maybe it wouldn't turn out like he'd just promised her it would. Maybe he wouldn't come back, but he'd let her live inside a bubble of happiness for as long as he could. Enough of her innocence had been lost in that throne room when she'd had to watch the murder of their parents. He'd do whatever it took to keep her from growing up in a world ruled by the Maraan Prince that had done that to her. So he'd go get Tava, and then they would stand with the Fae. The very beings who they'd feared for centuries. He might hate Scarlett for taking Tava across the Edria, but if fighting alongside her would give Eva that future he'd just promised, then that's what he would do. Even if he wasn't around to see it.

# CHAPTER 6
# CYRUS

"*Y*ou look sad."

Cyrus looked up to find a beauty with dark red hair smiling down at him. He hadn't heard her come in, too lost in thoughts of a town that sat at the edge of the sea. He reached for her, wrapping an arm around her waist and tugging her into his lap. She laughed softly, nestling against his chest where she fit perfectly against him.

"I could never be sad with you around, Red," he said, nuzzling into her neck and planting small kisses along the column of her throat.

"Eliza has red hair too, you know," she said breathily, her head tilting to give him better access.

"Thia, if I called Eliza 'Red,' she'd string me up by my balls," he deadpanned, pausing to look into her hazel eyes. The flecks of gold in them reflected the setting sun from the balcony of their room. "Besides, hers is more of a red-gold. Yours is true red. The color of flames."

"You've put a lot of thought into the shade of my hair, Cyrus," she said, amusement in her tone.

"I put a lot of thought into everything about you," he murmured onto her skin.

She hummed in response, letting him move down her neck to the hollow of her throat. Her fingers dragged through his hair, and he felt her curl them, gently tugging him back by the scalp.

"It is okay to miss him, Cyrus."

*"I don't miss him," he said quickly. "How could I miss anyone when I have you? You're all I need, Red."*

*"I know what day it is," she replied quietly. Her fingertips skated along his jaw, gently tilting his face up to hers. "It's okay to miss him, even if it is your fault he is gone."*

*"What?" he said, jerking back from her.*

*She looked down at him, that same serene smile on her face. "You could have done more to save Merrik."*

*"Thia, I…"*

*This wasn't right. Something was wrong.*

*Cyrus shook his head, clearing his thoughts. He must have imagined what she'd just said.*

*"What could I possibly have to be sad about when the Fates have gifted me you, Thia?" he whispered, pulling her down to taste her lips, suddenly desperate to feel her, to feel something.*

*"I wonder the same thing," Thia murmured against his mouth. "You certainly do not deserve me."*

*Cyrus froze. "I…I know I do not deserve you, Thia." He didn't know what else to say. He didn't know how to deal with the emotions crawling up from the depths of his soul. Thia always helped subdue them. She didn't do…this.*

*"I think the Fates made a mistake," he mumbled. "I don't deserve you, but they gave you to me anyway. What if they realize their error and try to take you back someday?"*

*"Of course they made a mistake," Thia sneered, her features twisting into something he had never seen on her face before. Cold. Disgusted. Cruel. "My prayers to the Fates are that they release me from this torment sooner rather than later."*

"Stop. Doing. That," Cyrus gasped. His hands were buried in his chestnut hair, and he tugged at the roots. The pain sometimes grounded him, helped him remember what was real.

It did not help this time.

*Of course they made a mistake.*

He lifted his face from his knees. He was huddled in the corner of the room as far away from the cell in the Underwater Prison as he could get. Not that it mattered. The Sorceress had his blood. He could be in the Fire Court, and she could still fuck with him. He'd tried to leave once, to go up the stairs that would lead to other areas of the prison.

She'd made him relive Thia's death over and over for hours.

He'd come out of that nightmare curled in on himself next to a puddle of vomit. He hadn't attempted to leave this space again.

Cyrus caught her violet stare, her lips curving up slightly as she watched him. She had always been as pale as a spirit of the After, but there almost seemed to be some color to her skin now, as if torturing him with his own demons fed her soul somehow. Her long, black hair hung around her shoulders in straggly strands. The beige shift she wore made the splatters of blood on it stand out sharply. Splatters of his blood from when she would dip her finger into the vial Alaric had given her. Small drops from when she would draw Marks on the wall that allowed her to see into his mind.

This is what she did now. She would dig and turnover all the darkest corners of his soul, searching for the things that haunted him. The things that would break him. Except she'd changed tactics the last few times. Instead of pulling the gut-wrenching memories to the fore-front of his mind and trapping him there, she had begun finding all the good ones. The Sorceress had started taking the treasured memo-ries, the ones that let him breathe when he felt like he was suffocating, and tainting them. The cherished memories of Merrik and Thia were becoming stained with grief and cruelty, and his greatest fear was that she would leave him with nothing. That there would be nothing good left in his mind of Merrik and Thia. The only good parts of himself. She was taking them all and leaving him empty and broken and lost in the darkness.

"Would you like to make a bargain, pretty Fire Fae?" the Sorceress asked.

"No," he gritted out.

*He stood in a small flat, everything they owned in this one room. Ratty old blankets were in a corner where they slept. A trunk with clothes they shared. A small table with mismatched chairs.*

*Cyrus took a deep breath, the smell of the sea filling his senses as the sun shone in through the window. Merrik would be back soon, and they'd be going out to pick pockets and steal some breakfast. At the thought, his stomach grumbled. They'd been too busy plotting a big job last night and had forgotten to nick dinner.*

*He heard footfalls on the stone steps a few moments before the wood slab they had crafted into a door creaked open, and Merrick came through it. A dimple appeared when he smiled, a mischievous thing that matched the glint in his green eyes. A hand dipped into his pocket, and he pulled out a handful of coin, tossing them onto the table.*

*"Good haul," Cyrus said, swiping up a coin and rolling it between his knuckles.*

*"It's all right," Merrik replied, pulling his tunic over his head and tossing it to the side before collapsing onto the blankets.*

*"Get up," Cyrus said, nudging him with his foot. "We got food to steal."*

*Merrik waved him off. "Bring me back some bread."*

*"You need more than bread," Cyrus deadpanned, nudging him harder. "Get up, Merrik."*

*"You don't need me to steal bread, Cy," Merrik grumbled, pulling the one flat pillow they had over his face.*

*"True. Maybe I just want you."*

*Merrik huffed a laugh into the pillow.*

*"To come with me, you perv," Cyrus said, nudging him again. "Get up. I'm hungry."*

*"I knew saving you that day was a mistake," Merrik muttered.*

*Cyrus rolled his eyes. "Stop bitching, and get moving."*

*Merrik moved the pillow off his face to look up at Cyrus. "You think I'm joking? You're a pain in my ass."*

*"Yeah, yeah."*

*"My life was better without you in it."*

*"Stop being a dick."*

*"You're always around. Always here. Always in my space."*

*"You wanted me to stay."*

*Merrik scoffed at him. "No one wants you, Cyrus. Your own mother didn't even want you."*

*Cyrus flinched. "Then why did you help me that day?"*

*"Good question. I ask myself that every time I drag myself back here, knowing you're waiting here. Momentary lapse in judgment that I'm paying for daily."*

*"Merrik—"*

*"Go get your fucking food, Cyrus," Merrik sighed, rolling away from him. "In fact, stay gone all day. I can at least pretend I found a way to go back in time and let those market guards have you."*

A string of curse words left this mouth when the Sorceress let him out of his mind this time. That wasn't how that memory had happened. They'd spent the entire day together. They'd stolen so much food they hadn't needed to leave their flat for three days. They'd ate and slept and fucked and somehow still managed to finalize plans for that job.

The job that would get Merrik killed just two weeks later.

"I thought we were becoming friends, Gehenna," Cyrus rasped, reaching for a waterskin. They brought him one when they brought them food, but it was sporadic. He didn't know if it was day or night. He didn't know if he'd been down here for one day or three. He lost track of all time while the Sorceress had her fun.

"Do not call me that," she chided. "You know not to do that."

"You're already torturing me, Gehenna. Not sure what else you're going to do from in there," he replied after taking a drink in an effort to clear his mind.

"Funny, funny Fire Fae," the Sorceress sang, moving up to the bars. Her fingers curled around them, and she pressed her face to the shirastone, a slight wince pinching her features.

"Doesn't that hurt?" Cyrus asked, tipping his head back against the wall. Sometimes he could get her to talk for quite some time. It gave him a much needed reprieve.

"Not as much as nightstone," she answered.

"What's the difference?"

"The Legacy created shirastone to contain Fae. Nightstone was created to contain those more powerful. It drains one's power instead of simply subduing it."

"Interesting."

"Quite."

"Is there anything worse than nightstone?"

"That is a matter of perspective."

"That seems to be a favorite phrase of yours."

The Sorceress smiled at him. "But it is true, yes?"

"Is there anything that *you* find worse than nightstone?" Cyrus amended.

"There is not much worse than nightstone," she answered, a finger beginning to trace one of the bars. "But deathstone does more than drain one's power. After it takes your magic, it drains your life-force. It is a specialty of the Firsts."

"Sounds like a painful way to die."

Her violet eyes brightened with the madness of being locked up for centuries. "Who said anything about death? It drains you to the very precipice of death, but never lets you cross into the After. Much can happen in the in-between."

"That is…horrific."

"Isn't it, though?" she sighed wistfully. Then her eyes narrowed on him, as if she had suddenly recalled who she was speaking with. "Are you ready to make a bargain?"

"No," he answered quickly.

"You know there are worse things than my bargains."

"I am aware," he muttered, trying to mentally prepare himself for the next memory she was going to taint.

"Many unnecessary sacrifices have been made in efforts to avoid bargains with me."

"Can't imagine why."

"Me either," the Sorceress said with a shrug. Her hand dropped to her side, fingers slipping into a pocket where she kept the vial of his blood.

"Wait!"

"Yes?"

"A story," he said, scrambling to hold on to this moment of peace a little longer. "You have not told me a story in a while. I quite enjoy your stories."

"You do?" she asked eagerly, hands coming back to the bars as she pressed herself as close as she could to them.

"Yes, of course," he answered quickly.

"I can tell you one of betrayal."

"That sounds…nice," Cyrus said, debating whether this was indeed a good idea.

"In all things there must be balance," she started, and he loosed a breath of relief when the story started the same way the others had. "When the balance tips, who must pay the price? She was supposed to be his, but she chose another."

"You fault Serafina for falling in love with Arius instead of Achaz?" Cyrus asked.

"What is love?" the Sorceress replied. "Love changes the course of the realms. It upsets the balance. *They* upset the balance."

"Arius and Serafina?"

"They upset the balance. They could have ended one war, and instead started another. And now they must pay the price to right it," the Sorceress continued. "He hunts them. All life they created— together and separately. He will not rest until not one remains, until dreams are gone and death is dead. Not until they have answered for their betrayal. But there are many realms. He could not find them all on his own, so he created new life."

"The seraphs?" Cyrus asked, trying to piece together everything she was saying.

"They aid him, but he created *more*," the Sorceress said, her smile widening. "He created the Hunters. Night and shadows thought she could hide them behind the mirrors, but she cannot outsmart him. Oh, no." She tipped her head back, an eerie laugh coming from her throat. "Her own flesh and blood let the Hunters into this world, into her own kingdom, and when the gateway is unlocked, they will return and tell him what they have learned. Then he will come for them all, and the Maraan Prince shall pay for his failure unless he can fix his errors before he arrives."

"Who are the Hunters?" Cyrus asked.

"*What* are the Hunters," the Sorceress corrected, her head tilting as she began studying him once more.

"What are the Hunters?" Cyrus agreed.

"You do not know?"

Cyrus shifted on the ground. "No?"

"But you were across the Edria," she said, watching him carefully. "The Cursed King did not tell you?"

"Tell us what?" Cyrus asked, unease creeping up his spine at her referring to Cethin as 'the Cursed King.'

Her lips tilted again. "Perhaps he will not need to come here after all."

Cyrus was silent, trying to think of how to pose his next question in a way that would keep her talking, but she spoke again first.

"Would you like to make a bargain?"

"No," he said immediately.

"I will tell you of the Hunters if you tell me where my spell book is," she continued as though he had not spoken.

"No," he repeated.

Her lips pursed, and her shoulders fell in disappointment. "We were having a pleasant conversation, and you ruined it."

He'd been nibbling on some stale bread while she spoke. He didn't eat a lot, never knowing what kind of nightmare she was going to throw him into next. At her obvious displeasure, he set the bread off to the side.

"Would you like to hear another story?" she asked suddenly.

And he could tell by the look on her face this was a bad idea. But would it be worse than her dragging him back into a memory or Merrik or Thia? He doubted it.

"Sure," he said, tipping his head back against the wall and closing his eyes. "Tell me a happy one this time."

"A happy one?" she repeated. "Like a story of *love*?"

"Fuck," Cyrus muttered. He should have known better.

"In all things there must be balance," she started, and he relaxed a bit when the story started the same way the others had. "Love is no different. It has the power to create balance, but more often creates chaos."

That…was actually a fairly accurate statement when he really thought about it.

"When the gods began to have offspring with the mortals, the Legacy came into being. Some said they loved their mortal partners. Others simply did not want the other gods to have something they did not. But as more and more Legacy were born, the gods began to fear being overthrown by their children."

"I thought this was supposed to be about love?" Cyrus said.

"I am getting to that part," the Sorceress hissed. "They put limits on the powers of the Legacy, and they made them dependent on others to maintain that power."

He knew this story, knew how the Fae came into being, but if she was talking, he wasn't suffering, so he let her continue.

"Together with the Witch Goddesses, the Fae were created and given their gifts in gratitude for agreeing to watch over and aid their children. But their gifts were not the only thing they gave to the Fae."

Cyrus opened his eyes at that, dipping his chin to see the Sorceress better. The faint smirk on her lips told him whatever she was about to say wasn't going to be good. If he'd thought a story would give him a reprieve from her torture, he was clearly mistaken. He sucked in a sharp breath, waiting for her to continue.

"They were given twin flames."

He released the breath in a rush. But he did so too soon.

"The twin flame bond was a *gift* to both the Fae and the Legacy. A bond of *love* to link the two together. Some found it a blessing, others a curse."

But that meant—

"Thia was Fae."

"Was she?" the Sorceress asked, that faint smirk growing wider.

"Yes," he said firmly.

"Then she was not your twin flame."

"The bond was Anointed. If she had not been my twin flame, the Anointing would have failed," he gritted out.

"Then she was not Fae," Gehenna sang lightly.

"Stop," he hissed. "You are lying."

He refused to let her take this from him. She could take his good memories and alter them. She could trap him in his nightmares and make him relive them over and over again, but not this. Even if she ruined every memory he had, he could still cling to the fact that he had once had a twin flame. Had once known love on such a deep level, there were no words in any language to describe it.

The Sorceress clicked her tongue at him. "I have not lied to you once, Son of Fire. Why would I start now? What do I have to gain from it?"

"I do not believe you," he said, trying to steady his breathing.

*"You need a Source, Cass. For all the reasons Cethin said and more. Scarlett is worried. We're all worried. If you don't want it to be me, fine, but we need to find you one."*

*Cassius ran a hand down his face. "Can we talk about this later? I just need some time to think."*

"So think with me," Cyrus said, moving to the small sofa against the wall and sinking down onto it.

Cassius sighed, settling back down at the desk without another word. But he didn't tell Cyrus to leave, which meant he'd eventually say something. Cyrus just needed to wait for it.

When he finally did speak a half-hour later, it was certainly not what he was expecting him to say.

"You know you never deserved a twin flame, right?"

Cyrus had been absent-mindedly tossing a ball of fire into the air and catching it. At Cassius's words, he dropped the damn thing, singeing the rug beneath his feet before he could put it out. He cursed under his breath.

"You're probably right," he replied thickly, prodding at the burn mark with the toe of his boot. "But we don't get to choose what we deserve. We only get to make the best out of what the Fates decide we get."

"Maybe," Cassius mused, and Cyrus heard him shift in his chair. "But you have to realize they made a mistake by giving you a twin flame, especially after how things ended with Merrik."

Something was wrong. This was...wrong. Cassius would never say something like this to him.

But he had told him to leave.

Cassius pushed to his feet, crossing the room in a few long strides. He stood over him, forcing Cyrus to tilt his head back to look up at him. "You call me self-sacrificing, but you? You just keep taking and taking from people because you think you are deserving of it."

"Stop." He meant to say it with some bite behind the word, but it came out as more of a pained rasp.

Cassius bent down, bracing his hands on the back of the sofa on either side of Cyrus, bringing his face inches from his. "Merrik and Thia were the cost of you claiming something you should have never had. Do you know what I've been researching in that book, Cyrus? Twin flames." Cassius's mouth twisted into a cruel smirk as he brought his face closer to Cyrus's. "Twin flames happen between an Avonleyan and a Fae. You claimed something that was never yours to have, and Thia paid the price. How many more people will you sacrifice? If you were anyone else, I would be selfish like you all keep telling me to be. But that's the thing. I am being selfish. I want a Source bond with anyone but you. And if you can't see that all you do is damage everyone around you, then I will keep reminding you until you believe it."

"Stop," Cyrus gasped, feeling the tears trail down his face. "Stop," he whispered again. "Leave those ones. Please."

The Sorceress hadn't done this yet. She had not touched one memory of Cassius. Not a single one. She had clearly been saving them for this exact moment. But the way she had just altered that memory was already sinking into his soul and taking root. It didn't matter how much he tried to rationalize with himself. The damage was already done.

*All you do is damage everyone around you.*

"You will let me play with memories of everyone but him?" she asked, her head tilting in curiosity. Her fingers curled around the bars once more. "I am intrigued, pretty Fire Fae."

He knew it seemed odd, but Merrik and Thia were in his past. He had once thought Cassius could be his future in some way or another. But now...

*You just keep taking and taking from people because you think you are deserving of it.*

He shook his head, trying to get the words out of his head, but they kept replaying over and over. And it was his voice he kept hearing say them.

*"Get out," Cassius said, his voice low and gravelly. His pupils had shifted, eyes glowing. "Get the fuck out."*

*Cyrus stared at him for a long moment before turning and stalking to the door, but right before he pulled it open, he looked over his shoulder. "I was coming here to tell you that after we got back from the Southern Islands, I wanted to go to Aelyndee with you. For the first time since Thia, you made me feel seen. I never want to step foot in Aelyndee again, but for you, I would have. I would have jumped through every godsamn hoop if you'd have let me."*

*"Get out," Cassius said again. "I want nothing to do with you. I never did. I used you for your blood, and I tolerated you for Scarlett. That is no longer necessary."*

"Stop!" Cyrus cried out, his chest heaving as he gasped for breath. He couldn't get enough air into his lungs. He thought he could hold out. He thought he could be strong enough to withstand her, to keep his family safe. But he wasn't. He was weak. He couldn't do this. Not if she started messing with those memories. He was already too far gone. Losing those memories would tip him over the edge.

"Are you ready to make a bargain?" Her voice drifted over to him, soft and coaxing.

All he did was damage everyone around him. They would expect nothing less at this point.

"Fae of Fire," she whispered again.

He opened his eyes, connecting with her stare. "Yes," he rasped. "I will tell you where your spell book is if you leave my memories of him be."

Triumph danced in her violet eyes. "Oh no, pretty Fae," she said, manic glee dripping in her tone. "The price to leave those memories alone is much steeper."

*Of course they made a mistake.*

*No one wants you, Cyrus.*

*If you can't see that all you do is damage everyone around you, then I will keep reminding you until you believe it.*

"Name the cost," he said hoarsely, fingers digging into his scalp, hating himself for those three words, knowing they would indeed damage everyone he loved.

# CHAPTER 7
# SCARLETT

Scarlett took a deep breath outside of the rooms that Cyrus had claimed at the Avonleyan castle. She stretched her neck from side-to-side before rolling her shoulders. She had been eating with Sorin when Azrael and Rayner had come back to their suite to go over a few things before they went to the continent to get Ashtine. They were still finalizing things with Sorin when she had excused herself to come find Cassius. She'd meet with them again in a few hours to see them off and get any last-minute updates. But right now her soulmate needed her, and she needed him to know she was here, that he wasn't alone.

Cassius. Then Ashtine. Then Cyrus and Neve.

She had to take things one step at a time. If she tried to think about everything at once, she felt like she was drowning.

Cassius first.

She raised her hand, knocking lightly on the door twice before she pushed it open.

"Cass?" she called softly, stepping into the room. She pushed the door shut behind her, leaning against it, her hands behind her back.

He was here, exactly as she'd known he would be. He sat on the sofa before the fireplace, staring blankly into the empty space. It was cold in here, and with a thought, flames sprang to life in the hearth.

He didn't even blink. There was an empty liquor glass on the small table beside the sofa, his eye patch lying beside it. His shaggy brown hair hung in his face, and he was shirtless, his tunic on the floor. It appeared shredded.

"Your wings appeared?" she asked quietly.

"I do not—" He paused, his entire body seeming to shudder. He released a long breath, steadying himself. "I do not have much control right now. He... He steadied me when things felt out of control. I was hoping being in his rooms would give me some of that, but it has not."

He still hadn't looked at her, but she nodded anyway. Silence fell again, and she looked around the space. It was clean and tidy. It looked like no one had even stayed in here. Other than the open decanter of alcohol near the window, it appeared to be a guest suite waiting for an occupant.

"He slept on the sofa in my rooms," Cassius said. "Or sometimes he'd take the bed, and I'd take the sofa."

Her attention darted back to him just in time to see his gaze shift from her back to the hearth.

She cleared her throat. "We're going to get him back, Cassius."

"We both know he will not be well when we do, Scarlett," he replied, reaching for the liquor glass and then seeming to suddenly remember it was empty. He clenched his hand into a fist, bringing it to the arm of the sofa. "Think of all the things Alaric did to us. You think he won't do the same to him?"

He wasn't wrong. Alaric could, and likely would, do all manner of things to Cyrus and Neve. She knew time was of the essence. But she also knew that until Sorin's power was back, she was weakened without a Source. She would have one chance when she went to get Cyrus. That mission would not be about killing Alaric. It would be about surviving him and getting her family back here safely. It was never that simple with Alaric though. There was no preparing for him because he was anything but predictable. The only thing predictable about the Maraan Prince was that you learned to be prepared for anything and everything, and even that was rarely enough.

But the next time she faced off with him? When Saylah fulfilled her end of their deal and Sorin was back at her side at full power?

Then she was bringing the war to her former Master, and only one of them was walking away.

She pushed off the door, making her way over to Cassius. "You're right," she replied, lowering down onto the sofa beside him. "We don't know in what state we will find him, but, having been on the receiving end of Alaric's wrath numerous times, we will know the best way to help him. We can remind him that we are here. You can remind him that..."

"That I love him?" Cassius supplied bitterly. "I told him to get the fuck out, Scarlett. He's not going to believe a damn thing I have to say. Why would he?"

"Do you?" Scarlett asked. "Do you love him?"

Cassius blew out a long breath, brushing his hair back from his face. "I don't know."

"Of course you know, Cassius," she scoffed. "You wouldn't take blood from anyone else. He stays in your rooms. He grounds you and helps you find control when you feel like you have none. You wouldn't take him as a Source because you didn't want him to feel trapped, but you refused to take anyone else."

"And look where that got me," Cassius interrupted. "Forced to take another Source."

"You're not taking another Source. Not if you don't want to."

"I don't have a choice."

"You do, Cass," she said, reaching over and taking his hand. "I am giving you this choice. I am sorry for trying to force you to do anything otherwise. We have had enough choices stolen from us. If Cyrus is the Source you want, then we will wait and see if he is still willing."

"I don't deserve him."

"That is for him to decide." Cassius made a noise of acknowledgment. She reached up, gently turning his face to hers. "But Cassius, coming from someone who is the farthest thing from being deserving of a crown, the loyalty of numerous Courts, and a twin flame, it will take more than a fight to drive Cyrus away from you. I know him. He does not walk away. It will be far harder to forgive yourself and accept his forgiveness if it's offered."

"We were never offered such a thing nor taught how to give it, let alone receive it," Cassius replied, turning away from her.

"I know. He molded us into the perfect specimens for his plans. Take without remorse. Avenge the smallest of grievances. Meet every problem with wrath and a dagger. We lash out at those who want us, and try to do everything ourselves. We were taught we were stronger alone, could depend on no one, and to not even trust ourselves. I won't deny how hard it has been to change. But Cass, you? You made sure the light never died, even when Juliette, Nuri, and I were nothing but the Wraiths he had trained us to be. I did not deserve you, and yet you stayed. Guardian or not, you stayed, Cass."

He had turned to face her fully as she spoke, and when she finished, he pulled her into him. She squeezed him back just as tightly. "Our entire lives we did not know who we were. For years we did not know where we belonged, and now we do. Now we fight to keep it. We get back up, and we fight because we are deserving of the good as much as we are deserving of the bad. So get up, Cassius. Cyrus needs us. He has been there for us when we needed him most, and we will not fail him now."

"When did you become so wise, Seastar?" he murmured into her hair.

She shifted onto her back, her head in Cassius's lap, staring up into his eyes— one chocolate brown, the other a milky white where Alaric had tortured him with shirastone. "I think it's the shoes," she answered, wiggling her feet. They were clad in gold silk shoes while the rest of her was adorned in black with numerous daggers and knives.

"You look ridiculous parading around in those with weapons strapped to you."

"They are incredibly comfortable though. I'll change into boots before we see the others off to get Ashtine."

A comfortable silence fell between them. Cassius had an arm stretched along the back of the sofa, the fingers of his other hand drumming every once in a while on the arm. It was a scene she was all too familiar with, and despite everything they were facing, it brought a sense of comfort to her. It seemed to silence all her doubts, and she drew a certain strength from him. This was a different kind of strength than what she gained from Sorin or the others. This was a strength born of nearly two decades together. He had been through nearly every storm, every step, and when it had hurt to get back up, he had been there, pulling her to her feet and telling her to keep going. A soulmate through and through.

"I met my mother," she said quietly into the room.

Cassius's fingers stopped mid-drum. "And?"

"She is a goddess."

"We already knew that."

"She…"

Saylah had said a lot of things in the short time Scarlett had been in Shira Forest.

"She says if she leaves this world, the Maraans and seraphs will follow. Achaz will require it of them."

"Alaric will not simply leave after all he has done to gain control of this realm," Cassius said.

"Agreed. If he does not leave willingly, she said Achaz will send more to bring him back to his home world to face judgment for his failure."

"So Saylah and Alaric must leave this world?"

"Something along those lines."

"What aren't you saying, Scarlett?"

She was fiddling with a small knife, lightly twisting the point against the pad of her finger, but at his question, she sheathed it in her belt. She sat up, pushing to her feet. "Nothing. It will all be fine," she said with a small smile. "We will kill Alaric and send Saylah from this world when I retrieve the lock."

"When you are ready to talk, I am here," Cassius said, watching her carefully.

"I know. You are all right?"

Cassius nodded, getting to his own feet. "I will bathe and meet you to see off those going to the continent. Then we can plan out the mission to get Cyrus." She nodded, heading to the door until, "Scarlett." She paused, looking back over her shoulder at him. "Being a queen suits you." She felt her cheeks flush at his words. "You were born for this, Seastar. You are constantly fighting your destiny, but I think you are exactly where you need to be. I think the Fates may have been on your side all along."

Scarlett rushed along the hallways. She'd been trying to find Eliza to speak with her before she left for the continent. Azrael had informed her that Eliza was going along as Razik's Source. Scarlett wanted to check in with her friend before she left, but she couldn't find her. Now they were leaving soon, and she was out of time. She was meeting Sorin in the entrance hall so they could see everyone off. Frustration coiled in her. When they got back, she'd make sure to seek Eliza out as soon as possible.

Rounding a corner, she nearly ran into Callan. Her hand flew to her chest, shadows springing from her skin and hovering in her moment of surprise. Callan's eyes were wide, and he took a step back from her.

"By the gods," she gasped, but then— "Why do you have a pack?"

Callan's lips pressed together, and a muscle ticked in his jaw as he adjusted the pack on his shoulder.

"Callan?" she pressed, pulling her shadows back into herself.

He stood a little straighter, something in his hazel eyes hardening. "I am leaving with the group going to the continent."

Her head tipped to the side as she studied him, recognizing the stubbornness setting in. "What?"

"I am going to the continent with the others. To get Tava and to fight with the mortals."

"Tava wanted to go, Callan," she said slowly.

"And I want to go get her."

"You will drag her back here? Against her will?"

"No. I—" His brow furrowed for a moment, but his features twisted back into the anger she knew was driving his actions. "I will not let her put herself in danger. Someone needs to fight for her."

"You think I sent her to the continent without protection? Drake is with her. Prince Briar is with her."

"You did this to get Ashtine back," he snarled. "You placed Ashtine and her babes' well-being above Tava and Drake."

"No," Scarlett said calmly. "You are wrong. I tried to talk her out of it. Both of them. I told them we would find another way. I just needed some time, but they were adamant."

"And now?"

"I am working on it, Callan. I just need some more time."

"And when this trade is done? When Briar is no longer able to protect her? When she and Drake are back in Balam's hands?"

"I have taken measures to keep them protected until we can come for them, Callan. Despite what you seem to think of me as of late, I did not sacrifice them. I did not deem their lives any less important than anyone else's," she said, her temper beginning to slip.

"You could have waited to take them over. No one forced you to take them that very night," Callan seethed. "You could have waited—"

"I owed it to Briar to take him back. The female he loves is being held captive. She is carrying twins. His children. If you think Tava would let Ashtine remain in that state when she could do something about it, you do not know the woman you love very well. She would have found another way. She is clever. So maybe, just maybe, I took her back so you would hate me instead of her. Maybe I was trying to spare you the hurt of knowing she willingly sacrificed her own happiness with you for innocent children," Scarlett said. "I am many things, Callan, but I am not the villain in your story. No matter how much you wish I was."

Callan stared at her. He opened his mouth to say something, but snapped it closed just as quickly. And she could see it all there, shining in his eyes. The anguish. The desperation. The need to do *something*, even if that something was brash and reckless and likely to get him killed.

"I understand who Tava is to you, Callan," she said, her voice softening. "I understand Tava is to you who Ashtine is to Briar. Who Sorin is to me. But Ashtine is in Alaric's hands, while Tava returns to Lord Tyndell's. It is not ideal, but he will not harm Tava. He has kept them safe for years. He will not stop now, even if we do not know the reason. She will be safe until we can get her back, and as I said, I have already sent more protection until we can make that happen. I know why you feel the need to go, Callan. I do."

"But you will not allow it?" he said, some of that bravado deflating.

"You are a king, Callan," she said carefully. "I cannot keep you from doing something, but…"

"But you think it is a terrible idea," he finished for her.

A ghost of a smile danced across her lips. "Isn't it?"

Callan shoved his hands into his hair, pacing in a tight circle in front of her. "I cannot just sit here, Scarlett. I cannot just… Not while she is there, risking her life, doing something. I cannot…" He stopped, facing her fully once more. A hopelessness shone back at her, stark and desperate. "In the last months, I have watched my parents and my closest friends be slaughtered in front of me. I have fled my home, abandoned my people. I have *killed*. I cannot lose another, Scarlett. I cannot lose her, and I cannot sit here, safe behind Wards, while my people are taking the brunt of the anger aimed at you."

She was pushing up onto her tiptoes, wrapping her arms around him, and he was clinging to her. "I know it is a lot to ask of you, Callan, but can you trust me? Can you trust that I will fix all of this?"

"Can you?" he countered. "Can you fix all of it?"

"I am going to try," she replied, taking a step back. "I am trying."

"And I am still to simply sit here? Safe and protected? The coddled mortal prince now king?"

"A mortal king who has killed. Who has lost. Who has sacrificed. Doesn't sound like he is very coddled anymore, your Majesty." Her features twisted into something sad and heavy. "Soon you will be back on your throne, Callan. Soon you will be making the difficult decisions of prioritizing one person's wellbeing over another. Remember you will not always get it right. And when you have to choose between the lesser of two evils, some will hate you for it, but you will hate yourself more."

The two stared at each other for a long moment in that hallway. So different from what they had been. Lovers to strangers to friends. Wraith and Prince to Queen and King. Two royals trying to navigate their new roles. Neither of them knowing if they were ever doing the right thing. Trying to balance the needs of those they love with the needs of those they had been charged to protect. Trying not to drown while keeping their people above the turbulent waters. But he had never had to learn how to keep going through grief and trauma. He'd never had to be told to get back up because he'd never been knocked down. Not like the rest of them had. He was right. He'd been coddled. *She* had coddled him. Tried to protect him at all costs.

Maybe she shouldn't have.

Because now he'd been tossed into the sea himself without having learned how to swim. Without knowing how to keep going when everything you knew no longer was. And now he didn't have time to learn. Now he either needed to swim or drown.

Callan could be reckless. Not her kind of recklessness. Her kind of recklessness was calculated chaos. His kind of recklessness was driven by passion. He loved fiercely, obsessively. She knew that asking him to stay behind was asking him to go against every instinct warring inside of him right now. He wasn't Fae, but he was still a man, driven by the need to protect what he saw as his. He would need all of that when he was back on his throne. She didn't want to kill his beautiful recklessness, despite how naïve it sometimes made him, but he couldn't jump unless he learned to fly.

Or, at the very least, fall gracefully.

So instead of flat out refusing his request, she said, "I will make a deal with you, Callan. If you wish to go to the continent, I will not stop you."

"You won't?" Callan asked, eyeing her suspiciously.

Scarlett shook her head. "You deserve to make your own choices, just as Tava does. You were forced to flee for the Fire Court. You were forced to flee across the Edria. I will not stop you from leaving, but I ask that once you have seen Tava is well, you return with the others."

"And if she will not return with me?"

"Trust me to keep her safe, Callan," she answered. She held up her palm, shadows swirling, and when they receded, a vial sat in her palm. She held it out to him. "You remember how to use this?" He swallowed thickly, nodding. "Tava and Drake each possess one as well." His gaze snapped to hers. "I did not send them there with nothing, Callan, and I have sent more protection. I will continue to do so. They are not expendable to me. Trust me, and trust *her*."

He reached out tentatively, taking the vial of swirling black shadows, his eyes never leaving hers.

"Can you agree to stay with the Fae? No matter what happens? Stay with Eliza and Rayner and Azrael, and when they return to Avonleya, you return with them, even if Tava stays behind. Swear it to me, Callan. I have enough of my family to save right now. I do not wish to add you to that list."

"You believe this to be reckless," he stated, tucking the vial into a pocket of his jacket.

"Reckless is my middle name," she said with a wry grin, but it slipped from her face just as quickly. "I wish it hadn't rubbed off on you quite so much. But perhaps... Perhaps Windonelle will need a little recklessness on the throne when this is all said and done."

"And what am I to do back here? Sit on my ass until you decide I am ready to go back?"

"No, Callan. Build a rapport with Hale. Teach him about our continent. Teach him about his kingdom, your kingdom. Share your plans. See what he envisions." She shrugged. "You're a king, so be one."

She turned and headed back down the hall, now even later than she was before. Callan fell into step beside her, and she snuck a quick glance up at him. He seemed to be thinking through something, and when he tried to sneak a glance at her, she held his gaze. "Yes?" she asked, a brow arching.

"I..."

But he was interrupted by Kailia, who appeared when they rounded the corner. Scarlett and Callan both paused at the Avonleyan Queen's sudden appearance.

"The others are growing concerned," she said, amber eyes studying them. Her bow was over her shoulder, her black dress flowing around her ankles, and her feet were bare as always.

"I know. I'm late," Scarlett sighed.

"You are," she agreed. "May I speak with you briefly?"

"As was already stated, I am late."

"It will not take long."

Her gaze flicked to Callan. "I can let the others know you are on your way," he said, glancing down at Scarlett in question.

She sighed again, waving him off with a hand. "Fine."

When he was out of sight, Kailia moved a few steps closer, ashy footprints left in her wake. "You are upset with Cethin."

"Yes," Scarlett answered, watching the female warily.

"Why?" she asked, her head tilting and black hair slipping over a shoulder.

"Because he did not tell me everything he knew."

"Did you tell him everything you know?"

"That is not the point," Scarlett said incredulously. "I am the one being asked to find the lock and… He is not the one being tasked with nearly impossible feats."

"Tell me, your Majesty, when you keep things from those you love, why do you do so?"

"No," Scarlett gritted out. "You will not turn this around on me. He should have told me."

"Will Sorin feel the same when you tell him what you have learned?"

"How do *you* feel about it?" Scarlett countered.

"Cethin has already made arrangements for us. You would do well to do the same," Kailia said. "But Cethin is…upset that you are angry with him."

"He should be," she retorted.

"Know that the things he kept from you were to protect me. He would be annoyed to know I am speaking with you about this," she continued, as though Scarlett hadn't said anything. "He is the farthest thing from perfect, but I believe you are discovering the burden of maintaining a balancing act. Lean too far towards your family, and your people suffer. Lean too far the other way, and your family suffers. He is trying to maintain that balance, Scarlett."

Kailia disappeared amid smoke and ashes, and Scarlett pushed out a harsh breath, leaning against the wall. She was tired. So godsdamn tired. She needed to sleep. Her power was pushing at her being, aching to be used, but she had to keep it all locked up. She had to save it all for when they went to trade for Cyrus and Neve, but there was so much thrumming beneath her skin. The bit used to go to Shira Forest had done nothing to take the edge off after taking so much from Sorin. She slid down along the wall, tipping her head back. She knew she was late, but she just needed a moment to breathe.

One thing at a time. That's what she needed to do. Focus on just one thing.

But that was becoming impossible. No matter how hard she tried to stay focused on one thing, other things kept demanding her attention. Cethin. Callan. Kailia. It was piling up, and Kailia had been right. She was trying to balance it all, but all she was doing was collapsing beneath the weight of it.

"Scarlett?"

The sound of his voice nearly made her sob.

She opened her eyes to find Sorin lowered to a crouch before her. His hand came out, brushing stray hair from her face. "Callan said you were speaking with Kailia."

"I was."

"Are you all right?"

"How do you do it, Sorin?" she asked, her chest tight as anxiety clamped down on her. "How do you balance everything and everyone that needs your attention?"

"You are doing it, Scarlett," he answered gently, sympathy and understanding shining in his muted amber eyes. "You put one foot in front of the other. You prioritize. You delegate like you are by sending Luan and Rayner to get Ashtine."

"It doesn't feel like enough," she whispered. "It never feels like I am doing enough. I feel too inadequate to be ruling over so many. First it was two Courts. Now it is four. And now…" She paused, Sorin waiting patiently for her to gather her thoughts like he always did. "I always said I was not the one for this. Not because I did not think I could do it—that was never truly the issue—but because I am too fearful of failing everyone."

Sorin shifted, moving into the space beside her. He took her hand, lips grazing her knuckles, before he pressed her palm to his chest

"Breathe, Love." And she did. She took what felt like her first full breath since she'd returned from speaking with Saylah. She could feel his heart beating steadily beneath her palm, her own breathing naturally falling into rhythm with his. After a few moments, he said, "Scarlett, the moment you think you are doing enough? That is when you start to worry. The moment you stop feeling fearful of failing them? That is when you likely already are. Nothing about it is easy. This will not be the last time you will question everything you are and everything you are doing." Fingers gently gripped her chin, turning her face to his. "But remember, my love, you are never alone."

He leaned forward, closing the distance between their mouths. Lips brushed against hers, and she wished they could simply go back to their rooms and hide from the world. "Cassius told me I was becoming wise, but he has never experienced your profound monologues," she murmured.

Sorin huffed a laugh, leaning back and flicking her nose. Then he got to his feet, pulling her up with him. She started down the hall, but he tugged her back to him. His fingers brushed along her jaw. "Like the stars love the night, Scarlett."

"All the way through the darkness," she murmured back, pushing up onto her tiptoes to kiss him again. He interlaced their fingers, leading her down the hall. "Everyone is waiting?"

"They are," he confirmed.

"I was trying to find Eliza, then ran into Callan. He plans to go with them."

"That seems…foolish."

"It likely is, but we came to a compromise of sorts. There will be several Fae with him, plus Razik. He is a king of the realm. We let Tava and Drake make their own choices. I suppose he deserves the same courtesy."

"True. We will not always agree with the choices of other rulers," he replied thoughtfully, pushing open a door and ushering her through. "Such a wise queen," he teased.

"I would like it noted that I have been called wise twice in one day by two separate people." Sorin snickered. "I would also like it noted," she continued, ignoring him, "that I achieved the status of 'wise queen' in less than a year, while it took you centuries to become a wise old sage."

She heard him muttering under his breath as she flitted away from him, making her way over to Eliza. The general saw her coming and broke away from the crowd to meet her off to the side.

"You look unwell," Eliza said, grey eyes sizing her up.

"I am tired. That is all," Scarlett replied with a smile she knew Eliza could see right through. "But I was trying to find you. To ask how *you* are."

"Niara cleared me," Eliza said defensively.

"I do not mean your wound, although I am glad to know you have recovered. I mean with, well, everything. Nakoa. Becoming Razik's Source. All of it."

Eliza adjusted a buckle across her chest. "I am...adjusting."

"You are sure you have rested enough to be going? I am assuming Razik drew from you to fill his reserves for this mission."

"He did, but as his Source, doesn't it make more sense for me to go with him? If he drains his power while there, he will need me."

Scarlett couldn't argue with that. She just wanted some time with her friend. Such luxuries were clearly a thing of the past for the time being. "Callan told me he plans to go with you all to the continent."

Eliza's brows shot up. "He told you?"

"You knew?" Scarlett countered.

"He came to me earlier in the day. Asked if he could go with us. He assumed you'd fight him on it. I tried to tell him he was being an idiot, but he insisted."

Scarlett sighed. "You will stay with him? Watch over him?"

"I'm not going to simply let him walk up to the Tyndell Manor," Eliza drawled.

"We are already late, and you are wasting more time," called an irritated Azrael.

Scarlett wrapped Eliza in a tight hug. "Stay safe. When you return, I request an entire day without males, huddled beneath a blanket with chocolates and wine."

"Who am I to deny a queen?" she replied, her embrace just as tight.

The females walked over to the others, Eliza moving to speak with Sorin. Scarlett's attention fixed on Rayner. "Please try not to rip out anyone's spleen unless I am around to witness such a thing."

The Ash Rider's lips twitched. "As you wish, your Majesty."

She scowled at him. "Seriously. Stop that." Her attention skipped to Azrael. "You good, Azzy?" It was the Earth Prince's turn to scowl.

Her taunting smirk fell from her face as she stepped closer to him. "Thank you. For taking the lead on this."

"We will be in and out. Back by this time tomorrow," he reassured her.

She nodded, stepping back to Sorin's side at the same time she saw Razik break away from Cethin. She hadn't spoken to her brother since returning from Shira Forest, and when their gazes met briefly, she quickly looked away.

One thing at a time. After this group left, her next focus was Cyrus. Then sleep. Then Cethin. Assuming nothing else came up in the meantime. But, at the rate things were going, that was unlikely.

Those leaving all gathered around Razik, who was taking them to Anahita's Springs where Sawyer and Briar would meet them. The last person she locked gazes with before they disappeared was Callan.

It had not escaped her that he hadn't sworn to return with the others. She knew in the depths of her being he would not step foot in Avonleya again, and she prayed to the gods she had not just let him go to his death.

# CHAPTER 8
## ELIZA

They appeared on the edges of the Springs, the surroundings falling silent at their sudden appearance. She immediately dropped Razik's hand, stepping away from him. Eliza scanned the area out of instinct, breathing deep. Home. Or closer to it. Back on their own continent anyway.

She'd only been to Anahita's Springs one other time— when Sorin had arrows imbued as a gift for her when she had agreed to become the Fire Court General. The same arrows Cyrus had begged her to take with him on the last mission to this continent. She'd argued with him because she'd been bitter about not being able to go. They obviously hadn't helped anyway. He was stuck here until Scarlett brought Talwyn back to trade for him and Neve. If she had been with them, would she have found a way to keep this from being the outcome? She and Nakoa had always had an agreement that they would take care of each other's people, and not only had Cyrus been left there, so had Neve. It was a failure, no matter how logical the argument was that she needed to heal. It was a failure nonetheless.

"Where are they?" Eliza asked, scanning the area again. Unease was growing in her gut. It was too…something. Quiet. Calm. As if the land itself was holding its breath.

"Sawyer indicated they would meet us here," Azrael answered, fingers flexing. He was feeling it too. She could tell by the way the grass was vibrating at his feet.

"You think something is wrong?" Callan asked. She was glad to see his sword in hand. He never used to be prepared for an ambush. Always had the thing sheathed at his side. It took her a good week to break him of that habit, constantly reminding him it was more than an ornament for a pampered prince.

"Something certainly does not feel right," she replied, calling flames to her other hand, casting a soft glow around them. "Stay close to the others, Callan."

"Nothing is amiss," Rayner said, appearing from ashes. "But I also did not find Briar, Sawyer, or the Tyndells."

"Let's make our way into the Springs," Azrael said. "We will be a little more hidden there."

Eliza nodded, herding Callan in front of her. Azrael and Rayner led the way, while Razik fell into step beside her. She said nothing to him, but her skin buzzed at his closeness. It was godsdamn distracting. Ever since he'd given her this Mark, it'd gotten harder to ignore the bond that was trying to form. He'd warned her the Source Mark would intensify things; she just hadn't realized quite how much. She'd told herself she'd be strong enough to handle it. That's what she'd spent her entire life doing. Making herself strong enough to face whatever the Fates threw at her— whether it be a father who disowned her, males who didn't believe she belonged in their army, or a Curse Mark she would never be able to dispel. She could deal with the intensity of this too.

They reached the center of the Springs a short time later, and Eliza pushed out a harsh breath at the sound and smell of the water. They immediately spread out some, and she put space between her and the dragon shifter, moving closer to Rayner. He glanced down at her, his brows pulling together.

"What are you doing?" he asked.

"What do you mean?"

"You are acting out of character."

"I am not."

He studied her a moment longer, but before he could say anything else, Callan's voice drifted over.

"Do you think there will be a significant impact if a new insect is introduced to this environment?"

What in the actual fuck was he talking about?

She ran her thumb and forefinger across her brow before turning to the mortal king. "What is this about, Callan?" He held up his hand, a blue and yellow wingless insect crawling along his finger. "Why would an insect affect anything?"

"It is a valid concern," Razik said from atop a rock he'd climbed and where he now sat leaning back on his palms, casual as fuck. "Transplanting different species of animals or plants can have drastic impacts."

"Why do you know anything about that?" Eliza asked in annoyance.

Razik shrugged. "One would think any time a new being is introduced to an established environment, it would have the potential to cause havoc."

She ground her molars together. "It's just an insect. I'm sure it will be fine."

"The color is unique. Blue and gold. I have only ever seen one like it in Avonleya."

"What?"

The growl came from Rayner, who came stalking over. His grey eyes were swirling faster than normal, and Eliza tensed. The Ash Rider was pissed about...an insect? This was turning into one of the most bizarre missions she'd ever been on, and she'd once accompanied Cyrus on a rather outrageous outing to the Shifter territory.

"What is wrong with you?" Eliza demanded, stepping closer to Callan. The mortal king may have insisted on coming with of his own foolish volition, but she would still protect him when she could. She'd promised Scarlett as much, and being on the receiving end of Rayner losing control was something few would survive.

"Where is she?" Rayner said, his features a mask of anger.

Eliza stared at him for a long moment before saying, "She? As in the insect?"

"Tula. Shift back. Now." His tone left no room for argument, but

Eliza was more focused on the little girl that had appeared amid a soft flash of golden light. Her head hung down, blonde curls shielding her face as she shuffled her feet. "Look at me, Tula."

The child shook her head, but she spoke. "I'm sorry, Rayner. I heard King Callan tell Princess Eva you were coming back, and I didn't want to be away from you. The bad men always come when you're gone." Eliza could hear the wobble in her voice, and when she finally lifted her chin, there were tears pooling in her baby blue eyes. "The dark is scarier when you're gone," she added in a whisper.

Rayner sighed, his anger almost immediately dissipating as he scooped her up. She immediately wrapped her arms around his neck and legs around his waist, and he brought his brow to hers. He murmured something Eliza couldn't hear, even with her Fae hearing, but the little girl nodded earnestly before burying her face in Rayner's neck. He sighed again. "Can you take her back?" he asked, turning to Razik.

"I can, but I cannot guarantee when I will be back," Razik answered. "I will have to track down Cethin for more blood and find Scarlett to get me back out of the Wards. "

"I don't want to go with him, Rayner," Tula cried into his neck.

"Shh," Rayner soothed, murmuring low into the child's ear again, his hand running up and down her back in calming strokes.

"Her other form is an insect?" Eliza asked, studying the Shifter child.

"It is any form she chooses," Rayner replied. "She is a Power Shifter."

"So she caught a ride on the mortal king to go with you?" Razik said.

"It appears that way," Rayner muttered.

Razik seemed rather impressed when he said, "Clever."

"How long has she been Shifting?" Eliza asked.

"We have been practicing with it for a while."

"How long is a while, Rayner?"

Rayner held her stare, and she heard Razik jump down from the rock. "Shortly after the ball that introduced Scarlett to Avonleya."

Her mouth dropped open. "And you didn't think to say anything to anyone?"

"I have been working with her."

"Rayner." And she didn't know what else to say to him. She knew why he was overprotective of the child. So did Sorin and Cyrus. The fact that Tula was clearly powerful didn't help matters. It would bring up a lot of unwanted memories for the Ash Rider. She finally added, "You should have said something."

Rayner's eyes flicked to Razik before coming back to her. "We have been constantly running interference for Scarlett and Sorin. I did not want Tula put in unnecessary danger because of what she can do."

"You cannot honestly believe Scarlett would use her like that," Eliza argued.

"Scarlett? No. But our supposed allies? I trust few and even less when it comes to her."

Eliza glanced at Razik, who was staring back at Rayner, his features hard. "Cethin and Kailia would never use a child for such purposes."

Rayner barked a harsh, humorless laugh. "Your king has been using Scarlett, and she is scarcely out of childhood."

"Their mother has been using her. Not my king," Razik snarled, baring his teeth.

"Your king has been going along with everything their mother demands," Rayner countered. "You cannot tell me if Saylah demanded this of him, he would deny her."

"And you think it is easy to deny a goddess?" Razik asked.

"When it comes to this child? I would deny Arius himself to my dying breath."

"Okay, let's just take a step back," Eliza said, sliding further in between the two when smoke started drifting from Razik's nostrils and ashes were flitting off of Rayner. "No one is going to use Tula. We are here to get Ashtine. Tula should be fine to stay with us, right? We can take her to the House of Water or something during the exchange."

"Probably not the best idea," Azrael cut in. He was leaning against a tree, watching them all with a bored expression, Callan having moved to his side. "With Alaric having infiltrated all the Courts, I wouldn't trust any of the capital cities right now."

"That's a good point," Eliza muttered.

"Siofra would be a better choice," Azrael added.

"Maybe. Can you make us a—"

She felt the air shift behind her before the warning came from Razik. Her sword was already lifted at her back, her arms trembling with the force of the hit she blocked. Eliza spun, fire flaring from her palm as she did. The flames slammed into the seraph that had appeared, forcing him back. Not just one seraph, but a small unit of them. They were surrounded.

"They Traveled in somehow," Razik supplied from behind her. She glanced over her shoulder. Azrael had one seraph wrapped tightly in vines, a dagger poised at the male's throat. Callan was keeping close to the Earth Prince. Rayner had a shield of ashes around him and Tula, who had—

Who had shifted into a small black snake. She was coiled tightly around Rayner's bicep, her blue eyes glowing faintly.

"The seraphs cannot Travel," Eliza gritted out, flames igniting down her sword. "Only the Maraans can."

"I don't know what to tell you," Razik retorted. "They appeared out of the air just like how I Travel."

She was still looking at Razik when she moved her sword to block the arrow that came straight for her. Razik's eyes widened slightly, and Eliza smirked darkly. "We will worry about where they came from later. Can we just kill them right now?"

"So bloodthirsty, *mai dragocen*," he said, his own dark smile appearing. "I get the one that just fired an arrow at you." His wings appeared. "Try not to get stabbed this time."

"I'm going to stab you if you don't fuck off," she snarled, turning her back on him to engage with the next seraph that was coming for her. She heard his dark chuckle as he shot into the sky. Irritation coursed through her, and she channeled it into each swing of her sword. She left Callan to Azrael, knowing they'd fought together at the Necropolis. Rayner wouldn't let anyone within ten feet of Tula, so it was just her and the song of death that she'd missed so greatly these last weeks.

Until her sword met two scimitars.

"Fuck," Eliza cursed, immediately recognizing the weapons.

"What kind of greeting is that?" came a voice of silk and honey. "I just came to talk."

"With a unit of seraphs? I somehow doubt that," Eliza gritted out, striking out with her sword. Nuri ducked with a laugh, meeting the sword with a scimitar again, before the two broke apart.

"The seraphs weren't my idea," she replied. Then she reached up, pulling down the cloth that covered her face, and let out a shrill whistle. All the seraphs stopped, heads turning to her.

"Neat trick," Eliza said, keeping her eyes trained on Death's Shadow. She wore all black, as usual. She blended in with the shadows, her honey-colored eyes dancing with mania and violence.

Nuri shrugged. "They listen like the trained dogs they are." Her gaze skipped over their company, a pointed grin curving on her lips when she said, "Pretty plant prince, good to see you again."

"Insufferable Daughter of Night," Azrael replied, a seraph still wrapped in vines before him. "I was hoping you were dead by now."

Nuri's grin turned into a pout. "Rude when I just stopped an attack on you and have information on your water friends." Her eyes slid to his right, and the grin returned. "The wanna-be king." She made a big show of appearing to search for someone else. "The Toreall Heir has not joined this escapade? Pity."

"You spoke of Briar and Sawyer, but what of Drake and Tava?" Callan called out to her.

"This is why I assumed the final mortal king would be with you. You sent Drake back. Now Callan is here. The next obvious foolish move is to deliver the final mortal heir into their hands," Nuri drawled. Her gaze moved over Rayner, pausing on the snake.

"We are not delivering Callan to anyone," Eliza gritted out.

Nuri only hummed, still studying Tula. Eliza glanced quickly at Rayner, his eyes swirling violently. They didn't need him expelling his magic unless absolutely necessary. It took him months to replenish it.

Eliza slid between Nuri and Rayner. "I would stop looking at him like that."

"Alaric will be upset to learn he has lost a Power Shifter," Nuri replied, apparently having overheard their conversations from the cover of the surrounding foliage.

"So don't tell him."

Nuri dragged her eyes to Eliza, looking at her as if she were indeed a moron. "I cannot keep something like this from him." Her eyes flicked up, and a moment later, Eliza felt Razik land behind her. "I was wondering when you were going to stop fluttering around up there."

Eliza choked on a laugh, glancing up at Razik, who was glaring at the Contessa, but Nuri was already focused back on Eliza. "Right then, I guess I deal with you. I always liked you. You are an actual challenge when we fight, almost as if you trained in the Black Syndicate."

"Trained in the Black Syndicate?" Eliza scoffed. "I picked up Scarlett's training where it had been left lacking. I am the one who trained her in the Fire Court."

Nuri tipped her head back in a laugh. "Well met, General."

"Can you explain to me why we are listening to you two chatter like females at high tea instead of killing the Fae and taking the mortal and Shifter to our prince?" one of the seraphs groused.

"I do not owe you any explanations," Nuri replied without bothering to look at him.

"We do not, in fact, answer to you, you know," he snarled.

Nuri went completely still, and Eliza found herself stepping back into Razik at the look that had come over the Night Child's face. Nuri slowly turned her head to look at the seraph.

"Say that again," she hissed.

The seraph turned, squaring off with her. "I said we do not answer to you," he repeated with a sneer, his lip curling up. "It is only a courtesy to our Commander that we stopped at your—"

But he was cut off by the fangs that were in his throat. Nuri had moved so fast, Eliza hadn't seen her go from one spot to the next. One moment she had been standing in front of her and Razik, the next blink she had been at the male's throat. It had been quite some time since she'd seen the speed of the Night Children this close.

Nuri didn't stop at just biting the male though. She ripped his entire throat out with her fangs, spitting it onto the ground. Blood was dripping down her chin when her manic eyes swiveled back to Eliza. "A little fire help here, General?"

Eliza didn't have the words to say anything as she tossed flames atop the now still seraph. Razik's wing was wrapped loosely around her, shielding her from Nuri.

"Anyone else want to question why you answer to me?" Nuri purred darkly to the other seraphs.

"Are we going to do anything about this?" Eliza muttered to Razik.

"Why would we?" he replied in a hushed tone. She looked up at him. "We want the seraphs dead. She's doing the job for us," he continued, his sapphire eyes fixed on Nuri.

He made a valid point.

"Sorry about that," Nuri said, walking back to Eliza as she adjusted her gloves. Blood was smeared across her cheek where she'd wiped it off her chin. The remaining seraphs had taken to the sky, leaving them alone with Death's Shadow. "Sometimes the dogs need to be reminded who's in charge."

"You cannot have Callan or Tula," Eliza said, getting right to the point. She shoved at Razik's wing to get it out of her way, ignoring the soft growl that emanated from him when she did.

Nuri rolled her eyes. "Clearly. Anyway, we were sent to ambush the Water Prince and his brother before the appointed meeting time, but they appear to have figured out our plan and left."

"How inconvenient for you."

"Quite," Nuri agreed. "But then you lot showed up. Tell me, is Scarlett getting dumber across the sea?"

"Watch it," Eliza snarled.

"She must be, because *why the fuck* is Callan here?" She took a step closer to Eliza, and the general felt Razik tense behind her. But he didn't move, didn't try to come between them.

"Callan is a *king*," Eliza retorted. "Scarlett cannot tell him what to do."

"So he is the foolish one?" Nuri asked, a brow arching as her focus shifted to the mortal king. "That fits. He was sharing a bed with an assassin for a year. Finally moved on then, *your Majesty?*"

"Is Tava with Prince Drayce?" Callan asked through gritted teeth.

"Why would I know that?" Nuri questioned, her head tilting.

"Because you know where Briar and Sawyer are."

"I never said that. I said they are not here. One would guess they are hiding in another territory."

"In the south, by chance?" Azrael drawled.

Nuri shrugged. "They are not as foolish as you all appear to be. I doubt they would hide in a Fae Court or in the mortal lands."

"When is the exchange to take place?" Rayner cut in.

"At sundown. They are to meet at the Windonelle Castle. The Water Prince and the Rydeon heirs for the Wind Princess and the babes," Nuri answered. In the next blink, she was standing in front of Azrael and Callan, unconcerned with the thorny vines the Earth Prince had winding around her legs. "The unborn younglings are not the only innocents being used right now, Mortal King."

"Do you always speak in riddles? You are like a godsdamn Oracle," Azrael muttered.

"Hush, plant prince. The king and I are speaking," Nuri chastised. Azrael bristled, but she ignored him, her focus once again on Callan. "She took his readily available innocents across the Edria, so he has found a new source."

"The Fae Courts?" Callan asked, shifting to see more clearly around Azrael.

Nuri shook her head. "He tried, but they are too protective, which leaves…"

"Mortals?" Callan said, lurching forward a step. "From Windonelle?"

Nuri took a few slow steps back. "I believe your betrothed often visited them."

"You speak of the slums," Callan said. "He is taking innocents from there and…doing what he did to the Black Syndicate orphans?"

"Why?" Eliza cut in. "He took orphans from the Syndicate because they had magic in their veins. Mortal children would give him nothing."

"Nothing but pure innocence," Nuri countered. "He would likely require more of them without magic in their veins."

"And you are doing nothing to protect them? Because they are not from your precious Syndicate?" Callan demanded with a sneer.

"What do you think I am doing right now?" Nuri hissed, her fangs snapping out. She whipped off one of her gloves, showing him her palm. Eliza couldn't see anything, but she assumed a Blood Mark adorned it. "This is the best I can do, Callan. My sisters and I are clever and cunning, but we learned it from him. I have nothing left to barter for their safety with. I would if I could. You wish to be their king? Then *be their king*, Callan. Stop making idiotic choices out of *love*, and make decisions as the ruler of a godsdamn kingdom." She slid her glove back on, turning to Rayner. "Keep her hidden, Ash Rider. I can only keep her a secret for so long."

The snake uncoiled from his arm, a soft flash of light leaving Tula standing beside him. He reached down, gripping her arm when she tried to move to Nuri. She tipped her head up to him. "Nuri won't hurt me, Rayner."

He gave her a tight smile in return. "I know, Tula, but we do not know when the seraphs will return."

Tula's brow furrowed at that, but she nodded nonetheless, stepping closer to his side.

"Aren't you concerned about the seraphs reporting you to Alaric?" Eliza asked.

"Let me worry about that," Nuri replied, stepping back further into the shadows of the surrounding trees. "And do tell Scarlett to get on with things already."

Then she was gone, disappearing into the vegetation. A tense silence settled over their company. Eliza looked up, trying to see if there were any seraphs lingering, but the dense canopy of trees only offered glimpses of the sky.

"Siofra then?" Rayner said, hoisting Tula up so she sat on his shoulders. She looped her little arms around his neck, resting her cheek against his ebony hair.

"That does seem like where they may be. The Witches would be a last resort," Azrael agreed. He lifted a hand and a swirling sand portal appeared.

"So much for this being a fast mission," Eliza grumbled under her breath, sheathing her sword down her back.

"We have only been here a few hours. We will still be back within a day," Razik countered as they watched Rayner, Tula, and Callan go through the portal first.

"You have clearly never met the Shifter siblings," Eliza replied before she followed the others through.

She stepped through the portal, unbuttoning her cloak as she went. The heat would be oppressive in Siofra. The House of Water was warm as well, but not like Siofra. The Shifter capital was more in line with the Earth Court climate. Arid and hot during the day, cool and comfortable during the nights. Since the sun was only just starting to set, however, stifling heat it was.

Eliza looped the cloak over her arm. "You couldn't get us a portal inside?" she accused Azrael.

"Some of us do not have the rapport Aditya has with the Beta," he returned.

"You have been offered that rapport many times, Azrael Luan," came a sultry voice. They all turned to find Arianna Renatus, Beta of the Shifters sauntering down the dusty path that led from the palace gates to a receiving chamber. Her tight braids hung down her back, the gold beads tinkling lightly as she moved. Her gown was lightweight and sheer across her stomach. The sleeves were just as transparent, and the slit up the sides of the dress showed off her dark skin with every step of her gold sandaled feet. A large tiger padded along beside her.

"Look, Rayner!" Tula squealed excitedly from where she was perched, pointing at the feline. "A tiger!" She was squirming, trying to climb down his back.

"That is Jamahl," Rayner answered, his hands clamping down on her legs to keep her seated. "A tiger is his other form, Tula."

"Oh," she sighed, disappointment ringing in her tone.

"Do you have a love child I am unaware of, Rayner?" Arianna asked in amusement, her olive eyes roving over the Ash Rider.

"No, Beta," he answered, reaching up and lifting the still squirming Tula from his shoulders. "This is Tula. She was an orphan in the Black Syndicate."

"And now?"

"And now she stays with me."

The Beta's head tilted to the side. "Even though she belongs with us? She is a Shifter. A powerful one. I can smell it on her."

"She belongs with me," Rayner replied, his voice low and carrying a promise of death as ashes flitted around him.

"What is her other form?" Arianna asked, ignoring the icy change in Rayner.

This was why Rayner had kept it such a closely guarded secret that Tula had shifted. None of them would attempt to use her, but he was right. Power shifters were rare. Any kingdom would do nefarious things to have one serve in their court. The Shifter siblings would want her to remain here, to live among her own kind. They would see it as their duty to protect her, to ensure she was not being used for her gifts.

"It does not matter," Rayner answered, gently tucking Tula behind him. "She stays with me."

"Are Briar and Sawyer here, Arianna?" Eliza cut in. Rayner had been on the edge of losing control since they got here, and the Beta's keen stare on Tula wasn't helping matters.

It took a moment, but Arianna tore her eyes from Tula and settled her attention on Eliza...and then Razik, where her gaze remained fixed as she spoke. "They are with Stellan, along with the Rydeon king and princess. I was sent to see who was at our gates. I will take you to them in a moment. Who is this?"

Eliza felt it then. The possessive nature of the bond that she was so adamantly trying to shove down. She rolled her shoulders, trying to shake it off as she cleared her throat. "This is Razik Greybane. He is the Hand-to-the-Avonleyan King."

Arianna's nostrils flared as she clearly scented him. "He is a Shifter."

Eliza folded her arms across her chest. "Yes," she gritted out.

"He is also powerful," Arianna continued, and Eliza could feel all eyes on her. Razik's eyes. Rayner's. Everyone except the Beta, who was fixated on Razik.

"He is Avonleyan. A descendant of Sargon," Eliza provided, cursing Razik in her mind for staying silent, yet also strangely satisfied that he wasn't speaking for her.

The Beta's eyes went wide. "A dragon shifter then."

Eliza nodded sharply.

"One form we are not permitted to take," Arianna murmured, new interest shining in her eyes.

"Why can you not take the form of a dragon?" Eliza asked.

"Because it was forbidden by Arius and Sargon," Razik supplied, and Eliza felt him take a step closer. Felt the heat radiating off of him against her back.

"There are other forms you are not able to take?" Rayner cut in.

Arianna hummed an agreement. "There are some beings created by the gods that are considered sacred. We are not able to wear those skins, even as Power Shifters."

"Can you take us to the Water Fae, Arianna?" Azrael interrupted. Eliza could hear the attempt at politeness in his tone, but she could tell he was agitated with this entire conversation. "Time is of the essence."

Arianna tilted her head, beads clinking. "Is it? You cannot go with them for the exchange. You have nothing but time until Sawyer returns with Princess Ashtine. Perhaps some rooms to rest while you wait?"

"Not necessary," Razik said. "We will leave as soon as the princess is retrieved."

"That's inconsiderate," Arianna said with a pout. "My brother will not approve of such manners. Surely your companions know this."

Eliza sighed. "Would you have extra rooms available so that we may rest for the night before we take our leave sometime in the next day or two?"

"Of course," she replied, her coy smile returning. "I am certain there is a room for you two near my chambers."

"We do not need a room together," Eliza quickly corrected, refusing to look back at Razik.

"No?" Arianna asked with a knowing lift of her brow.

"No."

"Interesting," was the Beta's response. "I am afraid there is only one room available near mine. The other available rooms are on the other side of the palace. You will not object to being so far from him then?"

Eliza tensed, her fingers tightening around her arms that were still crossed and nails leaving crescent-shaped indents in her skin. "No," she said from between clenched teeth. "He is free to room where he wishes."

She knew she shouldn't do it, but she glanced at Rayner, whose eyes were narrowed on her. If anyone was going to figure this out, it would be the busybody Ash Rider. Or Cyrus, who could read people better than anyone. Or Scarlett, who had an uncanny ability to figure out secrets. Or Sorin, who had known her for centuries.

Fucked.

She was so fucked.

In an attempt to save face and ward off the suspicion she could see in Rayner's eyes, she added, "As he is free to go to whomever he wishes."

Arianna's gaze flicked to Razik when he said tersely, "A room near my company would be preferable, my Lady."

Arianna looked between them again before she said, "I am sure such a thing can be arranged. Come. Callan is anxious to see Lady Tava."

"I haven't said anything," Callan said, his brows rising.

Arianna smiled knowingly. "Yes, but I can smell her on you as I could smell you on her."

"That is... Can you take me to her please, Arianna?" Callan replied, his cheeks reddening slightly.

Her gaze swept over all of them again, before she nodded and turned to head back down the path, Jamahl at her side. They moved silently along. Well, *they* were all silent. Tula chattered at Rayner the entire time, excitedly taking in the sights of the oasis palace in the middle of the desert Shifter territory.

They stepped into a colonnade that would take them to a building that housed several meeting rooms. The roof provided much needed shade, while sheer gossamer curtains fluttered lightly between the columns. They were nearing the next building when a large hand gripped her elbow, tugging her behind a column. Then her back was being pressed to the smooth marble, Razik's forearm braced above her head.

"I feel like we have discussed this already," Eliza bit out. "Just because I am your Source does not mean you get to haul me wherever you want."

"Not unless it suits your needs, right, *mai dragocen?*" he returned.

She glared back at him, ignoring the flash of heat that went through her at his words. "What do you want?"

"To make something clear." The hunger in his eyes shifted to anger, his pupils changing to vertical slits. "I am not going to push something you do not want." Her gaze darted to the side, but he gripped her chin, waiting until she met his sapphire eyes once more. "But do not imply to anyone that I will go elsewhere when you are right in front of me."

Flames shifted under her skin, reaching for him, and it took all of her to hold them back. To keep her magic chained and subdued when it clearly recognized its counterpart. The fact that his dragon fire had already charmed her own flames didn't help matters. Her magic wanted more as much as the bond she was trying to smother did.

"Eliza," he growled, thumb and forefinger still on her chin.

"I cannot give you what you want," she said. She wanted it to be a snarky bite, but it came out more of an anguished admission.

"As if you have any idea what I want."

She scoffed, jerking her chin free, and his brows arched.

"You have never asked. How could you know? You have only made it very clear what you do not want." He leaned in closer, his mouth inches from hers. "But that's not true either, is it, *mai dragocen*? I can feel your magic react to mine. Some of my magic lives in you now. Part of the Source bond you offered up. I warned you it would intensify this bond. You do not get to offer me up to the Beta, or anyone else for that matter, to try to make yourself more comfortable. You chose this. I would have let you go."

"Why?" she whispered, something inside her twisting at the words.

A harsh smile formed on his lips. "Because I am used to not being wanted. It does not bother me anymore."

She didn't know what she was doing until her lips were already on his. If he was surprised, he didn't show it. Instead, his hands gripped her face, and he deepened the kiss. Hot and intense and demanding. The kiss was everything Razik encompassed as his tongue slid between her lips and took control. Her fingers curled into the front of his tunic, and her flames sang at finally tasting him again. They broke through any restraints she'd had on them, brushing along his black flames. Her moan of pleasure mingled with his low groan of the same.

Razik pulled back first, his hands still framing her face. "You bound us together when you chose to be my Source. We could have walked away before."

His hands fell away, and he left her standing there, going to catch up to the others.

She tipped her head back against the column. Her lips still tingled with the heat from his mouth.

Fucked.

She was so fucked.

# CHAPTER 9
## CALLAN

E motion roiled through him with every step he took as he followed Arianna through her home. He had never been this far south in the continent. The beach by the Black Halls was warm, but not the arid heat of Siofra.

Callan had kept quiet when Arianna had shown up. The female was…peculiar. He didn't want her attention, but he had been anxious for any bit of news regarding Tava. Then to learn she was indeed here, and he'd had to stand there and listen to them all discuss Tula and Razik. But now that he was finally being led to her, his emotions were all over the place. Anger that she'd come to him that night knowing she would slip out and leave him in the morning hours. Relief that they'd made it before the trade. Anxiety at not knowing what he was going to say to her. Dread that this might be the last time he saw her.

And now this new urgency. People of his kingdom were being used in ways only the gods knew. He already knew he wouldn't be going back to Avonleya with the others. He wasn't sure how he'd tell Eliza yet, but he couldn't do it. His place was here. With his people. He'd left twice. It was time to stay.

Arianna turned the golden knobs on a set of double doors and threw them open unceremoniously, several sets of eyes swiveling to them. A male stood at the head of the table. He had to be Arianna's brother. He was tall and dark-skinned, the same olive eyes staring at all of them. A male and female flanked him. Prince Briar and Sawyer were also standing at one side of the table, while Drake and Tava were on the other. They were all crowded around a map that was spread out before them.

"New arrivals," Arianna announced, sweeping into the room ahead of them. There was a flash of golden light, and Jamahl strode beside her in his human form. His hand fell to his Beta's lower back as he guided her to a seat near the head of the table before he took up a spot behind her, hands resting on the back of her chair.

"Azrael," Briar said, relief heavy in his tone. "We had no way to get word to you. We received word of a trap——"

The Earth Prince held up a hand. "We heard. We were met by Death's Shadow and some seraphs. I cannot decide whose side she is on."

"Nor can I," Briar replied grimly. "She seems to be playing both."

Callan scarcely heard the conversation happening around him. His entire being was fixed on Tava, who was staring back at him with wide eyes. Her fingers went to her throat, searching for an amulet that was long gone, and perched on the back of her chair was a golden owl.

"What is Paja doing here?" Rayner asked quietly. "I saw him last with Scarlett in Aimonway."

"He appeared this morning," Briar answered. "Hasn't left the Tyndells since."

*I have taken measures to keep them protected until we can come for them.*

She had sent a spirit animal to keep them protected until she could come for them. She had already taken measures to protect those she viewed as hers while he had been…panicking and reacting based on emotion. It never ceased to amaze him that a girl raised to take life was more equipped than he was to be on a throne.

"I will be back in a moment."

Her voice tore him from his thoughts, and Callan found Tava moving toward him.

"We leave soon," Drake argued.

"We were almost done here," Tava countered. "You can fill me in at another time."

Her fingers interlaced with his as she passed, pulling him along behind her. The owl gave a disapproving hoot, but stayed put on the chair next to Drake. Razik and Eliza were coming through the door at the same time, Eliza's eyes narrowing on him.

"Do not do anything stupid," the general muttered to him. "I have enough to deal with right now."

Callan sent her a dry look over his shoulder, but she had already turned back to the others, going to the opposite side of the table of Razik.

"Tava," he said.

She was pulling him down the hall, but she didn't say anything. She wasn't in a dress as usual, but instead wore pants and a sleeveless tunic, her boots echoing off the marble floor.

"Tava, stop," he tried again.

She pushed a door open to what appeared to be a small study, and he followed her in. He started to say her name again, but she was shutting the door before pushing him back against it. Then she was on her toes, her mouth on his. He pulled her to him, one hand on her cheek, his other arm winding around her waist.

"I am sorry," she murmured onto his lips. "I am sorry, Callan." Her arms were looped around his neck, fingers in the hair at his nape. Frantic. Frenzied.

He spun them, and then he turned her away from him. She gasped as he pressed her front against the door. "I took my anger out on Scarlett, you know," he said harshly into her ear, pinning her hands above her head with one hand while the other stayed looped around her waist. He was probably being too rough with her, but a part of him didn't care. He *was* angry with her. He was angry with all of them. He was so godsdamned sick of everyone making decisions for him. He'd thought she, of all people, wouldn't do that to him.

Tava shook her head as much as she could. "It was not her fault, Callan. She let Drake and me make the choice."

"So she said. She tried to defend you. To keep my anger focused on her, to protect my feelings for you. She did a good job of it too," he continued. The arm at her waist tugged her tighter against him. "You should have told me."

"I knew you would have tried to stop me," Tava replied, twisting as he let her break his hold. He saw her own rage filling those ocean-blue eyes. "Are you saying those innocent babes are not worth it?"

"Of course that's not what I am saying," he retorted. His hands went to her shoulders, holding her back against the wood of the door. "You are noble and brave and so godsdamn selfless. Sometimes too selfless."

"They deserve a chance to live, Callan!" Tava cried. "I cannot let them be used because I refused to return to Balam."

"I *know*, Tava, but we could have found another way."

"I was not willing to risk it. You were not supposed to come here," she said. Tears were welling in her eyes. Hot, angry tears.

"So godsdamn selfless," he muttered.

"You are not angry with me," she hissed. "You are hurt by my actions, and rightfully so."

"Can it not be both?" he countered. They stared at each other, a stand-off of wills. He spit a soft curse before he said, "You once told me you could not handle only having me when I allowed it. That goes both ways, Tava. I cannot… There cannot be secrets. We cannot go behind each other's backs. I cannot do that again."

"I had to do this, Callan. I could not let you deny me," Tava whispered, the anger flaring in her eyes once more. Gods, she was beautiful like this. When she argued with him, challenged him. He could still see her flinging a teacup across her room in a fit of fury.

"I will never deny you a godsdamn thing," he said in a low snarl. Then he was kissing her again, hands running down her sides, clutching at her waist, slipping under her tunic. Her head dropped back as he worked his way down her neck. He pulled a hand from her tunic to tug at the ties on the front.

"Callan," she gasped. "I must go soon."

"Then we make this fast," he replied against her skin as his teeth scraped along her collarbone.

He thought she might argue, but she reached for his tunic instead, frowning at the buckles securing his various weapons. "Nothing about this will be fast."

Callan had never removed weapons from his body so quickly. Tava watched him unfasten buckles and toss daggers aside. Her brow pinched when she spotted dried blood on his arms. "Were you fighting?"

"Some seraphs," he answered breathlessly.

"Were you hurt?"

"Not by them." Her eyes flashed back to his. "Nuri showed up. She implied Alaric is using the people in the slums of Baylorin."

Horror crossed her features. "What?" He moved back to her, all weapons now discarded, and smoothed stray hair back from her face as she blinked up at him. "What are we going to do?"

His hands fell to her thighs, and he hoisted her up against him, walking them over to the settee along the back wall. "You are going to appease the man that raised you until Scarlett can come for you," he answered, lowering her to the settee. "I am going to figure out what is going on in the slums of Baylorin."

He reached for her feet, quickly unlacing her boots.

"How?" she pressed.

"Still working on that," he answered, removing her other boot. She lifted her hips when he reached for the band of her pants, letting him slide them down her legs.

"But you will do something, right? You won't leave them to suffer?"

He stilled, staring down at her. "They will not be forgotten, Tava. They will not be left in the background."

She surged up then, her arms coming around his neck once more and pulling his lips to hers. He'd never seen her like this. Urgency with every plunge of her tongue into his mouth. Hands roaming as though they could not touch him enough. He reached down, peeling the tunic from her body while she frantically tugged at his. Somewhere along the way, he lost his own pants, and she was straddling him on the settee.

"I did not wish to leave you," she murmured, fingers skating along his ribs and down his bare torso, his stomach caving under her touch. "You have to know that. I did not wish to hurt you, Callan, but I could not—"

Her words turned into a whimper as he palmed her breast, rolling a nipple between his thumb and forefinger. Her hips ground down against him, seeking any type of relief on instinct as her eyes fluttered closed, and he cursed, knowing they did not have the time to drag this out. Someone would surely knock on the door soon.

He gripped her hips, lifting her up to position her. Her hands fell to his shoulders, and her entire body tensed. He leaned forward, whispering into her ear, "Breathe, Little Fox."

He felt her suck in a breath, and when she released it, he pulled her down onto him, eyes falling closed at being inside her again. She shifted, and it was his turn to hold his breath while she adjusted. Fingertips brushed along his jaw that had him opening his eyes and meeting hers. Her lips were parted, panting staccato breaths making her chest rise and fall. Strands of golden hair fluttered in her face, her fingers flexing on his shoulder.

Holding her stare, he lifted her hips and pulled her back down, her eyes going wider at the movement. Then she started moving her hips on her own, experimenting as she rolled against him. He hadn't planned on this when he had set out to find her, but gods, he would be damned if this was the last time he got to watch her experience new sensations like this.

He reached up, brushing hair back, while his other hand roamed over her soft skin—brushing down her arm, chest, stomach—until it found its way to her center. He moved his thumb in slow circles, another whimper coming from her as she moved faster against him. "Here is what we are going to do, Little Fox." He gripped her chin, forcing her eyes to his. "We are going to fight for the innocent and the forgotten. We are going to make sure those with the least in our lands are cared for as much as those with the most." He grunted as she continued to move in rhythm with his thumb. His circles became tighter and firmer. "And when this war is over, we will continue to do the same from our thrones. You will be at my side. I am going to marry you, Tava Tyndell. When this war is over, you will become my queen at the first opportunity, and we will serve our people together."

A sob of some sort came from her, and he released her chin to grip her hip and move her faster against him. Her brow fell to his shoulder, and she buried her face in his neck as she held onto him. His own hips were moving now, thrusting up to meet hers with every pass, and when he knew she was close, he pressed down with his thumb. Her cry of pleasure was muffled against his skin, and he held her tightly as he found his own release.

For the next few moments, it was only the sound of their harsh breaths as they clung to each other. His fingers were brushing up and down her spine, and he was dreading the coming minutes when they would need to get dressed and say their goodbyes.

Tava sat up, a hand cupping his cheek and a thumb brushing along his lower lip. "Thank you," she whispered, "for letting me make a difference for Ashtine and Briar and their children."

"I meant what I said, Tava. I will never deny you anything."

"Then I will make another request of you," she replied, a soft smile appearing. She leaned forward, brushing a kiss against his mouth.

"Anything," he breathed onto her lips.

"I am going to hold you to what you said. Go be a king to your people and fight for them, but promise you will come back to me."

Tension hung thick in the air in the sitting room. They were all just... waiting. Callan sat in a chair, staring at the hearth. When the sun had dipped below the horizon, the temperature had dropped rapidly, and a fire had been started shortly after sundown.

They'd all congregated to watch them go, Tava's hand in his until she stepped through the water portal Briar had created. He'd watched them all go through, and it was Eliza who had gently touched his arm after the portal closed, stepping to his side.

"We will get them back. Scarlett won't let anything happen to them," she'd said softly.

"We all know even she cannot make such promises," Callan had replied.

"She will not fail you."

Callan had simply nodded, allowing himself to be herded inside and to this room. Food had been brought in, and Eliza had fixed him a plate herself. It sat untouched on a side table. How long had it been now? The exchange was supposed to happen at sundown. That had been at least three hours ago. Sawyer and Ashtine should have been back by now.

Azrael and Razik were murmuring quietly with Stellan and Arianna at a table. Rayner held a sleeping Tula in his lap where he sat on the sofa. Eliza was on the other end of the sofa, seemingly lost in her own thoughts.

All heads snapped up at the gust of wind that tore through the room, a portal appearing in the next moment. Sawyer came through with Ashtine at his side. The portal snapped shut behind them. Eliza was already on her feet, making room for Ashtine to sit on the sofa. The princess looked exhausted, her stomach far more swollen than Callan would have expected, despite knowing Fae pregnancies didn't last as long as mortal ones. Coupled with the fact she was carrying twins, she appeared to be as far along as a woman in her fifth month would be. She wore a gown the same color as her eyes, angry red marks adorned her wrists.

"How did everything go?" Rayner asked, while Eliza went to get Ashtine a glass of water.

"As expected," Sawyer answered, watching Ashtine carefully. "Lord Tyndell was there to collect Drake and Tava. Alaric slipped shirastone onto Briar's wrists before he removed the same from Ashtine. He did not allow them any time together before he Traveled them all out."

"Cyrus and Neve?" Eliza asked, passing the princess the water.

"Neve was there, but I did not see Cyrus," Sawyer answered, reaching for a blanket that was draped along the back of a chair. Eliza took it from him, spreading it over the Wind Princess.

"He allowed Neve to tend to me," Ashtine said in her usual lilt, although even that sounded tired. "Cyrus is in the Underwater Prison. He was left with the Sorceress."

"Alaric said we had three days," Rayner said tightly.

"He did," Ashtine agreed. "In what state Cyrus and Neve were returned was not negotiated."

"Of course not," Eliza spat, sparks flaring at her fingertips. Razik had moved closer to her at some point during all the discussion, and

Callan watched as he subtly shifted, his arm brushing against hers. She glared up at him, but her fire banked, and she didn't step away.

"How will he retrieve him?" Callan asked.

"He will leave him there until the trade is to be made, your Majesty," Ashtine answered.

"But she cannot do magic in there, right?" he pressed, trying to understand the gravity of what was going on.

"The Sorceress is not of this world. She was stripped of her physical gifts when she was imprisoned, but she retains her knowledge of ancient magic."

"Then why hasn't she used it until now?"

"Blood is required. It is blood magic," Rayner supplied. His gaze shifted to Ashtine. "Are you saying Alaric gave her blood?"

"Cyrus's blood," Ashtine answered.

"If she is released—" Stellan started.

"*When* she is released," Ashtine interrupted. "He will release her when Talwyn is returned."

"He cannot seriously believe he can control her," Azrael said. Ashtine remained silent. "He controls every Court but the Fire Court now," Azrael added grimly.

"That is inaccurate," Ashtine said.

"What do you mean? Talwyn was leading the Fire Court," Eliza cut in.

Ashtine shook her head. "When Talwyn attempted to defy him, he found someone new."

"Who?" Eliza and Rayner both snarled simultaneously.

"I do not know," she answered, wincing as she shifted on the sofa.

"That is enough for tonight," Sawyer said, taking a step towards her. He looked to the Shifters. "Can you take us to her room? She needs to rest."

"We need to go back and relay all of this to the others," Razik interjected. "It is no slight to anyone," he added when Eliza glared at him again. "We do not have time to waste."

"I cannot leave," Ashtine said.

"We will wait and go in the morning," Sawyer said, shooting a look at Razik that dared him to argue. Razik crossed his arms, annoyance clear on his features.

"You misunderstand," Ashtine said, exhaustion and defeat heavy in her tone now. "I cannot leave this continent."

"Why not?" Azrael demanded.

The Wind Princess reached up and tugged aside the neckline of the gown she was wearing, and Razik swore. Callan didn't know why. There was nothing there that he could see. Apparently none of the Fae could see it either. Only Razik.

The Avonleyan took a step towards her then paused. "May I?" Ashtine nodded, and he moved before her, leaning down to study... whatever it was he could see. Her head tipped back against the sofa, eyes falling closed. Razik's gaze flicked up to her face. "Did he say what would happen if you broke it?"

She didn't open her eyes, but her hands moved to rest atop her belly, and Razik cursed under his breath.

"What?" Eliza asked.

He straightened, looking over at her. "She has a Binding Mark. It has various purposes depending on how it is drawn. I cannot say for sure what this is binding her to—not without looking at a book I have at home—but the cost of breaking it is the lives of the babes."

"I am bound to these lands. I cannot leave," Ashtine repeated.

Silence fell again, the magic-wielders all glancing among themselves. Then Sawyer stepped towards her again, gently tugging off the blanket. "That is enough with the questions for tonight. I promised Briar I would look after her until he returned. She is clearly exhausted."

"I heard the winds again," Ashtine whispered, so quietly Callan almost didn't hear her with his mortal hearing.

"I am glad to hear that, your Highness," Sawyer said gently. "Come, you can rest."

"I will come and help," Eliza said.

"I am not sure if it is me they seek or the one in my womb," the Wind Princess continued as though no one else had spoken, her eyes still closed.

Azrael and Sawyer exchanged a look. "Can you speak with her?" Sawyer asked. "Briar..." He swiped a hand through his white-blond hair that matched his brother's. "He knows how to speak to her."

Azrael nodded. "Ashtine, did the winds tell you any secrets?"

"It is an odd thing," she answered, "to carry secrets you do not understand. But perhaps one simply wishes not to acknowledge such truths."

Azrael seemed to think this over, and Callan watched in fascination as everyone else waited for him to decide how to respond to that. He had little experience with the Wind Princess. The only other time he'd seen her was when she'd fought in the throne room, and then he'd watched her and Briar say goodbye.

"What secrets did they share, Ashtine?" Azrael finally asked.

"They spoke of other worlds."

"Avonleya?" Sawyer asked.

"They spoke of wars. Past. Present. Future." Her eyes opened then, sky blue irises landing on Sawyer. "They spoke of sacrifices to be made."

"Who?" Sawyer asked in a hushed tone.

She held his stare. "Too many to name."

Sawyer's lips thinned, a muscle in his jaw clenching as he understood something Callan did not. "Come, Princess," he said, bending to scoop her off the sofa. "You need to rest. We will figure everything else out in the morning."

As she settled against his chest, her eyes landed on Callan. "Thank you, your Majesty. For letting her come. Paja was with her. She will be safe." He nodded to her, not sure what else to say. Her eyes fluttered closed again, her head falling to Sawyer's shoulder as she murmured, "I hope the winds are wrong about many things, but they rarely are."

Eliza followed them out, and when the doors closed behind them, the Fae all released a collective breath.

"She is not well," Azrael said, taking the goblet that Sariah was passing to him.

"The rest in a safe place will help," Arianna said, but she appeared somewhat rattled by the state of the princess.

"If she cannot leave the continent, others should stay with her," Rayner said. "And we need to figure out who is leading the Fire Court."

"We should all rest for the night," Arianna said. "Things are often clearer in the morning."

"I also imagine Eliza will want to be a part of these discussions," Razik said.

They all stood and silently filed out of the room. Callan didn't hear Arianna fall into step beside him, lost in his own thoughts. "You did not eat this evening, your Majesty."

He glanced at her out of the corner of his eye, really not in the mood to deal with the Beta and her not-so-subtle suggestions. "I find myself without much of an appetite tonight."

"You have become a king since I last saw you."

"Yes."

"And you have found love."

"I have."

"You are in a foul mood," she added.

Callan pushed out a harsh breath. "I apologize if I am coming off as rude, my Lady."

A laugh burst from Arianna that had Callan pausing mid-step, turning to face the Beta. Jamahl had fallen back and followed them from several paces behind. She reached up, patting Callan's chest. "No need to apologize, your Majesty, especially if it is not sincere. It is not required of kings to do so."

Callan frowned. "A king should certainly apologize if he is in the wrong."

A knowing smile graced her lips. "And tell me, do your feet still follow the paths of others, or have they found their own path yet?"

"It is difficult when others think they know what path is best for you," he answered, too tired to adequately articulate his thoughts right now.

"Of course it is," she replied. "If it were easy, it would not be worth it. A word of advice, though, young king: I found Stellan more…amenable to me choosing my own path when I had a plan and was able to present it to him to justify my actions."

He sent her a dry look. "You left with Sorin while your brother was away to come to Baylorin when Scarlett was taken."

She smiled wryly. "True," she conceded, "but Sorin was the one doing the convincing in that instance. Not me. He came to me with a plan. He was inviting me down his path. It was not one of my own, but part of his." She stepped closer to him, her fingers slowly trailing up his arm. "Is that not what Tava did when she proposed the ruse all those months ago? She had a plan."

"Tava is not here," he bit out.

"No," Arianna agreed. "From what I understand, they went to Scarlett and Sorin with a plan. The king and queen listened to what was proposed, shared their concerns, but ultimately let them follow their own path." She shifted on her feet, her fingers dragging along his chest now. "Tava grounds you. Forces you to think before you act. Without her here, you must do that for yourself."

"She makes me better," he said quietly.

"I know," Arianna answered with a sad smile. "Destiny is a fickle thing, but it is also often demanding. You are still waiting, young king."

"Waiting for what?"

"For others to tell you what to do. Sometimes our path requires us to walk it alone for a while," she answered. She stepped towards him once more, reaching up to brush back a lock of hair from his brow. "Your path will cross with hers again, but for now? You must learn to be the king required of you, whether Tava is here or not." Her hand moved to cup his cheek. "You still look to others to guide your way. Eventually, you must find it yourself."

# CHAPTER 10
# ELIZA

There was a soft knock on the door, and Eliza looked up from her book as Azrael entered the room.

"How is she?"

"Sleeping," Eliza answered. "Alaric had her for a while. The early months of pregnancy are hard enough, and she has been by herself and then with him." She paused, trying to find the words. "It has taken its toll on her," she finally finished.

She would know. She had been with child three different times, and she had done it by herself too. While she had never made it as far into her pregnancies as Ashtine was, she had gone through the first few months before the curse took those lives from her.

"Rayner needs to speak with you," Azrael said after a moment. "I came to stay with her so you could go to him." His eyes darted to the door of the bedchamber. "I assume Sawyer is in there."

Eliza nodded. "Last I checked he was sleeping on the sofa."

"Go. I will stay. Rayner is in his rooms."

Eliza closed her book, tucking it under her arm as she got to her feet. She snagged her boots from near the door, carrying them with her rather than putting them back on. Trudging down the hall in her stockinged feet, she did not bother to knock when she came to Rayner's rooms next to hers.

He was standing before the fire, a glass of amber liquid in his hand. He glanced up at her before flicking his wrist. A swirl of ashes carried a glass of wine from a side table to her. She dropped her boots by the door and sent her book to a pocket realm in a burst of flames.

"Tula?" she asked, taking a sip of the wine.

"Sleeping in the bedchamber."

"You let the tiny child sleep in the giant bed while you take the sofa?" she asked, arching a brow.

Rayner simply shrugged and took a drink of his liquor.

"Are you going to the Fire Court?" she asked, moving to stand beside him while she swirled her glass of wine.

"Not until Tula is back in Avonleya, across the sea with Sorin and Scarlett."

Eliza looked up at him incredulously. "Rayner, we need to know who we are dealing with."

"I know this, Eliza," he answered. "But most of my connections are in hiding. I will need to do this myself."

"So go do it."

"I will not leave her here alone."

"Stellan and Arianna will not hurt her," Eliza said, rolling her eyes.

"No, but they will fight to keep her."

Eliza's lips pursed as she watched his fingers flex around his glass, swirling eyes fixed on the fire. He was always quiet and stoic, the voice of reason, but she never forgot what prowled beneath his skin.

"They will not do anything while we are here," she tried again. "This is necessary—"

"What is *necessary* is keeping her safe," he snarled, rounding on her. "Stop being naïve, Eliza."

She bit her tongue to keep from snapping back with a scathing reply. The last thing they needed was division among themselves right now. They were both worn out and on edge.

"You know as well as I do they have people watching our every move. It is the same thing I do when visitors come to the Fire Palace," he finally went on, his tone terse as he worked to keep control. "The moment they have an opportunity to claim her, they will."

"Arianna will not alienate herself from Sorin," Eliza argued.

"She will not give a fuck. Not when it comes to protecting one of their own. You know they have their own charters here. I want Tula out of this territory before they can invoke them."

"Rayner," she started slowly, knowing that she was toeing a very dangerous line. "Maybe it would be better if—"

"I swear to Anala, Eliza. If you are about to say it would be better for her to be raised among her own kind..." He trailed off, leaving the threat open-ended.

"For fuck's sake, Rayner! She is not Breya. She is not Aravis," Eliza said, exasperated with this entire conversation.

Ashes fluttered from his hand as he slowly raised his glass to his lips, holding her stare. He didn't say a word, and she knew she had lost him. He would not discuss this further. Not anymore tonight.

She set her half-empty glass of wine off to the side, wrapping her arms around herself. "If Ashtine cannot leave the continent, someone needs to stay with her. Sawyer will not be enough."

"Agreed."

"They will need Azrael for battle strategies and planning as he is a prince and knows the Wind and Earth Courts best, and you need to go back for...obvious reasons. I will stay with her. You two can go back tomorrow. Take Callan with you."

"And Razik?"

"What of him?"

"You are his Source."

"I am well aware," she grumbled.

"What else are you?"

She glared at him. "What is that supposed to mean?"

"You have been hiding in your quarters to avoid answering questions about this," he said, swirling his glass, ice clinking together. "You have been avoiding all of us."

"There is nothing to talk about."

"Nothing to talk about?" he repeated incredulously. "Did you think this through at all?"

"Of course I did."

"You did? What is the plan, then? You will stay with him in Avonleya when this is all over?"

"What? No." Her lip curled at the idea. "I will go home to the Fire Court."

"You are his Source, Eliza. You will need to be near him at all times. He is Cethin's Hand. He will need to be in Avonleya."

"He can Travel. He can come to me when he needs to."

"And if his power is too drained to do so? What then?"

"He will need to plan for such things."

"Eliza," he deadpanned.

"This is none of your business, Rayner."

"It is my business. It is Sorin's business because there is a very good chance you will need to challenge for the Fire Court throne."

She jerked back from him. "What? No," she said, shaking her head in denial. "Sorin lives. He has not abdicated—"

"And he no longer has any power. If whoever is running the Court right now challenges him, he will lose. There is no question. You are now the most powerful Fire Fae. Surely you have thought of this."

Her arms tightened around herself, eyes darting away from him. She hadn't let herself think about it. She did not wish to rule. She was perfectly content leading Sorin's forces as his general.

"And then what will you do, Eliza? How will you balance being both the Fire Court Princess and the Source of a powerful Avonleyan?" he went on.

"Don't be stupid. I'm not going to be the Fire Court Princess," she snapped.

Rayner fell silent, knocking back the last of his drink. For several minutes, the only sounds were the crackling logs in the fire. Eliza just wanted to get out of here. Go back to her own rooms and curl up with her book. Escape to places where she did not need to contemplate such things. As much as she loved reading, it was a necessity as much as it was for enjoyment.

"What do you want me to tell Sorin?" he finally asked.

"Tell him whatever you want."

He sighed. She knew she was in a mood now. Rayner did too.

"Get some sleep, Eliza," he said, setting his empty glass down on the side table before he disappeared into the bathing chamber, shutting the door behind him.

She stalked out of the room and past her own guest chambers. There was no way she could sleep right now. Not after all the things he'd just filled her head with. She wouldn't be able to concentrate on reading either. She would love to go into a sparring ring, but Rayner wouldn't spar with her. That would require leaving Tula alone. And they weren't at home, so it wasn't as if she could find an off-duty warrior to spar with either.

Which left sword meditation. She hadn't done it since Nakoa had died, mainly because he had been the one to teach it to her. A series of precise movements with a sword, specific body positions held for an extended period of time, and a concentration on breathing, the practice demanded all of her attention. It left no room for her focus to stray or she would lose her balance, which wasn't ideal while holding a sword.

Nakoa had taken over her training when she'd surpassed all those in the Fire Court armies. Most of the soldiers in Sorin's armies had come to accept her as one of their own. She'd more than earned their respect, but there were a few—some top commanders—who were still passive aggressive with her to this day. More than once, she'd had to put them in their place. The first few times, Sorin had been pissed, and she'd had to stop him from going down there himself. Cyrus had been the one to finally convince him she needed to handle it herself. That they would never truly respect her if Sorin stepped in and did this for her. But that had always been Sorin's nature. Fiercely protective of his people, and overprotective of his family. Just like Scarlett. They were the perfect rulers for the Fire Court. Not her.

Eliza crossed a stone patio, nodding at the small lynx that sat up at her approach. The shifter's luminous eyes watched her, but it made no movement of acknowledgement. She was sure there was an avian shifter flying around as well that would report her movements to Stellan.

She walked until she was at least half a mile out into the desert before she slipped her socks off. The sand was freezing beneath her bare feet, and she tossed some flames to the side, creating a good-sized fire that radiated with heat. She pulled her spirit sword from another burst of flames and planted her feet, inhaling deeply. The cool, night air filled her lungs, the stars looking on from above. She tightened her grip on her sword, and her eyes fell closed as she slid one foot out and raised her arms, controlling her exhale, forcing everything from her mind but her movement and her breathing.

She didn't know how long she had been going through the various poses when she felt him land softly. Irritation prickled at the same time her flames flickered under her skin, reaching for him. She opened her eyes just in time to see his wings disappear. He was shirtless—because of course he was—but his pupils were still vertical, irises glowing faintly.

"I can see better in the dark when my eyes are shifted," he said by way of explanation. She didn't need to ask how he knew what she'd been thinking. She already knew. This damn bond was trying to settle into place.

"By the gods," she gritted out, any semblance of calm she'd found obliterated when he'd literally dropped out of the godsdamn sky. "Can I not have one night of peace?"

"Your night hasn't been peaceful since Ashtine returned," he replied. Then she heard him grumble under his breath, "And mine haven't been peaceful since you stepped foot in Avonleya."

"You are the one who seeks me out," she shot at him.

"I am well aware, Eliza."

"Then stop."

"I can only ignore the sudden intensity of your emotions for so long."

"You can...feel that already?"

He gave a sharp nod. "The male usually feels the bond stronger in the beginning. It's a primal protectiveness."

"Great," she muttered, resuming her movements. She went through another few stances before he spoke again.

"Do you want to spar?"

"No," she bit out.

"Do you want to talk about what caused the spike in your emotions?"

"No." She began to move into her next position.

"Do you want to fuck?"

She tripped on her own feet, her foot landing in the wrong position in the sand, and she flung her arm out to keep her balance. Her eyes flew to Razik. He was staring back at her, arms crossed, that unimpressed look he gave everyone else on his face. The flickering flames of her fire cast shadows that danced across his features, and she saw his lips twitch the smallest amount.

"I want you to fuck off," she spat.

She heard his low laugh as she spun away from him, starting her routine over from the beginning. Refusing to look at him, she began going through all her stances again. She fell into the lull of the movements, and it was nearly an hour later when she finished. A faint sheen of sweat coated her skin, but she felt calmer. More settled. But more importantly, she was so exhausted, she should be able to fall asleep without her endless thoughts keeping her awake. She hoped that would be the case anyway, because she could still hear Rayner's words rattling around in the back of her mind, screaming for attention.

*There is a very good chance you will need to challenge for the Fire Court throne.*

No. That was exactly the life her "father" had wanted for her. Marry her off to the Earth Prince, rule a Court at his side. She had worked too hard at becoming the exact opposite to have to do that.

Turning to trudge back to the palace, she paused mid-step when she found Razik sitting next to the fire. His knee was bent, arm resting atop it while he leaned back on his other hand. Had he sat here this entire time?

"What are you doing?" she asked dryly, her sword hanging loosely at her side.

"Thinking about my cave at home."

She blinked, unsure of what to say to that. "Are you...talking about your study?"

He huffed a humorless laugh. "No, although I have some of my most valuable volumes at my cave."

"Your cave," she repeated.

"In the Nightmist Mountains."

She could do nothing. Nothing but stand there and stare at him because she was completely dumbfounded and confused and what in the actual fuck was he talking about? Razik was staring past her, out into the desert, and when she couldn't take it anymore, she said, "Is there something special about this...cave?"

"I keep treasure there."

She clicked her tongue, instantly annoyed. "You do not."

He brought his gaze to hers, tilting his head up to see her better. "I do."

She sent him a frank look. "What sort of treasure?"

He shrugged. "Various things." His eyes dropped to her sword. "If I had won that, it would be there."

She looked down at the spirit sword. She'd won it in a race through a hedge maze, beating Razik by mere seconds. Looking back at him, her eyes narrowed. "I suppose now you are going to try to convince me you let me win."

He gave a scoff of his own. "Eliza, I would never let you win anything. Remember when I spit fire farther than you?"

"How could I forget? You constantly remind me," she sneered.

"Exactly. I would have reminded you every fucking day if I had won that sword. Come to think of it, no. I wouldn't keep that sword in my cave. I would have it sheathed down my back at all times to rub it in your face. I would give that sword its own seat at the dinner table directly across from you so you would have to stare at it while eating."

A bark of laughter escaped her. She took a step towards him before she realized what she was doing and stilled once more. He had gone back to staring off into the night. She flexed her fingers around the sword hilt. He had to be lying.

"Do you really have a cave in the mountains?" she blurted.

His lips twitched again. Godsdamnit. How did he always know how to pull her into these stupid conversations?

"I do," he answered. "I usually sleep there."

"In a cave," she said dubiously. "You have rooms at the estate and the castle, and you expect me to believe you sleep in a cave?"

He nodded. "I fly at night, after Cethin and I are done with whatever has required our attention that day. I usually end up there and just sleep there rather than fly back. I rarely stay at the estate or castle."

"You could simply Travel back," she pointed out.

"If I wanted to."

"You *prefer* a cave?"

"It's a very nice cave," he answered without a hint of mirth.

Another laugh bubbled up. "I am sure it is if it's full of treasure."

"It's a dragon thing," he replied with another shrug.

She studied him, looking for any sign that he was jesting, but there was nothing. She honestly couldn't tell if he was lying or not at this point.

A few minutes later, she was still standing there when he met her gaze. He tipped his head to the spot beside him. "Come, *mai dragocen.* Tell me where you learned *serena sabre.*"

And damn it all to hell, she did. The sand was warm beneath her feet, heated by her fire, as she made her way to him. He reached up, gently taking the sword from her hand and setting it aside. She lowered down, wrapping her arms around her knees, and tried to dig her toes into the hard sand.

She was so sick of the sand. Beaches. Deserts. It was all the same. She wanted to go home to the mountains. Aimonway wasn't so bad in that regard, she supposed. It was nestled right at the base of the Nightmist Mountains. The next best thing to Solembra in a way. Sand had never bothered her before. She was just...homesick. Sorin had given her a home when she'd had nothing. She missed her own space where she could simply be.

*You will stay with him in Avonleya when this is all over?*

Fucking Rayner and his introspective shit.

She lifted a hand, small flames appearing at her feet. Toying with the fire, the flames mirrored the movements of her fingers. She saw Razik look down at her, and she could tell by the way a muscle in his jaw ticked that he had felt her shift in emotions.

"Who taught you *serena sabre?*" he asked.

"I don't know what that is," she sighed.

"It is what I just watched you do for an hour. With perfect form, I might add."

She turned her head to look at him, her temple resting on her bent knees. "You know of it?"

"It is an ancient art form. One not commonly found here."

"On this continent?"

"In this world."

She went silent again, contemplating that. "Then how do you know of it?"

"My... Tybalt taught it to me."

"Why don't you call him your father anymore?"

"It feels different. With his true son here now."

"He does not seem like the type of person who would replace you simply because he learned of Cassius."

"He is not that type of person," Razik replied, shifting so he faced her a little more.

"Then… Is this what he wished to speak with you about?"

"Some of it, I am sure," he muttered. "I will have to go speak with him when we return tomorrow."

She stiffened, the fire she'd been playing with at her feet flaring slightly. The entire purpose of coming out here was to *not* think about the logistics of how this Source bond would play out when this was all over, yet here it was. Already being thrown back in her face.

"*Mai dragocen,*" he said softly.

"Stop," she snapped. "Stop calling me that."

But a large hand wrapped around the back of her neck and pulled her to him. His lips landed on hers, and she was kissing him back. She let him deepen the kiss, his tongue demanding against hers, and then he was hauling her into his lap. Her knees dug into the sand on either side of him. One hand was still on her neck, holding her to him, the other slid down her back, fingertips tracing her spine until he gripped her hip. She leaned into him, his skin warming her better than any fire could. She felt his magic brush against hers, and she ground down against him on instinct, his black flames seeking both to comfort her and draw her to him. And she let them. She let him drive out the thoughts that had been plaguing her; the memories trying to haunt her.

"Come back to my rooms," he growled into her mouth. Then his lips were moving along her jaw, down her throat.

"No," she whispered, trying to pull back, but he held her in place.

"Then I will come to yours," he murmured.

"I am staying here when you return tomorrow," she blurted out.

He went rigid, his fingers tensing around her nape. He didn't say anything for a long moment before he ground out from between his teeth, "Can you repeat that?"

"Azrael, Rayner, and Callan will go back with you tomorrow. I am staying here with Sawyer. To stay with Ashtine," she answered, her tone hardening with each word.

"And what am I to do if I need you?" he snarled.

"If you need your power refilled, you can Travel."

She watched as so many emotions crossed his features, she couldn't decipher them all. She could tell he was holding back, biting his tongue on words he wanted to say. He sucked in a sharp breath, his entire body shuddering as he exhaled, but he was still rigid beneath her fingers.

She snatched her hands back when she realized they were resting against his bare chest. His lips pressed into a flat line and a faint trace of smoke rose on his next exhale.

"It is not that simple right now, Eliza," he finally ground out. "Leaving Avonleya requires getting blood from Scarlett and blood from Cethin to return. She has her own matters to tend to. I cannot be tracking her down for blood when needed. What if she is here collecting Cyrus?"

"That's not my problem," she retorted.

"Wrong, Milady," he growled again, moving his face inches from hers. "This became your problem when you volunteered to become my Source."

"When this war is over, everything will be easier," she said, shoving down the desire coursing through her. "The Wards will be down, and you will be free to Travel when needed. You just need to endure it until then."

"Endure it until then," he repeated.

"I'm sure you'll be fine," she replied, pushing against him to stand.

He let her go, getting to his feet just as quickly. She moved to retrieve her sword, sending it away in a burst of flame. When she turned back to him, she found his hands loosely fisted at his sides, and the faint outline of scales shimmered beneath his skin, reflecting the soft glow of the fire. They made his skin darker, and she briefly wondered what his full dragon form looked like.

"Are you going back to your rooms?" he asked tightly.

"Yes," she answered, wrapping her arms around herself, looking away from him.

"Straight there?"

"Does it matter?" she tossed back.

"It does."

She rolled her eyes. "It doesn't, Razik."

He studied her for a long moment, seeming to debate something, before he nodded curtly. His wings appeared, and he bent his knees in preparation for launching into the night.

"Where are you going?" she asked, lurching forward a step.

He gave her a mocking smile. "Does it matter?" When she stared back at him, her lips sealed tight, he said, "I didn't think so."

But she knew. She knew as she made her way back up to the palace that he was flying above her, making sure she got back all right. It was an instinct he couldn't fight against.

And she hated that it mattered.

# CHAPTER 11
# SCARLETT

The stars were dull tonight, blocked by the clouds. The world was too still. She could feel it all. Everything hanging in the balance.

Scarlett released a slow breath. The too soft grass swayed gently around her as she studied the map burning in the air above her. Thin lines of white flames created an outline of their continent and Avonleya along with the borders of the various territories. She studied the red and orange embers hovering in various places, moving some to new positions. Moving pieces into place. Setting up the game.

It was almost time.

She'd been forced to stay behind more times than she liked these past few days. She'd been hiding out in Avonleya out of necessity, but it hadn't been wasted time. Not when she'd been training every day with Cethin and learning to fight off the same draining magic Alaric had. Not when she had learned where she truly came from. Not when she finally, *finally*, had all the pieces laid out in front of her. Now it was making sure they were all where they needed to be. Making minor adjustments as Alaric made his moves.

As Saylah made hers.

But tomorrow?

Tomorrow when she saw Alaric things would be set into motion that could not be undone. The final game would start.

Sorin had gone to bed hours ago. It had been a long day, and he was still adjusting. She had spent the entire afternoon and evening planning with Cassius and Sorin. When Sorin was all but falling asleep in the middle of their discussions, she'd told him to go to bed and that she would be in shortly.

Cassius had stayed another three hours, then she'd come here two hours ago.

The Sutara Family country estate. A place she would have called home if things had been different. This was where Cethin had always brought her in her dreams when he would dream walk to her. There was some comfort in that, despite the things Cethin had kept from her. He may not have known everything Saylah had told her, but he knew enough. He'd kept enough from her to break that fragile trust that had been built. But Kailia had been right too. She had her own secrets. Could she fault Cethin for keeping his?

Her hands were stacked on her stomach, and she drummed her fingers as she let her thoughts have their way. Cassius was... Well, not better, but functioning again. There was a team collecting Ashtine now. They would be back tomorrow, and she would leave to get Cyrus. Then her focus could shift again. The Tyndells. The lock. Cethin. Sorin. More pieces that would be moved into place.

Moves and countermoves.

What would their world look like when this was over?

Would she be here to see it?

She lifted a hand, the embers on the map disappearing and far fewer ice crystals appearing, scattered in various places throughout the two continents.

Mirror gates.

There had to be others. Surely Pyry contained one or two. And what of the other continents in their world? Lands she'd only read about and territories unexplored?

Her magic strained beneath her skin. Shadows and flames pushing to be let out. She was keeping it contained, but it demanded more. She'd taken so much from Sorin and then had kept it locked up tight. It felt dangerously similar to when it would break through her tonic and that had never ended well, so she let her shadows out to breathe before they forced her hand. They coiled around her—brushing along her arms, throat, cheek—seeking to comfort her. She sucked in another breath, her eyes fluttering closed at the now familiar essence.

Until they thickened around her.

Her eyes flew open, and she pushed up to a sitting position. Her shadows were writhing, merging into two panthers prowling around her as she got to her feet. The gentle breeze had stopped, the grasses stilling.

Scarlett raised a hand, starfire flaring to life in her palm as she peered into the darkness. There was nothing around but the rolling fields and a small copse of trees. She should Travel back to Aimonway, but there was something watching her. She could feel its eyes on her.

The shadow panthers snarled softly, their eyes glowing orange embers. Pulling a dagger from her hip, she took another step. She was barefoot, clad in only loose pants and a thick long-sleeved tunic. Her silver hair hung loose around her shoulders, and she was debating sheathing the dagger and calling forth her spirit sword when she saw it.

The copse of trees was perhaps thirty yards to the left and drifting among it was...

Scarlett didn't know what it was.

It had a body, but it wasn't one of flesh. It shimmered against the dark, almost translucent. Almost, but not quite. A spirit of the After?

Scarlett took another step towards it, her panthers falling to her sides to flank her. The being stepped forward too.

No.

It glided.

Its legs moved as it took a step towards her, but it hovered a few inches off the ground. The entire being was pale. Pale skin. Short hair white as fresh fallen snow. White eyes with no pupils she could see from here.

She stopped, but the figure continued forward until it was no more than ten yards from her. Tall and lean with sharp, angular features, it was not mortal nor Fae. She could almost call him beautiful. This was a being she had never encountered, never read about. And there were definitely no pupils in the white eyes that glowed softly in the night. How did he see?

The figure tipped his head back, inhaling deeply. Scenting, she realized. Then he dipped his chin, soulless eyes settling on her.

And he smiled.

She felt it settle over her. The calm as she prepared to fight. The anticipation of a deadly game. The hunger for the kill. Something that had been ingrained in her very being.

Scarlett tilted her head, a wicked smile of her own filling her face as she sheathed her dagger. A flare of starfire had her spirit sword appearing in her hand, and one of her panthers let loose a warning snarl.

She should definitely go to get someone, but now Death's Maiden was waking up.

And she hadn't been out to play in far too long.

The being nodded, as if in agreement of what was to come, before his mouth opened. The thing exhaled. Scarlett could see his breath as though they were in the arctic climate of Pyry. Lifting a hand, he reached into the hovering puff of air and pulled out something gleaming gold.

A sword.

A godsdamn solid gold sword.

She planted her feet. Her grip tightened on her sword hilt as she waited to see what he would do next, and when he started gliding towards her again, she let starfire ignite down her blade. The being didn't falter. He kept moving forward smoothly, purpose and hunger set on his sharp features.

A hunter who had caught its prey.

One of her panthers lunged for him. His gold sword swiped through it, her shadows dissipating into nothing. He hadn't even paused, the movement like an afterthought as he continued towards her. Her remaining panther shifted in front of her with a deep growl, but he brushed it aside with his hand. She felt her shadows try to strike, to coil around him, but they dissipated too.

Definitely time to go for help.

But when she tried to Travel out, she found herself rooted to the spot. He lifted his sword, placing the tip of the blade beneath her chin and tilting her head up. She glared back at him, knocking his sword aside with her own. She felt the sting of the blade as it left a shallow slice along her throat.

His eyes went wide, flaring with white light, and he leaned forward, inhaling sharply.

"Blood of death," he breathed, and gods. His voice. It was unearthly. Raspy and icy and a whisper that latched onto her bones. It was as entrancing as a Night Child but so much stronger.

Scarlett had had enough. She couldn't move her feet, but she could move the rest of her body. The being was still leaning towards her, his tongue running along his lower lip, when she struck, plunging her sword deep into his gut.

Her starfire went out on contact, and her sword felt like it was pushing through…nothing. No flesh. No muscle or bone or insides. There was no resistance, as though the being really was nothing but wisps of faint white light.

She yanked her sword back, and the being straightened. His head cocked to the side. There wasn't a wound. No entry point where she had shoved her sword into his stomach. In fact, the only solid thing about the being seemed to be his own gold sword.

He reached for her, and she couldn't step back. His hand landed on the wound, his fingers flexing around her throat. Well, those felt solid enough. She swiped her sword up on instinct, but it drifted right through his arm. He leaned towards her once more, his nose brushing along her cheek.

"Not one of his here, but two," he breathed.

And then it was hissing and lurching back from her, releasing her throat and his hold on her. She stumbled back, her feet released from whatever power had been holding them in place. She tightened her grasp on her sword, but the creature was looking around wildly and that was an arrow protruding from his neck.

He reached up, yanking the arrow free with another hiss. It drifted away, becoming the same wispy light that he was. Except for the arrowhead. That fell to the ground, and he backed away from it quickly.

Another arrow came from her right, sinking into the creature's skull. His mouth fell open, a wail of rage ringing as white wisps poured out of it before the entire being faded into the dark.

"There are more."

Scarlett whirled to find Kailia standing behind her, bow raised and an arrow nocked. Where the hell had she come from?

"Magic does not affect them," she continued.

"No shit," Scarlett snarled as the Avonleyan Queen came to her side. "Why does an arrow work and not a sword?"

"Not any arrow," Kailia replied, pivoting sharply and releasing the string of her bow. She had another nocked before the wail sounded into the night to announce she'd hit her target. Scarlett spun, looking for the source of it, but found nothing.

"How many are there?"

"More than there should be," Kailia murmured.

And then they appeared.

They floated out from the copse. Two dozen at least.

"What are they?" Scarlett gasped, watching as they all drew swords of gold.

"We do not know." An arrow flew. Ashes swirled, and another appeared in her hand before she nocked it to the string. The beings were advancing, floating towards them, white eyes glowing specks in the night.

"How did you learn what could kill them?" Scarlett asked, feeling entirely useless as Kailia let another arrow fly.

"They got in my way," she answered, releasing two arrows at once. Amber eyes darted to Scarlett for the briefest of moments before she added, "When I tried to kill Cethin."

Scarlett forgot about the floating assailants for a moment. "You tried to kill Cethin?"

"Yes. Many times," she answered simply. "Keep them busy until I can get to them, and don't let their blades touch you."

"What?" Scarlett demanded, but she was already gone among ashes.

Kailia moved fast. As fast as Rayner had when he had ripped organs from bodies on the ship. The floating beings tried to ignore her.

Until they couldn't anymore.

She appeared in the thick of them, stabbing an arrow into the skull of one before yanking it free and firing it from her bow at another. One reached for her, and she dropped to the ground, disappearing into ashes. The rumble of frustration from the beings shook the earth beneath Scarlett's feet. She blinked, and another arrow whizzed past her face, sinking into the skull of a being several yards to her right. Three others skirted around it, white eyes fixed on her.

Kailia could have at least given her a couple of those damned arrows. She stooped down, swiping up the arrowhead left behind from the first being. The one that had cut her with his blade.

And what exactly was going to happen because of that?

And wait. Where the fuck was Cethin? He let Kailia come out here and fight these things alone?

Scarlett rolled her shoulders, stretching her neck. Then she raised her sword to meet a golden blade, shoving back against it. The being bared his teeth in a snarl, fangs like a Night Child appearing as it pressed forward. Her arm buckled under its strength, but as he lunged for her throat, her other hand came up. She plunged the arrowhead into its skull. His mouth fell open, his wail piercing the air, mixing with the cries of the ones Kailia was slaughtering.

A hand gripped her tunic, yanking her back. How could they grasp her when her sword slid right through them? She managed to keep her hold on the arrowhead as she was tossed to the ground, her spine screaming at the impact, and the air whooshing from her lungs. Two of the creatures stood over her. They all looked exactly the same. There was no differentiating between them. A third joined them, all of them inhaling deeply.

"Blood of death," one murmured.

"The same, yet different," another added.

One brought the tip of his sword to her chin, tilting her head to examine the cut along her throat. She tried to raise her own weapon, but something was wrong. The movement was sluggish. Her arm was too heavy. Her entire body was too heavy. Her movements were all in slow motion. The figures were blurring, shimmering on the edges. She blinked, trying to clear her vision.

A swirl of ashes had Kailia appearing near her head. She held two arrows, thrusting out with both hands into the heads of two of the beings. Scarlett blinked again, and she'd pulled her bow from her back, both arrows on the string aimed at the third who had backed away, hissing at her.

"You were cut," the Avonleyan Queen observed, releasing the arrows. "I told you not to let that happen."

"Where is Cethin?" Scarlett asked, struggling to sit up. Her voice sounded different. Shallow. Breathy.

"Trying to lead them away from you," Kailia answered. She dropped to a knee beside her, a small hand tilting Scarlett's head to the side to examine the wound. "How long ago were you injured?"

"Before you got here," she answered. She managed to raise a hand to her throat. "It is not deep."

"That does not matter. The sword blades themselves are poisonous."

"Fantastic," Scarlett muttered.

"It will not kill you. Just paralyze you," she added.

"Even better." It explained why holding her head up was getting difficult. "Are there any left?"

"No. Cethin will be here to get you as soon as he can. We will need Tybalt and Cassius with Razik unavailable." She plucked the arrowhead from Scarlett's hand, and it disappeared in a swirl of ashes.

Scarlett flopped down onto her back. "I think I need a Healer, not a dragon," she muttered.

Kailia was back on her feet, amber eyes watching warily. She had another arrow nocked and ready. "No. A Healer cannot help you."

"Is there an antidote?"

"No."

Her head was becoming too fuzzy for this conversation right now. Her magic was fading. She could feel the shadows and starfire slipping away, just like her consciousness was starting to do. Traveling was impossible.

Kailia glanced down at her again. "Stay awake, Scarlett."

It was the last thing she heard before she slipped into the darkness.

*"This is unexpected, my pet."*

Scarlett went rigid at the sound of his voice.

Her eyes snapped open, and she found herself in a study. It was early morning judging by the faint light coming through the two windows on one wall. She slowly turned to face him, finding Mikale Lairwood rising from a seat behind a large oak desk. His dark eyes raked over her, mouth twisting into a smirk.

She took a step back, bumping into the door. Her hand fumbled for the door handle, but when she yanked on it, it didn't move. Locked. She was locked in a room with Mikale, unable to access her magic.

A dark laugh came from him as he moved towards her. *"You have been most difficult to find these last weeks, my pet. Yet here you are. You came to me."*

*"I did no such thing,"* she spat, lifting her chin.

He laughed again. *"But you did, Scarlett."* He lifted a hand, a ring with a green stone shimmering on it. A finger traced along her jaw.

*"I wouldn't know how."*

*"Yet here you are."* His finger dragged along her throat. *"This is new."*

*"It will heal."*

He flashed her another mocking smile. *"I wouldn't be so sure."* Then his hand was around her throat, holding her in place while he pressed against her to speak softly into her ear, *"Where are you, Scarlett?"*

She shook her head, clawing at his hand that only squeezed tighter. *"You only make those you love suffer by drawing this out. Juliette. Nuri. Ashtine. Briar."* He paused, appearing to think dramatically. *"What is that other one's name? From the Fire Court?"*

*"What is he doing to him?"* Scarlett gasped, trying to pry his hand from her throat.

*"Absolutely nothing,"* Mikale said. *"The Sorceress on the other hand…"*

*"No,"* she rasped. She tried to bring her knee up, but he had a leg wedged between her thighs, pinning her to the door.

*"Yes,"* he whispered into her ear. *"How many more, Scarlett?"*

Then he was flying across the room, a strangled cry of surprise coming from him. He landed on a chair, knocking it over as he fell to the rug. Scarlett sucked in air, her hand coming to her throat, and she found her brother standing before her.

*"Who are you?"* Mikale snarled, climbing to his feet.

But Cethin turned his back on him. He took her by the shoulders as he said, *"He is not in control here, Scarlett. This is your dream. Not his."*

She shook her head, wincing. Between the cut from the gold sword and Mikale's tight grip, her throat was sore. "He controls them when he dream walks to me."

"You give him that control."

"I don't," she retorted.

"You do," Cethin insisted. "He is strong, but you are stronger, Scarlett. He stole his gifts. You are the daughter of a goddess. You let him have this power over you."

"No." She shook her head, tears beginning to well in her eyes.

"She has no control here," Mikale sneered.

"You can do something," Scarlett whispered. "You're here."

"This is not my dream, Scarlett," Cethin said. "I can only do so much. Just as you give him control, you limit mine."

"I'm not doing anything," she insisted

"Exactly," he answered, shaking her shoulders. "Do something."

She slowly lifted her hand, tried to bring her shadows forth, but there was nothing. No darkness or ember of starfire.

"This is it, Scarlett. The last place he controls you," Cethin said, urgency creeping into his tone. "You take this from him, and he has nothing left. Nothing."

"She came to me," Mikale taunted, moving cautiously into her field of vision. There was a cut along his cheek, a small bit of blood.

"Take back the control, Scarlett," Cethin said, completely ignoring Mikale. His hands shook on her shoulders.

"What is wrong?" Scarlett asked, brow furrowing.

"It is taking a lot of my power to stay here."

"That was never a problem before."

"My power is already greatly depleted. I am using the last of it to come for you."

"Why would you do that?" she demanded in horror.

"Because you are not a means to an end, Starfire. I wish..." He swallowed thickly. "I wish I could do this for you. I wish I could take on so many of your burdens. I failed as your brother before I even knew I was one, but you? Gods, Scarlett. You are stronger than this. Stronger than me. Stronger than him. And I do not mean your magic. I mean you are stronger. Take it back from him."

She held his stare for a long moment. In the back of her mind she knew it was odd that Mikale was not interfering more. It seemed he could not come any closer to them. He prowled around them, back and forth, agitated and muttering.

*"You are doing that," Cethin said softly. "You are keeping him back so we can speak. This is your dream. Your mind. You control it."*

*Her gaze slid to Mikale, and his dark eyes snapped to hers. "No," he snarled, his features twisting with fury. "No! You are mine."*

*A breath of relief left Cethin as his trembling hands slid from her shoulders.*

*"Go," Scarlett whispered.*

*He gave her a weary smile. "We will be waiting for you."*

*She blinked, and he was gone.*

*She was left alone with Mikale.*

*He straightened, adjusting his tunic. "Brother, was it? We have wondered who the Avonleyan King was. Just another card you have revealed in this game."*

*Scarlett cocked her head as she watched him. Felt his words try to claw their way into her being, but they didn't settle.*

*"You revealed a card of your own," she answered. "Tell Alaric I am coming for Cyrus and Neve at sundown. I expect him to uphold his end of the deal."*

*"And what of your deals?" Mikale asked, his lip curling back in a sneer. "Does your word mean nothing?"*

*Scarlett winced dramatically. "Do you mean the one where I promised death the next time I saw you but killed Veda instead?"*

*"The one," he gritted out, "made nearly two years ago. All of this could have been avoided if you had simply honored your word."*

*"All of this could have been avoided if you and Alaric were not trying to rule this realm."*

*"This realm is the prize," Mikale spat. "Not our objective." He paused, inhaling deeply and seeming to collect himself. He smoothed his hands down his tunic again. When his attention settled on Scarlett once more, he gave her a pointed smile. "So clever, yet you cannot see that he only wishes to save you. Without him, you will die with the rest."*

*"I will take my chances," Scarlett retorted.*

*"And risk millions of other lives in the process? Risk innocents? Risk those you think you love?" He took a step towards her, and Scarlett lifted her hand, shadows spilling from her fingertips. "You cannot kill me in a dream. Even you are not that powerful."*

*"No," she agreed. "But for every time you have come to them, I will drag out your death a little longer. Come to my dreams again, and I will find out exactly what I can do to you in my dreams."*

*Her shadows crept forward, a ring of starfire springing up around him, and Mikale flinched back.*

*"So be it. You could save the realm, instead you damn them all. How* benevolent *of you," he sneered.*

*She just smiled back at him, letting her crown of darkness and starfire take shape atop her head. "Be a good lackey and deliver my message to Alaric, Mikale," she purred. "Tell him our game continues."*

"Love?"

Scarlett groaned. Fingers slid gently into her hair. Lips brushed softly against her temple. Her eyelids were heavy as she forced them open, and her eyes locked with ones of muted amber. Relief flashed through Sorin's features, and she reached up, smoothing away the crease between his brows.

"Are you all right?" he murmured.

She nodded, then winced. Her hand went to her throat, fingertips running over raised skin.

"It will scar," Sorin said quietly, pulling her fingers away. "It wasn't deep, but the poison in the sword…"

"It's fine, Sorin," she whispered. "I'm fine."

"Truly?" he asked, pressing his brow to hers. "Mikale? Cethin said…"

She pushed up onto her elbows then, searching for him. They were back in her suite at the castle. She was on a sofa in the sitting room, Sorin sitting on the edge beside her. Cassius was hovering over the back of the sofa, his eyes shifted and glowing. She reached up, brushing her fingers along his that were clenched on the back of the fabric.

Cethin was in an armchair. He was pale. Tired icy blue eyes were locked on her, and he smiled weakly. Kailia was perched on the arm of the chair, and standing off to one side was Tybalt. His warm, kind eyes watched her.

"How are you feeling?" the Avonleyan Commander asked.

"Hot," she answered. Her clothing was sticking to her, and she noted the cloth on the floor.

"Is that normal?" Cassius asked, eyes flicking to his father.

"It is," Tybalt answered. "You did well, Cassius."

Sorin helped her sit up more, shifting so she could lean against him. "What happened?"

"You were cut with the sword of one of those beings," Cethin supplied.

"I remember that. And Kailia showing up. Where were you?"

"They have only ever been interested in me," Cethin said. "Until tonight."

"And you do not know what they are?" she asked, taking the glass of water Tybalt handed to her.

"No," Cethin answered. "Creatures created by Achaz. That is all we know."

She looked at Tybalt. "You do not know? Or Saylah?"

Tybalt shook his head. "I have been with Saylah since Arius and Serafina hid her and Temural away. We, admittedly, do not know as much about the more recent beings created."

"Then how did they get here?" Scarlett asked between gulps of water. She was still so damn hot.

"I unknowingly let them in," Cethin answered.

Scarlett slowly lowered her glass. "How?"

He pressed his lips together. "I will tell you, Scarlett. I swear. But I do need to rest. Walking into your dreams and working against Mikale's power drained me, and that is a conversation I want to be in a better place to have."

She didn't like it, but she nodded. "When I return from the continent then."

"Are you sure you should still go today, Love?" Sorin asked, picking up the cloth and pressing it to her brow. It was cool against her sweaty skin, and she leaned into it. "Maybe take a day to recover—"

"He is with the Sorceress, Sorin," Scarlett said quietly, sneaking a peek at Cassius. Her Guardian had stiffened, fingers digging into the sofa again. He exhaled a long breath, smoke spilling from between his lips.

"What do you mean he is with the Sorceress?" Sorin gritted out.

"I don't know. All Mikale said was that the Sorceress had him," Scarlett said. "We go today. I told him to tell Alaric we would be there at sundown."

"Your power?" Sorin asked tightly.

"Is there and at full-strength."

"Her power should not be affected with the poison removed from her veins," Cethin supplied.

"I thought there was no antidote?" Scarlett asked, reaching over her shoulder and grasping Cassius's hand.

"There isn't," Cethin answered. "There are only two ways that we know of to remove the toxin."

"Which are?"

"The creatures themselves suck it out from your throat."

Her face screwed up in disgust. "Like a Night Child?"

"Similar, yes," Cethin said with a nod.

"And the other way?"

"Dragon fire burning it out of your blood."

Her gaze swung to Cassius. "You did that?"

He nodded. "Tybalt guided me."

Well, that was…both amazing and slightly terrifying.

Cethin cleared his throat. "Razik usually does it, but with him across the sea…"

She twisted back to face him. "How many times have you been cut by their swords?"

Her brother drummed his fingers along the arm of the chair. "A few." Then he added, "It is how I know it will scar."

Her hand drifted to her throat again, but Sorin caught it, kissing the tips of her fingers. "If you are going to the continent tonight, you need to rest."

She had to agree. She had been tired when she'd Traveled to the estate grounds. After fighting and that dream, now she was completely wiped out.

Cethin, Kailia, and Tybalt were already striding for the doors, but Cethin paused. "Please let me know if you need something, Scarlett."

She held his stare for a long moment before answering, "I will."

They both knew it was a lie. They needed to have a conversation first, and even then…

Well, she might have to adjust a few plans is all.

She looked up at Cassius. "Go sleep, Cass. We get him back tonight."

He bent, pressing a small kiss to her cheek. "You are truly all right?"

"Perfect," she answered. "Thanks to you."

His hand ran down her hair affectionately as he straightened. "I will be back in a few hours. If Rayner is not back yet?"

"We still go," she answered. "We will figure something out."

Cassius nodded once more before leaving her alone with Sorin. He stood, reaching for her hands. "Come, Love."

"I am going to bathe real quick," she said, letting him pull her to her feet. "Can you get me some food?"

"Of course."

When she was settled in the bath—the water on the cooler side because she was still so godsdamn *hot*—Sorin left her alone to find her something to eat. She tipped her head back against the lip of the tub. With a thought, her map of starfire appeared, hovering above her. She reached up and slid an ember down to a new position.

Another piece moved into place in this dangerous game.

# CHAPTER 12
# CYRUS

"The spell is not working, Gehenna," Alaric seethed.

"Impossible," she replied coldly, her fingers wrapped around the bars of her cell.

"It is not working," Alaric repeated, stepping closer to her. He lifted a hand. What could he do? His draining power wouldn't work on her. There was nothing to drain. Unless he was planning to reach through the bars and wrap his hand around her throat, in which case Cyrus couldn't blame him.

Eyes fixed on his loosely clasped hands, he kept his gaze down. He sat in the same corner he'd been sitting in for hours, knees bent, arms resting atop them. He hadn't moved since he'd made the bargain with the Sorceress.

He'd heard the footsteps on the stairs, and he'd assumed it was someone delivering food again. He hadn't touched the last two trays they'd brought him. But then he'd heard two sets of footsteps. Alaric hadn't bothered to look at him when he'd entered the space, but Briar did. Briar's icy blue eyes had connected with his, and Cyrus had immediately looked away at the look that had crossed the prince's features.

Pity.

Pity he did not deserve. Not after what he'd done to keep the memories of Cassius out of her hands.

"You said it would lead me to the lock," Alaric was saying, his tone tight with barely leashed control.

"I said the lock would call to you," the Sorceress retorted, pushing off the bars and beginning to pace.

"You tricked me," Alaric spat.

"No, Prince of Failure," she chided. "We made a bargain. I fulfilled my end."

"Gehenna," he snarled, slamming an open palm against the bars.

"You brought the Fae of Water instead of the Princess of Wind," she said, ignoring Alaric's outburst. "She could have found your lock."

"I ran out of time."

"A pattern in your existence as of late," Gehenna said with a laugh. The same laugh she sometimes had when she'd let him out of his nightmares. "You had another way. You should not need the lock."

Alaric cursed, slamming a palm against the bars again. "That wretched girl destroyed it when she burned down my Fellowship. I have not needed the lock until now."

"That girl has ruined many plans," the Sorceress said darkly. "Not only yours."

"Cyrus."

His murmured name startled him. He hadn't heard it since he'd been down here. How long had it been now?

He glanced up to find Briar standing over him, concern filling his eyes.

"Ashtine is safe?" Cyrus rasped.

Briar nodded slowly.

"Good," he replied. "That's...good."

"They are coming for you, Cyrus."

Cyrus nodded mutely.

"You will... You are strong enough to endure this," Briar said.

A small, sardonic smile tilted on his lips. "If only I was that kind of male," he answered. "But it's already too late."

Briar's gaze darted to Alaric and Gehenna. They were face-to-face at the bars, heated whispered words being hissed between them. Good. If her focus was there, it could not be on him.

Briar sank to a crouch before him. "They will understand, Cyrus. Whatever you have had to do to survive her... They will understand."

"How long?" Cyrus asked.

"Soon."

He shook his head. "How long has it been? Since I have been here with her?"

"It has been three days since the encounter in the Southern Islands."

Three days.

It had taken three days for him to break. Only three days to give in to her. Only three days to betray his family, his Court.

And Briar wanted to tell him he was strong?

If he had it in him to laugh, he would have then. He was the farthest thing from strong there was. He didn't need to be reminded that he damaged everyone around him. It was something he reminded himself of every waking moment, and his nightmares reminded him while he slept. More than once he had thought that it would be better if they didn't come for him, if they left him here. But three days.

That's how many days Alaric had given them. If they didn't come today...

Well, what more could Alaric really do to him? Drain his power? He could fucking have it. Physically torture him? He deserved that and more. Keep him locked away with the Sorceress? There was nothing left of him anyway.

He'd told himself he would make it up to them. He would do better. This would be the last thing he did that would hurt those he cared for so profoundly. He would never be deserving of anything, but he would try. Try to not be the complete fuckup his mother had clearly deemed him to be. What he'd proven to be every day since. He would do better. Do more than he had done for Merrick, for Thia. He would be better.

*The room fell silent when Cyrus walked into the den. Eliza wouldn't look at him, her gaze fixed on her wineglass as she fiddled with the stem. Rayner was standing next to Sorin, trying to look casual and relaxed. Cyrus knew he was anything but. And Sorin? The Fire Prince had a grim look on his face, mouth set in a taut line.*

*His steps faltered. "What?"*

*Sorin pushed out a harsh breath, swiping a hand through his dark hair. Then he jerked his chin at the table. "Sit, Cyrus."*

*There were no cards waiting for them. No food spread. No drinks, save for Eliza's, but she was currently chugging the last of her wine.*

*"Just tell me what is going on," Cyrus said, moving to the chair anyway.*

*The three of them—his family—glanced between themselves again. Sorin took a seat, but Rayner remained standing next to him. Ever watchful. Cyrus sank unceremoniously into his seat.*

*"These last few years have been difficult," Sorin started, holding his stare.*

*Cyrus blinked at him. Difficult? These last five years had been agony. Five years since Thia had been killed. Five years since he'd lost his twin flame. Five years of mania. He scarcely remembered some months. Entire periods of time were simply blank.*

*"We have waited to have this conversation," Sorin continued. "You know we are here for you. Whatever you need."*

*Cyrus nodded, trying to figure out where he was going with this.*

*"We…" Sorin swiped a hand down his face.*

*"Just say it, Sorin."*

*"We want to give you an out, Cyrus."*

*"A what?"*

*"An out. If this is no longer what you want to do—if being my Second is no longer something you wish for—I want you to know you can walk away from it," Sorin said.*

*Cyrus stared at him. "You want me to leave?"*

*"No," Sorin said quickly. His gaze cut to Eliza, who still hadn't looked up from her glass. Rayner shifted slightly. Sorin blew out another harsh breath. "But perhaps it would be for the best."*

"Cyrus."

He blinked several times. Back in the prison. That's where he was. Briar still crouched before him, so much worry filling his features.

That wasn't how that conversation had gone. They had offered him an out, yes, but they had wanted him to know that he would still have a place in their family. The Fiera Palace would still be his home, but if he no longer wished for the role of Second, they understood. Eliza wouldn't look at him because she had tears in her eyes, not wanting him to go. Rayner had been agitated at the thought of him leaving, at the idea of having to bring another into their fold.

Sorin wanted to give him a choice, even though it pained him to do so.

But maybe they had wanted him to walk away? Maybe he had gotten it all wrong?

"Prince of Water," the Sorceress called, and Briar's eyes widened as he quickly rose to his feet. "Did no one teach you not to play with other people's things?"

A thing. That sounded about right at this point.

Alaric turned, cold amusement glimmering in his dark eyes. "Do not worry, Prince Drayce. Mikale delivered a message from my Wraith. She comes for him tonight."

"Then I will be freed," Gehenna gasped, clinging to the bars.

Alaric glanced back at her. "In time."

"In time?" she repeated in horror. "You said you would free me!"

"You said that spell would help find the lock," he replied with a shrug.

"You will regret this choice, Alaric."

"It appears you are already regretting yours," he retorted. He began striding for the stairs. "Come, Prince. We will come back for the Fire Second later."

Briar looked down at Cyrus, an apology written on his face.

"Go," Cyrus said. "It doesn't matter."

"Cyrus—"

"Go, Briar," he snapped. "Before you pay yet another price."

Briar gave him one last look as he murmured, "Soon you will be free of her," before he turned and followed Alaric up the stairs.

Cyrus could feel the Sorceress's eyes on him. He inhaled deeply, steeling himself to look at her. Be free of her? He never would be.

He lifted his head, meeting her violet stare. She tilted her head, a finger sliding up and down a bar. "We don't have much time left together, pretty Fire Fae."

"I would say let's make the most of it, but I would really rather you didn't."

She smiled, and he flinched back.

"Still so funny," she said softly. She began pacing slowly behind the bars, fingers dragging along them. "Our time will end, but you will not be free of me."

He knew that. Not only did he make a bargain with her, she still had his blood.

He'd had to give her more.

Just one part of what he agreed to in order to keep his memories of Cassius free of her ministrations.

*If you can't see that all you do is damage everyone around you, then I will keep reminding you until you believe it.*

He ground his teeth against the voice in his mind. Cassius's voice repeating those words. He'd saved the other memories. Smoking mugweed on a balcony at the Black Halls. Stealing that stupid mirror from Sawyer's cabin on the ships. Helping Cassius expel his magic when they first arrived in Avonleya. The sparring ring the first time Cassius had kissed him.

"Do not forget our bargain, Fire Fae," Gehenna called, pulling him from his thoughts.

"How could I?" he gritted out, pulling up the sleeve of his grungy tunic. Wrapping around his upper bicep ran a Bargain Mark, blood red against his skin. The Mark was three winding ropes. Three sacrifices to keep his memories pure. One of blood. One of betrayal. One of time.

"Will they want you back? Once they know what you have given me?" she asked curiously.

And the fact that he paused to consider his answer told him enough. The Sorceress had fundamentally broken something in his soul. Something that had always been fractured. Something he'd always barely held together.

"Yes," he finally answered. The word did not hold any conviction. He said it because he knew it was the right answer, not because he believed it.

She hummed an acknowledgment, her pacing becoming more erratic. "You get to leave while I stay locked away."

"Sounds like you'll be free soon enough, Gehenna," he muttered.

"Not soon enough," she snapped. "I have been in here for centuries, pretty Fire Fae."

"You did try to help the Maraans take over this world, so I can't really blame them," he offered.

"I was not helping the Maraans," she snarled, fingers pulling at her lank black strands. "Achaz sent me."

"To aid the Maraans."

"To further his own plans, not those of the Maraans," she spat.

Cyrus didn't say anything else. He didn't want to agitate her any further.

Gehenna whirled to him again, gripping the bars and pressing her face to them. "Do not forget what is required of you, Fae of Fire. Do not forget what the consequences will be for breaking your deal with me."

"I won't," he answered. "I can't."

"Good."

And she pulled him into another nightmare.

# CHAPTER 13
# TALWYN

Talwyn had just finished the small tray of breakfast food when she heard the door at the top of the stairs open again. She knew it was morning. Could Az really be back already?

No one else had come to see her yesterday. Only the guards that brought her food and water and changed out the waste bucket. It had just been her and her thoughts, Azrael's parting words rattling around in her skull for hours on end.

Setting the tray aside, Talwyn brushed her hands off on her pants. She'd managed to braid her hair into a plait, hissing and cursing at the sting of the shackles the entire time. She had been anxious for Azrael to return, eager to hear a report on Ashtine. Maybe, just maybe, he would bring her with him to see her. Her heart rate picked up in anticipation, and it was odd. It was a feeling she could never really recall having before. But it was not Azrael or Ashtine who stepped into view.

It was Sorin.

She sucked in a sharp breath, her eyes locked on his. There was something wrong. They weren't as bright as she remembered them being. Had she done that to him? She couldn't move. She could scarcely breathe. He had stopped Scarlett from taking her life, but he had not said one word to her. Not that she blamed her. He had been trying to calm Scarlett down, all of his attention fixed on his wife and twin flame. Why had he come here now?

He smiled. A small sad thing. "Hello, Talwyn."

Her mouth was too dry. She couldn't form words. She didn't know what to say to him. She didn't know how anything she could say would make up for nearly killing him, but she blurted, "I am sorry," as if that would mean anything.

Some deep understanding shone in his muted amber eyes. "As am I." He dipped his hand into the pocket of his black pants, pulling out a key.

"What are you doing?" she breathed.

"I came to speak with you. We are certainly not going to do so down here," he answered, fitting the key into the cell door. It creaked loudly as it swung open. Sorin stepped into the cell and produced another key. She watched, too stunned to do anything else, as he crouched before her and removed the ankle shackles. He was wearing a thick grey tunic. He only wore long-sleeves for formal occasions when it was required, and this was the farthest thing from that one could get.

He brought his gaze back to hers. "My agreement with Scarlett was that the wrist shackles stay in place." Talwyn nodded, and Sorin reached for her hands, gently pulling her to her feet.

He waited, making sure she was well enough to stand, before he motioned for her to follow him out of the cell. She followed him up the steps. Down some halls. Still unsure how or why this was happening. When they neared another door with two guards standing on either side, Sorin nodded to one who bowed and left down a side hall. Talwyn briefly wondered what that was about, but then Sorin pushed open the door. The sunlight that poured in drove all thoughts from her mind, and she couldn't keep the tears from pooling in her eyes.

Sorin glanced at her, that small smile forming once again, before he retrieved something from a bench near the door. A pair of shoes.

"I thought we could walk," he said, holding the shoes out to her. "I would offer to help you put them on, but—"

"I can put shoes on," she grumbled. His smile widened as she reached for the footwear. "What?"

He shook his head, handing the silk shoes over, but the smile slipped from his face when she winced against the wrist shackles as she worked the shoes onto her feet. When she finished, he stepped forward as if to help her up, then stopped himself. Ever the protector, trying to take care of those in his charge.

Except for the time he hadn't.

She cleared her throat, adjusting the shackles carefully, anxious to step outside.

"Thank you," Sorin said.

She turned to find him taking two bowls from the guard that had left a few moments earlier. She hadn't heard him approach, too excited at the thought of being outside. Despite her power continuously draining, she could feel the wolf prowling beneath her skin, as tired of being caged as she was. It was faint, but it was there.

Sorin passed her a bowl, and she looked down to find—

Chocolate frozen cream.

She slowly brought her eyes back to his, and he gestured to the open door. "Shall we?"

Talwyn glanced down at the bowl of frozen cream in her hands again.

"I won't melt it," Sorin said.

Her head snapped up to find a half-smile on his mouth. Her eyes narrowed on him a bit, but she moved towards the doorway and beyond.

Inhaling deeply, crisp mountain air filled her lungs, drowning out the stale air she'd been sitting in for days. A breeze caressed her face, stray hair escaping from her messy plait and fluttering across her brow.

Talwyn slowly took in her surroundings. They were at the base of towering black mountains. She'd been Traveled to a sparring ring when she was first brought to Avonleya. Then the Avonleyan King had taken her directly to the cells. Dark fog drifted along the ground, reminding her of the shadows that often trailed Scarlett. It was morning, but later than she had expected it to be.

"I have this for you."

She turned to find Sorin with a cloak in one hand, his bowl of frozen cream in the other.

"I did not know if you would need it or not," he added.

It was not overly warm, but it was mild out for a spring morning, even in the mountains. "I am fine," she answered slowly.

He nodded, looping it over his arm before bringing a spoonful of his own frozen cream to his mouth. Unsure of what exactly this outing was, she tentatively brought a bite to her lips, nearly moaning at the taste. She'd had nothing but bread, cheese, and apples for days. Still better than what Alaric had been serving her, but a sweet? It had been ages.

They moved down a rocky path, silent and side-by-side. No guards followed them, but she felt eyes on her nonetheless. She was sure there was someone watching them at all times. The Ash Rider perhaps.

"Have Azrael and Ashtine returned?" she asked after several minutes.

"Not yet. We expect them any time," Sorin answered, scraping his spoon along the bottom of his bowl.

Talwyn nodded, bringing another bite to her mouth. She was trying to savor it, not knowing when she'd be offered such a thing again. They walked on for another several minutes, and she took in more of the surroundings. A large castle loomed behind her. They'd come out of some side door. The path they were following had low stone walls on either side, and it led straight to the mountains. There were no side paths. You either went back in the same door or into the mountains. One could traverse the wall, she supposed, but she also assumed there were guards patrolling it.

"I am working on better...accommodations for you," Sorin said after more silent minutes passed between them.

"Why?" she asked. "I deserve to be in a cell."

"My wife would agree with you."

"Your wife believes I deserve worse than a cell, and she is not wrong."

He came to a stop, setting his bowl down on the low wall. Shoving his hands deep into his pockets and staring out at the towering mountains, he said, "I am sorry, Talwyn."

She laughed. A strangled, shocked bark of noise. "I tried to kill you, and you are apologizing to me?"

He turned to face her fully. "I should have been there. You had already lost so much, and then I..." He blew out a breath. "I should have been there for you. I am sorry that I was not. And for these past twenty years, for my part in the feud between us, I apologize for that too. For all of it."

She stared at him, utterly speechless. She had used her magic against him, struck him in the chest with a bolt of energy, nearly took him from this world, and *he* was apologizing to *her*?

He reached over, gently taking the bowl from her hands and setting it beside his own. "I know I am no longer needed to watch over you, but I will make sure that you are not placed back in that cell. There will be guards outside whatever room you are given, and I can make no promises about the wrist shackles—"

"Sorin, stop," she interrupted in a harsh whisper, and he fell silent. "Please stop…apologizing to me. I do not deserve such a thing, least of all from you."

He gave her another sad smile. "You deserve an apology, Talwyn. I made you a promise, and I broke that promise. I raised you as much as Eliné did. Knowing what I know now, she left you, yes. But she left you with me, and I failed you."

"I tried to kill you," she whispered.

"You succeeded."

"What does that mean?"

"It means I entered the After. For the briefest of moments," he answered, turning back to face the mountains once more.

"Then how do you stand before me?"

"That is a long story that involved Cethin bartering with Serafina from what I understand, and Scarlett…" A fond smile filled his features. "Being Scarlett."

"I do not understand," Talwyn said. "I hit you in the chest, Sorin. There should have been no coming back from that. I thought I had…" She trailed off, the entire scene replaying in her mind once more.

"I know, Talwyn," he said gently. "Even I do not fully understand what was done."

"And you are fine? You died, came back, and are completely fine?" she asked, scanning him from head to toe, but when her gaze went back to his face, she saw the wince.

"That does not matter," he answered. "What matters is that I am here. With her. No matter what the cost was."

But there was a cost, and Sorin, being who he was, was again trying to protect her. But she did not need him to protect her. Not because she thought she did not deserve protection. That wasn't it at all. She did not need to be protected from the consequences of her actions. If he paid a cost to come back from death, then she had forced him to pay it. She did not wish to be protected from that reality. She needed to face it, feel it.

"Tell me the price you paid."

"You have enough guilt and burden to bear, Talwyn. There is no need to add to it."

"I am not a child any longer, Sorin," she replied, lifting her hands to brush back stray hair. She scarcely felt the bite of the shackles. "I was not a child when you... I blamed so many, but what I have become? That is not your fault. That is not Eliné's fault. It is no one's fault but my own, and I wish to know what cost you have paid because of me."

Sorin studied her, seeing her in a way that no one else ever could. Azrael may have known of her as a child, but she rarely interacted with the Earth Prince then. Ashtine was her same age for all intents and purposes. But Sorin? Sorin had been Eliné's Second. He had always been around. Seeing him in the Black Halls was as natural as seeing her aunt. He would always know her in a way that others didn't. No matter how much they both changed, there would forever be some trace of Little Whirlwind and the Prince.

Whatever he was looking for, he must have found it, because Sorin finally spoke. His voice was low and quiet, as though he was trying to soften the blow he was about to deliver. "The cost was my magic."

Talwyn lurched back from him. "What?"

She could say nothing else. Her brain could not form any other thought because she could not comprehend what he had just said.

"I no longer have my magic," he repeated. "I cannot summon fire. I cannot create portals. I cannot..." He pulled his hand from his pocket and held it up. His left hand. Where a twin flame Mark should have been stark against his golden skin. Only a gold band was there. "I cannot have a twin flame. I am mortal with an extended lifespan. That was the cost. To correct the balance."

Talwyn Semiria sank to her knees and wept.

All those little things that had bothered her made sense now. The muted eye color. The thicker tunic. The offering of a cloak instead of his magic to warm her in the spring weather.

Tears streamed down her face, but she forced herself to look Sorin in the face when she rasped. "There is nothing I can say to make this right, Sorin, but I am so profoundly sorry for what you have lost because of me."

And Sorin, perhaps one of the few she had wronged more than her own people, knelt before her. He took her hands in his, careful of the shackles. "You are forgiven, Talwyn."

"You do not owe me such mercy."

"I give it to you anyway. It is your choice what you do with it." He squeezed her fingers. "I was proud of you, Talwyn. The day you took the throne. So many losses weighing you down, and yet you took on the burden of four Courts. I was so proud of you that day. I never told you. I wanted you to know."

More tears spilled over. He squeezed her fingers once more before he released them and pushed back to his feet. He moved over to the stone wall, sitting down beside the empty bowls. It was several minutes before she'd gathered herself enough to do the same.

They sat in silence, staring at the mountains. The sun was nearing its peak when Sorin spoke again. "I know this has already been an emotional day for you, but we do need to discuss what is to come."

She nodded. She'd been waiting for this. Waiting to hear what had been decided about her future. She would accept whatever it was as long as she did not need to sit in the unknown any longer.

"You will no longer rule, Talwyn," he said quietly. "Scarlett claimed your Courts after you were brought here. If you wish to have your throne back, you will need to challenge her, and you will not win."

"I think it is quite obvious that I am no longer fit to rule over anyone," she replied tightly, her fingers toying with the edge of her tunic. "Perhaps it was once my destiny to rule, but my time for that has come to an end."

She felt more than saw him glance over at her. "What do you wish to do then, Talwyn?"

It was a question that had plagued her since Azrael had left. A question she had pondered since he had challenged her to start thinking about what she would change if given the chance, and the truth was, she did not know. She had been raised to rule since she had entered this world. Had never entertained any other options. She would forever be remembered as the queen who had handed over her people to monsters for the sake of her own petty revenge. But perhaps she could do some good for a few people. Maybe they would remember her as something different, even if it was just one person.

"I wish to help," she finally answered. "In whatever I can and in whatever way Scarlett will allow me to do so."

Sorin stiffened a little beside her. "Alaric has Cyrus and Neve. He will only release them in exchange for a Fae Queen."

"But I am no longer that."

"Yes, but he does not know that," Sorin said. "Scarlett and Cassius will take you to the continent at sundown to make the exchange."

"But Ashtine will be here?" she asked. "And Azrael? He will stay with you."

Sorin turned his head to look at her. "Ashtine will be here and safe. Azrael will fight alongside us when the time comes."

Relief washed over her. "Good. That is what matters. If I can help by getting Cyrus and Neve back, then that is what I will do. If I can get you any information on their plans, I will do that too."

Sorin looked as though he wanted to say something more, but he kept his mouth shut.

"What?" Talwyn pressed.

He didn't answer for a long moment before he said, "I want to tell you not to put yourself in more danger than necessary, that trying to get us information could likely get you killed, but you are right, Talwyn. You do not need my protection anymore."

"This is war, Sorin," she answered. "Let me fight on the right side of it, if only for a little while."

He nodded, and she could swear there was the briefest glimmer of pride in those dull amber eyes.

Before either of them could speak again, two figures stepped from the air. Two silver heads of hair. Cethin's hand rested on Scarlett's shoulder, almost as though he was prepared to hold her back if necessary. The queen was rigid as she stared at Talwyn.

And Talwyn held her stare as she rose from the wall and sank to a knee before the Avonleyan royalty, then bowed her head.

"What is it?" Sorin asked, getting to his feet and striding towards them.

Talwyn lifted her head to see Scarlett dragging her eyes from her to her husband, but she was not the one who answered him.

"Our mother is here," Cethin said.

"Saylah is here? In Aimonway?" Sorin asked, looking back and forth between the siblings.

Scarlett nodded. "She has come to fulfill her end of the deal. She has come to tell us how to restore your power."

# CHAPTER 14
# SORIN

They made their way up the path to the front gates of the castle. Kailia and Cassius had met them when Cethin had Traveled them all here, but the Avonleyan Queen had been watching him with Talwyn for the last two hours. It was one of the compromises he had made with Scarlett. She would concede to him going to speak with Talwyn, but only if Kailia would be guarding him from the smoke and ashes she moved among.

That and the nightstone had to stay in place on her wrists.

Considering Scarlett had not demanded to join him, he counted only two conditions a win. He still wasn't certain if she had not made such a demand because she didn't wish to see Talwyn, or if it was because she was saving her strength for when she faced Alaric tonight. He did not need their bond to know how she was feeling. She hid it well enough, but he knew her tells. It was in the way she carried herself, more tense than usual. It was in the tight way she spoke. It was in the way she was with them physically, but her mind was elsewhere. Planning. Scheming. Preparing. Riding an edge where her control was stretched tight and Death's Maiden prowled just beneath the surface.

He knew her mother showing up was the last thing she wanted or needed right now, but she would deal with it. She would keep going, and when things were all said and done tonight, when she returned with Cyrus and fell into bed exhausted and spent, he would be there. He would be the one place she did not need to keep her masks in place. The one place she could breathe while saving the world. Together. Always together. If Saylah could not fulfill what Scarlett demanded of her, being that place for Scarlett would be enough. It would have to be.

Talwyn was being escorted by a guard behind them. He had promised she would not return to a cell, and he would not break another one to her. Her fate had not yet been decided, and Sorin had not broached the subject with Scarlett since their fight about it the day Scarlett had nearly killed her. Too many other things demanded her attention, but giving her back to Alaric? He knew it was their only option. Talwyn had said she wished to help, that she would not fight against this, but would the others trust her enough to believe she was on their side now? And after this was over, if she survived, he did not know what Talwyn's future would hold.

When he had said Talwyn was to come with them and not returned to the cells, Scarlett had held his stare for a long moment, fire dancing in her silver eyes as she pursed her lips. But then her gaze had slid to Talwyn, who was still kneeling before them.

"You once told me I needed to prove myself to my Courts," Scarlett had said coldly. "You were right, and I have. Now *you* need to prove yourself to *me*, Talwyn Semiria. Prove you are worthy of his mercy."

Talwyn had not faltered, poised and unreadable as she had been taught and trained to be. She had held Scarlett's stare, only nodding sharply once in response. Scarlett hadn't said another word. She'd just turned her back on Talwyn, grabbed his hand, and jerked her chin at her brother to Travel them out.

Their small group strode through the main doors and into the entrance hall at the same moment several others stepped from the air. Sorin froze, and Scarlett did the same beside him. Luan. Razik. Rayner with…Tula? Where was Ashtine? Sawyer? Callan? Where the fuck was his Fire General?

Razik's eyes ran over them all. The dragon shifter looked irritated. "Cethin, we need to talk. Now," he barked, already moving towards a side hall.

"Saylah is here," Cethin answered.

Razik stopped, his entire being going rigid. "Why?" The question was a gritted growl.

"Better question," Scarlett interrupted, her voice low and eerily calm. "Why have you again returned with fewer people than you should have?"

Razik turned, his eyes shifted and glowing as faint scales rippled across his visible flesh. "This was not my mission, princess," he sneered. "I was sent for the Traveling. That was it."

"Raz," Cethin warned.

The dragon's glowing stare shifted to Cethin. "And what the fuck happened to you? Why are you trying to draw power from me?" When Cethin didn't answer, his attention shifted again. "Lia?"

"He dream walked and drained himself," Kailia said simply.

"Where is Ashtine?" Scarlett demanded sharply.

"She cannot leave the continent," Rayner answered. Tula was hiding behind his legs looking unsure and slightly terrified. "Eliza and Sawyer stayed behind to guard her. They are all in Siofra with the Shifter Siblings."

"Callan?"

"Stayed behind as well. We ran into a unit of seraphs, and Nuri was with them. She relayed some information to him about his people," Rayner explained.

"Saylah is waiting," Cethin interrupted.

"Saylah can keep fucking waiting," Scarlett snapped at her brother before her attention went back to Rayner. "Why can Ashtine not leave the continent?"

"Apparently, Alaric has placed a Mark on her. Razik could see it, but it was not visible to the rest of us."

Scarlett was quiet, taking in the brief report Rayner was giving her. Cethin and Kailia had moved closer to Razik, the three of them having their own quiet conversation. Azrael hadn't said a word since appearing, but his gaze was locked on Talwyn.

"Why was Tula with you?" Sorin asked.

The Ash Rider's eyes flicked to the Avonleyans before he answered. "She caught a ride with Callan."

Scarlett's nose scrunched as she was pulled from whatever thoughts she was working through. "What does that mean?"

Rayner's lips pressed into a tight line. "She shifted and hid among Callan's things. To go with me."

"She shifted?"

"She is a power shifter. We can discuss this more later," Rayner said in a way that left no room for debate.

Scarlett's brows shot up at his address, but Sorin knew him well enough to understand the implied warning. He brought his hand to the small of her back and leaned in to whisper, "There is more to say, but he does not trust everyone in this room."

She nodded once, attention still fixed on Tula. "You are all right, Tula-Bug?" she asked, her tone softening.

The little girl peered out from behind Rayner, and she nodded. The Ash Rider reached back, gently ruffling her curls. His eyes met Sorin's again. "The Alpha and Beta know what she is."

Fuck.

Sorin expelled a harsh breath. That explained a lot of his hesitation at the moment. With the current accords and charters in place, they could demand that Tula be given over to them. She was an orphan Shifter.

"Tonight, when I return, I will need that explained to me," Scarlett said, her spine straightening. "But I need to deal with Saylah before we go get Neve and Cyrus." She glanced at Rayner once more. "Are you all right to go with me and Cassius?"

He nodded. "Let me get Tula settled, and I will rest. Unless you need me for—"

But Scarlett was already shaking her head. "Go. I need you prepared for tonight."

Rayner gripped Tula's hand in his, then hesitated. "Scarlett. Ashtine said that Cyrus is with—"

"I know where Cyrus is," she interrupted again, her tone strained and agonized. "We go at sundown."

Rayner nodded again before leading Tula to the stairs that would lead up to the guest rooms on their level of the castle.

Cethin cleared his throat. "It truly is unwise to keep her waiting, Scarlett."

Scarlett rolled her eyes and waved her hand dramatically in a gesture for him to lead them along.

Sorin kept his hand on her lower back as they followed down a hall. He bent to murmur, "Whatever information she has, whether or not this will work—"

"It will work," Scarlett interjected. "She knows what is at stake if she does not come through on what I have demanded."

He wanted to say more. He knew there were things she had left unsaid about her visit to Shira Forest, but now was not the time to push her. So instead, he leaned down and pressed a kiss to her temple as they came to a set of closed double doors.

Cethin looked at Scarlett. "Are you ready?"

She tossed him a mocking smile as her ornate crown of shadows and starfire took shape atop her head. "Of course."

Her brother seemed to hesitate, but then he pushed open the doors. They all filed into a grand sitting room. Tybalt stood near a window, and next to him was a goddess. There was no mistaking what she was. Unworldly beauty. A circlet of stars sat on her brow, and shadows flitted around the stars as if they were in the night sky itself. Long silver hair that matched her children flowed down around her shoulders, reaching to her waist, and misty shadows drifted around her, just as they often did her daughter when she let them out.

Saylah's silver eyes took them all in as they entered, and as one, they all dropped to a knee, bowing their heads.

Everyone except Scarlett.

If he could, he would be hissing to her down their bond and telling her to get on her godsdamn knee before the goddess of night and shadows, but when he chanced a glance at his wife, she stood there with her arms crossed and a bored look on her face.

"At least your company knows how to show respect to a goddess," Saylah said, her voice as cold as the shadows around her.

"Seeing as I am your god these days, perhaps you should be on a knee before me then," Scarlett retorted, and Sorin could hear the wickedness in her voice.

"Scarlett," Cethin hissed at her above the collective sharp inhale from several others in the room.

"Rise," Saylah said tightly.

They all got to their feet, and Scarlett moved in front of him and Cassius protectively. Two shadow panthers appeared, snarling softly while they prowled around the Fae. Tybalt's eyes widened, his fingers flexing as he watched the shadows.

Saylah tore her gaze from Scarlett, surveying them all once more. "Cethin."

"Hello, Mother," he said, stepping forward and pressing a soft kiss to her cheek.

"Your power is drained."

"It was necessary."

"Why have you not drawn from your Guardian?" Her silver eyes flicked to Razik.

"He only just returned from a mission across the Edria," Cethin explained.

"He should not be leaving your side," Saylah replied. "Certainly not right now with the state of things."

Sorin watched as a muscle feathered in Razik's jaw, but he dropped his gaze to the floor.

"Did you come to chastise them?" Scarlett drawled, moving casually to an armchair. She dropped unceremoniously into it as her shadow panthers continued to guard him and the other Fae. "Because if that's the case, I do not need to be here. I have matters to tend to, and your mistakes to fix."

Saylah stiffened, but she did not reply, instead shifting her attention to Cassius. "You were young when I last saw you."

"Ah, yes," Scarlett chimed in with faux wistfulness, an adder's smile on her lips. "The time you laid eyes upon Tybalt's son, but did not tell your Guardian of his existence."

The Commander started, but he also said nothing. He only looked at Cassius with remorse and sorrow at knowing how his son had grown up because that secret had been kept from him.

"I was hoping after our discussions in Shira Forest, you would have become a little less confrontational," Saylah said.

Scarlett hummed, drawing patterns on the arm of the chair with her finger. "I am a disappointment to many people who wished to use me. I will add you to that growing list."

Everyone in the room seemed to hold their breath while the two exchanged words, Sorin included. He could not decide if he should feel pride while watching Scarlett talk down to a goddess or fear for her life.

"Have you located the lock?" Saylah asked, a tinge of scarcely controlled fury entering her tone.

But Scarlett barked a harsh laugh. "Oh, *Mother*," she tsked. "Your lock is quite a ways down on a list of my priorities."

"Then perhaps your twin flame has just dropped on my list," Saylah replied.

Scarlett made a show of considering. "It is still well above proper mothering on that list, so I am not too concerned."

"Scarlett," Cethin hissed again when the shadows around Saylah thickened.

Still Scarlett sat, casual and bored in her armchair, finger continuing to draw on the armrest as she watched her mother. "Relax, Brother. She needs me as much as you do, and neither of you gets what you want from me unless she holds up her end of our deal."

Sorin frowned. Scarlett had spoken of this deal in passing, but he did not know the particulars. They'd had little time to speak privately these last two days, and there would be no more time to do so today.

Scarlett's features suddenly morphed from bored and aloof to wicked and cunning. "You lured me here with a promise of telling me how to restore Sorin's power. Get on with it. You are taking too much of my time the way it is."

Saylah turned and stared out the window for a long moment. Her gaze stayed fixed on the mountains when she said, "The balance was upset when he crossed the Veil and came back. Serafina warned you there would be a cost."

"And I told *you*, enough costs have been paid. This would not be one of them," Scarlett retorted, pushing to her feet.

"He cannot have his original power back."

"That is not our agreement, Saylah," Scarlett said, starfire beginning to slowly wind up her arms. Tybalt stiffened, again flexing his fingers, and Razik moved closer to Cethin, who had shoved Kailia behind him. But the Avonleyan Queen was peeking around him, curious eyes bouncing between Scarlett and Saylah.

"I cannot defy the balance, Scarlett," Saylah said harshly, finally turning to face her daughter once more. "His power crossed the Veil. We cannot bring another power into this world without sacrificing one of equal power or greater."

"How would we do that?" Scarlett pushed.

"You choose a powerful being to kill, and take their power before you do it," Saylah replied.

Scarlett did not move, and Sorin knew by the look on her face that she was about to say something both brilliant and terrifying.

"What if the power is freely given?" Scarlett asked.

"What?" Saylah said in confusion.

"What if the powerful being offered their power up freely? Death would not be required," Scarlett pushed.

"Transferring power from one being to another is not done for a multitude of reasons," Saylah said slowly.

"Like when it fits your own needs?" Scarlett asked, her head tilting. "Eliné's gifts were transferred to me. Those gifts are stronger than Sorin's were. Take them from me, and give them to him."

"No," Sorin, Saylah, and Cethin all said simultaneously.

"What do you mean no?" Scarlett seethed. "They are my gifts now, which would make them mine to give away."

"You need them to find the lock. You know this," Saylah admonished.

"Fuck your godsdamn lock," Scarlett said. "You will do this, Saylah."

The goddess took a step towards her, and the shadow panthers immediately snapped at her. The Guardians in the room all growled low warnings.

"If I do this," Saylah said, "you will not be able to uphold your end of the deal."

"I will find another way," Scarlett insisted.

"There is no other way," Saylah spat. "If there were, do you think I would have sacrificed my time with you? Do you think I would have made you carry this burden? If there were another way, this would have been finished centuries ago. This world would be at peace, your father would still live, and you and Cethin would know the love of the family you should have had."

The room went silent as mother and daughter stared at each other, neither of them willing to back down. Saylah's shadows thickened even more while Scarlett's shadow panthers stalked forward.

But it was Sorin who broke the stand-off. He moved to Scarlett's side, cupping her jaw and forcing her to look at him. "Love, I will not take your magic from you. You will need every advantage when you face Alaric. If this is our only option, we will not take it."

"We will find a way," Scarlett ground out, determination filling her eyes.

"And if we do not, it will be fine," he replied. "We will still be together. All the way through the darkness."

"I do not accept this," she whispered. "I will not."

"Would it work?"

Everyone turned to the person who had spoken.

Talwyn.

Luan was beside her. Sorin had forgotten they were even in the room with the Sutara family dramatics playing out in front of him.

Talwyn lifted her chin as the attention of the room settled on her. "Would it work?" she repeated. "To transfer power willingly given?"

"It is ancient magic of the gods, of those who can create new beings," Saylah answered. "The power must be as strong as or stronger than the original power. It can be forced, but the cost is much greater and comes with death."

"But if freely given? You could do it?" Talwyn pressed.

"Talwyn…" Luan started, but she stepped forward.

"You could take my magic—that is stronger than his was—and give it to him?" Talwyn asked.

"No," Sorin breathed.

"He could not rule the Fire Court with wind and earth magic," Scarlett cut in. "He would need to learn and master entirely new elements."

"It would not manifest as wind and earth magic," Saylah said, studying Talwyn. "You are Henna's daughter." It was a statement, not a question, and Talwyn nodded. "You look just like her."

Sorin saw Talwyn's throat bob before she said, "Why would it not manifest as wind and earth magic?"

"Because he was not born to harness such gifts. They would

change to a form his Fae body could harness. The magic he was born to possess," Saylah replied. "They would become fire."

"You are saying that he would essentially have Henna's power, but it would be all fire?" Luan asked, the shock evident in his voice.

"The Shifter gift she possesses as well," Saylah replied. "That would also manifest differently." Her silver gaze slid to Sorin. "You would essentially be as powerful as an Avonleyan, perhaps more so."

"Then why did I maintain water and fire when you transferred Eliné's gifts?" Scarlett cut in, her brow furrowed.

"Because you are not Fae," Saylah replied. "Your bloodline made you able to carry more gifts."

Silence fell as everyone contemplated what had just been shared, what was being offered. Scarlett bit her lip, glancing up at Sorin. Her eyes held his as she asked Saylah, "And our twin flame bond?"

"Would be reinstated, just as it had always been," Saylah answered, and Sorin could swear her tone had softened just a touch.

Scarlett stared at him, hope shining in her eyes, and gods, he was about to crush her all over again. He brought his hand up, cupping her cheek. His thumb swiped along her cheekbone. He smiled sadly, and her face fell because she could read him as well as he could read her.

Sorin pulled her to his chest, and she buried her face in his tunic as he looked at Talwyn. "I cannot ask this of you," he said thickly, running a hand down Scarlett's hair.

"You do not have to," Talwyn replied. "I am offering."

"I cannot accept."

"You can," she said sharply. "I am no longer on a throne. You are. You need this power. I do not."

He looked to Saylah, who now stood silently, waiting for their decision. "Can she keep one gift?" he asked. "The wind? Or the Shifter gift, since that is not Fae magic? Two of her gifts would still be more powerful than what I had."

Saylah shook her head. "The magic is intertwined. It is all or nothing."

"She will be mortal?" Luan asked, his arms crossed tightly.

"She would be as Sorin is now," Saylah answered. "A powerless being with an extended lifespan."

"Her Staying?" Sorin asked.

"Would remain for a time, as yours does," Saylah answered. "For how long, I cannot say."

Sorin rested his chin atop Scarlett's head, preparing to decline Talwyn's offer again.

"If it were not for me, you would not be facing this decision," Talwyn said. "So let me make it for you. I stole from you. From both of you. Let me give it back."

"Talwyn, we need to think about this," Luan said, stepping to her side. "You do not understand everything this entails."

She tipped her head back to look up at him, a brief glimpse of sadness crossing her features before she wiped the emotion away. "I think I do, Az."

"Talwyn—"

"It is stupid to keep debating this," Talwyn said, cutting Luan off and turning away from him. "This needs to be done before I am returned to Alaric."

"You cannot go back there powerless," Luan snarled. He turned to Sorin, helpless fury etched along his features. "You will allow this?"

"Stop, Azrael," Talwyn said coldly. "This is what is best for everyone."

"Except you," he countered.

Scarlett was still buried in Sorin's shirt, listening to the debate around her. She was still, scarcely breathing. He knew she would not contribute to the conversation. She did not need to. They all knew what she would say. Knew that, in this, she would side with Talwyn.

"This is my cost to bear. Not theirs," Talwyn replied. "You know this, Az. This is what is best for the Courts, the continent, the entirety of the realm."

"This is the sacrifice of a queen," Sorin said quietly.

"It is my choice what to do with the mercy I have been given," she replied. Her voice did not tremble. She did not flinch or show an ounce of hesitation.

Still holding her jade green stare, Sorin said, "So be it."

"You must maintain physical blood contact the entire time," Saylah said, drawing Marks into the dirt around Sorin and Talwyn. They had moved to one of the training arenas in the mountains. Saylah had told them they needed to be somewhere the power could manifest. It would fight being taken from one source, and because it would be stronger than his prior magic, he might not be able to completely control it right away.

"It will be painful for you, Daughter of Henna," Saylah continued, working her way around a circle. "A piece of you will be cleaved away. You must not lose contact with him."

"Understood," Talwyn answered. She was still shackled, Luan standing close to her.

The others were all gathered throughout the ring. Rayner had also caught wind of what was happening and had left Tula with the other children to be here. He and Cassius stood a few feet away while the Avonleyans stood on the other side of the arena. Sorin turned to Scarlett who was hovering near him. She was fidgeting, shifting her weight as her eyes tracked Saylah and the Marks she was drawing on the ground.

"You are anxious," Sorin murmured.

Her eyes flicked to him before going back to her mother. "Of course I am anxious," she clipped out. "If this does not work…"

"It will work," he said softly. Then he gripped her chin and brought her gaze back to his. "And when it does, this is enough, Scarlett. She will no longer rule, and she will no longer have her gifts. She has given enough. Her debt has been paid. Swear it."

Scarlett rolled her lips, but she gave a curt jerk of her chin. He dropped a kiss to the top of her head and pulled her close. "I love you, Sorin," she whispered.

"All the way through the darkness, Love."

"You two cannot be in the circle," Saylah said, and Scarlett pulled back to look at her mother. "If you remain, the power could try to come to one of you instead of him. It will draw out the process."

Sorin glanced at Talwyn, who was nodding at something Luan was murmuring to her, but her gaze connected with his. Still not a hint of regret or hesitation.

Scarlett pushed up onto her toes, kissing him softly and drawing his attention back to her. His hand slid into her hair, and she murmured onto his lips, "Soon we set the world on fire together, Prince."

He crushed his lips against hers once more as her shadows brushed along his throat, curling around his ear. She pulled back, a wry tilt to her lips as she walked backwards from him. She did not break his stare as she stepped out of the circle and to Cassius's side, her Guardian's arm dropping around her shoulders.

Sorin tore his eyes from her to look at Talwyn, who had moved to the center of the circle and was waiting for him. When he moved in front of her, she raised her hands, and Sorin reached into his pocket for the key that would undo her shackles. No one said anything as he fitted it into the lock, the shackles falling open. He tossed them outside the circle of Marks along with the key, and Talwyn turned her palms up, just as Saylah had instructed. Sorin drew a dagger from his side, slicing across both her palms before doing the same to his own. Then he placed his hands atop hers, gently squeezing her fingers.

"Thank you for this, Talwyn," he said quietly.

"It is the very least I can do," she replied curtly, eyes fixed on their joined hands.

He saw it then. Her chest began to rise and fall more rapidly. Her breaths became small, controlled gasps as she worked to keep control over herself. A gust of wind tore through the arena, but the Marks around them were already flaring. Saylah had already spilled her blood along them. She was speaking an ancient language Sorin did not know, but his entire being was fixed on the female before him.

"Little whirlwind," he said softly, and her eyes snapped to his. Tears pooled there. "Henna and Eliné would be so very proud of you."

A tear spilled over, sliding down her cheek.

And then she flinched.

Sorin felt it. The prickle of power that hit his palm at the same moment that Talwyn sucked in a sharp breath. He tightened his grip on her hands as more power flowed, small trickles of it that crawled along his palm as if seeking. Their mixed blood was seeping between their fingers, dripping onto the earth.

"Do not let the connection break," he heard Saylah warn. Then she spoke again in that ancient language, and Talwyn screamed.

He heard a roar echo around the arena, but he could not focus on it because his knees were buckling as power poured into him. He was gripping Talwyn's hands, lowering to the ground as she sank to it, still screaming in utter agony. The ground was trembling beneath them, small rocks shaking and the dirt swirling, and that was fire sparking in his veins. He may have been completely powerless for only a few days, but his power had been slowly waning since he had been brought back from the After. He had not had a full well of power since before that throne room. But this? This was staggering.

The sparks became embers, and the embers became fire. Pure wildfire that sang as it raced throughout his being. No longer a trickle of power moving from her to him, but a crushing wave of it. It was unyielding. He was sweating, this heavier tunic suddenly sweltering with the heat flooding his veins. His magic had been great, the strongest fire gift in this realm, but this power? If this was Talwyn's power, he could not fathom the power that flowed in Scarlett's veins.

He could hear the commotion going on around them, but he couldn't focus on it. It was a dull afterthought compared to the all-consuming power rushing over him, seeking a way out while simultaneously sinking deep into his soul.

And breaking through all of that was a hope that was not his. An anxiousness that was scarcely being suppressed. It was shadows and white flames, wildness and darkness. It was a star shining brighter than any other.

*Sorin?*

Her voice echoed in his mind, so tentative and full of hope. He whipped his head to her, finding her just outside the circle, two tears tracking down her cheeks. Her hands were clasped beneath her chin, but on one of those hands, stark against her ivory skin, was a Mark that flowed down her fingers.

Another burst of power surged into him, and he could not control it as flames flared out from him. But Scarlett had a shield of shadows up in the next breath, keeping his flames away from them all. He tried to pull them back, but they raged and burned and only flared brighter. So he let them burn. Let the magic get to know him, and when the last of it left Talwyn, and she sagged against him, he pulled her close while the fire burned.

She was shaking violently, her palms still bleeding while his were already healing. He ripped a section from the hem of his tunic, making two strips of fabric that he tied around her palms, all the while trying to rein in this mighty power.

"What do you need?" he asked gently as he tightened the second strip of fabric around her hand.

"I'm fine," she rasped. "Just get me Az."

It took another few minutes, but the raging flames finally died down. He suspected Scarlett was using some of her own magic to help. He could faintly feel it brushing up against his, but she was conserving most of it for later when she faced Alaric.

The others were all gathered around the edge of the circle, and Scarlett and Luan rushed forward. Luan dropped before Talwyn, pulling her away from Sorin. He smoothed her hair back, bringing his brow to hers, brushing tears away with his thumbs. She murmured something that was too low for Sorin to hear, even with his enhanced senses restored. Whatever she'd said had Luan's eyes closing briefly, a look of grief crossing his features as he gathered her close to him. She was still trembling. Luan rested his chin atop her head, and when he opened his eyes, they met Sorin's.

And in that moment, Sorin understood just how much Talwyn had sacrificed.

*Sorin?*

He looked up to find Scarlett standing over him, watching him carefully. Pushing to his feet, his left hand caught his eye as he did so. His twin flame Mark back in place, exactly as it should be. He looked at his right arm where a Source Mark had returned. His gaze lifted to Scarlett.

*Hey, Love.*

She leapt at him with a breath of laughter. He caught her as her arms looped around his neck, and she pressed her lips to his. Her legs wound around his waist, and he clutched her to him.

"It worked," she rasped onto his lips. "I cannot believe it worked." Another kiss. "How do you feel?"

"Tired," he admitted, and she pulled back with a frown. "Not a mortal kind of tired," he clarified. "The kind of tired you feel when you need to fill your power reserves."

He could still feel it all beneath his skin. A great well of power that he barely had leashed. He did need to rest, to get to know his magic in this capacity.

"You can rest while we go to the continent," she replied, lowering her feet to the ground.

He nodded in agreement. His attention went back to Luan, still holding Talwyn in the dirt. "Take her to your rooms, Luan. Let her rest as much as she can."

Luan did not look at them. Just Traveled from the arena without a word.

"Do you need to worry about them trying to run?" Cethin asked from where he stood next to Saylah.

"No," Sorin said. "Luan is loyal to Scarlett, and Talwyn will insist on going back to the continent."

Cethin nodded, but Sorin could tell he wasn't so sure. He turned and said something to Razik, who Traveled out a moment later.

Saylah stepped forward, and Sorin bowed his head while Scarlett stiffened and turned to face her mother. "I have fulfilled my end of our agreement. Can I trust you to now fulfill yours?" Saylah asked, keen silver eyes watching her daughter carefully.

"Are you questioning my word?" Scarlett asked, head tilting in that calculating way of hers.

"No more games, Scarlett," Saylah warned, taking another step towards her. Cassius was at Scarlett's side in an instant, and the goddess smiled in approval. "Remember what I told you must happen to save this realm."

"You mean what must happen to fix your mistake," Scarlett countered.

Saylah's lips pursed in disapproval. "Call it what you wish, Daughter. It does not change fate."

"Lucky for me, I make my own fate," Scarlett purred.

"This is not a game—"

"I know what this is," Scarlett snapped, cutting off the goddess. Sorin reached for her, but she shrugged out of his grip. "Do not speak to me of games when I am the center of so many. I gave you my word. It will be done. You are no longer needed here. I will send word when it is done."

"One would think gratitude is appropriate in this situation," Saylah said coldly.

"Do something worthy of my gratitude that is not done merely to fulfill a deal to further your own purposes, and I will consider it," Scarlett retorted.

The goddess stared her down for a long moment before her shadows rose up around her, and she was gone.

"Scarlett…" Sorin started.

"Later, Sorin," she sighed, her shoulders sagging. "I need to prepare for Alaric, and you need to rest." She grabbed his hand, preparing to Travel.

*You have secrets,* he sent down the bond.

She tensed but did not reply as she pulled them through a rip in the air, taking them to their rooms.

Still holding his hand in hers, she looked up at him and said, "When I return, I will tell you all of it. I just needed time to come to terms with what I have learned."

He slid a hand into her hair, cupping the back of her head. "We will face it together, Scarlett."

She smiled weakly, and he felt her dread down the bond before she blocked it. "That's what I'm afraid of."

# CHAPTER 15
# CYRUS

The entire room was shirastone. The walls. The floor. The ceiling. Shackles on his wrists and ankles really weren't necessary when he was literally sitting on the floor and leaning against the damn stone. The soles of his feet burned, cut up from traversing the Underwater Prison and these godsforsaken cliffs barefoot, and now they sat on shirastone.

Neve was standing nearby. She had shackles on her wrists and ankles too, but she had boots on. She'd been allowed to bathe as well from the looks of it. In clean fresh clothing, she stood well away from the walls, avoiding any extra shirastone, but her soft grey eyes were haunted. She'd endured something in her time with Alaric. Knowing how the bastard had manipulated Scarlett for years, he could only imagine what he'd done to the Water Court Third. Neve was often mistaken for being soft. Many often wondered how she had become the Water Court Third. Cyrus didn't need to wonder. He knew, and the fact she was that shaken told him enough.

He adjusted his arms around his bent knees where he sat curled tightly in on himself to avoid as much shirastone as possible. But when it came down to it, he would rather endure months of this room than sit in Gehenna's presence another day. She hadn't wasted a moment of the last of their time together, and before Alaric had finally taken him from that dungeon room, she had demanded another vial of blood from Cyrus. He'd had no choice but to oblige her. Alaric had only muttered impatiently from the bottom of the stairs. A seraph had escorted him out, the tall one with the deeply tanned skin and brown feathered wings. His black hair was tied up on top of his head, and his hard grey eyes scarcely glanced at him when he'd roughly slapped the chains to his wrists. Briar had been present, needing to be there for Alaric to enter the prison, but he'd clearly been instructed to keep his mouth shut after their last visit.

The door opened, and Alaric and Briar came into the room. Neve flinched back, and Briar's attention snapped to his Third. Still the Water Prince said nothing. Just like Ashtine had said nothing when they had come here before.

Alaric was cursing under his breath. Something about the lock and Gehenna's useless spell. From what Cyrus had gathered, he was hoping Briar could figure out what he was missing. Guess that didn't go well.

Cyrus noticed them first while the others remained oblivious. Probably because he was sitting on the ground. He saw the ashes creep under the door before instantly disappearing when they crossed the threshold. Those were Ash Rider ashes. Shirastone did not usually affect Rayner, but besides the shirastone, this room was warded extensively so that no magic could be accessed. The only room in the entirety of the cliffs from what Alaric said. That was why he had chosen here for this exchange. So that there would be no surprises from his protégé.

He sucked in a breath when the door started to open. It was not hope that filled him, though. It was dread. What would they say when they found out what he'd promised the Sorceress? Gehenna had asked if they would want him back. That question had plagued him since it crossed her lips. Would they? Could they forgive one more thing that he had done?

Rayner came in first, gripping Talwyn by the elbow. The former Fae Queen looked...different. Less... Just less. Rayner's swirling eyes went straight to Cyrus, but Cyrus could only hold his gaze for a fraction of a second before he was staring at the floor.

He heard them enter. Two sets of footsteps. One heavier, one lighter. But he couldn't do it. He couldn't look at them.

Couldn't look at *him* as his warped words echoed in his mind.

"My Wraith," Alaric said smoothly.

"Alaric," she replied coldly.

"I must admit that while I am relieved to see the Fae Queen here, I am disappointed in you that she still breathes."

Cyrus knew without looking at her that her head was tilted, an arrogant smirk on her lips, when she said, "Disappointing you is my greatest pastime."

Alaric tsked in disgust. "I trained you better than to leave someone alive who wronged you. I trained *both* of you better."

"Do you plan to kill me then, Alaric? For the times I have wronged you these last couple of years?" she asked.

Cyrus watched her boots move across the floor as she edged inside a little more, Cassius sticking to her side. Rayner had moved Talwyn off to the side as near to Briar as he dared.

"I should," he sneered.

"But you won't."

"What makes you so sure, Scarlett?"

"Killing me would mean you lose something you view as belonging to you. You would never willingly allow yourself to lose," she replied, boots sliding along the shirastone floor. "It does beg the question though…"

"What question?" Alaric gritted out when Scarlett forced him to ask by trailing off.

"How do you plan to convince Achaz to let me live when he desires the death of every descendant of Arius?"

Cyrus's head snapped up at that question, and the way Cassius and Rayner were looking at Scarlett told him they did not know what she was talking about either.

*He hunts them. All life they created—together and separately. He will not rest until not one remains, until dreams are gone and death is dead.*

The Sorceress had told him, had all but spelled it out, but he'd been too lost in his own head to comprehend what she was saying. Achaz would not stop at Saylah, but would come for Scarlett and

Cethin too. What else had he missed? What else had Gehenna revealed to him that he hadn't understood?

Another thing he had failed his family in. He was proving just how useless he was at this point, and—

A dark brown eye landed on his, the other hidden behind an eye patch. It pulled him from one spiral into the darkness and into an entirely new one. Cassius was in all black, but whereas Scarlett was in her witchsuit, Cass had on a fitted black tunic and pants. Vambraces were on his forearms, daggers and knives strapped to his weapons belt and thighs. His upper half didn't appear to have any weapons, likely on purpose in case he needed to shift. He had a black cloak on, though, that Cyrus was sure hid more weapons beneath it. But the look on his face?

Complete indifference.

Cassius looked away a heartbeat later when Scarlett took another step forward, and he moved with her. Because of course he would. He was her Guardian. She was what mattered most to him. Always had, always would.

"If you would simply do as you were trained to do," Alaric was saying, "I would have been able to deal with Achaz. If you would have followed through on the deals you made, none of this would be an issue."

"The deals?" Scarlett repeated. Then her eyes went wide. "Are you speaking of Mikale?"

"Did you think I gave you to him solely as a punishment?" Alaric sneered. He moved towards her until they were mere feet apart. "There is always a motive, Scarlett. Always a piece being moved into place in a bigger game. You know this."

That wicked smile curved on her lips again as she replied. "You have no idea."

She moved again. A clever, subtle move that appeared casual, but put her in between Cyrus and Alaric. A move of her own in this game between her and her former master.

"Let's get this over with," Scarlett said, turning to Neve and jerking her chin. The Water Third glanced between her and Alaric before tentatively taking a step.

"Wait," Alaric said, holding up a hand, and Neve immediately stopped, wincing. "I want the Fae Queen's shackles removed before this is done. I do not need her bound in chains I do not hold the key to."

"Then I want Cyrus and Neve's shackles removed."

"I can agree to that," Alaric replied, nodding at the seraph. He moved silently forward, removing Neve's chains first, then his. Cyrus rotated his wrists, rubbing at the red flesh left behind.

"Why can I not feel power from her?" Alaric demanded, his eyes narrowing.

Scarlett rolled her eyes. "Aside from the fact you insisted on meeting in a room made of shirastone, it is because the Avonleyans are more thorough than you are. She has been in nightstone chains, not shirastone."

"Nightstone?" Alaric repeated, his brow arching. "A little overkill, don't you think, my Wraith?"

She flashed him a mocking smile. "Like you said, she shouldn't be breathing. A little overkill was more than warranted."

"So, what now, Scarlett?" Alaric asked, watching her keenly. Cyrus and Neve still hadn't moved, and Rayner still gripped Talwyn's arm. "We go our separate ways until the next battle or prisoner exchange? Seems rather pointless, does it not?"

Scarlett stepped back and turned to Cyrus, reaching a hand down for him. She didn't bother looking at her former master when she clicked her tongue and said, "I am hurt that you have forgotten one of our most important conversations." Her silver eyes held his as he reached for her, smaller fingers wrapping around his and pulling as he pushed to his feet. She smiled softly, her grip tightening on his hand, before she turned back to Alaric. "Although that was a fairly eventful day for you."

"What are you talking about?" the Maraan Prince asked tightly.

"The day your Fellowship burned to the ground, I told you I was already so far under your skin, you didn't even know I was there."

"You have no idea what you cost me the night you burned that to the ground with your starfire," Alaric seethed.

But Cyrus did. Gehenna had told him what the Maraan Prince had thought he had lost.

Her tone had gone icy and vicious when she spoke again, ignoring his outburst. "And tonight? This is the start of the final game. I have already set things in motion."

Alaric's hand snapped out, but Cassius was before her in the next blink, gripping Alaric's wrist with a growl. The Assassin Lord's lip curled up in disgust. "If I had known what blood ran in your veins, I would have killed you the day I found you. Before this is over, I will make sure I have rectified that mistake."

"Instead, you trained us to kill, and in the end, that will be your greatest regret," Cassius returned, releasing Alaric's wrist with a shove that had the male stumbling back a few steps.

Alaric smirked at him. "You will not be the one to end me, Cassius. You were always one of the weak ones. It is why the girls were the Wraiths, and you were just there so they had something to practice with."

"You've wasted enough of my time," Scarlett snarled, shoving Cassius to the side. "Name your cost for Briar's freedom."

The Water Prince started, but he still said nothing. Alaric was straightening his tunic as he answered, "A Blood Bond from you, my Wraith. That is the only price I will accept."

Scarlett locked eyes with Briar, some unspoken agreement being said between them, and Briar dipped his chin the smallest amount in acknowledgment.

"Let me know when that changes," she replied, turning and making her way to the door.

"It won't," Alaric snarled.

Scarlett stepped to the side as she held the door open. "We will see, won't we? Rayner, release Talwyn and bring Neve," she said, an obvious dismissal of the Maraan Prince.

"Mordecai will escort you out," Alaric said, not even bothering to look at Talwyn as she traded places with Neve.

Scarlett batted her lashes at him. "No trust in your favored students, Alaric?"

"I am not stupid, Scarlett. I know we seek the same thing at the moment. I will not give you an opportunity to get to it before me," Alaric said.

"I have absolutely no idea what you're referring to," she replied so innocently Cyrus almost laughed. Almost. He wondered if the

Sorceress had ensured he'd forgotten how to do so. Her attention flicked to Cassius. "Let's go."

Cassius matched Cyrus's pace, their arms brushing once, and Cyrus moved a step away from him. If Cassius noticed, he didn't show it. Scarlett followed them out, the door clicking shut behind her. The moment she crossed the threshold, her shadow armor appeared, along with half a dozen shadow wolves that prowled around them. She moved to the front of the group along with Rayner, and Cyrus found himself herded beside Neve with Cassius behind them. No one looked at him or Neve. No one spoke to them.

Rayner and Scarlett were murmuring softly between themselves as Mordecai led them to the stairs and down the ten levels. After sitting on a cold stone floor for days, the trek up those stairs had been godsdamn miserable. The descent wasn't much better. But he knew they wouldn't be able to Travel within the cliffs. They needed to get outside to the beach.

The only sound as they crossed the cavernous main hall was the boots of the others. Rayner's ashes were moving subtly throughout the space. Cyrus had no idea what the fuck he was doing, but it seemed risky as fuck with Mordecai still in their presence. As terrible as it was to admit though, he also didn't particularly care at the moment. He just wanted out of here. Wanted to bathe and eat something that wasn't stale and sleep in a soft bed. Really, any bed would do as long as he wasn't curled up on a stone floor. He'd take the thin mattress and thread-bare blanket from the flat in Aelyndee for all he cared.

They finally stepped through the archway that appeared, Cyrus just catching the faint glow of the brand beneath Rayner's skin. Mordecai didn't say word to them. Only turned and headed back into the belly of the Cliffs.

It was dark, and the sand was cold beneath his bare feet. His fire instantly reacted, flooding him with heat, and he released a shuddering breath at feeling his magic again. He rubbed at his raw wrists, looking around and trying to get his bearings. He took in another sharp breath—

And the scent of the sea assaulted him.

He ran both of his hands through his hair, pushing out another harsh breath. If it wasn't the Sorceress, it was the sea. He was just exchanging one form of torture for another at this point.

"Just a little farther," Cassius muttered. "We want to make sure we're not being followed."

Cyrus didn't bother acknowledging him. Rayner led them up the beach and into trees so thick they blocked out the stars. And when he was sure his legs were going to give out after days of sitting and so little food, they finally stopped. Shadows and ashes speared out as if searching for something, and they all stood waiting.

"I sense nothing," Rayner said.

Scarlett sighed. "Same. But you got what you needed?"

"I gathered enough," Rayner returned. "Let's get the fuck out of here."

She turned to Cyrus and Neve. "Show me your palms," she ordered gently. Neve glanced at the others before holding them out to her. Scarlett inspected them closely before turning to Cyrus. "Are there are any Marks we need to be aware of before we go?" she asked, and Cyrus realized she was checking for Blood Bond Marks. She was making sure neither of them were sworn to Alaric as Nuri was. No surprises. Not this time.

"No," Neve whispered, and Cyrus shook his head. They didn't need to know about the bargain with the Sorceress. He couldn't face telling them yet.

The queen grabbed Rayner's hand and reached for Neve's. Rayner reached out a hand for Cyrus, and then Cassius grabbed his other, fingers flexing tightly around Cyrus's. Before Cyrus could do anything, they pulled him through the air.

They reappeared on one of the entrance islands off the coast of Avonleya. They were points that had been set up for those who knew how to enter the Wards. Scarlett pulled a vial from her pocket and dumped the contents into the black waters around them. Then they were Traveling once more.

This time when they reappeared, it was directly in the main room of her suite at the castle. The five of them stood there for a moment, just looking at each other, before Scarlett spoke, her voice thick with emotion.

"Hello, Darling."

Cyrus tried to smile, tried to work up any emotion really, but there was nothing. Just the numbness he'd clung to since Gehenna had started playing with his demons. Scarlett was in front of him in the next breath, her arms wrapping tightly around him, and he was clutching her back. A lifeline. A tether to who he was.

At least until she learned what he'd done.

"Sorin is resting," she whispered. "He wanted to be here when you returned. But something happened, and he—"

"It's fine, Scarlett," he murmured into her hair.

Another few moments passed before she said softly, "I'll drown with you, Cyrus. Whatever he let her do to you… I'll dive in and drown with you on the hard days."

He swallowed thickly. He didn't deserve a queen, a friend, like her. He didn't deserve to serve in her Court, let alone call her family.

He gently eased back, swiping a tear away that trailed down her cheek. "I need to bathe. It's been days. I smell like piss and vomit and nightmares."

A half-sob, half-laugh came from her. "You idiot," she muttered. "Food? I can see what I can make in the kitchens."

Cyrus winced. "Please don't."

Her face fell a little. "You're not hungry?"

"I'm fucking starving," he replied. "But I've cooked with you before. That cake was not edible."

"That was the middle of the night! We were both drunk after playing billiards," she said in outrage.

"Mhmm."

This felt…good. This was good. Some normalcy. At least for the moment.

"I won't cook," she promised. "Cold meats. Cheese. Warm bread."

He gave her a fake smile that he knew she could see through, but she didn't call him out on it. She worried her bottom lip for a moment, before giving him a weak smile of her own and heading for the doors. Cyrus moved to follow and go to his own rooms, but a hand gripped his arm.

Turning, he found the Ash Rider's swirling eyes fixed on him. His other arm was around Neve in a comforting hold. She looked as exhausted and haunted as Cyrus felt. Then again, he probably looked that way too, and that's why everyone was giving him these pitying comments and looks.

"We're here," Rayner said in a low tone. "You are not alone. Remember that."

Cyrus nodded, so many emotions beginning to swirl in his gut that he averted his eyes. "Neve, I'll walk you to your rooms."

"I can do it," Rayner said. "Go bathe. I'll stop by in a bit."

He nodded again and stepped from the room, heading down the long hall from the princess's rooms to the guest suites. Cassius was silent beside him, hands shoved deep into his pockets.

When they came to their rooms, directly across from each other, Cassius hesitated when Cyrus reached for the handle of his door.

"Tell me what you need, Cyrus."

"Nothing," he answered, keeping his back to him and eyes fixed on the wood door. "I just want to bathe, eat, and sleep."

He felt him step closer. Cassius leaned a shoulder against the wall. "I know what he does, Cyrus," he said, voice low and rough. "I know how he breaks someone."

Cyrus finally looked at him. "I was already broken. He just made sure I remembered how thoroughly."

"Cyrus—"

But he pushed through the door and closed it behind him. The room was as he remembered. Everything neat and tidy, waiting for a guest to stay. The only thing that seemed amiss was the decanter of alcohol on the end table. He'd never actually stayed in here. They'd always stayed in Cass's rooms. One on the bed. The other on the sofa.

He sighed again, raking a hand through his hair as he tossed a flame into the empty hearth. He'd add some logs later. Right now, he just wanted his magic to burn.

Moving through the bedchamber, he went straight to the bathing room, kicking the door shut and dragging his soiled tunic over his head. He started filling the tub, moving aimlessly around the room as he waited.

Until he caught sight of himself in the mirror.

Exhausted and haunted didn't even begin to cover it.

His normally bright amber eyes were muted and dull. Dead. His chestnut hair was disheveled, his skin sallow. He hadn't been gone long enough for the lack of sustenance to really affect him, but his magic being inaccessible, accompanied by the Sorceress's constant meddling…that had definitely taken a toll.

Three days.

Three godsdamn days to undo decades of healing. Or at least decades of learning to live with the memories.

His fist slammed into the glass, shards flying everywhere. He felt the sting as a few grazed his bare flesh— arms, chest, across his brow. But no one came to see what the commotion was. Because he was alone. As he was always meant to be.

Cyrus moved to the tub, not caring if he stepped on broken glass or not, kicking off his pants as he went. His magic heated the water to near scalding, and the new abrasions stung even more as he sank into the blessed warmth. He quickly washed—twice—before changing out the water, and then he sat, his head tipped back against the lip of the tub and his eyes fell closed. His magic was already working to heal the cuts from the glass, but the marks around his wrists and ankles from the shirastone were slowing down the process.

He lost track of how long he sat there, trying to shove all the trauma and damage back down to the depths of his being where he'd kept it locked away for years. But it refused to go back now that Gehenna had let those demons free.

Eliza. He'd find Eliza tomorrow and spar with her. She'd let him work out all this aggression and darkness. She wouldn't go easy on him out of pity, or think he needed to take it easy for a few days. She'd let him work himself into a state of exhaustion so he wouldn't be able to feel any of it for a while.

And if that didn't work, he'd find some mugweed and a new decanter full of alcohol since someone drank all his.

Finally dragging himself from the tub when he didn't think he'd be able to go another minute without food, he quickly dried himself off before remembering all his clothing was in Cassius's rooms.

Fuck it. Surely there was something in the various dressers and armoires of this guest suite that would fit him, even if it was just a pair of pants. He'd get his clothes after he'd slept.

He tossed the towel into the corner with the dirty clothing. Making an effort to avoid the shattered glass he'd worry about cleaning up tomorrow, he opened the bathing room door and moved to the bedchamber, pausing when he found his own tunic and pants lying on the bed. Not caring who had brought them in, he shoved his legs into the pants. Clean clothing. He'd nearly forgotten what a luxury such a thing was. He was reaching for his tunic when someone spoke.

"You have a new Mark on your arm."

Cyrus paused, the tunic halfway over his head, before he quickly pulled it on the rest of the way. "A new Mark on my arm and a thousand new marks on my soul," he muttered, not intending to say it aloud but too apathetic to care at this point.

"What kind of Mark is it?" Cassius asked.

Cyrus turned to find him sprawled in a chair before the bedchamber hearth, black flames crackling in it. His forefinger was steepled along his temple, and his eyes were glowing amber-red as he studied Cyrus.

But before Cyrus could think of something to say, Scarlett came through the bedchamber door, Rayner behind her carrying a tray piled high with food. Cyrus was swiping a piece of cold roast beef and cheese cubes before Rayner even set the tray down on a side table.

"Where's Eliza?" Cyrus asked around a mouthful of food.

"The continent," Rayner answered, his keen eyes watching him as carefully as Cassius was.

"What the fuck is she doing over there?"

"There is a lot to fill you in on, Cyrus," Scarlett said. "But it does not need to be done tonight."

"Who else is there with her?"

"Cyrus—" she started, but Cassius cut her off.

"Sawyer and Ashtine. Ashtine cannot leave the continent. They stayed to guard her. They're in Siofra with the Shifters," Cassius answered.

"And you gave him Talwyn?" Cyrus went on, swiping an entire loaf of bread and taking a bite. "You know he plans to release the Sorceress."

And he ate and listened while Cassius filled him in on what had happened in three short days. Sorin. Talwyn. Eliza. Saylah. All of it. Because Cassius knew he needed something to occupy his mind or his thoughts would consume him. Just as he'd kept him company in the dead of night on a ship, or on a balcony in the Black Halls.

When he finished, Scarlett was nestled on the bed, leaning against a stack of pillows. He could tell she was lost in her own thoughts, letting Cassius do all the talking. Cyrus flopped down next to her, finally full, and she reached over, grabbing his hand.

"I'm sorry I took so long to come for you," she whispered.

He shrugged. "Sounds like you were pretty busy, Darling."

Tears welled suddenly in her eyes. "You are my family, Cyrus. Do not think that you are any less important—"

"I didn't mean it like that," he interrupted. "This is war. I understand. I'm glad you got Ashtine out first. How is Neve?"

Scarlett blinked at the sudden change of subject, wiping at her damp eyes. "Sleeping. Do you know what…"

Cyrus shook his head as she trailed off. "They separated us. I do not know where she was or what she endured." Scarlett nodded, gaze dropping to her lap. Guilt. He could see it settle into her shoulders, adding to the weight she already carried. He squeezed her fingers still wrapped around his hand. "We're back now, Scarlett. That's what matters."

Until he had to tell them just how thoroughly he'd fucked them over. Because if the Sorceress was free when he fulfilled this bargain…

Silence fell, filled with a thick tension.

"There's no need to fret over me," Cyrus said, bringing an arm up to rest behind his head. "I'm clean. You've fed me. Now let me sleep."

"Are you telling us to get out?" Scarlett gasped in mock outrage.

"Yes," he answered, releasing her hand and giving her a light shove. "And for the love of your mother, please do not knock on my door before dinner tomorrow evening."

Scarlett got to her feet with an unimpressed glare. "I'll let that comment slide this time."

"I'll take full advantage of the pass," he returned with a wink. "Get your royal ass out of my rooms."

She smiled, features softening. "I'm glad you're back, Cyrus."

"Me too, Darling."

He could tell she wanted to say more, but she didn't, heading for the door. Rayner fell into step beside her, and they began murmuring amongst themselves again. Scarlett nodded at whatever Rayner was saying, her shadows appearing and trailing behind them.

Cyrus sighed. "You don't have to stay here. I know you prefer your own space."

"I'm fine here," Cassius replied.

He pushed onto his elbows, leveling him with a glare. "That was me saying get the fuck out."

"I know what you were saying, and I'm still fine here," he said, stretching his legs out and crossing his ankles.

"I do not need to be watched."

"I'm not watching you. I'm staying here with you."

"It's not needed."

Cassius shrugged, tipping his head back against the chair and closing his eyes.

"Fucker," Cyrus muttered, before he rolled onto his side away from the Avonleyan. He knew Cass had reopened his eyes. Could feel them searing into his back.

*Not watching me, my ass.*

But he didn't say anything else. It was probably selfish of him, but he welcomed the company. Maybe the nightmares wouldn't come for him with another here. Wishful thinking, he knew, but he was fresh out of hope, so denial would have to do.

# CHAPTER 16
# SCARLETT

H er fingers moved over the keys, the music stilted and methodical. Shadows drifted along her arms, keeping her company.

Rayner had left a few minutes ago after they had spent the last hour going over the layout of the cliffs again. They knew the lock was hidden there, but the space was huge and cavernous. It would take months to explore every nook and cranny of the place, even with Rayner's extensive knowledge of it. There were hundreds of places she could have hidden it, and there could be just as many the Ash Rider did not know of. Rayner had sent his ashes searching while they were there, but they hadn't had much time. On top of that, she had absolutely no idea what she was looking for. Saylah had told her the lock could change forms, and that Moranna, the female who had hidden it, had likely disguised it somehow. That female was also apparently Alaric's mother, and Rayner had killed her.

Gods, she wished she could have seen that.

She'd plan more with Rayner tomorrow. Or rather later today, she supposed, knowing it was closer to dawn than the dead of night. Maybe they could go visit Ashtine. See if she knew anything.

Her song kept flowing as she switched focus. How long would it take for Sorin's power reserves to be replenished? Knowing him, he would insist she draw from him the moment he woke, even though she hadn't used that much of her own magic. What would his power look like now?

Then there was Callan. Rayner had filled her in on the things Nuri had said, but he didn't know what had been said between Callan and the others to make them agree to leave him behind. He had been guarding Tula and keeping her hidden away. Something about the Alpha and Beta trying to lay claim to her.

Another thing to add to her list.

Scarlett hadn't seen Azrael since she had left with Talwyn. The Earth Prince had escorted Talwyn to the entrance hall where they were all departing from, but he hadn't said a word to anyone other than Talwyn.

She sighed. She needed to smooth things over with him. He was a prince, older than almost all of them. He had also become a valuable member of their company, and there couldn't be discord among them. Not now that she had started putting her plans into motion. She knew he understood strategy and war, but Talwyn had not been the only one to pay the cost for this.

The door to the den opened, pulling her from her thoughts, and her brother walked in. Her eyes narrowed as he moved silently to the liquor cart, pouring measures into two small glasses before swiping them up and setting one on the piano before her. He looked better. Rested. Although his eyes were an icy blue like hers had been for years. How long would it take him to refill his reserves? Rayner had taken nearly two entire months, and he was only half-Avonleyan.

Cethin lowered onto the nearby sofa, sipping his drink.

"I do not wish to speak right now," Scarlett said.

No, she wished to be left alone with her thoughts and her plans. She could have gone to her rooms, would have likely avoided this exact situation, but Sorin was sleeping. She could feel him down the bond. If she woke him, even unintentionally, he would want details of everything and would want to go see Cyrus. So she came here to not disturb him.

"That is fine," Cethin answered. "I can do the talking."

"I would rather you didn't."

"Too bad," he shrugged, taking another sip of his drink.

Scarlett rolled her eyes, but she stayed put, her fingers never missing a note.

"I did not learn I could control what entered the Wards until our parents were gone. Saylah was on your continent, and our father had sacrificed himself to allow that to happen. When Saylah returned, she informed me that the gift had manifested when you entered the world. Two parts of the same key, you and I. But while she was gone, I thought…" He paused, taking another sip of his drink. "I did not know of you. I did not know where Saylah had gone or why. She does not share her motives or plans without purpose. The games of the gods are just that—dangerous games. We just happen to be caught in the middle of the chain reactions.

"When I learned I could control who entered the Wards, I thought I could fix things for my people. They had been locked away here, separated from the Fae. I did not wish to fix things so we could use the Fae to feed our magic, but to work with them as we had since the beginning. There had long been a balance from my understanding, and that balance was upset when the Wards went up. It affected more than us being able to leave our kingdom. Farmland stopped producing as well. The seasons got more intense. I think even the Avonleyans were surprised at just how much was affected by being cut off from the Fae. The lack of magic source became the least of their concerns. Many people moved east of the Nightmist Mountains, abandoning the lands farther inland where we have far more space. You have not seen those places or those who continue to try and make their living there."

Scarlett's song had slowed, but her fingers kept moving as she listened to him. She made no other sign of acknowledgment, but he kept speaking.

"I knew of the Maraans across the Edria. I had been told the story of the Great War since I was a youngling. Our parents tried to ease the burden on our people, and Saylah…" He trailed off, as if trying to find the right words. "I remember her disappearing for days, back to Elshira to comb through texts she keeps there. She has tried to find ways to change what is to come. For centuries. But even the gods cannot change fate, not entirely, once it is set in motion."

Her fingers stumbled at the words, but she quickly recovered, her melody changing to minor chords.

"I thought if I could do something from here to ease the burden of my people, it would not matter how long it took for the Wards to come down. If I could get word to the Fae that they could seek refuge here, not be trapped behind the wards they'd put up, I could help more than just our people until Saylah was ready to make her move. So I figured out a way to get word out through Blood Magic." He glanced over at her. "I did not understand the cost. And when I started practicing with the ability to let people into the Wards, I did not realize it was not only these Wards that I could allow passage through. There were other enchantments around the realm, and beings outside of our world got my message too."

Silence fell as her fingers stilled on the keys, a final chord echoing in the room. "The things that attacked me?"

Cethin nodded. "Among others. But those? Those are why I am called the Cursed King. They have only ever come after me. Until last night."

"Why the secret?" she asked, reaching for the glass of liquor.

"Because while they seek me, they have also captured Kailia and tried to take her beyond the Wards. To bring her to Alaric."

Scarlett nearly dropped her drink. Her gaze whipped to Cethin in horror. "Why?"

He hesitated, but when her eyes narrowed, he said quickly, "Her story is not one of light and beauty, but it is her story to tell, Scarlett. Surely there are things Sorin knows about you that he would never share."

He wasn't wrong. Sorin would never tell another of what happened the night she had been forced to kill Juliette. Sorin was the only one who knew every detail of that night and the days that followed.

"I will do whatever is necessary to protect her," Cethin went on. "Explaining the creatures that hunt me would have meant explaining so many other things. How we learned of them to begin with. How Kailia is the only one with the means to end them. And when we were just meeting and learning to trust each other outside of dreams? I could not risk word getting back to Alaric that she is here."

"Has she met Alaric before?"

Cethin nodded. "He held her captive for a short period of time. She is incredibly adept at escaping. But then she found her way here." He smiled then, almost wistfully. "To kill me."

"She mentioned she has tried to do that a few times," Scarlett said, taking another sip.

Cethin only nodded, as if amused.

"All of that is fine. I understand you wanting to keep Kailia safe. But none of that is the greatest thing you kept from me, Cethin," she said. "How could you keep from me that I would need to leave this world in order to save it?"

He blew out a harsh breath, shoving a hand through his shoulder-length hair. He studied his empty glass for a long moment before speaking again. "I have known for centuries that I would eventually need to leave this realm. There have been plans in place to do so for just as long. The plans have been altered numerous times over the decades, but it always involved our parents and me, along with Tybalt and Razik as our Guardians. Kailia was added to those plans after a time. For nearly two decades it has just been us. Me, Kailia, and Razik. We do not create other relationships. We do not have other close friends because we know that eventually we will leave.

"I watched you through your dreams, but I could not truly learn of your life. Dreams are often skewed and unreliable. I knew of Sorin, of course. And Cassius, although I did not know his name until you found the mirror gate. I assumed they would come with us when the time came. But then you arrived on these shores with a number of ships. With children who adore you. With friends. With family. And I… I did not know how to tell you that you would need to leave them. Cyrus. Eliza. Rayner. The Water Prince. Juliette and Nuri. I did not know how to tell you that you—who has already been forced to give so much—were going to be forced to give even more. And the more I watched you and got to know you, I thought that maybe, just maybe, you would find another way. That maybe it was a heartbreak I could spare you from. I know you do not need me to protect you, but if I could save you from this pain, I would, Scarlett."

Her fingertips glided over the tops of the smooth ivory keys before her as she processed everything he'd said. She didn't like it, but she understood. It was the same reason she hadn't mentioned it to the others yet. She knew they would be asking after the comments she made to Alaric at the cliffs earlier that evening. Knew she needed to talk to Sorin before that other conversation happened. She just wanted him to have a few moments to enjoy having his power back before she heaped another pile of shit onto their already full plate. She'd wanted to have some sort of solution to offer when she told them. Even if it was scarcely a plan, it would be something instead of just more...impossibilities.

"Why can't you leave the Wards? How did that happen?" she asked after several minutes.

Cethin had refilled his glass while he'd let her think, and he took a sip before he answered. "When our mother returned from the continent, she was...upset."

"Saylah bound you to the Wards?" Scarlett said in horror.

"Yes, but she had little choice. My actions had inadvertently opened a rift in the enchantments, allowing other beings to enter. It is how some of the Maraan Lords got here. The cost to close it was my ability to let people in all together. In order for me to still control the Wards, I had to be bound to them. If I leave, the Wards fall and take my life with them. It leaves my people vulnerable. Without being able to refill their reserves quickly, they would not survive long in a war, no matter how well trained they are in combat. Against mortals, yes. But against those with magic? Night Children? Seraphs? They would be slaughtered."

"But what will happen when the Wards come down? What will happen to you?"

He shrugged. "The Wards will no longer be needed. Since I am not the one taking them down, the binding will be severed."

Her nose scrunched. "That doesn't seem right. Are you sure?"

"No," Cethin said tightly. "It is simply what we are hoping for."

She blinked, unsure of what to say. "Taking down the Wards could potentially kill you?"

He nodded, bringing his drink back to his lips. "Razik seems confident it won't. He is very knowledgeable when it comes to ancient magic and Marks, but the possibility still exists."

After several more beats of silence, she said, "Thank you. For coming to speak to me tonight."

"I do not know what Saylah shared with you, but know that I am here, Scarlett," he said. "I will help in whatever way I can. The Avonleyan resources are at your disposal. *I* am at your disposal."

She nodded, fiddling with her empty glass.

"My intention has never been to use you," he added quietly. "Please know that."

She nodded again, setting the glass back onto the piano. When she began playing once more, Cethin quietly stood. She could feel him watching her, but after a few moments, he left the den, leaving her alone with her thoughts.

This changed some things. Many of her plans would stay the same, but some of them… Some pieces would need to be moved around.

She played until her fingers hurt. She could hardly keep her eyes open when she dragged herself up to her wing of the castle. Stopping at Cyrus's rooms first to check on him, she found him fast asleep in bed, and Cassius passed out in the winged armchair he'd claimed. She'd known Cassius wouldn't leave him tonight, even if he craved the control of his own space and rooms. She could never ask Cassius to leave this realm and leave Cyrus behind. *She* could never leave Cyrus behind. Or Eliza. Or Rayner.

Sighing heavily, she pulled the door shut behind her and made her way to her rooms. After quickly washing up and changing into nightclothes, she slipped into bed. Sorin immediately reached for her, his arm draping over her waist and tugging her into him.

"Love?" he murmured.

"I'm here," she whispered, brushing dark hair back from his brow.

"Cyrus?" he mumbled, eyes never opening.

"Safe and sleeping," she answered, pressing a small kiss to his temple. "Go back to sleep."

"Be here in the morning," he breathed.

Scarlett smiled softly as she settled in. "Okay."

His shift in breathing told her he'd slipped back into a deep sleep. But as exhausted as she was, she couldn't shut her mind off. Replaying conversations. Sifting through information. Making adjustments to plans.

Moves and countermoves.

Dangerous games indeed.

What would the gods and Fates do when they learned she did not play by their rules?

# PART TWO
## THE FOUND

# CHAPTER 17
# ELIZA

"Left side!" Eliza yelled at Callan as he blocked Ilyas's saber just in time. "Clean up your footwork," she added.

She couldn't deny that Callan was doing well though. He'd been training for months, and despite the break while she was recovering, he'd obviously kept practicing. She may have just chided him for his footwork, but it was nearly perfect. Too bad she demanded actual perfection from those she trained. Her time was valuable. If she was going to take the time to train someone, she would accept nothing less. Not only that, if he was going to follow through on this plan to go to the slums of Baylorin, he needed every second of extra training he could get.

Callan and Ilyas, one of Stellan's personal guards and lovers, had both lost their shirts with the sun beating down on them. Callan had been given a pair of lightweight, looser-fitting pants that the Shifters wore in this arid climate, and she had forced him to train for the better part of the last two days. They hadn't quite worked out how he was going to get back to Windonelle. The time not spent training was spent strategizing. Admittedly, she was better suited to planning battles. Strategy and scheming were more Cyrus and Sorin's areas of expertise with Rayner providing movements of those being plotted against. Stellan and Arianna had been ruling the Shifters for centuries though. Their father had been one of the first to receive Shifter gifts when stripped from the Sorceress, but they hadn't maintained their seat of power by blood right alone. They were cunning and ruthless when needed.

It was why all the Fae royalty made sure to stay on good terms with the siblings. It was also why they had been sequestered away to the south when all the Wards had gone up. The Witches didn't want to interact with others in general, so they didn't particularly care that they had been sent to the eastern part of the continent. They were more upset about not having the freedom to leave, and that *males* had dictated their fate. The Night Children were driven by instinct and hunger, but the Shifters, in a way, were more dangerous than the other two bloodlines.

Eliza was getting ready to do her own sparring with Sawyer when Arianna stood from where she had been sitting with Ashtine on the veranda overlooking the sandy training pit. Ashtine nodded to the Beta before Arianna shifted into a red-tailed hawk and took to the sky. Sawyer gave the princess a questioning look from where he stood.

"There are visitors at the gates," Ashtine replied.

Her usual lilt was stronger. These last few days of rest and safety had done her well. Her skin was still paler than usual, and she spent the better part of her days sleeping; but she had insisted Sawyer escort her outside for fresh air today. When Sawyer had still seemed hesitant, she'd told him she needed to feel the wind—both for her and the babe with wind gifts in her belly.

"Do you think we should take her inside?" Sawyer murmured to Eliza, turning so Ashtine would not be able to read his lips. Not that it mattered. The winds carried his words to her anyway.

"That will not be necessary," Ashtine replied, coming up behind them.

"You should not be on your feet," Sawyer chastised.

"Those here will not harm me or you," Ashtine said. A small vortex of wind formed at her fingertips, tiny ice crystals dancing around it. She closed her eyes as a look of relief crossed her features. She was carrying so much power. Her power was mighty in itself, but twins of two of the strongest Fae in the realm? Eliza had seen her siphoning off that power numerous times since being here. Having it

LADY OF STARFIRE

restrained by shirastone had been the only form of torture Alaric had
really needed for the Wind Princess. It would have slowly driven
her mad.

Sariah appeared after a moment, making her way to Ilyas, who
had shifted to his wolf form and was watching them all from the edge
of the training area. He got to his feet at her approach, shifting back
when she neared and dipping his head so she could speak into his ear.
The two were the personal guards and lovers of the Alpha, and while
Sariah was pleasant enough, Ilyas was openly distrustful of all of
them.

Eliza propped the flat of her blade on her shoulder while her hand
went to her hip as she watched the two shifters. "Who is here?" she
asked Ashtine.

"Azrael and Razik."

"What?" Her head whipped to the princess, and her stomach
tensed. "Why are they here?"

"I suppose we will learn shortly," the princess answered, the small
vortex of wind and ice still spinning in her palm.

"Can we spar, please?" Eliza grumbled to Sawyer, moving into a
defensive position.

Sawyer's brow arched. "Now? Surely they will be here any
moment."

No sooner did he finish speaking and they came into view. Eliza
huffed out an annoyed breath, but then she paused.

"Why is Maliq with them?"

The giant black wolf was the spirit animal of Celeste, goddess of
the moon. He had also been bonded to Talwyn. Eliza wasn't sure if
the wolf still was or not, but she had not expected to see him at
Azrael's side. The Earth Prince had his own spirit animal already
bonded to him.

"He was sent by Scarlett," Ashtine answered, her magic disappearing as they approached. Azrael went straight to her, brown eyes
looking the princess over from head to toe.

"You appear a little better," he said, folding his arms over his
chest.

Ashtine smiled faintly. Maliq had moved to her, nudging her hand
with his nose. She slid her fingers into his thick fur, scratching behind

205

an ear. "I am feeling well," she answered. Then her head tilted. "You have much to share."

Azrael gave a sharp nod, but it was Razik who spoke next.

"You can get his report after I take my leave," he said. "I don't need to be here for it."

"Then why *are* you here?" Eliza asked in irritation.

His gaze slid past her. Hardly a glance. "I need to refill my reserves." He was already walking away from them.

"Right now?" she demanded.

He didn't stop. Didn't acknowledge her. Simply kept walking.

"He has been in a mood since we left. Not much different from his usual temperament, but a mood nonetheless," Azrael supplied.

Great. Broody dragon attitude was not what Eliza wanted to deal with right now.

Flames flared, taking her sword to a pocket realm. "I will find you all after I take care of this," she gritted out.

She had half a mind to make him wait. To not follow him and let him brood alone while she got a report from Azrael, but she knew Stellan could be back any moment. When the Alpha returned, she wanted to speak with him immediately and without interruption. It appeared her best option was to get Razik out of here as quickly as possible, even if it did feed into this mindset he seemed to have that she was at his beck and call.

Forcing herself not to stomp as she followed him, Eliza made her way into the palace. He had already disappeared inside, but she caught a glimpse of him rounding a corner. Heading to the guest suites then. Her room, she assumed.

Her irritation climbed higher with every step she took, and by the time she made it to her rooms—her door wide open—the leash on her temper was taut. Taking a deep breath to try to dispel some of the simmering fury, she stepped into her room. She hadn't even turned back from closing the door when Razik was crowding her against it and reaching for her arm.

"What are you doing?" she snapped. She tried to yank her arm back, but he held firm, pulling a dagger from his side.

"I told you," he growled, sounding as irritated as she felt. "I need to refill my magic reserves."

"How did you drain them so quickly?" she asked, still trying to wrench her arm away from him.

"Does it matter?" he countered, tossing that question from a few nights ago back at her yet again. "Hold still so I don't cut too deep."

Eliza cursed him up and down, but she stilled. There was something off about him. Not his mood. He was usually pissy and surly, but now he was almost frantic, his sapphire eyes wild. Even though he was clearly in some kind of heightened agitated state, he was still as gentle and quick as possible when he sliced the dagger across the Source Mark on her forearm. He made quick work of his own palm, placing it over the Mark. His fingers dug into her skin. He gripped her so tight she almost winced as she felt her magic flow into him. His dragon fire called to it, and her flames went without hesitation.

He was rigid, his jaw tight, as he wordlessly drew from her. Without conscious thought, her other hand drifted up, landing on the side of his torso. Her fingers curled slightly into his tunic, and she realized his skin was cooler. Not cold by any means, but not the blazing inferno he usually was. She could usually feel heat emanating off of him through his clothing.

"Don't," he snarled, shifting slightly so her hand fell away from him. His fingers dug in more, his hold on her arm becoming bruising, and there was a vicious yank on her power. She couldn't hide her wince this time, but he still wouldn't look at her, so he didn't see it.

But apparently he felt it.

His grip instantly loosened, and he tipped his head back, exhaling sharply through his nose as if trying to get control of himself.

"Tell me why your power is so low," Eliza said quietly.

"It's not low. It's nonexistent," he gritted out. "The Earth Prince Traveled me here."

"What happened?"

"Doesn't matter."

"I think it does," she scoffed.

"You're wrong."

Her mouth fell open at the finality of his tone, as if the conversation was over. "That's all you're going to say?"

"This is how you want it, Eliza," he retorted.

"What is that supposed to mean?"

"It means if you want a report on things that have happened, you'll have to ask someone who answers to your queen."

Her lip peeled back in a sneer, and she made to push off the door. But his other hand came up, wrapping loosely around her throat and holding her in place. That frenzied gleam was still in his eyes, and she couldn't decide if the move was a primal instinct to stop his current source of power from slipping away, or if it was a calculated move. Perhaps a bit of both, but he finally met her stare.

"You have made it clear this is what you want," he said tightly. "Avonleyan and Source. That is all that we are. I needed my power refilled, so I came here. That is the extent of the information I owe you when that is all this relationship entails."

She didn't know what to say to that because he was right. This is what she'd demanded of him. She shouldn't be asking him what was going on across the Edria. She shouldn't be looking to him for anything.

His thumb brushed along her pulse point. Then he did it again. And again. He still held her by the throat, but the hold was loose. She could easily break it if she wanted to. Razik knew that too. Knew she was allowing him to hold her that way. She could tell he knew it by the way his thumb kept making those light passes on her neck. By the way his gaze had zeroed in on her mouth. How that frantic mania that had been in his eyes was shifting to something else despite everything he'd just said to her.

And her power kept going to him. Her flames almost entranced the way a Night Child could entrance another. That was an ability unique to the Night Children, but they were descended from the Legacy. The Night Children had been cursed by Arius for continuing to feed on the blood of Fae instead of taking Sources, but what had happened to that entrancing ability in the Legacy and Avonleyans?

"Are you going to take it all?" she asked hoarsely.

"If you'd let me, I would take everything."

Her breathing stuttered, air getting stuck in her throat that he was still caressing with his thumb. She could tell he hadn't meant to say that aloud.

"Razik," she whispered.

His eyes snapped to hers, as if suddenly remembering where he

208

was. He cleared his throat. "I was completely drained. Even taking all your power, my wells still will not be fully replenished."

"So you *are* going to take it all?" she repeated, her knees weakening. She'd like to think it was completely from being drained of her magic, but his godsdamn thumb was still moving.

"I will leave some," he replied. "But I will need to draw again when your reserves have refilled. Before I can go."

"If you drain it this much, it'll take a few days to get to that point."

"I am aware. I had a Source before."

Her lips pursed. As if she could forget that.

"It was nothing like this," he added as an afterthought.

"I don't care," she snapped.

"Of course you don't."

That mocking smirk made an appearance, and Eliza yanked her arm from his grip. "If you're going to draw from me again, that is enough for now."

It wasn't lost on her that she'd forced him to release her arm and not her throat.

*Godsdamnit.*

His gaze dipped to her mouth again, his lips parting slightly, before his hand slipped from her neck, and he took a measured step back. She couldn't move though. Mainly because she was sure she would stumble from losing so much power so quickly, and she'd be damned if he would witness that. So she stayed pressed to the door as though he were still holding her there.

"This is not going to work," he said tightly, folding his arms across his chest and eyeing her.

"What?"

"That I have to Travel here when my power is low."

"What do you plan to do then? Stay here?" she asked, dread coiling through her at the thought.

"I cannot stay here."

"You're here now."

He tensed even more. Apparently filling his empty power wells hadn't been enough to ease that tension he'd arrived with. "I did not have much of a choice, just as I do not have much of a choice as to whether or not I stay here."

"Says who? Cethin?"

"Saylah," he ground out. "How long are you going to pretend that door isn't the only thing keeping you on your feet?"

She leveled him with a glare. "What do you mean Saylah says you cannot stay here?"

"I am Cethin's Guardian. I need to be where he is. You know. To *guard* him," he replied. He took a step towards her, but she held up a hand.

"I don't need your help."

He sighed, looking towards the ceiling as if asking the gods for patience. "Come sit down, Eliza. I should not have taken so much at once. I apologize."

Her brows shot up. "I'm your Source. Isn't that my purpose?"

That muscle ticked in his jaw. "Come sit down," he repeated, stepping to the side and out of her path.

She sucked in a breath to steady herself before moving as quickly as she dared to the sofa in front of the hearth. She sank down onto it, holding in her sigh of relief. That would take some getting used to. She rarely let her power get this low. Only when she had forced herself to train with low reserves. She could do it, but it was uncomfortable and jarring.

Razik didn't make any move to help her, but she heard him mutter under his breath something along the lines of "so damn stubborn."

"You're one to talk," she retorted.

"It's not supposed to be like this," he said, ignoring her small outburst.

"Like what?"

"We are not supposed to be separated by an ocean, Eliza."

Eliza. He hadn't called her any of his pet names since he'd returned. Not once. She should be relieved. Instead, she was irritated that she even noticed.

"When you offered to do this, I assumed you understood we could not be separated. Part of that lifelong commitment we discussed," he was saying.

She tipped her head back to look up at him. "You thought I would *stay* in Avonleya? Why would you think that?"

He stared at her. "Again, because of that whole lifelong commitment thing."

Instead of replying, she leaned back into the sofa, resting her head against the back and letting her eyes fall closed. She was tired after he'd drained her magic, and—

"I'm staying in your rooms while I am here."

Her eyes snapped back open at that. "You most certainly are not."

He was prowling towards her now, and she was pressing herself into the sofa even more as he lowered down beside her. "If you are not coming back with me, I'm staying near you. This relationship is supposed to be a give-and-take, Eliza. You give me power; I give you protection and care in return. I have nearly drained you of your magic. It is instinct for me to watch over you when you are vulnerable."

"I'm not vulnerable," she muttered.

"You were holding yourself up with a door."

"I was adjusting. I will be fine in a few minutes. I've trained for this."

He huffed out another harsh breath of frustration. "I did not mean to imply that you are weak. I know you are anything but."

"You know nothing about me," she retorted.

"I know more than you think." His eyes dipped to her chest, to where a Curse Mark adorned her skin beneath her tunic, before he met her gaze once more.

"Who told you about that?" she hissed, the sting of betrayal making her ears ring.

"I've seen it before. That night you reacted poorly to the Healer's tonic."

"I know you've seen it. Who told you what it was?"

"No one. I have studied ancient magic and Marks for decades. The first time I saw it, I knew what it was." His tone had gone impossibly soft for the male she knew him to be. Her gaze went to her lap because she didn't want to see the sympathy shining in his. "Who gave you that Mark, Eliza?"

"You need to leave." Her chest was tight, breathing too difficult, as the memory of receiving that Mark surged to the forefront of her mind.

At a blade being dragged across her mother's throat.

At men holding her down while the male she'd known to be her father gave her the Mark.

Curse Marks were just that. A curse. From the moment they were given. They burned when etched into one's skin. She'd never experienced the pain of a burn until that day—not with fire in her veins—and this one seared her very soul.

Then there was being abandoned, left to fend for herself. Having to learn to trust again, and still not letting anyone really see all of her.

"I know those feelings, *mai dragocen*."

She'd forgotten he was still sitting there with the flood of memories. Her emotions had to be screaming at him down the bond she did not want.

"Who gave you that Mark, Eliza?" he repeated.

"It does not matter. It's done. Please leave."

"I'm not leaving. Not after I all but drained you of your magic." She turned to look at him. His body was angled towards her, his arm draped along the back of the sofa, fingers resting near her shoulder. "It's not supposed to be like this," he said again.

"None of it is supposed to be like this," she replied. "But life does not give a shit about how things are supposed to be."

"That is a fair statement," he conceded. He shifted his arm along the back of the sofa, bringing his hand up to rest his temple against his fist as he studied her. He didn't say anything else, a comfortable silence settling between them.

Finally, Eliza said, "You can stay in my rooms under two conditions."

"I cannot wait to hear what they are," he replied dryly.

"You're sleeping out here. On the sofa."

A brow arched. "We have shared a bed before. Was I not behaved?"

She scowled at him. "You said we never needed to discuss that again. Stay out here, or find another room."

"We can circle back to this topic. What is your other condition, Milady?"

"We are not 'circling back' to this, Razik," she said indignantly. She would have said more, but he was leaning closer now, and her thoughts had scattered at the small smirk on lips that were all sorts of distracting.

"The second condition?" he pressed.

She held his gaze when she said, "You never speak of the Mark I bear again." He went still. "Never again, Razik."

He opened his mouth, but before he could say anything in response, there was a knock on her door. "General?"

And just like that, she slipped back into her role of Fire Court General. She got to her feet, shoving aside the uncomfortableness of not having even semi-full reserves. Pulling the door open, she found a Shifter. "What?" Eliza asked.

"The Alpha has returned. He has requested your company."

"Thank you for informing me."

The Shifter stepped aside as she exited the room. Razik was already at the door, following her out. The Shifter cast him a wary look, to which he flashed his teeth in a challenging taunt, and Eliza elbowed him in the ribs. "Stop being an ass. They are our allies."

He didn't say anything, but his features became the bored, uninterested face he usually wore.

When they came to the meeting room, they found Stellan and Arianna seated at either end of the table. Sariah was pacing back and forth in her jaguar form near the Alpha, while Ilyas sat to his right. Ashtine, Azrael, Sawyer, and Callan were already here and seated as well. Eliza slid into a chair next to Callan, Razik taking the remaining one beside her.

"I have news of the Fire Court," Stellan said, cutting right to the thick of the matter.

It was one of the reasons he'd been gone. With the wards down and the Shifters able to move about freely, he had been out gathering information.

"You traveled all the way to the Fire Court and back in three days?" Callan asked.

"He flew to the Earth Court," Arianna explained, smiling serenely at Jamahl as he placed a goblet of wine on the table before her.

Azrael tensed across the table, his lip curling in a silent snarl.

"Did Tarek reveal when the armies are to move?" Ashtine asked, her head tilting in curiosity.

"The armies? What is she talking about?" Ilyas asked, looking at his Alpha.

"The winds are speaking more willingly these days," Arianna commented, swirling her goblet.

Ashtine graced her with a small smile. "They speak of things in passing."

"Tarek indeed leads the Earth Court. Ermir has kept them out of the Citadel, but the seraphs have taken over the rest of the Wind Court," Stellan said. Ashtine did not react, only nodding once at the information. "I thought Prince Drayce may be seen as a figurehead in the Water Court, but Alaric appears to be keeping him hidden. A seraph with water gifts has assumed control of that territory."

"And the Fire Court?" Eliza pressed.

"A Fae by the name of Bastien has assumed the throne."

"Are you fucking with me?" Eliza growled, the wood of the table beneath her palms beginning to smolder.

"I do not know that name," Arianna commented.

"He is a lower commander in the Fire Court forces," Eliza answered. "Strong gifts, but too brash and conceited to be given greater responsibilities."

"The perfect puppet for Alaric then," Sawyer said grimly.

"The forces are being gathered at seemingly random places in the Courts. There are no significant towns or strongholds," Stellan continued. "The mortal armies are also preparing, and there are a great number of seraphs in every territory."

The room fell silent as he finished telling what he had learned in his time away.

"Where would all the seraph forces have come from?" Azrael asked after a moment. "Scarlett closed all the rips with the keys. She essentially locked the realm."

"That is a question with no answer," Ashtine said. "But one would assume they wait for the Sorceress to obtain her freedom."

"Is Talwyn returned to him then?" Eliza asked, realizing she hadn't been given any type of report after being preoccupied with Razik.

Azrael had clearly already filled in the others as he told her everything that had happened since they'd left Siofra two days prior. Scarlett being attacked. Cethin draining his magic. Saylah appearing. Talwyn sacrificing her magic for Sorin. Sorin getting his magic back. The exchange of Talwyn for Cyrus and Neve.

"What is the plan then?" Eliza demanded. "If Sorin has regained his magic and is even stronger than before, he can feed Scarlett's power. The two of them together…"

She trailed off, because good gods. Those two mighty powers together? They could literally burn the world to ash. Add in the ability to communicate down their twin flame bond, and they would be virtually unstoppable.

"Scarlett wants to find the lock first," Azrael said. "She has been planning with Rayner. They will come for it soon. When she has it, the Wards around Avonleya can come down, allowing their forces to cross. When she returns, she returns with an army."

"And until then?" Callan asked. "What do the mortals and the Fae do until then? How long will she make them wait?"

"She understands that time is not on her side, your Majesty," Ashtine said kindly. "Until then, we turn to our allies. They prepare to aid us until she can come."

"The Witches were preparing," Razik cut in. "When we were there, the High Witch had stockpiles of potions and said they had been training."

"The Witches on their griffins could be an aerial host to combat the seraphs in the skies," Eliza said, leaning forward as her mind immediately began planning battle formations. "And any avian Shifters?"

She looked between Stellan and Arianna. It was the Beta who nodded. "Those who have larger forms will fight. The smaller Shifters are trained in stealth. We stand with the true Queen of the Continent."

Queen of the Continent.

What would Scarlett say to that?

But it was true. She could take it all. *They* could take it all. No one would be able to challenge her and Sorin. Not anymore. Arianna had all but said they would bow to her.

"And the mortals?" Callan pressed. "What are they to do? Any mortal host will be carrion in this war."

"Alaric does not care. They are chattel to him," Stellan said.

"So who does care for us?" Callan asked.

"Scarlett does," Azrael answered. "It is why I am here. I am to go with you to Baylorin, to aid you and your people in whatever way we can."

"They will not trust you," Arianna said, chin propped in her palm. "You are Fae. Everything they have been taught to fear. They are being told this is all *because* of your kind."

"She is right," Callan said, a finger tapping absent-mindedly on the table. "It will be difficult enough persuading them to trust me, let alone if I show up with a Fae Prince."

"I think you will find your people a little more willing to trust you than you think," Ashtine commented. "It is interesting what light and dark can accomplish together." Sky blue eyes settled on the mortal king. "Angel and Wraith."

Callan lurched forward. "Tava is already risking enough. She is not to be part of this."

Ashtine only smiled faintly. "You will find that is not true. She has always been a part of this. Just as you have always been a part of this."

"So the Earth Prince and mortal king will go to Windonelle," Stellan said, rolling out the map Ilyas had retrieved for him. It covered half the table, and they all leaned towards it. "The Wind Princess will stay here along with the Water Second and Fire General."

"What if I didn't?" Eliza said, the plan already taking shape as she spoke. "What if I went to the Fire Court on Sorin's behalf? I could regain control of my forces. Alaric would be down at least one Court then."

"It could make the other Court armies pause," Azrael said, rubbing at his jaw. "They will see you making a stand. It will spark hope that we are still fighting and cause some unrest among their ranks."

"Exactly," Eliza said, pushing to her feet to see the map better. "We take back the Fire Court, and Windonelle and Rydeon have protection from the north. Toreall and the Wind Court have the Witches to the East. The Shifters can take the Water and Earth Courts. The Fae and mortals at least stand a chance then. We hold the lines until they can get here."

"This could go poorly," Arianna warned from where she still leisurely lounged down the table. "Alaric could simply decimate them all if they try to rebel."

"We have to try," Eliza retorted. "It is better than doing nothing."

"I am not saying we do nothing. We will always fight against injustice and for freedom," the Beta answered. "I am saying be prepared for all the possibilities. You never know what rebellion will cost you."

It was late, the stars having long since appeared in the night sky. She should be sleeping. She needed the rest to refill her power reserves. After she refilled Razik's magic and sent him on his way, she would go with Azrael and Callan to Baylorin. Azrael would eventually Travel her into the Fire Court, and she would make Bastien regret ever thinking he could run the Fire Court.

The male had always disliked her. It had probably started the day she'd handed him his ass in a sparring ring when she was still a grunt. Now she was his superior, and he had continuously toed the line of insubordination. In short, he was a pain in her ass, but his power was one of the stronger in the Court so she put up with him.

Yet here she sat, propped against the headboard of the bed with her knees bent and a book balanced before her instead of sleeping. The candle on her bedside table was burning low. She'd likely need to get another one soon.

Eliza saw him in her periphery. He was leaning against the doorjamb, arms crossed, barefoot, and, of course, shirtless. The same way he'd stood while he'd watched her retch on a bathing room floor weeks ago.

She didn't bother looking at him when she asked, "Do you have an aversion to fabric?"

She saw his brow furrow. "No. Why?"

"You seem to find any reason possible not to wear a shirt."

The slight frown disappeared. "What are you reading?"

"A book. Go away."

His eyes shifted, glowing a faint blue. "Not just any book."

She sighed, turning her attention to him. "No. Not just any book. Can you see better with your eyes shifted? Better than normal for an immortal?"

Her senses were spectacular as a Fae. She couldn't imagine them being even more enhanced.

"I can see farther away. When I am flying, I can see things on the ground clearly," he answered.

That made sense.

Her focus returned to the book she was studying. It was the one he'd given her in his study back in Aimonway, and she was currently trying to figure out how to read the Avonleyan language. Even though it was a book meant for younglings, it was still incredibly complicated.

"Why is it so difficult to understand?" she asked absent-mindedly.

"It is a sub-sect of the Celestial Language," Razik answered.

"What is that?" She tilted the book. There were two words that were nearly identical. Like the Marks, writing a word slightly different changed the meaning entirely, and she could not figure out how these two differed.

"The language of the gods." She looked up at the nearness of his voice, finding him standing beside the bed. He pointed to the two words. "Here. The angle of this part is different."

She saw it then. It was different, but barely. No wonder Sorin had been struggling to learn it. Scarlett had seemed to pick it up easily enough though. It had taken her a matter of months when she'd sneak down to the chamber beneath the Fire Palace library.

"Does it come easier for you? With the blood of a god in your veins?"

"In theory," he answered. "Move over."

She did so without thinking, sliding over a bit to give him room to sit beside her. Turning the book so he could see it better, she pointed to another set of words. "What about these two?"

For the next two hours, Razik entertained her questions and taught her the basics of the Avonleyan language. It was only when the candle had indeed burned all the way down and the words on the page blurred that Razik gently closed the book in his lap.

"You need to sleep," he said. She was nestled against his side where she had been leaning to see the book better as he'd explained things to her.

"I do," she murmured, eyes already closed. A palm ran down her hair. "I want you to stay," she added in a whisper.

"I know, *mai dragocen*," he answered, the whisper of lips brushing against her temple.

And when she woke the next morning with her head on his chest and his arm curled protectively around her waist, holding her to him, she couldn't bring herself to regret asking him to stay.

# CHAPTER 18
## TALWYN

Fucking bars.

Again.

They had waited in that room in the cliffs until the seraph had returned to report that Scarlett and her company had indeed left the Southern Islands. Alaric did not acknowledge her the entire time. Briar stood next to her but also did not speak. When Mordecai had returned, he'd taken her arm, and they'd all gone down to the beach where Alaric had immediately Traveled them out. Then the seraph had escorted her down here while Briar had been taken elsewhere.

Talwyn tipped her head back against the wall of the dungeon she was once again sitting in. Not in Windonelle. No, this time she was graced with the Water Court cells. Musty, dank, and cold, the mist of the sea seemed to seep into her clothing. Shirastone shackles were still on her wrists, but they didn't burn. Not anymore. Not without magic in her veins that would react to the stone. The open cuts and bruises from the nightstone shackles were still there though. She'd heal as a mortal now. She turned her hands over, the slices along her palms scabbed over but still red and raw. At least she was in clean clothing, she supposed, and she'd had a bath. Her eyes fell closed at the memory. The only bit of warmth her soul could cling to right now, and even that was bittersweet.

Azrael had been holding her tightly to his chest when Sorin had told him to take her to his rooms. She had heard him, heard Azrael's roar when she had started screaming. The pain of having her magic ripped from her being nearly overpowered the agony at knowing what price she was forcing him to pay alongside her.

She'd figured it out during her many hours behind bars. Finally saw what had been right in front of her all this time. What she'd been too lost in anger and grief and hurt to see.

What Tarek had taken advantage of.

She hadn't been wrong. Not entirely. She'd felt a twin flame bond. But it hadn't been Tarek.

*"Why didn't you tell me?" she asked.*

*Azrael still clutched her to him as he began filling a tub with hot water.*

*He didn't answer. Didn't say anything as he peeled her grimy and sweat-drenched clothes from her body before helping her into the tub. With a care she was certain no one else had ever seen, he washed her hair for her, rinsing it thoroughly.*

*It was when he was wiping dried blood from her skin that he said, "I wanted you to be happy, Talwyn." His voice was low and soft, just as gentle as he was being while he washed away traces of the last several weeks. "And if he... When you came to me, you were so lost. You were hurting. You felt abandoned and betrayed, and after all of that, all you had endured, I just wanted you to experience happiness. True happiness. And you did. With him. For a little while, at least. I could feel it. I wasn't about to take that away from you."*

*"You chose me," she whispered.*

*"I have always chosen you. Even when choosing you meant having to step back and let you choose your own path. Perhaps I should have—"*

*"I wouldn't have listened," she interrupted, sinking further beneath the water. It was the first time she'd been warm in ages.*

*"I know," he replied. He was kneeling beside the tub, arms resting atop the edge and water dripping from his hands.*

*A somber silence fell as all that could have been hung between them.*

*"When did you know?" Talwyn asked, barely audible.*

*"Not right away," he answered. "I began suspecting some months after you had appeared at the Alcazar. We had not spent much time alone together before then. After that day, though, we spent nearly every day together. But if you are asking if I knew before I found you on that veranda with Tarek the first time, the answer is yes."*

*She nodded, letting the quiet engulf them again.*

*When she was finally ready to get out of the bath, Az helped her out and wrapped a towel around her shoulders before using another to wring the water from her hair. He tossed the damp towel aside when he was done. One hand on the nape of her neck, his other came up to cup her cheek, tilting her face up to his.*

*"I am sorry, Talwyn. I should have protected you from so much."*

*"Why is everyone apologizing to me for the consequences of my actions?" she replied, searching his brown eyes. "I am sorry, Az. For making you endure watching me with another. For not..." A tear slipped free. "I am sorry. For all of it."*

*He gathered her close, towel and all. His chin rested atop her wet hair as she let more tears fall. "You didn't have to do this, Talwyn," he murmured. "You know that, right?"*

*She pulled back, looking into his eyes once more. "I did, Az. I could have stood there. I could have stayed silent. I could have let everything stay the same and committed the same sins I have been committing for decades. Or we could change one thing that will hopefully contribute to some good. I have to believe that giving this up was worth something. Right?"*

*Her tone was almost desperate as she spoke. She needed him to tell her this had been the right choice. That she had done* something *right. She needed him to tell her he understood why.*

*"The fate of this world is more important than what we could have been. Things could stay the same, or we could be part of changing it all," she added.*

*His thumbs swiped across her cheeks, wiping away tears as he brought his brow to hers. "I love you, Talwyn Semiria," he said, and her heart was both healed and broken all at once with those words. "I do not need any type of bond to choose you."*

*Azrael walked her out to his bedchamber, where he pulled one of his tunics from the armoire and slipped it over her head. Then he led her to the bed. She crawled under the blankets, and he slid in beside her, pulling her back against his chest.*

*"Know that while I understand why, I wish you were not going back to Alaric," Az murmured into her hair.*

*She swallowed thickly. "I know, Az."*

*"So much could go wrong."*

*Vulnerable. He was never vulnerable, but his being so now made this moment all the more intimate.*

*She twisted in his hold so she was facing him across the pillows. Reaching up, she slid her fingers into his hair. "We will see each other again. We might not survive this war, but I will see you again. And maybe then—" Her voice cracked, her words getting caught in her throat. "Maybe then we can have what should have been."*

*He kissed her then. Soft and tender and full of the sorrow that was consuming them both.*

She'd slept, a sense of safety she hadn't felt since the last time she'd shared a bed with Azrael falling over her despite what she would face mere hours later.

He'd helped her dress when the messenger had come to his door to tell them their party would be leaving in thirty minutes' time. A courtesy of the others to not come themselves, but to give them these private moments together. She didn't know if they'd figured it out or not, but she appreciated it nonetheless. He'd watched while she'd braided her hair back, no longer able to simply summon her leathers and weapons and be ready to face whatever came for her. That would take some getting used to. He'd passed her a leather band to tie off her hair, and then they'd walked side-by-side to the entrance hall. Azrael hadn't acknowledged anyone else, and when it had been time for her to go, he'd taken her face between his hands and looked into her eyes.

"You can do this, Talwyn. Magic was not all that made you powerful. You are not weak. Do you understand?"

She'd reached up and gently pulled his hands from her face. "Meet me on the battlefield, Prince."

He'd held her gaze as the nightstone was put back onto her wrists. His eyes were still fixed on hers when she'd been pulled through the air to a humid beach on the Southern Islands. Cassius had escorted her until they were outside the cliffs and the archway was appearing after Rayner had summoned it with the brand beneath his skin. As she was handed off to Rayner, Scarlett had cleared her throat.

"I don't know that I can ever like you, Talwyn Semiria, but thank you. For what you did for Sorin," she'd said curtly, tugging down the sleeve of her witchsuit to her wrist. Her twin flame Mark was covered with gloves due to the room they would be in not allowing for glamours. She'd lifted her eyes to Talwyn. "For what you have sacrificed and what you are doing now, thank you."

Talwyn hadn't said anything. There wasn't anything to say anymore. She'd been entirely focused on her task, and now here she sat, waiting to see what would happen next. When would Alaric realize Scarlett had once again tricked him? When he did, Talwyn knew the odds of her surviving his wrath were slim. Knew the probability of seeing Azrael or Ashtine again on this side of the Veil was unlikely, and she'd made peace with that. She hoped she'd done enough. She hoped she'd made enough of a difference to matter.

It had been nearly three days since the exchange. Something would happen soon. She could feel it in her gut, so she wasn't surprised when two seraphs appeared outside her cell a few hours later and escorted her to Alaric. She sat at a table, the Maraan Prince not sparing her a glance as he pored over a map spread out before him.

"Fae Queen," Nuri greeted with a mocking bow when she appeared in the doorway taking a bite from an apple.

"Do you even need food?" Talwyn asked sharply.

Nuri paused, the apple halfway from her mouth in her gloved hand. "Do you need those shackles?" When Talwyn narrowed her eyes, Death's Shadow only laughed, tossing the apple to her. "If you wanted a bite, all you needed to do was ask."

Talwyn caught the apple, the chains on her wrists rattling, and she remembered to let out a hiss to feign discomfort. Alaric flicked his eyes up when Mordecai came into the room.

"Is everything ready?" Alaric asked.

The seraph only nodded in confirmation, moving to his side to study the map. Nuri flopped into a chair opposite him. "The Water Prince isn't here?"

"He's in his cell until needed," Mordecai answered.

She sighed in disappointment. "I enjoy looking at him."

"Why are you here, Nuri?" Alaric asked in annoyance. "Do you not have somewhere else to be?"

She smiled at him. A smile that even Talwyn knew was far too sweet and devious. "Not yet. I thought I would accompany you. Just in case Scarlett is waiting for you."

Alaric's features tightened. "Do you know of her plans, Nuri?"

The Contessa scoffed. "How would I possibly know of her plans? I only mean that she seems to be a few steps ahead of you these days. Maybe an extra set of fangs is warranted."

"The vampyre has a point," Mordecai said, turning the map to see it better.

"She is not a few steps ahead of me," Alaric snarled.

"Everything is going to plan then?" Nuri asked, elbows on the table and chin propped between her hands.

"Mikale has things under control in Windonelle, and the mortal and Fae lands are now all under my rule. Balam is pacified with those mortal offspring returned, and he is back on task. Tarek controls the Earth Court and has all the Fae forces ready and waiting. I have the Fae Queen back and a Water Prince to get me into the prison. Today we free the Sorceress. In a few days' time, this will be over. But if you insist on joining us, Nuri, then by all means," Alaric replied tightly.

"No need to rant," Nuri replied with a dismissive wave. The same casual arrogance and impassiveness that Scarlett had displayed when speaking with her former master.

"I swear to Achaz, Nuri," he muttered under his breath. "Go get the Water Prince and be useful."

"Of course, Master," she replied, that same faux sweetness in her tone as she pushed to her feet and sauntered out of the room, tossing a wink to Talwyn as she went.

"She is insubordinate," Mordecai said, drawing Talwyn's attention back to the males.

"She strains against the leash, but she is under control," Alaric replied dismissively. "She has no choice but to be."

A look of what seemed to be concern crossed the seraph's face, but he shrugged and pointed to something on the map. "After this is done, you plan to travel here?"

"Yes. When Gehenna is at my side, we can work on finding the lock. They won't dare try to come there. Not right now."

Mordecai looked up, his feathered wings shifting behind him. "And then?"

Alaric's lip curled back in a feral sneer. "And then we rip the Wards down and take what's mine."

She walked silently beside Nuri, Briar and Mordecai ahead of them with Alaric leading them all along the corridors. Talwyn had never come to this area of the prison. She'd never interacted with the Sorceress at all. The Sorceress was the bedtime story that caused nightmares. Fae children feared her as mortals feared spirits of the After. Talwyn knew of her history. That was all she'd needed to know. She had never planned on interacting with the female. Her bargains were dangerous, and her knowledge was deadly; yet here she was, about to be revealed in front of the being.

She'd known full well when she stepped inside the prison it was likely the last time she would see the sky. She'd breathed deep, taking the fresh air into her lungs, and letting the warmth of the sun dance across her face before going beneath the sea. The corridors seemed to get darker as they went deeper beneath the surface, no windows in the halls to even show the mer-guards who patrolled beneath the waves.

"Do I really need to come down here?" Nuri groused. "The Sorceress is unnerving."

Talwyn turned to her, nearly gaping at the female. She was Death's Shadow, and she called the Sorceress unnerving?

"You wanted to come with," Alaric growled from the front of their company. "Now you complain about being here?"

"No," Nuri countered. "I said you should have another with you in case Scarlett had something planned. How would you know if we are all beneath the sea?"

"I have seraphs in the skies," Mordecai said, eyes fixed straight ahead.

"As far as I know, Scarlett is the only one of them who can fly with that shadow dragon," Nuri drawled. "Besides Cassius, I suppose. And the dragon shifter. But the others are all stuck on the earth."

"Nuri!" Alaric snapped, whirling to face her. Everyone else stumbled to a halt. Mordecai and Briar stepped to the side as the Maraan Prince stalked towards them. "You have succeeded in getting on my last nerve earlier than usual today."

"I will note the accomplishment in my daily report later this evening," she replied.

Alaric's hand shot out, the slap across her face echoing in the corridor. Briar winced. Mordecai's wings rustled. And Nuri? Her maniacal laughter echoed too.

"Leave, Nuri," Alaric gritted out. "I do not want to see you the rest of the day. I will deal with your insolence tomorrow."

She sketched a mocking bow before she turned on a heel and disappeared into the shadows of the prison.

Great. Now Alaric was in a foul mood, and it was about to get worse when he realized Talwyn couldn't release the Sorceress. Before, he might have simply killed her. Now, he was likely to take out all his frustration on her and draw it out.

Alaric prowled back to the front, barking an order to follow. Mordecai fell back to walk beside her, and Briar cast a troubled look over his shoulder before turning and following Alaric.

She worked to steady her breathing when they began descending the steps to the Sorceress's cell. She may not have been to this area of the prison before, but she knew the layout. Even if she didn't, Briar had gone even more tense in front of her.

The Sorceress was not what she was expecting when she finally laid eyes on her. She was at the bars, her fingers curled around the shirastone. Violet eyes watched them all curiously as they filed in, and they stopped on her and Mordecai, her head tilting with interest. Dark inky hair slid over her shoulder, and a smile that reminded her of Nuri's insane grin tilted on the corners of her dry and cracked lips.

"More gifts?" the Sorceress asked, gaze sliding to Alaric.

"Have I not given you enough?" Alaric asked, his tone lighter and conversational now.

"You know what I desire, Prince of Nothing," she answered, her focus shifting to Briar. "Prince of Water." Briar said nothing, mouth in a taut line. The Sorceress's smile grew, and she pressed herself closer to the bars. "Father of those who should not be. There will be consequences," she sang. When he still said nothing, her smile morphed into a pout. "I prefer your lover. She at least spoke to me."

"She is far more tolerant than I am," Briar said pointedly.

Her smile returned at getting a response from him, and seemingly satisfied, she moved on to Mordecai. Her brow furrowed in confusion. "You smell of the one of other worlds."

Talwyn looked up at the seraph. He hardly blinked at being addressed. "I am not from Halaya."

Halaya? That name nudged at a memory, but Talwyn couldn't remember where she had come across it before.

The Sorceress shook her head, her smile going serpentine. "No, Seraph of Chaos. You smell of another who smells of other worlds."

"Enough of this, Gehenna," Alaric interrupted, stepping into her line of sight. "I am sure the Commander takes whatever pleasure he desires when needed. That is not why I am here."

The Sorceress studied Mordecai a moment longer before she looked at Alaric. "I am unsure why you *are* here. I will do nothing else for you until you free me."

"Why do you think I am here?" he retorted, obvious annoyance in his tone. "I should think you would be more gracious in this moment."

The Sorceress blinked at him, then she broke into a fit of shrill laughter. "You do not know," she finally managed to say. She began moving in front of the bars, her fingers dragging along them, clanging lightly with each pass she made. "The Daughter of Saylah has made a fool of you yet again."

Alaric went entirely still. It was the same preternatural stillness Fae possessed right before they lost control. "What do you mean?"

Talwyn was so focused on the scene playing out in front of her, she didn't realize she was edging towards the stairs. She might not have Fae senses anymore, but her self-preservation instincts were still intact.

"Only a Fae Queen can free me," the Sorceress said. She was in the center of her cell now. She lifted her arms and began turning in a slow circle as she sang, "There is no Fae Queen here, Alaric."

"Talwyn Semiria is the daughter of Henna and niece of Eliné," Alaric snapped, pointing his finger at Talwyn. "She is the Fae Queen of the Eastern Courts."

The Sorceress stopped her spinning and leapt for the bars, her face pressed to them. "*Was* the Fae Queen of the Eastern Courts. She has no power. Not anymore."

"She was in nightstone shackles," Alaric argued. "Then shirastone.

Her power was drained and has not had a chance to replenish. That does not matter."

"There is no earth or wind in her veins. Her wolf slumbers, never to rise again," the Sorceress continued, dropping and beginning to draw in the dirt at her feet. "Even if she did, your Wraith of Deceit challenged her and won. She is not Fae. There is no longer a Fae Queen. Not in this world."

The silence at her words was deafening.

Slowly, Alaric turned to face them. Fury emanated off every part of him. Every movement was a careful stilted motion, his entire body tense with scarcely restrained rage. "You knew," he hissed in a deadly whisper to Briar. "Your lover and unborn will pay the price for this deception."

"No," Briar said, lurching forward a step. "I did not know. I did not know what fate was handed to her. When I came to you, it was still being decided."

He was begging, pleading. For Ashtine. For the babes.

"And you," Alaric snarled, turning to her and ignoring Briar's pleas. "You did not think to mention this?"

Talwyn lifted her chin, looking down her nose at him. "We are no longer allies, and as such, I owe you nothing."

"That conniving little wench," he spat. "When I get her back—"

"You won't," Talwyn interrupted. "You won't get her back. She warned you in the Southern Islands. Nuri warned you mere hours ago. She is so many steps ahead of you, you won't realize you have lost until you are staring at your death."

"How poetic," he sneered. "*You* standing here. Defending *her* to me. When all you sought for decades was revenge. You forget *I* am the one who taught her everything she knows."

"Revenge against those responsible for the death of my family. Revenge against those who orphaned me. Revenge against those who took advantage of me when I was vulnerable," Talwyn replied. "She will accomplish all of that when she comes for you."

"Too bad you will not be on this side of the Veil to witness it," Alaric replied coolly, so much violence glimmering in his dark eyes. "Mordecai, escort her and the Water Prince out. I will be along after I am through here. You know what to do."

The seraph jerked his chin at Briar who rushed to her side, and they were shoved roughly towards the steps. Briar was taking them two at a time. Talwyn knew why. She had seen Alaric lose his temper. Knew he could call them back at any moment. But she was still adjusting to her muted senses. She couldn't move as quickly or as gracefully, and her feet didn't feel like her own as she slipped and stumbled up the stairs.

"Faster," Mordecai hissed at them, which was odd in and of itself.

When she tripped again, the crack of her knees when they slammed into the steps echoed around them. Briar reached down and gripped her arm, hauling her back to her feet. He kept a hold of her, tugging her along. "What the fuck has happened?" he asked.

"Not now," she whispered. She was breathing hard, a combination of exertion and nerves, while Briar was barely winded.

Nothing else was said as they raced through the prison. Alaric might not be able to access his magic down here, but he could still hurt them. Kill them. Worse.

They reached the entrance where magic would normally return to her, and Briar held out his hand to the seraph who quickly swiped a dagger across his palm. He let his blood drip onto a Mark carved into the stone, and a moment later they were all in a courtyard outside the Black Halls. The entrance and exit to the Underwater Prison.

"Now what will you do, Majesty?"

Talwyn whirled, trying to catch her breath. Nuri stood near Mordecai, toying with a dagger. "Where the fuck did you come from?"

She shrugged. "Caught a ride out with you lot."

By the gods.

Nuri sauntered forward. "You finally learned to play the game."

Briar stepped closer, trying to come between them. "Whose side are you truly on, Nuri?" he said in a tone Talwyn rarely heard from the male. It was icy and full of promised threats. It was why he was the Water Prince.

"The side I have always been on," she replied.

"That is not an answer," Talwyn spat.

"No?"

Talwyn straightened, her breathing evening out, and the emotions she'd been shoving down spilling over. Fury. Sorrow. Agony. Grief. She'd sacrificed and gave, and it might never be enough, but at least she was godsdamn trying.

She took a step towards Nuri as she said, "I think this truly is all a game to you. I think you enjoy inciting dramatics purely for amusement. I think you are *entertained* by keeping secrets and watching what happens when they are discovered. I don't think you truly care about anything."

Nuri's features went positively wicked. "So many insights," she purred, prowling closer.

"Nuri," came a low warning from the seraph.

"Hush, Cai," she replied, her grin growing. "Didn't you hear? I *enjoy* dramatics."

"Nuri, please," Briar said, trying and failing to shield Talwyn. "I do not know what has happened, but—"

"New game," Nuri said suddenly, cutting Briar off. "Let's see how quickly you learn to play this one, *your Majesty*." Her fangs snapped out, and she dropped into a crouch.

"Nuri!" Mordecai barked again. "Not like this."

"You know what to do, Cai," she crooned. Then her honey-colored eyes locked onto Talwyn. "As for you, I would run."

"What?"

"Run, Talwyn," she repeated. Then she started counting down from twenty.

Talwyn looked at Briar, his icy blue eyes wide. "Run, Talwyn!"

"What about you?"

"I cannot risk Ashtine and the babes. Go!"

Nuri was at fifteen when Talwyn took off.

She was at ten when the insane female started laughing.

She was at five when male hands scooped Talwyn up and hauled her into the sky.

# CHAPTER 19
# SORIN

"Hey, Prince," Scarlett chirped as she flounced into their rooms. She took a bite from the pear she held, eyeing him with bright silver eyes. Sorin slowly set aside the note he'd been reading from Eliza that Razik had brought back with him. His general had told him of Bastien taking control of the Fire Court and the plan they had come up with, along with the Shifter siblings. It was a good plan, even if he didn't like her over there alone. He knew Eliza was capable. Call it his Fae male protective nature, he supposed. Keeping his Inner Court safe and unified had always been one of his highest priorities. One he felt like he was failing at as of late.

Now his attention was fixed on his twin flame. Her eyes danced with mischief, and the same radiated down their bond. She was in casual attire— fitted black pants, a long-sleeved white tunic, only two visible weapons rather than the usual assortment, and those gods-damned gold shoes she insisted on wearing whenever she could these days.

She took another bite of the pear as she draped herself across the armchair, her feet swinging over one side. He had filled her power reserves after he'd slept for two entire days. Then, much to her dismay, he hadn't let her accompany him to a training arena. There was no way he was risking having her—or anyone, for that matter—around while he worked with the new depths of this power. It felt like his, but it felt...wilder. More chaotic. After centuries of having his fire firmly under control, it was a touch unsettling. So every time he'd gone to train with it, he hadn't let her come. One time she tried to be sneaky, but their newly reinstated bond gave her away as soon as she was within a few miles. And the way she was acting now had him narrowing his eyes at her in suspicion.

"How was training?" she drawled, not attempting to hide her irritation with him.

He stretched his legs out and propped an elbow on the arm of the sofa, resting his chin on his fist. "It was good," he answered casually.

The glare she sent him had his lips twitching into a lazy smirk.

"Have you seen Cyrus today?"

That had his smirk fading. Cyrus hadn't left his rooms since he'd returned. As soon as Sorin had awoken, he'd gone to see him. His Second had been sleeping. Cassius had said he'd woken a few times, but only to eat and use the bathing room. He'd hardly spoken since his initial return. Sorin had checked on him multiple times each day since. Most of the time, he was resting, but the times he'd been awake... Sorin knew that look on his friend's face. It's how he had looked when Rayner had finally tracked him down as a thief. It's how he'd looked for years after Thia's death. He knew what was coming next.

Sorin sighed. "This morning and when I returned from the training arena," he answered. "I stayed with him for a bit while Cassius bathed and got fresh clothing."

Scarlett nodded, fiddling with the half-eaten pear. "What do we do?"

"The same thing we always do, Love. We sit with him in the dark until he's ready to fight for the stars."

She nodded, taking another bite. "How many times are you going to read that note?"

Her change of subjects yet again had him blinking at her. She was avoiding something.

Razik had returned late in the night, power fully restored and pissy as hell. He'd shoved the note at Scarlett before he'd stalked off to find Cethin.

"I do not like us all separated," Sorin said. "It is happening far too often these days."

"Eliza is more than capable of handling this. Their plan is sound."

"I know this. It does not mean I have to like it. It does not mean I do not wish we could do more from here."

That deviant glint returned to her eyes. "Care to go on an adventure with me, Prince?"

Finally. She was finally ready to let him in on this.

"Do I need to change for this outing?" he asked, sitting up a little straighter.

She shrugged. "We may encounter a few of those things that attacked me."

"The beings only Kailia can kill?" he replied dubiously.

"Mhmm."

He rubbed at his brow with his thumb and forefinger, knowing if he said no, she'd go off on her own anyway. "And where exactly are we going?" Scarlett waved a hand, and a map of starfire appeared in the air between them. Avonleya and their own continent with a few ice crystals scattered across them. "What am I looking at, Love?"

"Locations of mirror gates," she answered, finishing off the last of her pear.

"The mirror gates," he repeated.

"Yes." She pushed to her feet, moving to toss the pear core in the rubbish bin. "I suspect there are more. There has to be, right? Pyry? Other continents in this world that we do not know of?"

He studied her burning map for a moment, trying to figure out where she was going with this. "I suppose there could be. How did you learn of these? We knew of the two on our continent and the one your mother took you to, but the others?"

Her eyes darted to the window in a way that told him she was about to reveal something that would alter everything, and Sorin braced himself for it. He leaned forward, elbows resting on his knees and hands loosely clasped. "Love?" he prompted.

"Saylah told me of them. That night in Shira Forest. But even she does not know if these are all of them in this world," she answered. "They were once all gateways, as the one in Shira Forest is."

He stared at her, knowing there was more. But she didn't offer it, so he said, "And what is your interest in them? Why do they matter?"

"If they once were that, could they not be that again?"

He got to his feet but didn't move towards her. "Why would you want that? Are we not trying to keep Achaz and others out?"

"Yes, but…" She trailed off, biting her lower lip. "When this is over, maybe it wouldn't have to stay that way. Maybe beings of other worlds that wish to visit would be able to."

"What aren't you saying, Scarlett?"

She finally met his gaze, and he could feel her trying to keep control of her emotions down the bond. "Because if I cannot change fate, I will be forced to leave this world, and I would like to think I could come back some day."

"What do you mean you will have to leave this world?" he demanded, moving to stand in front of her. She tipped her head back to look at him and crossed her arms. He gripped her shoulders, needing to touch her, as if she were going to disappear at any moment and leave him behind yet again.

She held his gaze as she said quietly, "Achaz will not stop, Sorin. This is an ancient war. Even if we defeat Alaric and the Maraans here, Achaz will still come. He will not leave this world in peace as long as a descendant of Arius still lives in it."

"But that would mean Cethin—"

"Will leave too. Kailia and Razik with him."

"He knew? This entire time?"

She nodded mutely.

"Where will we go?"

Tears pooled in her eyes. "We?" she whispered.

Sorin pulled her closer, one hand cupping her face. "Always together, Scarlett."

"I cannot ask you to leave…everything," she replied, a tear slipping free.

"I once told you I would cross deserts and oceans for you. I would cross the realms for you. I choose wherever you are. That has not changed."

"But your people—"

"*Our* people," he corrected.

"They can't lose both of us," she argued. "One of us has to stay."

"A you and a me is not an option, Scarlett. Not ever."

"This is bigger than you and me, Sorin. It has to be."

"I will not accept it, Scarlett. If you try to leave me behind, I will come for you. I will find you. I will always find a way." He brushed away more tears with his thumbs. "So instead of making me do that, tell me of your plans and let me scheme with you, Princess."

She huffed out a laugh. "What makes you think I've been scheming?"

He gave her a frank look. "You are always scheming."

"True," she said with a small smile. "Let's change and scheme then, Prince."

"Just to clarify," Sorin said, reaching down to haul Scarlett over the edge of the rocky incline they were climbing up. "You knowingly Traveled to snowy terrain, and now you are complaining about the cold."

"No one *likes* the cold, Sorin," she retorted irritably, adjusting the hood of her fur-lined cloak.

"And you wanted to explore Pyry for a mirror gate? You wouldn't have lasted more than five minutes," he teased, reaching over to flick her nose.

She batted his hand away with a scowl. "Need I remind you that Cassius and I spent plenty of time in Pyry a few months ago?"

He chuckled, sending heat into her cloak, and the moan she let out was godsdamn orgasmic. "You have your own fire magic, you know," he said, his voice gruff as ways to elicit that same sound tonight started forming in his mind.

"I know," she sighed. "I just prefer yours." She was peering around when she added down the bridge of their bond: *I've missed it.*

This was the first time he'd used his restored power around her. It was the first time he'd felt like he had enough of a grasp on it. She'd tried to coax it out of him a few times, her shadows and starfire calling to his flames, but he'd only let the smallest amount of magic answer.

*I've needed time to readjust. That is all, Scarlett.*

*I know,* she replied, beginning to walk into the snowy expanse before them.

They were somewhere between a mountain range on the west side of the continent and some expanse of cliffs and canyons that reminded Sorin of the Wind Court. The cliffs seemed to connect the Nightmist Mountains with the other mountain range and ran along the northern part of the continent. And somewhere around here, there was supposed to be a mirror gate.

Sorin set off after Scarlett, falling into step beside her. "Which other mirror gates have you visited?"

"None across the Edria," she replied.

"And in Avonleya?"

"I found one other one. In the southern part of the continent."

"And you've kept it a secret because...?"

"Because I don't want Cethin thinking I need to be followed everywhere. I am not entirely sure how much I trust him right now. If I happen to find something unexpected, I want to be in control of if and when he learns it," she answered.

"Kailia hasn't followed you?"

"I've had to be more strategic since the attack at the estate, but no. She does not follow me. That way," she said, pointing to the right.

She turned, starting down a small decline. He knew she was using a Mark she had drawn on the palm of her right hand to guide her. How it worked, he had no idea.

"There is nothing guarding the mirror gates?" he asked.

"I never said that."

"Scarlett..."

"I'm fine, aren't I?"

"By the gods," he cursed under his breath. "What guards them?"

"My shadow panthers took care of them."

"Scarlett. What were they?" He reached out, tugging her to a stop.

"I don't know what they were, Sorin. Some type of serpent creature." She swiped a gloved hand down her face before her eyes fixed on the ground. Then she was dropping down and wiping away the small smattering of snow that had fallen. "Sorin, do you see this?"

He crouched next to her, seeing nothing but barren grey ground. He'd long since learned that didn't mean anything, though. "I do not," he answered, looking over at her. "What do you see?"

She pulled a glove off, her finger tracing along something. "I can't make out what it says," she murmured. She used her other hand to clear away more snow. "This isn't Avonleyan."

But he was only half-listening to her now. Something felt…wrong. He scanned the surrounding area. There was nothing out here but snow and rock and grey skies. Pulling one of the short swords strapped to his waist, he pushed to his feet and turned in a slow circle.

"I feel it too," Scarlett murmured, still studying the ground. Shadows pooled, her panthers forming and beginning to prowl around them. "I can't figure out what I'm missing."

"Perhaps we go figure it out somewhere else then come back," Sorin muttered. "Something is not right here, Scarlett."

"Just a few more minutes. It has to be here," she replied. She pricked her finger, now tracing whatever she saw with her blood.

Then the ground began to shake.

"Scarlett," Sorin snapped, gripping her elbow and hauling her upright and into his side. "What did you do?"

"I think my blood activated the Marks," she whispered, a slight nervousness in her voice.

"And what are those Marks going to do?"

She bit her lower lip, gaze fixed on the Marks he couldn't see. "Hopefully take us to the mirror gate?"

"By the gods, Scarlett," he growled, clutching her tighter as the ground lurched beneath their feet.

But the air around them was shimmering. The various towering cliff sides and ledges were shifting as the earth shuddered again. Scarlett had a wall of starfire around them in the next breath, and her shadows covered them like a second skin as she shielded them from whatever was about to happen. Still the world shook around them.

"Travel us out," Sorin gritted, another violent tremor making them both stumble.

"A little longer."

"We can come back, Scarlett," he insisted.

"There's something bigger, Sorin. We're missing something so much bigger. It has to be connected to the mirror gates."

Before he could argue further, everything stilled. Scarlett looked up at him in question. He sighed, his lips forming a tight line. He didn't like this. He didn't like that he had no idea what they were walking into, what danger she might be in. But she was including him. She was finally letting him in on her plans.

Sorin gave her a tight nod. Her shadows tightened around them as she slowly lowered her starfire. Then the white flames disappeared altogether, and they stood gaping.

There were doors and balconies. There were *buildings*. Bridges spanned between various levels, a network of paths connecting it all. They spanned farther than he could see. Up, down. Left and right. They seemed to be standing in the very heart of whatever this was. Everything was stone, and there were several places where the rock was crumbling or gone all together. Ancient and lovely and—

"Ruins," Scarlett whispered. "These are the ruins of a city."

"It would make sense if a mirror gate is hidden here," Sorin replied, still trying to take everything in.

Scarlett looked down at her palm where the guiding Mark she'd drawn was still stark against her skin. "This way I guess."

She stepped from his hold, her shadows going with her and swirling until two panthers stalked at her sides. She had a dagger in her other hand, and Sorin adjusted his grip on his short sword as he followed her deeper into the ruins.

They came to a decrepit fountain a few minutes later, and she turned, starting down a ramp that led into a crevice. Bits of debris crumbled as the ramp became a bridge, winding down into the dark. There were no railings or sides on the bridge. Just a fall to one's death. Two glowing flames appeared above them, and he couldn't help but marvel at her effortlessly using so many facets of her magic at once these days. Natural. A fate she had fought for so long.

"I feel you looking at me," she muttered. "Stop thinking such silly thoughts."

"What thoughts?"

"That you believe I've followed fate more than I care to admit."

"All evidence does seem to point in that direction."

She hummed in response. "I suppose we shall see who wins in the end."

Once he would have said the Fates always win, but now?

They finally reached the base of the winding ramp, and Scarlett made the guiding flames flare brighter. She sucked in a breath. "Sorin?"

"I see them, Love."

Doors. Giant onyx doors stood before them. Numerous Marks were etched into the doors, but in the center were three that were bigger than the rest: Arius, Achaz, and another he did not know. A triangle inside a circle.

But there were others he had never seen before as well, and it was these that Scarlett was tracing with her finger.

"These are the same as the language we found in the snow," she murmured.

She swiped the dagger across her palm before placing it on the door, directly over the Arius symbol. There was a faint click, and she pushed, the ancient door grinding against the stone floor.

On instinct, Sorin tugged her back to him, his sword raised, but her shadows swept inside. They were both holding their breath, and it took a minute before she released hers. "Empty. There's nothing in there."

She gave him another shaky smile, and Sorin stepped forward, pushing the door open farther. "The others are going to kill us for going here without them."

"Probably," she muttered. She let the fire flare again, and Sorin saw it before she did. A ledge that ran around the perimeter of the room. He sent an ember from her flame to it, and the oil he suspected was there caught light, the chamber suddenly cast in a warm glow.

And at the end of the corridor was the mirror gate.

Scarlett rushed forward, setting her dagger down on a cracked stone table as she went. The same symbols surrounded the mirror, and she again began tracing them with a slight frown.

"You know," he ventured carefully, "Saylah would likely know of them."

The frown became pursed lips, her hands coming to her hips. "I know."

"She is your mother."

"Eliné was my mother," Scarlett said sharply.

"I know, Love," he said, stepping closer. "All I am suggesting is maybe if we were a little more…cooperative, she might be willing to give a little more."

To his utmost surprise, she murmured, "Maybe."

She continued inspecting the mirror. For what, he didn't know, but he watched her pace back and forth in front of it.

He took in the rest of the chamber. There was nothing. It was completely empty save for the table in the center of the room. No other markings. No books like in the chamber beneath the Wind Citadel. He turned back and froze.

Scarlett stood directly in front of the mirror, and someone was on the other side.

It was a male with clean cut brown hair that matched his russet colored eyes. His hands were shoved into the pockets of pants from material Sorin had never seen before. He had a thick wool shirt on and some type of large satchel slung across his chest. The male tilted his head, watching Scarlett curiously as he rocked back on his heels.

"Where are you?" she asked cautiously, bringing her fingertips to the mirror.

The male glanced between them, then shook his head as if to tell her he could not hear her. He lifted the flap on his bag and pulled out some paper. Sorin stepped to her side, and they both watched while he wrote on it.

He held it up in the mirror. There were various lines written, all in languages Sorin did not recognize except for one.

"This one," Scarlett said, tapping on the one written in the Avonleyan language.

The male looked at which one she'd pointed to, then back at her in surprise. He flipped the paper over, scribbling on the back, before holding it up again.

"What does it say?" Sorin asked, not nearly as proficient in the language yet as Scarlett was.

"He is asking if we are Legacy," she said with a frown.

She gave him a tentative nod, and he quickly began scribbling on the paper again.

"Which god," Scarlett read when he held the paper back up.

Looking around helplessly for something to write on, she finally settled for drawing in the air with her starfire. She drew Saylah's symbol, and confusion passed over the male's features. But then his attention went to something else wherever he was at. He gave them a small smile with a quick bow before he stepped out of view.

"No! Wait!" Scarlett cried, pressing her palms to the glass.

They waited several minutes in silence before Sorin said gently, "I do not think he is coming back, Love."

She slammed a palm against the smooth surface. "He knew something. He knew about the mirror gates."

"We can come back."

Her brow fell against the glass. "I am running out of time, Sorin."

"We will figure it out, Scarlett."

Then they both went rigid. There was a dragging sound. Claws on stone.

Starfire flared, and Scarlett was holding her spirit sword in her hand. Sorin pulled his short swords, and they both scanned the chamber before starting back to the doors.

The sound came again, and Scarlett had her shadows forming into wolves that surrounded them as they stepped through the onyx doors.

Sorin didn't know what he was looking at.

Creatures lined the ledges, staring down at them. They were as large as tigers, but they had long canines protruding from their upper gums. The claws on their feet were razor sharp. Their coats were golden, even in the darkness of the crevice, and their eyes glowed white.

That scraping sounded again, and two of the creatures prowled from the shadows to their left. Scarlett wasted no time, starfire whipping out from her palm. The creatures snarled as the fire wrapped around their throats before consuming them in their next breath, leaving nothing but scorch marks on the floor.

"Effective," Sorin said, glancing at the dozens more appearing on the various levels. "But let's just Travel out."

"Good plan," she agreed, grabbing his wrist.

He waited for the pull, but it never came. "Travel, Scarlett," he gritted out as several of the creatures began hopping among the cliff sides and coming closer.

"I can't," she hissed. "I can't Travel."

"What do you mean you can't?" he retorted, raising his sword. Would steel even work against them?

"Exactly what I said," she snapped. She sheathed her sword before lifting her palms. Starfire flared across several of the ledges, taking out a dozen of the creatures at once. "Maybe it's the doors," she said, her breathing slightly labored as her fire died out. "Maybe if we get back to the top?"

"And if not?" he demanded, her shadow wolves beginning to move up the bridge they had come down.

"I guess we'll figure something else out," she replied, more starfire appearing in her palms. "Let's focus on getting up there. Only take them out if we need to."

They ran, racing up the winding incline as quickly as they could, but it didn't take long for the creatures to figure out what they were doing. Soon the bridge was shaking as the creatures leapt to it, taking chase.

"Faster, Scarlett," he muttered, having sheathed his swords long ago. Her starfire was keeping them at bay behind them, the shadow wolves making short work of those in front. Blood as golden as their fur splattered across their path. She'd tried sending orange flames to conserve some of her Avonleyan power, but the creatures were unaffected, which meant his fire would be useless.

"They're strong," she rasped, stumbling on a crack in the stone. "It takes a lot of my magic to kill them. If I keep doing this, I won't be able to Travel out when we reach the top."

The bridge lurched as several of the creatures landed on it again. They both fell to the side, Sorin gripping Scarlett's arm before she went over the edge.

"Fuck," he ground out. "They're going to bring down the bridge before we get back to the top."

Another flare of starfire. More snarling and howling as the creatures were destroyed.

"We have to keep going. Run, Sorin!"

They made it another hundred feet before the bridge shook violently again. Sorin pulled a dagger, slicing it clean through his tunic and dragging it across the Source Mark. He could give her more power so they could get to the top. He reached for her hand, still running along beside her.

And then the creatures seemed to collapse in on themselves. One would still, its white eyes flaring bright in surprise, maw opening and fangs bared, before it became ashes starting from the chest and splintering outward. The snarls became cries and whines of agony. One by one, they fell. Over and over.

"What is happening?" Scarlett gasped, breathing hard beside him, her hands braced on her knees.

They'd skidded to a halt when it had happened to the first few. Sorin still gripped her arm, dagger still poised to slice across her palm. Blood from his arm was dripping to the ground as he answered. "Rayner is here."

She straightened at that, silvery-blue eyes darting around, searching. But Rayner was moving too fast. He *was* smoke and ashes. As soon as a creature made a movement toward them, it was ash in the next blink. Sorin took the opportunity to cut Scarlett's palm, letting some of his magic flow into her. She was still looking for Rayner as she stepped into him, fingers flexing around his forearm.

"That's all I need," she said after a few moments, pulling her hand away as the last of the creatures were destroyed.

"That can't be all," he argued, trying to tug her back.

But then ashes swirled before them, and Rayner stepped into view. His hands were black with soot and ash. Golden blood mixed amongst the blacks and greys, and streaks of the same covered his face. His eyes were swirling slowly as they fixed on them.

Furious.

The Ash Rider was pissed.

"What. The fuck. Were you two thinking?" Rayner demanded. This wasn't a rage-filled bellow. This was a low, deadly demand for an answer.

This was the Reaper before them, and Scarlett knew it too as she shrank back into Sorin.

"How did you find us?" Sorin asked, tucking Scarlett behind him as his Third worked to leash his fury.

"I've been searching for godsdamn hours," Rayner replied, lethally calm. His gaze moved to Scarlett. "You could have been a little more detailed in your whereabouts, *your Majesty*."

Sorin looked down at her. "You told him?"

"I left him a brief note. In case we weren't back by a certain time."

"A very vague note," Rayner gritted out.

"There are a lot of busybodies in that castle," she replied, lifting her chin. She gestured towards Rayner. "Besides, you figured it out."

"Scarlett!" he snarled.

"Let's discuss this back in Aimonway," Sorin cut in. "Can you Travel with them gone, Scarlett?"

A moment later, she shook her head. "Something still isn't right."

"Maybe we just need to be back at the top like you said," Sorin replied, taking her hand and beginning to walk up the bridge again. He knew that likely wasn't the case, but it was their only option right now.

"Where the fuck are we?" Rayner grumbled, falling into step on his right.

Scarlett was on his left, Sorin still not comfortable letting Rayner that close to her while he was riding the edge of control.

"Scarlett found some Marks in the snow, and when she let her blood drip onto them, an entire godsdamn ancient city appeared," Sorin answered.

"Great," Rayner muttered.

Scarlett snorted a laugh. "So grumpy, Rayner."

"I'm not speaking to you right now."

Another bark of laughter. "At least I left a note this time."

"I swear to Arius, Scarlett," Rayner grumbled again.

"Speaking of Arius," she said, perking up a bit. "Do you know whose symbol this is?"

She drew the triangle in a circle in the air with her fire.

Rayner begrudgingly glanced at it. "No."

"There was nothing in the Southern Islands with it?"

"No," Rayner snapped in annoyance. "We can discuss this later, Scarlett. When I don't want to throttle you."

"Fine, fine," she muttered, falling silent in a way that told Sorin she was trying to work something out.

No one spoke again. It took nearly fifteen minutes to make it back to the top of the winding bridge, and when they stepped back onto the flat ground, Scarlett muttered. "Well, that explains it."

Beings surrounded them. Exactly as she had described them. White as moonlight. Solid, but not. Razor-sharp features. Unearthly grace. Pure white eyes. Gold swords.

"What's the plan now, your Majesty?" Rayner gritted out. Ashes were spilling from his palms, encasing them in a shield.

"Those won't work," she said. "Just like I can't Travel."

"Suggestions then?" he retorted, the beings gliding closer. "Or did you leave an unclear note for Kailia, and we just need to survive until she gets here?"

"You know, I think I like this snarky side of you," she replied. Then she looked up at Sorin. "Try your fire?"

His head whipped to her. "If your power does not work against them, what makes you think mine will?"

"You're stronger now, right?"

"You are still stronger, Scarlett!"

"Blood of death," one of the beings breathed, his eerie voice raking along Sorin's bones.

"Ugh," Scarlett drawled. "Again with this?"

"Scarlett, this is not the time for your dramatics," Sorin chided. "You told me you had a plan if they showed up."

"I do," she replied, twirling the dagger she had pulled. "Use your fire."

One being glided closer, his golden sword slicing easily through Rayner's shield of ashes.

"Now, Sorin," Scarlett said, her back straightening with the demand.

A command from a Queen.

Rayner glanced at him sidelong, his features tight. He nodded, moving closer to Scarlett, preparing to shield her if necessary.

Sorin stepped away from her before he let his fire out to play. His eyes fell closed as he worked to control the raging wildfires in his veins. He couldn't let it run wild. Not with her so close.

"All of it, Sorin," Scarlett demanded.

"Scarlett—" Rayner started.

"He said it himself," she interrupted. "I'm still stronger. He's not going to hurt me."

Then her shadows raked down his soul, calling to his power. Taunting it. Any control he had snapped. His fire exploded out. He felt Rayner's shield shatter at the impact. In a panic, he opened his eyes.

And found Scarlett smiling wickedly at him.

"There it is," she purred. Flames of red and orange, yellow and blue, reflected in her silver irises. "Keep them burning, Prince."

Before he or Rayner could stop her, she was tossing starfire and freezing it in the air. Godsdamn steps that went higher and higher into the sky.

The beings were hissing, their swords cutting through his flames as they pushed forward, but his fire flared right back to life. He was scarcely scratching the surface of his power well.

"Be ready to catch her," he snarled at Rayner.

"Already prepared," he muttered, his eyes fixed on the queen leaping from flames in the sky.

When she was a good seventy feet in the air, she lifted her arms, all the frozen steps of flame coming to her and creating a stage in the sky. Her braid was floating among shadows that were thickening and swirling around her, strands of silver falling from the plait. Her gaze connected with his, and she fucking winked at him as she unclasped her cloak and let it fall from her fingers, the black material fluttering to the ground.

Then, as if she were pushing them down, her shadows plummeted when her arms dropped. Darkness crashed into his flames, and he staggered under the weight of it. Her shadows latched onto his fire, merging with it. She was walking along her platforms of ice, leading the dark flames along. He'd seen her use this before with her own fire. Shadowfire she had called it, but she'd had to split her power between shadows and flames. Now, though? Now she could put her full strength into her shadows, and their twin flame bond let her combine them with his fire.

His fire magic was now more powerful than an Avonleyan.

"Holy gods," Rayner murmured.

Where she pulled, the shadowfire went. She was a dark goddess that could claim the world for her own or burn it to nothing.

The beings were screeching, golden swords clattering to the ground as the shadowfire consumed them. And while he kept his focus on his fire, making sure it flared back whenever one of the beings cut through it, he could hear her laughing in delight. From her vantage point, she could see every one of them.

"She is terrifying," Rayner muttered again.

Sorin chanced a glance up at her and found her staring straight at him. Her crown of shadows and starfire sat atop her head, that same wicked grin in place.

And he grinned back as a crown of flames flared above him.

"Drop your shield, Rayner," he ordered.

"Sorin—"

"Do it."

His ashes disappeared, letting Sorin clearly see the beings remaining. He yanked on the flames, and he saw her stumble a bit before she tipped her head back and laughed again. She let him have control of the shadowfire, giving him free rein of her shadows, and as he dragged it around and finished off the few remaining beings, she spun atop her stage of frozen starfire, dancing to a dark song only she could hear.

His breathing was ragged as the last being was burned among shadow and fire. The air was filled with ash that did not belong to Rayner. It drifted down to the ground like gently falling snow, and Scarlett was floating amongst it all atop one of her frozen flames. She was still ten feet in the air when she leapt from the ice and into his arms.

"Fucking hell," Rayner muttered when Sorin caught her with a bark of laughter that mixed with her own. They were covered in a fine layer of ash, but her mouth crashed into his. Her legs wound around his waist, and she was pure darkness as her tongue met with his.

*You planned this,* he said down the bond.

She pulled back, unable to hide her smirk. *You wouldn't let me near when you were using your power. You left me no choice, really.*

*How did you know it would work?*

She shrugged. *I didn't, but I had a backup plan.*

His brow arched as he slowly lowered her to the ground.

*We'll save it for another time,* she said with a wink. *Wouldn't want you to get bored.*

Sorin shook his head in awed disbelief, but he couldn't keep the smile from his face as he tugged her back to him and kissed her deeply.

"Why didn't you do that in the crevice?" Rayner asked when they finally broke apart.

"I didn't know how much space we would need in case things got out of control," she answered. "And I wanted to know if combining our power would work on these beings. I could kill the other creatures on my own."

"It is why you didn't take more power when I tried to fill your reserves," Sorin said as Scarlett nudged one of the golden swords with her boot.

She glanced up at him from beneath her lashes. "I knew you'd only access it around me if my life was in danger."

*Cunning, wicked goddess,* he sent down the bond, feeling her desire spike at the words.

"That was..." Rayner trailed off, still surveying the destruction they'd wrought. Finally, his grey eyes settled back on them. "The two of you can bring this world to its knees."

"This world doesn't have to worry," Scarlett said darkly. "Only those who should have never come here."

# CHAPTER 20
# CYRUS

C yrus refilled his glass with liquor after knocking back the first. He sipped on the second, aimlessly pacing back and forth in his bedchamber. This was the longest he'd been awake at one time since returning. He'd bathed and cleaned up a bit, ate some food, and now here he was. Just being.

He wished he were still sleeping.

In sleep, he couldn't dwell on the promises he'd made and the vows he'd broken.

Then again, in sleep, his nightmares found him more easily. The memories the Sorceress had altered played on repeat, one after another. He suspected it was her, making his life a living hell from thousands of miles away. Reminding him she was waiting for him to fulfill his bargain with her. It had to be her because the last memory, the final nightmare that always jolted him awake, was the one memory she'd altered of Cassius. Cyrus knew it for the threat it was. If he failed in this, she would take every memory he'd sacrificed so much to save and ruin him.

He knocked back the liquor again, his fist clenching around the glass so tightly it was a miracle it didn't shatter.

Someone had cleaned up the glass on the bathing room floor. It had been gone when he'd awoke the first time. A new mirror had not appeared yet, and he was secretly grateful for that. Although, he had a feeling the male who rarely left his rooms was responsible for both cleaning up his mess and making sure he couldn't see the mess he'd become.

Cassius wasn't here now, though. Neither were Sorin or Scarlett or Rayner. One of them was always here. Now they weren't even in the sitting room. He was completely alone. At first he had been relieved, but now... Alone meant his thoughts went places he knew they shouldn't.

Setting the glass aside, he slipped on boots and headed out of the room. Pausing, he looked at Cassius's door for a moment. He toyed with the idea of checking to see if he was in there, but he was obviously doing something important. He didn't need to bother him.

Cyrus made his way down the various halls and stairwells until he found himself outside a decent-sized den, much like their own back in Solembra. There were two billiard tables off to one side, and with nothing better to do, he grabbed a cue and racked the balls.

He was sinking the last two balls when he heard footsteps approaching. He didn't need to look up to know who was leaning in the doorway across the room.

"What?" Cyrus said, setting his cue aside and beginning to collect the balls from the pockets of the table.

"I've been looking for you," Cass replied.

"For what?"

"You left your rooms."

"Glad to see all that assassin training made you such a keen observer," Cyrus replied, rolling a few more balls down the green felt.

"I did not mean to be gone when you woke."

"As I have repeatedly told all of you busybodies, I do not need to be watched," he replied, gathering the balls to rack them.

"Are you going to look at me? Or just speak to the table?"

Cyrus stilled, breathing suddenly difficult. He raised his eyes, connecting with two glowing amber-red ones, pupils vertical slits.

"Why are your eyes shifted?" he asked quietly.

"I was flying," Cass answered, moving into the room. "With Razik

251

back, I wanted to get in some training in the sky before he leaves again."

"Is he leaving again?"

Cassius swiped up the rack that was set off to the side and began placing the various balls inside it. "He hasn't said anything, but with Eliza across the sea, I'm sure he will."

Right. Because Eliza was Razik's Source. Cyrus hadn't been able to ask if Cassius had taken one. That had been his plan before he'd gone to the Southern Islands. Not that it really mattered anymore. He'd need a Source before they went to fight.

Cassius finished racking the balls in silence, then held the cue out to Cyrus. He took it, watching while Cass went to grab another.

"Where is everyone else?" Cyrus asked.

"Scarlett and Sorin have been gone for quite some time. Rayner is trying to track them down."

"We don't know where they are?"

Cassius shrugged, but Cyrus could see the tension in his limbs he was trying to downplay. "They'll turn up. She always does," Cassius muttered. He gestured to the balls on the table. "You break. We'll clean it up together."

Cyrus held his stare for a brief moment before he pushed past him and lined up his shot. The crack of the balls was loud in the silence that had engulfed them. Neither of them spoke through the first game or the second. Razik appeared in the middle of the third. It was the first Cyrus had seen any of the Avonleyan since returning.

"How's Eliza?" Cyrus asked when the dragon shifter stalked into the room.

"Infuriating," Razik grumbled, crossing his arms and watching Cassius take his shot.

Cyrus snickered. "Is that all? She's infuriating on a good day." He watched as Cassius sank ball after ball. "When is she coming back?"

He saw Cass glance at Razik, his lips pressing into a thin line, before he went back to lining up his next shot.

"She is likely not," Razik answered tightly. "You will meet up with her across the sea at some point I assume."

"And after this is said and done?" Cyrus asked while Cassius proceeded to clear the table. Gods, he swore billiards was part of their training at the Fellowship. Cass and Scarlett always won. So much so, the others didn't allow them to be on the same team anymore.

A muscle in Razik's jaw feathered. "No one can say what the world will look like when this is all said and done."

"Fair point. You in?" Cyrus asked as Cassius started racking the balls again. Razik shrugged, but reached for a pool cue.

Razik broke the balls, and as he began working the table Cyrus asked, "But Eliza is all right?"

Razik's gaze flicked to him for a moment. "She is healed and well, Cyrus."

"I lost her arrows."

They'd bickered before he had left. It was nothing new. They always did. He'd insisted on needing her Fiera arrows, and she had finally given in with a threat to never come to his aid again if he lost them. He knew it for the empty threat it was, but he still felt terrible about losing them. He'd have to get her a new set, he supposed. It was the very least he could do.

"I assure you, she does not care about the arrows," Razik replied in that bored tone he always spoke in. He hit the cue ball towards a striped ball, sending it into a pocket.

"Did you know it took her years to say more than five words at a time to me and Rayner? She would snap at us, of course, like she does at others in the forces, but truly talk to us?" Cyrus shook his head as he trailed off, heading to a liquor cart in the corner. He poured three glasses of alcohol, passing them out.

"That seems fitting," Razik said, lining up his next shot.

Cyrus nodded. "She'll either be your greatest asset as your Source if you can get past her defenses, or the biggest pain in your ass. Either way, probably both." Razik huffed in a way that had Cyrus thinking he knew exactly what he was talking about. "Does she? Talk to you, I mean?" he asked curiously.

"Not like she should," he answered roughly. "Legacy and their Sources are not meant to be separated by thousands of miles." He hit the cue ball, but it ricocheted at the wrong angle. He didn't seem to care as he swiped up his liquor glass and drank the liquid down. "She does not seem to care how things are meant to be," he added, his words laced with a growl.

Cyrus snorted a laugh, setting up his shot. "She never has. How do you think she became the Fire Court General?"

Two hours later, the three males all paused at the sound of laughter. Rayner came stalking through the door looking more than irritated, grey eyes swirling slowly but violently. The Ash Rider went straight to the liquor cart, and Cyrus caught a glimpse of his hands smeared with...black and gold?

A minute later, Scarlett and Sorin burst into the room, and Cassius and Cyrus both straightened at their appearance. Both of them had eyes bright with exhilaration, but the rest of them...

There was dried blood on various places— arms, necks, faces. Scarlett's hair was half out of her braid, and their clothing was torn in random spots. A fine layer of what appeared to be ash covered every inch of them. Sorin's ebony hair was speckled with grey from it.

"Where have you three been?" Razik asked, his eyes narrowed.

"Out," Scarlett said far too sweetly for Cyrus's liking. "I want in the next game."

"My team," Cyrus said immediately.

Scarlett smirked, flopping down on her back onto the sofa. Some ash fluttered to the ground at the movement. Sorin took a seat next to her, and she rested her head on his thigh. Lifting a hand, shadows appeared, and she let them flow and coil around her fingers.

"Are you going to tell them where you were? Or do I have to?" Rayner asked, his low tone cutting through the room.

"Oh, you can," Scarlett sighed dramatically.

"They were in some rocky lands. Looking for a fucking mirror gate," Rayner muttered, taking a sip of his drink.

"There is no mirror gate in the Nightmist Mountains," Razik said sharply.

"Not those," Scarlett answered bitterly. "These had snow. Or the mountains to the west did. The cliffs we were in just had small bits of snow here and there, but it was still miserably cold."

Razik went rigid. "You were in the Runic Lands?"

"Is that what they're called?"

"If you were between the Olwen Mountains and the Nightmist Mountains, then yes," he snapped. "And you're lucky to be alive. Cethin is going to be livid."

"We killed some of those floating beings with the gold swords," Scarlett said with a smirk.

"Only Kailia can kill them," Razik retorted. "If you think they are dead, you are wrong. They will come back." Then his eyes widened. "Wait. Is that what is all over you? You think you burned them to ash?"

"Those and some other creatures," she answered with a shrug. "Is there food? I'm starving."

Razik cursed colorfully. "You brought them back here? Do you know how hard we have worked to keep them from this side of the Nightmist Mountains?"

Scarlett pushed up onto her elbows. "No, actually, I don't," she snapped. "Because you lot decided to keep it from us, even though they apparently come for me as much as they do for Cethin."

"We didn't know that," Razik countered.

"And we would have never figured it out if I hadn't gone to the estate that night alone. Even then, we weren't sure if it was merely coincidence or not."

"It is most definitely not coincidence. Not after what I saw today," Rayner muttered. "But I have to agree with her. They combined their power to take them out. It was unlike anything I have ever seen."

"They are not gone," Razik insisted. "We have tried everything. Fire has never worked. Only the dark stone Kailia can conjure kills them."

"Dark stone?" Rayner asked. "Nightstone?"

Razik shook his head. "This is different."

"Like deathstone?"

Everyone turned to look at Cyrus who had been watching and listening to everything play out. Being gone for three days, and then sleeping for nearly five, he felt like he had nothing to contribute to current conversations or planning.

"How do you know of deathstone, Cyrus?" Rayner asked, and the way he said it—like he was seconds away from destroying someone—told Cyrus he'd struck a nerve.

He grabbed the rack to busy himself and began collecting balls, even though they were in the middle of a forgotten game. His eyes were on the green felt of the table as he said, "The Sorceress told me of it."

The others fell silent. The only sound was the light clinking of the balls as he dropped them into the rack.

After several awkward moments, Rayner said, "Moranna had some deathstone. Not much. A few items at most."

"What does it do?" Scarlett asked, her tone soft.

Cyrus shrugged. "She said it was like nightstone in that it suppressed and drained power, but when the power was gone, it drained your life-force. Never actually killed you. Just held you in the in-between."

He felt Cassius move closer to him, but he didn't acknowledge it. The balls in position for a new game, he lifted the rack. He didn't want to be thinking of any of this. He'd come down here to keep his mind busy, and it had been working until now.

"Kailia can conjure deathstone?" Rayner asked, and when Cyrus glanced at him, he looked as if he'd just put something together.

"Yes," Razik said. "It is the only thing we have found that truly kills the things that come for Cethin. And apparently Scarlett."

"You're talking about the Hunters, right?" Cyrus asked, lining up his shot to break the balls. He hit the cue ball, the other balls scattering. Straightening, he studied the layout, trying to decide which ball to try to sink next when he realized no one had answered him. He looked up to find them all staring at him. "What?"

"Who are the Hunters, Cyrus?" Sorin asked. Scarlett was sitting completely upright now, silvery-blue eyes pinned on him. How much magic had she used?

Cyrus cleared his throat. "Not who. What." He looked at Razik. "You don't know what they are?"

Razik shook his head, arms crossed over his chest. "Explain."

The solid purple ball. That one would be the easiest to sink. Except it was violet. Like Gehenna's eyes. And he could feel them on him as she'd told him of the Hunters that day. So he lined up a shot for the striped green ball instead as he cleared his throat. "Achaz created them. Their sole purpose, according to her, is to hunt the bloodline of Arius, and any beings created by him or Serafina. She said there are some here, and when they can leave, they will report back to Achaz what they discovered. She wouldn't tell me anything else about them."

He hit the white cue ball, but he hit it too hard. It bounced up over the side of the table, and Cassius shot out a hand to catch it. "My shot," he said with a smirk.

Cyrus moved out of the way, swiping up his drink.

"But there are no twin flames over here, right?" Scarlett piped up.

"That is random," Razik muttered.

"It's not though," she said, pushing up onto her knees and leaning over the back of the sofa to see him better. "You said you've tried everything, but if there are no twin flames over here, you wouldn't know if our combined power could kill them. And Sorin's magic is... Well, it's stronger now."

"There are not twin flames here because we are separated from the Fae," Razik replied, rubbing his jaw in thought. "But I suppose you could be right. There is not much research on the twin flame bond. The gods keep the specifics of it hidden from most."

"Why would it matter that you are separated from the Fae?" Cassius asked, and Cyrus felt his stomach plummet.

Razik paused, his drink halfway to his lips. "Because a twin flame bond occurs between a Legacy and a Fae."

"What?" Scarlett asked, lurching forward and nearly falling over the back of the sofa. Sorin reached out a hand and grabbed the back of her tunic.

Razik sighed heavily, as if having to explain this to them was the worst thing to happen to him all day. "The basic history is that the twin flame bond was given to the Legacy and Fae as a gift. A gift to the children of the gods, and a gift to the Fae who watch over them and provide them with power."

"So that's why it is so rare to find your twin flame?" Scarlett asked, her nose scrunching. "Because the Avonleyans were separated from the Fae?"

"Yes and no," Razik answered. "Finding your twin flame is still rare, but not as uncommon as it is here in this world. It was another cost of the Wards."

"But you wouldn't need to be full-blooded Avonleyan, right? To have a twin flame."

That question came from Cassius and had Cyrus averting his gaze to the night sky out the window.

"The pull is not usually felt right away or as strongly when the Legacy line is not pure, but no. Any amount of Avonleyan blood would allow one to have a twin flame."

"How do you know all this?" Scarlett asked, falling back down onto the sofa, her head once again resting on Sorin's thigh.

"I read a lot," Razik muttered. Then he added, "I need to go find Cethin and Lia." He paused, looking back over his shoulder and catching Cyrus's gaze. "They are going to want to speak with you. About your time with the Sorceress and what you learned of these Hunters."

"I already told you everything she said."

"Regardless."

"Another day," Cassius said curtly, sending a solid yellow ball into the pocket.

Razik nodded once before he left the den, leaving Cyrus alone with his family, minus Eliza.

The quiet was thick and uncomfortable. Cyrus was about to announce he was going to return to his room when, in usual fashion, Scarlett broke the tension with an absurd statement.

"I just want you to know that if I had met Rayner first, you and I would likely not be together." Everyone's head whipped to her. She was looking up at Sorin, batting her lashes.

Sorin blinked back at her.

"All I am saying," she went on, "is that Death's Maiden and The Reaper sound like they belong together."

Cassius chuckled as he went back to clearing the table yet again. "How long have you been contemplating this, Seastar?"

She shrugged. "It just fits. Don't you think?"

"I find myself suddenly suspicious of all these murmured conversations the two of you have been having as of late," Sorin said nonchalantly, his fingers winding into her hair, clearly unfazed after the initial shock of what she'd said.

"Maybe after we save the realm, I'm ready to explore more of your *experiences*, Prince," she replied innocently.

Sorin's amber eyes darkened, and Cyrus saw Rayner's lips twitch as he took a sip of his liquor.

"You lie," Sorin retorted, his voice gravel.

"Me?" she teased, pushing up to a sitting position. "I would never."

Then her cheeks flushed bright red, and a satisfied smirk tilted on Sorin's lips that had Cyrus chuckling as Sorin clearly spoke to her down their bond.

She cleared her throat, getting to her feet, and there was a slight quiver in her voice as she said, "I believe I called next game."

Cyrus teased her relentlessly over the next hour, Sorin sipping his alcohol and smirking every time her cheeks went red again. It was well into the dead of night when they started the trek up to their wing of the castle.

When he stopped outside his rooms, Scarlett pushed up onto her toes and pressed a soft kiss to his cheek. "It was nice to see you out of your rooms. Even if you were an ass the entire time."

"Let me know when to expect my invitation to the *experiences*, Darling," he retorted.

Sorin clapped him on the shoulder when Scarlett scowled, her face flushing yet again. "I hate you all. I need Eliza to come back," she grumbled under her breath, jerking out of Sorin's reach.

The two continued down the hall, Sorin slinging an arm around her shoulders and bending down to whisper something in her ear that had her shoving him away yet again. His laughter echoed down the corridor.

Rayner bid them goodnight and disappeared among smoke, likely going to check on Tula, and Cyrus turned to his door. "Good night," he said stiffly to Cassius, pushing into his room, but of course, Cassius followed him in.

"Sleep in your own room tonight, Cass," Cyrus sighed. "I'm just going to bed. Surely you're sick of sleeping in an armchair."

"You're not going to sleep," Cassius said, kicking the door shut behind him. "You're going to lie awake and let memories torture you. You don't need to be alone for that."

He wanted to snap some sort of witty retort, but he didn't. He just sighed in resignation and made his way to the bedchamber, where he grabbed loose-fitting pants and went to change in the bathing room.

When he emerged shirtless, Cassius was waiting, arms crossed in a state of semi-dress. He'd changed into his own lightweight pants and still had his tunic on. At some point that evening, he'd put his eye patch back on, and he was barefoot, his boots discarded near the armoire.

"You need to talk about it at some point, Cyrus."

"No. I don't," Cyrus said pointedly. He made to move to the decanter of alcohol, but black flames blocked his path. "Fucker," he hissed, whirling on Cassius.

"Why did you appear to already know what Razik was going to say about twin flames?"

"Because I know more about twin flames than you do. I didn't need a history lesson," Cyrus sneered derisively.

"Get as nasty as you want with me, Cyrus. I'm not leaving." Cassius came towards him, stopping a few feet away. "No one else knew about twin flames being between Legacy and Fae. You are telling me you have known that this whole time? I call bullshit."

Cyrus held his stare, mouth pressed into a thin line.

"So do you have Avonleyan blood then? Or did Thia?"

"Do not push me on this right now," Cyrus growled, fire flaring unbidden at his fingertips.

Cassius raked a hand through his hair, frustration lining his features. "Come on, Cyrus. I need you to meet me halfway here."

"If memory serves," he replied coldly, "you told me to 'get the fuck out.' I do not need to meet you anywhere."

Cassius's eye fell closed, clear regret washing over him. "I didn't mean that. I shouldn't have said it."

"Doesn't matter. It's fine. You were right anyway."

His eye flew open. "Right about what?"

"I wasn't ready to be your Source. To be your anything really. I'm far too broken for you."

"Stop," Cassius snarled. "We are not doing that."

"Doing what?" Cyrus scoffed. "Speaking truth?"

"Of course I want you to be honest with me," he retorted. "But I know how Alaric works. I know how he breaks people—"

"Alaric?" Cyrus asked with a bark of harsh laughter. "Your *master* did nothing to me. Nothing but give my blood to the Sorceress."

"I don't know what that means," Cassius said, desperation in his tone. "I do not know enough about her to know what she does. I need you to tell me, Cyrus. Tell me so I can help you."

"Don't you get it? There is no helping me. This is what I am deserving of."

"No. None of that is true."

"No? Here's a truth for you," Cyrus sneered with a cruel curl of his lip. He took a few steps forward, embers left in his wake. "I never had a twin flame. I'm Fae. Thia was Fae. I was a fool to think I was deserving of such a thing. The Fates would never find me worthy of such a gift."

Cassius was shaking his head, hands fisting at his sides. "I don't believe that."

"Believe it or don't. Your beliefs don't change truth," Cyrus said with a shrug. "I have failed everyone I've ever loved." He pointed to the Bargain Mark on his arm that he'd been keeping hidden from everyone else. "This is just further proof. I'm a thief, Cassius. I always have been. I take what I want, no matter what it costs someone else. Selfish and callous. I damage everyone around me. You were right to tell me to get out. To not tie yourself to me by letting me become your Source."

He turned to walk away from him, done with this conversation, but a large hand clamped around the nape of his neck and hauled him back. Then there were lips on his, and he was so startled, he froze. Cassius pulled back, his brow resting against Cyrus's.

"What are you doing?" Cyrus rasped.

"Reminding you what you are deserving of," he answered, his voice rough.

There was a moment, one where neither of them dared to

breathe, and then, because he clearly enjoyed torture, Cyrus kissed him back.

He was smoke and heat and a warmth that had been missing from his soul. His hand was still clasped around the back of his neck, and his other dropped to Cyrus's side. His fingers brushed along his bare torso, calluses from years of training rough against his flesh.

Cyrus gripped his tunic, keeping him close, and the rumble that came from Cassius had him echoing with a low groan of his own. Tongues tangled and teeth clashed in a heady desperation that was scarcely being restrained. Cassius walked him backwards until his back hit the wall. Cass's lips moved to his jaw, and Cyrus tipped his head back. He could feel the stubble on Cass's face. Could feel every one of his harsh breaths. Could feel him pressing against his stomach.

"You were deserving of Merrik and Thia," Cassius murmured against the space beneath his ear. The hand on his nape slid up into his hair. "You are deserving of the family that loves you."

Cyrus's eyes fell closed.

*Of course they made a mistake.*

"You were deserving of a twin flame. Thia *was* your twin flame."

*No one wants you, Cyrus.*

"You are deserving of being Second of the Fire Court."

*If you can't see that all you do is damage everyone around you, then I will keep reminding you until you believe it.*

"Look at me, Cyrus."

He inhaled deeply, focusing on the feel of Cassius against him. Cass gave him the minute he needed before he could open his eyes. They locked on a brown one, the other hidden behind his patch.

"You are deserving of being wanted, Cyrus. You *are* wanted." The hand at his hip began moving, sliding along his abdomen. "I'll tell you as often as you need to hear it." His hand dipped beneath the band of his pants, and Cyrus stopped breathing entirely. "And when words aren't enough, I'll show you."

He paused for a moment, waiting for Cyrus to object, but Cyrus couldn't think around anything as Cassius's fingers grazed his length. Cassius kissed him again before his mouth moved to his neck. Nips and bites that made Cyrus gasp as much as the hand curled around his cock did.

But when Cassius's lips moved lower—across the hollow of his throat, his chest—and then lower still, when Cassius started lowering to his knees, Cyrus gripped his forearm. "Cass," he rasped, Cassius never stopping the movement of his fist up and down his length. "You don't—"

"I know I don't. I *want* you, Cyrus." His voice was nothing but gravel and lust, and when he went to get on his knees again, Cyrus let him.

Cassius held his gaze as he pulled him from his pants, and when the flat of his tongue ran over his tip, Cyrus hissed out a curse. All coherent thoughts left his mind when Cass's lips closed around him, sucking gently before taking him deeper into his mouth. He couldn't think about how he didn't deserve to have a male on his knees before him, let alone Cassius. He couldn't think about the memories the Sorceress had altered. He couldn't think about anything except Cass and his mouth and, gods, the way his tongue felt as he ran it along the underside of his cock.

Cyrus slid a hand into Cassius's shaggy brown hair, fingers tightening in the strands. Cassius was dragging the tips of his fingers up and down Cyrus's exposed thigh, barely touching him. His other hand was still wrapped around his base, stroking in time with the bob of his head, and fuck. Cassius never looked away from him, and the look in his eye never left. Want. Desire. The need for more.

Cass took him deep again, and Cyrus slammed his palm back against the wall. He was so fucking close. "Godsdamnit, Cass," he rasped. Cassius's hand squeezed his thigh where he held him, a glimmer of male triumph in his eye.

Without thinking, Cyrus pulled the eye patch off, tossing it off to the side. "I hate that thing," he muttered. Cassius huffed a laugh around him that had Cyrus bucking his hips forward at the same moment Cass's eyes shifted to amber-red. His grip tightened on Cass's hair. "I'm serious, Cass," he ground out, thrusting again out of pure need. "I'm about to lose it."

Cassius gave him a wicked grin around his cock as he pulled back and swirled his tongue around the head before he sank back down on him again. And that was it. Any shred of control Cyrus was clinging to was shattered. His other hand slid into Cass's hair, his hips snapping forward. He tried—gods, did he try—to take it easy on him, but Cassius had steadily worked his way through every layer and defense Cyrus had.

And damn it all to hell, Cass took it all when release found Cyrus. His head tipped back against the wall, his eyes falling closed as he jerked and emptied down Cass's throat. Then Cyrus was tugging on his hair with a growl. "Get up here."

He hauled Cass's lips to his own, tasting himself on Cassius's tongue, but when he reached for the band of his pants, Cassius caught his wrist. "Not tonight, Cyrus," he murmured onto his lips.

The pleasure-haze of release immediately evaporated. "You don't want—"

"Fuck, of course I want," Cassius interrupted, mouth hovering over his. "I'm not as selfless as you believe I am. I want, and I take. But tonight, this time, was just you." His hand came up, cupping the side of Cyrus's neck while his thumb swiped along the edge of his jaw. "You deserve to be wanted without being required to give something in return."

He swallowed the emotion building in his throat. "Cass," he rasped again, his fingers flexing where they sat on Cassius's hips. He could still feel him hard against his body. "Don't ever tell me to get the fuck out again."

"Don't tell me to sleep in another room again," Cassius retorted.

"Don't sleep in the armchair anymore," he tossed back. Cassius's amber eyes flared brighter, and Cyrus flicked his gaze over his shoulder. "Are your wings about to appear?"

Cassius rolled his eyes. "Fuck off, you ass."

He made his way to the bed as Cyrus reached for his pants and followed.

The candles were blown out, the night permeating every inch of the room when Cyrus said into the dark, "Can you promise me something, Cass?"

"Depends on what it is."

They were both on their backs. Cyrus had a hand propped behind his head, the other resting on his stomach.

"When you learn what I've done..." He loosed a long breath, trying to find the words.

Cassius reached over, his fingers intertwining with the hand on his stomach. "It will not matter, Cyrus. We have all done things to survive."

Cyrus didn't reply, and it was minutes later when Cassius said, "Cyrus?"

"Yeah?"

"If you break, we clean it up together."

# CHAPTER 21
# ELIZA

S he had been awake for hours when the first bits of dawn started
dancing through her window. Something was coming. She
could feel it in her bones.

Eliza paced back and forth in her room. Window to veranda doors
back to the window. She was dressed, leathers in place, sword sheathed
down her back. She couldn't explain it. Maybe she'd just go through
her routine early. It couldn't hurt.

Razik had left days ago, and she'd slept like shit since. Which was
just great. She'd known better than to ask him to stay. This godsdamn
bond had latched onto that moment of weakness, and she'd been
fighting it ever since. It was nothing she couldn't work out in a sparring ring.

She waited another ten minutes before she stepped from her
rooms and headed out to the training sands. It would be a good hour
before Callan would meet her. When she reached the training area,
she found Maliq still sitting, facing the north. Still waiting. His ears
twitched at her approach, jade eyes settling on her when his head
cocked to the side. She bowed her head, and the wolf huffed before
turning its attention back to the north.

"You feel it too."

Eliza turned, finding Ashtine walking up the path. One hand

rested on her belly, the other had water taking different shapes in her palm. A flower. A fish. A horse. A hawk.

"Has Nasima returned yet?" Eliza asked.

Ashtine's small smile faltered. "No."

"Will she?"

"Perhaps," Ashtine murmured, the water vanishing when Maliq came to her side. She reached down, scratching between the black wolf's ears.

"Do you know what is coming?" Eliza asked.

"Many things come, General. Some from the north. Some from the west. Some from the east."

"At least we don't have to worry about the south," Eliza muttered.

"There is that," Ashtine agreed, not catching Eliza's sarcasm. "We shall leave the south to the others."

"Does Sawyer know you are out here?"

"He sleeps. He worries too much about me. A promise he made to his brother." Eliza shifted her weight, glancing down at the wolf. "You are restless," Ashtine noted. "I will let you be."

"Do you need anything?" Eliza asked before Ashtine turned away.

"I am well," she answered, moving to the settee on the veranda she usually occupied when she came out for fresh air. Maliq followed, dropping to his belly at her feet, ears perked up and listening.

Still waiting.

Callan appeared before their usual time, Azrael with him. Eliza was still working through her own routine. The mortal king moved to sit next to Ashtine, while the Earth Prince took up a position across from Eliza and drew his sword. She didn't question him, eager for a chance to spar and work out her edginess.

They'd only been sparring for a few minutes, and she was burning through a vine Azrael had cast in an attempt to distract her from his attack when the first warning came. Avian Shifters flocked to the palace. The cries of hawks and screeches of eagles filled the air, and she and Azrael both lowered their weapons, looking to the skies. Moments later, a tawny-colored wolf came racing up, shifting mid-stride. Ilyas stood before them, face grim.

"Winged beings. From the northwest," was all he said before he shifted once more and took off.

"Seraphs," Azrael ground out.

"You and Callan need to go," Eliza said, striding towards the princess and the king.

"We weren't going to put things into motion for another few days," Azrael replied tightly, sheathing his sword down his back.

"Things change. On the very small chance Nuri has not reported Callan's return, we need to maintain that element of surprise. The seraphs cannot see him or you here," she retorted. "If you go now, you have a bit of time to gather a few things. Sawyer and I will stay with Ashtine."

"How will you get to the Fire Court?" Callan asked, already on his feet as they approached.

"I can create a wind portal if needed when the time comes," Ashtine said calmly. Maliq had sat up, and she was idly dragging her fingers through his thick coat.

"You two need to go now. Before they can track you," Eliza snapped. She turned to Callan. "Don't die. Scarlett will kill me." He barked a dry laugh, nervously fingering the hilt of his sword at his side. She could see the unease in his hazel eyes. "None of that," she said, knocking his hand away. "I have been training you for months now. You saved me from a powerful Witch. You have slaughtered seraphs and have survived hours of being knocked on your ass by various beings. You have stood up to a Fire Prince and stared down a terrifying Fae Queen. You have a sister to fight for. A love to fight for. A kingdom to fight for. You are a king of this realm, Callan Solgard."

"You truly believe I can do this." It was a realization, not a question.

"I would not have wasted my time training you if I did not think you could do this," she said, pulling him into a tight hug. "Be quick. Be smart. Be fierce. Don't forget about your left side, and for fuck's sake, watch your footwork."

He huffed another breath of laughter, returning her embrace. "Thank you. For everything, Eliza."

"Yeah, yeah," she muttered, shoving him away lightly. "Go be a king." Her gaze cut to Azrael. "Send a message when you can."

He nodded once before he turned, and the two set off for the palace. They no sooner rounded a corner when Sawyer and Arianna appeared around another. The Water Second rushed to Ashtine's side, handing her twin daggers. Neither of them would let her fight, but they weren't stupid enough to leave her unarmed either.

The Beta had lightweight golden armor strapped to her forearms and shins, along with a chest plate. Twin swords were strapped down her back. Her many braids were tied up, and her eyes were shifted to that of a bird of prey as she watched the sky.

"Stellan has dispatched some fighters to try to weaken them before they arrive," she said, Jamahl prowling into view in his tiger form.

"If we can drain them of any magic, it will help," Eliza said, tightening buckles and straps on her own leathers. She began pulling various weapons from a pocket realm, sheathing some and handing others to Sawyer. A bow and quiver came last.

"You should go inside, Ashtine," Sawyer said, sliding a bandolier of throwing knives over his head and fixing it to his chest.

"I will be better served to stay here," she replied, pulling up one side of her dress. "Do you mind?" she asked Arianna, holding out one of the daggers and its holder. The Beta crouched down, quickly strapping it to the princess's thigh, making sure it was within easy reach. The other dagger Ashtine kept in her grasp.

"Ashtine, will it not be safer for the babes if you are inside?" Sawyer tried again.

"You argue with the winds, Sawyer."

"The time for debating is over anyway," Arianna cut in, attention returning to the skies. "They're here."

"Ashtine stays in the middle at all times," Eliza said as they moved a little more into the open. The last thing they needed was to get trapped in an enclosed space. "If you get a seraph down, it needs to be burned to keep it that way. I'll do my best to keep up."

She reached over her shoulder and grabbed an arrow from the quiver, wishing for the hundredth time it was her Fiera arrows. These couldn't be imbued with her fire, but they could certainly do some damage to feathered wings. She nocked it to her bow and waited as the first dark specks appeared in the sky against the morning sunlight.

When they were still two hundred yards away, she glanced over her shoulder at Ashtine, who nodded. Eliza raised her bow, took aim, and let the arrow loose. Unnatural winds kept the arrow airborne, and its path true. She had expected it to bounce off a shield, but the arrow struck its target, a bellow of fury sounding that could be heard from where they stood.

"They did not expect her to be out here," Arianna said, adjusting the armor on her forearms as she waited.

"Then let's take advantage while they scramble with their defenses," Eliza said, already releasing another arrow.

Six more arrows found their marks before the seraphs got their shit together and shields started blocking them. Eliza managed to take three of the beings from the sky before that happened. Ashtine didn't stop working against them either, her winds making some of the seraphs use their own magic to keep them on course. When a small unit of seraphs finally landed before them, Eliza felt good about forcing them onto the defensive while maintaining the advantage of this being lands they did not know.

Arianna stepped forward, her armor gleaming under the already hot sun. Jamahl stalked in front of her, a low snarl sounding from him. "I am Arianna Renatus, Beta of these lands. You have come here uninvited and unannounced. By our charters, that is cause enough for us to claim your deaths."

There was a male at the front of their company. His off-white wings were nearly the same color as his ivory skin. Blond hair was tied back at the nape of his neck, and his navy blue eyes were hard as he looked the Beta up and down. Jamahl snarled another warning, his hackles rising, but Arianna held up a hand to stay him.

"There are others coming to speak with you," the seraph finally said. His gaze moved over the rest of them, instantly dismissive, until they landed on Ashtine. "I am only here to collect the Wind Princess."

"A deal was made," Sawyer cut in sharply. "Three lives for three lives. Or does Alaric not stand by his word anymore?"

The seraph blinked at him, his lip curling slightly. "My prince demands payment for the false queen that was returned to him. That payment is the return of the Wind Princess."

"Those terms were not agreed to," Eliza interjected.

"I do not deal with low-level grunts," he sneered.

Eliza only smirked, memorizing every line of his face. She would be the one to send him to the After.

"You do not get to come to my lands and disrespect the family of my sovereign," Arianna said. Solid and unflinching. Fierce and demanding. That was who the Beta had always been. She took another step towards the seraphs, Shifters beginning to slink into view. Feline and lupine. Fangs and claws.

"Where is your Alpha?" the male retorted.

Arianna went utterly still, and Eliza realized in that moment, she may have to relinquish the male's death to the Beta.

Until a spear came flying out of nowhere.

It pierced the seraph right between the eyes. The male stumbled, dropping to a knee. Before he raised his hand to reach for the spear, Eliza had his wings alight with flames. Sariah and Ilyas stalked forward in their Shifter forms, while Stellan appeared in his human form, armor in place that matched his sister's and a feral rage emanating off him. He held another spear in his hand, and his opposite hand had claws. The look on his face said they were done talking. Bloodshed it would be then.

The flames that had started on the seraph's wings were suddenly out, his body twitching on the ground. He would heal. They healed faster than the Fae.

"There are wind wielders here," Ashtine gasped, her lilt tight and strained. "Several of them. They are working against my power."

"Shit," Eliza cursed. The unit had kept their own element of surprise. They'd let some of their own fall to keep them from knowing what gifts they had. "Cut off their wings. Keep them grounded. We get them down and bleeding, then we end them all at once."

There was murmured agreement. Soft golden flashes of light had the Alpha and Beta shifting. A sleek black and white tiger stood next to Jamahl, and a massive lion standing between the jaguar and wolf roared his challenge.

Eliza twirled her sword in her hand, the bow and quiver discarded. She locked eyes with Sawyer. "They do not get near her."

Sawyer nodded.

The Shifters attacked.

Blood sprayed.

If a seraph made it past a Shifter, they met Eliza.

Not one made it to Sawyer.

Sounds of battle filled the air. The snarls of animals. The bellows of men. The clanging of metal and steel. It was a song that filled her veins as Eliza fought with blade and fire. She felt the winds suck the air from her flames over and over. That was fine. If they stayed focused on her fire, they weren't focusing on the others plunging blades through chests and sinking fangs into limbs.

Her sword had just sliced across an abdomen, warm blood splattering across her arms and leathers when Sawyer's warning cry reached her.

She whirled to find a handful of seraphs that had gotten airborne and were circling around to come for Ashtine from behind. Maliq was snarling, his teeth bared as the winged-beings landed feet away. Eliza raced for them, but a gust of wind slammed into her, knocking her onto her back. She hit the ground hard, the air forced from her chest, but a moment later there was more oxygen finding its way into her lungs.

She rolled, pushing onto her hands and knees, and found Ashtine with one hand extended towards her. The other had water pouring from it, a wall of ice forming between her and the seraphs as Sawyer added his own water, freezing it at the same time.

Eliza was on her feet with the next breath she sucked in. She sheathed her spirit sword, pulling a dagger from her side instead. Flinging out a hand, fire flared, melting a small portion of the wall. Big enough for her to get through, but too small for the seraphs. She let a ball of flame grow in her palm, then she looked back over her shoulder at Ashtine. The princess nodded, her face already paling from the exertion of using so much power at once. With a mighty surge of wind magic, the flames in Eliza's palm exploded through the hole she had melted.

She heard the cries of the seraphs as she clamored through. A rope of fire wrapped around the neck of the nearest one. Eliza yanked, forcing him to his knees while her dagger went across his throat. On this side of the ice wall, she found herself facing seven other seraphs alone.

Shaping her flames into knives, she launched them at the seraphs. One after another. A knife of steel followed each one. The first four found their targets. By the fifth, they'd caught on, but that was fine. She wasn't aiming to take them down. She wanted to know what magic they possessed, what she was up against. Two shielded with water. One created a shield of sand. Three had wind. And the last?

Eliza swallowed her cry of surprise as her hands were wrenched behind her back.

*Shit.*

*Shit, fuck, shit.*

This one had the power to move things with his mind, just like Scarlett and Callan had said Veda had.

She was being forced to her knees a moment later, but fire still flared around them, forcing them to split their focus. She set wings and clothing alight. While the other seraphs were combating her magic, she sent flames winding around the one who was holding her to the ground. He sneered at her, a victorious smirk lifting on his lips.

Until those flames went up his nose. His mouth opened on a silent scream, and her fire went down his throat. Her invisible bindings released, and Eliza was on her feet in the next moment. Her spirit sword was burning as she plunged it into his gut with a vicious snarl.

She was panting and sweating, her magic starting to wane, but she turned to face the other seraphs who were already recovering from her onslaught. Sucking in a deep breath, she hefted her sword up again.

And then sagged in relief as they all went up in black flames.

She knew those flames, and while she could have held her own, she was really fucking glad when she felt him land behind her.

"Make sure that one is dead," she said between gasping breaths, pointing to the one who had forced her to her knees.

"As you wish, Milady," came his taunting drawl.

She finally turned to look at him and almost went to her knees again. His black wings were out and splayed wide, the talons at the end sharp and deadly. Brown hair was a mess from flying, falling into his glowing sapphire eyes that raked over her, pausing at the blood splatters. His nostrils flared as he scented whether it was her blood.

Then the corner of his mouth tipped up in a taunt, and he *spat* black flames onto the seraph she had pointed to.

With a growl, she flipped him off before swiping up a few of her knives and shoving them into sheaths. She tossed fire at the wall of ice, a signal to Sawyer that it could come down, and moments later, water was rushing across the sand, turning it into a muddy mess.

The battle still raged, but there were more seraphs bleeding than Shifters. Razik looked her over one more time, before he was back in the sky to combat the few seraphs that had been able to get airborne and were raining arrows on their company.

Eliza rejoined the fighting, conserving her magic and feeling confident leaving Sawyer and Maliq to guard Ashtine.

Until Maliq let out a piercing howl that ripped through the sounds of battle.

Instinctively, her attention went to the sky, where two griffins were approaching, flying fast and hard. They were still airborne when the females on their backs leapt into the fray. Eliza immediately recognized one as Arantxa. The dark-skinned Witch was the High Witch's Second. The Witch rolled when she hit the sand, two daggers flying as she flipped to her feet then drew her swords.

The other was Talwyn Semiria.

Leathers in place, hair braided back, and the same impassive mask she always wore, Talwyn drew her blade and fought alongside the Witch. The female may not have a drop of magic in her veins anymore, but she had trained with weapons longer than she had trained with power. She was as deadly as the Witch beside her, even if she was no longer as quick or graceful.

Having Razik in the sky aided them to the point where there were only a few seraphs left when a male voice boomed across the din of the fighting.

"Stand down!"

The seraphs instantly stilled, weapons dropping to their sides. The Shifters all began looking around in confusion, Eliza doing the same. Razik landed beside her a moment later, an arm gripping her elbow. She saw why at the same moment an agonized cry came from Talwyn.

"Ashtine!"

Maliq was on his belly, whining softly. Sawyer was beside the spirit animal on his knees, gaze pinned on the Wind Princess.

Because there was a dagger at her throat and one poised at her rounded belly.

And Death's Shadow was holding both of the blades.

A seraph stood next to Nuri, and this one Eliza recognized. Mordecai. The commander of the seraph forces. "Do not move," he snarled at Sawyer and the wolf.

Eliza tightened her grip on her sword, preparing to start swinging once more. Mordecai's grey eyes slid over her in a way that had Razik growling low and tugging her back into his chest. But the seraph walked right past them, his grey wings shifting slightly as he moved.

There were three seraphs left alive. Stellan, Ilyas, and Sariah were near one. Arianna and Jamahl, along with a mountain cat shifter, were near another. The third still had his blade in the chest of a female on the ground, shifted back to her human form when death had claimed her.

Eliza's mouth fell open as she watched Mordecai draw his own blade. He drew it across the throats of the seraphs faster than Eliza could track, and as the males slumped to their knees, his blade sliced the wings from their backs. He looked over his shoulder at her and Razik. "Some flame." Then his gaze swept over all the fallen seraphs, and he added, "All of them."

Not about to argue with him when it would accomplish their own goals, Eliza sent some flames to the nearest fallen seraphs, while Razik took care of the rest. When there was nothing but ash left, Mordecai sheathed his sword, his shoulders slumping some.

He turned to Talwyn and Arantxa. "You were not fast enough."

"One of the units you warned us of changed course. We barely managed to get away. I still have Witches fighting them in the skies," Arantxa retorted with a cold violence.

"Ashtine," Talwyn said, her voice cracking as she took a step toward the Wind Princess.

"What the fuck is going on?" Eliza demanded, looking from the seraph to Talwyn to Ashtine. "Someone start talking. Now."

Flashes of light had the Alpha and Beta shifting along with their lovers.

"They sent us to warn you. That they were coming for her," Talwyn said, two tears slipping free. "But we got caught in an ambush. We are too late."

"Too late for what? How did you know they were coming?" Stellan asked.

Talwyn didn't say anything else. She just stood with silent tears tracking down her face.

Eliza shrugged out of Razik's grip, turning to the Contessa. "Nuri?"

There was regret shining in her honey-colored eyes. The first time Eliza had ever seen such an emotion from the female. "The unit you all fought was sent to retrieve Ashtine. Mordecai and I were to come after to speak with the Alpha and the Beta about relations. I was not told until right before we were to leave that should the outcome not be in our favor, I was to kill Ashtine. As a message to Scarlett and to the realm."

"No," Eliza gasped, shaking her head in denial. "No. You don't have to——"

"She does," Mordecai said solemnly. "It was an order given through the Blood Bond. She has no choice but to obey it." The sound of his boots in the muddy sand was the only sound as he moved back to Nuri's side. "We sent word as soon as we heard. Talwyn and the Witch were to get her out before we arrived. If Ashtine was not here, she would have been unable to fulfill the command. It would have been out of her control."

"So she leaves now," Arianna said. "No one here will say anything. Unless you two have loose tongues?"

"She cannot let me go," Ashtine said softly, her hands resting on the sides of her stomach.

From where she stood, Eliza could see Nuri's hands trembling with restraint as the magic of the Blood Bond tried to force her to fulfill what had been ordered of her.

"There has to be something we can do," Eliza said, sheathing her weapons.

"Am I to understand the two of you are on our side?" Stellan asked, eyes narrowed on Nuri and Mordecai.

"Yes," Talwyn said. "They always have been, but they've had to work within the constraints of their positions."

"If a message must be sent, make it me," Sawyer said from where he still knelt before the Contessa and the princess.

"It cannot be," Nuri ground out. The dagger at Ashtine's throat pressed a little harder, a small amount of blood beginning to pool.

The princess closed her eyes, her breathing getting shallow. "It must be royal blood."

"Mine," Talwyn said, lurching forward. "I am the daughter and niece of two Fae Queens. I have royal blood."

"It must be powerful. A sacrifice of royal power. That is what Alaric demanded of me," Nuri whispered.

"Then me," Sawyer insisted. "Those babes are not yet born. I am the current heir to the Water Court as Briar's brother."

Ashtine loosed a shuddering breath, and Eliza realized she'd known. She'd known the entire time that this moment would come.

*I hope the winds are wrong about many things, but they rarely are.*

Those are the words she had spoken the night they had retrieved her from Alaric.

Her eyes opened, filled with sorrow and tears.

"It will work," Sawyer said softly. "The winds told you."

Ashtine swallowed thickly before she nodded. "I did not know when. Only that a choice would be made. A Prince of Water would fall. There were three." Her hand rubbed at her stomach. "I didn't know…"

"Then I am glad it is me, Ashtine," he said gently.

"It does not have to be," she whispered through her tears.

"I promised him I would keep you safe," Sawyer answered. "Let me keep that promise." He lifted a hand, his palm resting on her stomach. "Let me do this one last thing for the people I love most in this world."

"I am sorry," Nuri said, her voice thick with emotion. "I cannot wait much longer."

"Can it be him?" Mordecai asked. Eliza scarcely noticed the hand he brought to Nuri's lower back.

"It can," she answered.

"Then step away from her."

With a shaky breath, Nuri moved from Ashtine to Sawyer. The daggers had barely cleared her when Ashtine dropped to her knees before the Water Fae, clasping his hands in hers. "They will know of you, Sawyer. The realm will know of you."

"Tell Briar it was duty to serve as his Second, but it was an honor to call him brother."

A choked sob escaped from the Wind Princess, and she nodded, bringing her palm to his face. "I will, Sawyer. I will."

"I'm sorry," Nuri whispered. "I will make it fast. That is the only mercy I can offer."

Talwyn had moved to stand behind Ashtine. Eliza tried to move closer, but Razik was holding her back. From where she stood, she could see the dagger Nuri had poised at Sawyer's neck, right where the spine met the skull. The move would kill him instantly and painlessly, just like she'd offered.

"You served this life well, Sawyer Drayce," Ashtine whispered. "I was blessed by the Fates to know you. Thank you for this gift of life."

Nuri struck, and the cry that ripped from Ashtine had Talwyn dropping down beside her and pulling her into her arms. Sobs shook her small frame to the point she was gasping for breath.

Mordecai caught Sawyer as he slumped forward. He gently lowered his body to the ground before he carefully pried the dagger from Nuri's hand as she stared blankly at the blood pooling on the ground.

"We do not belong here, Cai," Death's Shadow whispered, pulling her hood up over head.

She said nothing else as Mordecai scooped her into his arms. But before he launched into the sky, he turned to face them. "Know that she is not the monster Alaric turned her into."

No one spoke when they were gone. The only sound was Ashtine's gasped sobs as Talwyn held her friend. And when there was a piercing, sorrowful cry and a silver hawk came to rest on the ground between Ashtine and Sawyer, the princess's cries became inconsolable.

"You need to breathe, Ashtine," Talwyn ordered softly. "For the babes, you need to breathe."

"I need Briar," Ashtine cried. "I need to tell him! I need Briar! I want for nothing else. Only him."

"We need to go," Arantxa said grimly.

It was only then that Eliza realized everyone had formed a small circle around them. Arianna. Stellan. Jamahl, Sariah, and Ilyas. All the Shifters were on a knee, heads bowed for the sacrifice made.

"Go where?" Stellan asked.

"The High Witch awaits our return. We have Wards prepared to keep her Highness protected."

Talwyn looked at Arianna and Stellan. "Thank you. For letting her stay here."

"She will be safer behind Witch Wards at this point," Arianna replied, Jamahl helping her to her feet. "But should you need aid, send word. Stellan and I are swift with wings."

Arantxa nodded, stepping forward. "She needs to ride with me. Your griffin is still becoming accustomed to you."

Talwyn nodded, then looked back at Stellan. "Can you carry her, please?"

The Alpha's brows rose at the word, but he moved to lift Ashtine.

"Wait," Ashtine said, throwing out a hand. A gust of wind made the Alpha grunt when it hit him. "I apologize," she whispered. Her pain-filled eyes landed on Eliza. "Can you... Your fire? Please, Eliza? I will take his ashes. So Briar can perform his Farewell."

Eliza nodded mutely, orange flames igniting as everyone stepped back from Sawyer. How many more friends was she going to have to do this for? She could feel Razik, a solid presence at her back. The ashes were gathered and stored in a glass box clutched tightly to Ashtine's chest as she was set atop a grey and black griffin, a silver hawk at her shoulder. Arantxa deftly hoisted herself up behind her. Talwyn was astride a golden-tan creature, and when they were nothing but specks in the sky, Maliq disappeared in a flash of soft green light.

And when she had aided the Shifters in honoring their dead, when the sun had long since set, Eliza still had not said a word.

She trudged through the palace to her rooms. Not wanting to dirty any of the furniture with her soiled clothing, she went straight to the bathing room. She did not undress. Instead, she climbed into the dry porcelain tub, curled in on herself, and finally let the tears come.

It wasn't long before she heard the door of her room open, the muffled footsteps on the ornate rugs. He did not bother undressing either as he climbed into the tub with her. Large hands pulled her to him, and she buried her face in his bare chest as he pulled the tie from her braid and unwound what was left of the plait.

"I am sorry, Eliza," he murmured.

"This is war," she said, her voice hard as she wiped angrily at her face. "Death is part of our duty during these times."

"Death still hurts, even when met with honor."

She wiped at her tears some more, hating that he was seeing her like this yet again. No one got to see her like this.

A finger hooked under her chin, forcing her face up to his. "You do not need your armor with me."

"I need my armor with everyone," she whispered harshly. "Especially you."

"You can grieve, Eliza. You need to grieve. You do not need to do so alone."

"Ashtine is the one who has lost yet again. Ashtine and Briar. The Water Court." Razik reached to wipe her tears this time. "I should be preparing to go to the Fire Court. I should be planning and preparing. The sooner this is over, the fewer sacrifices to be made."

"The grief will still be there. You cannot outrun it. Their loss and heartache does not diminish your own."

"I do not need the words of a sage right now," she snapped, pushing his hands from her face.

"Then what do you need?"

She ground her molars, lips pursing. She needed to not think about Ashtine or Sawyer. Her gaze flicked to him for a heartbeat. "Do you believe Nuri and the seraph? You don't know them like we do. As an outsider, do you believe them? That they are on our side?"

"It is hard not to believe them after what I witnessed today."

"I guess," she murmured, looking out the nearby window. "I never know what to make of Nuri. She is like Scarlett, but different. I think Alaric truly loves Scarlett in some twisted way, but Nuri? She has always been a true means to an end for him."

"That sounds plausible from what I have seen and been told."

It took a moment before she realized he was slowly undoing all the buckles and straps of her fighting leathers and carefully setting aside weapons. She was too tired to fight with him anymore tonight.

"Did it seem like she and Mordecai were...something?" she asked when he gently tugged on her foot so he could get at the laces of her boot. She shifted, sliding back some.

"Only someone who has been forced to commit the same atrocities she has could see her for what she is," Razik answered.

"More profound wisdom," she murmured, propping her chin on her hand. He reached for her other boot. "What are you doing here anyway?"

"That is a rather broad question," he answered, and she shoved at his chest with her now bare foot.

"In Siofra. Your power was clearly not drained when you arrived."

"I was sent."

"By Saylah?"

"By Cethin," he said, plopping her other boot onto the floor outside the tub.

"Why?"

"To aid in whatever way I can. Since they cannot leave the Wards yet."

"Soon?"

Razik shrugged. "In theory."

Eliza rolled her eyes. A comfortable silence settled over them, and she couldn't help the snort of laughter that escaped her. What a sight this must be. A grown-ass female and a broody dragon sitting in a dry tub covered in blood and grime.

"I need to bathe," she finally sighed after several minutes.

"And then?"

"And then I need to sleep," she replied, gripping the sides of the tub and pulling herself to her feet. She stepped out, and Razik did the same, not looking back as he left the bathing room.

She took a long, hot bath, and alone among the steam of the water she kept heated with her remaining power, she let the tears come. Not the shaking sobs of earlier, but the tears of loss at yet another she had called her own crossing the Veil. What would Nakoa think of her now?

She let out another sigh as she dried off before tossing the towel in the corner and heading to her bedchamber. She didn't stop moving when she saw him waiting for her, sitting on the edge of her bed. He went unnaturally still. She'd known he was out here, had scented him.

Had felt him down this stupid bond.

She moved straight to his pack that he'd set on a settee. Pulling one of his shirts from it, she slipped it on, the hem reaching her knees, before she climbed under the blankets.

There was a long, tense silence before he said with a low growl, "You are not wearing pants."

"You're too fucking hot at night."

"You're going to make me sleep beside you when you are only wearing my shirt?" he ground out.

"No one said you had to sleep beside me. The scent of your shirt will be enough for me to sleep just fine."

Another bout of silence before he huffed loudly. "If I sleep beside you tonight, this will not be like other times, Eliza. This will not be something we never speak of again."

"I know," she whispered.

"We will discuss everything in the morning."

"I know."

"I am going with you to the Fire Court."

She sighed loudly. "I know, Raz."

There was another long stretch of silence before she heard him move, and the bed dipped. He didn't reach for her, didn't touch her at all as he settled in. Then he said quietly, "Only Cethin and Lia call me Raz."

"Sorry," she muttered.

"No. I… No one else ever cared enough to call me by a nickname."

She went still, letting his words settle into her soul, before she said softly, "Good night, Raz."

# CHAPTER 22
# CALLAN

Callan shuffled through the papers of scribbles and notes and maps they had crudely drawn. The flickering fire in the center of the cave was his only source of light, and Azrael was currently adding more kindling to keep it burning. He'd never imagined having to hide in his own kingdom, yet here he was, tucked as far back in a cave as they could get.

Azrael had Traveled them just outside the tunnel system that ran under Baylorin. It was an expansive network that made moving about the city easier. It had also been proven time and again that others knew the network of tunnels better than the king's men. They could only assume Alaric and the Maraans knew the tunnels just as well, so they'd agreed to avoid them all together. Scarlett and her sisters had used the tunnels numerous times for their jobs, not to mention it was Scarlett's primary way of getting in and out of the castle when she would come to him.

Gods. That was a lifetime ago. That was a prince who knew nothing of sacrifice or loss and who was denied nothing, and a girl who knew nothing but sacrifice and loss and an unending, simmering fury.

For two days, he and Azrael had stuck to shadows and back alleys. They had scouted and watched as men Callan did not know patrolled the streets of the capital city of Windonelle. There were seraphs on street corners and in the skies. There were curfews in effect. Taxes had been increased to pay for the extra protection from the Fae, and if you could not pay, you were assigned extra duties at the castle.

So no one was batting an eye at the slums slowly being emptied of its residents as they were carted away to pay off their debts owed to the kingdom. After all, they were getting the same protection as everyone else. Of course they should be paying for it. That was the murmurings Callan picked up in taverns and on the streets.

After spending the days in the city gathering information, they came back here, to the caves along the sea. There was a pier a ways down the beach that Callan knew was a popular location for revelry among the upper and middle-class citizens, but they rarely wandered this far down the beach. Not with the towering cliffs that blocked the way farther down.

Callan had spent every moment of his time with Azrael learning how he had worked with all the people in his Court— the wealthy and the commoners, the males and the females. They'd also discussed how he'd handled relations with outside Courts. That had been interesting. His Court obviously got along fine with Ashtine's Court, but navigating the Fire and Water Courts had been tricky. Callan didn't anticipate issues with Rydeon or Toreall, but it was useful knowledge for the future if any disagreements ever arose.

But the mortal kings needed to reclaim their thrones before they worried about that.

And first they needed to earn the trust of their people.

Azrael moved back over to him, dropping onto the ground. They'd grabbed bedrolls when they'd hastily gathered their belongings in Siofra. Thankfully, he'd been somewhat packed, but they hadn't been planning to leave for another few days. As such, he only had a change of clothing. That had aided their cause, he supposed. They blended in more in dirty clothing, even if it was still of finer make than most had. Other than that, Callan had a cloak and the items in his pocket he refused to leave lying about anywhere.

"You are ready for tonight?" Azrael asked as Callan passed him some of the bread and dried meat they'd purchased in the markets earlier that day.

284

"If we can get even one person in the poor districts to talk to us, we will count tonight a victory," Callan replied, taking a bite of his own meal.

"And you still believe this Mary Ellen woman will aid you?" Azrael mused, studying the vague maps before them. Callan could count on one hand how many times he had been in that district of Baylorin.

Shame crawled through him at the thought.

"Out of all the people I have encountered there, which admittedly is not many, she was the most knowledgeable of the happenings. She was also the most accepting. Her place seemed to be some sort of haven for them," Callan replied. "She is our best bet at learning anything new tonight."

Azrael nodded. "Then we start there."

They sat in silence, finishing their meals and waiting until the hour they would venture out again. He was sure the prince's thoughts were on a female that had been given over to Alaric, wondering if she still breathed. Callan's own thoughts were on Tava, as they always were in the quiet moments.

There had been no word on the streets of the Tyndell children returning home, but he supposed there wouldn't be. Lord Tyndell had done his job thoroughly in keeping them sequestered. Tava always said she was in the background, and Balam had made sure that's where she'd stayed. He'd effectively done the same with Drake in a way. He wondered if many even realized that Drake and Tava had been gone. Drake, perhaps, with his lower position in the kingdom's forces, but Tava?

The thought of trying to get her a message somehow had briefly crossed his mind, but he knew they couldn't risk it. If Lord Tyndell was trying to keep their return a secret, someone showing up with a note would certainly make him suspicious.

When their fire had burned down to embers, Azrael put it out the rest of the way after they'd donned their cloaks. Faces obscured deep in their hoods and weapons—mainly daggers and knives to allow for faster movements if they needed to run—hidden just as well, they set off, sticking to the outskirts of the city as long as possible. When they finally crossed into the city proper, they passed through back alleys and side streets. It took nearly an hour to get to the poor districts with this roundabout maneuvering.

One hand positioned on a dagger beneath his cloak, they slowed their pace when they finally made it to the streets of the slums. The streets were completely empty. No one was on the corners or in the alleys like he had witnessed before. The curfew had effectively cleared every area of the city. He knew Azrael was taking in every detail as they moved. They'd debated coming during the day, but had decided they'd rather risk having to make an escape than being recognized in the daylight.

"Which way?" Azrael murmured.

Having only been to the woman's house once, Callan wasn't entirely sure. He'd only been here at night, but that didn't help him navigate the place now. The clouds obscured the moon, and there were no candles in the windows of the run-down houses. They ended up starting on the left and working their way through the various streets. It took several blocks before Callan recognized the alley where they had found Ivan. There were no people gathered around fires or huddled in coats and blankets this night though.

"Do you think they have all of them?" Callan asked in a hushed whisper as they turned another corner.

"The hunted become highly skilled at hiding," Azrael replied in a flat tone. "And those who are already used to being ignored are even more adept at moving about unseen. It is all they know."

Callan didn't say anything after that.

Minutes later, they found themselves on the creaking porch of Mary Ellen's home. It was as dark as every other building, and they waited a few extra minutes after Callan tried knocking a few times. The door was locked, and, surprisingly, the lock held.

They were debating if Azrael should use his magic to break in so they could at least see if anyone was in there, when the Earth Prince was whirling with a long knife drawn. Callan turned to find a group of six guards stalking up the street towards them. They were completely in black, their faces beneath hoods. Callan didn't know if he knew these men from the castle or not. He doubted it would matter either way.

Azrael and Callan waited as they approached. Azrael shuffled a little closer, preparing to Travel if necessary, but they didn't want to reveal a Fae was here if they didn't have to.

"Are you unaware there is a curfew in effect?" one man near the front snarled at them. His arm shifted under his cloak, no doubt thumbing free his sword.

"We are aware of the curfew," Callan replied. "We are searching for a friend of ours. This is her home. It is dire."

One of the other men snickered. "*Dire*, is it?"

"Yes," Callan answered through gritted teeth.

"What's her name? This friend?" the first man asked. He sounded vaguely familiar. If Callan could see his face, he might recognize this one.

"Mary Ellen," Callan said. The guards seemed to pause at the answer, so he pressed, "Do you know of her?"

"What's your business with Mary Ellen?"

"None of yours," Callan retorted. All the men stiffened, and Azrael shifted, his hand clamping around Callan's wrist. "Wait," he hissed at the Earth Prince.

"Your companion does not speak?" another of the men sneered. "Show your faces."

"Show yours first," Azrael replied, somehow making the three words drip with challenge and violence.

"You are not from here," the first man said, stepping forward.

"Do you know where Mary Ellen is?" Callan asked before Azrael could reply.

"Not if you don't state your business with her, we don't," another guard chimed in.

Callan glanced at Azrael, but with the dark and the hoods, it was pointless. He sucked in a sharp breath, knowing this was likely to get them nowhere, before he said, "The angel sent us."

"Bullshit," one man said.

So they knew of Tava then.

"Take us to Mary Ellen," Callan said, an order that had all the guards straightening.

There was a tense moment of silence before the first man swaggered forward, pulling something from his cloak. "Sure thing." Callan could hear the smirk in his tone. "But if you're lying, I'll be cutting out your tongue."

"Callan," Azrael said in a tone so quiet he almost didn't hear him.

"You can Travel us out if needed, right?" Callan murmured out of the corner of his mouth as the men came forward.

"Not if they separate us," Azrael replied.

It was a risk, but what wasn't these days? It would be worth it if they truly knew where Mary Ellen was. It would be worth it if it got them any information on how to aid his people.

"Put 'em on," the guard said, tossing something to Callan while another did the same to Azrael. Hoods to go over their heads, he realized a moment later. "And hands behind your backs."

Callan did as ordered, rope being wound tightly around his wrists. That would be fine. Azrael's earth magic could get them out of any bindings.

Once they were bound and unable to see, they were led back down the streets until they were shoved into a carriage.

"Wait a minute," Callan barked around a wince as his face crashed into something hard, but there was the slamming of a door, followed moments later by the creaking of wheels that had him lurching forward.

The hood was yanked from his head. Callan couldn't see Azrael in the pitch dark.

"We are in a godsdamn prisoner wagon," the Earth Prince growled in annoyance.

"I guess we will see where it goes," Callan murmured, shifting so he could sit against the side.

"A prisoner wagon generally leads to dungeons or death."

"This is the first decent lead we've had since we got here," Callan argued. "You saw those streets, Azrael. No one is there. Either Mikale and Alaric have all of them, or..." He trailed off, jarred with every bump and rut in the road.

"Or what?" Azrael gritted out.

"You said it yourself. They're good at staying hidden. This might be our only chance at finding them."

"You honestly believe these men know where this Mary Ellen is?"

No. He wasn't sure what he believed. But these men seemed to know who Tava was, and he couldn't ignore that.

He had no way of calculating how much time had passed. It had to be at least an hour, likely closer to two, before the wagon began slowing. They quickly replaced their hoods, Azrael using his magic to get their bindings back in place, before they were hauled from the back of the wagon.

A short walk later, they were being forced to their knees onto damp earth that seeped through the material of his pants. Their hands were left bound, but their hoods were removed. Cool air kissed Callan's face as he blinked against the sudden light.

There were several fires throughout the space, and tents. Rows and rows of tents. This was a camp. He turned his head from side-to-side, taking it all in. The woods north of Baylorin. That had to be where they were. It was a good two-hour ride to get this deep into the trees. People moved among the fires and tents, calling out to one another and…laughing. Despite clearly being displaced, they were joking with each other.

Two of the guards stayed beside him and Azrael, three others peeling off and greeting some other men by a fire. The final man had disappeared.

"Is Mary Ellen here?" Callan asked, looking up at the guard nearest him.

"Shut up," he snarled. It was the first man. The one who had spoken the most. And why did he sound so familiar?

Azrael shifted, inching closer. The guards glanced at him but didn't say anything.

"Finally," the guard next to Callan muttered some time later, stalking forward.

And then Callan felt the world fall out from beneath him as he beheld who he'd been waiting for.

There were two women moving through the trees and heading in their direction. One had red-brown hair braided over her shoulder. She moved with lethal grace and had more weapons strapped to her than Callan could count. She was wearing a suit just like the one Scarlett often wore. Holding a book open in her hand, she was showing something to the other woman.

Who had a golden owl perched on her shoulder.

That was Tava. In a godsdamn witchsuit that fit her like a glove. Her hair was also braided over her shoulder, and she was listening intently to whatever the other was saying. And the other?

That was Juliette.

Angel and Wraith.

Tava looked up, smiling softly at the guard—was he a guard?—as he approached. She hadn't noticed him and Azrael kneeling on the forest floor yet, but he knew the moment the man mentioned them. Her eyes went wide, snapping to them, her hand covering her mouth in as much shock as Callan was in.

"Oh my gods," she rasped, shoving past the man and rushing forward. Paja gave a disgruntled hoot at her sudden movement, swooping up to a low-hanging branch. "I am so sorry, Callan," Tava said. He could feel her fingers trembling as she tried to work the knots in the ropes.

"Azrael," Callan muttered, and a moment later, the bindings fell away. He was twisting around to grab her in the next breath. Her arms wound around his neck, and he breathed her in.

"Are you all right?" he murmured into her hair.

She gave a choked laugh as she leaned back. "Am I all right? You were transported here in a prison wagon. Are *you* all right?"

"I am fine, Little Fox," he said, tucking a piece of hair behind her ear. "Confused as hell, but fine."

"My Lady," he heard Azrael say, and Callan looked over his shoulder to find him bowing to Juliette. It took him a minute to remember that she was the Oracle.

Juliette gave him a crooked smirk, and she winked as she said, "Plant Prince." Azrael muttered something under his breath too low for Callan to hear, but Juliette gave a small laugh as she added, "I am the least vexing of the three of us, I assure you."

"In that case, I think some explanations are in order," Azrael replied.

"Prince?"

They all turned to find the man who had approached the women, standing with his arms crossed.

"Callan," Tava said. "I do not know if you ever met Ezra, but—"

"You are Sloan's son," Callan said, staring at the young man. That was why he'd recognized the man's voice. He took after his mother in a lot of ways, but he had Sloan's pale blue eyes and blond hair. Sloan had always kept his hair cropped short. Ezra's was a little longer, curling slightly around his ears. Callan had known Sloan had had a family, but he'd only met his wife a handful of times. And his kids? Ezra was a few years younger than he was. Closer to Tava's age than his and Drake's. He knew Ezra had three younger sisters as well. He had been the only boy, older than his sisters by several years. Sloan's wife had become pregnant when she and Sloan were both so young, but Callan knew Sloan had regretted nothing about his life with her.

Ezra surveyed him, hand still on his sword.

A sword that had once belonged to his father.

And then Callan bowed to him.

When he straightened, Ezra was staring at him wide-eyed, his hand fallen slack by his side.

"Your father gave his life protecting my family. Protecting me and Eva. I can never repay the debt that is owed to you and your family," Callan said thickly, emotion welling in his throat. "He was a man I was honored to call a friend."

Ezra glanced at Tava, and Callan could see her smiling softly out of the corner of his eye. Then the man cleared his throat. "Tava says you are on our side. That you did not flee, but that you have been gone all this time finding help."

"I have," Callan replied.

"Let's take this to another place," Juliette suggested, gesturing back the way they had come.

Tava's fingers intertwined with his, and she led them through the array of tents until they came to a larger one in the center. Ezra pulled the flap aside, Juliette and Azrael entering first, followed by Callan and Tava. The inside was spacious, candles and lanterns spread out and casting everything in a warm glow. There was a bed to one side, along with various trunks and a small washbasin. In the center was a long table with maps atop it. Drake and a few other men Callan did not recognize were standing around them. They looked up at the interruption, and Drake straightened when he saw Callan.

"What are you doing here?" Drake asked, rushing towards them.

"I could ask you the same thing," Callan replied.

"There are many stories to share," Juliette said, plopping unceremoniously onto a stool near the table. An elbow rested on the surface, and she propped her hand on her chin. "You will definitely want to sit, your Majesty."

Several of the men excused themselves so that it was just Juliette, Azrael, the Tyndells, Callan, and Ezra in the tent. Callan turned to Drake and Tava and said, "Start from the beginning. How are you here? Does Balam——"

"Balam does not know we are here," Tava interrupted. Her hands were in her lap, back straight and poised. Still a Lady, even in a godsdamn witchsuit.

"Where is here? Who put this together?"

"It is a safe site of sorts," Juliette chimed in, chin still propped, watching them all curiously. "It has been in the works for quite some time. Set up by those who opposed your father's rule."

"My father's..." His eyes widened in realization. "This was being planned *before* Alaric and Mikale took over?"

Juliette nodded, straightening some. Her eyes flicked to Drake.

"Yes and no," Drake said. "It was originally being set up to aid those seeking refuge from Rydeon and Toreall. They kept your family in the dark about much of the happenings in those kingdoms, especially after the new rulers took the thrones. Balam made sure certain happenings were never reported to King Theodore. But word got out to the poorer people of Windonelle, and well..." He scratched at the back of his head. "There were a lot of unhappy people in the kingdom, Callan."

He knew that. Well, he hadn't known that at the time. Not until Tava had taken him to the poorer districts that first time. There would always be those discontent with how things were run, but this had been different. This had indeed been a people who felt invisible to their king. Who felt their king did not care if they lived or died, let alone cared about their quality of life.

He turned to Tava. "How long have you known about this?"

Her eyes were down, and she was worrying her bottom lip, but it was Juliette who spoke.

"I learned of it first," she answered. "When we were searching for answers about the children in the Black Syndicate."

"Scarlett knew?" he asked sharply.

Juliette shook her head. "Even then I had...abilities. I did not fully understand what they were yet, but I always *knew* things. Which path to take when we were tracking a target. When the best time was to sneak from the Fellowship...or into a castle. I found myself inside the right tavern at the right time one night and overheard a group of men from Rydeon speaking with some men from the king's forces."

*From the king's forces.*

Callan's gaze jumped to Drake. The Rydeon king was staring straight at him.

"You were part of this? This whole time?"

"For years I begged my father to give me more responsibilities, to train me as his replacement. He refused. I was passed over time and time again. At first, it was a foolish, youthful rebellion against my father, but when I saw what was happening in the slums, to Windonelle's own people... I couldn't sit back and do nothing. I tried talking to my father about it once. He brushed me off. Told me to keep my head down and do as I was told. I started watching more, noticing more things that weren't right, and when no one who could do something about it stepped up..." He rubbed at the back of his neck again. "Yeah, Callan. I was working with Rydeon and Toreall rebels. Have been for years. I was worried that what was happening in their kingdoms would happen here. We were trying to be prepared. I didn't realize that we would be following in their footsteps quite so closely."

"And you were part of this?" Azrael asked, looking at Juliette.

"Not then," she said. "Not as long as Drake has been. I had just put everything together shortly before Scarlett met Callan."

"When she left me that first note," Callan clarified.

Juliette nodded. "My sisters knew I was keeping something from them. We had fought about it. I had wanted to tell them, but I was just beginning to earn the rebels' trust. I didn't even know Drake was involved at that point. That's why she was in that clearing that day. We had fought, and she had left to work off her temper. I eventually told Nuri, but Scarlett got close to you. We needed that for the Black

Syndicate children, and a part of us hoped..." She cleared her throat. "I knew she would be a queen. One of those things I just knew. I had always assumed she would be your queen, based on how everything was unfolding. We had hoped that when she was at your side, she would help you see the forgotten in the kingdom. That the two of you would be the change the kingdom needed, and that eventually that would carry over to Rydeon and Toreall."

"Then why did Scarlett start taking Tava to the slums if she was not part of this?" Callan asked.

"The three of us had always been involved in the slums," Juliette supplied. "When I was no longer here, Scarlett kept going."

"I caught her sneaking out one night," Tava said quietly.

"*You* caught her sneaking out?" Azrael asked, his brows high.

"She sees what everyone else misses," Callan said, gaze on Tava. She slowly raised ocean blue eyes to his.

"She'd been a spirit of the After for weeks. I had promised Cassius I would keep an eye on her. When I heard her door open well into the night, I followed her down to the study she liked to sneak out of. I demanded to know where she was going; and when I would not drop it and threatened to send word to Cassius, she finally told me to change into godsdamn pants and get a cloak. She said if I got her caught, there'd be hell to pay."

"And you did not know your brother was involved?" Azrael asked.

She shook her head. "I did not know Drake and I were working towards the same goal until the night everything fell apart. When they tried to abduct me for Veda."

"But when did Drake meet with them?" Callan asked, still trying to piece this all together.

"He was always out with other men from the forces," Tava said. "I did not learn until later that he usually excused himself early to come home. Instead of returning to the manor, he would meet with the rebels."

"It was why I was unaware Tava was sneaking out. The night you brought her home and she was upset—" His gaze flicked to his sister with regret. "I did not know of Veda's plans, but I also did not know Tava was sneaking out. It was why I did not know she was gone that night." His focus came back to Callan. "After you spoke with her, I went up to her room to find out what had happened. That was when I told her of my involvement."

"Why has no one said anything about this?" Azrael demanded. "We were on a ship for weeks. Together in Avonleya. Neither of you thought it would be wise to disclose this information?"

Tava lifted her chin, holding the Earth Prince's stare. "These people have long been at the bottom of every priority list, even that of their own kings. We have worked tirelessly to gain their trust. I was not about to betray that until I knew what kind of king Callan was to be."

"Wait," Callan cut in. "The ruse? That was a test to—"

Her head whipped to him. "No, Callan," she said in a rush. "That was not some ploy to be used in this matter. The ruse was only ever to save you from Veda. To give you that choice. It became more than a ruse for me the first night you insisted on accompanying me to the poor districts. The first time I witnessed you truly seeing your people. *That* was when I knew you could be different from your father, if given the chance. And you have become that king. More and more every day. That you sit here with us now proves that. You did not have to come. You could have waited for Scarlett to fix this. We all could have, but…"

There were tears glimmering in her eyes as she trailed off.

"They deserve rulers who care for them as mortals. Not magical beings whose first priority will always be their own," Callan said, echoing words she had said to him what seemed like a lifetime ago. "Someone has to fight for them."

Tava's throat bobbed as she worked to control her emotions.

"The point is, we did not know who we could trust," Drake said. "We did not want it getting back to our father or Alaric and Mikale that there were people working against them. We knew it would lead to immediate extermination. The things that have happened in Rydeon and Toreall to squash the smallest show of rebellion… We could not risk it."

"Not even for those we love," Tava added quietly.

"You thought we would leave the mortals to fend for themselves?" Azrael asked in a harsh demand.

Tava leveled him with a look that Callan had never seen on her face before.

It was cold and unforgiving.

It was fierce.

It was the look of a queen defending her people.

"We have been left to fend for ourselves for centuries," she replied, her tone as icy as her glare. "Where were the Fae when Hale's family lost their throne? Where were they when our true parents were slaughtered? You have not cared about the affairs of mortals for decades. It may have been a lie that the Fae were our enemies, but it was one easily believed because there was no effort made to show yourselves as anything else. Why would we assume you would start caring now?"

"We were locked behind wards——" Azrael started, but Tava cut him off.

Her palms were planted on the table in front of her as she leaned forward, her voice low and vicious. "Sorin was here. For three years. Eliné was here for years before that. The Fae Queens could Travel. *You* could Travel. All of you came for Scarlett when she was taken by Tarek. The wards were in place then too. Do not use them as an excuse for not aiding those beneath you when you were in every position to do so. You were still far more skilled than any mortal forces, even without access to your magic. You chose not to care about mortal affairs. You knew there had been a change in monarchs in Rydeon and Toreall. None of you cared to look into why or how it happened. None of you cared."

Azrael blinked at her. Everyone else had gone still. He said nothing. What was there to say to any of that? She could say the same thing to Callan. She *had* all but said as much to him in various conversations.

The Earth Prince nodded his head once in acceptance of her words.

"When Scarlett dropped the wards containing the Shifters and Witches, I was able to come back and help. Other Witches come when they can. We have wards around many of the rebel camps. It is harder with so many people and larger areas, but it is something," Juliette said after a moment. "And when we learned that Drake and Tava were the Rydeon heirs?"

"The rebels have been rallying forces in our absence," Drake said. "There are camps like these across the kingdoms. Men are being trained. So are women. There are soldiers and guards training them. Juliette is training them. *Witches* are training them. We have people on the inside. Men close to the kings' inner circles. Women who serve in the castles and hear things. We have an army. Unified forces. It is small, and it might not do much, but they would rather fight and die than continue as things have been. They've just been waiting for the right time."

"This is why the two of you wanted to get back to the continent so badly," Callan said, looking between the siblings.

They had been in the perfect position for this. Lord Tyndell had worked so hard to make sure they were in the background. Unseen and unnoticed. They'd sat in meetings with the leaders of the realms, quiet and absorbing information, listening to plans and strategies. Tava played the perfect role of the demure, docile Lady. And Drake? No one had ever really given him a second thought. A Lord's son. Nothing special or extraordinary. Not even worthy to take over his father's position when the time came.

And all this time, he'd been part of organizing a rebel movement across the entirety of the continent.

All this time, he'd been unknowingly proving himself to his people.

"No. I mean, yes," Tava amended. "We would have done so for Ashtine either way. Those unborn babes are as innocent as the people we are trying to help. Someone must fight for them too. But yes, we were anxious to return to help in whatever way we could. They knew we would come back. They knew we would never abandon them."

"How do the Maraans not know you are here?" Azrael asked, avoiding Tava's gaze.

"That's where I come in," Ezra said. He'd been so quiet, Callan had forgotten he was here. He had a knife and a piece of wood in his hand. He'd been carving on it the entire time they'd been speaking. "I am Tava's newly appointed personal guard."

Callan couldn't help the bark of disbelief that came from him because that was the definition of irony.

"When it was reported the Tyndell siblings had returned, I offered to be her personal guard. They still believe I am loyal to the throne."

"Why?" Callan asked.

Ezra leveled him with a pale blue stare. "Because when I

learned of my father's death, I pretended not to care. Because when they told me of his *treason*, that he and Finn had been implicated in the deaths of your parents, I pretended like they got what they deserved. When Mikale told me my father had been killed while attempting to murder the king, I *thanked* him for taking him from this world. I keep up the façade because my mother and sisters still live in that city. It will look too suspicious if we leave now. We would be accused of being unhappy with the king and all that he is doing for us."

Callan thought he might be sick. *That's* how Mikale had spun the story of their deaths? That Sloan and Finn had been traitors to the crown? Somehow involved in the deaths of his parents?

He swallowed thickly. "No one questioned you volunteering to be her guard?"

Ezra had gone back to carving the block of wood. He didn't look up when he said, "I have known Tava for years. We grew up together. Met one day at a castle banquet. She was always ignored at such events. Lord Tyndell knows we are friendly. It was no surprise that I volunteered for the position."

Callan glanced at Tava and found her eyes on her lap again, fidgeting with her fingers.

For several moments, the only sound was Ezra's knife on the wood. Then he spoke again repeating words he'd said earlier. "She says you've been gone all this time finding help."

"I have been," Callan agreed.

"Where is it?"

"It's coming. Your king has been working with the leaders of the other kingdoms. He has built relations with Fae and Avonleyans, Shifters and Witches," Azrael said. He met Tava's gaze. "The Fire Court is preparing to defend Windonelle and Rydeon. The Witches will defend Toreall, and once I have my Court back, we will defend your lands as much as we defend our own. Our queen will not fail you. The Fae will not fail you again."

Ezra didn't reply. Instead, he slid his knife into his boot before he stood and slipped the piece of wood into his pocket. "We need to be getting you back, Tava."

She nodded, getting to her feet and running her hands down the sides of the witchsuit. "Can you retrieve my dress? I left it with Mary Ellen when I changed before going to scout with Juliette."

Ezra nodded once, slipping from the tent without another word.

"I can show you to an empty tent that you and Callan can share for the time being," Juliette said pointedly to Azrael, jerking her chin to the tent entrance as she stood. A clear signal for him to follow.

The Earth Prince sent her a bland look. "I know they want a moment alone before Tava must leave."

"Oh, good," Juliette chirped, already striding for the exit. "Perhaps you are not as simple as Nuri claims you are."

"For fuck's sake," Azrael cursed, following Death Incarnate out of the tent.

"Do not be long, Tava," Drake said, stopping to press a kiss to her cheek.

"You will be back at the manor before dawn?" she asked.

He nodded. Then he clapped Callan on the shoulder before he left too.

Tava slowly turned to face him as he pushed to his feet. Her hand went to her throat before she moved it to her braid, fiddling with the end of it. Callan slipped his hands into his pockets, feeling the items he refused to leave lying around anywhere.

"Say something," Tava whispered after a lingering silence.

"I am in awe of you."

Her face flushed, eyes fixed on the ground. "You are not upset? That I kept this from you?"

"No, Tava," he answered softly. "Do I wish you would have told me? Of course. But I understand why you did not. I did not deserve the information. Not with who I have been these last few months. Not with who I have been my entire life, really."

"I wanted to tell you," she replied. "But you were grieving after everything that happened, trying to find your way through all that pain and grief. Trying to come to terms with who you had been raised to be and who you wanted to be. I couldn't tell you. Not until I knew for sure that you would fight for them. And then you showed up in Siofra, and now you are here—"

She stopped her rambling when Callan hooked a finger under her chin, tilting her face up to his. "Thank you."

She blinked at him. Once. Twice. "I do not understand."

"Thank you. For believing in me when I did not believe in myself. For caring for the people of this kingdom when I did not. For fighting when I did not know there was something to fight for. For showing me the light. Thank you, Tava."

"You will make a remarkable king, Callan," she whispered, eyes searching his face.

"Because of you."

She shook her head, reaching up and brushing back a piece of hair from his brow. "It has always been there. I helped you find it, but it has always been you."

Callan lowered his mouth to hers, savoring every second of the moment they were about to lose. He inched back just far enough to look into her eyes. "I went to Siofra for you; I came here for my people. I will fight for both. No matter the cost."

Her arms looped around his neck. She pulled his lips back to hers as she murmured, "You already have me. In this life and the next. Now we fight for our people together."

# CHAPTER 23
## SCARLETT

"I am going to Elshira," Scarlett announced.

Everyone at the breakfast table went silent. Food paused halfway to mouths. Cethin and Tybalt exchanged stilted glances.

Cethin slowly lowered his fork back to his plate. "Why are you going to Elshira? And when? And does our mother know?"

*Mother.*

Scarlett held back her eye roll.

"You said there are ancient texts there. That Saylah would spend days locked away studying them," Scarlett said, reaching for a roll. Sorin immediately took it from her, spreading jam atop it.

"I can see if Saylah is open to this," Tybalt ventured carefully.

Scarlett waved her hand dismissively. "No need. She does not need to be there."

"We did discuss speaking with Saylah," Sorin added casually, passing her the breakfast roll. "Perhaps we should accept Tybalt's offer."

"*Perhaps,*" she mimicked, not bothering to hold back her eye roll this time.

Sorin smirked, picking up his glass of fruit juice.

"I'm just glad she told us where she was going this time," Cyrus drawled from down the table.

"No shit," Rayner muttered.

"Honestly, Rayner. I thought we'd moved past this." She sighed dramatically, then barked a laugh of delight when the Ash Rider flipped her his middle finger.

Cyrus snickered again, popping a slice of bacon into his mouth. Cassius sat beside him, cutting off a piece of ham and stacking it on his fork with some eggs. Cyrus had seemed a little better the last few days. Both of their scents had shifted. Everyone at the table knew it, but neither Cass nor Cyrus had acknowledged anything.

"When are we going?" Cyrus asked.

Her brows rose. "I didn't think you'd want to come."

That was the truth. He rarely left his rooms. That day they'd returned from the Runic Lands to find him playing billiards with Cass and Razik had surprised both her and Sorin. When Cass would go train with Tybalt, Cyrus insisted on resting or bathing, not wanting to talk to anyone. In fact, this was the first time he'd joined them for breakfast since returning. She had a feeling based on the way he'd dragged his feet coming into the dining room that Cassius had forced his hand today.

"Your Guardian is becoming as big of a mother hen as your twin flame," Cyrus said. "I need to leave my rooms to make him happy."

Cass sent him a flat look as he took another bite of eggs.

"Perhaps they should start a club," Scarlett mused. Then she added, "This afternoon sometime. I need to check in with Hale."

The Toreall King had been graciously helping with all the children. He'd even gone so far as to arrange for private tutors to come in so the children could attend lessons. Neve had been going to the estate to help more and more these days as well, and both she and Auberon had been helping Hale with the history of their own continent.

They all started when a silver hawk came swooping in the open window, all chatter around the table dying down. Nasima flew straight to Scarlett, dropping a rolled piece of parchment directly atop her eggs and fruit before she went right back out the window.

Scarlett frowned as she reached for the parchment. She hadn't seen Nasima since she'd left Ashtine's side months ago. Even when

Scarlett took control of the spirit animals, she didn't *control* them. They just answered to her instead of Saylah. She hadn't quite figured out how all that worked yet. Her desire had never been to rule over the animals, but Saylah certainly didn't deserve to have them at her beck and call when Scarlett was doing all the godsdamn legwork.

"Who's it from?" Cyrus asked around a mouthful of biscuit.

She gently unrolled the message, sitting back in her seat. "Talwyn," Scarlett murmured, confused as to how *Talwyn* had found Nasima. Quickly scanning the message for the important bits, she'd go back and reread it more thoroughly, but a line near the end drew her entire attention. She forgot everything else she had read. She forgot everything else entirely.

Sorin's head whipped to her, clearly feeling her drastic shift in emotions. "What is it?" he demanded, his fork clattering to his plate.

Oh gods. She had been prepared to comfort him if Talwyn had been killed when Alaric realized how he had been tricked again. A part of her had even been prepared to mourn for the female after what she had sacrificed for all of them. But this?

She hadn't been prepared for this. She didn't know how to tell him.

*Briar.*

How was she going to tell Briar?

"Scarlett," Sorin said sharply.

He tried to grab the paper from her, but it was bunched in her hand, clutched too tightly for him to pry it from her fingers.

"Scarlett?"

That was Cassius.

Everything was impossibly loud, but their voices were muffled.

Her fault.

This was her fault.

There were hands on her face. Golden eyes boring into hers.

*Scarlett.*

The voice in her mind was a snarled order. A mate calling to his twin flame.

Her cheeks were wet. She was crying.

She was vaguely aware of everyone crowded around them, of

Cyrus trying to force the note from her hand, but all of her attention was on Sorin.

"He killed him," she whispered, her breakfast roiling in her stomach.

"Who? Who killed who, Scarlett?"

"Alaric," she gasped, breathing too difficult. "He had Sawyer killed."

"What?" Cyrus demanded, his fingers stilling on her hand. "How? Why? We made the exchange."

"But it was a trick. We tricked Alaric with Talwyn," she said, eyes still on Sorin who had gone so still, she wasn't sure if he was breathing. "He sent Nuri after Ashtine." Her voice broke as she whispered on a choked sob, "Sawyer took her place."

"Fuck!"

That was Cyrus cursing. Cyrus who had been tortured by the Sorceress and who had now lost yet another friend.

"Sorin," she whispered. "I'm sorry, Sorin. I'm so sorry."

"I just…" he rasped, hands still framing her face. "Just give me a moment, Scarlett."

His hands were trembling against her skin.

She'd known Alaric would retaliate. She should have seen this coming. Should have known he wouldn't go after Talwyn. Talwyn would be too easy. The effect wouldn't be the same.

Her fault.

This was her fault.

She wanted to go. To run. To the sea. To the country estate. Anywhere. Anywhere but here. She needed to breathe, but her family needed her more. Sawyer had been her friend, yes, but the others had known him for centuries. Family. The Drayces were part of their family. She had done this.

Her movements felt heavy and slow as she turned to her family. Cassius had Cyrus in a tight embrace. Rayner was staring down at the ground. Sorin was still holding her face.

She sucked in a sharp breath, shoving the note into her pocket. Then she gently pulled Sorin's hands away before she wrapped her arms around him and pulled her husband close. He buried his face in her neck, and she reached over and grabbed Rayner's hand, squeezing his fingers tightly in hers.

Everything else was forgotten. They summoned Neve, and Sorin broke the news of another loss for the Water Court. They spent the day in a cozy den, Cethin and Kailia giving them space, but also bringing them anything they needed throughout the day.

And when the day was over, when everyone had gone to their rooms and Sorin was fast asleep, she slipped from their bed. She tugged on her pants and tunic, not bothering with shoes before she Traveled to a section of beach south of Aimonway. Pulling the note from her pocket, she read it over and over. It wasn't much. Talwyn had clearly been in a rush. Short, scribbled words that gave the barest details of what had happened, and where she and Ashtine were now. Scarlett memorized every detail before she let the note go up in white flames. Her eyes fell closed, the sea breeze kissing her face. All she could see was the last line of that note in Talwyn's elegant scrawl.

*Get Briar here now. Or it was all for nothing.*

With fire warming her veins, Scarlett walked straight into the waves, and when she could no longer touch the bottom, she swam out a little farther. She cast an air pocket and sank beneath the water, letting the sea wash away her tears.

Then she started planning.

The stars were fading when she emerged, using her fire to dry her clothing before she was back on the dry sand. She sent a message off amidst a swirl of shadows as she moved, ignoring the person waiting on the shore.

It wasn't Sorin or Cassius. It wasn't even Cethin.

It was Saylah.

"I do not have the time nor the energy for you right now," Scarlett said with a quiet snarl.

Her mother was still. Her entire being seemed to have a faint silvery glow about her. "You are very much like your father."

It was Scarlett's turn to still.

"You take after him more than me," Saylah added. Scarlett stood gaping as the goddess lowered to the sand. "He would spend hours listening to the waves. Said it was a song that soothed his soul."

Scarlett swallowed thickly, not knowing what to say.

Her mother looked up at her, eyes shining as brightly as the disappearing stars. "You have suffered another loss in all of this. I am sorry."

"His death should not have happened," Scarlett replied in a harsh whisper. "My people are continuing to pay the cost for your failures."

"Many have paid the price for my failures. I pay the cost for the failures of others. It is a vicious family cycle, I am afraid," Saylah answered, her gaze going back to the sea. "I wish it had been me to pay the cost to get you outside the wards. Tethys would have been better suited to raise a king and queen of this realm. He was one of the most treasured things in my long, immortal life, aside from you and your brother."

For some reason, Scarlett held back her sharp retort. She couldn't picture it, though. She couldn't see the goddess sitting in the sand as anything but the cold, demanding being she had been from the moment Scarlett had set foot unbidden in the Shira Forest.

"I need to be getting back," Scarlett said, turning to walk up the beach and Travel. "Sorin will wake soon."

"Cethin is making sure he knows you are safe and well," Saylah replied, hands clasped and resting atop her bent knees.

"That isn't necessary."

"I know of sacrifice and loss, Scarlett," Saylah said. Her long silver hair shifted in the slight breeze, but otherwise she sat unnaturally still.

"Forcing others to sacrifice for you and experiencing loss are not the same thing," Scarlett retorted.

Saylah's sharp gaze slid to Scarlett. "Do you think I have lived for thousands of years and not experienced loss?"

"I think living for so many years has made you callous."

"Experiencing so much life has a way of hardening one's soul,"

Saylah agreed. "But you would understand that, wouldn't you? Even in your short years."

Scarlett fell silent, crossing her arms. Her attention fixed on the waves gently rolling to the shore. After several moments of silence, she asked, "Would he have gone with you? When you left this world?"

"Yes," Saylah answered softly. "He would have. The gods do not have twin flames—not like the Legacy and Fae—but he would have gone with me. With us."

Scarlett nodded.

There was another extended silence before Saylah said, "Some gods are selective in who they physically create offspring with. Like Sargon."

"That is an incredibly callous way to speak about having children," Scarlett muttered.

Saylah let out a sharp sigh. "I did not mean it to sound as such. I did not wish to have children. Knowing the kind of life they would lead because of happenings outside of their control. It seemed cruel to bring them into existence just to be hunted by others."

"And yet here I stand. Are you asking for a thank you for the gift of life?"

Saylah ignored her sarcasm as she said, "Tethys was the only one I have ever wanted something more with. Thousands of years, and there was only ever him."

Scarlett may not have lived for thousands of years, but that last part? She understood that in the depths of her being. She may tease Sorin about his past experiences, but there would never be another. He was it. No one else, and she wasn't about to share him with anyone either. It would only ever be him.

"When I first came to this world, I stayed hidden with no one but those who had traveled with me. We discovered there were Legacy here after a time. They called themselves Avonleyans after the kingdom they had built. They once ruled the entirety of the realm. Avonleyan, Fae, and mortal. All living in harmony. This world had been a secret from many. We thought it would stay that way. A sanctuary hidden among the stars."

Scarlett had lowered to the sand as Saylah spoke, hugging her knees close to her chest and resting her chin atop them.

"I was forced from hiding when the Everlasting War found its way here," Saylah continued. "Tybalt arranged a meeting with the then Avonleyan King. He was your father's uncle. We wanted to spare this world. Protect it. The Fae Queens were sent across the Edria to lead that continent, knowing who and what we would be facing. The Fae Courts had long been ruled by an Avonleyan and a Fae, and the mortal kingdoms were once one, ruled by a mortal king and queen, but aided by the Courts whenever required. Our aid was welcomed, and for a time, we appeared to be triumphant in our efforts. Until Esmeray betrayed us all and joined forces with Deimas. That was when I left to get more help."

Scarlett sat up straight. "You left?"

Saylah nodded, still scarcely moving. "I returned with the spirit animals this world knows of. I did not know that while I was gone, Gehenna was sent here. I did not know that she had stolen the lock and brought it here for Moranna. I did not know until it was too late. Not until it was decided to put up the Wards.

"The Wards had been part of our plans. We would regroup. Give the Avonleyans a moment to breathe. Then we would bring the Wards down and claim victory. I would see this world restored to peace before I left for good. The Avonleyan King gave his life as part of the enchantment to enact the Wards, willingly paid the cost for his people. He did not have children. His husband was killed in the war, as was his brother. Which left his nephew to assume the throne.

"Except Gehenna had learned of our plans while I was away. She altered the enchantment, and when the Wards went up, the gateway was sealed. I could not leave. The spirit animals could not leave. I could no longer spare this world, and more than that, we did not know how to take down the Wards. They were only meant to be up for a year, two at most, while we prepared. The Avonleyans became separated from the Fae, weakened to a point of sure surrender. The Fae that were here Faded early, part of the enchantment that Gehenna had altered. The spirit animals could move among the Wards because of what they are, but even their power is a fraction of what it used to be. And my power? The gods emerged from the Chaos. That is where our power comes from. By being stuck here, I am cut off from the most powerful sources of Chaos. My power is not as mighty as it should be.

"The spirit animals were bonded with the Fae Royalty to give them as much protection as I could. The Sorceress was found and imprisoned, but she would not tell Eliné and Henna of the lock. The Shifters and Witches were given gifts to aid the Fae because we could not, and, again, for a while, it seemed they would be victorious. Until Deimas created his own wards, giving his life to do so. But even then, with Deimas gone, there were several decades of quiet after that. The mortals rebuilt, creating the three kingdoms you know now. Esmeray had seemingly disappeared, assumed to have died with Deimas. The other territories settled into their own way of life. And your father and I? He did not know what I was. My secret had died with his uncle, but he knew I was something other. He was relentless, digging until he learned the truth. Another trait I am told you also have."

Scarlett's chin was resting on her knees once more as she listened to Saylah's story. She didn't look up when she spoke of her father. Just kept her eyes fixed on the sea before her.

"Tethys was strong-willed and uncompromising in so many ways, but he was loved by his people. He knew how to lead, how to fight, how to love. He was everything. We became something more. The world seemed to have calmed. The realm was locked. No way in, and no way out. For the first time in my long life, I wanted more and did not feel foolish for wanting it. Cethin was born, and with his birth, we learned how wrong we had been about everything."

Scarlett hugged her knees tighter, so many thoughts and feelings going through her, she couldn't sort them all out. It was enough turmoil to rouse Sorin as his voice echoed down their twin flame bond.

*Love? Cethin said you are with Saylah.*

*I am. I'll be back soon.*

*Are you all right?*

It took her a moment before she could answer. *I don't know.*

Saylah began speaking again after a moment. "As you know, things escalated when Esmeray reemerged and killed the Fae Royals. We learned Alaric had found a way in and was bringing more. Tethys and I knew we needed to do something, and I spent many decades searching for answers. We wanted to leave. To draw the war from this world, hoping the Maraans would follow. I was what they were after. Me and my own. But we could not leave without the lock. The day I learned you were growing in my womb was the day we became desperate. Your father would have given anything to keep you and your brother safe. He *did* give everything."

"Why did I have to be on another continent for this?" Scarlett asked in a hoarse whisper. "Why was it necessary to get me out?"

"I needed to find the lock. It was, and still is, the only way to get you and Cethin out. The one person who knew where it had been hidden was locked away beneath the Black Halls. I went to see Gehenna. She is the one who told me how to find the lock."

"So how am I the only one who can find it now?"

She felt Saylah's gaze fix on her again. "You know the answer to this. I told you when you came to Shira Forest. But you were right that night too, Daughter. You are a god here. Not my god, like you claim. Not like Anala or Silas or any of the others. But to this realm? You may as well be one. There is no one more powerful aside from me."

"And if I do not wish for such a thing?"

"It is already done. When you took your first breath. It is why you were delivered with the Witches."

"And I had to be left there alone because?"

"I did not leave you there alone. I left you with Eliné."

"My mistake," Scarlett retorted bitterly.

"You were not meant to be left there as long as you were," Saylah said. "There was a plan to awaken your gifts when you reached age sixteen. She was to help you find the lock, and then return here. But when Eliné died…"

Scarlett glanced at Saylah when she paused. She could swear there were tears glimmering in her eyes.

Saylah lightly cleared her throat. "When I learned of Eliné's death, I assumed you had met the same fate. I had no way of knowing otherwise. It was not until Cethin unknowingly found his way into your dreams that I learned you still lived, and by then, everything had changed."

"Why?"

"Because the Maraans had you. Knew what you carried."

"I don't understand," Scarlett said, digging her toes into the sand. "What do I carry?"

"That is enough for now," Saylah replied. "Your heart is already too heavy this night."

"So you decided to add to it and leave me with more questions? What was the purpose of this visit, Saylah?"

"To let you know I understand sacrifice and loss. To help you understand why all this is necessary," she answered. "To tell you of your father, who was pure goodness and light. He cared deeply for his people. You and Cethin got that trait from him. I will not pretend that any of that goodness came from me. But I am glad you still feel, Scarlett. It is a dreadful thing to become so numb to loss that you no longer feel the cost of such things. I am glad you found your way back before you lost that light for good."

"I am more dark than light," Scarlett murmured. "My stars are my light."

"Retrieve the lock, Scarlett, and I will tell you more," Saylah said, gracefully rising to her feet.

"Oh, Saylah. You were so close to actually being a mother," Scarlett drawled, eyes going back to the sea.

"I have not survived this long by sharing all my knowledge at once. Secrets are the currency of the gods," she replied, silver gaze fixing on Scarlett as the first light of dawn touched the sand. "But you already know the value of cunning secrecy. That particular trait, Scarlett, did come from me."

Her words echoed in Scarlett's mind long after her mother had disappeared amidst her shadows.

# CHAPTER 24

# TALWYN

"She needs to eat more," the High Witch said, her violet eyes studying Ashtine intensely.

"I am getting her to eat as much as I can," Talwyn replied tightly. They'd had this same conversation multiple times over the past few days.

They had flown for nearly two days straight when they'd left Siofra. They'd only stopped twice, pushing their griffins to their limits, and finally arriving at the High Witch's residence at twilight on the third day. Another Witch had taken Ashtine from atop the griffin and brought her to this room. The princess hadn't left it since. She was curled on her side, head in Talwyn's lap, where she gently ran her fingers through Ashtine's silver hair. Talwyn had convinced her to wash up at one point, the princess allowing Talwyn to use a cloth and warm water, but she had refused all suggestions of a bath.

Hazel Hecate, the High Witch herself, was overseeing Ashtine's care. In the four days they had been here, it wasn't until the second day Talwyn had convinced Ashtine to eat anything. The princess had hardly eaten anything on the flight here. That was also the day she had sent a message to Scarlett with Nasima. Ashtine needed Briar. There was no way around it anymore. As if the stress of a Fae pregnancy coupled with all she had been through these last months hadn't been enough, Sawyer's sacrifice had pushed her over an edge. Talwyn didn't know the first thing about being a decent friend, but she knew that without Briar, Sawyer's sacrifice would be for nothing. Even if Ashtine hung on until the babes were born, if Briar did not survive this war, neither would the Wind Princess. Talwyn refused to let that be the outcome after everything the princess had forsaken.

Hazel came forward. Nasima gave a soft, warning cry from where she perched near the window. The High Witch placed her hands on Ashtine's rounded stomach. Soft light flared, and Talwyn held her breath like she did every time Hazel did this.

"They are still fine, but she needs to eat more," Hazel said again. "Their power drains her. She needs to keep up her strength, or these last months of carrying them will be even more difficult."

"I know," Talwyn gritted out, fingers stroking through Ashtine's hair again. Ashtine didn't acknowledge either of them. When her eyes were open, she stared at nothing, but for the most part, she slept.

"She needs to siphon off power too," Hazel added.

"I know," Talwyn snapped, before taking a deep breath to ease her temper.

Hazel stepped back, leveling Talwyn with a cool glare. "I have news for you as well."

"What is it?"

"We received word that King Callan and Prince Azrael have returned to Windonelle. They have found their way to some of the rebel camps. Arantxa leaves to travel there at first light tomorrow. If you wish to go, this is your chance."

Go.

She could go back to Azrael.

But she couldn't leave Ashtine. Not until Briar found his way back to her.

"I will stay with her," Talwyn said.

Hazel nodded at the same moment there was a quick knock on the door. A Witch with bright red hair entered, her pale violet eyes scanning over Talwyn and Ashtine. "The tonics, my Lady," she said, holding out her hand. There were three vials in it.

"Are more being prepared?" Hazel asked, the glass tinkling as she swiped the vials from her hand.

"Yes, my Lady."

"With Arantxa going to be with Juliette, I want you to take over her patrols, Jetta," Hazel said, moving to a side table.

"Already done," the Witch answered.

"Is there any other news from Juliette?" Talwyn asked.

"The Oracle said nothing else," Hazel replied. "And we have not received any news from Death's Shadow."

Nuri. The wicked, cunning female who had been playing her master from the very beginning. Who had somehow found the one seraph who was doing the same.

She was still fucking insane.

After Nuri had told her to run, Mordecai had scooped Talwyn into the sky and taken her to some hideaway in the Dresden Forest on the Toreall and Witch Kingdoms' border. Because somehow, inexplicably, the seraph could Travel. Talwyn had sat for nearly three days until Nuri had returned with him.

"Sorry for making you wait," Nuri had said, gliding into the hidden clearing with Mordecai behind her. "You'll be happy to know it wasn't for the sake of dramatics."

"No," Talwyn had sneered. "The dramatics were making me think you were going to chase me."

"You could say thank you."

"Thank you?" Talwyn had repeated incredulously.

Mordecai had been removing a few weapons before taking off his jacket and beginning to roll back the sleeve of his tunic. Quick, efficient movements. He was every bit the warrior he'd been trained to be.

"Yes. Thank you," Nuri had replied, pulling her hood back and removing her gloves, tossing them atop Mordecai's jacket. Her hands went to her hips. "You're alive. You're free of Alaric. You're welcome."

"You told me to run so that you wouldn't have to lie to Alaric?" Talwyn had asked in realization.

"I can't lie to him."

"But you told me to run."

She'd rolled her eyes, appearing to fidget in agitation. "I can't *lie* to him. I told him you ran. Not that I *told* you to run. Again, this is where you say thank you."

"What of Briar?"

"The Water Prince is safe for now," Mordecai had replied, grabbing Nuri's elbow as she'd begun to pace in a tight circle. He'd lifted his now bare arm with the sleeve folded up to the elbow, and Nuri's fangs had immediately sank into it with a feral moan as he'd gently tugged her closer. "Alaric is withholding blood from her as punishment for losing you," Mordecai had said at Talwyn's arched brow.

"You were not punished?"

"Of course I was," he'd retorted, one of his wings curving protectively around Nuri.

"And I am to believe the two of you are working against him?"

Talwyn had then listened to a tale that she would not have believed if she had not witnessed so many of the moments herself. It explained everything. How Nuri had always known where to be and when. How she'd always known exactly when and how to rile her master. How they'd worked closely with Juliette—who would warn them of things she had seen—and in turn, the Witch Kingdoms. How Nuri would play her master with just the right words to work around her Blood Bond most of the time. How they'd been part of preparing a rebel army of mortals and Witches and Shifters to fight alongside Scarlett and the Fae when they returned. How Mordecai had a small band of rebel seraphs helping in all of this too.

Yet despite all their cunning and secrecy, they had still been forced to commit their own atrocities to keep their cover. The Blood Bond. Killing the Contessa. Fighting in the various battles and slaughtering those they were trying to aid.

Suddenly Nuri's insanity was a bit more understandable. How did anyone stay sane when forced to do so much evil against their will?

She'd fed the entire time Mordecai spoke. He'd eventually lowered them to the ground, and slowly her limbs had relaxed.

"Has he starved her this whole time?" Talwyn asked, eyeing the vampyre.

"Yes," Mordecai said darkly. "This is the first time I have seen her since the prison. He has had her locked away in a room of sunlight to drain her even more."

They'd sat in silence after that while Nuri had fed, and when she was finished, Mordecai had Traveled Talwyn to the Witch Kingdoms before he and Nuri had to return to Alaric. Juliette had warned them the next day of the impending attack on Siofra. That they had two days to prepare, and when they were getting ready to depart, that was when the warning about the order to kill Ashtine had come.

That was when Talwyn had learned just how much time the Witches and Shifters had been buying for Scarlett, trying to hold the lines while she went for aid in Avonleya.

Hazel approached the bed, one vial uncorked in her hand. "She needs to take this. If she will not eat, the babes need extra sustenance."

"I will see that it is done," Talwyn replied tightly, reaching for the vial.

"You also need to go see your griffin," Hazel added. "The bonding is imperative if you wish to fly with him in battle."

A griffin. She had a godsdamn griffin. Sort of. She wouldn't if she didn't train with him. It had been a rough flight to Solembra. She was sure the griffin had only followed orders in the end because Arantxa's griffin made him fall into line.

"I cannot leave Ashtine alone right now," Talwyn replied.

"If you wish to be of continued use in this war, you will go see your griffin. I can stay with the princess until you return," Hazel retorted. "Or perhaps a better idea would be to convince her to go with you. The winds would do her some good. I will return shortly."

The High Witch turned on her heel, striding from the room with Jetta behind her. Talwyn sighed. Asking Ashtine to be strong yet again hurt. She shouldn't have to be strong. Not right now. Her only worry should be those babes. Briar should be doing this, and even though she was here now, caring for her friend until he could, it did not ease her guilt.

"Ashtine," she said softly, squeezing her shoulder. "You need to take this for the babes. Then perhaps we can go for a walk outside."

"Has Briar arrived?"

Talwyn froze. They were the first words she had said since leaving Siofra, and the pieces of her heart that may have been mashed back together by Azrael fractured a bit more.

"Soon, Ashtine," she said, stroking her hair once more. "But maybe the winds know something."

"The winds know everything and nothing."

She had never been so happy to hear Ashtine's nonsensical jargon.

"Can you take this, Ashtine? Please?" she asked, holding up the vial.

Ashtine pushed herself up to a sitting position, taking the tonic and tipping it into her mouth. Then Talwyn was scrambling up when the princess moved from the bed faster than expected. Nasima swooped to Ashtine's shoulder a moment later. She reached up, dragging her fingers along her feathers, and the bird nuzzled into her hand.

"I have missed you, my friend," Ashtine whispered.

"Do you want to eat something while we walk?" Talwyn asked, pulling open the door and grabbing a cloak for Ashtine from a hook nearby.

"No."

"All right."

Later. She would work on that later. Ashtine was up and speaking. This was progress.

Hazel was rounding a corner when they came to the end of a corridor, approval flashing in her eyes when she spotted them.

"It is good you are up, your Highness," she said, looking the princess over keenly.

"Thank you for the tonic," Ashtine replied.

"Are you going to the pens? If so, I will accompany you."

The High Witch did not wait for an answer. She just turned and led the way. Talwyn stuck close to Ashtine's side as they made their way across the castle grounds. She seemed steady on her feet, but Talwyn wasn't taking any chances.

Nearing one of the pens, there were several surrounding enclosures. Aeries was more like it. Nearly all the enclosures were covered, providing shelter from the elements, but they rose into towers where the griffins could come and go from the air, apparently trusted to return on their own.

"I will get Thorne," Hazel said over her shoulder before striding away and into an aery.

"We should probably stay back," Talwyn said when Ashtine began moving towards one of the tethered griffins.

The princess continued as though she hadn't heard her, Nasima clicking her beak at her shoulder. The dark grey griffin she was approaching cocked its head, eyeing the hawk. Talwyn tensed when Ashtine reached up and rested her hand on the creature's beak. Its wings rustled, but other than that, it stood perfectly still.

Talwyn stood back, giving the princess room. She didn't need to be hovered over. Not with Nasima back at her side and winds whispering in her ear.

"You did well."

Talwyn turned at the sound of Hazel's voice to find her leading Thorne over. The griffin clicked his beak in agitation, raking his talons along the ground.

"I did nothing," Talwyn said curtly.

"You have not left her side, and you convinced her to get up. That is something."

They stood silently for a moment, watching the princess and the griffin. "The babes are truly doing well?" Talwyn asked.

"They are, but she needs to eat more."

"So I hear," Talwyn muttered.

"You should take Thorne for a flight," Hazel said. "Get to know him better."

"Tomorrow perhaps."

"Still stubborn, I see," Hazel said. Talwyn turned her head to look at the Witch. "I detested working with you when you were queen."

Talwyn took a moment, leashing the irritation that climbed up her spine. Hazel had refused to work with her when she had been queen. The few times they had spoken, the meetings had never ended well. "I am well aware of what you thought of me, my Lady."

"No, you are not. You would have made an excellent Witch. I often found it ironic that you were given Shifter gifts rather than Witch gifts when you are so much like us," the High Witch said.

Talwyn studied her. The straight back and lifted chin. The perfectly intact braid and the witchsuit. "If those were your thoughts of me, why did you insist on working with Sorin?"

Hazel was quiet for a long moment before she said, "Mostly

because he had worked closely with Eliné, but also because you reminded me too much of myself. I would not have stayed with my friend, though. I would have found other things more important. I could not stay with my own child let alone a friend and her young. For that, Talwyn Semiria, you are better than I could ever wish to be."

With that, Hazel handed off Thorne's lead and strode away. Talwyn stared after her until Ashtine's approach drew her attention.

"This one is yours?" the princess asked, running a palm along his neck. Thorne let out a low huff of sorts, lowering his head to peck at something on the ground.

"He is. If we can bond enough," Talwyn answered.

"Did you choose him?"

"No. I was told to walk through the aeries until one came to me. It took nearly two days. I think he only approached because I carried an apple, and he wanted it."

Ashtine huffed a small laugh. She brought her hands together, cradling her belly. "I know that I have appeared weak these last few days."

"You are the farthest thing from weak, Ashtine," Talwyn said as they moved along a path, Thorne trailing behind them.

"I simply wish for you to know that I do care. For the babes."

"I never once doubted such a thing. Everything you have done is for them. To give them a world different from what we know. That is not weakness. And even if it were, I am the last person you need to explain yourself to."

They continued on in silence, Ashtine pulling her cloak tighter around herself. After a while, she said, "I should have let Eliza take Sawyer's ashes to the sea."

Talwyn stopped short. "Why? Briar will be grateful that you waited for him."

"And if I find myself with two sets of Water Prince ashes? What am I to do then, Talwyn?" Ashtine turned to face her, unshed tears glimmering in her eyes.

Talwyn swallowed. She couldn't promise everything would be all right. She couldn't lie and say she knew they would see Briar well and whole again before this was over. So instead, she dropped Thorne's lead and stepped closer to Ashtine, drawing her into an embrace.

"In my time spent behind bars these last weeks, I have come to realize that sometimes all we can do is breathe," Talwyn said softly. "Sometimes that has to be enough for the moment."

"I thought I could do this, but I cannot," she whispered. "I cannot do this without him by my side."

"You can, and you will not do it alone. If the Fates take Briar from you, I will still be here, Ashtine. You will not be alone."

Ashtine nodded into her shoulder, reaching up to brush away her tears. "I fear for them."

Her voice was so quiet, Talwyn hardly heard her with her now mortal hearing.

"Briar is strong. Scarlett will not fail at this, Ashtine."

"Not him. I fear for him, yes, but…" She trailed off, her hands rubbing along her belly. "They will be hunted, and I fear I do them a disservice to even bring them into this world."

Talwyn placed her hands over Ashtine's, feeling the babes move beneath their fingers. "They will be protected more than any others."

"If Briar and I are not…"

And Talwyn knew. She knew what the princess was asking her. Because they had both grown up without mothers and fathers. But they had grown up with each other. The gods knew she'd likely make a shit mother, but if Briar and Ashtine could not be there, those babes would never feel abandoned. Not for a single moment of their lives.

"They will know love, Ashtine," Talwyn said. "The unconditional kind. The kind you showed me. They will be loved fiercely."

Ashtine nodded, a small sad smile coming through her tears before the princess turned and continued walking along the path.

And as Talwyn followed, she had a feeling the winds had spoken to her friend again.

# CHAPTER 25
# CYRUS

"Y ou do not have to do this, Thia," Cyrus said as he watched her buckle on her fighting leathers.

"We can handle this, Cyrus," she replied, her irritation with him over this seeping into her tone as she slid a knife into the sheath on her thigh.

"I do not doubt your skills," he said. "I know you can handle this. What I am saying is something does not add up. Please don't go. Help me convince Sorin to wait just a little longer."

Thia sighed heavily, turning to face him. She flicked her red braid over her shoulder as she moved towards him. She took his face in her hands, and his palms landed on her hips, tugging her closer. "When this is all over, you will see you worry for nothing," she murmured, brushing her lips along his jaw.

"What if he's wrong?" Cyrus said in desperation.

"What if he's right?" Thia countered. "What if Eliné is indeed right across the border? We cannot walk away from this, Cyrus."

"I'm not saying we should. I'm saying we need to slow down—"

She kissed him deeply. The kind of kiss that stole his breath and had his hands sliding to her ass and hoisting her against him. Thia pulled back, nipping his bottom lip lightly. Hazel eyes stared into his, her fingers sinking into his hair.

"Please, Thia," Cyrus begged.

"This is happening, Cyrus," she replied, brushing her thumb along his lower lip with her other hand. "And I hope Sorin is wrong."

321

"*What?*"

"*I hope Sorin is wrong. I hope this is a trap. I hope when I step outside this tent, it is the last time I see you.*"

*Cyrus shook his head, trying to clear his thoughts, to wrap his mind around what she was saying.* "*If something happens to you, I will break, Thia. I do not know how I will come back from that.*"

"*Good,*" *she breathed, letting her long legs slide down his body.* "*It will be no less than you deserve.*"

"Cyrus."

*It will be no less than you deserve.*

"Cyrus, look at me." A warm hand on his face. "Open your eyes, Cyrus," came a whispered demand.

He blinked, finding Cass leaning over him. It was dark in their room, but Cyrus could make out the concern on his features. His thumb brushed across his jaw. Cyrus swallowed thickly, his mouth too dry as he tried to pull himself out of that memory. Trying to remember how things had actually happened. But Gehenna had forced him to relive this particular memory so many times, truth and lie blurred together.

"Hey," Cassius said quietly. "It was a dream, Cyrus. It wasn't real."

"It wasn't a dream," Cyrus rasped, pushing his hand from his face and pressing the heels of his palms into his eyes.

"What do you mean?" Cass asked, sitting up when Cyrus slid from the bed.

Cyrus didn't answer, moving out to their sitting room and pouring a measure of liquor. He knocked the entire thing back, relishing the burn of the alcohol, letting it calm his racing heart. He set the glass back down roughly, bracing his hands on the cart and letting his head hang down.

She was growing impatient.

"What do you mean it wasn't a dream?"

Cyrus lifted his head, looking over his shoulder to find Cass leaning in the doorway. His arms were folded across his bare chest. The low fire in the hearth reflected in his eyes. He'd stopped wearing that godsdamn eye patch.

Cyrus straightened, dragging his hand through his sleep-addled hair. "It was nothing," he finally said, letting his magic stir the fire to life a little more. He moved to the sofa. There would be no going back to sleep now. "I'm sorry I woke you."

"I woke you," Cass replied. He came to sit beside him before he added, "You were dreaming of Thia."

"It wasn't..." Cyrus released a harsh breath. "Forget it."

"I'm forgetting nothing."

Cyrus leaned back into the sofa, gaze fixed on the flames. He lifted a hand, letting his magic play with the embers. The silence around them was loud, and his chest was so tight, he couldn't speak above a whisper when he said, "It wasn't a dream. It was a memory."

"Okay..." Cassius said when Cyrus didn't go. "Tell me why the difference matters."

"Because she changed them."

"Who did?"

"Gehenna." Then he added, "The Sorceress," when Cassius didn't react.

He felt Cassius stiffen beside him then. "What do you mean she changed them?"

Cyrus drew the flames out into thin tendrils, absent-mindedly looping them through the air. "Exactly that. She changed my memories. Altered them. Made me relive them but changed the details. So many times that I..."

*Of course they made a mistake.*

*No one wants you, Cyrus.*

*If you can't see that all you do is damage everyone around you, then I will keep reminding you until you believe it.*

*It will be no less than you deserve.*

"You what, Cyrus?" Cassius pressed.

Cyrus glanced at him out of the corner of his eye. He was leaning forward, arms crossed and braced on his knees, watching the flames Cyrus was toying with.

Cyrus cleared his throat. "She did it over and over. Kept me trapped in some for hours. The reality and the lies are mixed together so thoroughly. She altered them all, Cass. All the good. The things that reminded me the stars were worth fighting for? She took it all and—"

Cassius was pulling him into his chest, arms wrapping tightly around him and a hand cupping the back of his head. Cyrus hadn't realized he'd started crying.

"I'm sorry, Cyrus," he murmured.

"Don't be," Cyrus muttered. "Don't feel sorry for me."

Cassius stiffened again. "Why would you say that?"

Cyrus gently shoved him back, sliding away from him. "Because she broke me in the end, Cass," he sighed. "Instead of staying strong, outlasting her until you all came, I gave in when she——"

He stopped, rolling his lips. The fire he'd been playing with faded away.

"We'll clean it up together, Cyrus," Cassius said into the now dim room.

"None of you will be saying that when you know…"

"Try me," Cassius said sharply. "I swore not to tell you to get out again. This won't change that."

He may as well get this over with. He'd been selfish long enough, stealing moments with his family and nights with Cassius, just wanting a few good memories to cling to. Ones the Sorceress hadn't touched. But they needed to know. He could go, and they could figure out how to work around what he had cost them.

"She altered them all," Cyrus finally said. "Merrick. Thia. Memories of my family. All the good ones are tainted now, but then… Then she came for memories of you." He heard Cassius suck in a sharp breath. "She altered one, and I begged—*begged* her, Cassius—not to touch any more. To let me keep those, because I could live without memories of my past, but you were not my past. You were…everything I did not deserve in the future."

"Cyrus——"

"So I made a bargain with her," he pushed on, speaking over Cassius. He brushed his fingers over the Bargain Mark that wound around his bicep. "Everyone knows you don't do that. Everyone knows to deal with her is to make a fool's bargain. *I* knew it was foolish and could ruin so much for everyone else, but you? You were the one sacrifice I was not willing to make. Merrick and Thia were already gone. But you were here. And you made me feel again. And the thought of her twisting your words? Of carrying memories of you looking at me with derision? I couldn't——"

"There is nothing you could do that would make me look at you like that, Cyrus. *Nothing*," Cassius said vehemently. "How could she even do this? Because Alaric gave her your blood?"

Cyrus nodded mutely. He could say that, but he still didn't know—

And then Cassius was in his face, forcing him to look into his eyes. One brown, one pale and white. "I will never look at you with derision, disgust, or hatred. Never, Cyrus. Do you hear me? It is impossible when I love you."

Cyrus stopped breathing because he couldn't have heard him right.

"Say it again," Cyrus whispered.

Cassius gripped his face in his hands. "It will not matter what you traded to the Sorceress because I love you, Cyrus. Whatever you promised her, we will figure it out."

Cyrus wrapped a hand around the nape of his neck, closing the distance between their mouths. His other hand ran down his chest, fingertips sliding along the muscled indents and grooves of his abdomen. A low rumble came from Cassius, and he pulled back after a moment, his breathing ragged and eyes glowing. "We need to finish talking about all of this."

That was the absolute last thing Cyrus wanted to do at the moment. Not with Cassius pressed up against him in nothing but loose pants that could be taken care of far too easily.

"Cyrus," Cassius growled, a knowing look on his face.

He let his hand fall from Cass's neck and sat back with an embellished sigh. "Fine." He swiped a hand down his face, trying to calm the want racing through his blood. "We should wake the others."

Cassius stood, and Cyrus saw just how hard it was for Cassius to stop this right now.

"We should change," Cass said.

"Why?" Cyrus asked with a smirk and a pointed look.

But what Cyrus had intended to be a taunt had Cassius's eyes glowing brighter as he leaned over him in a move that had Cyrus tipping his head back against the sofa to see him. "Remember what I said, Cyrus," he said, his tone rough and low. "I'm not as selfless as you believe me to be. I want, and I take."

Cyrus scoffed, despite this doing nothing to calm him down.

"You're the most selfless person I know. Except maybe Tava. She might have you beat."

Cassius said nothing, but the corner of his lips tilted up in a knowing smirk. He brushed his knuckles across Cyrus's cheek before his thumb brushed along his mouth. Cyrus found himself trying to remember how to breathe. Do you take air in first? Or out?

"Make no mistake, Cyrus," he murmured. "I'll take what's mine."

Well, fuck.

That was all he could think as Cass straightened and started heading back to the bedchamber to change.

"Cass," he called out, his voice a hoarse rasp.

Cassius paused, looking back over his shoulder.

"I love you too."

"You could at least put on pants," Sorin grumbled as he emerged from his room behind Scarlett.

She waved him off with a yawn. "If I'm going to be dragged from bed with the sun, I'll wear whatever I please."

While Sorin had put on pants and a tunic, Scarlett had only slipped on a dark silk robe that scarcely came to her knees over her nightgown. Or at least, Cyrus assumed there was a nightgown under there. The way Sorin was fretting over her attire, he wasn't so sure.

"Morning, Seastar," Cassius said, ruffling her hair while simultaneously pressing a pastry into her hand.

"Thank you," she grumbled, taking a bite.

"You think I would wake you at dawn and not feed you?" he teased, crossing the room and taking a seat beside Cyrus on the sofa. Cass's hand landed on his thigh, and it was only then that Cyrus realized he'd been bouncing his knee with his nervousness.

Sorin was eyeing him. So was Rayner, who had only bothered to put on pants and was drinking a cup of tea. The male looked exhausted. Granted, he was still recouping the power he'd used to save Sorin and Scarlett from those feline-type creatures. In fact, Rayner was the main reason Scarlett hadn't gone for the lock yet. But this was a different type of exhaustion. As if the mere idea of putting on a shirt was too much.

Cyrus arched a brow in question at his appearance. He was the early riser of the group. Him and Eliza. They were always up before the sun.

"When I checked on Tula in the middle of the night, she was not in her bed," Rayner muttered.

Everyone stopped and turned to him at the words. He had recently been given a two-room suite. Scarlett had insisted when he kept sleeping on the sofa so Tula could have his bed. Tula had been absolutely smitten to have her own room.

"I found her. Nearly two hours later. As a godsdamn mouse nestled deep under the blankets at the foot of my bed," Rayner continued, tipping his head back against the chair, his eyes falling closed.

Scarlett slapped a hand over her mouth, but it didn't stifle the sound of her laughter.

"She'd had a nightmare and didn't want to wake me, so that was her solution," Rayner went on. "When I woke her and demanded she Shift back, she refused to go sleep in her own room."

"Rayner," Scarlett said around another laugh, "please tell me you did not spend the night on the sofa again."

"She wouldn't leave my side," he sighed. "I let her stay in my bed, and when she fell asleep, I tried to go to her room. She woke because she was clutching my fingers and felt it every time I tried to disentangle them. Every godsdamn time. I finally tucked her in tightly among the blankets and tried to sleep atop them, but she's a restless sleeper. She kicks in her sleep."

Scarlett didn't bother trying to hide her laughter this time. "How is her training going?"

"Clearly fine. She seems to be able to Shift at will into whatever she chooses," Sorin said with a grin as he ushered Scarlett to another chair. He tried to cover her with a blanket, but she scowled and shooed him away, tucking her legs beneath her. Cassius chuckled under his breath as Sorin gave her an unimpressed look.

"She does well with small forms," Rayner said, taking a drink of his tea. "We haven't worked up to larger ones yet."

"How will that work?" Scarlett asked, her nose scrunching. "She can't shift into a full-sized tiger, can she?"

"No," Rayner answered. "She'd shift into a tiger cub, but even those forms are too large right now. So we stick with smaller forms."

"Anything with wings?" Scarlett mused.

Rayner's eyes went wide. "Fuck no. Never anything with wings. She can keep her feet, paws, scales, whatever, on the godsdamn ground."

Scarlett huffed another small laugh at that, batting her lashes at Sorin when he handed her a cup of tea. He took a seat on the arm of her chair, and Cyrus looked away when his gaze settled on him.

"Cyrus," he said, his tone the same one he used when they spoke of Thia. "What is this about?"

He'd been so careful to keep the Mark on his arm covered. Cassius was the only one who knew about it. He didn't know why Cass had never told them, but that wasn't true either. Even if Cassius had known what kind of Mark it was, he wouldn't have betrayed his trust like that. So when Cass flexed his fingers against his thigh, Cyrus pulled the sleeve of his tunic up over his shoulder, gaze fixed on the floor.

No one spoke for a long moment. Not until Sorin said, "What are the terms?"

"In exchange for keeping particular memories untouched, I agreed to…give her a few things," Cyrus answered.

"Explain that," Sorin said calmly.

Cassius's hand did not leave his thigh while he told them what Gehenna had done with his blood, how she'd altered his memories, and how she'd made him relive his nightmares over and over. He didn't share every detail, not like he had with Cassius, but he shared enough. Or he hoped he had. He hoped he shared enough that they understood why he'd made the bargain with the Sorceress. That they wouldn't completely hate him for it.

Cyrus chanced a glance up at his king and queen. There were silent tears tracking down Scarlett's face. Sorin's face was that of his friend who understood the desperation it took to make a deal with her. There was worry and sorrow there. Some guilt perhaps, but not anger. Not disappointment.

"What do we need to do, Cyrus?" Scarlett asked, a fierceness in her tone that told him she was descending into that place where she would do whatever was necessary to protect her own.

"You do not need to do anything," he said hoarsely. "I will do it. I can buy you time before I do, but——"

"Name the costs," Sorin said. A demand from the Fire Prince.

Cyrus rubbed at the back of his neck. "There were three. One of blood. One of betrayal. One of time. I had to give her more blood. I have to keep supplying her with blood until I fulfill the bargain. She can reach me, even here. She said…" He glanced at Sorin. "She said to tell you that one was because your bargain was fulfilled by deceit."

"By deceit?" Sorin asked, his brow furrowing. "How so?"

"Because you technically died?" Rayner asked. "Did that nullify the Bargain Mark?"

Sorin was studying his arm where a Bargain Mark had once been to solidify the deal made when he had needed to get to Scarlett in the mortal lands. "All of my Marks came back as before, but not that one. That doesn't make any sense."

"No," Cyrus said, shaking his head. "She said it was because of Scarlett. That she had ruined everything."

Scarlett suddenly gripped Sorin's arm. "What if it was fulfilled before you died? With everything else going on, we just didn't notice the Mark was gone? It's not like it was front and center."

"I don't know, Love——"

"When we went there and got the key. Don't you remember what she said? 'You have ruined everything. I have nothing anymore. No more debts to call in. Nothing.' What were you to bring her?"

"The blood of a god," he answered.

"Which flows in my veins," Scarlett said. "I spilled my blood across her Marks to find the key. Technically, you fulfilled your end of the deal."

"But you're not a god," Rayner said, rubbing at his brow with his thumb and forefinger. "If you go by that logic, any Avonleyan blood would have been payment."

"Perhaps with a goddess as my mother?"

Rayner and Sorin didn't seem convinced, but it didn't matter. "Somehow it was fulfilled and not the way she wanted," Cyrus said.

"And that was why she demanded one of my payments be unlimited access to my blood until the bargain is fulfilled."

"And the one of betrayal?" Scarlett asked. Her chin was propped in her hand as she watched him carefully, already calculating and clearly still thinking through Sorin's fulfilled bargain.

"I am to deliver her spell book to her."

Scarlett straightened. A moment later, a shadow panther appeared, a book in its maw. She took the spell book and tossed it unceremoniously atop the low table before them.

"Done," she said. "What else?"

Cyrus gaped at her. "Just like that? You cannot simply give that back to her."

"Actually, I plan to do just that. She just provided me with a reason to do so," she replied. "What else, Cyrus?"

"I…" This was not how he had envisioned this conversation going. "I have to get something for her from the Black Syndicate."

That had both Scarlett and Cassius going unnaturally still.

"Absolutely not," Scarlett said. "How is that a sacrifice of time?"

"It will take time for me to find what she wants. Time and planning," he said, fiddling with the seam of one of the sofa cushions.

"What does she want from there?" Cassius asked. His hand had tightened around Cyrus's thigh, and Cyrus was sure he hadn't realized it.

"Apparently, Alaric had something that allowed him to communicate with another realm. He believes it was destroyed when the Fellowship was burned, but Gehenna said it couldn't be destroyed. Not by starfire alone," Cyrus explained. "I am to find it and bring it to her when I bring her the spell book."

Scarlett stood, beginning to pace back and forth. "What is it you are supposed to find?"

"I am not entirely sure," Cyrus said. "Alaric mentioned it once when he was there. Was pissed you destroyed it."

"She did not tell him it was not destroyed?" Rayner asked.

"Why would she when she wants it?" Sorin said. "But why? What does it do?"

Cyrus shrugged again. "Lets him communicate outside the realm, I guess."

"Like a mirror gate?" Scarlett asked, still moving.

"There wasn't a mirror gate at the Fellowship, Seastar," Cassius said, his grip on Cyrus's thigh finally relaxing some.

"In his rooms maybe?" she pushed.

"We were never allowed in there."

"I know," she murmured, speaking more to herself at this point. "I was in there twice. Once as a child and once when I burned the Fellowship down. I suppose I would have noticed a giant mirror, even as an eight-year-old." She frowned, tugging her robe tighter around herself.

Cyrus cleared his throat. "She's growing impatient."

"It's only been a few weeks," Scarlett grumbled. "She's been locked up there for centuries. You'd think this wouldn't be a big deal."

"I need to start working on this," Cyrus said. "If she thinks I'm backing out on this bargain…"

"You cannot break a bargain," Rayner said. "The Mark will force fulfillment after a time, and if it is physically impossible to do so, you will be cursed."

"I'm aware, Rayner," Cyrus sighed.

Not to mention the Sorceress would take her own revenge for failure. He was fairly certain he'd rather cross the Veil than live with any of that.

"Okay," Scarlett said. "This will be…okay."

"How do you figure that?" Cassius demanded.

"You and Cyrus can go find this…thing the Sorceress requires. Or, at the very least, figure out what it is."

"He is your Guardian," Sorin cut in. "He cannot simply leave you in the middle of war."

"He can," she insisted.

"It goes against the Guardian Bond," Cassius argued.

"Only if I am in danger," she countered. "You two can go, but after we get the lock. We need a second Traveler with us when we go. Just in case." Her gaze shifted to Cyrus. "Can you wait? Until Rayner is back to full-strength, and we accomplish this?"

"I mean, yeah, but I can go. This is my mess I created. I can fix it—"

She stopped pacing, turning to face him fully. "We are a family. We choose each other. We claim each other. You said something. Now we face it together. You taught me that, Cyrus."

He swallowed thickly before nodding his head, eyes falling to his lap.

"You deserve a family, Cyrus," Cass said before the voices could start up in his mind again. "You deserve people who fight for you."

"This might be better in the end," Scarlett said, heading towards her bedchamber. "I was already altering our plans a bit. This isn't a big deal."

"What do you mean the plans are changing? Scarlett, where are you going?" Sorin asked, getting to his feet.

She sent him an incredulous look. "I cannot very well scheme in a *robe*, Sorin. It's incredibly indecent. I'm going to get dressed."

Rayner tipped his head back, his eyes falling closed again at the same time Sorin muttered, "That godsdamn tongue."

They disappeared into the bedchamber, the door snicking shut behind them.

"I'm going to sleep for a few hours. I'll meet you all later," Rayner muttered, immediately disappearing among smoke and ashes.

"Cyrus," Cass said.

"Yeah?" he muttered.

"We're still here. None of us looked at you with derision or contempt. No one told you to leave. We're all still here."

Cyrus slowly lifted his gaze to meet Cass's eyes, that patch still gone as it had been for days now.

"We'll help you remember which memories were real. The ones we can anyway, and we'll create new ones to help you remember that you deserve this. To help you breathe when you feel like you're suffocating."

Cyrus said nothing. He just leaned forward, erasing the space between their lips, and kissed him deeply.

# CHAPTER 26
# SCARLETT

"**A**re you ready to go train, Love? We have the next two days to spend in here."

Scarlett looked up from the text she was reading through. Or trying to read through. The language was Avonleyan, but it also wasn't. It seemed to be a mishmash of a couple different languages, and she'd spent the better part of the last week frustrated. Which worked out, she supposed. Because while they spent the mornings in these damn catacombs in the Elshira castle, they spent the afternoons training, and she could work out all of that frustration.

Rayner's power was nearly back to where it needed to be. He hadn't completely depleted his reserves when he'd come to the Runic Lands, so it hadn't taken nearly as long as it had after the battle on the ships. In two days they were going to the Southern Islands to find this lock. Tonight she would draw from Sorin, and for the next two days, no one was touching their magic. This would give everyone time to replenish any lost power and tunnel down to whatever place they needed to be to carry out this mission.

Hell.

For her, that place was hell.

It was tunneling down to the place where Death's Maiden dwelled.

For what she was going to do in two days, Death's Maiden was who she needed to be.

She brushed the stray hair back from her face, blowing out a harsh breath. There was so much here, and Saylah refused to say anything else until she retrieved this godsdamn lock. Any almost-bonding they'd done on that beach had been negated by the goddess's complete lack of help right now. But some of the things she *had* said that night...

"Love?"

Scarlett shoved back from the table, stretching her arms above her head. "That depends. Are you going to actually use that mighty power today?"

Sorin sent her a dry look as she arched her back to stretch her spine. "That power does not need to be unleashed unless necessary."

She rolled her eyes, unclasping her cloak. It was cold down here, and Saylah refused to let fire near the ancient texts. The little light they had down here was small flames in enchanted globes, but she'd be plenty warm soon enough. "I want to play with that power, Sorin. We need to train with all of it. I cannot believe I'm having to explain this to you."

"Scarlett, there is no need to endanger everyone."

"You do remember a week ago when we killed Hunters with our combined power, right? I'm still alive. Rayner's still alive. We're fine."

Sorin dropped an arm around her shoulders, guiding her to the stone stairwell that would lead up and out of the catacombs. Saylah had impassable wards around the place. Once they reached the main levels of the castle, Scarlett could Travel them out.

"As I have repeatedly told you, it is impossible for me to use the full extent of my power against you. The twin flame bond simply does not allow it. Only if your life is in danger would I be able to fully access it around you."

She sighed. "Yes, yes. I know."

"Did you find anything interesting today?" he asked, passing her a pear she begrudgingly took from him.

This elicited another huff of irritation. "Yes and no. There are entire passages about Chaos that I cannot decipher. Saylah said that is where her power comes from. But if the power of the gods comes from Chaos, wouldn't that mean *all* magic comes from Chaos in some way or another?"

"That sounds reasonable," Sorin agreed. "Anything about the mirror gates?"

"No. How did they come to be? Who put them in every world created? Are they even in every world created? Are there worlds without them?"

"We will figure it out, Love."

"Maybe," she murmured, taking a bite of the pear. "I did read something interesting about the Runic Lands, though."

"Oh?"

Cethin had told them he and Razik had been searching for the Runic Lands for decades but they had never been able to find them. Even when Scarlett went back with them, they couldn't see the strange marks on the ground. Even stranger, the city had again disappeared, as if some glamour kept it hidden from the rest of the world. She'd again had to spill her blood across the marks to get the city to emerge.

"According to the texts, it was the first city in this world," she answered Sorin, climbing the steps. "The being that created this world lived here for a time, and the Runic City was their home."

"Did it say which god or goddess created this world?" Sorin asked.

Scarlett shook her head, taking another bite of the fruit. "No, but that's not the most interesting part," she went on excitedly. "The being that created this world has the power to truly lock it. Something about their essence being so intertwined with the world they created, they have the power to keep others out if they wish. The only exception would be a god or goddess of equal or greater power."

"Are you saying if a First created this world, then they could keep out all others except for the other First gods?"

"If I translated everything right, yes."

"That is interesting," Sorin replied as they neared the top of the stairs.

"If I could connect any of that history back to the mirror gates, that would be great," she grumbled.

Sorin chuckled softly. "It sounds like we have much to look into these next few days."

"It feels utterly pointless right now."

He pulled a door open at the top of the stairwell, waving her through, but when Scarlett reached for his hand to Travel, she found herself backed against the stone wall. He had a hand on her hip, the other was tipping her chin up, and his golden eyes were molten as he leaned in close.

"What are you doing?" she gasped around her surprise, heat flooding her and her stomach dipping.

"Taking a moment. With you," he answered, lowering his mouth to hers. Cloves and honey assaulted her when his tongue dipped between her lips. She curled a hand in his tunic, dragging him closer, somehow remembering she still held a pear in her other hand. The hand on her hip slid down, hoisting her thigh up and allowing him to come impossibly closer.

The pear thudded to the ground.

All thoughts of mirror gates and Chaos, of the lock and the Southern Islands, were gone as Sorin kissed her deeply, lazily. As if they were not running out of time. Not facing an impossible task. Not leading entire continents into war.

When he pulled back, his fingers tangled in her hair and lips swollen and glossy, it was pure love shining in his golden eyes.

A love she would burn the world to ash for.

A love she would save the world for.

A love that promised her the world.

There weren't words that needed to be said, so she didn't speak as she steadied her breathing and then Traveled them to the training arena in the Nightmist Mountains.

They were still staring at each other when they appeared in the center of the ring, and Cyrus whistled low under his breath. "You two sure you don't want to finish whatever this was?"

Sorin's smirk was sinful as he replied, "I will certainly finish this later."

Scarlett's lips lifted coyly, her shadow armor sliding into place. "Perhaps I'll come up with a new use for my tongue, Prince," she chirped as she slowly backed away from him.

His eyes darkened. *I'm holding you to that, Love.*

*Use all that power today, and I'll come up with two,* she purred back.

Starfire flared and her spirit sword appeared in her hand at the same moment she sent flames at Rayner, who she'd sensed appearing behind her a moment before. She whirled, a dagger at his throat when his shield of ashes faded away, and the Ash Rider blinked in surprise.

"Well done, Scarlett," he said after a moment.

She slowly lowered her blade. Rayner had been training her hard on this. They did not know who or what they would face in the Southern Islands. They did not know if Alaric had a seraph with Ash Rider gifts. Perhaps a seraph had the same gifts as Kailia. She wanted to be prepared for all of it. Rayner and Kailia had been ambushing her at random moments for days now.

"I should hope so," she huffed, sliding the dagger back into her belt. "After Kailia knocked me on my ass multiple times, I had better be improving."

Rayner was somewhat careful with her, always catching her before her face hit the ground or she took a hit to the gut. The Avonleyan Queen didn't have such qualms.

"Are we ready?" Cethin asked.

He was there to help Cassius and her utilize their Guardian Bond more. She wished he could keep training her to defend against his draining power—the same magic Alaric had—but he was still replenishing his power after using the last of it to dream walk to her. She had wondered if he would find a Source when the Wards were down and the Fae and Avonleyans would coexist once more. But as Kailia appeared at his side, and he looked at her the same way she and Sorin had been looking at each other moments ago, Scarlett knew he wouldn't.

The next hour was grueling. Their group trained hard with magic and weapons, knowing this was the last time they could do so before they left on their mission. Cassius was in the sky with Tybalt. She was shielding against Sorin's fire, while Cyrus and Rayner were assaulting him with counterattacks. Her world was fire and darkness, ashes and ice. Cethin was barking commands at her, at Sorin, at all of them.

"More, Sorin," she ground out, purposely letting his wild flames get closer. He immediately backed off, as he had been doing the entire time.

"The bond won't let him, Darling," Cyrus panted, appearing at her side and throwing up a shield of flame when Kailia sent an arrow at him. The fire didn't stop the deathstone arrow, but it did slow it enough for Cyrus to catch it in midair before it found its mark.

"I know," she ground out in frustration. She glanced up at the sky, still in awe at seeing a dragon flying around. Tybalt couldn't half-shift like Cassius and Razik could. It was either his human form or his dragon.

And the dragon was magnificent.

Smaller than Ranvir, the spirit animal of Sargon, he was still huge. His charcoal scales seemed to absorb the sunlight as he soared above them. Black wings flapped as dragon fire spewed from his mouth with a roar that forced Cassius to back flap and guard at the same time. Cass would never be able to shift fully into a dragon due to his Witch blood, but Razik could. Scarlett hadn't seen it yet, but she was sure it was just as spectacular.

"We should take a break before—" Cyrus started.

"No," she interrupted. "No breaks."

"Scarlett. I still don't think—"

"We're doing this, Cyrus," she retorted, catching Cethin's eye. Her brother nodded in understanding.

Kailia sent an arrow into the sky. The signal they'd all agreed on as Tybalt turned sharply and began to dive straight for her.

They'd all agreed Sorin needed to lose control. For centuries, he'd had his fire mastered. He was training with his new gifts, sure, but she needed him to be ready faster. She needed *him* to understand what he was capable of now, because if she was reading those scrolls in the catacombs correctly... Well, if she was, neither of them truly knew what they were capable of.

In the Runic Lands, he'd only given in when they were in danger. Even then, he'd waited until she had leashed his power with her shadows. She understood the twin flame bond thing. She truly did.

Which is why there was currently a dragon flying straight for her. Tybalt could protect himself with his dragon fire, and Scarlett had already leashed Sorin's fire once. She could do it again.

Cyrus and Rayner were keeping Cassius busy. Despite knowing the plan, the Guardian Bond would still try to force him to come to her aid. Everything was going to plan.

Except when Kailia appeared directly in front of her, a wicked glint in her amber eyes, as she slipped a band onto Scarlett's wrist before disappearing amidst her ashes.

Scarlett looked down as she felt her starfire thrash in her veins. Her shadow armor vanished. Her fire and ice slipped away to nothing.

And when Tybalt hurled dragon fire in her direction, she was left with only her training and wits, and that did fucking shit against gods-damn dragon fire.

She ducked and rolled out of the way seconds before the fire hit directly where she had been standing. She tried to reach Sorin down their bond, to tell him what was going on, but there was nothing. There was silence in her head. Deathstone killed *everything*. It nullified her Marks. She could feel her power draining, a steady trickle from her soul.

She clawed at the band on her wrist as she ran, but it was stuck. There was no removing it.

"Rayner!" she screamed, ducking when Tybalt swooped low again. Rayner knew about deathstone. He'd know what to do.

But the deafening boom of flames colliding with dragon fire drowned out her scream. She was thrown back by the meeting of those two powers, and the breath was knocked from her lungs as she landed hard on her back. Not only that, she'd landed wrong, and her ankle was screaming in pain.

She was going to kill Kailia for this. She didn't care if the female was her brother's wife or not. She didn't care that the female was a queen.

Coughing, she rolled onto her stomach and pushed herself up onto her hands and knees. A low snarl she felt in her bones had her lifting her head as she tried to suck down air, but the air got caught in her throat.

Sorin was striding towards her, and he looked like a god of fire. There was no other way to describe him. Flames of orange and red and blue wound around him. Glowing embers sparked with every furious step. His golden eyes were pure flame as they zeroed in on her, and there was nothing but primal wrath on his features.

"Sorin," she gasped, trying to push to her feet, but her ankle gave out.

Another roar drew both of their attention to the sky where Tybalt was diving once more, but a wall of flame erupted that had the dragon banking hard to avoid colliding with it.

And then Scarlett was gaping as that wall of flame took on a new shape.

One with a tail and wings and scales of embers.

A fire dragon.

A godsdamn dragon of pure fire was sweeping past, and Sorin was throwing a rope of blue wildfire around its neck before he leapt atop the thing and took off into the sky after Tybalt.

*Shit.*

*Shit. Shit. Shit.*

"Rayner!" she screamed again, and the Ash Rider was there, crouching before her. "Get it off! Get it off!" Scarlett cried, thrusting her arm at him.

His eyes went wide at the band, and he uttered a vicious curse as he tore the deathstone from her wrist. She was already running, ignoring the agony in her ankle. Her shadows shuddered as they broke free, and she immediately had them forming into her shadow dragon beneath her. It cried a roar of its own as it took flight, racing for Sorin, who was gaining on Tybalt with every flap of flaming wings.

*Sorin!* she screamed down their bond. *Sorin! Stop!*

She had seen him like this only one other time, and she barely recalled it. From what Eliza had told her, Scarlett hadn't seen the worst of that time when Talwyn had surprised them in the Fire Court courtyards. Scarlett had broken her arm and acquired cracked ribs, and while Beatrix had healed her just fine, Sorin had been blinded by primal rage at his twin flame being injured. They'd only drawn him out of that state when Briar had put her in his path of destruction as he'd sparred with Eliza on the front grounds.

His power had been grand then. Now? It would be catastrophic.

*Faster,* she urged her magic, but she wasn't going to make it. She was close, but not close enough. She wasn't fast enough to avoid the blast of the impact when dragon fire and Sorin's upgraded flames collided again in the air.

Scarlett was thrown from her shadow dragon, and she hissed a curse, grasping for her magic as she free-fell through the air. But Cassius was there, scooping her out of the sky, and she clung to his neck as he shot to the ground, holding her close. His grip was still tight as he set her on the ground, and she gave a cry as her ankle barked in pain again.

But Sorin had seen her falling, and he'd immediately come after her too. His fire dragon disappeared at the same moment Sorin's feet hit the ground, and he was tugging her from Cassius's grip.

"Are you all right?" he demanded. His voice was a guttural snarl, and his eyes were still flames.

She reached up, cupping his cheek. "I am fine, Sorin. I'm sorry. I am fine."

"You are not fine," he snapped, dropping to a knee to examine her ankle.

"It will heal before we go."

"Their Healer can manage it faster," he said sharply, pushing back to his feet and pulling her into him once again. His heart was beating rapidly beneath her ear, but he was eerily calm as he held her to him.

"Sorin," she whispered tentatively.

"Don't, Scarlett. Not right now."

"We needed to know. *You* needed to know."

"We could have found another way," he retorted.

She didn't move, didn't try to push back from him knowing he needed to feel her against him, but she said, "We don't have time for you to experiment, Sorin. We leave in two days. We will face seraphs and Maraans and who knows what else in the Southern Islands. Better to know now then to be surprised by a godsdamn fire dragon inside the cliffs."

"She has a point," Cassius said.

Scarlett had forgotten he was there. She'd forgotten entirely that they were standing in the middle of a training arena surrounded by others.

"You were all in on this?" Sorin demanded. Scarlett lifted her head to find the flames in his eyes had banked some. Now they just glowed like hot coals.

"Like she said, you needed to know," Cyrus said, coming up beside Cassius. "If this had been someone else, you'd have done the same thing, and you know it."

"Not like this," he snarled, his grip on her tightening involuntarily. "Not with her in the mix."

"It was the only way to draw it out," Cethin said.

Her brother's voice reminded her—

"What the fuck was that?" Scarlett spat, spinning to face Kailia.

The Avonleyan Queen tilted her head, her bow and quiver slung across her back. "You said to do whatever it took. I simply sped up the process."

"With godsdamn deathstone? Sorin and Tybalt could have been seriously hurt, or worse," Scarlett cried.

"Were the desired results not achieved?" Kailia asked with a shrug.

At Sorin's growl, Cethin was stepping in front of Kailia. "How about we all head back and take some time? I can send Niara to look at your ankle, Scarlett."

When no one answered, Scarlett Traveled with Sorin, leaving Cassius to worry about Cyrus. Scarlett wasn't even sure her feet had landed on the ornate rug before Sorin was scooping her up and setting her on the bed. Then he dropped down before her to gently remove her boots. She hissed as he pulled off the one on her sore ankle, and his mouth tightened.

A knock on their chamber door had them both looking up in confusion. Sorin pushed back to his feet and strode to the door, stepping aside when he found Rayner.

"What is it?" Sorin asked tightly, already back at her side and removing her weapons for her. She let him. Let him take care of her in whatever way he wanted, knowing it was pure instinct to do so right now.

"I wanted to…" Rayner let out a sharp breath, carving his hand through his hair. Scarlett had never seen him so…unsure. "Don't be too upset with Kailia," he finally said.

Scarlett's brows shot up, and Sorin went preternaturally still.

"Repeat that?" Sorin said in a voice that made Scarlett far too nervous. "Because she used deathstone against your *queen*, Rayner."

"I know what she did, Sorin," Rayner said. "She was acting on our queen's behalf."

"I did not tell her to use deathstone," Scarlett admonished.

"No, but you did say we needed to do whatever it took to get his magic to surface, and that's how things were done beneath the cliffs," Rayner countered sharply.

Sorin and Scarlett glanced at each other. Rayner rarely spoke of his time on the Southern Islands.

"When they were trying to force gifts to emerge, they used whatever means necessary. And those of us trained for killing purposes? Our training was grueling. Deathstone was likely used against her, and she was likely forced to use it against others. She knew it would accomplish what you wanted," he continued.

"Did you know her?" Scarlett asked. "Before we came here I mean?"

"No," he answered, striding for the door. "But I know what she faced beneath those cliffs, and I know how she was trained there. This would have seemed mild compared to that."

As Rayner was walking out the door, Niara was coming in, a small satchel in her hand. "Cethin asked me to stop by," she said, attention already fixing on Scarlett's ankle, as though she could sense the discomfort. "May I?"

"Of course," Scarlett said, scooting back on the bed. Sorin was hovering like the mother hen he was as Niara gently laid a hand on her ankle, faint light flaring. "Thank you again for everything you did for Eliza," Scarlett said around a wince as the Healer rotated her ankle.

"I am glad I could be of service," Niara said. "This is a deep sprain. Your own magic will heal it in a day or so, but I assume that is undesirable?"

Scarlett nodded. "We leave in two days' time."

Niara stood, reaching into her satchel and producing a tonic. "Take this. It will speed the healing, but will also make you sleep."

She tensed. "For how long?"

"Likely into the evening."

That wouldn't be so bad. The mention of taking a tonic to make her sleep had memories surging of a tonic that had made her sleep for days while forcing her magic to slumber. It had not even been a year ago, but felt like another lifetime.

"Thank you," Sorin was saying as he escorted Niara out. She had already downed the tonic and was settling in among the pillows when he returned to her side.

"You are not even going to change?" he asked, a brow arching.

She was asleep before she could answer.

When she did wake hours later, it was indeed well into the evening. There were candles burning throughout their room, and she had shifted onto her side at some point. Sorin was propped against the headboard beside her, one knee bent and a book balanced on it. She studied him as he studied the text, referring every once in a while to what she assumed were notes set off to the side. She could see the book was in Avonleyan, and while he was steadily becoming more proficient, he still struggled to translate some of it.

Shifting a bit, she tucked her hand beneath her cheek, drawing his attention to her. He immediately set the book aside. "How are you feeling?"

"Fine."

"Your ankle?"

She rotated it a few times beneath the blanket he'd draped over her. It was a little stiff, but nothing like the agony of earlier.

"Fine," she replied again with a small shrug. He huffed a chuckle and reached for his book. "What are you reading about?"

"I am trying to find information about this name Beatrix told me before she Faded."

She perked up at that. "Did you come across it?"

"No," he grumbled. "But it has been guarded for centuries. I did not think it would be easy to find."

"True," she murmured. After several moments of silence, she said, "You created a fire dragon today."

Sorin kept his gaze on the text, but his lips lifted into a small smile. "I did."

"You couldn't have come up with something more creative? I already did the shadow dragon thing."

He was tossing the ancient book aside and moving atop her in the next blink. "You and this godsdamn tongue today," he murmured into her neck as his lips began making their way down her throat.

She arched into him the moment his hand slipped beneath her tunic, warm, calloused fingers dragging along her ribs. "Sorin," she rasped, one of her hands sliding into his hair. "We should eat."

He glanced up at her from beneath thick lashes, his golden eyes nearly glowing once more. "I intend to."

"Sorin!" she admonished around another rough laugh as he tugged at the ties on her tunic. She was about to argue that they truly did need to eat so she could draw from him and refill her reserves, and then he could sleep and refill his own. But the heat coursing through her at the moment drove all those thoughts from her mind, and it took her a moment to realize the heat wasn't entirely from want.

Sorin's flames were slowly licking along her flesh, starting at her toes, moving up her legs, and across her torso, burning away her pants and tunic.

"Stop burning all my clothing," she chided breathlessly. "I am going to have nothing left to wear soon."

"Perhaps that is the plan, Love," he rumbled against her skin as he kissed along her navel.

"Then I want to hear no more complaints when I attend meetings in nothing but a robe."

He paused, glancing up at her. "Good point."

She gave him a taunting smirk. Which he returned before nipping along her inner thigh. His gaze had dipped between her legs where he watched as his thumb slid across her center. Liquid fire shot through her, and her hips bucked forward of their own accord. His eyes lifted to hers, and he held her stare as his tongue swept out and licked the pad of the same thumb, a low groan escaping him.

And then starfire was flaring, burning his clothing away without nearly the same sensual flare he had used. He chuckled darkly when Scarlett surged forward, wrapping her arms around his neck and kissing him deeply. His hand came up to cradle the back of her head, fingers digging into the strands to hold her close to him, to keep her at his mouth when he sent his flames licking along her flesh again. Her gasp became a moan as she let her shadows out to tangle with the fire, and then it was Sorin's turn to groan as his grip around her waist turned bruising.

"Let go," she murmured onto his mouth. "Your power will not hurt me. You've said it yourself. It can't. We are designed that way. For each other." She pulled back just enough to look into his eyes. "You speak to me of fate and destiny? *You* are the only fate I will ever accept."

Sorin slid his lips along her jaw before she felt his canines drag along her throat. And then she was swallowing another gasp of surprise as he flipped them and thrust into her with one hard, fast movement. Fire danced across her stomach and up around her breasts. Hot. She was hot and wanting, and gods, she needed him to—Fuck, she just needed him.

She lifted her hips, grinding against him as he bent down and took one of her peaked nipples into his mouth, his fire flitting among the strands of his hair. He reached down, hooking one of her legs around his waist as he sank in impossibly deeper.

"Fuck," Scarlett moaned when he sent another wave of flames over her. Sorin huffed another dark laugh that had her impatience tipping over the edge. "Damnit, Sorin. *Move. Please.*"

He sat back then, hands grasping her hips and tilting them up the smallest amount to allow him to drag himself slowly out before he thrust back into her hard.

"Thank the gods," Scarlett gasped when he did it again.

"Not the gods, Love," he growled, tilting her hips up even more and slamming into her again.

She sent her shadows raking down his chest, his arms, his back. Felt him arch into her, hitting that spot that made her see stars. He spit out a curse when she sank those shadows into his flames, and then sent her starfire to mingle with the shadowfire. Reaching up, she curled her hand around his neck to haul herself up to him. She coiled a tendril of starfire around his ear and heard him suck in a ragged breath as she whispered, "*We* are the gods now, Sorin."

She felt his growl in her soul as he hauled her up and shifted beneath her so she was in his lap. He yanked her back down onto him, another sharp gasp forced from her lungs. Her hands were on his shoulder, nails leaving indents in his flesh. His hand slid up her spine, embers left in its wake as he wound his fingers into the length of her hair and pulled, forcing her head back to look into his eyes. She found pure lust. Primal desire and need.

She took over the movements as his other hand snaked around her belly and down to play with those nerves. There was no rhythm. There was no rhyme or reason to their push and pull, not as he drove her to the edge of pleasure with his thumb on her center, his tongue in her mouth, and his cock buried deep inside of her. Their magic swirled around them— fire and shadows, light and dark. It was power she had never felt before. It was them. Fierce and raw and wild.

And when release slammed into her, when she tipped her head back in pure pleasure, Sorin followed, hauling her into his chest and clutching her tightly as his movements slowed.

Their breathing was erratic as they clung to each other, clung to this moment. Sorin eventually pulled back, tenderly brushing his lips along her brow, her temple, her mouth before there was a burst of flame and a dagger appeared in his hand. They said nothing as he cut across the Source Mark, and she held out her palm for the same. He only pulled her back to his chest, letting his magic feed hers. The same way he fed her body. The same way he fed her soul.

And later, when her power was brimming and after they had eaten with their family, when Sorin was deep in sleep restoring his own power reserves, Scarlett slipped from their bed yet again. She pulled on pants and a loose tunic, along with some silk slippers, before she slipped from their rooms.

She made her way up one level of the castle, to the entire floor that was Cethin and Kailia's. When she rounded a corner that would take her to the main doors of their suite, a swirl of ashes and smoke appeared before her, just as she'd known it would.

Kailia stood there, amber eyes narrowed and an arrow nocked loosely in her bow. "What are you doing here?"

"Looking for you, actually," Scarlett said. Then she jerked her chin at the arrow. "No need for that. I've had enough deathstone for one day, thank you."

Kailia eyed her, leaving the arrow in place. The female certainly didn't trust easily, but that was to be expected, she supposed, given where she was raised.

"I came to see if you wanted to come with us in two days."

At that, the queen jerked back a step. "No. I will never step foot there again."

Scarlett held her palms up placatingly. "I can understand that, but our plans have changed slightly, and I think... I think you may just want to be part of them."

Slowly, Kailia removed the arrow from the bowstring, and it disappeared among a swirl of ashes. She looped the bow across her back as she met Scarlett's gaze and said, "I'm listening."

# CHAPTER 27
## SCARLETT

"There are seraphs everywhere," Rayner said before he'd fully stepped from his ashes. "In the skies. Around the perimeter."

That was fine. Not ideal but fine. They'd expected as much. Scarlett knew it had been too much to hope for anything else.

"And the entrance?" Sorin asked, arms crossed as he surveyed the dense foliage around them.

"Easily a unit of forty," Rayner answered, grey eyes swirling. The Ash Rider was tense. Simply being here put him on an edge that Scarlett rarely saw from him. Kailia was in the same state. The Avonleyan Queen was rigid, her grip on her bow so tight her knuckles were white. She always wore a black gown, but today she was clad in tight fitting black pants and a black tunic. She had fighting leathers in place, a quiver at her back, and Scarlett was fairly certain the dagger in her belt was a deathstone blade that she would be asking about if they all survived this day.

"Kailia?" Scarlett ventured tentatively.

Amber eyes snapped to her. "I can take care of a good number of them from a ways back, but once the initial surprise wears off, it will be more difficult."

"That's not what I was asking," Scarlett said softly. "You know you do not have to do this, right?"

"I am aware of my freedom," she answered, eyes sliding back toward the cliffs.

Scarlett was fairly certain that if Cethin had had any semblance of his full power, she would have found her shadows locked in a battle against his darkness when he learned she had approached Kailia about coming with them.

"She will never breathe the air of those islands again. I promised her that." Cethin had snarled, advancing on Scarlett when she met with him the morning after she'd spoken with Kailia.

"Stop right there, Cethin Sutara," Scarlett had said sharply, holding up a hand. "If you make me tap into my power right now, I swear to Arius, I will make you regret it. It will fuck up everything."

"I cannot believe you went behind my back and asked her to do this," Cethin had said, his fists clenched at his sides.

"I asked her to do nothing," Scarlett had retorted. "She deserves the opportunity to be part of this. Have you ever thought that maybe she *needs* to do this?"

"I cannot go with her," he had all but roared at her. "Do you have any idea how hard it is to have to sit back and watch all of you go and fight while I can do nothing? How do I protect her from across the fucking sea?"

"You trust she can do this. She is one of the fiercest females I have ever met. I have watched her fight the Hunters, Cethin. You think she cannot do this?"

"You have no idea what she was forced to do beneath those cliffs, Scarlett. What happens if being there triggers something, and she freezes? What happens if she is captured by Alaric again? Answer me that," he'd returned, taking another single step towards her. "If anything happens to her—"

"It won't," she'd interrupted. "Trust your wife, Cethin."

"I trust Kailia with everything I am. It is everyone else I have no faith in," he'd said before he'd turned and stormed out of the room.

"You are sure about this?" Scarlett asked Kailia now, finally letting her shadows out to breathe as they slithered over her witchsuit to form her shadow armor.

"I would not have come if I was not sure," Kailia replied. She looked at Rayner. "You control the wards now. Where do we enter?"

"There is a hidden balcony on the side facing the sea," he answered. "But we will need to climb."

Scarlett still did not understand why he could not just let them pass since the wards around the cliffs were now tied to him, but after he'd explained for the third time it was simply the magic of the wards, she'd given up. They would Travel to the base of the cliffs and then climb. They'd debated flying in, but they were hoping not to be detected until they were inside. After that…

Well, they'd survive this part first and then worry about the rest. Cassius and Cyrus would stay outside to keep watch and discreetly take down seraphs when possible, while she and Sorin went in with Rayner and Kailia.

Scarlett closed her eyes, breathing deep. She rolled her shoulders back, stretching her neck from side-to-side, and when she reopened her eyes, she found everyone looking at her, waiting for instruction.

"Let's start a fire," she purred darkly.

Cassius Traveled Cyrus, while she grabbed Sorin's hand and did the same. Rayner and Kailia moved among their ashes and smoke. It took nearly three hours to reach the hidden balcony, and it would have taken longer if Cyrus and Sorin hadn't used their fire gifts to help keep everyone dry. This included their hands and boots to prevent them from slipping on the cliff-side that was drenched with spray from the sea. The sun hadn't reached this side of the cliffs yet, so they were already partially concealed. Scarlett used her shadows to hide them even more.

Rayner was helping Kailia over the ledge, and they all took a moment to catch their breath and regroup. No one spoke, and she nodded to Rayner after a moment. Ashes spilled from his hands, seeping under the glass doors as they all stuck to the shadows.

"Two inside," Rayner said in his low tenor.

"Does the Reaper get them or Death's Maiden?" Scarlett asked with a wicked grin.

Rayner's own smile was just as dark. "You can watch, your Majesty."

Scarlett stuck her tongue out at him. Cyrus and Cassius moved forward to check the doors, and when they found them locked, Cyrus used his fire to melt the handles.

"Be careful, Seastar," Cass said as the rest of them prepared to enter.

She winked at him. "You know better, Cass."

He sighed. "I do. See you when this is over."

She nodded again, and the two pulled open the doors. Rayner was already moving among his smoke, and Scarlett darted inside to see him standing between two seraphs. His hands were deep in their chests, and when he pulled them back, he held a heart in one hand and a lung in the other.

"How do you do that?" she demanded, the seraphs dropping to the ground before they could utter a sound.

The organs faded to ash in his palms, and Rayner bent to wipe the blood from his hands on some of their clothing. He shrugged. "The same way you make your shadow pets."

"They are not shadow pets," she scoffed. "But are you saying I could rip out—"

"No. You couldn't," he interrupted. "This way."

Rayner strode towards what appeared to be a closet, and Scarlett looked over her shoulder. Kailia was idly wandering around the large suite. Every once in a while, she'd run her hand along a surface or the wall, ashes left behind. She glanced at Sorin, who nodded, and Scarlett followed after Rayner.

The Ash Rider was swiping his bloody palm along a wall, and Scarlett stood back as a doorway appeared. His ashes and her shadows speared into the dark passageway, seeking any sign of life, and when they found none, Rayner took the first step inside.

Sorin and Kailia appeared behind them as Scarlett followed Rayner into the stairwell, and Sorin sent small flames into the air to light their path. It was a winding staircase with landings that branched off every once in a while, and Rayner eventually took one.

Wooden doors lined the stone corridor. Rayner walked past them all. Scarlett couldn't help but wonder how many times he had done this. How many times had he traversed these halls? She knew the bare minimum of Rayner's history, but his knowledge of these cliffs had been invaluable to their planning.

At the end of the hall were two heavy stone doors etched with intricate carvings. While Rayner sent ashes to the other side before they entered, Scarlett traced along one of the carvings. It was the same language she'd been struggling to decipher in the Elshira catacombs.

"Do you know of it?" Rayner asked, the first words any of them had spoken since entering the hidden stairs.

"I'm trying to, but no," Scarlett answered. "You?"

Rayner shook his head. "Ready?"

She nodded, looking back at Sorin and Kailia. "Were you ever in here?"

"No," Kailia answered. She offered nothing else. Scarlett couldn't blame her.

Rayner pushed open the doors, and when Scarlett stepped through them, she felt the wards bending as Rayner allowed them passage. Sorin sent more flames into the air to light up the space, and they all just…stopped. Tables of papers and potion supplies littered with dust took up most of the space. The room smelled musty and stale.

"When was the last time someone was in here?" Scarlett mused aloud, stepping further into the room.

"The day I killed Moranna," Rayner answered. "Do you need anything else before Kailia and I go to the other levels?"

"I don't think so," Scarlett said, watching the dust filter through the rays of the soft glow of the room. She glanced back at Rayner. "Send a message if you need us. Otherwise, we'll see you outside as planned. Make sure you have enough magic left to travel from here if necessary."

"Be mindful of what you touch," Rayner said. "She could have enchanted anything."

When the heavy doors had closed behind them, Scarlett faced the apothecary room once more, planting her hands on her hips. She had no idea what she was looking for with this lock, but apparently this was the best place to start looking. Rayner had said that if the Baroness had wanted to hide something, it would most likely be here. According to Saylah, Moranna had also been trying to experiment with it, so having it nearby in her workroom seemed logical.

"I still find it hard to believe Saylah has no insight as to what this lock looks like," Sorin said, moving deeper into the room with her.

Scarlett hummed in agreement. "Apparently, it has taken on different forms since its creation."

They moved among the tables, Scarlett scanning the items as they went. Empty vials. Empty cauldrons. Books. Some closed, some lying open. She paused and blew the dust off one, studying the page. A book on herbs and plants. She moved to another, her head tilting as she studied it.

Then she flipped the book closed and sent it to a pocket realm.

"What are you doing?" Sorin asked, his tone wary.

"It seems silly to leave such interesting reading material just lying around," Scarlett quipped, sending another book off in a puff of shadows.

"You are going to steal from the Baroness?"

"A *dead* Baroness," Scarlett corrected. "And isn't that what we are already here to do?"

There was a long pause before, "I suppose you are right."

She picked up a vial, holding it up to the flame above her. A reddish-gold liquid swirled inside of it.

"Stop touching everything," Sorin said, snatching it out of her hand and placing it back on the table. "You heard what Rayner said. The last thing we need right now is to deal with a curse of some sort. Or for you to summon some ancient city."

She stuck out her tongue at him, continuing to browse the tables and shelves. One cauldron had residue in it, as though the potion inside had long since evaporated. Another made her wrinkle her nose when she found solidified brown sludge inside.

"Do you remember what I said the other night? About us being gods?" she asked after several minutes of silent searching had passed.

Sorin looked over at her from across the room where he was rifling through a cupboard. "Of course I remember that."

"Would you want to be one? If you could?"

He turned back to the cupboard, pulling out small drawers and shoving them shut again. "What would I be the god of in this scenario?" he teased.

"Hmm. Since fire is already taken by Anala, I suppose you'd have to be the god of mother hens," she retorted, sending another book to the pocket realm.

He threw her a dry look over his shoulder. "And what would you be? The goddess of wicked tongues?"

"You would certainly benefit from such a thing. Just think of the possibilities," she sighed wistfully.

He barked a laugh, returning to his searching. "Let's focus on getting out of here today, then we can discuss your tongue and its various possibilities all you'd like."

She rolled her eyes. "Fine. Help me push some tables back."

Carefully, they slid several tables off to the side until she had a decent-sized space in the center of the room. She pulled a dagger and pricked her finger before crouching down and beginning to draw in the dust and dirt covered floor. It was a locating Mark, but one she had been working on altering in small ways based on the differing texts she'd read and notes in the Sorceress's spell book.

When it was done, she stood back, making sure it was perfect. Sorin had been quiet while she'd worked, flipping through more papers and books. She was fairly certain he'd sent a few to a pocket realm of his own.

"Are you ready?" she asked Sorin, shaking out her hands to ease some nerves.

"Not even remotely," he replied, looping an arm around her waist and leaning in to kiss her soundly.

She smiled up at him when he pulled back. "What's the worst that could happen, right?"

Golden eyes narrowed. "Let's get this over with."

He stepped back as she raised her hands before her. Shadows and starfire in one palm. Fire and ice in the other.

Powers of the gods and of the Fae. All in one vessel.

That's what Saylah had said. Why it had to be Scarlett and no one else. One born of the gods who could harness the elements of the Fae.

She brought her hands side-by-side, letting the powers merge, and then she sent them to the Mark on the floor where her blood was still drying. It flared so brightly that Sorin was dragging her back, tucking her head into his chest to shield her eyes.

After a moment, she peeked out, and then she sighed. "I don't think it worked."

"It did something," Sorin said, his hand still resting protectively on her back. "Magic does not react like that for nothing."

She stepped closer to the Mark once more. It was still glowing faintly. She reached for it, her fingers nearly touching her blood when she heard it. A faint chiming? No. A lilted whispering? It was constantly changing.

Her head cocked to the side. "Do you hear that?"

"Hear what?"

"That..."

She didn't know how to describe it. It wasn't a song, although it reminded her of music. It was a beckoning of her soul.

"Is someone approaching?" Sorin asked, hand on a sword and eyes darting to the door.

"No, it's not—"

It had gotten a touch louder when she'd pushed to her feet. The lilting had become a humming so deep it felt as though her very essence was vibrating.

"Scarlett, what is wrong?" Sorin demanded, tense and worried.

She waved a hand to shush him, taking a step forward. The humming became a lulling melody, then the sound of waves lapping at the shore. She took another step, then another. When she moved to the left, the sound lessened, fading away.

So she followed it, that ever-changing sound she could barely hear. She let it guide her across the expanse of the room, the sound fading if she veered too far off course. She followed it to a rack full of instruments, scales, and other contraptions. Dragging her fingers along the various shelves, the sound became a lover's caress.

In the center of a shelf was a model of some sort. Scarlett didn't have the faintest idea what it was supposed to be depicting, but next to it? She knew in the depths of her being what that was.

It was a sphere as dark as deathstone. Symbols and glyphs were fading in and out, moving across the surface in varying colors. Symbols that matched those on the door and those in the Runic Lands.

"Sorin?"

Her voice sounded odd. Mesmerized. Entranced.

"I see it, Love."

He was right beside her, and she hadn't even noticed.

Her hand lifted, reaching towards it, but Sorin brushed it aside.

"If anyone is going to get cursed by the thing, it'll be me," he muttered, hand closing around the sphere before Scarlett could argue.

The moment he came in contact with it, the symbols faded away. He was left holding an ordinary light grey orb, nothing more than a weight to hold papers in place.

"Anything?" Scarlett asked, eyes fixed on the sphere.

"No, but that does not ease my worry of what will happen when you touch it."

"It's why we're here, right?" she said, holding out her hand.

"You believe this is it?"

"Even if it's not, it's clearly something important." She saw his fingers tighten around the orb. "It has to be me, Sorin," she said softly, extending her hand. "It's always had to be me. Fate and all that nonsense, right?"

He huffed a harsh laugh before his other hand came to her chin, tilting her head back. "All the way through the darkness, Love."

He set the orb in her palm as he spoke. They both sucked in a sharp breath.

And nothing happened.

The sphere remained an inanimate object held between them.

"You have to let go, Sorin."

"I know, Love," he replied, his other palm sliding to cup her cheek. "But I also know that this is about to set so many things into motion."

"The end," she whispered. "It sets the end of all this into motion."

His thumb swiped across her cheek before he inhaled another deep breath and stepped back from her. The moment his fingers fell from the orb, the glyphs reappeared, brighter than stars. The sphere became warm in her hand, and the entire thing darkened back to the darkness of deathstone. Shadows seemed to swarm among the glyphs, and she could see… She didn't know what she was seeing in its depths. Whatever it was, it was moving and shifting too fast for her to decipher.

"How do you feel?" Sorin asked tentatively.

"Fine," she said after a moment. "I feel fine."

"You are sure this is the lock?"

"Sure as I can be," Scarlett said. "Let's go. Rayner and Kailia must be almost done by now."

Scarlett took one last look around the apothecary room, making sure they hadn't overlooked anything. There would be no second chances.

When they were both satisfied after sending a few more books and papers to a pocket realm, they stepped from the room, the heavy doors thudding shut behind them. Scarlett had tried to send the orb to a pocket realm, but it wouldn't go. Her shadows couldn't take it, nor her starfire. Her Fae gifts couldn't touch it, and none of her pockets on the tight-fitting witchsuit were large enough to hold it. So she was left clutching it tightly in one hand, which wasn't an easy task. It fit easily in Sorin's large palm, but it was awkward in her smaller one.

Sorin grabbed her other hand, leading her down the stairs once more. This was the way Rayner had directed them to go. He'd told them there would be a hidden door at the bottom that would lead to a chamber. From that chamber, they could follow a small stream out of the cliffs without having to use the main entrance...assuming the boats there weren't rotted away to nothing from disuse.

When they reached the bottom, Sorin sliced his palm, dragging it along the stone wall until it hit the enchanted doorway. They rushed through it, heading straight to the dock where several small boats were indeed tied off. They didn't have time to take in the chamber. Not if everyone had completed their tasks. Finding the lock was the least dangerous part of their mission here.

Sorin was inspecting the boats to see which one was safest when a voice had them both whirling.

"Sorin? Scarlett?"

Sorin had flames igniting the chamber in the next breath. It was cavernous and dank, some of the walls covered in moss. Not at all the pristine cleanliness of the rest of the cliffs. Cells lined an entire wall, all empty except for one.

One that contained a Water Prince.

"Briar?" Sorin said in shock, rushing to the cell, Scarlett on his heels. "What are you doing here?"

"I do not know. I was being kept in Earth Court cells until a few nights ago. Alaric showed up and brought me here," Briar answered. "How is Ashtine?"

"She is with the Witches," Scarlett answered, studying the bars. They were shirastone, and the same was on Briar's wrists.

"That is not what I asked you."

She met his icy blue eyes. "I know." She stepped forward, starfire flaring and melting the lock of shirastone. The door creaked open. "You are here because of me."

"What?" Briar asked, stepping out of the cell. Scarlett was already reaching for the shackles, starfire flaring once more before they fell away too.

"I may have sent a coded message to the Shifters that got intercepted," Scarlett said, a small smile on her lips as two daggers of ice appeared in Briar's hands.

"To have me brought here?"

"Something along those lines," Scarlett said. "However, I was not expecting to stumble upon you like this. Alaric is here, then?"

"I do not know," Briar answered, falling into step beside them as they headed back to the dock. "Some seraphs brought me here. I have not seen anyone in three days."

"Food?" Sorin asked tightly. Briar shook his head, which had a curse flying from the Fire Prince's mouth. "How are your reserves?"

"Fine," Briar said. "I have not been able to use them in weeks."

"Good. Then you can freeze this stream. These won't keep a child afloat, let alone the three of us."

Minutes later, they were moving carefully along the ice, Sorin gripping her arm while she clutched the lock to her chest should she slip and fall. They put the fire out when they approached a tunnel, not wanting to alert anyone to their presence on the outside. If things had gone well, most of the seraphs were inside the cliffs searching for them now. If not…

But she knew things were going far too smoothly. Briar being here confirmed that Alaric had indeed intercepted the "message" she'd sent to their allies in Siofra asking them to be prepared to house them should things go terribly wrong after she retrieved something of value. She knew Alaric would not leave Briar behind. The Fae Prince was bargaining power, and the Assassin Lord knew she valued the prince as one of her own. She had been prepared to feign a bargain with him to see Briar released. Finding him alone was pure luck, but such good fortune never came for free.

Sorin was tugging her to a stop as they neared the cave mouth. "There are others out there."

She sent her shadows creeping along, staying close to the cave walls, but they weren't like Rayner's ashes. His magic could somehow sense *what* was there. All she could feel was life. It could be Rayner and Kailia as planned. It could be others.

She turned to Briar, speaking low and quick. "Once we are outside the wards of the cliffs, you need to go. Create a water portal and go to the High Witch's Keep. Ashtine is there with Talwyn. She is not well, Briar. She needs you."

"Ashtine is with *Talwyn*," Briar repeated.

"She sides with us now. She is how Sorin's power was returned. They can fill you in, but we are not your worry at the moment. Getting to Ashtine is."

"But if I can help—"

"Go to her, Briar," Scarlett interrupted. "Before it is too late."

"We will send word when it is safe to do so, but Talwyn and Ashtine know much of our plans," Sorin said, clapping a hand on his friend's shoulder. Scarlett shifted as she glanced back to the cave mouth and the bit of daylight she could see shining through. They had agreed not to tell Briar of Sawyer. Not here. His focus needed to be on getting to Ashtine, but she felt like a shit friend for keeping the information from him. He could grieve when he got to safety, though. He could have the time he deserved to mourn his brother, and he could be with Ashtine after being separated from her for so long.

She looked up at Sorin as he readjusted his grip on her arm. "We stick to the plan. No matter who is on the outside of these walls," she said.

"Scarlett—"

"We stick to the plan, Sorin," she interrupted. "Make sure Briar gets through a portal."

Sorin did not argue further. Only gently tugged her forward. She encased the lock in starfire, freezing it around the orb before adding a layer of shadows too. They kept their footfalls quiet on the ice, letting their eyes slowly adjust to the daylight as they neared the cave entrance.

When they finally emerged enough to see properly, they found no one on the ground, but there were at least twenty-five seraphs in the sky. Rayner and Kailia were nowhere in sight, and neither were Cyrus and Cassius. Either something had gone very wrong or very right. The seraphs hadn't appeared to notice them yet, but the moment Briar opened a water portal, the sound of rushing water would surely alert them.

She gave the Water Prince a sad smile before she jerked her chin. He hesitated for the briefest of moments, but then she heard the portal.

And so did the seraphs.

Five were diving for Briar in the next breath, but Sorin had a wall of fire erupting to the sky while Scarlett worked to maintain the frozen water below their feet.

"Go!" she screamed at Briar, her shadows taking shape behind her. Giant eagles of shadows that met more seraphs in the sky as she and Sorin ran in the opposite direction from Briar. Her feet slid out from beneath her as she ran. She could do nothing to catch herself while she clutched at the lock, but Sorin had a band of fire setting her upright before she hit the ice.

"Keep the lock safe, and do not touch your power again," Sorin growled at her.

And as Sorin erupted with power, she knew she hadn't been too far off that night. Saylah had said she may as well be a god in this world, and Scarlett was staring at another. He may as well have been flames himself with the way the fire moved with him. He kept a wall of flame around her, while he sent fire into the sky. The seraphs that made it to the ground met his short swords wrapped in wildfire. And this? This was the general who had trained her in Baylorin. This was the Fire Prince that made his Court feared. This was what she'd needed him to know he could harness.

He moved faster than Scarlett could track. Whips of fire wrapped around wings and throats, taking seraphs to their knees before his blades went through their chests. He left the bodies burning in his wake as embers trailed behind him. A few of the seraphs, those who also had fire gifts, made it to him. She felt each hit Sorin took, her grip on the lock tightening as she forced herself to stay put. She couldn't touch her magic. Not yet.

Until her name being bellowed from the sky changed everything.

Cassius was there, diving for her. Panic was clear on his face, even from this far away. Before she could argue, he was scooping her off the ground and hauling her up.

"No!" she cried. "Go back! We can't leave him there!"

"Scarlett, Alaric is here," Cassius hissed.

"I know! We're coming! Go back! Now!" she commanded, trying to wrestle out of his hold without dropping the lock.

"He has Cyrus and Kailia atop the cliffs, Scarlett," Cassius snarled.

She went utterly still. Because Sorin was fighting alone, but Alaric had Cyrus and Kailia. And she had the one thing that would convince him to let them go.

*Sorin…*

*What is going on?* he demanded down the bond. He was breathless, even in her mind.

*Alaric has Cyrus and Kailia atop the cliffs.*

There was a long pause where he said nothing, and then, *I will come for you.*

She felt him take another hit to his side, a piercing, sharp strike that had her screaming his name as Cassius continued to haul her higher up the cliff-side.

*Listen to me, Scarlett,* came a snarled order down the bond. *I will come for you. Do you understand? We follow the plan. Go do what needs to be done, and I will come for you.*

*I love you.*

*All the way through the darkness. He does not own you, Scarlett. Remember who gets to consume you. It is not him.*

Cassius must have felt the shift in her demeanor, because his bruising grip on her lessened as he landed on the hidden balcony where Rayner was waiting. Ashes were drifting around him, and his eyes were moving mildly, not the violent swirl they usually were.

"Do you have enough left to get out?" she asked.

Rayner nodded, eyeing her closely. "Where is Sorin?"

"He will come. He's following the plan. Briar got out."

His brows rose. "You found him?"

She nodded. "Tell me what is happening."

"Cyrus and I went to the top when we got Rayner's signal," Cassius said. "But Alaric somehow knew we were coming. They had a trap set for Rayner, but they caught Kailia instead. And Cyrus…" He clenched his jaw, a muscle ticking. "He shoved me out of the way and took an arrow to the shoulder. Whatever it was, it's stifling his magic."

"And he demanded to speak with me?" Scarlett asked, tossing the lock to Rayner as she allowed shadows to coat her hands like gloves. They seemed to shudder at finally being fully let out, and she gritted her teeth with the effort of holding them back.

*Just a little longer.*

"Keep that hidden," she said to Rayner, the lock a lifeless grey sphere once more. "I do not care who falls today. I do not care if everyone lies dead around us. I do not care if Alaric has me and does not release me. Keep it hidden and get it out of here. Take it to Cethin and no one else."

His eyes went wide. "Scarlett—"

She shook her head. "I would tell you to leave now, but he will be suspicious if you do not appear with me."

"And Sorin?" Rayner asked.

She sucked in a sharp breath, her chest tightening. "He will find his way to us."

Lifting her palm, shadows swirled again, forming a sphere she encased in ice. Just like the shield she had formed around the lock. She'd let her magic study it, learn every detail of the thing.

And now her magic formed a perfect replica in her hand.

"Everything else is ready? You and Kailia accomplished the task? Most seraphs are inside the cliffs?" she asked as smoke and ashes thickened around Rayner to hide the real lock.

"Yes, but if we are atop the cliffs, we cannot go through with this, Scarlett."

"So we will not be atop them when the time comes," she replied, more shadows sliding into place along her body. "Stay on guard. Keep your weapons out. Travel us up, Cass."

Cassius grabbed her outstretched hand, his other hand clamping onto Rayner's shoulder. When they stepped from the air, her shoulders were back, her chin high, and her shadow panthers were stalking along at her side.

Before Alaric had a chance to open his godsdamn mouth, two of his seraphs were burning with starfire, their screams echoing in the air.

Her former master stared at her impassively, his lips pursing the smallest amount. His dark hair was tied back at the nape of his neck, cloak billowing behind him in the breeze. "You always did throw a tantrum when things did not go your way."

Scarlett's gaze went to Kailia first. She was huddled with her knees drawn to her chest. Her hands and feet were bound in what Scarlett was sure was nightstone. It had to be to keep her from moving among her ashes. Cyrus still had an arrow embedded in his shoulder, blood steadily streaming from it. She could see it on his leathers, his tunic, dripping to the ground where he was on his knees. A seraph stood behind him, a sword in hand.

"Release them. Now," Scarlett gritted out.

And even Alaric had the good sense to pause at her dark tone.

"Why would I do that when you have reneged on our agreement, my Wraith?" he asked, taking a single step towards her. "I am told my Water Prince is no longer in my possession."

"I am simply following the example of my benevolent former master," she retorted. Then she let starfire flare in her eyes. "How *dare* you come after Ashtine and her babes."

"Oh, I *dare*, Scarlett Monrhoe, because you sent me back a false Fae Queen," Alaric spat, taking a few more steps towards her. "You thought you could play me, and there would be no consequences?" He clicked his tongue in disappointment. "You know there are always consequences for disobedience."

Cassius and Rayner stepped closer to her, a force of power at her back, and her panthers snarled a warning.

Alaric simply gave her a small smile. Cassius went to his knees with a curse.

"Cass!" Cyrus cried, lurching forward, but the seraph had the blade at his throat in the next blink.

"Release them all, or you will never have this," Scarlett snarled through clenched teeth, lifting the fake lock into the air before them.

Alaric's dark eyes fixed onto the object, Cassius sucking in a sharp breath as their former master released his magic from the hold of his draining power. "I knew you would be the one to find it," Alaric said, taking another step towards her.

"And you will never see it again if you do not release Cyrus and Kailia. Now," she said in a deadly hiss.

"I am to trust your word after all of this, Scarlett? I think not," Alaric said, moving closer still. Her panthers snapped at him, but she held them back. And when Alaric lifted a hand to touch the lock, she snatched it back from his reach.

"Terms, Alaric," she said. "I give you this lock; you let us all leave. Alive."

He smirked at the added caveat, and his raised hand came to her face instead. She made herself stand there. Let him drag his fingertips along her jaw until he gripped her chin. "You are such a godsdamn pain in my ass, and yet I find myself so incredibly proud of you. You are exactly what I envisioned you becoming."

She swallowed, holding his dark stare. "Are we in agreement?"

"No."

Scarlett blinked. "No? Is this lock not worth more to you than all of our lives?"

He tilted her chin even more. "That lock is only valuable to me if I can wield it. Something you can clearly do if you were able to find it, my Wraith. So no, I am not agreeable to your terms. I will let everyone *else* leave alive. You and the lock stay behind. And together?" His other hand trailed up her arm. "Together we will keep this world safe. Is that not what you desire most?"

She clamped down on everything roiling through her. Her eyes fell closed as she breathed it all in. The anxiety of what she was about to do. The fear of knowing she might fail. The revulsion at having him touch her. Of knowing if this failed, Mikale would touch her next.

She felt Sorin's snarl of rage ripple through her as he felt all her emotions.

*Mine, Scarlett. The crown is yours. This world is yours. But you? You are mine.*

She opened her eyes, connecting with Alaric's once more. "Yes," she said, letting her voice soften. "Yes, that is what I desire most."

"Then we have an agreement?"

"I give you this lock and stay to wield it. You let everyone else leave alive without further harm," Scarlett said.

"Agreed." A victorious smile tilted on Alaric's lips, and he nodded to the seraphs to release Cyrus and Kailia. The Avonleyan Queen was gone among ashes in the next blink. Cassius was racing for Cyrus, but Rayner stayed at her back.

"Go," she snarled at the Ash Rider.

"I cannot leave you here, Scarlett," he argued.

"It is an order from your queen," she snapped in reply, locking eyes with him. She could tell this went against everything he was, to leave her behind, but he did it. With a muttered curse, he was gone.

"This could have all been avoided if you had come to my side to begin with," Alaric chided, again reaching for the lock she held.

"This could have all been avoided if you hadn't come for a world that is not yours to take," she retorted.

"But it is mine," he said calmly, lifting the sphere from her hand and holding it up before him. Her magic swirled, just as the glyphs on the real thing had. "It has always been mine, just as it was always my father's. When the beings who created this realm were defeated by Achaz and his armies, they lost their rights to this land. To the victors go the spoils, Scarlett. You know this."

"Serafina and Arius were not defeated," she countered, dragging up her starfire as quickly as she could.

"Ah, but nor did they create this realm," he replied. He held the sphere out to her, the false glyphs fading in and out. "And this? This tells of all worlds, Scarlett. Every one that was, is, and is yet to be." He turned, striding away from her as he continued speaking. "And this is how I will save you from Achaz's wrath. With this, he can truly eradicate those who tipped the balance. His own princes can rule the realms, and he can finally rest."

"All of this because Serafina chose another?" Scarlett asked, feeling her veins begin to crackle.

"That is only part of the story, Scarlett," Alaric said, passing the false lock to a seraph. He turned back to her, extending a hand.

366

"Come. Your sister will be glad to see you. The two of you can convince Juliette to come home, and with the three of you back at my side—"

But the gurgled cry of a seraph had him whirling around.

The seraph he'd passed the lock to was slumping to his knees, an arrow through his throat.

An arrow with a deathstone tip.

The false lock tumbled from his hand, jolting her magic. It was already unstable as she'd had to split her focus to dredge up every last bit of her starfire. The false lock shattered apart at the same moment Kailia appeared again, another arrow going through the skull of the seraph who'd held a sword to Cyrus's throat. Then she was once again gone in smoke and ashes. The seraphs went up in flames of orange as two others fell from the sky encased in black flames.

She looked up at the same time Alaric did, finding Cassius setting another alight. She spun. Cyrus was at the cliff edge, the arrow gone from his shoulder and fire in his palm.

"The agreement said nothing about *his* people," Cyrus said, that mischievous smirk that often mirrored her own on his lips.

Then he leapt from the cliff. Before she could utter a cry of concern, Cassius appeared in the air, snagging Cyrus's outstretched hand and Traveling them both out. They were gone. Her family had gotten out.

"That was not the lock," Alaric snarled in a voice that was not of this world.

"But it was the lock we agreed on," she replied, finally releasing her shadows. They rose up around her, a flood of darkness that blanketed the entirety of the cliffs. She shrugged. "And I suppose agreements can always be undone. You taught me that."

She felt Alaric's magic reach for her. Felt it trying to latch onto something.

And she let it.

She let it latch onto her Fae fire and water, and she let her Fae gifts bite back, sinking in just as deeply.

"How?" Alaric demanded.

"I think you should be more concerned with how you will survive this day," she replied, starfire flaring to life in her hands so brightly, Alaric cried out a curse, turning away to shield his eyes.

"It will not be enough to end me, Scarlett," he bellowed at her.

He was right. His draining magic would not let her end him. Not yet. She knew that from training with Cethin. When she came for Alaric, everything would be in place.

But this day had been about the lock.

It had been about Briar.

It had been about destroying these godsdamn cliffs forever.

She dropped to her knees, and with everything she was, she slammed her hands to the rock, sending every bit of her starfire into the depths. Into the pristine halls and forgotten passages. Into the rooms of nightmares and horrors. Into the places that had haunted Rayner and Kailia and so many others. Into the hell that had stolen so much innocence and life.

Into the walls that Rayner and Kailia had already weakened with their ashes, decaying so much inside, that when her starfire collided with it, it gave out completely. The cliffs swayed beneath her, a groaning sounding from deep within.

"You foolish girl," Alaric snapped, reaching to grab her arm. But the minute he touched her skin, her shadows bit into flesh, and he jerked back with a bellow.

She only smiled as she sent one last blast of starfire into the belly of the cliffs. The last of her magic.

Then the world tilted.

She was thrown into the sky as the rock and stone exploded, dust and debris filling the air. The cliffs crumbled, the sound deafening, but they'd done it. She'd promised Rayner and Kailia they would destroy this place when they left today, and they had. They'd gotten Briar out, sent him to Ashtine. The lock would get to Cethin.

It was enough.

She'd given enough.

The raining rock slammed into her arms, legs, torso. Jagged stone tore through her witchsuit, sliced her flesh, and she fell.

She fell and fell to the sea below and the rocks within. She had nothing left. The Water Prince was not here to save her. She would not be able to breathe beneath the waves. The impact into the water alone would likely kill her.

She was not panicked or remorseful like she thought one would be moments before crossing the Veil. They'd gotten out. They'd all gotten out. Sorin lived. She could feel him down the bond. He would make sure they'd find a way to save this realm.

She'd given enough.

Those were her thoughts when a large rock slammed into her temple. Her vision went black as she tumbled down and down.

*No, Scarlett. Not like this.*

She blinked, trying to keep conscious. The world was blurry as it raced past.

The world was on fire.

She blinked again. No, it wasn't on fire.

But the dragon coming for her was.

Claws of flames wrapped around her torso, hauling her back up. Her stomach lurched at the sudden change in direction.

*Scarlett. Reach, Love.*

She blinked her eyes open again. She wasn't sure when she'd closed them.

Sorin was hanging off the side of his fire dragon, hand outstretched, fingers reaching.

*You...you came...*

*Always, Love. Reach.*

But she couldn't. She had nothing left to give.

And as her eyes fell closed again, she saw Sorin let go of his fire.

She felt his arms wrap around her as they fell.

And Sorin pulled them through a rip in the air.

# CHAPTER 28
# ELIZA

"What are you doing?"

Razik glanced at her before he returned his attention to whatever he was looking at. It appeared to be a...bowl.

The thing was gold with various small gems of red, green, and blue inlaid along the rim. It sat atop a pedestal in the hall outside one of the dining rooms at the Siofra palace.

Razik's arms were crossed, his head tilting as he studied the bowl. "This is very old. From before the Great War," he answered.

"Fascinating," she mumbled. But when Razik continued to stare at it, she narrowed her eyes. "Are you planning to steal this bowl?"

Sapphire eyes slid to her. "No."

"Are you sure? You seem rather intrigued by it."

"It is very valuable."

Her eyes went wide. "You want to take it to your cave. You really have a cave, don't you?"

"Why would I lie about that?"

"Who has an actual cave, Raz?"

His eyes seemed to darken at the nickname. "I told you, it's a dragon thing."

"Cassius doesn't seem to need a cave," she countered.

"He cannot shift fully into a dragon."

"Does Tybalt have a cave?"

"Yes."

Laughter bubbled from between her lips, and he turned to face her fully at the sound. Her mirth died out as he held her stare. Always so intense.

"You haven't braided your hair yet," he said.

Her brow furrowed. Her red-gold hair hung in sweeping curls, flowing over her shoulders. "I'll braid it before we leave." He just hummed, still watching her. "Are you ready to go?" she finally asked, turning away and beginning to walk down the hall.

He fell into step beside her. "I've been ready to go for a week now."

So had she. They were leaving for the Fire Court today. They'd been waiting, and now they were finally going. She'd refilled his power reserves, then she'd needed the time to refill her own. They'd been in communications with the Witches, had been filled in on the rebel movements in the mortal lands being led by Juliette—and apparently Nuri—and now the Tyndell siblings, along with Callan and Azrael. They knew Scarlett and the others were going for the lock soon, so they'd waited. Everything needed to be timed perfectly, and with Rayner sending word that the lock had been retrieved yesterday, they could finally put their own plans into motion.

Despite Razik's warning that they would discuss him sleeping in her bed, he hadn't brought it up the next morning. Or the next, or the next. In fact, he hadn't said one damn word about the bond. He'd continued to share her space and sleep in her bed, but he did not touch her when he climbed beneath the sheets. She knew on the mornings that she woke up nestled into his side, it had been her seeking him out in her sleep and not him initiating anything.

Which was just great.

But still, he said nothing, and she wasn't about to bring it up. Even if she was finding herself watching him more over the top of her book when they'd retire to their sitting room in the evenings. Even if she found herself wondering where he was when she didn't see him for a few hours.

Even if she *liked* having him in her bed at nights.

Godsdamnit.

She did not want this. Not in the slightest. A bond like this meant building a life together. She didn't want to give that much control of her life over to anyone. Not only that, bonds like this tended to lead to building a family, and she couldn't give him that. She couldn't give him children. She couldn't give him all of her. It wasn't fair to him. It wasn't fair to her, even if she did want this.

Which she didn't.

So she'd resolved to stop thinking about it. If he wasn't going to bring it up anymore, she certainly didn't need to waste precious time worrying about how she was going to respond to him about what they were and what they weren't. He'd obviously figured it out, and that was good. Great even.

Razik could only Travel to places he'd been to before, which left them pretty limited for options on the continent. Actually, it had left their only options the Necropolis or Anahita's Springs, both of which were not acceptable options at all. They'd spent a few days planning how they were going to enter Solembra and the Fiera Palace. She didn't want Bastien to know she was there until she was walking into that godsdamn throne room with her fire wrapping around his throat and dragging him to his knees.

In the end, they'd had to wait on Azrael. She had tried Ashtine first, but Talwyn had sent a pointed message telling her the princess was not doing well and to figure something else out. She had used more colorful language, but that had been the general gist. Azrael had sent an earth message letting her know he could come and get them a portal, but not right away. Not until they got a few things under control in the mortal lands. But he'd finally sent a message last night that he'd be here mid-morning.

The Earth Prince met them outside the front gates. He hardly said anything, creating them a portal and all but shoving them through as he muttered something about needing to get back to Windonelle. Eliza didn't even have a chance to ask him for an update on what was happening with Callan and the rebels. At least they'd said their good-byes to the Shifters while they'd been waiting for Azrael, and as the portal snapped shut behind them, she wondered if she would see them all again on this side of the Veil.

The portal had spit them out exactly where she'd wanted it too—

a few miles outside of Lightmere along the Tana River. It was a trading town nestled in the Fiera Mountains, but more importantly, it ran ferries to and from Solembra. That was how they were planning to get into the capital city unnoticed. They would catch a ride on the next ferry, get a feel for how things were being handled in Solembra, and make their final plans from there.

Eliza took in a deep breath of mountain air. So much better than the arid heat of Siofra. It wasn't just the mountains either. It was *home*. It was the Fiera Mountains, and soon she'd step foot in Solembra.

Razik was looking around keenly, his eyes shifted to vertical slits allowing him to see even farther than she could. She took the opportunity to take her cloak from her pack. Slipping it on, she quickly clasped it before raising the hood and tucking her hair back. Razik would have to do all the talking and interacting. She was too recognizable, and word would surely reach Bastien if she was spotted in the territory.

"Are you ready?" she asked, crouching to close up her pack once more. When she stood, Razik was reaching for it. "I can carry my own pack," she muttered.

"I know you can," he said, taking it from her hand anyway. Then he reached for her once more, tucking back hair that she had missed. She ignored the way her skin burned when his fingers brushed along her neck as he pulled them back from beneath her hood.

Slipping his own cloak on and pulling up his hood, he picked up both packs and gestured for her to lead the way. They had gone perhaps a half mile when he said, "With arriving in Lightmere well into the day, do you still think we will get a ferry today?"

She held in her sigh because no, they wouldn't be able to catch a ferry today. "They leave every hour, beginning at dawn until mid-morning. The trip upstream takes most of the daylight hours. Around dusk, they will return with people from Solembra and goods from the businesses. Tomorrow they do it all over again."

"We will board the first ferry then?"

She nodded. "We can buy passage today to ensure our place on the boat."

Razik made a sound of acknowledgement, then asked, "What are we to do for the rest of the day?"

"If the town is busy enough that we will easily blend in, I'd like to see if we can pick up any interesting information. We can get rooms at an inn for the night."

He glanced at her momentarily. "We have shared a room for a week, and now you feel the need to have separate ones?"

She kicked a rock on the path, watching it skitter and bounce along, trying to decide how to answer him. "Perhaps it would be a good idea," she finally said. "To make sure we are not..."

When she didn't finish, he said in a low rumble, "Are not what?"

She didn't hold back her sigh this time. "To make sure we are not getting too used to something that will not continue when this war is over."

Razik didn't say anything else for quite some time. The only sound was their boots on the stone road, small pebbles and debris crunching. But the smell of the mountains and the gentle rushing of the Tana River had Eliza not minding the silence. She'd never minded silence or being alone.

"Do you have family in Solembra? Blood relatives, I mean. That you are looking forward to seeing again?" Razik asked after a time.

The question had her drawing up short. It had been so long since she'd been asked about her blooded family. She wasn't prepared for the grief and pain of losing her mother, or the fury and hatred of the man who'd thought himself her father.

"No, I do not have blooded relatives in Solembra, nor any other part of the Fire Court," she replied curtly. "My mother died when I was in my second decade of life. I do not know of my father."

She had stepped from the path and stood facing the Tana now, her arms wrapped tightly around herself. They were perhaps a mile from Lightmere. Soon they'd be able to hear and see the bustling of the trade town.

Razik still stood on the path. She could feel his eyes on her again, studying, watching.

She hesitated before she said, "Obviously your parents are not..."

How did a person phrase this and not sound like an insensitive ass?

"Do your blooded parents still live? I know Tybalt raised you, but—"

"I do not know if they still live," Razik interrupted. She heard his boots scrape against the road, then crunch on the grasses beside the river. "They left me with Tybalt when I was seven years."

"Left you with him? Where did your parents go?" she asked softly.

He pushed out a long, harsh breath. "I was not born in this realm. We did not come here until I was four."

"What?" she gasped, turning to face him fully. She knew her mouth was hanging open, but how else was she supposed to react to that kind of statement?

"I am older than Cethin by three years. When he was born—" His hands curled and uncurled at his sides. "It took Tethys and Saylah nearly a year after he was born to figure out that he had the ability to not only let people in the Wards, but also into the realm. Granted, entering the realm cost more than a vial of Cethin's blood, but it could be done if the right cost was paid. Not anymore, but at the time, it was possible. Before they bound the gift to his Avonleyan magic to reawaken at a later time, my parents entered this world with me."

"And your father was Tybalt's brother?"

"Yes. He is also Temural's Guardian."

That was...new information. It was information that she wasn't entirely sure why he was sharing with her.

"Guardian bonds are much like Source bonds or twin flame bonds. They operate outside of the normal bounds of magic to a certain extent. It is incredibly complex, and I have studied it for centuries."

"To find your parents?" Eliza asked.

"Fuck no," Razik spat. "I was left here because they had never wanted me, but when I was born? Another direct descendant of Sargon?" He released another harsh breath. "We are coveted across the realms. Guardian bonds are stronger with direct descendants. *We* are stronger, more powerful, and, of course, we can summon dragon fire at will."

Eliza had slid her hands into her sleeves, her fingers curling around the ends. "I do not understand. They brought you here to hide you? To keep you safe?"

"They brought me here for several reasons. One of those reasons was to be left with Tybalt."

She wanted to ask the other reasons, but the harshness of his features and the flare of his nostrils told her this was not the time.

Then she asked herself when she had come to know him well enough to know how to read him like that.

But after an extended silence, she did ask, "Where were you born, Raz?"

"It was once called Noidrir, but now it is known simply as The Requiem." Before she could say anything else, he turned and strode back to the road. "We should keep moving. I suspect you will be getting hungry soon."

She glared at him as she made her own way back to the road, but he wasn't wrong.

They crested a hill a few minutes later, and Lightmere was spread out before them. A tall wall of stone surrounded the trade town. She could see warriors patrolling along the top of the wall…and there were a few seraphs among them. Fuck.

Hands on her shoulders were spinning her to face him, and Razik tucked her hair back farther before tugging on the hood to hide her features even more. "I know it will go against every instinct in you, *mai dragocen*, but you need to let me do the talking."

"I know that," she retorted as he pulled her cloak tighter around her too.

Fretting. He was fretting over her.

"You don't think you won't stand out more? Especially if your eyes shift?" she countered.

"We will secure our ferry passage first, and then get some food," he answered, starting down the hill.

"You don't even know where you're going," she snarked, hurrying to keep up with his long strides.

He gestured to the town before them. "I'm assuming we need to first enter Lightmere before I am in need of detailed directions."

Eliza muttered a foul name under her breath, and she saw his lips twitch the smallest amount. Gods, he really was an ass.

They entered Lightmere without issue, and Eliza was forced to adopt a role of appearing to be a timid female visiting the trade town with her partner. This was worse than when she'd had to pretend to be a servant in the Tyndell manor. She murmured directions and instructions to Razik as they moved around the town, his hand resting on her lower back and keeping her tucked in close.

Just as he'd said, they immediately purchased their passage for the first departing ferry of the morning, and then he was telling her to find them some place discreet to eat. A tavern of some sort seemed their best bet at picking up gossip and information, so they wandered until they found one not completely off the beaten path but not too popular. Razik secured them a table in the back, and they kept their hoods in place while they ate. His general air of annoyance with everything kept others from bothering them, despite the curious glances they were receiving.

Eliza dug into her bread and stew, listening to the various chatter. Incoming goods. Passing thoughts on the brewing unrest with the mortal lands. New trade agreements with...the Earth Court?

That had her spoon pausing halfway to her mouth. There had long been tension between the two Courts. It had been exasperated by Sorin's feud with Talwyn, but the turmoil between Fire and Earth predated Sorin and Azrael. She didn't even know when it had fully started or how, only that both Courts continued to feed it. Her own history hadn't helped matters.

But new agreements? That would mean Bastien was working with Tarek and that couldn't mean anything good.

She didn't hear anything else about it, but there were mentions of more and more seraphs appearing in their towns. Solembra, Aelyndee, and Threlarion in particular. The three largest cities in the Fire Court. There was division, it seemed, as to the fate of the Inner Court. Some still believed Sorin was dead and the rest of them had fled. Some believed the "silver-haired female" that had been seen briefly in Solembra was responsible for all of this. Still others said they were waiting for the opportune moment to strike back, while others said they'd all left like cowards, Sorin included.

Eliza tried not to let it affect her, but when it was again muttered that "maybe the Fire Royal and his most-trusted had never truly cared for their Court," she was ready to go. She didn't bother finishing her meal. She muttered something about the bathing room to Razik, but instead, she slipped out onto the street, needing some air.

She tipped her head back, breathing in deep. A seraph passed by overhead, and the sound of footsteps had her turning to her left. A group of warriors—*her* godsdamn warriors—were ambling along, far too inebriated for this time of the day. She was choking down the feral growl in her throat as she forced herself to turn away to avoid being seen.

And she turned right into a hard wall of muscle.

"Gods," she gasped, Razik's hand landing on her waist to steady her. "Why are you standing so close?" Then she noticed the large bag in his hand. "What is that?"

"You hardly ate anything," he said. "It is late afternoon. Let's find an inn. You can eat properly and rest before tomorrow."

"You have enough reserves?" she asked, wondering what food he'd ordered to bring with them. It smelled like roast beef and bread and— "Did you get chocolate cake?"

She couldn't see his face beneath his hood when he said, "I am not going to draw from you when you are to fight for your lands tomorrow. I've hardly used my magic since refilling it days ago." He stepped to the side, nudging her down the street. "There was an inn down the way."

"Not that one," she muttered, shoving him lightly in the other direction.

"My mistake, Milady."

She rolled her eyes even though he couldn't see it and directed him towards an inn closer to the Tana. It would certainly be pricier, but if she was spending the night in the Fire Court, she wanted to see the Twilight Wildfires tonight.

Ten minutes later, Razik was unlocking the door to their room (of course, he only got one room) and ushering her through. She'd insisted on a room facing the river, and when she saw he'd gotten one that not only faced the river but had a small balcony as well, her chest did the exact thing she didn't want it to do.

It tightened, and her stomach flipped, and that godsdamn bond sparked to life, her flames swirling in excitement.

There was a small table and two chairs set near the balcony doors, and Razik was there, setting the bag of food down after he'd placed their packs near the small armoire. There was an attached bathing room with a privy and a small tub that Eliza would scarcely fit into, let alone Razik. That was fine. They'd bathed that morning before they'd left Siofra, and it's not as if they'd done anything straining aside from the short walk to Lightmere.

Eliza pushed her hood back, undoing her cloak and looping it over a chair. Razik immediately picked it up and hung it on a hook near the door. She always forgot how tidy he was.

She was emerging from the bathing room where she'd changed into more casual attire and taken her hair out of her braid, when there was a knock on the door. Razik answered it, and a moment later, he turned back to her with a bottle of wine and two glasses.

"I don't drink the night before a mission," she said with a slight frown as he moved back to the table.

"Great. This is for me," he answered.

"Really? With two glasses?" she replied dubiously while he uncorked the wine and poured a glass.

"I didn't want to hurt your feelings by only getting one."

She clicked her tongue, finally unpacking the bag of food. Razik had been using his magic to keep everything warm, and she devoured the roast and bread before pulling out what was indeed a slice of chocolate cake. She hadn't even noticed the small cheese tray that Razik was eating cubes off of. She took her cake out onto the balcony. The sun was dipping low, and she knew the fires would start any moment.

Leaning on the balcony railing, she was halfway through her cake when the sizzling rush of the wildfires reached her moments before the flames zipped along the surface of the water. The Tana seals leapt among them, and the wildfires bathed the land around it in a soft glow she had missed. It was odd. She'd seen these fires nearly every day for decades, had taken them for granted. But watching them now made her think of the first time she'd seen them. Alone and scared out of her godsdamn mind before Sorin's people found her.

She watched the wildfires until her cake was gone. She knew it was a risk to spend too much time out here, and she turned to head back in, only to find Razik leaning in the doorway, his wine glass dangling in his fingers.

"Your homeland is beautiful," he said softly, the wildfires reflecting in his sapphire eyes.

"Do you remember much of Noidrir?"

He beckoned for her to come through the doorway, and he closed the doors behind her, drawing the curtains closed. He'd poured the other glass of wine and left it sitting on the table, and she swiped it up. One glass wouldn't hurt.

Plopping down into a chair, she sipped on the wine as Razik took the other chair. He'd cleaned up the rest of the table, because of course he had. The only thing remaining out was the small platter of cheeses.

"I only remember small details of Noidrir. I was only a few years old when we left, and considering my age now…" He shrugged. "It is just glimpses of things."

"The book with the weapons?"

"Came from Noidrir."

"Do you have other books from there?"

"Not many, but a few, yes."

She took another sip of wine, her nail tapping on the glass a few times. "The Fire Court is not my homeland."

Razik's glass paused for the briefest of moments as he raised it to his lips before he said, "Oh?"

Her nail tapped again. "I was born in the Earth Court. My mother had Earth gifts."

"Cross-breeding is frowned upon among the Fae here," Razik said in confusion.

"Indeed. It will be interesting to see how the Courts react to the news of Ashtine and Briar."

Razik hummed an acknowledgment.

"Anyway, I was supposed to marry the Earth Prince. The pairing had been arranged before either of us were born," she went on.

"Prince Azrael?"

She nodded. "My mother and her husband were both powerful Earth Court Fae. I got that power, but it was fire."

"Her husband was not your father," he said quietly in under-standing.

Eliza nodded, draining the glass of wine. Razik was already reaching with the bottle to fill her glass, emptying the last of the wine.

"He forced you to leave?"

She huffed a harsh laugh. "Something like that, yeah."

Neither of them said anything for several minutes, and she was reaching for a cheese cube when she said, "If your...father?" She glanced up at him. "Is that what you want me to call him?"

"I don't want you to call him anything," he said, settling back deeper into his chair. His brown hair curled around his ears, a few stray strands hanging forward and brushing along his face. He seemed relaxed, despite the topic she'd just brought up. His legs were spread, arm resting casually atop the table, and his fingers were loosely curled around the stem of his glass.

"Okay, well, if he is Temural's Guardian, why did he come here? Why wasn't he with Temural?"

"I already told you. One of the reasons he came here was to leave me with Tybalt."

"But...why?"

"Does it matter?"

"Yes."

"Why?"

She didn't know. She didn't know why she cared or why she was asking. So she said, "Because I'd like to think that if I wasn't who I was, hadn't experienced what I have, that this would be different. That you wouldn't need to be questioning why I care enough to ask."

His sapphire eyes held hers, and she saw it in the depths of them. Saw what should have been. Saw what he wanted. Saw what she couldn't give him.

He didn't say anything, and she couldn't blame him. He owed her nothing. If he didn't want to tell her about his father or why he'd been left behind, that was fine. She finally broke his stare and stood, using the bathing room once more before she climbed into the bed. Razik hadn't moved. Was still sitting at the table, his eyes tracking her every move.

She was opening her mouth to bid him good night when he spoke first.

"He came here for several reasons, but they all revolved around me."

Eliza rolled onto her side, tucking a hand beneath her cheek so she could see him. He seemed to be searching her face, looking for something. Apparently, he found it because he continued speaking.

"He brought me to Tybalt. To keep me hidden. That's what he said anyway, but I'd heard them one night. Him and Tybalt arguing. Tybalt wanted them to take me with them so that I could stay with them until Cethin was of age."

"Of age? For what?" Eliza asked.

"I was brought here to be his Guardian."

Eliza tensed. "You were forced to become his Guardian?"

She remembered Tybalt speaking of the Guardian Bond at dinner one night in Aimonway. He'd said it wasn't a burden, and that no one selected as a Guardian was against it.

"I eventually chose it on my own, but not when they wanted me to. I was supposed to become bonded to him when his power was awakened. I refused. For decades. Centuries. Tybalt tried to persuade me. Saylah threatened me numerous times. But Tybalt would not allow it to be forced. Repeatedly argued with her that forcing a bond would work against what it was meant to be."

"Why did you eventually choose it?" she asked quietly.

"I hated Cethin. For decades. I hated being around him. Hated being in Avonleya. Hated being in Halaya."

"Halaya?"

"That is what this world is called in other realms," Razik said.

"You read so much to escape," she said in realization.

"No," he countered. "I read so much because I believed that someday Saylah truly would force me into a Guardian Bond. I wanted to find a way to break it. So I studied magic and bonds. I studied beings in this world and others. I read any book I could on the subjects. I read any book I could get because you never know when or how such knowledge might be useful."

"Did you ever find a way?"

"No."

"But you still chose it?"

He shifted. The first time he'd moved the entire conversation. "Cethin and I eventually realized we are soulmates. That as much as I resented him, we got along remarkably well when I wasn't being a prick, and he wasn't being an entitled ass. As much as I hated being left here for such a purpose, it appeared fate had other plans."

"Do you regret it? Fighting it? Accepting it?"

His sapphire gaze came back to hers. "No, *mai dragocen*. But I know what it is to have a bond forced on you, to be pressured into accepting something you do not want."

Her stomach twisted at what he was implying.

"You think I am being foolish? To fight what fate has destined for me?" she asked.

"No, Eliza. It takes a special kind of strength to fight fate. Even if you eventually accept it, it will be on your terms, and I am okay with that. Because I know that forcing fate would work against what it was meant to be."

Eliza swallowed, her mouth suddenly dry. She shifted, rolling away from the intensity of his stare, but not before she said, "Good night, Raz."

"Shit," Eliza muttered, tugging on Razik's arm.

"What's wrong?"

His arm slid around her, pulling her in close. Instinct or because he could, she didn't know. She'd woken curled into him again this morning, and when she had stirred, his arm had wound tighter around her. He'd still been sleeping. She could tell by his breathing, and it was foolish of her, but she stole a few more minutes of what could have been if she had been a different person.

She'd nudged him awake a few minutes later, and they'd grabbed some pastries from a street vendor before boarding the ferry to take them to Solembra. Now they were nearing the docks, and Eliza realized they were checking papers. Sorin had randomly ordered the same, usually when they were needing information or trying to track someone down. She didn't know if this was standard practice with Bastien or not, but the fact remained that they didn't have identification papers on them. Furthermore, she wouldn't need them. The moment they saw her face, she'd be reported to Bastien.

"Travel us to shore. Now," she hissed.

Razik didn't question her, and a moment later, they were standing on a rocky ledge, partially hidden but still able to see the docks. She explained what was happening, and Razik crossed his arms, monitoring the scene below.

"I can see the city proper from here," he said. "We could Travel in."

"There are wards around the city. Bound to the city guards. Few can Travel here. In fact, until Scarlett, there were only two known Travelers—Talwyn and Azrael. Until recently, they were not people we wanted in Solembra unannounced," Eliza explained, hands on her hips as she tried to come up with a plan.

"There must be other entry points besides the docks," Razik said.

"Of course there are. But what if they are requiring papers at those points as well?" She looked at the surrounding mountains. "What we need is a place to lie low for a few hours so I can work out a plan."

"Like a cave?"

"Oh my gods," she moaned, swiping a hand down her face, but… "Yes, like a cave," she sighed.

"There is one farther up the mountain," he said, grabbing her hand before she could protest.

Sure enough, she found herself at the mouth of a cave he had somehow spotted. Razik was already striding inside. She could still see Solembra, but she couldn't make out any buildings aside from the Fiera Palace north of the city proper.

Perhaps she was studying the city too hard. Perhaps she'd become too reliant on having Razik with her. Perhaps a seraph had some magic she was unaware of. Whatever the case, she didn't hear the whizzing of the arrow until it was too late.

Shirastone went straight through her shoulder, exactly where she'd been injured before, her flames guttering with the arrow still lodged in her body. Her anguished cry ripped through the air as she fell to her knees. Where the fuck was Razik?

She opened her mouth to scream for him, but a gag of vines

appeared, winding down around her throat and squeezing, scarcely allowing her enough air.

"None of that, *daughter*."

The world fell out from beneath her as three seraphs dropped from the sky, and with them was a male she had not seen in centuries. She had not known if he was alive or dead. She hadn't cared enough to keep tabs on him.

She should have cared.

The male was tall and thin, his sharp features filled with disgust as he stood over her. Sandy blonde hair hung to his shoulders, and his tanned skin told her he still spent time in the sun of the Earth Court. There was pure loathing in his pale green eyes as he reached out and gripped her jaw hard. His other hand clamped around the arrow shaft, driving it in deeper, and causing her to scream around the gag.

Varlis. Her mother's husband.

"Scream all you like, Eliza. The dragon cannot hear you." He gestured towards a seraph. "Keres has wind magic and currently has us all encased in a soundproof vortex."

*Razik!*

She screamed it. She screamed his name down a bond she had been so adamantly pushing away. Perhaps she had pushed it away too much. Perhaps it was too weak because of it, but she screamed down it anyway. Trying to reach him.

*Razik!*

"Did you honestly think you would not be recognized the moment you entered this Court, Eliza?" He huffed a sharp noise of disbelief. "We have been following you since you were spotted outside a tavern in Lightmere. We assumed it was only a matter of time before you tried to enter Solembra."

*Razik! Please!*

Varlis pushed on the arrow again, twisting as he did. His smile was cold and depraved. "I have so often regretted not killing you that day, especially when I heard you became the Fire Court General." Venom dripped off the words as he spoke. "I killed your whore of a mother. I tracked down the male who had fucked her and killed him too." Eliza's eyes flashed up to him, and his smile grew. "I was never quite sure why I had never finished the job and simply dealt with you in the same manner, but now? Your existence has actually proven useful."

Her confusion must have been evident on her face. She could hardly track what he was saying through the pain as tears streamed down her face.

*Razik!*

Varlis leaned in close, the arrow sinking in another inch. "You brought us the dragon."

Panic.

That was pure panic and dread that flooded through her alongside agony as Varlis snapped the arrow off, leaving the shirastone tip embedded deep in her shoulder. "A token from Bastien," he said with a sneer. "Should you survive the night, you can crawl back to your dethroned Fire Prince. Or you can die up here alone, and prove you are not a complete disgrace."

*Raz! I need you!*

The roar that echoed from the cave shook the entirety of the mountain.

And she felt rage. So much wrath and fury that was not hers.

He was coming.

He had heard her.

He was coming.

She had seen Tybalt in his dragon form, but the dragon that swooped out of the cave was larger. His scales were black as night and seemed to absorb the sunlight. Two horns protruded from the diamond-shaped head, and a spiked tail thrashed in the air as he soared up, banking hard. Blue glowing orbs locked on her as his wings gave a mighty flap. His neck stretched out, and black flames spewed from his mouth when he released another roar. Two seraphs were nothing but ash.

He was diving, coming straight for her then, his head rearing back for another onslaught of dragon fire. Careful. He was being careful of her because she could not shield against his flames.

But the roar that came from him was not one of wrath and vengeance. It was one of agony, just as her scream had been when the arrow had struck her.

Because that was a bolt protruding from his chest, right above one of his front legs. A bolt as dark as his scales. Nightstone or deathstone. She couldn't tell from here.

She was screaming. Screaming around that gag so loudly she thought she might blow out her vocal chords.

*Razik!*

She tried to push to her feet, but Varlis shoved her back down. All rational thought left her mind when she saw Razik beginning to fall from the sky. She surged against Varlis again, needing to get to him. She didn't know what she was going to do, but she needed to get to him. That was all she could think.

His wings splayed, trying to balance his weight and slow his fall.

But that was another bolt going straight through his right wing.

Her scream mixed with Razik's roar.

That was the last thing she heard when Varlis's vines tightened around her throat.

And the last thing she saw through her blurry vision as she struggled to breathe was Razik plummeting to the rocky mountainside.

# CHAPTER 29
# CALLAN

"She's nearly here," Juliette said, sticking her head inside the tent that Callan shared with Azrael.

They had entered a rather odd daily routine. With Drake and Tava only able to make their way here in the dead of night, Callan found himself getting a few hours of sleep in the evenings and then falling back onto his bedroll in the hours before the sun rose. Tava and Drake weren't able to come every night, and Drake had far more freedom than Tava did. He had been here last night, but it had been three nights since he'd last seen her. Not that he'd had much time to think about it. If he wasn't getting those few precious hours of sleep, he was training with Azrael or Juliette, attending endless strategy meetings with rebel leaders, or just helping around the camp wherever he could.

It had taken a few days for the rebels to even come close to him, and it took Ezra talking to some of the men the second night to get them to discuss their plans around him. Callan couldn't blame them. The third night, when the Tyndells were able to return again, it had only taken seeing *them* to include him without worry, and suddenly they welcomed him into the fold without another word said about it.

Callan grabbed his cloak and swung it around his shoulders as he

388

ducked out of the tent, Azrael passing him a tin cup of some watered-down stew as they moved through the camp.

"Did you get enough rest?" Callan asked him.

"Enough to bolster my reserves for the night, but after this meeting, I do need more to fill them completely," he answered.

They'd spent all of last night rescuing a group of people being brought in from outlying villages. With the poorer districts all but emptied, they were seeing more and more people being brought into the capital in wagons. The rebels in the city would report that they were being brought in to work since they could not pay their share of the newly increased taxes. But there were never any wagons taking those same people back to their homes. The wagons always left empty and returned full. Men. Women. Children. It didn't seem to matter.

Azrael had to be exhausted. He was using his magic to create diversions, cover tracks, whatever he could really. He was training mortals in the camps, and this morning he'd had to leave to go create a portal for Eliza. It had been a fast trip. He'd only been gone a few minutes, but the distance drained him more than anything.

Tonight they were meeting to discuss what they were going to do with their growing numbers. They couldn't keep everyone here, and many of the people couldn't fight. The women and children being rescued. The elderly. With so many people, they would surely be discovered soon. Juliette had wards around them, but they were being stretched thin.

They had just stepped beyond a copse of trees and into a semi-private clearing when Azrael cursed soundly.

"Watch your mouth. There are *children* nearby, Plant Prince," admonished a voice of silk and honey.

"This is not the 'her' I thought you were referencing," Azrael said tightly to Juliette.

Nuri was leaning against a tree, flipping a dagger in her hand. Mordecai stood nearby, arms crossed and eyes constantly scanning... everything. Their surroundings. The sky. His wings rustled slightly, and his gaze skimmed over Juliette.

"Where is the other Witch?"

"Arantxa is collecting the Tyndells," Juliette answered. "Nuri, a moment?"

Death's Shadow paused her dagger-flipping, eyeing her sister curiously as she pushed off the tree and followed her into the trees.

"Do you know what that is about?" Mordecai asked, eyes narrowed on the spot where the two had disappeared.

"Do *we* know what *they* are up to?" Azrael asked, his lip curling slightly. "I am certain they do not even know what they are doing half the time."

The seraph didn't answer.

"I did not know you and Nuri were to join us today," Callan ventured, keeping well away from Mordecai. They may have explained how they had been working on the inside all this time, but the male was…unnerving. Callan had seen a lot of immortal beings at this point—Fae, Avonleyan, Shifter, Witch—and despite that, there was something about Mordecai that he couldn't quite put his finger on.

"We bring undesirable reports," the seraph commander said.

"Did something happen?" Callan asked.

Mordecai nodded once, his gaze going back to where Juliette and Nuri had disappeared.

"Are you going to share the reports?" Azrael asked, crossing his arms and glaring at the male.

"When everyone has arrived," Mordecai said. "I do not like to repeat myself. It is inefficient."

"And what, exactly, is efficient about the three of us just standing here?" Azrael countered.

The seraph's wings rustled again, flaring slightly.

"You're annoying him, Flower Fae," Nuri chided, stepping back into the clearing. "It's rude."

The hoot of an owl had all of them stilling. It sounded again a moment later. Paja swooped overhead, flying to a low branch. Arantxa stepped into view, Drake, Tava, and Ezra behind her.

The dark-skinned Witch had arrived a few days ago, along with news of Sawyer's death and reports of Ashtine and Talwyn. The former was not doing well, and Talwyn had been offered the choice of coming here with Arantxa, but had stayed to tend to the Wind Princess.

The Witch surveyed them all shrewdly before striding to Juliette.

Tava reached for a satchel Drake was carrying. She met Callan's gaze, giving him a soft smile, before she also moved to Juliette.

"I have those herbs you requested," Tava said, untying the bag as she went. She wasn't in a witchsuit tonight, but she was in tight-fitting pants and a close-cut tunic, her cloak billowing out behind her.

"Did you two find anything on your scouting the last few days?" Drake asked, coming to stand with Callan and Azrael. "Rumors are beginning to spread about rebel camps. We need to get people moved out of here."

"We found some decent areas farther north in the forest. It took us a good day's ride. With so many people, it'll take a few days," Azrael said.

"Wouldn't it be wiser to take them even farther north? Even a day's ride is too close at this point. They are spreading forces out to the northeast to cover all the towns and villages. Two camps that close together will be noticeable," Drake said.

"If we go much farther north, I worry about the camps getting too close to the Fire Court border," Azrael said. "Until we know if Eliza can take that seat from Bastien—"

"Eliza won't fail at that," Callan interjected. "We just need to give her time. You took them there this morning. She's obviously going to be making her move soon." Callan pulled a small, folded-up piece of paper from his pocket. He'd drawn a crude map of Windonelle on it to take with on their scouting to mark areas of interest. "I'm not saying we need to set up camps right on the border, but if we can get them a little farther north, when Eliza does take back the Fire Court, the people will easily be able to cross the borders into the Court and safety."

"What makes you think they'll be safe in a Fae Court?"

They all turned to Ezra, who was standing a few feet away. He reminded Callan a lot of Tava. Always quiet and blending into the background. Hearing and seeing everything.

He stepped forward. "You think they will suddenly welcome mortals into their lands?"

"They will," Callan said. "I've spent nearly a year building a rapport with all the Fae Courts. I know each of the sitting royals well, including the one standing with us right now."

Ezra's eyes flicked to Azrael. "He is Earth Court, not Fire."

"I spent months in the Fire Court."

"Chasing a woman," Ezra countered.

Callan's lips pressed into a thin line. Yeah, he'd deserved that. He'd expected this. To have to prove himself to his people, but the need to prove himself to Sloan's son was an extra heavy weight on his soul.

"That's fair," Callan conceded. "But that is clearly over, and that same woman is one of the most powerful beings in this world and is now the wife of the Fire Prince. They will welcome us across the border once they regain control of their territory."

"And until then?"

"We hold the lines with the allies we have in Rydeon and Toreall, as well as the Witches and Shifters," Callan said firmly.

"Is everything all right?" Tava asked, coming up behind them.

Ezra didn't look convinced in the slightest, but he didn't say anything else, turning to face her. "Fine," he relented. "What do we need to do tonight?"

"All those plans need to be put on hold," Nuri interrupted, shuffling closer to Mordecai. "We have news, and then we need to go. Alaric has been in a rage since Scarlett destroyed the cliffs and stole Briar back."

"Briar is back?" Azrael asked.

"We do not know where he is, but he did not return with Alaric from the Southern Islands," Mordecai said. "The Maraan Prince is certain he did not perish in the desecration of the cliffs."

"Which leaves Scarlett," Nuri said with a shrug.

"What are these reports then?" asked Arantxa, her voice carrying the same icy edge Hazel always spoke with.

Nuri's eyes darted to the surrounding vegetation, and it was Mordecai who said, "Two of your camps were discovered in Toreall, along the Wind Court border."

"When?" Drake demanded.

"I do not know how long the Maraans have known of it. I was informed of their discovery while Alaric was in the Southern Islands. We were in discussions of how to handle the camps, but when Alaric returned in his rage..." Nuri trailed off, eyes fixed on her boots.

"He had them all killed today. Some Wind Fae crossed the border and attempted to help. They were also slaughtered," Mordecai said. There was no emotion in his tone. A warrior reporting facts.

"Were you there?" Juliette asked cautiously.

The seraph's grey eyes met hers. "Yes. We both were."

Juliette's lips pursed, her gaze lingering on Nuri. "Anything else?"

"They plan to attack the Wind Court. We have been kept out of the Citadel. Alaric wishes to kill any resistance left in the Court."

"If they knew of those camps, what are the odds they also know of the others? Of this one?" Tava asked.

"The patrols who found the Toreall camps reported to me in the presence of Mikale and Orvyn. There was nothing I could do," Mordecai said.

"What were Mikale and Orvyn doing in the same place?" Callan asked. Orvyn was the Maraan Lord who was on the Rydeon throne. Idris was acting as the king of Toreall.

"We were discussing moving forces closer to the Fire Court border," the seraph answered. "There were rumors of the Fire General planning a siege."

"Shit," Azrael muttered, and Callan was fairly certain the ground shook the smallest amount.

"Indeed," Mordecai said. "But with the Wind Fae attempting to aid the Toreall rebels, attention has shifted. Bastien sent word he could handle the Fire General if she showed."

"I do not know who this Bastien is, but Eliza is the most powerful fire Fae after Sorin. She will win that fight," Azrael said.

Mordecai shifted, reaching out and pulling Nuri into his side. She pulled her hood up, not looking at any of them. "I have no other information on that front. We must go."

They were gone in the next blink, and Tava turned to face Callan, Drake, and Azrael. "What do we do?"

"We go forward with our plans," Drake answered. "We figure out a way to spread out the people. That way, if they discover one camp, it is small and minimizes losses."

"We cannot have several camps spread out everywhere, Drake," Tava countered. Callan saw her hand lift, about to reach for her throat, before she crossed her arms instead. "How would we possibly provide food, safety, and other necessities? We can scarcely get provisions to this one camp, let alone more spread across Windonelle." Drake glared at his sister, but she only added, "You know I am right about this."

"So you propose keeping everyone together. Then, if they are discovered, they can all die together? You find that to be a better alternative?" he argued.

"Some of these people will not survive a several days' journey through this forest," Tava hissed, stepping forward and poking Drake hard in the chest. "Some are sick. Many are too frail to travel. The children are already exhausted. If you move the men, you take them away from those who can train them. I have been against this from the beginning."

Drake blew out a harsh breath, looking at Callan and Azrael. "Any input here?"

"There will be no best solution," Azrael said, his usually harsh tone having softened just a touch. "These are the hard decisions of rulers. You have watched Scarlett, Sorin—all the Fae Royalty—make these choices these last months. Now it is your turn as the leaders of your people."

Callan, Drake, and Tava all exchanged glances.

"We have to do what is best for the majority," Drake said, his face full of pity as he looked at Tava.

"And tell the others what?" Her voice wavered as she spoke. "That they matter, but not quite enough to be saved and protected?"

"Tava, that is not—"

But she was already turning on her heel, striding away in the direction of the camp. Ezra gave them a grim look, and when Drake jerked his chin, the guard followed after her.

Drake sighed, running both his hands through his golden hair.

"This is an adjustment. For all of you," Azrael said. "Sometimes there is not a good choice. Only two equally bad ones, but a choice must be made nonetheless."

"I will go talk to her," Callan said. "In the meantime, see what you two can come up with."

"If the Wind Court is going to be attacked, I will need to go be of aid there," Azrael said. "For Ashtine and Talwyn."

"Understood," Callan said. "Discuss options, and we will figure out how to move forward."

He turned to head the way Tava had when Juliette called out to him. Looking back over his shoulder, he found her standing with Arantxa. They had been speaking with their heads close together, murmured whisperings while they'd let Callan and the others debate. Juliette didn't tend to offer much, and when she did, it was always obscure and hard to decipher. Arantxa was just...formidable. If asked to do something, she would, but mostly she stuck close to Juliette.

"Yes?" he said to Juliette.

"Did you know that in some realms, I would be known as a priestess?"

Callan's brow furrowed. "No?"

"We are known by many names among the realms. Priestesses. Witches. Sages. Divines." At that, his brows shot up. She just gave him a small smile. "I thought that may be of interest to you. For future reference."

Then the Oracle was turning back to Arantxa, resuming whatever discussion they'd been having.

It took him a few minutes to make his way back to the camp, and when he got there, Tava was rummaging through a crate they must have brought with them.

"What are you doing, William?" she called out, not even looking up from the crate.

A boy of around eight or nine years skidded to a halt at being addressed. After a pause, he said, "Nothing, my Lady."

"Mhmm," she answered, finally lifting her head to look at him. "You are not on your way to put a small creature in your sister's bedroll?"

The boy looked down, shifting on his feet. "How do ya know abou' that?"

Tava gave him a firm smile. "Go release it."

William trudged to the edge of the clearing and knelt down, opening his hand. A small frog indeed hopped out, escaping into the trees.

"Apologies, Lady Tyndell," he mumbled.

"Come here."

Dragging his feet, the boy made his way back to her. She had pulled something from the crate and was now crouched down before him. "Can I entrust you with a very special mission?"

At that, William perked up. He lifted his head, brown eyes brightening some, and he nodded eagerly. She held up a sack. "Can I trust you to make sure that all the children get a fair share of what is in here?"

"Is that...candy?" William whispered, his eyes going wide.

Tava's smile grew. "It is, and I believe I can trust you to ensure all the children receive some, right?"

"Oh, yes, my Lady," he said, eyes fixed on the bag.

"And I can also trust you will stop putting frogs in your sister's bedroll?"

"Yes, Lady," he murmured, cheeks going pink.

"Good boy," she said, standing and scuffling his brown hair.

She held out the bag, and the child took it eagerly. "I swear to be fair about it, Lady Tava."

"I trust you, William. Off you go."

The boy took off again, head high and chest puffed out at the responsibility she had just given him.

Tava turned back to the crate, her face falling as she began pulling out extra blankets. She looked up when she heard him approaching, giving him a sad smile before going back to what she was doing.

"Can I help?" he asked, reaching to take the small pile she was holding.

"You should be conversing with Drake and Azrael," she said tightly, but she let him take the blankets.

"You need to be part of those conversations, Tava."

"I do not think I can make those types of decisions, Callan. That is better left to kings."

"And queens," Callan countered.

"Of which I am not one."

"You are already their queen, Tava. We simply need to make it official." Her hands stilled in the crate, a blanket halfway out. Callan reached for it, adding it to his pile. "Are we taking these somewhere?"

Tava cleared her throat, pulling the remaining blankets out. "Some of the newer arrivals needed them."

"Lead the way."

"I can handle this, Callan."

The sound of footsteps crunching on branches and leaves had them both turning, and Ezra appeared carrying another crate. He glanced from Tava to Callan, his lips thinning.

"Thank you, Ezra," Tava said. "You can set it there. I will come back for it."

Ezra nodded. "Do you need me to accompany you?"

"Not necessary," she answered, eyeing Callan for a long moment before nodding and heading deeper into the camp.

"How have things been at the manor the last few days?" Callan asked as they walked.

"Fine."

"Has Balam said anything?"

Her lips pursed. "Only that this was necessary to keep us safe. That someday, we would understand. When Drake pushed for more, he refused. He knows he makes us uncomfortable, so he keeps his distance."

They spoke little after that. She was on edge, still clearly upset about what had been said in the clearing, but the moment some of the people noticed her, word quickly spread that she was here. Soon, they were surrounded by people calling greetings. Callan watched as her entire being relaxed. Tension eased. Her real smile returned.

The people glanced at him, eyes widening in recognition, but Tava put them at ease all the same. She passed out blankets and asked about various people by name. She would discreetly fill Callan in on the families. She knew them all. Knew which children belonged to which parents. Knew who had been ill, who had been looking for soap, and who had been needing a few extra pairs of socks. She introduced him to all of them. He'd never remember them all. Not right away. He'd try, and he'd feel terrible when he fumbled names and information, but he also knew she'd be there too. That it truly was no longer his people, but their people. They'd always been more her people than his anyway.

Later, when they were taking a moment to themselves before they rejoined Drake and Azrael, they were wandering beside a small stream when he said, "I have something for you."

The only light was the moon, shining brightly in the cloudless sky. She turned, her hair fluttering in the breeze. The soft smile she gave him made his chest tighten. "You being with me tonight was enough, Callan."

One hand was intertwined with hers, and he dipped his other hand into his pocket, fingering the three items he carried with him everywhere. He pulled out one of them and held it up before her. The chain was silver and hanging from it was an amulet of white sapphire. Three interlocking circles side-by-side. Falein's symbol.

Tava sucked in a sharp breath. She lifted a hand as if to reach for it, but then drew it back, fingers covering her mouth instead. The moonlight reflected off the sapphire, and with it, he could just make out the faint, shimmering silver dust contained within.

"What is that?" Tava breathed.

He smiled, extending the necklace to her. "Arianna calls it energy. I simply call it magic."

Callan had asked the Beta to make him the piece of jewelry. When he had explained to Arianna what he wanted, she had taken him to a room in their palace full of finery. She'd gone straight to a cabinet full of jewels and told him to pick one, that she would shape it into whatever he desired. He'd chosen a white sapphire, knowing she wouldn't want the flashiness of a diamond, but needing something white and pure that would reflect her light. Arianna had shaped it as he'd asked, and when she'd slipped it onto the silver chain and handed it to him, she'd said, "I made a few enhancements. I hope you do not mind."

"What does it do?" Tava asked, tentatively reaching for the necklace again.

Callan shrugged. "As far as I can tell, it simply adds the Beta's flair to her creation."

Tava laughed softly. "It is beautiful, Callan."

He motioned for her to spin, and she lifted her hair so he could clasp the necklace around her neck. She turned back, fingers already sliding the amulet back and forth on the chain.

"Thank you," she whispered, pressing onto her toes to kiss him.

His fingers tangled in her hair as he slid a hand to cup the back of her head. "I meant what I said earlier, Tava," he murmured onto her lips.

She pulled back a little to see him better. "About what?"

"You are already their queen." His hand dipped into his pocket again. "We simply need to make it official." She took a step back, eyes wide as she stared at the ring he held between his thumb and forefinger. A sapphire of the deepest blue was flanked by two diamonds on either side, all set in a band of gold. Arianna had made this for him as well. "I spoke with Drake last night," Callan said. "He gives his blessing."

"Callan, we cannot—"

"I know I said when this war was over I would make you my wife at the first opportunity, but I realized that is ridiculous. You are already their queen, Tava," he repeated. "What is the point in waiting?"

"There is no way to get a union sanctified," she said, fingers fiddling with the amulet at her throat. "We cannot approach a Divine. Not with the state of things."

His lips curled into a grin. "Juliette can do it."

Divines were the priests who were said to be able to communicate with the gods and unite two souls in marriage. Callan didn't know if the Divines of the mortal lands could truly do such a thing, but Juliette, as an Oracle, certainly could.

"This is madness, Callan," she said.

"Is it?" he countered. "I know you cannot wear it at the manor. I can keep the ring here with me, but we would know. Drake would know. Juliette and Azrael. You would still need to be crowned, of course, but so do I. We can hold the coronations together. When this is over." She said nothing, eyes going from his face to the ring and back again. "If you want a grand ceremony, we can do that later as well," he added.

"I do not wish for that," she said softly. He'd known she wouldn't want such a thing. In fact, he knew that a small, intimate union would be exactly what she'd want.

"What do you wish for?" he asked, taking her hand and pulling her back into him.

"You," she whispered.

"Done," he replied, brushing his lips across hers. "What else?"

She huffed a small laugh. "You think there is more I desire?"

"I told you, Little Fox. I will never deny you a thing."

An hour later, a thick gold band with small alternating sapphire and diamonds inlaid along the entirety of it was on his finger. He'd asked Arianna to make him a set, and the Beta had again taken his request and made it her own.

Juliette had randomly appeared by the stream—conveniently with Drake, Azrael and Arantxa in tow—and here they stood. The union complete. He had a wife and a queen.

Drake was hugging his sister, murmuring congratulations into her ear. Then he reached to shake Callan's hand. The moment their hands touched, Juliette sucked in a sharp breath. Startled, they all turned to face her, Callan reaching to tuck Tava into his side.

Juliette was staring beyond them, but when Callan glanced over his shoulder, there was nothing there. Her eyes were a vibrant violet and were nearly glowing.

"She sees things she does not understand," Arantxa said, stepping between Juliette and the rest of them, a hand on the dagger at her hip. "Glimpses of truth. Glimpses of what could be."

"Is it like the winds speaking to Ashtine?" Tava asked.

"No," Azrael said. "This is different. The winds are wild and whisper of whatever they please. The Fates use Oracles to speak for them, to push for a destiny they desire."

Juliette blinked. The faint glow of her eyes receded, but they remained a darker shade of violet. She swallowed, her throat bobbing with the motion. "When Scarlett took the wards down around the mortal lands…"

Everyone went utterly still.

Her gaze settled on Drake. "Your once-father said you do not understand the cost."

"I recall," Drake said slowly.

Juliette looked between the three mortals. "It would be wise to learn that cost before nothing can be done."

# CHAPTER 30
# TALWYN

"Come on," Talwyn muttered, tugging on the tether around Thorne's feathered neck.

The griffin had the audacity to squawk at her. Fucking *squawk*. He dug his back paws into the ground, his front talons making an awful screeching as he dragged them along the stone path.

"Idiotic beast," she snarled, glaring at him.

He glared back.

She propped her hands on her hips, the rope still in hand. Huffing, she blew stray hair from her face.

She'd been out here for nearly three hours, arriving before the sun rose. Now it was above the horizon, bathing the world in the first day's light. Ashtine had been sleeping soundly when she'd left. The princess had been... Well, not better, but not quite as sullen, perhaps? She still didn't eat much, but she took the tonics Hazel prepared for her without argument. She still slept much of the day, but she accompanied Talwyn down to the aeries every day too.

Talwyn wasn't entirely sure what she was supposed to do with the griffin. The High Witch just kept telling her she needed to spend time with him to strengthen their bond.

The bond they absolutely did not have.

She was sure at this point the creature had only approached her that day because it had wanted the apple she had been eating.

The plan had been to go for a short flight this morning, but that wasn't going to happen when Thorne wouldn't let her close enough to touch him. It had taken her an hour to even get the tether around his neck. It was the first time she had truly missed her magic. Conjuring a vine to use as a lead would have been so much easier than swinging a godsdamn rope above her head and tossing it at him over and over until it finally looped around his neck.

Then there had been getting him to even leave the fucking aerie.

In the last two hours, they'd made it a whole fifty feet from the doors. She was exhausted, sweaty, and irritated as hell.

Not that the griffin gave any sort of fucks.

"Fine, you overgrown buzzard," she growled. "We'll just sit here and take up space."

With that, she plopped down onto the ground. Thorne blinked at her, his head tilting in that avian way birds do. Then his wings rustled, and he began pecking at the ground and digging at the dirt with his talon.

Godsdamn dick of a beast.

And that was how the High Witch found her.

"Why are you sitting in the dirt?"

Talwyn looked up, startled out of her thoughts. She hadn't heard the Witch approach, and the griffin certainly hadn't given her any type of warning. No, he had moved off the path as far as his lead would let him, now digging for whatever the hell he was looking for.

She quickly pushed to her feet, dusting off the back of her pants. Hazel stared back at her expectantly, waiting for an answer.

"We were going for a walk together. To bond," Talwyn gritted out, yanking on the lead. Thorne didn't even look at her. When she turned back to Hazel, she could have sworn there was the briefest glimmer of amusement on her face, but if there had been, it was fleeting.

The High Witch walked over to the griffin, Thorne raising his head at her approach. His wings shifted, feathers flaring slightly, but when Hazel lifted a hand, he bowed his head and allowed her to run a hand along his broad neck.

Dirty godsdamn traitor.

"Do you know why the griffins were banished to our kingdoms?" Hazel asked, continuing to stroke Thorne's neck.

"The Witches were the only beings who could control them," Talwyn replied.

"And do you think that is what we do? Control them?" Hazel countered.

Talwyn blinked at her, knowing this was some kind of trick question. "Is that not what you do with any animal?"

"Did you once control your wolves?"

"They were not mine to control."

The High Witch arched a brow. "No?"

She pursed her lips, fists clenching at her sides.

Hazel's attention returned to the griffin. "Most griffins select their riders when they are fledglings."

"What?" Talwyn demanded. "If most Witches *raise* their griffins, how am I supposed to bond with a full-grown one?"

"Thorne was once bonded with another."

"What happened to his rider?"

"She was killed by Alaric, but she left Thorne long before that." When Talwyn stared at her in confusion, she added, "Thorne was Eliné's griffin."

Talwyn opened her mouth, then closed it. She tried to speak again, but nothing. Hazel continued stroking the griffin's neck.

"After your mother's death, Eliné did not visit nearly as often. The responsibilities of running four Courts and caring for you took all her time, as they should have. The last time she visited was when Scarlett was born here. She said goodbye to Thorne, and he has not let anyone ride him since." Hazel's violet gaze connected with Talwyn's. "Until you."

Talwyn still didn't know what to say. She'd always known her aunt was close with the Witches, but close enough to have a bond with a griffin? She hadn't known that Eliné had once visited the Witch Kingdoms so often that she'd flown in the skies with them.

"We cannot force a bond. Griffins value control as much as a Witch does," Hazel continued.

"He did not exactly choose me," Talwyn grumbled, crossing her arms.

"Of course he did. I just told you he has not let another ride him since Eliné left him behind."

"So, what am I supposed to do?"

Hazel stepped back from the griffin. "It is not my bond to work out."

"You have no instruction to offer?" Talwyn gritted out.

"Spend time with him."

"What do you think I have been doing?"

"Bonding with a griffin is not done sitting in the dirt," Hazel said curtly.

She glared at the High Witch. "Why are you down here? Did you need something?"

Likely not the smartest move to speak to the High Witch in such a manner, but after three hours of battling wills with a griffin, she had about as many fucks to give as Thorne did.

Hazel's eyes flicked over Talwyn's shoulder at the same time Thorne lifted his head and clicked his beak. It was answered by the cry of a hawk.

"She has news from the west," came a lilting voice.

Talwyn turned to find Ashtine behind them, Nasima soaring above her and circling in the sky. Talwyn frowned at her appearance. She still looked unwell, despite everything. Still pale. Still exhausted.

"You should not be out here yet, your Highness," Hazel said. "The mornings are cold in these lands, even in the warm months."

Ashtine had her cloak clutched tightly around her, the hood up and her hands shoved deep in the pockets. She wore silk shoes that could not possibly be keeping her feet warm. With a weak smile, she said, "They remind me of my home. High in the cliffs."

"Can you take Thorne back to the aerie?" Talwyn asked Hazel. "I will escort Ashtine back."

"The winds summoned me," Ashtine said, moving closer to the griffin. "What news do you carry, Lady?"

"I received word last night that Scarlett visited the Southern Islands two days ago as planned," Hazel answered, stepping back more to give Ashtine room to pet Thorne.

"Did she find what she was seeking?" Ashtine asked.

"I do not know that, but I do know she left the cliffs in ruins."

Talwyn couldn't contain her small gasp. The power it would have taken to desecrate those cliffs would have been astronomical.

"She had a trap set. Most of Alaric's forces that had accompanied him were inside the cliffs when she destroyed them. He returned to the continent upset."

"That is nothing new," Talwyn muttered.

"He retaliated," Ashtine said softly.

Talwyn stilled because she was right. When Scarlett had tricked Alaric by trading him a powerless once-queen, he had retaliated by coming after Ashtine. He would have retaliated out of fury again.

"What did he do?" Talwyn asked.

Hazel's keen gaze was on Ashtine, whose own eyes were fixed on the feathers she was smoothing down on Thorne's neck. The beast bent his head, shuffling closer to her.

"It was reported that mortal rebel camps were discovered near the Wind Court border in Toreall. They were attacked, and some Wind Court Fae crossed to defend them. They were all killed, but he now plans to attack the Court. To solidify his holding there," Hazel said.

Ashtine's hand had stopped, fingers curling into Thorne's feathers. She was trying to hide her trembling, but Talwyn could see it.

"Ashtine?" she asked tentatively.

She could already see all the progress the princess had made since coming here beginning to drain away at this news. The winds were picking up, piles of dirt swirling in the gusts. Nasima let out a disgruntled cry, shooting higher into the sky.

"Ashtine," Talwyn tried again. "Ashtine, let us walk a bit."

Hazel had taken Thorne's lead, urging him to back up.

"Ashtine."

Talwyn reached for her, but a gust of wind slammed into her so hard she was thrown backward, landing hard on her back. She scrambled up onto her elbow to find ice swirling around Ashtine, her winds creating a swirling mass of the crystals, obscuring her from the rest of the world. There was nothing Talwyn could do. She couldn't counter the wind and ice. She couldn't reach Ashtine to try to calm her. She was utterly helpless as she watched her friend break all over again.

Talwyn couldn't hear anything outside of the howling winds. They continued to swirl violently, but the ice—

The ice was being pulled from the vortex the princess was cocooning herself in. Ice shards were collecting in the air as if someone were piling them up, and then they melted, water cascading to the ground. Ashtine's winds caused it to spray, and Talwyn felt the cold drops splatter on her face and hands. She lurched to her feet, trying to figure out the cause. Hazel had managed to get Thorne back to the aerie, but it wasn't a Witch Talwyn's gaze settled on.

It was Briar.

When the Water Prince had gotten here, she did not know. She did not care when or how, only that Scarlett had done it. She had come through and freed him from Alaric and sent him here.

He did not look at Talwyn when he moved past her, walking straight into the heart of Ashtine's heartache. Talwyn stood and waited. One second. Two. Three.

The winds stopped as if the world itself had lost its breath.

And as the dirt settled, she found Briar and Ashtine kneeling on the ground. Her face was buried in his chest, and he was clutching her tightly, one hand running down her hair over and over.

"It is a wonder they are not twin flames," came Hazel's hushed voice from behind her.

Talwyn murmured an acknowledgment, continuing to watch the prince and princess. Briar framed Ashtine's face with his hands, pulling back enough to brush his lips across her brow, the bridge of her nose, her mouth. Ashtine's eyes were closed, continuous tears rolling down her face. The prince brought his brow to hers. Talwyn saw his mouth move but could not hear the whispered murmurings. Whatever he said had Ashtine nodding before he pulled her back into his chest.

"Perhaps it is something purer this way," Talwyn said, as Briar stood, scooping Ashtine up with him. "They did not have a bond drawing them to each other. It is pure love that they managed to find despite all odds."

"High Witch," Briar said, bowing his head. "Thank you for allowing her to stay. It is not a request that I will be staying with her."

His tone left no room for argument. He was not asking if he could stay in the Witch Kingdoms as a male, but commanding that Hazel allow him to do so.

"Understood, your Highness," Hazel replied, her voice softer than Talwyn had ever heard it. "Talwyn can show you to her room. Should you require anything, speak to me or Jetta."

"Thank you, my Lady," Briar replied, turning to Talwyn. He gave a jerk of his chin, telling her to lead the way.

Talwyn nodded, averting her gaze and beginning up the path that would lead back to the High Witch's Keep. Ashtine was nestled into his chest, a hand curled tightly into the material of his worn tunic.

"Tell me everything," Briar said in a tight command.

"I think there are some things she will want to tell you herself," Talwyn answered, wondering if he knew of Sawyer's sacrifice yet.

"Then tell me what you will."

By the time she had finished telling him what she knew of the happenings in Avonleya and what had happened since she had been traded for Cyrus and Neve, they were crossing the threshold into the room she had been sharing with Ashtine. She quietly closed the door behind them as Briar moved to lie the princess on the bed. She had fallen asleep on the walk back, and when Talwyn glimpsed her face, it was the most at peace she had seen her friend in months.

Briar moved to step back, but Ashtine's fist curled tighter in his tunic. "My heart," she murmured, her brow pinching in sleep.

"Hush, my dear," he soothed, running a palm along her hair again, but he climbed atop the bed, never breaking contact with her. It took a moment, but he got himself positioned against the headboard, Ashtine's head in his lap. He unclasped her cloak, gently maneuvering it off her. Talwyn grabbed a blanket to spread across her, and when she stepped back, she couldn't help the emotion that swelled at the back of her throat.

Briar now sat where she had been for the last several days. And he should. That had always been his spot, not hers. She had stolen that from him, but... She had been so quickly replaced. Ashtine no longer needed her. Her Courts no longer needed her. She was no longer needed to make some trade with the enemy, or to give her power to right a wrong. Looking after Ashtine had given her purpose and kept her mind busy, but now...

"Talwyn?"

Briar's voice was tight, but a thread of concern broke through.

She met his icy stare. There was a hardness there that she deserved. He knew she had stolen moments from him. That while she had been caring for Ashtine, she was also part of the reason she was in this state to begin with.

"I am sorry, Briar," Talwyn said thickly. "For forcing her to make a choice she should have never had to make. For making her feel she had to prove her loyalty to me when it was never mine to demand. For taking so much from her. From you."

"Looking after her does not atone for that theft, Talwyn," Briar said, and Talwyn winced. She deserved that, and he deserved to reject her apology.

"I did not stay with her to atone for anything," she replied. "She is perhaps my only true friend. I am only now learning what it means to be a friend in return. She has my love, and those babes have my love, Briar. I do not know if that means anything at this point, but they have it nonetheless."

Briar stared at her, some of the hardness of his features having softened while she spoke.

She cleared her throat, beginning to gather her few belongings. A few extra tunics and pants. A cloak.

"I tried to get here sooner," Briar said into the room.

"I know," Talwyn answered, reaching for a hairbrush.

"Scarlett freed me in the Southern Islands nearly two days ago, and I could not get here. I could not get to her."

There was so much frustration and angst in those last words that Talwyn turned back to face him once more.

"My reserves were full after not being able to use my magic for weeks. I made a portal, but— I cannot explain it. I do not know if they laced the little food they gave me with something, but it was as if each portal could only go so far." His gaze fell to Ashtine, and he laid a palm on her belly. "All I could think was that I was finally able to come to her, and I could not get here. Scarlett had told me she was not well, and I could not get to her. I could not get to them."

"You did not fail them, Briar," Talwyn said, fingers flexing around the items she held. "You protected them the way any mate and father would. You sacrificed yourself. There is no greater love, and if that is failure, then I hope I am as big a failure as you at some point before I cross the Veil."

Briar went quiet again, and Talwyn returned to gathering her few things. She moved to the door, to go where she wasn't sure, but she wanted to give Briar and Ashtine their privacy.

"Thank you, Talwyn. For watching over them for me," Briar called out when she reached for the door handle. She glanced back over her shoulder to find him toeing off his boots so he could settle down better beside Ashtine. She nodded, pulling the door open. "Can you come back in a few hours? I need to bathe and do not want her left alone."

"Of course. Send a message when you want me to return," she answered.

Talwyn crossed to the room opposite Ashtine's, finding it empty and claiming it for her own. The Witches could move her if they didn't want her there. Not knowing what else to do with herself, she went back down to the aerie.

Thorne was standing by a fence, and he let out another squawk of what she could swear was annoyance as she neared.

The feeling was mutual.

"Why would you pick me if you want nothing to do with me?" she grumbled, stopping a few feet away.

The griffin blinked, bright amber avian eyes studying her.

She sighed, pulling an apple from her cloak pocket that she'd grabbed on the way out here. She held it out to him, moving closer. "Here."

He blinked again before his wings rustled, and he swiped it from her hand in a move so fast Talwyn almost missed it. She jerked her hand back, watching him devour the fruit in a few mighty crunches of his beak. He stared at her expectantly.

"I am not giving you another one," she snapped. "Not until we figure this thing out between us. I have been trying to fix all my shit. You don't get to ruin it."

One of the griffin's talons scraped against the ground, making them screech.

"Don't be a prick," she barked, taking another step closer so she was nearly nose to beak with him. "The High Witch says we need to bond. So what will it be, Thorne? Are we bonding over being abandoned by the same female? Over the fact that she chose others over us? Although, I guess she chose me over you, didn't she?"

A sound that was a cross between a growl and a screech came from Thorne.

"Is that why you chose me? To see what was so great? Because I assure you, there is nothing special here," Talwyn said, absent-mindedly reaching up and stroking a hand down his beak. He huffed, the breath hot against her palm. "What have you been waiting for?" she murmured.

His wings flared slightly, and he took a step back, tilting his head to see her better.

Crossing her arms, she rested them atop the fence rail. "Listen, I don't have much of anything to offer you, Thorne. But we are at war." He blinked, as if telling her to go on. "I don't have people to call my own anymore, but I still plan to fight beside them. You are a stubborn shit. Battles need that kind of strength."

The griffin huffed again.

"So that is what I can offer you. The freedom to be a dick to whomever you want. I know you already do that, but there would be a purpose behind it. Can we bond over that? Over being stubborn fools who are just trying to figure out their purpose after…everything?"

The two stared at each other. Beast and powerless mortal.

Thorne moved towards her, and she took a step back, wondering if he was about to peck at her yet again. Instead, he lowered his head, nudging at her cloak pocket.

She sighed, pulling out another apple. "I guess apples. I have those to offer too," she muttered.

He crunched it down in two bites before he nudged at her chest with his head.

"Stop it," she barked around the oomph as she stumbled backwards, falling on her ass from the force of the beast.

The sound of boots crunching had her turning her head, and Hazel dropped a set of reins in her lap. "Take him flying."

That was all the High Witch offered before she strode away. Talwyn turned back to Thorne to find his head already lowered in the way she'd seen him do for Arantxa when they'd prepared to fly to Siofra.

Slowly, Talwyn got to her feet, and smoothed a hand along the top of his head, feathers soft beneath her fingers. An acceptance. Of her as she was.

"Okay," she whispered, lifting the reins. "Let's fly."

# CHAPTER 31
# CYRUS

C yrus shoved bits of egg and fruit around on his plate, an elbow propped on the table and his temple resting against his fist. He wasn't hungry, but if he didn't at least pretend to eat, Cass would throw a godsdamn fit.

But Cass wasn't here. This morning he sat at the breakfast table alone. Scarlett still had not woken up. It had been three days since they'd gone to the Southern Islands and the female had shaken the very realm. They'd all met up on one of the islands outside the Avonleyan Wards as they'd planned. Cyrus wasn't sure what was more surprising: the fact that they'd all survived or the fact that Sorin had somehow Traveled.

Kailia had poured a vial of Cethin's blood into the sea, and Cassius had Traveled them all back to Aimonway. They'd all slept. He and Cass had slept an entire day. The Ash Riders and Sorin nearly two. Rayner's power wasn't anywhere near replenished. He hadn't seen the Avonleyan Queen to know how she fared. Sorin had managed to refill Scarlett's reserves before he'd fallen into the deep sleep needed to restore their gifts, and Cyrus had given Cassius extra blood when he'd woken.

Cyrus had been awake for nearly two hours this morning when the knock had come on their door. With Cass still sleeping, he'd been surprised to find Tybalt on the other side.

"Do you have news from Razik?" Cyrus had asked, stepping aside so the Avonleyan Commander could enter.

Tybalt had shaken his head, features tightening some. "I have not heard from him in quite some time."

"Should we be worried?"

Tybalt had flashed him a tight smile. "Razik is resourceful, and he will not leave Eliza right now. I am sure the two of them together are a formidable pair."

Cyrus had nodded. He had a point, but still...

All right, fine. He missed Eliza. He hadn't seen her in weeks, and before that she'd been healing. He wanted some sense of normalcy, and that included her snark.

Tybalt had cleared his throat then. "I was hoping to speak with Cassius about a few things."

As if he'd heard his name, Cass had come through the door that led to their bedchamber. Barefoot and shirtless, Cyrus had looked him up and down. Cass's lips had rolled to hide his smirk, but his focus was fixed on his father.

Cyrus had left them to their daddy-son bonding session and wandered down to the dining room, finding the breakfast spread ready and waiting. So here he sat. Alone with the same thoughts that had him up before the sun.

The same thoughts that had kept him from sleeping much at all last night.

Now that Scarlett had the lock, he needed to go start looking for this thing the Sorceress wanted from the Black Syndicate. He had a feeling she might be looking to collect more blood from him soon too. So many of their plans now had to be timed perfectly. This little quest was no different. If things went well, everything would fall into place. If things didn't...

Well, they had back-up plans for their back-up plans at this point.

Footsteps sounded and his gaze flicked to the door, Tybalt and Cassius coming through a few moments later. Cyrus sat up straighter at the look on Cassius's face. The tense jaw, lips in a thin line, a slight furrow between his brows.

There was something...not wrong, necessarily. But it was something that bothered him, and Cass was trying to hide it.

His gaze met Cyrus's, and he moved to the seat next to him, reaching for the plate of toast. Tybalt moved to a chair at the head of the table, his demeanor the same as Cassius's.

"What's going on?" Cyrus finally asked as the two wordlessly filled their plates.

"Nothing," Cassius said too quickly, scooping fried potatoes from a bowl.

Cyrus looked at Tybalt, the same warm brown eyes as Cassius had already staring back at him.

"Cethin said he visited with you all last night," Tybalt said.

"Yeah..." Cyrus said in confusion. They'd all been in the princess's suite with Sorin. With Scarlett still unconscious, Sorin rarely left the space. They'd gathered in their sitting room to hash out final details for the next phase of their plans. Although that was rather pointless when Cyrus really thought about it. Scarlett would wake up and likely change everything anyway.

"His power has been restoring over these past weeks," Tybalt went on.

"Doesn't it take Avonleyans quite a bit of time to do that?" Cyrus asked, glancing at Cass who was giving his father a pointed look.

"Yes, especially when completely drained as Cethin was," Tybalt answered. "His circumstances are...a little different."

"Because Kailia isn't his Source?" Cyrus asked. He'd found it odd that she wasn't. He couldn't imagine Cethin having that kind of bond with someone else.

"Kailia is not Fae," Tybalt said, shaking his head. "Cethin does not have a Source, nor will he ever take one. As I said, his circumstances are different."

"Different how, exactly?" Cyrus asked, settling back in his chair and crossing his arms. "And what do you mean Kailia is not Fae?"

Tybalt cut off a piece of sausage. "These are questions you should ask Cethin."

"Cethin hasn't exactly been forthcoming with information, so I am asking you," Cyrus said, his tone softening into a dark demand that even had Cassius pausing and turning to look at him. It took a lot to get under Cyrus's skin, and he knew his personality often made people forget he was the Fire Court Second. Good-natured and easy-going to hide the cunning. It was a skill he'd perfected with Merrik. Rayner might rip out organs, and Eliza might get extra stabby with pointy objects, but Cyrus?

He didn't need the fancy tricks. He preferred to simply burn things, and smile at the carnage left in his wake while sipping on a glass of liquor and smoking some mugweed.

But they were in the middle of a godsdamn war. There shouldn't be secrets at this point. All cards should be on the table. Saylah keeping information hostage was enough. They didn't need to be doing it to each other.

Tybalt cleared his throat, setting his silverware off to the side. "We do not know what Kailia is. Cethin and Razik have been searching for answers for decades, but without knowing where she came from—"

"I thought she was raised in those cliffs like Rayner," Cyrus interrupted.

"As far as she can remember, yes. But her ancestry? Parents? We have nothing to go on. Only her gifts, which seem to mirror that of Ash Riders but are also different," Tybalt explained. "And with Cethin being able to detect power levels, he can tell she is not Fae."

"And even if Fae were more accessible, he would not take a Source?" Cyrus guessed, Cassius still suspiciously quiet while he listened to their conversation.

"Correct. Saylah refills his gifts faster when she can, but her strength is not what it should be, having been trapped here for so long," Tybalt went on.

"Does he need blood then?" Cyrus asked. He'd been supplying it to Cassius since he'd returned. Neve was the only other available Fae option at this point, and she'd started providing for Auberon. For either of them to supply Cethin? It would take a lot for such a powerful being.

Tybalt shook his head again. "Cethin will not drink. He…" Tybalt paused, clearly searching for the right words. "It would require a large amount for him at this point. But Cethin is not who we should be discussing right now."

Cyrus propped his elbow on the arm of his chair, his finger steepled along his temple. "You brought Cethin up."

"Yes, because he spent some time with all of you last night. With his power returning, he can once again sense power levels," Tybalt said, eyes flicking to Cassius.

Cyrus sat forward, understanding exactly what Tybalt was saying this time. "You haven't been taking enough," he snarled at Cass.

Cyrus knew he'd needed more. He'd been giving him blood twice a day, but it had apparently still not been enough.

"It has been enough," Cassius said, turning to face him, his features a mixture of frustration and... Cyrus couldn't tell what else was there. "Or it was until we returned from the Southern Islands."

Cyrus placed a palm on the table as he said, "Just to make sure I have this right: instead of saying something and telling me you needed more, Cethin had to tell your daddy who, in turn, had to tell me?"

"Fuck off with that daddy shit," Cassius snarled, eyes shifting and glowing softly.

"No, you fuck off, Cass," Cyrus shot back. "Did we not have this exact argument weeks ago?"

"Things have obviously changed since then," Cass retorted, stabbing a piece of sausage onto his fork.

"Not really. Still found out from someone else that you are not properly refilling your reserves."

Cassius's fork clattered to his plate, and he turned to face him fully. "That's not fair, Cyrus."

"What's not fair is you not keeping your magic wells full at all times when others are counting on you in a godsdamn war. Gods! Why is this so hard for you and Scarlett to understand? Why did we practically have to beat this same concept into her?" Cyrus spat.

"Could it possibly be because it was *literally* beaten into us not to be dependent on others?" Cassius bit back through clenched teeth.

"Bullshit," Cyrus said, settling back in his chair again. "You two are ridiculously co-dependent on each other."

"Perhaps I should let you two have some time—" Tybalt said, starting to get to his feet.

"No need," Cyrus interjected, sliding his chair back and standing.

"Maybe you can talk some sense into your son. Whatever I say to him clearly doesn't sink in."

"Cyrus," Cassius sighed, rubbing at his brow with his thumb and forefinger.

Cyrus paused in the doorway, resting his hand on the doorjamb as he looked back over his shoulder, already feeling the guilt over his part in this. "I know, Cass," he sighed. "Just…find me when you're ready."

He wandered back up to their rooms, but then he kept going to Sorin and Scarlett's. He knocked once before going inside. It was quiet, but Sorin came out of the bedchamber a moment later.

"Cyrus? Everything all right?"

"Fine," he muttered, looking past him into the room. "She still sleeping?"

Sorin raked a hand through his hair. "Yeah."

"But you can still feel her and everything down the bond?"

He nodded, pushing out a harsh breath. "Niara checks in multiple times a day. She says everything is healing as it should. We can only wait."

The Fire Prince had begun pacing as he spoke, and the corner of Cyrus's mouth tilted up. "Were you like this when you first brought her to the Court, too? When you kept us all locked out?"

Sorin paused mid-step, letting loose another sigh. "Yeah. Yeah, I was."

Cyrus snickered, plopping down on the sofa.

"Are you sure you are all right?" Sorin asked, lowering into an armchair.

"Cassius needs a Source."

Sorin went still for a moment. "Did he ask you?"

"No."

"Did he ask someone else?"

"Not that I'm aware of."

"I feel as though I am missing something here, Cyrus," Sorin said, studying him in that knowing way of his. Like he could see past all the bullshit. He'd always looked at him like that. Ever since Rayner had dragged him to the Fiera Palace, and Cyrus had met the Fire Prince for the first time over a game of cards and a drink.

Cyrus quickly filled Sorin in on the conversation he'd just had with

Tybalt, and when he was done, Sorin asked, "Is it something you are still willing to give, Cyrus?"

And wasn't that the question of the day?

It was late evening when he heard the door to their suite open. He'd been on the balcony for almost an hour now. Thinking. Waiting.

Drinking and smoking mugweed.

The sun was nearly set, and he had small orbs of flames floating above the balcony. Avonleya loved the night. Their odd schedule had been fine for a time, but he was ready to go back to their continent.

He swirled his glass of liquor, the ice clinking as he brought the mugweed to his lips and inhaled. He heard him stop at the doorway. Knew if he turned to look, he'd be leaning against the doorframe, trying to decide what to say.

Pinching the mugweed between his thumb and forefinger, he held it above his head in offering. A moment later, footsteps sounded before Cassius was taking it from his hand.

Cyrus shuffled down the sofa, making room, and Cass took a seat, blowing smoke into the darkening night.

"I'm sorry, Cyrus," he said after a moment. "I did not intend to keep it from you."

Cyrus nodded, taking a drink.

"I did know my power wasn't refilling as much as it should, but I didn't realize…" He leaned forward, elbows on his knees and arms crossed, mugweed still pinched in his fingers. "Tybalt came to me this morning because if I ask you for more, if I start drinking more each day, I'm slipping into dangerous territory. Night Child kind of stuff."

Cyrus reached for the mugweed, taking another drag. "You need a Source."

"Yeah, Cyrus. I need a Source."

"Glad you finally figured that out."

They sat in silence. Cyrus didn't care. He was more relaxed than he'd been in weeks. They could sit and stare at the sky all fucking night for all he cared.

Finally, Cass said, "That's all you're going to say?"

Cyrus shrugged. "Not sure what you want me to say."

"Something. Anything."

He took another drag. "Neve is really the only option now, isn't she?"

"Neve," Cassius repeated.

Cyrus tipped his head back, exhaling the smoke. "Eliza is tied to Razik. Sawyer is... Unless you want to track down Luan when we get to the continent? But he's got Avonleyan blood so not sure how that will work. Briar will literally drown you if you ask Ashtine, and Briar is about to be a father."

When Cassius didn't say anything, he went on. "Neve is not as powerful as the others, but she is probably a good choice. She won't want anything physical, even if the bond pushes for it. She prefers females." He tossed the last of the mugweed roll to the ground before he incinerated it. "You should probably figure it out before we go to the continent, though."

Cyrus moved to rise from the sofa, but a hand on his shoulder kept him seated.

"We're not done talking about this."

"I told you my thoughts. This is your decision, Cass," Cyrus said, shrugging his hand off his shoulder. "If you don't want any of them—"

"I don't."

"Then there are some Fae on the continent, but they'll be hard to track down right now with everything going on. I can get a list written up though. Get Sorin's thoughts, too, before you decide who to ask."

"And if I ask you?" Cassius asked in a low rumble.

Cyrus flexed his fingers on the glass he still held.

He'd thought about this. All day. Talked about it with Sorin. Tried to sort through his thoughts.

His eyes were fixed on his glass when he said, "Maybe you've been right all along, Cass. Maybe it shouldn't be me."

He couldn't look at him. But this topic had been a source of contention between them since they'd come to Avonleya. They'd argued about this more than anything else. They'd had godsdamn fights over this. Maybe if it was taken out of play...

"Are you saying you will be fine if I create this bond with someone else?" Cass finally asked.

No. He hated the idea, but he'd failed so many others. Merrik. Thia. He could spare Cassius from that.

"Because I'm not fine with it," Cass said when Cyrus didn't answer. "Look me in the eye and tell me you'll be perfectly fine if I take another Source."

"Of course I will not like it," Cyrus snapped, shooting to his feet. "But this isn't about me. It's about you, and what's best for you."

"What's best for me is you," Cass answered, gaze following him as Cyrus paced in a small circle, dragging both his hands through his hair.

*If you can't see that all you do is damage everyone around you, then I will keep reminding you until you believe it.*

"Cyrus."

His fingers tightened on the strands, tugging at the roots.

*No one wants you, Cyrus.*

"Cyrus."

His eyes closed.

*If you can't see that all you do is damage everyone around you, then I will keep reminding you until you believe it.*

Hands on his face.

A brow pressing to his.

"Talk to me, Cyrus. If you don't want to do this, I understand. I get it. I understand if what I said to you was too unforgivable."

"What are you talking about?" Cyrus rasped, fingers still tugging at his scalp.

"I will not ask this of you if it is not something you want anymore. I understand, Cyrus," Cassius said again, a hand reaching up and pulling his own from his hair one at a time.

"You think I do not want to?"

"I think I hurt you and do not deserve to ask this of you anymore," Cass answered. "And I do not want you to feel guilty over that."

Cyrus's brows pinched together. "Then what will you do? Take another?"

"No."

"You need a Source, Cass."

"If I have learned anything, it's that there is always a workaround—"

"This is not that," Cyrus interrupted. "This is… You need this. I thought you understood that."

He stepped away from him in frustration.

"I understand, but I can't give that control to anyone but you."

"It can't be me!" Cyrus said, the words raw and agonized as they clawed up his throat. "Can't you see that?"

"Cyrus…"

But now that he'd said it, he couldn't stop. The mugweed and the alcohol loosened his tongue, and his thoughts spilled out before he could stop them. "I can't ruin you like I ruined them, Cassius. You speak of being deserving? You deserve so much more than what I can give you. I couldn't save Merrik. I made Thia believe we were twin flames, convinced her to offer up a piece of her soul—"

He was cut off when he was pulled through the air, Cassius grabbing his hand and Traveling them. When he blinked, he stood in the foyer of the Greybane manor. Before he could ask what they were doing there, a woman stepped into view.

"Lord Cassius? I did not know we were expecting you tonight," Magdalena said, wiping her hands on her apron. "If you give me a few moments, I can get your rooms prepared."

"Thank you, but that will not be necessary. Is my father in?" Cassius asked, hand still wrapped tightly about Cyrus's.

Magdalena's brow furrowed. "Yes. I believe he is in his study. Would you like me to fetch him?"

"No, thank you. I will find him," Cassius said, tugging Cyrus after him as he started down a hall.

"What are we doing here?" Cyrus asked in a hissed whisper.

He didn't know whether to be pissed, hurt, or relieved that Cassius had Traveled them in the middle of such an important conversation.

"We need to settle something," Cassius said.

"At this exact moment?"

"Yes," he answered. He rapped twice on the double doors of Tybalt's study, pushing them open as soon as they heard Tybalt's greeting.

The Commander got to his feet when he saw them, surprise and worry crossing his features. "Cassius?"

"What do you know of twin flames?" Cassius asked, finally releasing Cyrus's hand.

"What?" Cyrus hissed, rounding on him.

Tybalt blinked in clear surprise at the topic, but said, "A fair amount, I suppose."

"Razik said a twin flame bond occurs between a Legacy and a Fae," Cassius said.

"Yes. That is true," Tybalt agreed, eyes moving from Cassius to Cyrus and back again.

Cyrus shoved his hands into his pockets. He didn't want to hear this. Didn't need to hear the truth of the matter again. That he and Thia had not been twin flames.

"But one does not need to be a full-blooded Legacy to have a twin flame, correct?" Cassius asked.

"Yes, that is correct. The bond is not usually felt as strongly and can be harder to recognize," Tybalt said.

"And if two people take the Marks, but they are not twin flames, what would happen?" Cassius pressed.

"The Trials would not be completed, and the bond could not be Anointed," Tybalt answered. "Eventually the Mark would fade, and the piece of the soul that was offered is lost in the voids between the stars."

"To be clear, a bond cannot be Anointed if the two are not twin flames, yes?"

"Yes. What is this about, Cassius?" Tybalt asked, coming around his desk and leaning against it. "Do you believe the two of you are—"

"No," Cassius interrupted. "I love him, yes, but Cyrus had a twin flame. They recognized the bond the moment they saw each other. She was killed."

Kind eyes slid to Cyrus. "I am sorry to hear that, Cyrus."

"She wasn't—" Cyrus started.

"Did the two of you complete the Trials?" Cassius snarled, rounding on him.

"Yes, but—"

"And was your bond Anointed?" Cass demanded.

"By Beatrix, but—"

"But nothing," Cass interrupted again. "How much more proof do you need, Cyrus?"

"Thia was Fae!" Cyrus snapped. "I am Fae. It could not have been a real bond. The Sorceress said—"

"That godsdamn Sorceress," Cassius growled, his eyes shifting. Smoke furled when he exhaled, his hands fisting at his sides. His features darkened, violence simmering in his glowing eyes, and Cyrus almost took a step back. "If I accomplish only one thing before I cross the Veil, it will be to witness her death. I will consider myself blessed by the gods if I am the one to bestow it."

"If I may," Tybalt interrupted, hands still braced on the desk behind him. Cyrus glanced at him, and he could tell the Avonleyan now understood what was happening here. "Cassius is correct. The bond would not have been completed and Anointed if it were not a true twin flame bond. The Marks would have rejected the Anointing. Even completing the Trials would have been near impossible if it were not a true bond. One of you had Avonleyan lineage. Even a trace of it would have been enough. But if you both recognized the bond immediately while both of you believing yourselves fully Fae..." His lips tipped up in a small smile. "I would consider you profoundly blessed, Cyrus. Fate clearly wanted you together, even if just for a time."

"You were deserving of a twin flame, Cyrus," Cassius said, his tone having softened. Cyrus lifted his gaze to his, only then realizing a tear had slipped free. Cass's eyes were still shifted and glowing, but gods. It was love that stared back at him. Raw and unbridled and pure. "Not only were you deserving of a twin flame, but you have found real, true love two other times. You have found a family. The Sorceress stole from you. She stole your memories and made you question that love. That's not your fault, but do not give her this too, Cyrus. Choose to believe those who love you over her. Choose us, Cyrus."

"I will be in the den if you need me," Tybalt said quietly, Traveling from the room.

Cassius reached out, grabbing the front of Cyrus's tunic and tugging him forward. His other hand came up and cupped Cyrus's jaw. "I will not take another Source, Cyrus. It will be you or no one. It does not need to be tonight. It does not need to be tomorrow. It will be when you are ready, and if that day does not come? That is okay, too. We will figure something out. And if we do not? I choose a powerless existence with you over power with someone else. You deserve love, Cyrus. I'll say it until you believe it, and then I'll say it so you remember it."

"I don't know how to fix this. How to fix me," Cyrus replied in an agonized whisper.

"You don't need to fix a godsdamn thing," Cassius replied, bringing his mouth to his. It did exactly what Cassius had once said he'd do. When words weren't enough, he found another way. The kiss was slow and thorough, and Cass pulled back first, keeping his lips a breath away when he said, "You need to choose it, Cyrus. After that, we clean it up together."

Cyrus reached up, wrapping his hands around Cassius's wrists. "What's best for me is you."

The hand fisted in Cyrus's tunic loosened, fingers sliding down his torso and landing on his hip. "You took that mugweed from my rooms, didn't you?"

"Yeah," Cyrus sighed.

Cass's lips tipped up. "I have more I hid from you."

"Thank fuck," Cyrus muttered a moment before Cassius pulled them through the air.

They were back on the balcony, Cassius already striding for the door to get the mugweed.

"Cassius, wait," Cyrus called after him. Cass paused, turning back. Cyrus rubbed at the back of his neck. "We should find Cethin or something. Have him give the Mark. Probably shouldn't do that while we're fucked up on mugweed."

"I said it didn't need to be tonight, Cyrus," Cassius said slowly, moving as if to take a step but then staying where he was.

"I know what you said," Cyrus answered. "But it's something you need, and despite what you said, it does need to be done sooner than later. We need to go to the continent, and you need to have your magic at its strongest when we're there. And I just…"

"We don't need Cethin, Cyrus."

Cyrus dropped his hand to his side. "We don't?"

Cassius shook his head, still rooted to that same spot. "I'm Avonleyan. Same as Scarlett and Cethin and Razik."

"Marks have to be drawn precisely, Cass."

"I know. What do you think I have been studying in those books all this time?"

Cyrus's brows rose. "You've been studying the Source Mark?"

"I've been studying the Marks in general, but yes. I've been practicing the Source Mark more than the others."

"So you can…" Cyrus trailed off.

Cassius nodded. "But only if you're sure, Cyrus."

The thing was, Cyrus didn't know if he'd ever be completely sure. Not with everything Gehenna had done to his memories. He would forever question if it was the right choice. If he was hurting the ones he loved. Some small part of him would always grapple with distinguishing the lies she'd sewn.

He blew out a harsh breath, hand tugging at his strands again. "It won't be a twin flame Mark, but it will be something. To help ground me when her words are threatening to overtake my reality. To remind me that you're still here. That I chose this, and you chose me. Despite it all."

Cassius didn't say anything. Just turned and walked back into the room. Cyrus sighed, pushing his hands through his hair again before he followed. Cassius was already coming back in from the other room, flipping through the pages of a book until he found the one he was looking for. Uncertain eyes lifted to his.

"This is it, Cyrus," Cass said. "It's a lifetime."

"That's what we're going for, isn't it?" Cyrus asked, trying to muster up his cocky grin.

"You know what I mean," he retorted, scanning the page. "Last chance to say no."

"What's best for me is you," Cyrus answered. There was no hesitation when he said it. No second guessing himself or questioning the truth of those words.

"From what Scarlett and Sorin have said, this will be…uncomfortable," Cassius said, setting the book on their bed.

"Yeah, yeah," Cyrus replied, moving closer and flopping down onto the blankets. "I'm familiar with uncomfortable, Cass. Let's do this."

Cassius retrieved a dagger from across the room, and Cyrus propped a hand behind his head, bending a knee and getting comfortable. Cass snickered when he came back, and Cyrus felt the bed dip when he sat on the edge of it.

"Where do you want the Mark?" he murmured, pulling the book closer and studying the page once more.

"Whatever's easiest," Cyrus answered with a shrug. "Forearm? Like Sorin's?"

"That would be fine, but I was thinking the back of your hand. Your right hand," Cass added quickly, twisting to face him fully.

"That's fine, but any particular reason?" he asked curiously, studying him. His eyes were already shifted to an amber-red, and he reached for Cyrus's right hand where it was resting atop his stomach.

"Because you said the Mark would ground you," Cass answered, his thumb swiping across the back of Cyrus's hand. "Seeing it would remind you that you're wanted, even if I can't be there to say it at the time. This way, it's visible at all times."

Cyrus swallowed thickly, rotating his wrist so their fingers intertwined. "Yeah, Cass," he rasped. "Back of the hand is good."

They didn't speak after that.

Cassius dragged the dagger across the back of Cyrus's hand, holding it in his lap while he carefully drew the Mark with his finger. Cyrus watched him. Head bent low. Hair hanging in his face. Entirely focused on the task. In complete control.

When he was done, he compared it to the Mark in the book for a long moment until Cyrus said, "I'm sure it's perfect, Cass."

"I'm not taking any chances," he murmured back, eyes darting from the book and back to the Mark again.

"Let's go, Cass," Cyrus urged, stretching out his leg. "The sooner we do this, the sooner we find that mugweed."

Cassius huffed a laugh, reaching for the dagger again. He held it over his palm. "Last chance."

"I'm all yours," Cyrus answered with a wink. Cassius huffed another laugh, but when he sliced his palm and started to bring it to the Mark, Cyrus said, "Cass?"

Cassius froze. "Yeah?"

"I love you."

The corner of his lips tipped up. "I love you too, Cyrus."

Then his hand was on the Mark, their blood mixing, and Cyrus was cursing.

"Fucking fire of Anala," he gasped when heat blazed through him, and not the fire he was used to. This was the same heat that had steadily burned through his shield in a training arena the first time Cassius had kissed him. He'd known if that dragon fire touched him, it would hurt like a motherfucker, and he'd been right because *fuck*.

His own fire flared to life, rising up to protect him, and he tried to pull his magic back, to make it submit to Cass's power. It was useless. That's not how magic worked, not when its bearer was being directly attacked. This had to be done between their power, not their will.

He barked another curse when Cassius sent more magic into his veins, and Cyrus tried to pull away on instinct alone. Cassius held his hand in a vice grip though, and at the movement, a growl came from him that had Cyrus falling still. His magic stuttered for a moment too. There was nothing of the watchful, kind-hearted male on Cassius's face. This was just pure want and primal dominance at something he viewed as *his* trying to be taken from him.

"Let me have it, Cyrus," Cassius demanded, his voice low and rough, and the way Cyrus wanted to do just that—

"Fuck!" Cyrus snapped when another wave of black flames slammed into him. He couldn't just lie here. His Fae nature wouldn't allow it, even if he consciously knew what they were doing. He surged up, flipping them so he was on top of Cassius, his teeth bared and fire slamming up against his black flames.

"Godsdamnit, Cyrus," Cassius snarled, his eyes glowing brighter. He'd managed to maintain the grip on Cyrus's hand, and his fingers tightened. "If we break this connection, we have to start over."

Cyrus heard him, even understood the logic of that, but his primal

Fae maleness didn't give a fuck. He snarled back, leaning in close. His elongated canines were getting dangerously close to Cassius's throat when it was Cassius surging up. They were both on their feet, and Cassius was forcing him back and back. His wings ripped free, and smoke appeared on his next exhale as Cyrus's back hit the wall hard.

"Cyrus." His name was a feral order on his lips. A primal claiming. A demanding possession that again had his fire stuttering, and Cassius took the opportunity to wind his black flames around Cyrus's magic so tightly, it had no choice but to give in.

Cords of orange and black erupted between them, twining together until there was no way to tell where one started and the other began before they flared a bright gold and settled into them. Cyrus felt it in his soul. This connection was different from what he'd had with Merrik. Different from the twin flame bond he'd had with Thia.

This was theirs. Solely theirs.

They were both breathing heavily, bodies still tense. Cyrus tugged his hand from Cass's grip, reaching out to tug the remains of Cass's tunic from his chest. It had torn when his wings had appeared. Of course, now it was just taut muscle for Cyrus to look at. He tossed the shredded tunic aside, immediately reaching back to run his fingers along bare skin, but Cass caught his wrist before he could.

"You're mine," Cass said, his voice nothing but gravel as his fingertips brushed over the Source Mark on the back of Cyrus's hand. His eyes followed the movement, transfixed on the black Mark. Cyrus could hear it in his voice, feel it in the tremble of his hand as he gripped his wrist. As his chest continued to rise and fall too rapidly.

He was on the brink of losing control. He was doing everything he could to keep it.

It struck Cyrus then that dragon possessiveness might rival Fae possessiveness. Not only that, Cassius was part-dragon, part-Witch. Both bloodlines were notorious for being dominant and controlling. If he lost that control, it would shove him into his own dark place, but if Cyrus *gave* him that control…

"You said you take what's yours," Cyrus said into the space between them.

"I do," Cass said gruffly, slowly dragging his eyes up to meet his, but they snagged on Cyrus's mouth. Cass's tongue darted out, running along his bottom lip as he stared.

Cyrus reached out, tugging him forward by the band of his pants. "Prove it."

With another growl, Cassius's hand snapped out, gripping the back of Cyrus's neck and hauling him forward. Their mouths slammed together, and a new battle for dominance took place. This one with lips and tongues and teeth rather than magic and flames.

Cassius pressed Cyrus back into the wall once more, sinking his teeth into the line of his jaw as his hips rolled forward into Cyrus's, making them both groan.

"Fuck," Cyrus spat, his brow falling to Cass's shoulder. Then he cursed again when Cass wedged a thigh between his legs, parting them enough so that when his hand pulled Cyrus's thigh up to wrap around his hip, Cyrus could feel the friction everywhere it mattered.

A hand fisted in Cyrus's hair, tipping his head back, and Cassius licked a long line up his throat before he brought his mouth to his ear and said, "On your knees, Cyrus. Make it sloppy so I can take what's mine."

That was the moment all coherent thought left.

As he sank to his knees, Cass pulled Cyrus's tunic over his head, burning away the rest of their clothing, before planting a palm on the wall above them. His hips rolled forward again, his tip brushing along the seam of Cyrus's lips. And because he was who he was, Cyrus smirked up at him before he flicked the tip of his tongue over his crown.

Cassius growled what Cyrus thought might be his name, but Cyrus was already taking him deep. The growl became a curse. Cass's other hand slid into Cyrus's hair again, cupping the back of his head as he thrust forward. Cyrus did as he'd ordered, sucking and licking and taking every surge of Cass's hips.

"Cyrus," Cass groaned, fingers flexing in his hair, and Cyrus knew what he wanted. He didn't need him to say it. He had one hand on Cass's thigh, and he trailed his other hand up his torso, until Cass snatched his wrist. He took two fingers into his mouth, sucking hard, and Cyrus moaned around him as Cass's tongue lapped over the digits. The moment Cass released him, Cyrus was reaching around himself and getting ready for him the same way he was getting Cass ready.

The string of curse words that left Cassius had Cyrus huffing a laugh around him, but it turned into a moan a moment later, the sensation of his own fingers working himself open and Cass in his mouth almost too much.

Cass gave him the time he needed, but Cyrus could tell his control was slipping as his fingers fisted tighter and tighter in his hair. He had hardly pulled off him when Cassius was hauling him up and spinning him around to face the wall.

Then it was Cyrus cursing as he felt him press in slowly. Torturously slowly. Cyrus tried to press back, wanting more, but Cass hissed, holding him in place.

"Stop," he snarled into his ear. "It's been a while. For both of us."

"Stop being so selfless," Cyrus retorted on a gasp, trying to press back again. "You think I don't know how to prepare myself for this? Take what you want, Cass."

But still the prick refused, instead peppering small kisses along his shoulder, between his shoulder blades, up the back of his neck. Teasing. Coaxing. There was the soft sound of spitting before one of Cass's hands slipped around, gripping Cyrus's length. Then Cyrus was groaning as Cass slid in further while moving along his length at the same time.

"You think you need to fix yourself," Cassius murmured into his ear. "But you're perfect, Cyrus. Godsdamn perfect."

Cyrus couldn't help the shudder that rolled down his spine at the words, or the carnal groan that came from him when Cassius finally filled him completely. Cass's face was buried in his neck, sucking along it as he continued to move his fist.

Cassius was wrong, Cyrus realized, getting lost in the sensation of everything. He wasn't perfect. *This* was perfect.

It was perfect when they found themselves on the bed, Cassius above him, wings flared out as his hips punched forward in perfect rhythm with his fist wrapped around Cyrus's length. Each movement was precise and controlled because it was Cass, and he couldn't lose control even in this.

It was perfect when they both found their pleasure at nearly the same moment.

It was perfect when they were laying together later, legs tangled beneath blankets and facing each other in the dark of the room.

It was perfect when Cyrus realized he didn't have the slightest desire for a drink or mugweed, because this was enough to keep his thoughts at bay.

It was perfect when, instead of hearing the Sorceress in his head as he drifted off to sleep, he heard Cassius's words.

*What's best for me is you.*

And he believed them.

# CHAPTER 32
# ELIZA

Cold.

That's the first thing she comprehended as she slowly came back to consciousness. She was cold. Freezing actually.

Eliza blinked her eyes open, her lids heavy. The world was blurry, and bits of ash were falling from the sky.

No.

Not ash.

Snow.

That was snow gently falling above her. Not much. It melted as soon as it touched the ground. Because she was in the mountains where it didn't care if it was supposed to be spring.

The sky was dim, either with the first light or the last light of the day. How long had she been out?

She shifted slightly, then bit down on her scream of agony.

And with that, everything came rushing back— coming to the Fire Court, Razik, Varlis, the shirastone left in her shoulder, a dragon falling from the sky.

They'd used her to get to him. For what, she didn't know. They couldn't have gotten far trying to haul a huge dragon somewhere in the mountains. Not unless they had a Traveler with them.

Gods, she hoped they didn't have a Traveler with them.

Unless Razik had shifted back.

But they would have had to remove the bolts they had shot him with, and if he had enough power to shift, he'd have enough power to burn them to nothing. They would be stupid to risk it.

Which begged the question again of how fucking long had she been out? How thoroughly had Varlis knocked her unconscious to ensure she didn't wake up for hours, possibly days? The shirastone he'd left embedded deep in her shoulder didn't help matters. There was only one way she'd be able to find Razik now, and to do that, she needed to get the arrow tip out of her body.

A string of unending curses left her mouth as she worked herself into a sitting position and then to her feet. She would have preferred to crawl, but there was no way her shoulder was supporting any kind of weight right now. So she stumbled her way to the cave behind her, hoping to the gods that Varlis and the seraphs hadn't been smart enough to search it. That the two packs Razik had carried in here were still waiting.

She dropped to her knees when she was deep enough inside the cave to not be spotted by anyone flying overhead. Pressing her hand to the wound, it came away wet with blood. If she could still function, she hadn't lost too much blood yet, which meant it was likely evening of the same day. To be honest, Varlis leaving the arrow-tip embedded in her shoulder was probably staunching the blood flow for now.

Eliza forced herself back to her feet, feeling in the dark for the wall. It had to be a good hour, if not more, before she tripped over their packs after fumbling along, feeling with her feet and hand. Or maybe it had just felt like hours because she had to force every step, every breath. She constantly had to stop when her legs trembled too much with the effort to keep her upright, or the blackness of her vision became more than the darkness of the cave. She couldn't stop the tears that leaked from the corners of her eyes as she landed hard on her side, trying to protect her injured shoulder as her feet got wrapped up in the packs. It took everything in her not to vomit from the pain.

She took a moment, breathing through her teeth.

She knew.

She knew the pain she was feeling wasn't just her own, which told her Razik was in just as rough of shape as she was in, likely worse.

Bracing herself, she pulled a pack to her and began to unpack it. She couldn't just dump it out and risk losing valuable items in the dark, so she painstakingly took things out one by one. She lined them up beside her, sorting them out by touch alone. This was her pack, thank Anala. She knew how she'd packed everything, so when her fingers found the small knife she was searching for, she let out another shaky breath.

That had been the easy part.

Sybil had yanked the dagger from her when she'd been stabbed before. She didn't want to think about the fact that the male who had raised her was crueler than a godsdamn Witch.

Or the fact that such cruelty had likely saved her life.

She'd pulled out her leathers before she'd found the knife, and now she grabbed the closest one, placing a strap between her teeth and biting down.

Then she screamed, as she sank a finger into the wound, trying to figure out just how deeply he had broken off the arrow shaft. She could feel the splintered end of the shaft, but there was no way she was going to be able to dig it out with only one finger.

Yanking her hand back, Eliza spit out the leather and vomited, the pain too much. She didn't know if she could do this. Cut out the shira-stone. Pack the wound enough to hopefully let her Fae blood heal it to the point that she could use her magic. A shirastone wound would require a Healer, but she just needed to access her fire. If she could do that, she could figure out everything else.

She righted herself, tipping her head back against the wall. Her hairline was damp with sweat, face wet with tears. She took a drink from a waterskin, rinsing the vomit taste from her mouth, before she bit down on the leather once more and brought the knife to her skin.

Razik's roar of fury as he flew out of this cave.

His cry of agony when the bolt hit him.

Falling from the sky.

Not knowing where he was.

Knowing he was in unbearable pain.

Those things were what she focused on as she cut and dug and screamed until, finally, she threw the arrow piece across the cave, hearing it clatter as stone met stone. She had a tunic ready and waiting, and she pressed it to the wound, her chest heaving as she panted. Her vision was blurry, not that she could see anything in the darkness of the cave. Her entire body was cold and clammy.

But it was out. The shirastone was out. Now it was a waiting game.

Turning to look at the cave mouth, she found it just as pitch dark beyond. She'd been right. She'd woken in the evening.

She had lain everything out as she'd unpacked it— the tunic, jars of antiseptic and ointment she always traveled with, bandages. She'd even managed to cut strips off another tunic to tie around the wound once she cleaned it.

Her hands were trembling violently when she was finally done, and she slumped back against the wall. With the last bit of strength she had, she reached for Razik's pack, dragging it across the cave floor. There was no careful unpacking this time. She shook the pack out, hearing various items scatter across the ground. She was trying to find a spare tunic to pull on, having had to cut her tunic off to bandage the wound as best she could. Her fingers brushed against a cloak. He must have removed it while he'd been exploring the cave, trying to decide if it was a good one. What the fuck made a cave a "good cave" anyway? What was so special about his cave in the Nightmist Mountains?

That was her thought as she tugged his cloak over herself, closing her eyes.

But those weren't her last thoughts as unconsciousness finally won out.

No, those thoughts were of Varlis.

Dead.

Varlis was dead.

Sorin, Cyrus, and Rayner had all offered, at one point or another, to track the male down and kill him for what he had done to her. She'd declined, not wanting to waste another moment on the piece of shit. She'd built herself a perfectly fine life despite what he'd done to her. That had been the best form of revenge she could think of, and it had worked. It had clearly infuriated him to no end that she not only lived, but thrived. That she had risen to such a level of power within the Fire Court with the flames the male loathed.

But that had never been the real reason she had denied them his death.

She didn't need a male to avenge her or go after the Earth Fae.

If anyone was going to kill Varlis, it would be her, and she would make damn sure she looked him in the eyes when she did it with her fucking fire.

She drifted in and out of consciousness. At one point, she glimpsed blue sky at the cave entrance through bleary eyes. The next time she remembered anything, it had been dark again. This time, it was either early morning or late twilight, a few stars visible.

But that was a spark in her blood, and thank Anala for that. With a shuddering breath, she managed to drag up enough power to warm her body and start a small fire.

Then she slipped into nothing again.

The cry of a hawk jolted her awake, and she cursed under her breath as she shifted. Her entire body ached. Her shoulder from the shiras-tone and the digging and cleaning she'd done to the wound. Her head from dehydration. Her ass and back from sleeping against a cave wall. Why Razik willingly chose to sleep in a cave over his rooms most nights was beyond her. There was no way in the realms that was comfortable, even if he slept in his dragon form.

That was sunlight shining into the cave though. Between that and the fire still burning, she could make out the general layout of the space. It wasn't overly large. It would have actually been perfect for what they'd been looking for. A small hidden area to come up with a plan.

Tucking her chin, she could see the make-shift bandage around her injury. The tunic was just starting to show spots of blood. Which was good. She'd clearly slept for at least two days, if not more. If blood was just now reaching the outer layers of the bandage, she'd packed the wound well in her semi-lucid state.

Gathering the supplies close to her once more, she cleaned it out and applied a new dressing before searching for food and the water-skin. She worked Razik's cloak around her shoulders, her torso still bare from the waist up, save for the band around her breasts. Then she forced herself to get up and walk around a bit while she chewed on dried meat and nuts, her stomach revolting a little at the food. Small bites. Protein for energy. Little sips of water to rehydrate. Just like before.

Only he had been there taking care of her before. He'd never made it obvious that's what he was doing. He had this way of taking care of her without her realizing that's what he was doing until long after he'd drawn her into some stupid conversation and she'd eaten half a piece of chocolate cake. It was annoying and foolish and the only way she'd ever let a male care for her in that way. That he'd figured that out so quickly...

She bit off another piece of meat, and her gaze fell to the Source Mark on her forearm. She brushed her fingers over it, chewing slowly. So many Marks on her skin, but none as important as the one she was about to give herself.

Her knees beginning to tremble told her she was pushing herself too much, and she made her way back to the packs, lowering back to the ground. She dug through Razik's items she'd dumped all over the place, finding a grey tunic that she managed to get on after a few minutes of hissing and cursing. Taking another drink of water, she let fire flare in her palm, calling forth an item from a pocket realm.

A black ashwood scion.

The end turned bright red as she heated it. She wished she had some alcohol to steady herself. She'd like to say it was from the trauma of the past few days, but she knew it wasn't. It was nerves and anxiousness at what she was about to do.

Propping her left hand atop a stack of various items, she bent forward and began to work. At least her Earth ties were good for something, allowing her to be able to bestow the Markings of the Fae. And when she was done, sitting back and letting out the breath she'd been holding, the Mark swirled along the back of her hand and down her thumb. She'd given that Mark to only three other people. She'd never expected to ever be Marking her own skin with it.

Taking the Mark without a companion mark was a risk. It wasn't lost on her that nearly a year ago she'd been arguing with Sorin about this exact thing when they'd stood in the back room of a tavern in Baylorin, the Fire Prince demanding she give him this Mark. She'd told him he was an idiot for doing this.

That about summed up this plan, she supposed. Complete idiocy.

Sucking in another shuddering breath, she murmured the Claiming Rite. The Mark flared brightly, and then her breath caught in her throat as she felt Razik's anguish down the twin flame bond. Physical pain, yes, but so much more. Anguish about…so many things. His father. His past. Her.

*Razik.*

Something stirred down that bridge between their souls, but until he had the Mark, it wouldn't be complete. It wouldn't initiate the Trials. But it had to do something. Sorin had found Scarlett this way, so it clearly worked.

She closed her eyes, concentrating on that stirring.

*Raz, give me something to find you.*

*Cave.*

Godsdamnit. Fucking cave? That's all he was going to give her?

*We're in the mountains, Razik. I need more than that. Something useful.*

*River.*

She tipped her head back in frustration. If they were near the Tana, then they had a Traveler with them. There was no way they could have made it down the mountainside otherwise.

She was so fucked.

And she needed at least another day. Without a Healer, the shiras-tone wound wouldn't heal properly. Her magic would never get to its full strength. She'd need to be strategic about how she fought when she found them. More weapons than magic, which meant taking out as many as she could before they realized she was there.

Eliza rotated her shoulder, trying to keep it from getting too stiff, eyeing two vials she'd set off to the side. They were two tonics she was saving, but gods, taking one of them was really godsdamn tempting right now. The tonic was a powerful, pain-numbing potion. It was usually given to someone to help them sleep while healing. She was saving it to take when she started out to find Razik.

Tomorrow.

One more day of rest, or it would all be pointless.

Curling up beside her small fire, she whispered down the bond, *I'm coming.*

"Fucking son of Silas," Eliza muttered as she slid down an embankment. She caught herself before her face hit the rocky ground. She wouldn't have felt it. Just like she couldn't feel the pain from her shoulder that should be crippling her at the moment, but she was certainly going to be feeling it when the tonic wore off. She prayed to Anala she wasn't doing irreparable damage.

When she'd woken up, the sun had just crested the horizon. She'd slept nearly another entire day, but an early morning start was perfect. She'd sent a few things to a pocket realm before she'd taken the tonic. Once it had taken effect, she quickly donned clothing that actually fit her, along with her leathers. She had a number of weapons strategically strapped to her, but not as many as usual. She didn't want to be weighed down by them as she traversed the mountainous terrain. Some weapons she sent to the pocket realm, but she didn't trust that in case she got hit with shirastone again and was unable to access them.

She'd tried to reach Razik down the twin flame bond again, but there'd been nothing this time. She knew he still breathed, but that was about it. So she'd started down the mountain, feeling the tug of the bond guiding her as she went. At this rate, it was going to take her three days to reach the Tana River at the base.

It was mid-afternoon when the bond began to hum a little more violently in her chest, as if it sensed Razik nearby. But that couldn't be right. She wasn't even halfway down the mountainside. What if she'd been reading this stupid bond all wrong? Had she just completely fucked this all up?

The sound of voices had her scrambling behind some larger rocks, ducking behind them as two seraphs came into view. They'd been with Varlis. Not the one with wind gifts, though. She didn't know what kind of magic these two seraphs possessed.

"Where is the backup that was promised to us two fucking days ago?" one grumbled. "I cannot keep the dragon out much longer."

"You keep that fucker knocked out cold, Ramses," the other seraph griped. "He nearly tore my entire godsdamn wing off. That can't be healed in this realm. I have to wait until we can go back to—"

"It is not as if I have a plethora of Fae up here to keep my magic wells filled," the other interrupted with a snarl. "Varlis should have let us keep the female to feed off of."

Eliza shifted slightly, trying to get a better view of the two. Sure enough, one's left wing was almost completely shredded. Her lips curled involuntarily into a sadistic grin as she studied Razik's handiwork.

"He completely fucked this up. Too shortsighted about the female. The Fae here are undisciplined," the injured one grumbled. "Allowed too much freedom."

"Once this is over, that'll change," came the response as they kept moving out of sight.

She waited, not wanting the sound of her boots on rock to give her away. She was surprised they hadn't scented her. Then again, she'd been sleeping in Razik's clothing. She probably smelled like the dragon they were keeping unconscious.

She rolled her eyes at the thought of smelling like him.

After a few minutes, she rose from her crouch, moving silently along the same path the seraphs had followed. She'd thought of killing them both right there, but she needed them to lead her to wherever Razik was. If the one was using his gifts to keep Razik unconscious, they couldn't be far. It explained why he wasn't giving her more down the bond.

She went a little farther until she realized there was a ledge ahead that dropped off to...somewhere. Dropping to her stomach, she once again thanked the Witches for the tonic that allowed her to crawl on her belly and not feel her shoulder. She made her way to the edge and peaked over.

And saw a massive black dragon curled up. The bolt was still in his wing, splayed out and lying lifelessly on the ground. His other wing was tucked back along his sleek black scales. His eyes were closed, no sapphire orbs glowing brightly. The way his neck was curled and head sitting, she couldn't see if the bolt they'd struck him with in the chest was still there. But there were pools of blood beneath him, whether from the bolts or the damage he sustained when he'd fallen from the sky.

The fury that filled her blood was the song of death itself.

Dead.

All these fuckers were dead.

That grin tipped on her lips again.

Until she heard the wings rustle behind her.

Flipping onto her back, she found the seraph with the wind magic standing over her. Keres. That's what Varlis had called him. He'd obviously used his gifts to conceal the sound of his movements.

"Valiant effort," Keres said with a sneer. He strolled casually forward. "Varlis said we didn't need to monitor you, but you didn't become the general of a powerful Court for no reason, did you? I imagine even in this world, it requires more than spreading your legs to reach such positions of power."

Eliza said nothing, watching how he moved, sweeping his body for weapons. Her fire wouldn't do much. His winds would suck the air from it, and it would waste her already weaker-than-normal reserves.

"I flew over that cave a few times a day, not surprised to find you gone after the first one," Keres continued. "It is interesting that such an archaic way of thinking still exists in some worlds. That females are still considered the weaker beings. Varlis certainly seems to think so." He stood over her now, looking down on her. A mixture of amusement and victory written on his features.

"What is interesting," Eliza said, shifting her weight slightly to her injured side, "is that you just acknowledged that males are arguably weaker, and yet you stand over me as though you have won."

"Females may be stronger than males in many ways, but I am still a seraph. And you are still just a Fae," Keres retorted.

"A Fae with fire," she countered, flames flaring to life.

Keres scoffed, the fire instantly dying at the power of his winds, but it provided the distraction she'd needed. Rolling to her feet, she grabbed the dagger she'd seen shoved down the inside of Keres's boot. She felt him pull the air from her lungs, leaving her gasping, but she'd already thrown the blade with force, lodging it deep into his side.

He bellowed a curse, hand dropping to the hilt, and he lost the grip on his magic, oxygen flooding into her system once again. She'd been prepared for that move, had already been holding her breath when he'd stolen her air. While he was yanking the dagger free, she was pulling her knife from her belt, throwing it at the hand wrapped around the dagger. Keres cursed again, dropping the dagger.

"You bitch," he snarled, eyes full of rage narrowing on her, before he hissed another curse as he jerked around, putting out the fire she'd set on his feathered wings.

She felt the air sucked from her lungs again, but she stayed on her feet, ignoring her body's demand for oxygen as she drew the spirit sword from the air. Kere's eyes went wide when he spun back around, the apparent shock making his gifts falter, and she sucked in another breath.

"We were told that sword was with the queen across the sea," Keres said, eyes fixed on the blade.

"She has her own spirit sword," Eliza replied, trying to regulate her breathing again, preparing for the next time he took her air. "This one is mine."

"How is it that *two* Swords of the Requiem are in this realm?"

Eliza's gaze darted to the sword, then she shrugged as flames wound around the blade. "Maybe that question will be answered while you rot in the Pits of Torment."

Keres growled, hitting her with a blast of wind that sent her flying back. She managed to keep her grip on her sword, her head hitting the rocky earth hard. The tonic kept her from feeling the pain, but black spots still filled her vision. She closed her eyes, focusing on the sound of his wings rustling. The crunch of his steps. The movement of the world around her. The press of his boot on her wound. The feel of the blood seeping out as he opened it back up.

He stole her breath—slowly, torturously. She felt the air stir, knew he was bending over her now.

"Pathetic," he sneered. "You cannot even look your death in the eyes."

Her lungs were burning, her brain screaming for oxygen now, but he was certain he'd won. Just like all those times males in the armies thought they had bested her. She opened her eyes, the edges blurred and Kere's face swimming before her.

"So you do have some honor," he said with a cruel smirk.

A smirk she mirrored on her own lips. She saw the pause. The sudden worry that he had missed something.

And then she slammed her hand into the still bleeding wound on his side, sending flames into his body the same way he was sucking the air from hers.

Keres lurched back, a scream of pure agony ripping from him. If Varlis and the other seraphs hadn't heard them before, they certainly did now. Gulping down oxygen, she gave herself five seconds.

One.

Keres was still bellowing, having turned his magic inward now. She could feel it battering against the fire burning away at his insides.

Two.

She pushed to a sitting position as his wild gaze landed on her again.

Three.

He rushed her, winds slamming into a thin shield of flame she'd managed to get up.

Four.

She raised her blade, fire igniting around it once more.

Five.

She took in one more deep breath, all that time learning to control her breathing with sword meditation coming into play. Eliza pushed to her feet at the same time she felt Keres rip through her shield.

And she plunged her burning sword into his chest. Keres didn't have time to lurch back before she was yanking it back and swiping it across his throat. Then she spun, popping up behind him to slice both wings from his back in one clean swing.

Less than a minute.

That's how long it had taken her to have the seraph dying at her feet.

Less than a minute was also how much time she had before another seraph was in the sky and diving for her. The same one that was keeping Razik in slumber. That had to be using all of his power, which meant he had nothing left to combat hers.

Her dark smile grew as her fire wrapped around his limbs and yanked him to the ground. The sound of him hitting the mountainside echoed around them. Eliza stalked forward, already feeling her power starting to wane. That was fine. Blades would do.

"You are the one keeping him asleep?" she asked too calmly, crouching beside him and pulling a dagger from her side.

The seraph groaned, trying to push himself up on his arms and collapsing once more onto his front.

"Wake him up," Eliza demanded. When she was met with another groan, she slammed the dagger into a wing, dragging it down the feathers.

The seraph howled.

"Wake him up," she ordered again.

"Can't," he rasped, thrashing on the ground, trying to move away from her.

"What do you mean you can't?"

"It'll...wear off," he panted.

"Then I have no use for you," she replied, pushing back to her feet. She cleaved his wings from his spine one-by-one before she separated his head from his body, leaving it all burning behind her.

Stalking to the ledge once more, she found the seraph with the damaged wing armed with a bow, a shirastone arrow trained on her. She laughed as she leapt from the ledge at the same moment he let the arrow fly. She'd feel the impact of that jump when the tonic wore off, but now she landed on her feet in front of him. He didn't even have his next arrow nocked before she was plunging her spirit sword through his throat, twisting as she withdrew it.

She turned her back on him as he fell, fire already burning away his existence. Blood was splattered across her. Hers. The seraph's. It was on her face, her clothing, in her hair.

None of it was the blood she wanted.

In this moment, she understood on a soul-deep level why Sorin had lost his mind when Scarlett had been injured all those months ago. How Thia's death had driven Cyrus nearly insane. She understood why it had been so godsdamn hard for Scarlett to let Talwyn live and what that would have done to her when Sorin made that request. Razik wasn't dead, but he was greatly injured. Their bond wasn't even a full bond, and yet it demanded payment for harming him.

And she was all too happy to bestow it.

"Varlis!" she screamed, spinning in a slow circle as she searched for him. He'd be nearby, hiding like the fucking coward he was. "You should have killed me," she cried again, sheathing the sword down her back.

His death would be completely by the fire he loathed.

The fire that had caused the death of her mother. Her father.

The fire that had loved her when no one was left to do so.

She heard the crunch of gravel beneath a boot before she spotted him. He had been slinking towards Razik's still form, another bolt in his hand. Close-up, she could see it was nightstone. She heated the bolt, letting it absorb her fire until Varlis dropped it with a yelp.

With slow, measured steps she approached him, his tanned face leeching of all color as she burned away the vines he tried to subdue her with. He was powerful, but even in a weakened state, she was more so.

"Eliza." He said her name with venom, taking a step back with every step she moved forward until he was getting far too near to Razik.

"I would stop right there," she said in a dark calm. "Any part of you that touches him will be cut from your body, set on fire, and shoved down your throat."

Varlis stilled, but the condescension on his face didn't waiver. "You are involved with the dragon," he sneered in realization. "You truly found every possible way to disgrace your lineage, didn't you?"

"There is no doubt in my mind that my lineage is about to smile as I burn you alive," she replied, fire flaring at her fingertips.

"Your father was nothing but a mill-worker near the Xylon Forest," Varlis spat. "Worthless, with half the power of your mother."

"And yet..." Eliza said with a half-grin as she flicked a flame at him. He cursed, batting at the hole she'd burned into his fine jacket. "I am still more powerful than you."

"You are *nothing* compared to me," Varlis sneered, taking a step towards her despite the way her fire flared. "You won't kill me."

She barked a laugh. "What in the realms makes you believe that?"

"Because if you do, you will never learn how to lift that Curse Mark," Varlis said, eyes dropping to the place where the Mark was etched into her skin beneath her tunic. "That is the reason you have left me alive all this time, is it not?" He frowned in mock sympathy as he took another step towards her, standing almost toe-to-toe with her now. "Hoping that someday you could convince me to relieve you of that burden?"

Then his eyes went wide in shock. There was a strangled groan and blood bubbled at the corner of his mouth. Slowly he looked down, seeing the flaming dagger she had shoved into his gut.

She'd been wrong.

She did want to use a blade for this.

Making the fire burn hotter, she slowly dragged it up his torso, feeling the Fiera steel slice through muscle while she melted her way through bone. Varlis tried to stumble away from her, but she gripped his jacket with a burning fist, sinking the dagger in further, just as he'd done with the arrow.

"Let me be very clear," she hissed in a voice so wicked she could have been a descendant of Arius rather than a Fae of Anala. "I left you alive all these years because I did not have one single fuck to give about you." She yanked the dagger higher, reaching his sternum. "The only time I thought of you was when I was having a shit day. When I would remind myself it could be worse. I could share blood with an actual piece of shit." She halted the dagger, knowing she was nearing his heart. "And I would rather live with this Curse Mark the rest of my life and know it was *my* flames that ended your immortal years than let you take another breath on this side of the Veil."

She yanked the dagger up, watching as the last of his life left his pale green eyes, before she stepped back and let him fall to the ground. She stood and watched as she burned every last bit of him to nothing.

When the ashes were fluttering away in the wind, she turned to find glowing sapphire eyes pinned on her. He didn't move other than to blink. She took a few moments to gather herself before she approached him, figuring out her next course of action.

Those bolts needed to come out.

She stopped next to his head. This close, he was...

*You're drooling.*

Her eyes snapped to his, and a weak huff came from him.

"Shut up, or I'm leaving those bolts in place," she snapped, planting her hands on her hips and surveying the damage. His massive body moved some, as if he were trying to...do what? Get up?

"Stop moving," she chastised, moving closer to the bolt at his chest. She glanced at the one near his wing, studying the end of it. It was barbed, which meant it was going to do even more damage coming out. She'd have to pull the one in his wing all the way through, but this one...

Right. Get these out, then figure out the next steps. She adamantly ignored the stiffness starting to creep into her bones. The tonic was wearing off. She needed to get on with this.

Unclasping her cloak, she tossed it to the side, before pushing back her sleeves. She quickly re-braided her hair to keep it out of her face. She felt his eyes on her the entire time.

"Wing first?" she asked uncertainly, stepping closer to the black wing splayed out on the ground. It shimmered in the sunlight that was getting closer to dipping behind the mountains. They couldn't be out here when night fell. There were things that prowled these mountains at night that she was in no condition to fight off. They would need to find shelter.

Razik's massive form tensed again when she reached for the bolt, as if bracing for the pain, and she paused.

"Caves are shit," she blurted.

Razik blinked his luminous eyes at her.

"I've spent the last few days in a cave, and it was awful. How you can possibly prefer that over the comfort of a room in the castle or the estate is beyond me."

A low rumble came from his throat at the same time she grabbed the bolt and tugged.

The rumble became a roar, and she was grimacing around her own twinge of pain as her shoulder screamed at the movement.

Razik's head snapped up, his large snout coming close to her shoulder and inhaling sharply. Another growl came from him.

"I'm in better shape than you," she retorted, shoving his face away from her, briefly marveling at the feel of his scales beneath her fingers.

He huffed again, his lip curling back and baring a row of large, pointed teeth.

"Gods. You throw worse fits than Cyrus," she barked, tossing the bolt to the side as she moved back to the one at his chest. The thumping of a large-spiked tail had her lips twitching.

Taking a deep breath, that small smile fell. Gripping the bolt, she yanked it out. Fast and efficient.

But the roar that sounded made her chest tight. She didn't know when she'd moved from his chest to his head, or when she'd dropped to her knees, but a large, diamond-shaped head was in her lap, his breathing hard and heavy as she saw blood pouring out of the wound.

"I'm sorry. I'm sorry," she was murmuring. There were tears on her face. She slid her hands beneath this massive jaw, forcing him to lift his head so she could look into his eyes. "I need you to shift, Razik. I need you to shift, and then hopefully the little magic I have left will be enough for you to Travel us somewhere safe." His eyes fell closed, and she *felt* his heartbeat stutter. "No," she snarled, fingers flexing and nails trying to dig into his scaley hide. "No, you open your godsdamn eyes, Razik Greybane."

His eyelids lifted, but only halfway.

"I did not dig shirastone out of my shoulder and sleep in a fucking cave for the last three days to have it end here. Do you hear me?"

Something akin to a low keening whine came from him. She didn't even know dragons could make that sound.

*You...chose...the bond.*

His voice was strained and weak, bouncing around in her mind.

"No," she said, her voice breaking as she felt his heart stutter again. "I chose *you*, Raz. Please. Just shift. I can do the rest. Please."

*Mai dragocen...*

448

"You drive me mad!" she cried. "You're so godsdamn infuriating. You've ruined me!"

*Eliza*—

Tears were flowing down her face, dripping onto his scales and glistening in the setting sun. "I hate that you know I like chocolate cake and that the promise of books can get me to do anything. I hate that you sleep in my bed but won't touch me because you're just that godsdamn respectable. I hate that you make everything with me a competition because you know I won't back down from you. I hate that you get two glasses and extra food, even when I tell you I don't want any, because you know I'm lying before I do. I hate that you're tidy and always picking up after me. I hate that you called me one of Scarlett's Ladies-in-Wait, even though you knew damn-well I wasn't. You fuck with me every chance you get. And you have wrecked everything I have made of my life, but in the best way possible. I hate that I love that you have ruined me. Shift, Raz. Fucking shift."

The soft black glow was the only warning she got before Razik was before her in his human form. His wings were still out, smaller and one ruined, but he had shifted. She swiped the dagger from her boot, slicing the Mark on her arm and then his palm. His dragon fire took greedily, and she let out a small cry as it sank into the little magic she had left. He tried to pull his hand back, blinking his eyes open, but she held on.

She pulled a tunic from the pocket realm, pressing the fabric to his chest where the wound was still steadily losing blood. When she had given him all of her fire, she reached for the hidden pocket in her leathers, fishing out the other vial of tonic.

The one she'd saved for him to take away his pain. At least for a little while.

She pulled the cork out with her teeth before bringing it to his lips. "Drink," she whispered.

He obeyed, and she could tell the moment the tonic took effect because his eyes flew open. Which was good because her tonic had completely worn off, and she was feeling all of it: the slips and slides down the mountainside, the blows from Keres, the leap from the ledge, the strain on her injuries.

Razik was pushing himself onto his knees, pulling her into him. He bent his head, inspecting her shoulder.

"I'm fine," she mumbled, trying to push his hands away from her. "We just need to get somewhere safe."

They were Traveling in the next breath, Razik holding her tightly to him. They were on the islands outside the Wards, and Razik was pulling a vial of blood from somewhere, dumping it into the sea. Then they were in the warmth of…a cave.

A godsdamn cave.

But this wasn't like the cave she'd spent the last several days in.

This cave was stunning and warm and…a home.

There were stone steps off to one side that wound up to what she had to assume was the entrance. It was one large space. A kitchen of sorts was towards a back corner with a dining set nearby. Sofas and chairs were off to the left with a glass fire pit in the center of them. At the back there was steam rising from something, and off to the left was a large bed. Bigger than his bed in the Aimonway castle. It was low to the ground and piled with pillows and blankets. It was more of a nest.

And treasure. There was gold and silver, gems and trinkets, paintings and books artfully arranged everywhere.

She twisted in his arms. "You actually have a cave."

He tried to smile, but it fell flat. There was sweat on his brow. Despite the tonic, he was still losing blood.

"What the fuck happened?"

Eliza twisted again, finding Cethin, Kailia, and Niara standing near the fire pit.

"How did you know—"

"I felt him at the Wards," Cethin interrupted, stalking forward. "When he didn't come to the castle, I figured he came here. Kailia suggested bringing Niara. You need to let him go, Eliza."

"What?"

Kailia reached out, her small hands landing on Eliza's and gently prying her fingers from Razik's bloody tunic where she'd been clutching it.

"Niara needs room to work," the queen said softly. "Come."

She tried to stay awake, but the weight of everything had her nodding off on the sofa while Niara worked on Razik. It wasn't until the Healer began unwrapping her wound that she forced her heavy lids open.

"Raz?" she murmured, trying to sit up.

"Wait, General," Niara said, Kailia holding Eliza down. She was strong for such a petite female.

"He sleeps," Kailia said. "Cethin is watching over him while Niara tends to you."

"He'll be all right?"

"Eventually. If he takes the necessary time to heal," the Healer said. "You, however…" Niara's lips pursed. "If you do not take the proper precautions, this wound will not heal a second time."

"As long as Razik will be all right," Eliza said, letting herself sink back into the sofa while Niara cleaned and stitched the wound.

When Niara was done, Kailia helped her over to the bed where Razik was indeed sleeping. Looking at Cethin, Eliza said, "Please do not tell the others we are here."

His brows shot up. "Scarlett might actually kill me if I keep this from her."

"I know… I…"

"We will tell them in a few days' time," Kailia cut in.

"Kailia—" Cethin started.

"They need time to adjust, Cethin. We will stay while they sleep. Niara wants to monitor them anyway. When one wakes, we can discuss this again."

Cethin didn't look convinced, but he nodded, and that was all Eliza needed.

She climbed in beside Razik and nestled into his side. Her hand settled on his chest right beside the bandaged wound where she could feel his heart beating steadily, and she let the rhythm lull her to sleep.

# CHAPTER 33
# SORIN

Sorin sat back in the chair he'd been sitting in for the last few hours, rubbing at his eyes. He'd been studying the few books and papers he'd taken from the cliffs, but it was slow going. Half of it was written in a language he didn't know. The part he could translate wasn't much help. The books Scarlett had taken would probably be of use, but he couldn't access them until she woke up.

Six days.

It had been six days since they'd gone to the Southern Islands. Niara insisted she would wake. The Healer told him multiple times a day that her body would let her wake when it was ready. But six godsdamn days?

He'd given her power when they got back. She'd already been unconscious, and he'd fallen into a deep restorative sleep as soon as he'd given her his last ember. He'd woken fully restored two days later. It was odd, in a way. He had all the power of an Avonleyan with these gifts but didn't need to depend on another to refill his reserves. The best of both worlds.

He assumed the Traveling gift had transferred from Talwyn. She had been able to Travel, a gift separate from her wind and earth and shifting. It was the best explanation they'd been able to come up with as they'd all conversed in these rooms. He still didn't know how he'd managed to do it in the air. He'd been planning to catch them on his fire dragon, but instead, he'd found himself on the islands outside the Wards.

It had been quiet the last few days though. Cethin and Kailia had been scarce. Cethin only stopped by once a day to check in, and Cyrus and Cassius had left for the continent yesterday. They'd all agreed he needed to start looking for this thing the Sorceress wanted, and it was wasting valuable time to just sit around here. He knew they'd finally completed the Source Mark. That eased his mind a bit, but he still didn't like them going back to the continent alone.

He absent-mindedly rolled flames along his knuckles while his other hand tapped the pencil he held against the desk surface. Cyrus had also promised to check in with Eliza when he got to the continent. It had been far too long since they'd heard anything from her and Razik. He was about to send Rayner over there to track them down just to make sure they weren't in trouble. He'd be the fastest one to find them.

Eliza had been with Sorin the longest. He'd never forget when he'd received a message from the border patrols telling him about a female they'd detained. He'd portaled straight to the border to find an abrasive, ill-tempered female with fire gifts who'd been raised in the Earth Court. She'd tried to hide it, but panic had filled her eyes when she saw him. He didn't realize why until later. That she had thought he'd want to use her for her power. She'd kept the true strength of her magic a secret for quite some time.

He tossed his pencil onto the desk a little too hard, watching it bounce off the surface and roll across the floor.

"Am I interrupting a tantrum, Prince?"

Sorin bolted from his chair at the sound of her voice. How had he not heard her? Felt her?

But there she stood, leaning against the doorway of their bedchamber with her arms folded across her chest. She had on one of his tunics, the garment hanging nearly to her knees. Silver hair hung loose and lank around her shoulders. Her eyes were glowing a bright silver, but she still looked tired. Not in a physical sense, but in a soul-weary way.

He was across the room in a few long strides, pulling her into him, breathing in the scent of her—citrus and embers, lavender and night.

"Why are you acting like I was dying?" she murmured into his chest, but her arms were wrapped just as tightly around his waist.

"You were plummeting to your death after you destroyed the cliffs."

"Yes, but then this beautiful creature saved me."

He leaned back, pushing the hair off her brow. "Beautiful now, am I?"

"I meant the fire dragon, but you'll do."

He flicked her nose, leaning down to brush his lips against hers. She obliged him, but only for a moment before she asked, "How long have I been asleep?"

"Six days."

"That explains the urgent need for the bathing room," she mumbled. "Which is why you didn't feel me when I woke up," she added. "I didn't need a mother hen running around the room."

"For the love of Anala," he muttered. "Six days, Scarlett. I have been going mad."

"And throwing things," she added, crossing the room and retrieving the pencil, his shirt riding up her thighs.

"Pants," he growled. "We need to work on this no-pants issue."

"If memory serves, your master plan was to burn all my clothing," she replied, tossing the pencil onto the desk. Then she noticed what he'd been poring over these last few days. "Did you learn anything?" she asked, flipping open one of the books.

"Not really," he answered, watching her flip pages. "You should eat."

She hummed in response, closing the book and opening another. "Does Rayner still have the lock?"

"Yes. He has been keeping it hidden."

"Who else knows we have it?"

"Only those of us who went to the Southern Islands."

She glanced up at him. "Cethin hasn't asked about it?"

Sorin shook his head. "Not once."

"Interesting," she murmured, closing the book and shuffling

through the pages of Moranna's notes. Then she was pulling one from the stack, eyes moving rapidly over the page. "Sorin?"

"What is it?" He came up behind her, peering over her shoulder.

"Cethin said when we got here that the spirit animals are not from this world, and Saylah told me when she left to get help, she came back with them."

"Yes," Sorin said slowly.

"Why would she go get them to aid in a war against Deimas and ultimately Achaz? Why the spirit animals?"

"I am going to need more to go on here, Scarlett. What are you figuring out?"

"He thought they were myths," she murmured, flipping the paper over to find the other side blank. "But they weren't. They've been here the entire time. It fits. If I'm reading this right, and if what I found in the Elshira catacombs is true... It all fits."

"Love..." Sorin said, reaching out and tipping her chin up to get her attention.

"They're World Walkers, Sorin," she said excitedly. "Callan read about them in passing in the libraries at the Fire Court. He thought they were myths, but this?" She held up the parchment. "They weren't always animals."

"Are you saying that Amaré and Shirina once had another form?"

"Yes," she said, stepping around him and heading back to the bedchamber. "We need to go to the catacombs. Then we need to go see Saylah."

Sorin dragged a hand down his face, glancing at the clock on the desk.

Thirteen minutes.

She had been awake for a whole thirteen minutes and had already figured out something profound.

He followed after her. "Scarlett, you need to bathe and eat."

"This is important, Sorin," she called out from the large closet.

"Important, yes, but not time sensitive."

She came out of the dressing room, a pair of pants and tunic in hand. "It is kind of time sensitive," she argued.

"Not as time sensitive as a bath and food," he countered, pulling the clothing from her hands and setting it on the bed.

"Are you implying that I smell?"

"Six days, Love," he answered, dropping a kiss to the top of her head before steering her towards the bathing room. "Not to mention you are covered in dirt and debris from falling through the sky. We could only get you so clean."

She gave a disgruntled sigh but pulled the tunic over her head as she moved, giving him all that bare skin to look at.

*By the gods.*

She glanced over her shoulder, giving him a coy smirk. "Come tell me what has happened these last few days while I bathe."

"I still think you should have given her some warning we were coming," Cethin muttered as he led the way through the Elshira Castle. Sorin and Scarlett had really only seen the catacombs of the place, Scarlett having no desire to explore the building.

Scarlett waved a hand dismissively. "She'll be fine. She *loves* it when I just drop in."

Sorin and Rayner exchanged a look. They'd only had one experience with the goddess, and it hadn't exactly been a pleasant one.

"What does she do all day anyway?" Scarlett went on, her shadows drifting around her.

"Guards the mirror gate," Cethin answered.

"Hmm," was her only response.

"If the realm is locked, what would she need to guard?" Rayner asked.

"It is the main way into the realm," Cethin said. "If someone is going to find a workaround, it would be there."

"And?" Scarlett pressed, lifting a hand and watching snowflakes drift above her palm.

"And what?"

"She speaks to others through it."

Cethin stopped mid-stride, turning to face her. "You cannot speak through the mirror gates."

"We did," she countered.

"But we were in the same realm." His eyes narrowed as he studied his sister. "What do you know, Scarlett?"

"More than she should."

They all turned to find Saylah at the end of the corridor. Everyone dropped to a knee.

Everyone except Scarlett, of course.

"Saylah," Scarlett said tightly.

"If you are here, I assume you have found the lock," Saylah said.

"Or we just came to chat," Scarlett replied.

Saylah leveled her daughter with a silver glare before her gaze shifted to Cethin. "I will meet you all in the council room."

She was gone amidst her shadows as everyone got to their feet.

"She would be more amenable if you at least tried, Scarlett," Cethin chided.

"I highly doubt that," Scarlett retorted. "You bend over backwards for her, and it does not seem to make a difference."

"I would mind how you speak to him," Kailia said calmly, stepping to the side so Cethin could open a set of doors they had come to. "I have killed others for less."

The Avonleyan Queen swept into the room, Cethin behind her.

"I really do like her," Scarlett said after a moment.

"Of course you do," Rayner muttered. "She has a penchant for stabbing first and asking questions later."

"Nuri and Juliette would like her too," she added, heading into the room.

Rayner and Sorin exchanged another look.

"She is not herself," Rayner said in a hushed tone.

"I am aware," Sorin answered.

"How did she react to hearing Cassius had left?"

"She didn't," Sorin muttered, stepping into the room and moving to sit by his wife.

Who had made a statement by taking the seat at the head of the table.

Something had been off since she'd woken, and Sorin couldn't quite place it. She'd been quiet while he'd filled her in, hardly commenting on the fact that Cyrus and Cassius had left. That's when he'd known something was wrong. Perhaps not wrong per se, but she was lost in whatever she was working out. She'd shared a little more with him, but that had left him with as many questions as she had.

"Have you heard anything from Razik?" Sorin asked the Avonleyan royals.

"Communication with Razik has been limited since he left for the continent," Kailia answered, attention flitting to the window at the cry of an eagle. Altaria appeared a moment later, his beak clicking as he landed on the back of Cethin's chair.

Scarlett's head tilted, studying the eagle. "He is Temural's, yes?"

"Yes," Cethin said slowly, still studying her suspiciously.

Scarlett hummed, her fingers drumming on the table.

Before anyone could say anything more, the doors opened again, and Saylah strode in with Tybalt at her side. The Commander smiled warmly at them all before taking a seat next to Kailia.

Saylah did not sit, but stood opposite Scarlett at the other end of the council table. "Do you have my lock?"

Scarlett's brow arched, her chin resting lazily in her palm. "*Your* lock?"

"You know what I mean," her mother answered.

Not breaking her stare, Scarlett said, "Rayner."

The Ash Rider reached into an inner pocket on his cloak, ashes and smoke obscuring the orb he pulled free. He leaned over Sorin, stretching to hand it to Scarlett.

"Give it to me," Saylah demanded.

Rayner ignored the goddess, placing it in Scarlett's outstretched hand. The moment Scarlett touched it, Altaria gave a shrill cry that had all of them flinching.

"You defy a goddess?" Saylah asked, her voice as dark as the shadows drifting around her.

"He obeys his queen," Scarlett replied in a tone that matched her mother's.

"Scarlett," Cethin said in a tense whisper.

"Who created it?" Scarlett asked, ignoring her brother's warning.

The orb had instantly sprung to life the moment Rayner had ceased to touch it. The glyphs faded in and out, and Scarlett watched them as she waited for Saylah. The goddess remained silent for so long, Sorin wasn't sure she was going to answer.

Scarlett's eyes flicked to her. "Come now, *Mother.* I've come to deal in your currency of choice."

Sorin didn't know what that meant, but Saylah clearly did, judging by the way her eyes narrowed on Scarlett.

"Serafina created the lock," Saylah answered tightly.

Scarlett stilled, sitting back in her chair. Sorin could feel her shock at that revelation. Out of all the possibilities they had discussed of who had created it, Serafina had not been on that list.

"What is it?" Scarlett asked.

"The power to unlock the mirror gate," Saylah said.

"We are not trading half-truths," Scarlett retorted sharply, her shadows breaking free of their constraints. "I have retrieved the lock. The payment for that service is answers to my questions."

It was unnerving how still the goddess stood. Fae could go preter-naturally still, but this was something else. This was as if the goddess controlled the stillness of the aura around her. It was another full minute before the goddess spoke again.

"You and Cethin are the product of two bloodlines. Arius and Anahita. Because the Arius blood is more powerful, those are the gifts you inherited. Gifts of Arius and Serafina, myself and Temural. Those bloodlines are all essentially one. Temural's and my gifts are an extension of those of Arius and Serafina.

"Anahita is a Lesser god, but all the power of the gods comes from the Chaos. That is what makes us stronger than other magical blood-lines created. That is why we rule the realms. The more Chaos in one's being, the stronger the god. That is why the Firsts are the most powerful. They came directly from the Chaos. They *are* Chaos. Arius's darkness is Chaos, just as Achaz's light is Chaos. Chaos is what is used to create new worlds. Chaos is what is used to create new bloodlines."

"Are my shadows Chaos?" Scarlett asked.

"No, but Cethin's darkness is. It is why he finds it wilder and harder to control," she answered.

"What?" Cethin demanded, twisting to fully face his mother.

Saylah's gaze slid to him, something shifting in her eyes. "You were born with some Chaos. All magical beings are. Because your father was Legacy, you also have some mortal blood. Mortal blood weakens the Chaos."

"Then how does he possess it?" Scarlett asked, the lock still in one hand resting atop the table. "How would any Legacy maintain their power if mortal blood weakens Chaos?"

"Chaos is the undercurrent of all power. It is Chaos that determines how powerful one's gifts are." Saylah answered.

"Not Fate?" Scarlett drawled.

Saylah stared at her in a way that had Sorin shifting closer.

"Chaos and Fate are not the same, but they do create the balance."

After a moment, Scarlett muttered, "I do not know if that is helpful or not."

"But Cethin's Chaos is more than he was born with because I gave him some of mine," Saylah said, again having everyone go still with surprise. "He let beings in that should not have been. In order to save him, I needed to give him more."

Scarlett turned to Cethin. "What is she talking about? The Hunters?"

Cethin shook his head, Kailia placing a hand on his. "I told you there were other beings who received my message about entering the Wards. Beings from beyond the realm."

"So Cethin is what? A god? Because he has more Chaos than he should?" Scarlett asked, shifting her attention back to her mother.

"No. He does not have nearly enough Chaos for that. He has more Chaos, but only just enough to enhance his gifts. Just as the Chaos you carry is enough to enhance your gifts."

Scarlett lurched back in her chair, and Sorin was snatching up the lock that nearly tumbled to the floor as more shock spiked down the bond.

*Breathe, Love. In and out.*

*If we are right about the lock, Sorin, this means that—*

*I know, Scarlett. Let's see what other answers she has.*

"You asked why the gifts Sorin was given would not manifest as anything other than fire. Fae cannot possess more than one gift. The Fae Queens were different. They were enabled to carry more than one element by Taika," Saylah explained. "It is why you were born in the

Witch Kingdoms. The High Witch is a descendant of Taika. She had the ability to transfer the Chaos from Eliné to you. In order to transfer gifts, Chaos must be given. It is the cost. To give you Eliné's gifts, to have them intertwine with your soul and become part of you, it needed to be done when you took your first breath. To give you the ability to not only carry your own gifts but also hers, you needed more Chaos. Without it, the magic would have consumed you long before you were ready to wield it."

"You gave me some of your Chaos?" Scarlett asked in a hushed tone.

"Yes," Saylah replied. "More than Cethin has. It weakened me greatly. It prevented me from returning to Avonleya as quickly as I would have liked. The mirror gate was left unguarded too long. Those you know as the Maraan Lords found their way in during that time."

"If Chaos must be given to transfer gifts...?" Sorin started, trailing off when the weight of Saylah's gaze settled on him.

"What you are thinking is correct. I had to give up more Chaos to transfer those gifts to you. It will not be as effective as it was for Scarlett. It is why you find it unnerving to wield such power at times, because it has not been a part of you from the beginning."

The conflicting emotions he could feel coming from Scarlett mirrored his own. Saylah had sacrificed some of her power to give Scarlett what she had demanded. Had sacrificed it to keep her children safe. Had protected them in the only way she knew how.

"Is that how I am able to Travel?" Sorin asked.

"No. That gift would have simply transferred to you during the process. All Fae have a trace of Chaos. It is how they can carry their elements. The more Chaos in a Fae, the stronger their gifts. The gods created them that way to balance their Legacy but to never be more than them," Saylah said. "But Chaos is unpredictable. Some things are out of even the gods' control, despite our best attempts."

"What does that mean?" Scarlett asked, watching her mother carefully.

"The Fae will never be equal to a god, but if the right bloodlines were united, they could be stronger than a Legacy. This is why some realms keep the Fae under close watch. It is why contention around crossing the bloodlines is strategically sewn in some realms. Other worlds simply pass decrees forbidding it. The Fae that become too powerful are sought after for a number of reasons," Saylah replied. "Blood has been shed to keep them."

"This history lesson is fascinating," Scarlett cut in, drumming her fingers atop the table. Despite her sarcasm, Sorin could see her mind working, putting things together. "But what does any of this have to do with the lock?"

"Because the gods were not the only beings to emerge from the Chaos, and wars over powerful Fae are not the only reason blood has been shed."

"You speak of the World Walkers," Scarlett said, sitting up straighter, Saylah finally getting to what she was most interested in. They had spent the last few hours discussing the World Walkers. Scarlett was convinced they were the missing piece to figuring out the mirror gates, and whatever information Saylah had would determine if they moved forward with their plans or not.

Saylah only gave a sharp curt nod.

"That is all? A nod?" Scarlett asked incredulously.

"What else would you like?"

"What the World Walkers have to do with the godsdamn lock," Scarlett said, embers of starfire mingling with her shadows now. "And do not tell me nothing. There is a connection."

Saylah's lips pursed again, but she said, "The Great War here is simply a battle in the Everlasting War, just as every other battle in the realms is. Arius, Serafina, and Achaz were meant to end the war, instead they re-birthed it."

"The war was not originally because of Arius and Serafina?" Sorin asked, still holding the orb while Scarlett and Cethin both drummed their fingers simultaneously. They glanced at each other and pulled their hands into their laps.

"No. It was between the gods that you know and the World Walkers." She held up a hand when Scarlett opened her mouth. "And before you ask, I do not know the specifics. This was before my time. Before Arius and Serafina upset the balance. I do know that when the gods emerged victorious, they gave some of the World Walkers the choice of death or serving one of the gods. The spirit animals you know chose the latter. They were the original Shapeshifters and became bound in their animal form."

"But who were they? Before?" Scarlett asked, looking at Altaria still perched on Cethin's chair.

"That I do not know. I know they followed a World Walker named Korra. She was one of their high rulers. It is her Chaos in that lock. It is her power that can unlock the realm. She gave that power in exchange for her people to be able to make the choice of binding themselves to a god or going to the After where Arius would cast judgment," Saylah answered.

"Why does it respond to me and not the others?" Scarlett asked.

"It responds to the Chaos in you."

"You just told us all the immortals have some form of Chaos. It does not respond to them," Scarlett countered, gesturing to the orb Sorin still held.

"It responds to you because of the kind of Chaos you carry. Not only that with which you were born, but that of Eliné and what I gave to you. Chaos is drawn to its own power. It is why those born of it crave more. It is why the more one possesses, the more one desires it."

Scarlett's lips tilted in that way that made Sorin brace himself for what she was about to say, because she had clearly figured something out. "And you? Do you desire more of it?"

Sorin was fairly certain the entire room stopped breathing at the question.

"It would restore what I have given, as well as allow us to leave the realm," Saylah answered tightly.

"And would it be drawn to you as it is to me?" Scarlett asked, reaching over and taking the orb back from Sorin.

The glyphs sprang to life, the Chaos swirling violently within. Saylah's gaze snapped to it, and for the first time, she was not still. She seemed to tremble with restraint.

"No," the goddess gritted out. "I may carry more Chaos than you, but it will seek you."

"It's why Alaric wants me so badly, isn't it?" Scarlett asked, rotating the lock in her hand.

"Yes."

"Does he know what this is? What it can do?" Scarlett pressed.

"Yes," Saylah said again. "Achaz would have told him. He sent Moranna here to find a way to release the Chaos to be used for his own gain."

"Does Alaric know what *I* can do with it?"

"The same thing I can do. Unlock the realm," Saylah said, eyes sliding to her daughter.

Scarlett shrugged. "That might be all *you* can do with it."

That unearthly stillness returned to the goddess. "Explain yourself."

"I would but…" Scarlett got to her feet, tossing the lock into the air and catching it with a grin that would rival Nuri's insanity. Then she godsdamn *winked* at her mother. "Secrets are the currency of the gods."

# CHAPTER 34
# SCARLETT

"Scarlett, we need to use the lock to take down the Wards," Cethin said. She could tell by his tone he was trying to be careful, to balance his support between her and their mother. Not for the first time, Scarlett wondered what he had experienced to make him so submissive to her.

"About that," Scarlett said, beginning to trace a few of the glyphs with her starfire. "Tell me about the mirror gates."

"The mirror gates?" Cethin repeated. "What of them?"

"We were discussing them before we were interrupted. Who created them?" she asked, moving to another glyph.

"Serafina and Taika created the mirror gates along with the lock. Just as new worlds and new beings cannot be created by one god alone, nor could something like this," Saylah answered. "What are you doing?"

Scarlett had begun tracing another glyph, this one with ice. She flicked her eyes to her mother before focusing on the orb again. "Exchanging currency. Why did she create the mirror gates?"

"I do not know all the history, Scarlett," Saylah said. "It all happened before my time. I was told some, but my existence was kept a secret until it could not be hidden any longer. Because of that, my knowledge is limited."

She could hear the irritation in her tone at not having the upper hand here, despite being the most powerful in the room.

"Tell me what you *do* know of the mirror gates," Scarlett said.

Saylah exhaled a harsh breath, and Scarlett was certain it was the most mortal thing she had ever witnessed from her, aside from sitting in the sand that night on the beach.

"The beings that emerged from the Chaos all have different gifts, just as the various beings and bloodlines created do. The gods can Travel within one realm, but they cannot move among the worlds. That was a gift of the World Walkers. The gods did not wish to lose such magic when the World Walkers were conquered. Some of their Chaos was harnessed and used to create the mirror gates to allow the gods to travel among the realms," Saylah explained.

"And the lock is connected to them?" Scarlett asked, tracing another glyph with her shadows.

"Not all of them. Some mirror gates are used for communication. Some are used for crossing the stars," Saylah replied. "Now, Daughter, if we are exchanging secrets, it is time you share one with me."

Scarlett paused, slowly dragging her eyes back to her mother. "I did not say I was exchanging currency with *you*." She lifted the orb a little higher. "I find— What was her name? Korra? I find her secrets far more interesting than yours."

"What does that mean?" Cethin cut in.

"If Chaos has to be sacrificed to transfer power and create new beings, tell me how the gifts were taken from the Sorceress," Scarlett replied, ignoring Cethin and returning her attention to the orb. She began tracing a glyph in orange flames.

"If I am going to share things with you, it only serves you do the same," Saylah retorted, and Scarlett knew she was pushing the goddess.

Cethin obviously knew it too because he tensed, getting to his feet as though he thought he would need to intervene between the two. "Scarlett, she has answered every question you have asked."

"She *owes* me every godsdamn answer, Cethin," Scarlett snarled, whirling on him. "She owes both of us every answer. We were both used. Both given information only when she deemed it necessary. You said it yourself: she is a goddess first and a mother second." Then she scoffed. "I would say calling it second is generous, considering the *real* reason she desires this lock."

"Everything I have done is for the two of you and to save this realm," Saylah hissed, Cethin and Scarlett both turning to look at her.

Scarlett had been wrong.

The silver pooling in her eyes? *That* was the most mortal thing she had seen from the goddess.

"Tell me," Scarlett said, her tone low and vicious, "would you have still given up so much of your power—to me, to Cethin, to take from the Sorceress and create the Witches and Shifters—if there was not the guarantee of getting it returned?" She lifted the orb as she said it.

Saylah might be the most powerful in the room, but barely. Not with all that Chaos she'd given away trying to fix her mistakes. Power she clearly planned to reclaim with the lock.

"Yes," Saylah answered immediately.

"She cares, Scarlett," Cethin implored. "She cares in the only way she knows how to."

"Then she will not fight me when I tell her she does not get this lock," Scarlett answered, holding Saylah's stare.

"What?" the goddess gasped. "Without that lock, this world falls. Achaz will find another way. He has been close before. He will not stop. The only way to save the realm is to leave it, Scarlett. You know this. His attention will follow wherever we go. He will leave this world in peace as long as we no longer inhabit it."

"I read some *fascinating* things in the books below this castle," Scarlett said, beginning to move casually throughout the room. Her eyes connected with Sorin's, and she dipped her chin, feeling his fire crawl along her skin a moment later. She sent her shadows to it, letting them merge. Then she began tracing a glyph in shadowfire.

"Scarlett, what are you doing with that thing?" Cethin asked, concern growing in his voice. Kailia hadn't said a word, but she was watching Scarlett with curious eyes.

Rayner and Sorin stayed seated, both waiting. Because the moment Saylah had told them whose Chaos the lock contained? It had been the last piece of their puzzle.

"Did you know that the being who created a world has the power to truly lock it? That their essence is so entwined with the world itself, they can keep out all others if they wish?" Scarlett asked. "The only exceptions are those of equal or greater power."

"What does that have to do with this?" Cethin asked. "This world is… How would we even know who created it?"

Scarlett raised the orb before her again. "Korra has so many secrets," she said with a manic grin.

"Are you saying the World Walkers created Halaya?" Kailia asked, speaking for the first time.

"Not just any World Walker. This one," Scarlett said, gesturing to the lock. "The same essence contained in this lock. The funny thing is, Moranna was so close to figuring it all out. She knew the World Walkers were connected. Had pages and pages of notes on them. But she could never create a being powerful enough to get the lock to respond." Her eyes bounced from Kailia to Rayner. "No matter how hard she tried."

"No," Saylah said, taking a step forward.

That one movement had both Sorin and Rayner standing as her mother finally realized what Scarlett had been doing.

"Now, correct me if I'm wrong, but what I've gathered from today's history lesson is that the high rulers of the World Walkers would be the equivalent of a god or goddess. They would be as powerful as a First," Scarlett said, tracing another glyph with starfire.

"No," Saylah said again, panic seeping into her voice.

"How many were there, Saylah? How many high rulers?" Scarlett asked.

"I do not know," Saylah answered, lurching forward another step as Sorin pulled a dagger from his side. "Do not do this, Scarlett. You do not understand the cost."

"No?" Scarlett asked, holding out her palm to Sorin. "I am doing exactly what you asked of me. Find the lock. Save this world."

"Not like this!" Saylah cried, tears slipping free now.

If she had the time, she would marvel at it. At seeing a goddess cry for her.

But she didn't have the time because if she stopped, she would lose her nerve.

*Scarlett?*

She looked at him, her hand still cradled in his palm where he'd drawn the dagger across it. He smiled softly, but she could feel the same trepidation radiating off of him.

"What is going on?" Cethin demanded, Kailia on her feet as well.

But Scarlett could only see him.

*You'll find me? Among the stars?*

*Always, my love.*

*You remember what to do?*

He gently turned her hand over, guiding it to the lock. *I will not fail you.*

So she placed her bloody palm atop the glyphs swirling with her power and his power. The power of a Fae Queen and a Witch. The power of a goddess and a World Walker.

And Chaos erupted.

# PART THREE

FATE

# CHAPTER 35
# SCARLETT

S he was among the stars.
It was the only explanation.
So much darkness and light swirling about.
So many worlds.
So much power.
So much Chaos.
Her mother thought she did not understand the cost of this.
She did.
She knew what taking the power of a World Walker would cost her.
She knew it was no longer solely Fae Courts she was responsible for now.
No longer just her world.
But all worlds.
The only High Queen of the World Walkers.
The only World Walker left outside those bound to an animal form.
A World Walker with the gifts of the gods and the Fae.
A threat to not only Achaz, but Arius. Serafina. Anala, Falein, and Celeste.
All the Firsts. All the gods.
A Goddess Queen to stand between them and her world.
So she welcomed the Chaos.
Let it take her.

*Let it break her.*
*Let it consume her.*

# CHAPTER 36
## SORIN

He'd Traveled them the moment Scarlett had touched the lock with her blood. She'd done it. Shown the Chaos within what she could give it. How much power she had to offer. What they could create.

Because at its core, that's what Chaos did. It created and shaped, broke and remade.

Scarlett had found texts about it in the catacombs, but it wasn't until they'd learned of the World Walkers that they had figured out what the lock was. Why it could unlock the realm. What Scarlett could do with it— a secret not even Saylah knew.

Saylah had been right. The Chaos in the lock was drawn to Scarlett more than her. Scarlett carried Chaos from multiple different magical bloodlines. That alone made the lock seek her out more than others. It was why Alaric wanted her so badly. The power she could not only wield but create—just like she created shadowfire and a new Mark to take her to Shira Forest. It was something written in the pages Sorin had grabbed from the cliffs that made them come up with the idea of showing the Chaos all the power it could have to shape and break and create.

But the lock would also be drawn to her because the Chaos within recognized its own. Because while Scarlett had Chaos from Fae and Witches and a god, she also had Chaos from a World Walker.

Shirina had breathed it into her one day on a beach when Sorin had had a foot in the After, and Scarlett had screamed to the stars that she was done. She and the others had assumed it had just made her sleep so Cethin could dream-walk to her, but it had done more than that. According to the research Scarlett had translated, Shirina had been the daughter of a powerful high ruler. Whether or not that had been Korra, they couldn't know for sure, but still the panther was powerful. How she had transferred the Chaos, they did not know, but Sorin ventured to guess it had connected to Chaos that Scarlett already possessed.

Whether Scarlett wanted to admit it or not, the Fates had been walking beside her in more ways than one.

Now he and Rayner stood dumping a small vial of her blood atop the spot where Scarlett had summoned an ancient city. The same city a High Queen had once inhabited after she'd created this world. The three of them had Traveled here before they'd gone to Elshira to meet with Saylah. Scarlett had marked the spot that neither of the Fae could see.

They didn't know if their plan would work. They didn't know if she'd be with them or not. It ended up being not. When her blood had touched the orb, darkness had erupted, throwing them all back from her. When it had receded, the lock was gone and so was Scarlett.

If the Chaos had taken to her like they'd thought it would, she was likely between worlds right now.

Among the stars.

"This is going to work," Sorin said, the ground trembling beneath them as he and Rayner raced for the descending bridge that would lead to the mirror gate below.

Rayner didn't reply because they had no idea if this was going to work or not, and if it didn't...

They ran down the winding bridge, grateful to not find any of the feline creatures waiting for them. Hopefully that remained the case when they left. By the time they reached the base, the world had stilled. Sorin drew another vial from his pocket, smearing Scarlett's blood across the doors, and when they creaked open, he was shoving inside.

He threw flames into the air, casting the entire room into a soft glow and rushing to the other end of the chamber where the mirror gate stood. Pulling the final vial of her blood from his pocket, he studied the symbols and Marks around the mirror. The symbols of the gods, yes, but there were others. Scarlett called it the Runic Language, but they both knew it was more than that.

"Which one?" Rayner asked, coming to a stop beside him.

That was the real question.

Which symbol would call her back to this world?

He could still feel her down their bond. She was alive. That fact alone was keeping most of his panic at bay. As long as she lived, he could find her.

"I don't know," he answered. "It can't be one of the gods. It would call to the wrong being."

"So one of these then?" Rayner asked, brushing fingers along various symbols Sorin did not recognize.

Sorin nodded, pulling paper from his other pocket. Scarlett had listed out various symbols and their meanings, but none of them surrounded the mirror. Learning that an actual World Walker's essence was inside that lock had altered things. He'd promised he would not fail her, and he wouldn't, but they were running out of time. It would only stand to reason that the longer she was gone, the harder it would be for her to find her way back.

*Scarlett? Love?*

There was no arrogant voice replying in his mind.

"Can we eliminate any of them?" Rayner asked, crossing his arms while he continued to study the symbols. "Maybe process of elimination can help us narrow it down."

Sorin passed the paper to his Third. "None of these are listed there," he said, looking helplessly around the room for anything that might help.

"She gave you nothing else?" Rayner asked, flipping the page over and finding the back blank.

"This book might help."

They both whirled to find Cethin and Kailia at the chamber

entrance. Cethin held a book in his hand, and he was flipping pages as they closed the space between them.

"It is one we used when trying to find this city. Razik had figured out a few things, but most of the knowledge evaded even him," Cethin explained, holding the book out.

"What is this?" Sorin asked, reading through words Razik had translated.

Devram.

Nordrir.

Orlandria.

Waelore.

Siadrin.

"The best we could come up with was that they are other worlds," Cethin answered. "But some symbols appear to correlate."

Sorin glanced up to find he was right. There were several symbols around the mirror that matched the ones in this book. The problem was, none of them were translated. Rayner and Cethin crowded around him.

"This is not going to help," Sorin said in frustration, continuing to study the book, hoping something would jump out at him. He had an entire vial of blood. Maybe he simply needed to start trying symbols, and pray to— Well, maybe not the gods. Not anymore. But pray to the Fates that he didn't summon something he shouldn't.

"Perhaps she can help," Kailia said.

They all turned to the Avonleyan Queen, who perched on the table that ran the length of the room. She nodded towards the mirror, and Sorin slowly turned back.

There was a female standing there. She appeared to be in her mid-twenties, but that didn't mean anything if she'd gone through her Staying. She had arched ears, and long red hair so dark it was more burgundy than red. It was pulled back and tied high on the top of her head. She was of average height, and she was sipping something from a cup as she studied them. Her blue pants hugged her legs and hips, and the tunic she wore was too short, exposing her torso. She had Marks along her arms and across her chest, and what appeared to be some type of jewelry in her navel and nose, as well as her ears. But none of that was what had Sorin taking a step back.

No, that was her honey-colored eyes.

Eyes that he would recognize anywhere. The female he was staring at might be shorter and have a different hair color, but those eyes danced with the same amusement and slight insanity of another.

The female smiled at him, and that was the same as another too. She pulled something from her pocket. It was a small box of some sort, her thumb moving rapidly across it. Then she held it up.

Sorin stepped closer. There was an even smaller screen on the small box, and he peered closely to see what was on it. A Runic Symbol, if he was seeing it correctly.

His gaze darted back up to the female's. "How do you know where she is?" he asked, not sure if she could hear him or not. The last being they'd seen in this mirror hadn't been able to hear them.

She could though. Not only that, she could understand him.

"She has taken from him. He is not very pleased," the female said, casually taking another sip from her cup. It looked like it was made of paper.

"You speak of Achaz?" Sorin asked.

The female nodded. "I hear he is in quite the rage."

"How does he know already?" That panic he'd been keeping at bay was starting to surge up.

The female scoffed at the question. "When a power like *that* is released, the entirety of the universe knows it. Hope she is strong enough to harness it."

Sorin shifted uncomfortably at the words. "What world are you in? His?"

She shrugged. "The Light King thinks they're all his."

The small box in her hand suddenly lit up, and she glanced down at it. Her smile fell, replaced with something akin to dread. Her thumb moved quickly across the box again. Then she held it back up, showing him the screen once more.

"This one. It will call her to this gate," she said. "But hurry. He knows too."

"How do I know I can trust you?"

That manic grin returned. "You don't, but you called me here, so..."

"How did we do that?" Sorin asked, his brow furrowing. "How do you know all this?"

"Not important. What *is* important is that more than her blood will be needed to call her back."

Then with a wink, she was gone, as though she had Traveled. His own reflection once again stared back at him. He turned back to the others. What the fuck did that mean?

"She could be lying. What if she works for Achaz?" Rayner said immediately.

"I do not think we have much of a choice," Sorin replied, turning back to the mirror. It took a moment, but he found the symbol near the bottom on the left side of the mirror.

"And if you summon something else?" Cethin asked.

Sorin glanced at him as he pulled the vial of blood from his pocket. "I suppose you have experience with that. We'd have to figure something out."

"Anyone ever tell you that you are an ass?" Cethin deadpanned.

"Your sister. Daily," Sorin answered, tipping some blood into his palm. He could smell her in it. Embers. Citrus. Lavender. Jasmine. Taking a deep breath, he crouched before the mirror. He didn't let himself second guess it as he traced the symbol with her blood.

They were silent, waiting. For what, he had no idea. Would she appear in the mirror? Out of the air like Traveling?

"Your blood too," Cethin said after a moment.

Sorin glanced at Rayner, who shrugged. "It couldn't hurt."

Sorin sliced his finger before tracing over her blood on the symbol.

"She said it would take more," Kailia chimed in, still perched on the table. "Blood of the same blood perhaps?"

Cethin lowered beside him, taking the dagger and slicing his finger to trace the symbol.

Still they waited, and still there was nothing.

"Family blood too," Kailia said, jerking her chin at Rayner.

"But I am not blooded family," he argued.

"Chosen family is often stronger than blood," Kailia countered. "You know this, Ash Rider. Love, blood, and family."

Sorin pushed to his feet, stepping back to give Rayner room. "How do you know of this?" he asked the Avonleyan Queen.

She shifted cool amber eyes to him. "Some knowledge is learned. Some is innate. Some is both."

She spoke as nonsensically as an Oracle at times.

"Sorin."

Rayner's voice was tight and drew his attention back to the mirror. Where all the symbols and glyphs around it were now glowing.

"Shit," he murmured, Cethin and Rayner backing away.

The mirror was no longer reflecting the room back at them. There were images whirling past too quickly for Sorin to make them out. They were simply blurs of color, morphing from one to the next.

"Different worlds?" Rayner asked.

"Likely different mirror gates," Cethin said, tucking his wife protectively into his side. "What is her plan, Sorin?"

"If things work out, she will alter the mirror gates," Sorin answered, looking for any flash of silver hair among the swirling images.

"What do you mean alter them?" Cethin demanded, his eyes fixed on the mirror gate too.

"The theory is if a World Walker's power was used to fuel the mirror gates, a World Walker's gifts could also alter them. If it were powerful enough," he explained.

"The theory?" Cethin deadpanned. "You are placing the fate of the realm and your twin flame on a theory?"

"I know you do not know your sister well," Rayner muttered. "But she bases nearly every plan on a theory. Just be grateful she shared this one with some of us before putting it into motion." Then he added, "Somehow, they usually play out in her favor."

"Usually," Cethin repeated.

"More than half of the time," Rayner amended.

"Those are good odds," Kailia commented.

"By the Fates," Cethin muttered, dragging a hand through his hair.

Sorin glanced at him, his trepidation growing at Scarlett not returning yet. "She has a theory about you and the mirror gates too."

At that, her brother froze. "What does that mean?"

"She thinks that if you travel through a mirror gate, you are not technically crossing the Wards. You would be able to leave without taking them down."

"Even if that were true, my people would still be trapped here," Cethin argued.

"Yes, but you could fight. The Wards could come down after the Maraans are defeated, so that—" Sorin cut himself, realizing how insensitive this was about to sound. Perhaps now wasn't the time to discuss this.

"So that Avonleya will be safe, even if the Wards coming down takes my life," Cethin finished for him.

Sorin nodded, glancing at him out of the corner of his eye. He was bent down, murmuring into Kailia's ear. She shook her head, and he took her chin, turning her face to his. Sorin returned his attention to the mirror gate, trying to give them some semblance of privacy.

Then he felt her. Shadows and stars, wildness and darkness. But also something more.

Still the mirror before them swirled.

*Scarlett.*

"Sorin," came Rayner's warning.

He hadn't realized he'd taken a step towards the mirror.

*Scarlett? You're close, Love. Come home.*

*Home?*

His breath caught. *Yes, Love. Home.*

*I can't… It's too much. It wants too much. Demands too much.*

*No,* he snarled down the bond, placing his palm on the mirror. *It does not get to have you.*

*I'm sorry, Sorin. I tried.*

*No! Only I get to consume you, Scarlett! Me. Not the Chaos. Not the Fates. Me.*

*I love you like the stars love the night.*

"No!" he bellowed, slamming both palms against the glass.

There was no way. There was no way they had come this far, gone through everything they had, to have it end here.

"We knew this was a possibility," Rayner said quietly, his hand landing on Sorin's shoulder. "We need to go through with the plans."

"No," Sorin retorted, shaking his head. "No."

It was the only thing he could think to say.

"Sorin, you promised her—"

"I know what I promised her," he spat, shrugging Rayner's hand off of his shoulder. "I promised her I would find her among the stars. I promised her I would always come for her. I promised her I would not fail her."

*Scarlett! Love, answer me. Now!*

And when no answer came to him down the bond, he slammed his palms against the mirror again before he took a step back and hurled flames at the glass. Not a small flicker of embers, but a stream of fire that had Cethin throwing himself over Kailia and Rayner putting up a shield of smoke and ash.

When the flames receded and Sorin's chest was heaving, the symbols around the mirror were glowing brightly, as if the mirror itself had absorbed the power. The symbol where they'd smeared their blood was glowing the brightest, a brilliant white. The same color as Scarlett's starfire.

*More than her blood will be needed.*

That's what the female had said.

"Power," he said, turning to Rayner, who was glaring at him over his loss of control. He still had a thin shield of ashes swirling about himself. "It requires more than blood."

"So we have to give it magic? What if it keeps it, Sorin?" Rayner asked doubtfully. "This is Blood Magic and matters of the gods we should not be messing with."

"I will mess with it if it brings her home," Sorin snapped.

"Your power will not be enough."

They all spun around as Cethin said, "Mother?"

"You are right in your assumption, Prince," Saylah continued, moving towards them. Her ethereal grace made it appear as though she were floating. "The blood of the three of you called to her, but power calls to power." She stopped before the mirror, shadows beginning to pool in her hand. "Your flames alone will not be enough to call to her Chaos. Others in the universe know this. They will try to call to it too." She nodded at Rayner. "Your smoke with his flames. My shadows with Cethin's darkness and Kailia's ashes."

An Ash Rider.

A Fae Prince.

A goddess of shadows and night.

An Avonleyan King.

Some unknown power only Chaos would recognize.

Would it be enough?

Saylah sent her shadows spearing towards the glowing symbol that the female had shown him, and Sorin followed suit. He glanced at Rayner. The Ash Rider's jaw was tight. Sorin could tell he still wasn't sure about this, but he lifted a hand and smoke joined the shadows and flames. A moment later, there was darkness and ashes mixing among it all.

Sorin could feel it. Their powers all twining around each other, being absorbed by the mirror gate, and for the briefest moment, he wondered if Rayner was right. Were they all giving power that they wouldn't be able to get back?

"That's enough," Saylah said sharply enough that it startled him, his flames stuttering. Everyone stopped.

Everyone except Saylah.

Her shadows kept flowing to the symbol, around the mirror, obscuring the reflective surface.

Sorin glanced at Cethin, who was watching his mother closely.

And then a dagger appeared in the goddess's other hand. Before any of them could react, she had sliced her palm and was drawing a Mark on the glass of the mirror.

"Mother?" Cethin asked cautiously.

The goddess seemed to stumble before she sank to her knees, and Cethin lurched forward. Kailia's hand on his arm had him pausing.

"Look," Kailia whispered.

As the shadows receded, she stood there, her mother kneeling at her feet. Slowly, she lifted her eyes to his. Silver and glowing, wisps of shadows swirled faintly among them. Her shadows wound around her arms, starfire embers drifting among them. She was different. He could feel the power radiating off of her.

"Scarlett?" he said tentatively.

Her head tilted as she studied him. It took a moment. An excruciatingly long moment, where it seemed as though she were trying to remember why she knew that name.

Sorin swallowed thickly. *Love?*

Her lips tilted into a wicked smirk. His chest tightened, and he knew.

"Hello, Prince."

He was moving, stepping around Saylah, where she still knelt on the ground, and taking her face in his hands.

"I was trying," Scarlett said, her eyes swirling with shadows the same way Rayner's swirled with smoke and ashes. "I was trying to come back to you. I heard you calling, and I—"

But she was cut off by his lips landing on hers. His tongue forced its way in, taking her mouth as he slid it along hers. One hand slid into her hair and tilted her head, angling it so he could take the kiss even deeper. His other hand slid down to her waist, pulling her into his chest, and she melted against him.

He pulled back a moment later, brushing light kisses along the corner of her mouth, her cheek, her temple. "I would have come for you," he murmured into her hair.

"I know, Sorin," she whispered, clinging to him. "I know."

"How?"

She knew what he was asking. How had she done it? How had she found her way back? What exactly had she seen among the stars?

But before she answered, her gaze slid back to her mother, still kneeling on the ground. Saylah's breathing was ragged, and Cethin was crouched beside her.

Scarlett swallowed, turning back to Sorin. "I could hear you calling to me. I felt...you and Rayner and Cethin. But the Chaos..." Something in her eyes shifted to fear. He could feel it down the bond, and it had him tightening his hold on her. "It wasn't enough," she whispered.

"What do you mean it wasn't enough?" Cethin asked, looking up at them.

"We were right in assuming that the Chaos would be drawn to me because of the various kinds of Chaos I possess, but we were wrong in assuming that I would have enough to contain it," she answered.

"But you *are* containing it," Rayner said. "I can feel it. We can all feel it. The power in you is..."

"More than Saylah ever had," Kailia said from where she stood beside Cethin.

"More than she has now," Cethin added, clearly feeling her power wells with his own gifts.

"What does she have now?" Scarlett asked, twisting in Sorin's hold to face them.

"Nothing," Cethin said. "She has nothing left. Whatever she did to bring you back took it all."

Saylah finally lifted her head, looking straight at Scarlett. Her eyes were dimmer, and when she lifted a hand to brush back her hair, Sorin noted a slight tremor.

"It won't replenish, will it?" Scarlett asked quietly.

"What?" Cethin demanded. "Her reserves will refill. It will just take months because she has nothing left."

Scarlett shook her head.

"You don't know that," Cethin said harshly.

She raised a hand. Darkness swirled with starfire drifting among it. "She gave me her Chaos so I could control this. It was too much without it. I was trying to come back. I could hear you all calling me, but the Chaos… It wanted to go somewhere else. There are so many worlds, and they were all screaming at me. I didn't…" She ran her hand down her face, and Sorin was tucking her into his side a little more. "It took notice when it felt all of your power, but even still…"

"The Mark she drew on the mirror transferred her Chaos to you," Kailia said softly.

Scarlett nodded.

"So she is like Talwyn?" Rayner asked.

"I don't know," Scarlett admitted.

They all fixed their attention on Saylah. "I can Travel," the goddess said. "I was born a goddess. To give up all of my Chaos would kill me. I retain a small amount. I will eventually be able to summon a shadow, but nothing like I once was."

"Why?" Scarlett rasped.

"Everything I have ever done is for you and Cethin. This was no different."

It was different though. Sorin knew it. Scarlett knew it. Before she had given away her Chaos believing she would restore it with the lock. Saylah had known she was weakening herself, but it had been temporary. This was permanent. This was willingly given to spare her son and save her daughter so she could save a world.

"I assumed you wanted the lock to take its power for yourself," Scarlett said thickly.

"Power does call to power," Saylah answered breathlessly. "I told you the most powerful crave more power. But the moment I realized what you were doing… I knew it would consume you. You were too fast. I couldn't explain the cost. That the Chaos would use you. That it would take control of you and not the other way around."

Scarlett was sinking to her knees beside the goddess and her brother.

"I know you find me callous and unforgiving, but I know of sacrifice and loss, Scarlett," Saylah said. "When you live for centuries, you learn that sometimes to avoid the losses, you must make sacrifices. Sometimes you learn the same in two short decades. I wish you had not been forced to learn that lesson yet. Losing either of you has never been an option. It is why your father sacrificed his life. It is why I sacrificed knowing you as you grew up. It is why I have sacrificed pieces of my power. It has always been for the two of you."

"You have always been a mother," Scarlett whispered. "In the only way you knew how."

"I do not think the gods know how to truly love," Saylah said. "Nurturing is certainly not some innate thing to us. But I like to think that I have learned how to love, at least to some extent, in my centuries of life. From your father. From…" She cleared her throat, smoothing her hands down her dress. "There is not a sacrifice too great for you or your brother, Scarlett. If it would have required the entirety of my Chaos to save you, I would have given it. There would not have been a question."

"I know," Scarlett said quietly, reaching up and wiping at her cheeks. "I know, Mother."

Cethin gave her a tight smile as he helped Saylah to her feet, and Sorin reached down to do the same for Scarlett.

"I will take you to Elshira," Cethin said, reaching for Kailia with his other hand.

"Before we go, you should know," Kailia said, sliding her fingers into Cethin's waiting palm. "Your fire general is safe and in Avonleya."

"What?" Sorin, Rayner, and Scarlett all said together.

"She is with Razik," the queen answered simply.

"Where?" Sorin demanded.

"She asked us not to say anything until—"

"We will let her tell you the story," Cethin cut in. "Let me take Saylah to Elshira, and then I can take you to her."

They nodded, and the moment they Traveled, Sorin was spinning Scarlett back to face him again. "You are truly all right?"

"I am, Sorin," she said, reaching up to cup his cheek. "A little more powerful. That is all."

"A little," Rayner deadpanned.

Scarlett winked at him.

"You saw other worlds?" Sorin asked while they waited for Cethin, trying not to worry about Eliza. Why hadn't she wanted them to know she was back?

Scarlett nodded, worrying her bottom lip. "It is an odd thing. I just…know where they all are now. If I wanted to go to one, I could. I caught glimpses of them. It was as if the Chaos couldn't decide where to go."

"Are you going to be able to alter the mirror gates?" Rayner asked.

"We will go see Eliza," Scarlett answered, the shadows in her eyes swirling a little faster. "Then we move forward with our plans."

# CHAPTER 37
# ELIZA

She was waiting for them all outside the cave. Razik was still sleeping. He hadn't woken up yet.

Then again, that wasn't entirely true. Kailia had informed her he had been awake once while Eliza had been sleeping. She'd woken plenty of times, but apparently not when he did. Kailia had told her that Razik had insisted they let her sleep. In fact, he'd gone so far as to threaten them if any of them attempted to wake her.

Males and their godsdamn overprotectiveness.

She had been awake more and more these past two days. The Avonleyan King and Queen had filled her in on everything that had been happening, and she hadn't needed Sorin worrying about her while Scarlett still slept too. They had agreed that when Scarlett was awake and fine, they would tell the others that she and Razik were here. Kailia had sent a message that she had done just that. They would be arriving at any moment.

So she'd quickly dressed in loose pants, a sleeveless undershirt, and a tunic, slid on some silk shoes the queen had brought her, and climbed the steps to the cave entrance.

She tsked under her breath.

*Cave.*

Sure, it was inside a mountain, but this was nothing like the cave she'd spent time recovering in. The entrance to Razik's cave was hidden among rocky cliffs and ledges. How he'd even found it, she had no idea. He had wards all around it, and there were steps that led down into the belly of the mountain. The large main room was only the beginning. The steam she'd glimpsed towards the back was a large hot spring. There were a few other passageways leading off the main room as well, but she hadn't wandered down them, not wanting to pry into his personal space.

Eliza wasn't sure how he was going to react to her taking the twin flame Mark. Yes, he'd made it obvious he wanted the bond, but to make the decision without talking to him felt...wrong. She didn't like people making decisions for her, and she didn't particularly like making them for others.

Niara had been pleased her wound was healing faster than last time. Likely because she actually stayed in bed curled up next to Razik and gave her body the time it needed. It would be another day or two before Niara cleared her, but she could move her shoulder without issue.

Her hands were curled in her sleeves as she paced back and forth on the ledge, her unbound hair fluttering in the mountain air. She had slept more than enough to fill her reserves, and her fire kept her plenty warm; yet she still felt slightly chilled. She scowled. Damn dragon fire.

"Eliza."

Her name had her spinning to find Sorin, Rayner, and Scarlett standing there, the Fire Prince's eyes sweeping over her. He was the one who had said her name, but Eliza's eyes were fixed on Scarlett.

She was different.

Eliza couldn't place it, but she could feel it.

"What happened to you?" she demanded, sweeping her gaze over her queen the same way Sorin was eyeing her.

"What happened to me?" Scarlett retorted, stepping forward. "What happened to *you*? Kailia said you've been up here for days." Her eyes darted to the cave entrance. "Is there a reason you are staying in a cave instead of the castle? Or estate? Or anywhere else, really?"

"The cave is deceiving," she muttered defensively.

"Where is Razik?" Rayner asked. His ashes were roaming around him, seeking out whatever they could learn for him.

"Sleeping," she replied with a dismissive gesture behind her.

"In a cave," Scarlett deadpanned.

"It's not—" She huffed out a sigh as she pulled a hand from her sleeve and rubbed at her brow.

Unthinkingly, she did so with her left hand, and of course, Sorin zeroed in on it.

"You have a new Mark, Eliza," Sorin said carefully.

And Scarlett was darting forward, snatching Eliza's hand and running her fingers over the Mark that wound down her thumb and forefinger. "He is your twin flame?"

Eliza jerked her hand back, pulling it back into her sleeve. "He... I..."

"What happened, Eliza?" Sorin asked, he and Rayner coming to stand by Scarlett. They all stared at her expectantly, waiting for an explanation.

So she told them everything. How she'd known for quite some time who he was to her. How she'd known before she took the Source Mark. She told them of Siofra, of Sawyer's death, and of Nuri and Mordecai. She told them what had happened in the Fire Court. How she'd taken the twin flame Mark to find him. How she'd killed Varlis.

When she finished speaking, they all just stared at her. Not even Scarlett had some witty thing to say.

Sorin finally held out a hand, and Eliza pulled her left hand from the sleeve again, letting him examine the Mark. "He does not bear the companion Mark yet?" Eliza shook her head, and Sorin glanced up at her. "But he will take it?"

"Of course he's going to take it," Scarlett interrupted. Then her eyes shifted to Eliza, black wisps swirling among the silver irises. She bit her bottom lip. "Right?"

"He will take it," Rayner said. "You two have not witnessed them together. All of *this*," he gestured to the twin flame Mark, "explains a lot."

Eliza jerked her hand back again, muttering a curse at the Ash Rider under her breath. Rayner smirked at her.

"Tell me what has happened with you," she grumbled, crossing her arms tightly.

By the time they were done, it was Eliza's turn to stare at them with nothing to say. She looked between the three of them, coming back to Scarlett before she finally got out, "You are essentially a First goddess?"

"I guess so," she sighed. "A High Queen of the World Walkers with a little something more." Her shadows appeared, thicker and darker than before, white embers drifting among them. Scarlett frowned. "A little something more…chaotic."

"Let's go get something to eat," Sorin said, taking her hand. "We can discuss plans and go from there."

"I will still go reclaim the Fire Court," Eliza said. "As soon as Niara clears me—"

"Time is running out, but we can all take a minute to rest and breathe," Sorin said. "Let's reconvene tomorrow. Agreed?"

Eliza nodded, the bond in her chest stirring. She looked over her shoulder, half expecting to see Razik standing at the cave entrance. He wasn't, but it was the most she'd felt the bond move since she'd given herself the Mark.

When she turned back, Sorin and Scarlett had knowing looks in their eyes.

"Today we rest. Tomorrow we save the world," Scarlett said decidedly. "I need the day to figure out this Chaos, and you need a day to… figure things out with Razik."

"Whatever," Eliza muttered, crossing her arms once more. "Just come back tomorrow."

"Send a message if you need anything," Sorin said, worry still etched into his features.

Scarlett was right. He was a mother hen.

"I will see you all tomorrow," she said, turning and heading towards the cave entrance.

"Eliza," Scarlett called after her.

She glanced back to find a slow smirk spreading across Scarlett's face.

"Sorin and I only got one night for our Joining Trial. I know we're about to fight for the world and all, but I'll try to give you at least a full day," Scarlett said.

Eliza was already walking away again, flipping her off over her shoulder.

She felt the wards brush along her already too hot skin as she descended the steps back into the cave. What was he going to say when he woke up? What was *she* going to say?

She'd said things in a blind panic in the Fiera Mountains.

Too much.

She'd said too much. She'd meant it all, but she'd never meant to tell him all of that.

Her gaze fell onto her hand where the Mark swirled down her pointer finger, the Rescuing Trial already completed.

She slid her hands into her sleeves, balling them around the ends as she reached the bottom of the stairs, and then she froze.

Razik was not only awake but up and moving around the space. His back was to her as he did something in the small kitchenette area. His wings were still out, the right one with faint silver lines spider-webbing out from where the bolt had been embedded. Niara had told her wings heal differently. They would scar, unlike his chest.

The area the bolt had been was still raised and a little red, but there was hardly a mark on his skin. It didn't even require a dressing anymore. His Avonleyan blood healed him faster than her Fae blood. She scowled at the thought, instantly annoyed that his more extensive wounds would take less time to heal than hers.

Irritation that he apparently felt because he turned to face her fully. Bright sapphire eyes swept her up and down—twice—before he crossed his arms and leaned back against the counter, wings shifting behind him.

They just...stared at each other for a long moment before Razik said, "Come here."

Eliza clicked her tongue, ignoring the way relief flooded through her at hearing him speak for the first time since that day in the Fiera Mountains.

She also ignored the way her stomach dipped and heat pooled at the mere rumble of his voice. She had to actively hold back her magic from reaching out for him. His eyes seemed to darken as he felt her internal struggle.

"Come here," he growled again.

She took a single step before she managed to stop herself. She clenched her fists tighter, feeling her nails dig into her palms. "We should talk about this."

Razik's eyes narrowed. "Did you accept the bond solely to save me?"

"What? No, but I…"

"You what, Eliza?"

She couldn't think with him looking at her like that, knowing exactly what was going to happen if she obeyed his order to go to him. She could feel it all down this damn bond.

"Do you regret it?" he asked when the silence lingered.

"No," she whispered. Then louder, she added, "But it is not something we discussed beforehand. I do not want you to feel forced to accept this if it is not something you want."

"Why would you think I do not want this?"

"You said it yourself. I have no idea what you want," she shot back in annoyance. His lips twitched, and she wanted to punch him. "All I am saying," she gritted out, "is that you deserve to not have this forced on you, and I will understand if—"

She stopped speaking when Razik lifted his left hand, turning it so she could see the back where the twin flame Mark stood stark against his golden skin. "Come here."

"But your injuries—"

"I swear to the Fates, Eliza, if you make me say it again—"

But she was already moving, all but running to him. When she was within reach, his hands grasped her face, fingers sliding into her unbound hair and his mouth crushing against hers. And this kiss—Gods, this kiss was everything the others had been and more. Hot and desperate and all-consuming. He didn't wait for her to let him in. His tongue invaded her mouth, taking whatever he wanted from her.

"I meant what I said," she panted into his mouth. "You've fucking ruined me."

"I know," he rumbled, hands leaving her face to grip her thighs and hoisting her up. Her legs wrapped around his waist, arms looping around his neck.

"You're so godsdamn arrogant," she snarled as he carried her to the dining table, setting her atop it and peeling off her tunic.

"I know," he said again, hand cupping her face and tipping her head back so he could take her mouth once more. Her teeth sank into his bottom lip at the comment, and something between a groan and a laugh came from him.

Leaning back, his eyes dropped to her nearly healed wound. He brushed his fingertips over it, and it sent a shiver down her spine. He met her gaze as he said, "I am sorry I could not get to you."

She was shaking her head before he'd finished speaking. "It wasn't your fault."

His fingers skated along her skin to the Mark over her heart. "He was the one who gave you this."

It was a statement, and she only swallowed thickly before nodding once.

"Did you believe killing him would make it fade?"

"No," she whispered. "I've always known it was forever. That even his death would not free me of it."

"Do you wish to be free of it?"

She'd dropped her hands to the edge of the table, and her fingers curled around it, eyes darting to the side. "I have accepted it, but if it is not something you can accept, I understand. It is why I had wished to speak with you before you took the Mark."

"I already told you I know what this Mark means, Eliza," he said, guiding her gaze back to his.

"I know, but I didn't want you to feel obligated—"

"Obligation was the very last thing I felt when I had Cethin give me this Mark, *mai dragocen*."

She felt her cheeks flush, and she absolutely hated it. "I suppose we should figure out what we're going to do then."

"The only thing I want to figure out is what you taste like," he replied, reaching for the fitted undershirt.

"Raz, we're still healing," she said, the argument as weak as her voice when she said it.

"Me being on my knees is not going to affect any of our wounds," he replied in that same matter-of-fact tone he said everything else in. "Arms up."

His fingers skated along her ribs as he dragged the shirt up her torso. She was obeying the command and lifting her arms before she even realized what she was doing.

"So you can follow instruction," he said with a smirk, his hands coming to her breasts and thumbs sweeping across her nipples.

That flush in her cheeks spread throughout her entire body.

She arched into his touch. "I believe I told you if it suits my needs, I follow orders. It's simply rarely worth my while."

His eyes heated, shifting to vertical pupils and glowing softly. One of his hands slid to her throat, grasping it loosely and tugging her forward. She tilted her head back to look up at him, and his mouth was hovering over hers when he said on a soft growl she felt in her core, "You'll be begging me for orders by the end of this, *mai dragocen.*"

She scoffed, a snarky reply on the tip of her tongue, but the hand at her breast was moving lower down her belly and beneath the band of her loose pants. He didn't slow as he dragged a finger over those nerves before sinking it deep inside her. She let out a gasp when he slowly dragged the finger out before plunging back in.

"Feet up."

"It's a table, Razik," she said on a breath as he kept working that finger in and out.

"I'm aware of the furniture type. Bend your knees, and bring your feet up," he growled, pulling her forward by the throat and pressing a bruising kiss to her lips. By the time he pulled back, her feet were braced on the table. She didn't even know when she'd done that.

"Lose the pants."

"I can't with your hand down them," she tried to snap, but he was pushing a second finger inside her, and she was burning away her remaining clothing.

"Open your legs," he ordered.

"People eat on this table," she argued.

"Perfect. I've been starving for weeks," he replied, releasing her throat and pushing one of her knees wide.

And it was the way he said it—in that casual-as-fuck tone he always spoke in—that had her mouth hanging open as he dropped to his knees and tugged her forward. She fell back on her elbows.

"Seriously, Raz. We can't—" But then her head was tipping back and her eyes were fluttering closed when he ran the flat of his tongue across her center.

"Eyes stay on me, Eliza," he said, nipping at her inner thigh. "I'll stop every time they're not."

Her head snapped up, eyes flying open. She glared at him as he looked up at her from between her legs. His hair was disheveled and eyes dark with hunger.

Holding her gaze, he flicked his tongue against her again, and when she didn't look away, he went back in for more and more. He alternated between tight sweeping circles with his tongue and sharp sucks that had her writhing on the table. Anytime her eyes started to fall closed or her head dropped back, he would slow his motions and have her hissing curses at him.

She was right there when she couldn't do it anymore. When she was about to tip over the edge and her arms were trembling from holding herself up. Her eyes fell closed a moment before she was about to find her pleasure—

And he stopped. Just like he fucking said he would.

Her eyes flew back open. "Razik!" she snarled, her gaze transfixed on his swollen lips.

"For someone who claims to follow instruction when it suits her needs, you're terrible at it," he said, dropping open-mouthed kisses along the crease of her thigh.

"I swear to Anala, if you don't get your mouth back on my—"

And then she was crying out when his teeth clamped lightly around those sensitive nerves at the same moment his black flames swept over her, hurtling her into bliss.

She was still trembling from release when she was scrambling towards him, reaching out to touch skin and muscle that had taunted her for weeks in her bed, but he snatched her wrists in one hand before she got close.

She growled at him, and he smirked. Bracing one hand on the table beside her hip, he brought his face so close to hers, strands of his hair brushed along her cheek. "What do you want, Eliza?"

Her breath mingled with his, eyes holding his sapphire stare. Challenge glimmered there, and she pushed forward so her lips brushed across his when she whispered, "You, Raz. I want you."

Her words shattered whatever semblance of control they were pretending to have. Everything was desperate and needy. Razik released her wrists as his hands landed on her hips and tugged her forward so she was balancing on the edge of the table where her legs now dangled over the side. Bare skin brushed against bare skin, and she only had a moment to wonder when in all this he had lost his own pants before he was pushing into her.

"Gods," she gasped, feeling him stretch her. She could only cling to his shoulders, nails dragging down his arms as her mouth explored his jaw, neck, chest.

When he'd worked himself all the way in, he stilled. Fingers wound into her hair, tightening and pulling her head back. But gods, she didn't want him to stop. She needed him to never stop moving, and she bucked her hips forward, creating her own friction. Something deep in his chest rumbled as he held her stare, and she did it again.

"Move, Razik," she rasped, winding her legs around his waist and digging her heels into his ass, trying to get him to do godsdamn anything.

"You're not about to beg, are you?" he asked with a smug grin.

"Not even close," she retorted, leaning back on a hand. His brow arched as she brought her fingers to the hollow of her own throat. She began dragging them down her chest, between her breasts. A smirk of her own curled as he watched every movement, his wings shifting behind him. "I told you," she said in a heated rasp, her fingers gliding over her navel and making their way lower. "Others rarely make it worth my time. I can do it better myself anyway." As she said the words, her finger slipped between her legs that she'd let fall open, letting him see everything. Where they were joined together. What she was doing with her own fingers.

And she held his godsdamn stare the entire fucking time.

Then he was scooping her up from the table. Before she could blink, he was dumping her onto the bed, and she let out a godsdamn whimper at the loss of him being inside her.

"You're such a liar," he growled, flipping her onto her stomach as he crawled up the bed behind her. "Trying to tell me your fingers are better than me when you make *that* sound."

"Fuck off," she spat, pressing back against him when he hauled her hips into the air. Then she was moaning as he thrust back into her in one hard movement.

This time, he didn't stop. He gave her no reprieve as he drove into her over and over, each time seeming to go deeper than before. His hand slid up her spine, before pressing down between her shoulder blades, holding her in place in a way she had never let another male have her while he did exactly what she'd demanded of him.

He made it worth her while.

His hand slid up farther, sliding around her neck to grip her throat once more, and he was hauling her up, pressing her back to his chest. He bent one of his knees, planting his foot beside them. Tilted his hips, he hit a spot inside her that drew a sound from her that was pure sinful pleasure.

"Say it, Eliza," he said.

She knew what he wanted to hear. It wasn't that she'd been lying to him about her fingers being as good as his cock because that was the farthest thing from true, and he fucking knew it. It wasn't even some declaration of love. That would come in time. But he wanted her to say something she had never said to another male. Something no one else would ever hear come from her lips, and something more primal and permanent among the Fae.

His fingers flexed around her throat, just enough to restrict airflow in the best way, as he withdrew all the way before punching back into her again and then stilling, keeping her back secured to his chest.

"Yours, Raz," she gasped. "Only yours."

"*Mine*," he snarled in a way that could only be described as a dragon's growl, before his movements become erratic, sending them both careening into pleasure.

They flopped down together, a sweaty heap of limbs and ragged breathing. Razik stayed on his stomach, not wanting to lie atop his wing, but he rolled her onto her side. The filthy look he gave her had her breath seizing all over again.

"We're not done," he said.

"Never done," she agreed, hauling his mouth back to hers.

Eliza had no idea what time it was when they lay tangled with each other in the bed. They'd fucked and slept and then fucked some more. Now she was on her back, Razik's arm over her waist while he slept on his stomach with his face nestled into her neck. The wing with the scarring was splayed across her too, and when she dragged her fingers through his hair, he stirred enough to let her know he was at least partially awake.

"Can I touch your wings?" she whispered.

"You can touch whatever you want whenever you want," he murmured into her neck.

She huffed a laugh, gently running a finger along the wing draped across her. She had expected it to feel thin and fragile, but it was thicker like leather and rougher than she thought it would be. And it was cold. Not hot like the rest of him always was. She ran her fingers along it again, then stilled when he made a sound.

"Did you just…purr?"

"Dragons don't purr."

"It sounded like you purred."

He lifted his head enough to peer down at her through bleary eyes. "Do you want to talk about all the sounds I have heard you make in the last several hours?"

She snapped her mouth shut.

"Why are you awake?" he grumbled, settling back down. "You should be resting."

"*I* should be resting?" she admonished. "You were hurt worse than I was, and you're the one who keeps starting things."

"I heal faster than you," he mumbled, his words distorted against her skin where he'd once again buried his face in her neck. "And you have started things every time."

Her mouth fell back open. "I have not."

"You're starting this argument right now."

She rolled her eyes, huffing loudly, and she felt him smile against her flesh.

"Bastard," she muttered.

She should be exhausted after everything, but she wasn't. She knew she could get up, but... All right, fine. She liked being in a bed with him and being able to touch him and have him touch her without having to worry about what it would mean later.

Eliza lifted her hand above her head, studying the Mark that had wound its way down another finger. Then her gaze started bouncing around the cave lit up by the soft glow of her flames.

"So this is all the treasure?" she asked, eyeing the various trinkets and gold around the room.

"You were expecting more?"

"The way you spoke about it? Yes. You almost stole a bowl, for gods' sake."

He heaved a loud sigh. "I was not going to steal that bowl."

"Now who's the liar?"

Razik lifted his head again, giving her a frank look before he pushed himself up into a sitting position.

"What are you doing?" she asked, propping herself onto her elbows, eyes dragging down his bare torso to where the blankets pooled in his lap.

He stretched his arms above his head, muscles rippling with the movement and wings flaring out slightly. "Deeper in the cave, there is an entire room with piles of treasure."

"There is not," she tsked.

He leaned over her, reaching out and cupping the back of her head as he brushed a lingering kiss across her lips. "There is. I'll fuck you on top of all the gold later."

Razik moved to climb out of the bed, and she gripped his forearm. "Where are you going?"

"To get you food. You're restless."

"I'm not—"

Okay, yeah, she was both restless and hungry.

She watched as he made his way over to the kitchen area, opening the icebox and pulling out various items.

"Do you always cook naked?" she asked, sitting fully upright.

He glanced up at her before he went back to what he was doing. "It's my cave."

Eliza hauled herself up and out of the bed, dragging on one of his tunics as she crossed the space. Then she hopped up on the counter, the surface cold against her bare ass through his shirt, and watched as he chopped an onion and pepper.

His eyes flicked to hers for a brief moment. "People eat on this counter."

"Shut up," she grumbled, drawing her sweeping curls over her shoulder.

He was dumping the onions and peppers into a pan with eggs and moving it over a small flame on the stove when she said, "Razik?"

"What?" he asked, reaching for a utensil to flip the eggs.

"What does *mai dragocen* mean?"

He went completely still, keeping his back to her. She had slid her hands into the sleeves of his tunic, curling her fingers around the end.

"That was the deal, right?" she asked, her tone soft and small. "I tell you of the Curse Mark, and you tell me what that name means?"

"It is a term from Nordrir," he answered after a long stretch of silence. "That world was once inhabited by dragon shifters. Or so I have read."

She said nothing as he flipped the eggs he was making.

"My penchant for collecting treasure is nothing compared to a full-blooded dragon shifter. But their most valued treasure? It was called *dragocen*. *Mai* is a variation of 'mine' in that language, and while they do not have twin flames, they do have mates. They called their mates *mai dragocen*. My most treasured. It was a sacred term to them, only used between mates."

Eliza could hardly speak around the emotion clogging her throat. "That is why Tybalt reacted strangely when I asked him of it."

Razik didn't say anything else as he plated the eggs and sautéed vegetables. Finally turning to face her, he set the plates off to the side before he planted his hands on either side of her, caging her between his large frame.

"It was not something I called you lightly," he said. "It was not something I would have called you unless it was true."

"The only place I do not need my armor," she whispered, her hand coming up to cup his cheek, eyes searching his.

"Never with me, *mai dragocen*."

# CHAPTER 38
# CYRUS

"This is the Black Syndicate?" Cyrus asked, taking in the various shops and buildings along the main street Cassius was leading him down.

Their faces were hidden deep within hoods, but he felt Cassius look over at him. "What were you expecting?"

He shrugged. "I don't know. Something more sinister? I've only been here in the dark when we came in to get you and Scarlett. Didn't really have time to take in the sights. It's so…nice. Not like a place where the foulest of the realm are trained and then released to wreak havoc."

He could practically hear Cass's eye roll. "Come on," he murmured, steering him to a side street.

Cassius herded him down a few more streets before they were scaling a wall to the rooftops. Cyrus followed wordlessly, knowing this was Cass's domain and not his. Cassius had been tense and withdrawn about coming here for the past two days, despite everything that had transpired between them. But Cyrus had watched as he'd slipped from the role of Hand-to-the-Queen to lethally trained assassin. He donned a mask the same way Scarlett did when she became Death's Maiden, and Cassius as…*this* wasn't the same Cassius he'd spent the last couple nights tangled up with in bed or the last months helping learn to hone his magic. This Cassius was cold and calculating.

Cyrus had watched him strap on weapons so methodically, he could tell he'd done it hundreds, if not thousands, of times. Something in his chest had twisted at the knowledge that Cassius was only in his mid-twenties, and so many of those years were spent as...*this.*

"There are four people tailing us and more observing us from various vantage points," Cassius said quietly, standing perfectly still.

"You said we would be watched before we even entered the Syndicate," Cyrus replied, noting two figures on a warehouse roof down the street.

"Until we figure out *who* is watching us, we cannot go near the remains of the Fellowship."

"We can't just...take care of them?" Cyrus asked casually.

Cassius slowly turned to him. "If we strike first, it's as good as declaring a war against them."

"So we have to wait for them to attack us? I prefer to be on the offensive, not the defensive," Cyrus said, watching the people move about on the street below.

"Stick to the plan, Cyrus."

"We don't know what we're even looking for," he retorted. "We don't have time to waste on waiting them out."

"I thought we already had this argument," Cassius grumbled.

They had. A few times during their planning. Cyrus had always relented, telling Cass he knew the place best and would follow his lead. But now that they were here? He really just wanted to get this over with.

"We at least need to figure out where they are hiding out with the Fellowship gone. Then we can monitor their movements, get a feel for their routine—"

"We don't have weeks to plan a fucking mission, Cass," Cyrus interrupted.

"You don't just walk into the Black Syndicate and start killing people, Cyrus," he countered begrudgingly. "You do that, and you're the one that ends up dead."

"Doubtful," Cyrus muttered.

"Let's go," Cass gritted out.

"Go?" Cyrus repeated. "Go where? I thought we were monitoring movements."

"We are," Cass said, moving back to the roof edge they'd climbed over. "But we also need to scout out the underground passages that will lead us into the halls beneath the Fellowship."

"*Or*," Cyrus said, drawing out the word as he followed Cass down off the rooftop and into the alley below. "We detain one of the fuckers following us and see what he knows."

"It's like working with the Wraiths," he heard Cass grumble from beneath his hood.

Cyrus was still debating if he considered that a compliment or not when he heard it. The release of a bowstring. The stirring of the air. He caught the black ashwood arrow an inch from his chest, incinerating the thing in his palm a moment later. Five figures emerged from the shadows of the alley.

"Now that they have fired the first shot, can we please take care of them?" Cyrus ground out, fire already beginning to wind its way down his arms.

"Try to leave one alive," Cassius replied, drawing a sword.

A dagger came flying at them, Cassius stepping to the side a second before it grazed his cheek.

"Not that one. He dies," Cyrus said darkly, fire flaring from his palm. The man who had thrown the dagger was screaming the next moment as flames engulfed him.

"Fae bastard," one spat, pulling a shirastone dagger from his side and cocking his arm back to throw it.

But it was black flames that had him screaming, the dagger clattering to the stone alleyway.

Black ashwood arrows came from above, forcing them to shield and allowing those on the ground to advance. "Take care of them, Cass," Cyrus said as he reinforced his shield to deflect more arrows. "I'll cover you."

Adjusting his grip, Cassius moved forward, bringing his sword up to meet that of another. His opponent had a shirastone dagger that Cassius blocked with one of his vambraces before he brought a foot up, landing a clean kick to the guy's gut. An *oomph* sounded from beneath the hood as the guy stumbled back, and Cass wasted no time swiping his blade across his throat. He spun in time to meet another sword, but this guy was better, already jumping back and circling around Cassius again.

Cyrus watched, keeping the barrage of arrows from striking them. More archers had joined the others, and he had no choice but to focus on keeping his shield intact.

"Cass! There's one running!" Cyrus shouted as the final man on the ground turned and took off down the alley, but they couldn't take chase with the constant arrows firing. "Travel to the rooftops and fry these fuckers!"

"And leave you down here?"

"I'll be fine," Cyrus retorted. "Go!"

Cassius was gone in the next blink, and Cyrus moved into the shadows along the wall, keeping his shield in place. He could hear the screams of those Cass was taking out with dragon fire, and he glanced down at his hand, wondering if he would need to fill his reserves right away or if he could wait. They were still getting a feel for how the whole Source-thing worked.

Another scream echoed.

Only this one was his.

*The scent of blood hit him, and he whirled, falling to his knees at the body that was at his feet. Blood pooled around the female. Red hair the color of flames was flecked with mud and gore. There were puncture wounds at her throat, on her arms, on her stomach. Puncture wounds from fangs. Lifeless hazel eyes stared unseeingly at the roof of the cave they were in.*

*"Thia!" he cried, tears already wetting his face as he reached for her limp body. Blood coated his hands when he slipped them beneath her shoulders, pulling her into his lap. He buried his face in her hair, saying her name over and over. "No! No! No!"*

*The others were still fighting. Someone was tugging at his arm telling him they needed to go, but he couldn't go. His entire world was lying in a pool of blood.*

*"We need to go," someone said again. Sorin? Rayner? He didn't care as he jerked out of their hold, clutching Thia to his chest and brushing his lips across her brow, her temple.*

*"You're running out of time, Fae of Fire."*

"Cyrus, we need to go," Cassius was saying urgently, his voice low and coaxing. "Come on, Cyrus. Look at me."

Cyrus blinked in the darkness. He had no idea where they were, only that he was on his knees and doubled over. His entire body was shaking, fingers wound into his hair and pulling at the roots.

"Cyrus," Cassius said again, softer still as he closed his hands over Cyrus's fingers, trying to pry them out of his hair.

"Where are we?" Cyrus rasped.

"I heard you scream," Cass said. "I found you like this in the alley and Traveled us to an old building in the Syndicate. We'll be safe here, but we can't stay."

"That was really inconvenient timing for Gehenna to send a reminder," Cyrus muttered, straightening some and shifting so he sat on his ass rather than his knees. He bent one, dropping his brow against it as he tried to steady his breathing.

Cassius had been kneeling before him, and he shifted too, his shoulder brushing against his. They sat in silence for several minutes, Cyrus trying to plant himself back in the here-and-now.

"When this bargain is fulfilled, this shit stops, right?" Cass asked into the dark.

Cyrus closed his eyes, but immediately opened them again when all he could see was Thia lying in a pool of blood. Sure, the Sorceress wouldn't be able to force him to relive memories whenever she was looking for some fun, but the nightmares she'd already sown? Those wouldn't simply disappear.

He could lie to him. Maybe he should, but he said, "I don't think so, Cass, but having the bargain fulfilled should help some."

"When you're ready, I'll Travel us to the Fellowship ruins."

Cyrus turned his head to look at him, brow still pressed to his bent knee. "What happened to the plan?"

"The plan sort of got fucked when that mercenary got away. He'll report to Alaric we are here."

Shit. He'd forgotten about that part of the plan. Not leaving anyone alive who knew who they were. It was his fault the plan was already fucked.

"Don't do that, Cyrus," Cassius said, stopping the spiral before Cyrus could dive down it. "You didn't ruin anything."

It was another fifteen minutes before Cyrus felt in control of himself again. It was dusk, the sky a darkening grey when they appeared across the street from the burned Fellowship. The last time Cyrus had been here, it had been a towering building of four floors with an impeccably manicured lawn and gardens. Now it was nothing but charred rubble. But even from across the street though, he could still feel the wards around the place.

"Can you get past them?" he asked Cassius in a hushed tone.

"I've been training with wards," he replied. "Studying them as much as I can. These were put in place by Sybil. Since she's dead, they'll be weakened enough that it shouldn't take me too long."

"Tell me what you need me to do," Cyrus said.

"We need to be closer. I need to be completely focused, so I need you to tell me if you see anything suspicious."

"Got it."

"I'm serious, Cyrus. Anything. Even if you think it's nothing."

"Yeah, yeah. Go do your fancy Witch tricks."

"You're such an ass," he grumbled, as they pulled their hoods back up and quickly made their way across the street.

Cassius was right. It didn't take him long to create enough of a gap in the wards for them to slip through. Rubble crunched under their boots as they made their way across the ruins until they came to a spot where stairs descended underground. The debris had been cleared away, others having clearly been down there. Alaric had surely been one of them in his attempts to recover this thing the Sorceress desired.

Cyrus kicked at some of the rubble, rocks and dust scattering, and then he was throwing out a hand to stop Cassius from taking the first step down the stairs.

"What?" Cassius asked.

"There are Blood Marks here," Cyrus answered. He glanced around them, seeing no obvious observers before he conjured a small flame to illuminate the ground as he crouched down. "Don't suppose you know what these mean?"

"No," Cass said. "Well, yes and no. They are a stronger ward marking. I can't say for sure how to counter them."

"So we're back to needing to gain entrance from the underground passageways?" Cyrus asked.

"Assuming they aren't warded the same way."

Cyrus extinguished the flame, holding out a hand to Cass, and a moment later they were in the back storeroom of a shop. Cass had told him it was an apothecary shop that the emergency tunnel led to, with a disguised door in the floor here. Within minutes, Cass had stones removed and a hatch open in the floor. Cyrus did a thorough sweep of the floor, making sure there were no signs of Blood Magic, before they lowered themselves into the tunnel.

Cyrus had another flame kindling in his palm, but Cassius didn't appear to need it as he led the way down the tunnel. And thank fuck he did because there were so many passages branching off, Cyrus would have been lost for hours.

He didn't know how long it had been before Cass said, "Up ahead are the dungeon studies. It would have been where you found us that day."

Cyrus had hardly known Cassius then. He'd come to the Fire Court once for half a day, but all of that time had been spent with Scarlett. At that time, he'd been more worried that he was a threat to Sorin before he'd figured out Scarlett and Cassius were soulmates and nothing more.

"Did Alaric have a main study? Or is there some place else he would have kept something valuable?"

"It's hard to say," Cass replied, his steps slowing as they neared the end of the passage. "If it was something he didn't want anyone else seeing, he'd have kept it in his private rooms. No one was ever allowed in there, but if it was something valuable enough that he kept near him at all times, then a study. Did the Sorceress give you anything to go on? Is the item large? Small?"

Cyrus shook his head. "She only said I would be able to find it. I would know it when I saw it, and Scarlett's starfire could not have destroyed it."

"I guess since most viable options were destroyed, we start with the dungeon studies," Cass said, pulling his hood back and coming to a stop at a dead-end wall. He ran his palm along it, searching for what Cyrus was assuming was a switch of some sort to release a hidden door. A moment later, there was a faint clicking sound, and they were stepping into—

"Holy fuck," Cyrus breathed. "She doesn't do things by halves, does she?"

The underground halls were barely passable, the stench of smoke and decay thick in the air. Rubble and remains from the building above filled the passages and cells. It wasn't just stone and furniture either. Bones. Bodies. Scarlett had been a real wraith at that point. Sorin had been back, but her wrath had needed some place to go, and she had taken it out here. She hadn't told anyone of her plans to take down the Fellowship. The stone walls were scorched and entire chunks were missing, which didn't make him feel very good about the stability of the place.

"I guess just find *any* room to start in at this point," Cyrus said, pulling his own hood back and setting flame glowing above them to light their way.

It took longer than he'd ever imagined to pick their way through the debris, and when they finally came to one of the dungeon studies, they'd spent another hour clearing away stones and rubble to get inside it.

Sacrifice of time indeed.

They ended up crawling through a hole to get inside the room. If anyone else had been in here, they'd covered their tracks well.

Cyrus stood, pointlessly brushing dirt off his cloak and pants while he surveyed the area of yet another wreckage of his queen. This had definitely been a study at one point. The walls had bookshelves set into them. Half of a desk stood in the center, splintered remains of chairs around it. The floor was scorched black, but he could tell he was standing on what had once been an ornate rug.

Cassius and Cyrus looked at each other, both at a loss for where to start with this insanity. They were never going to simply stumble across something.

Cassius scratched his jaw. "I guess you take the bookshelves, and I'll take the...desk?"

Cyrus shrugged, because what else was there to say?

They worked in silence, scouring every inch of the space. Feeling for hidden compartments. Digging through ash and soot and more debris. And hours later, they had nothing but cracked and bleeding hands and fingers.

Cyrus sank down against a wall, wiping sweat from his brow. He could feel the smudge of dirt the movement left behind. Cassius wasn't any better off. Ash stained his brow, his cheek, his jaw. He was still sifting through what they thought was the remains of a cabinet of some sort.

This was going to take time they simply did not have.

They had thrown around the idea of using a tracking Mark like Scarlett had used to find the mirror gate in the Runic Lands, but she had known what she was looking for. They didn't, which made using the Mark even riskier.

Cassius turned to him, huffing a sigh as he raked a hand through his hair. "I guess we dig our way into another room?"

"Yeah," Cyrus said, arms resting atop his bent knees. "But food first."

Cassius nodded, making his way over to him and holding out a hand to pull him to his feet. "I know a place."

They made their way back through the passages, pulling themselves up through the hidden hatch, and then Cassius had him back on the rooftops. Eventually they dropped down over an overhang, swinging themselves through the upper window of a tavern, and both coming to a halt as they beheld the person sitting at the table, drinking from a mug of ale.

"Nuri," Cassius said carefully.

Her hood was down, gloves off. She winked at them as she took another drink of her ale.

"What are you doing here?" Cassius asked.

She tipped her head, studying them. "I suppose you two have no way of knowing, do you?"

"Knowing what?" Cass asked, angling his body so he stood between her and Cyrus.

Cyrus just watched Death's Shadow. There was something different about her from all the other times he'd interacted with the Contessa.

She looked...tired.

"Nothing," she replied, sipping from her ale again. "Find what you were looking for at the Fellowship?"

"Do you know what we were looking for there?" Cyrus countered, and her honey-colored eyes flicked to him.

"Do *you* know what you are looking for there?"

"Nuri," Cassius sighed. "Are you going to let us leave, or are we going to have to fight our way out?"

She shrugged. "I'm not going to fight you. Not right now, at least."

"What does that even mean?" Cyrus asked.

"Obviously at some point I'm going to need to fight you. Blood Bond and everything." She shrugged again. "But that day is not today."

"Why?" Cassius asked.

"You're annoying as hell, but I don't want you dead."

There was a patterned knock on the door, and Cassius went rigid. "Who is that?"

Nuri pushed to her feet, sauntering to the door and pulling it open. The person who entered was tall and broad, a hood in place hiding his features. But when he pulled it back—

"Fucking hell," Cyrus said, fire already flaring in his palms and a shield in place around him and Cassius.

"Relax," Nuri said with an eye roll, taking one of the mugs of ale the male held. "He brought you something to drink."

"Not a chance," Cassius retorted, sword drawn, focus bouncing between her and the seraph commander.

Mordecai turned to her. "You didn't tell them?"

"Tell us what?" Cassius gritted out.

The seraph shook his head, shooting Nuri a look to which she smiled mockingly and made her way back to the table.

For the next twenty minutes, they listened to the seraph and Nuri try to convince them they had been working against Alaric as much as they could. Cyrus had so many questions, but he held them back, evaluating every word they said. It made sense when he really thought about it, but even so, he couldn't risk trusting them based on their word alone.

When he said as much, Mordecai nodded. Nuri appeared bored out of her mind, head resting in her hand that was propped on the table and her eyes closed. Cyrus wasn't even sure she was listening at this point. Maybe she had actually fallen asleep.

"How, exactly, do you plan to prove any of this to us?" Cassius asked. Neither of them had touched their ale.

"Because I know how to find what you are looking for," Nuri said, eyes still closed.

"How could you possibly know that?" Cyrus asked.

"Because I already found it. Sort of."

"Again, how could you possibly know what we are looking for?" Cyrus repeated.

Nuri finally opened her eyes, reaching over and pulling Mordecai's half-empty mug of ale to herself. The seraph didn't appear to care when she took a long drink from it.

"We were sent in to search the Fellowship," Mordecai answered. "It took days for Scarlett's flames to finally go out, but the moment they did, we spent nearly two weeks searching through the rubble."

"If you found it, why doesn't Alaric have it?" Cassius asked, his gaze also fixed on Nuri, who had shifted so she was angled towards Mordecai now.

"Because my orders were to search for it until I found it. Which I have not," Nuri answered.

"I thought you said you already found it," Cyrus said skeptically.

"No. I said I know *how* to find it."

"You really have been working against him?" Cassius asked, eyeing her carefully.

And that thing Cyrus had glimpsed in her eyes shifted again, something haunted flickering across her features. She had them schooled again just as quickly. "I am many things. He has made me into many things. But that does not mean I wish to be those things," she finally answered.

Mordecai's wings rustled, one lifting and curving around her.

"So where is it?" Cassius asked.

"Better yet, *what* is it?" Cyrus countered.

"About that..." Her eyes dragged to Cassius. "You're going to need your mommy's help."

Cassius jerked back from the table. "What?"

"Her mother created them. Since it was her enchantment, your blood can find it. Relations and all that. But I don't know how your magic tricks work, so you're going to need her help," she said, fingers beginning to drag up and down Mordecai's forearm.

"I'm going to need you to cut the bullshit," Cyrus said. He was tired, hungry, and if she had information to make this whole thing go faster, it was high time she spit it the fuck out, especially if she was on their side as she claimed.

"It is my understanding they are known as the Semiria rings," Mordecai said, eyes flicking down to where Nuri had started dragging a nail along a vein.

"The rings that let the Fae access their gifts inside the mortal wards?" Cassius asked.

"There are only two Semiria rings," Cyrus said. "Eliné and Henna each had one. Alaric never had one."

"But at one time there were *three* Fae Queens," Nuri said. "Surely you've realized by now the third was a jealous thing and felt slighted for being given the mortal territories to rule over, while her sisters got the powerful Fae Courts."

"The rings were nothing special when they first came here," Mordecai said, hand coming up to still Nuri's fingers. She scowled at him. "They were simple family crest rings, but they were created into something more when they were used to hide a portal key."

"What the fuck is a portal key?" Cyrus asked, rubbing at his temples. He really was not in the mood for a history lesson.

"They are similar to the mirror gates in a way. They can create portals between the worlds. Deimas had one. It was how he got here," Mordecai explained. "I do not know all the details of what happened. Only Alaric's version of the events. But from what I can gather, Eliné and Henna became suspicious of their sister before her betrayal was fully revealed. They somehow stole the portal key and Esmeray's ring and took them to the then High Witch. She used an enchantment to split the key into three pieces, hiding them within the rings. Divided, the power of the stone is diminished, but he was able to use the ring to turn any mirror into a mirror gate to communicate with Achaz."

"And if the three rings were reunited, say by a powerful Sorceress…" Cyrus gritted out, piecing together exactly why Gehenna wanted her spell book and this ring so badly.

"The portal key could be restored with the right enchantment. But to fully destroy the portal key, the pieces must be reunited as well. It is why it could not be destroyed with the Fellowship, even with starfire," Mordecai answered.

"So what you are essentially saying is we need to get all three rings," Cassius said.

Nuri shrugged. "That's what I would do."

"The other two rings that Alaric already possesses," Cyrus deadpanned.

"Yes. He only held all three for a brief period of time," Nuri replied, fidgeting in her seat. "He had planned to have the Sorceress restore the portal key when he freed her, but Scarlett set the world on fire before he could fulfill that part of his plan. It is why he searched the rubble so adamantly for weeks."

"Anything else we should know?" Cassius asked.

"No," Nuri said. "Now leave so I can eat."

As she said it, she slid into Mordecai's lap, straddling him and brushing aside his shoulder-length hair. He was already tipping his head to the side, his hands landing on her waist.

"You can't drink from a glass?" Cassius said dryly, getting to his feet.

"Night Children only drink from the throat if they are lost to bloodlust or they are drinking from a lover. I don't think bloodlust is the case here," Cyrus murmured, tugging Cass to the window they'd entered through. He often forgot how little Cassius actually knew of the various bloodlines.

They were back on the rooftop before Cassius said, "That was unexpected."

"Which part?" Cyrus muttered, scanning the street below for a tavern that was open at this time of the night. He also needed to eat if he was going to refill Cass's reserves anytime soon. Holding those shields against ashwood arrows had been draining.

"All of it, I guess," Cass answered.

"We'll eat, sleep, and then go see the High Witch," Cyrus said.

Cass nodded. He was quiet the rest of the night.

# CHAPTER 39
# CALLAN

Callan took the hit he saw coming. He knew it was going to hurt. The Earth Prince was as brutal as Eliza was when it came to training and sparring. Then again, so was Arantxa when the Witch joined them.

So he took the blow to his ribs, leaning into the hit and doubling over.

To grab the knife from his boot.

He sucked in one quick breath before he snapped back up and threw the knife straight at Azrael. The prince's eyes widened slightly. It was the only surprise he let show as he managed to twist to the side at the last second, the knife grazing along his shoulder and drawing blood.

"Good," was all the Earth Prince said as he swiped at the blood before wiping it on his pants. The cut would heal in an hour or two.

The bruise on Callan's ribs would not.

But he'd long since learned he would never be stronger than the Fae. He would never be faster. He would always be outmatched, so he had to be smarter. Use distractions and technique to his advantage.

They were about to start another round of sparring when a sharp whistle sounded that had them both turning to the trees. A moment later, Mordecai and Nuri appeared. The seraph was in fighting leathers, and Death's Shadow was in her hunting attire.

"We don't have much time," Mordecai said by way of greeting.

Nuri stood beside him, still as the death she looked like she was about to bestow. Her hood was up, mask in place. Only her eyes were visible as she scanned the surroundings.

"One of your camps was discovered in Rydeon," Mordecai continued. "Instead of killing them all, they were taken to the Necropolis."

"For what?" Callan asked, the grip on his sword tightening involuntarily.

"I told you the innocent were being used," Nuri said. Her voice didn't carry the usual arrogance, but there was an edge of accusation.

"We are doing the best we can," Callan replied.

"Then your best is not enough."

"She's coming," Azrael said. "Scarlett is coming."

"And she will be too late," Nuri said simply.

"If you two want to come with us, I can take you. Drop you in a secluded area, but we need to go now," Mordecai said.

"Go to Rydeon?" Callan repeated.

The seraph nodded. "Not sure what you'll be able to do, but I'm told you know the Necropolis better than most."

"I have only been there a handful of times."

"Which is likely a handful more than the rebels being held there," Nuri replied. "They'll never find their way out on their own. They'd at least have a chance with someone there to follow."

"We should get Drake then. He is their king," Callan said. "He should go with us."

"Drake is not available," came Juliette's voice as she appeared with Arantxa and—

Ezra?

Callan took a step towards him. "Is Tava here?"

The guard shook his head. "It's why I am here. Drake and Tava have been locked away at the Lairwood house."

"Excuse me?" Callan said, and even he didn't recognize the viciousness that rang in his tone.

"The Rydeon and Toreall kings are here to discuss the growing rebellion with Mikale, Alaric, and Balam," Ezra explained. "Balam refused to have Drake or Tava at the castle or the manor. He didn't want them anywhere near the other Maraan Lords. Mikale offered to have them kept at his home, where they are now locked below. Balam is growing suspicious, and refused to let me accompany Tava."

"Are you saying he has them locked in a cell?" Callan asked.

"Yes. I came here to get you. See if the Earth Fae can possibly Travel there to get them," Ezra said, glancing between Callan and Azrael.

"Are they in danger?" Azrael asked. "Aside from being locked in a cell?"

Ezra appeared to hesitate, scratching at the back of his head. "I don't know. There has been tension at the manor. Drake and the Lord have been arguing a lot. I've overheard bits and pieces. Something about wards and costs. Things have gotten heated on more than one occasion, and I was ordered to escort Tava from the room. I think the disagreements have contributed to the Lord's suspicions. What's more, Alaric and Mikale have picked up on the tension. I think Mikale offering his home is a cover, but I don't have proof."

Callan had to use every ounce of control to clamp down on the surge of panic that rose up in him. The thought of Tava in a cell. What he knew Mikale was capable of. What he knew all the Maraan Lords were capable of.

"We have to go," Mordecai said, holding out a hand for Nuri to take.

"Make a choice, Callan," Nuri said.

And he felt every pair of eyes settle on him.

The woman he loved or innocent lives in a kingdom that was not his.

He'd like to think he would have made the same choice a year ago, but he knew that wasn't true. A year ago, he would have chosen the woman he loved. He *had* chosen the woman. The choice would have been easy.

It was easy now too, but not in the way he expected it to be.

"Rydeon," he said. "We go to the Necropolis."

"What?" Ezra demanded, mouth gaping. "She is a princess."

"And it is her people we go to save," Callan replied, taking the weapons from Azrael that he was pulling from some pocket realm. "She would make the same choice. They both would."

"And what of her? The woman you supposedly care so deeply for?" Ezra asked, his face reddening with anger.

Callan paused, turning to face him fully. "You can question my motives and my character. Frankly, you should. But never question my feelings for my wife again. Am I clear?"

"Your wife?" Ezra stammered, jerking back a step. "She never said... When?"

"Not important," Callan said, taking the cloak Juliette had gone to retrieve for him. "I need you to go back and learn as much as you can about what is happening at the Windonelle castle. When we return, we will figure out our next move."

Ezra was still staring at him in shock. "You expect me to leave my queen locked up?"

"No. I expect you to gather information so that we can figure out the best plan to retrieve her when we return. Can I entrust that task to you, Ezra?" Callan asked, moving to stand next to Nuri.

Ezra stared at him a moment longer before giving a sharp nod.

In the next blink, Callan was standing in one of the passages of the Necropolis. Mordecai and Nuri were gone before he had a chance to ask where exactly they had dropped them.

"Thoughts?" Callan asked Azrael, scanning the dark alcove and trying to get his bearings.

"I can scent them," Azrael said. "Mortal and immortal scents alike."

"Lead the way," Callan gestured, palming a dagger to have at the ready.

They crept along the passages, and it took far longer than he would have liked to figure out which part of the Eternal Necropolis they were in. North of the royal crypt if he was calculating right, and the farther Azrael led him on, that's exactly where they were heading. The only plausible explanation Callan could come up with for why they were there was the mirror gate.

He didn't know much about them, but he'd spent some time trying to research them in Avonleya. The task proved rather difficult with most of the books written in languages he did not know. But from what he'd picked up from their various meetings and from Scarlett, they could connect to other places in the realm and possibly other worlds, which would explain why Alaric would want to use it. It did not explain the people being herded here though.

They stopped when they came to a passage that would lead directly to the center. The sounds of the people growing louder. Crying children. Women trying to console them. Men demanding answers. Guards and seraphs barking orders.

"Can we get closer?" Callan whispered.

"Not without being detected," Azrael murmured back.

"Nuri and Mordecai are there. They have to know we are coming," Callan argued. "They will provide a distraction of sorts."

"You are going to put our fate in the hands of Death's Shadow?" Azrael deadpanned.

"She has cared for these people longer than I have," Callan said, ignoring the sting of truth at those words. "She came to get us to help in the only way she could work around her orders."

"Valid point," Azrael said.

"Let's get closer. If things go to shit, you Travel us out and we regroup," he urged.

They changed positions so that Callan was leading the way now, sticking to the walls as much as they could. When they neared the end of the passageway, Callan realized they would have a perfect view of the mirror.

Until a seraph stepped into their path.

Azrael was yanking Callan back by the shoulder, but they both immediately relaxed when they realized it was Mordecai. The seraph's gaze connected with theirs for the briefest of seconds before he turned his back on them. His wings flared, blocking the view of the passageway and effectively hiding them.

"We are not wasting innocent blood until we have figured out what is wrong with the mirror," the commander said.

"Maybe innocent blood is needed to fix it," argued another seraph.

"Are you arguing with your commander?" came a silky purr.

"No, Contessa," the seraph immediately replied.

"Have you not already wasted innocent blood? Is that not how we discovered the mirror gate had stopped working to begin with?" she demanded.

"Yes, Contessa."

"Then why are you suggesting we continue to waste finite resources?"

"We have tried everything else—"

Nuri's laughter rang out through the chamber. "Somehow I doubt that."

"We have. And they're not finite. We can get useless mortals from anywhere."

Callan could hear the seraph's temper rising in his voice.

"Perhaps we try your blood," Nuri said. "Maybe that will fix it since we appear to be fine experimenting with useless beings now."

"Touch her, and I will personally pour your blood on the mirror glyphs," came Mordecai's dark warning. Callan could only assume the seraph had made a move towards Nuri.

There was a tense silence. Even the mortal children seemed to have picked up on it and quieted.

"Explain again what happened," the commander finally said.

"The Prince got word that a few more seraphs were prepared to come though the mirror gate. It takes more mortal blood than magical blood, but after fifty, the mirror gate was still doing nothing."

Fifty.

They had killed fifty people trying to do something with the gods-damn mirror gate?

"Why did you kill fifty? It has never taken more than ten at one time unless children were involved," Mordecai asked.

And his tone was a warrior demanding information. No emotion behind his words. Just a commander assessing a situation.

Callan thought he might vomit.

"I told him this would happen," Mordecai said. "The cost would grow greater and greater."

"So we do simply need to spill more blood?" the seraph asked.

Mordecai shifted suddenly and then Nuri was in their view, the seraph clearly holding her back.

"We do not need the mortals more restless than they already are," Mordecai said. "You ripping out his throat will upset them."

"I thought Scarlett locked the realm with the keys," Callan whispered to Azrael. "How is this possible?"

"Scarlett closed all of the Maraans' current rips in the realm. She altered the keys so that they locked the spiritual planes being used, but there are always workarounds. Alaric apparently found one using the mirror gates," Azrael answered grimly. "But whatever he was doing appears to have stopped working."

The pointed look Azrael sent him had Callan saying, "You think this is Scarlett?"

"Someone fucking with Alaric's plans? There is no doubt in my mind it is Scarlett," he answered.

"Even if we manage to get all these people out, what do we do from there?" Callan asked. "Can you Travel with that many?"

"It will drain me to move that many so far."

"But you can do it?"

"Yes, but I also need to be able to Travel to the Wind Court when the time comes."

Callan nodded, trying to sort through options and scenarios. He didn't know the Rydeon Kingdom well enough to know where to hide the people. Maybe they would know somewhere to go? But they'd never be able to outrun the seraphs.

"You could create a portal though, right?" Callan said suddenly.

"And send them where?" Azrael asked.

"Siofra? Or the Witch Kingdoms?"

Azrael shook his head. "They will not go if we tell them that is where they are going."

But another idea was forming. "What if you took them to the Wind Court? You want to be there to help fight anyway. You go there to help them prepare, and take the mortals with you."

"You want me to take mortals to a Fae Court that is about to be attacked?" Azrael repeated, shooting him an incredulous look.

"Behind a Fae Citadel would be safer than a rebel camp in the woods. Is it not what we are planning to do once Eliza has the Fire Court?" Callan countered.

"I do not have the time to deal with this shit," Mordecai suddenly said loudly, drawing Callan's attention back to them. "There are rumors the Witches are assembling to fight at the Wind Court. I need to be preparing for that, not overseeing this nonsense."

"What do you want us to do, Commander?"

"Do not waste resources until you have figured out what is wrong with the mirror gate."

"But how do we—"

"Are you too inept for your position?" Mordecai interrupted.

"No," the seraph gritted out.

"Then get it done. I want this figured out before Alaric shows up here himself."

"What do we do with the humans until then?"

"Do you need to do anything with them?" Nuri asked.

"I suppose not," the seraph relented.

Azrael was tugging Callan back down the passageway. Once they rounded a corner, Callan said, "What?"

"If what Mordecai said is true, the Citadel will be one of the safest places for the mortals to be. If the Witches have been told of the plans and are coming to aid in the fight, the battle will be well met," Azrael said.

"So you will do it? Make a portal for them? Make sure they are taken care of?"

"What will you do?"

"I need to go back to Windonelle and my people," Callan answered.

"How will you get back there?"

"Don't worry about the king, Grumpy Gardener. Cai and I will make sure he gets back to Baylorin," Nuri said, appearing from a shadowy corner.

Azrael gave a full body sigh of irritation. "Stop doing that."

"Death's Shadow," Nuri drawled. "Have we met? This is what I do."

"How do you plan on getting Callan back without issue?" Azrael asked through gritted teeth.

"We got the two of you here, didn't we?"

"My wellbeing is not the issue here," Callan interrupted. "How are we going to get all those people through a portal unnoticed?"

"Oh, I have an idea for that," Nuri said.

"Care to share?" Azrael asked when she didn't continue.

The smile that filled Nuri's face mirrored one Callan had seen on Scarlett numerous times. Then his eyes went wide when Nuri said far louder than she should, "What is this? A mortal king and Fae Prince?"

"What the fuck are you doing?" Azrael hissed.

"This is the part where you run. Or rather, do that cute little disappearing thing," Nuri replied. "The mortals are closest to the southern passageway."

"For fuck's sake," Azrael grumbled, gripping Callan's arm and Traveling them.

When they reappeared at the southern passage, the central chamber was in utter chaos. Mordecai was barking orders and sending seraphs to search the northwest passages, effectively clearing out the main chamber. And once again, Callan was left to contemplate how someone could be both insane and so godsdamn clever.

As the last seraph went down the opposite passageway, Callan and Azrael made their way into the chamber. There were two guards remaining with the mortals, but their attention was fixed on the opposite passage.

Which left them open for Azrael to have their wings bound in vines before they even realized it was happening. He and the Earth Prince strode forward, swords drawn and plunging through the seraphs' backs. As they sank to their knees, they were drawing the same blades across their throats.

There was screaming and crying as Callan asked, "How are we going to keep them down without fire?"

"I think we can leave that for Mordecai and Nuri to deal with," Azrael answered, an earth portal appearing. "Convince them to go through."

Callan turned to face the frantic mortals behind him, quickly picking out three of the men who had clearly been part of the rebel movement and weren't refugees of any sort. Callan pointed at them, "Help me get everyone up. We have minutes, if that."

"For what exactly?" one of the men asked.

"We have a safe place for you to go in the Wind Court. Prince Azrael will take you there," Callan answered.

"You want us to go to a Fae Court?" a woman cried, terror at the idea evident in her voice

"I think we'll take our chances here," one of the other men said, crossing his arms.

Callan glanced over his shoulder at Azrael, who jerked his chin at the mortals. "They're your people. Convince them."

Right.

He turned back to the mortals. "We just killed the people holding you all prisoner. We are clearly on your side. Why would we send you into more danger?"

They seemed to pause at that, but still none of them were moving.

"Look, I do not know if you know who I am—"

"I know who ya' are," came a voice from the back. "The Crown Prince of Windonelle. Or ya' was."

"Yes," Callan said, his grip tightening on the sword he still held. "I was that. Now I am the King of Windonelle. I have been with the Fae for the last several months. They are our allies. More than that, *I* am your ally. Your rightful king and princess are in my kingdom. I am here on their behalf. If you cannot trust the Fae, trust me. And if you cannot do that, trust Drake and Tava Middell."

"You know of them?" one of the men said, his arms dropping to his side.

Callan shook his head. "I am working with them and the rebels there. We both are. So are the Fae and Witches. We have help coming, but the safest place until they get here is with the Fae."

"You have been assembling armies?" another man asked, trying to get to his feet. He was older, likely in his late sixties, and had clearly done hard labor for much of his life.

"Yes," Callan said, stepping forward to help him to his feet. "Help is coming. We just need to hold out a little longer. We have a safe place for you to do so. Prince Azrael can take you. I cannot force you to go, but I can promise you certain death if you choose to stay."

The people looked at each other, soft murmurs coming from them that he couldn't decipher, but the man he'd helped to his feet straightened some.

"Thank you, your Majesty."

Callan smiled warmly. "Go. You can trust the Fae where you are going." He stepped to the side so the man could make his way to the portal, and as he did, more people got to their feet.

"I will go through first to receive them," Azrael said. But before he stepped through, he added, "See you soon, your Majesty."

Callan nodded before he began helping more people to their feet and ushering them to the portal. The three men were the last to go through, and one stopped before Callan.

"There are more of us. Throughout the kingdom," he said.

"I know," Callan answered. "Help is coming."

The man nodded, and Callan sent him through with a message to tell Azrael he could close the portal. He was planning to go back down the passage and wait for Mordecai and Nuri, but when he turned to head that way, he found a seraph standing there.

"A mortal king," the seraph sneered, and Callan immediately recognized his voice as the male who had been arguing with Nuri and Mordecai.

Callan had sheathed his sword while helping the people, but he had it drawn with his next breath, instantly falling into a defensive stance that Eliza had drilled into him.

The seraph huffed a laugh. "Mortals really are the lowest form of intelligence, aren't they?"

"There are not mortals where you come from?" Callan asked, moving with the seraph as he began to circle.

The seraph smirked. "My world is not a place for mortals. They are not even worthy of menial tasks there."

"Then it seems to me you should not be making assumptions about a people you know nothing about," he replied, noting that the seraph's left wing appeared slightly injured, and he favored his left side.

The seraph scoffed. "Mortals rarely have purpose. You, however, are in luck. You do serve a purpose today."

"Is it rescuing innocent people? Because if so, that purpose has been achieved," Callan retorted, still tracking the seraph.

"I will let my commander deal with you for that stunt," the seraph gritted out.

"So you do nothing then? From what I gathered earlier, you simply follow orders."

"On second thought, I'll detain you myself," the seraph snarled, drawing his own blade. "Then maybe I won't have to answer to the commander anymore."

Callan knew he wouldn't be able to keep the male talking for long, but he had succeeded in getting under his skin. It made him impulsive with his attacks, which also made them easier to predict. He dodged the first swing, spinning to the right. The momentum of the swing kept the seraph propelling forward, and Callan was able to bring his blade down on the injured wing.

The seraph let out a cry of pain, the wing dragging as he whirled. "You are dead," he said with a growl, and he rushed him. He was too fast for Callan to avoid this time, and he was thrown to the ground, his head cracking on the stone ground, black spots appearing in his vision.

The seraph tossed his sword to the side before kicking Callan's weapon out of reach as well, clearly not deeming Callan a threat anymore. He wasn't wrong, but before he could drag in another breath, a shadow was at the seraph's throat.

Death's Shadow, to be exact.

She tore his throat clean out, spitting it to the ground a moment before Mordecai appeared, severing wings and head.

"Nice work, your Majesty," Nuri said, reaching down to help him up.

"Nice work? I would have died if not for you," Callan rasped, the room spinning slightly.

She waved a hand dismissively. "I was watching the whole time. All that training has paid off."

"You couldn't have intervened sooner?"

"Noting the weak wing and capitalizing on it? Perfection," Nuri went on wistfully.

Callan blinked at her, his vision still blurry. "Can we get out of here, please?"

"Agreed," Mordecai said, reaching for them.

A second later he was back in Windonelle, and his stomach was revolting against all the Traveling of the day. He sank down on a nearby log by the fire, his head dropping to his hands.

"Callan?"

He lifted his head to find Juliette making her way towards him.

"Is there word on Drake and Tava?" he asked.

Juliette studied him in that unnerving way of hers. She'd come to a stop directly in front of him. He often forgot she was raised the same way Nuri and Scarlett had been. She seemed so much...more sane, even if she did speak in odd riddles at times now.

She called to a nearby woman and asked her to bring warm water and a cloth.

"I am fine," Callan said. "Tell me an update on Drake and Tava."

"I do not believe Balam will harm them, Callan. However, the other Lords are growing impatient with their prince. You are bleeding."

"What?"

She lifted a hand, touching it to his head. When she pulled it back, there was red staining her fingertips. "You have a cut on the back of your head."

"No. What do you mean the other Lords are growing impatient?" Callan said, nodding in thanks to the woman who had brought the supplies to clean his wound.

"They were sent here with purpose," Juliette answered, moving behind him. "They either succeed or face repercussions for failure, whether at the hand of Scarlett or another. Alaric is not the only one with something to lose in this. Tell me what happened at the Necropolis."

While she tended to the wound, Callan filled her in on everything that happened, and as he was finishing, Mordecai and Nuri returned along with two others.

Arantxa and Drake.

Callan shot to his feet. "Where is Tava?"

Drake met his gaze, his features tense. "There was a deal made between Balam and the other Lords."

"Where is she?" Callan repeated.

"She is at the castle."

"How are you here?"

Drake ran both hands through his hair, tipping his head back and pushing out a long breath. "We suspected Balam was becoming suspicious. We had talked about lying low. Not coming out here as often. But he was not the only one who had taken notice. Mikale shared concerns with Alaric. The other Lords confronted Balam about it at their meeting, accusing him of working against them. As a show of good faith, Alaric demanded a deal. We could be released from the Lairwood house, but we had to stay at the castle."

"Then how are you here?" Callan demanded.

"Ezra," Drake answered. "They transported us to the castle. Ezra has connections to the castle guards. It was too risky for both of us to come, so Tava stayed behind. As long as she remains there, she is safe. But..." He dragged a hand down his face. "I learned the cost of taking down the wards. It was why he sequestered us when the other Maraan Lords showed up. I cannot go back. Not now."

"You cannot leave her there alone," Callan said in outrage.

"I did not know the cost when she agreed to stay behind. The fact that I learned it at all was purely by chance."

"Or fate," Juliette said calmly from where she had taken a seat next to Arantxa.

"I do not give a fuck if it was chance or fate," Callan said sharply. "What is it? What is this cost?"

"Taking down the wards bound our lives to the Maraan Lords on the thrones respectfully," Drake said.

"You mean if Mikale is killed, then I die too? And vice versa?"

Drake nodded.

"Then doesn't that mean we are safe?" Callan asked. "If they kill us, the Maraan Lords die."

"Yes, but it also means they want us kept close. Locked in cells to ensure we do not find a way to end ourselves and thus them," Drake said. "It is why I cannot go back."

"Why would we end ourselves?"

"Because as long as there are Maraans here, Achaz has a way in," Mordecai supplied. Callan had forgotten he and Nuri were still there. "Arius and Serafina have heavy protections around their children. It is why Achaz has not been able to come here yet, but Alaric is close to finding another way to let Achaz in. The only way to stop what he has planned is to kill all the Maraan Lords and the Maraan Prince."

"Are you saying that to truly end all of this, Drake, Hale, and I have to die?"

The silence that greeted him was answer enough, and yet he didn't care. All he cared about was that they had his wife, and it had just become infinitely harder to get to her.

# CHAPTER 40
# TALWYN

The flight from Hazel's castle to the Wind Court Citadel took from sunup to after sundown. It was well into the night before Thorne was landing on the cliffside overlooking Ashtine's home. Talwyn had flown with Jetta and a small unit of Witches. All together there were thirty in their company. They were the first unit to come this way. More would follow as they prepared to help in the Court.

There had been no other news from Arantxa about the attack they'd been warned of, but it had been days now. Knowing what she did of Alaric, he was patient until he wasn't. Scarlett was pushing him to an edge, and he'd take out innocent people to punish her. Talwyn hoped he waited until more Witch units could join them, but luck had never been kind to her, so she didn't count on it.

"This is the place?" Jetta asked, looking around the ledge they'd landed on.

"Down there," Talwyn answered, pointing to an area of stables near the main building. "But we'll need to relocate the horses. I doubt they will tolerate griffins." Thorne twisted his neck around, snapping at her ankle, and she shoved at him with her boot. "I barely tolerate you," she muttered.

But they had come to some kind of truce. They flew multiple times a day now, allowing Talwyn to get a feel for being in the air and staying in the saddle when Thorne decided to randomly dive after a rodent or small animal for a snack. The first time he'd done it, she'd screamed so loudly, Jetta had come running. She was fairly certain if griffins could laugh that's what Thorne was doing with the odd trilling sound he made. But he'd started coming to her without making her chase him all over the aerie, and he'd stopped pecking at her until they were done flying, so she counted it as progress.

She and Jetta flew down to the stables, leaving the other griffins and their riders on the cliff ledge until they had helped move the horses. Once the griffins were all settled, they started making their way to the Citadel. Ermir met them at the front entrance hall, a smile on his weathered face as he bowed to Talwyn.

"That is not necessary any longer," she said, looking around the foyer. Nothing had changed.

"It is my understanding you have been taking care of Princess Ashtine," Ermir said. "I will certainly bow to you for that."

"Who told you that?" she asked, distracted by what appeared to be mortals milling about.

"Prince Luan."

That had her attention snapping back to the Wind Court Second. "You have word from Azrael?"

Ermir smiled. "He is in one of the council rooms with the General formulating defense strategies."

"Can you show Jetta and the others their accommodations?" Talwyn asked, already striding for the hall that would take her to the meeting rooms.

"Of course," Ermir replied.

She forced herself not to run, but her steps were hurried as she made her way down the corridors. The first three council rooms were empty, but the fourth—

Everyone's eyes darted to her when she threw the door open, but her gaze was fixed on the Earth Prince, who was already striding for her. "I will be back in a moment," he said to the room. His black hair was tied up atop his head, and his patented stoic expression was on his face. But the relief and want and shock she saw glimmering in his eyes made her breath catch in her throat.

She was backing up as he neared, and he pulled the door shut behind him before he had her back against the opposite wall, hands framing her face and lips on hers. Her hands fisted in his tunic, keeping him close, as his tongue swept against hers greedily. She let him take control. She always had. He had always been the place she didn't need to have control. This thing between them had always been the one place no one was looking to her to make decisions or have opinions. She'd always left it all up to Az, taking the momentary freedom it had always offered. And now, even when she had control over nothing anymore, she still wouldn't have it any other way.

"What are you doing here?" he murmured against her lips, his tongue delving back in before he let her answer.

She was all but panting when he finally let her come up for air, his fingertips brushing across her brow before tucking stray strands back that had come loose from her braid during flight.

"I am here with the Witches. To fight with them," she answered breathlessly. "What are you doing here? I thought you were fighting with the mortals."

One of his forearms was braced above her head. His other hand was settling on her hip, thumb making sweeping circles. "When I was informed that there would be a siege on the Wind Court, I came to help knowing Ashtine was in the Witch Kingdoms."

"Briar as well," Talwyn said, realizing her hands were still clenched in his tunic. She quickly released them, arms falling to her sides.

"They know of the coming attack?" Az asked, eyes dipping to her lips again.

"Yes. Ashtine has not been well. Briar will not leave her side right now, and I do not blame him."

"Nor do I," Azrael said.

They stared at each other for several moments before Talwyn cleared her throat. "Did I see mortals here?"

"Yes. I brought them from Rydeon. I have much to fill you in on."

"Later. You have a meeting to finish, and I have Witches to get settled," Talwyn said. "I also need to go check on my griffin once more tonight. Make sure he's not being a pain in the ass."

Azrael's brows knitted together. "You have a griffin?"

Talwyn felt her face heat and silently chastised herself. "He is not really mine. I mean, he sort of chose me, but… The whole thing is rather stupid."

The intensity of his stare made her look away from him. "I do not think it is stupid at all," he finally said. His hand slid from her hip, and he took a step back from her. "You will stay in my rooms?"

"I did not want to assume—"

"We are past that, Talwyn. I will meet you there in an hour."

"All right."

With a last lingering look, he slipped back into the council room. She took a few deep breaths, still trying to get her racing heart rate back under control, before she went to find Jetta and the others.

She was tucked into Azrael's side when she felt it. It jolted her from sleep, her entire body tensing. She didn't know what it was, but before she had a chance to sort it out, Azrael was rolling her onto her back and hovering above her.

"They are coming, Talwyn," he said.

She swiped her hand down her face, trying to wake up fully. She'd checked in on the Witches after she'd left Azrael at the council room and then gone out to see Thorne. He'd glared at her, not at all happy with the small and cramped quarters of a horse stable, then he'd tucked his head under his wing and pointedly ignored her.

Every step she'd taken back up to Azrael's rooms had her stomach doing a weird fluttering thing she wasn't sure what to do with. She'd hesitated outside his door. Was she supposed to knock? Just go in? Knock and then go in without waiting for a greeting? She'd hated that she suddenly found herself having to evaluate these things.

But she hadn't had to think on it too long. The door had been wrenched open, Azrael standing there shirtless and barefoot, his hair down from the knot it had been tied in.

"Why are you standing out here?" he'd asked, looking her up and down as if he'd missed something.

She'd pursed her lips, not sure how to explain her thoughts on things.

But he'd known. He'd always just…known.

Which made complete sense now that she knew everything too.

But she hadn't gotten a chance to say any of that. He'd stepped to the side, holding the door open for her. Then he'd been kicking it shut behind her before he'd all but thrown her over his shoulder and dropped her on the bed.

"Nothing has changed between us," he'd said. "You may not have Courts to rule. You may not have any magic. You might not be a queen to anyone else, but you are still my queen, Talwyn Semiria." He'd methodically removed her boots and her weapons as he spoke. But then he'd paused, bracing himself above her and holding her stare. "I am yours, and you are mine. I choose you, above all others. Always."

The Claiming Rite. Words that would do nothing for a twin flame Mark that she could no longer bear or initiate any Trials, but she still felt the claiming in her soul.

"And if my Staying does not hold?" she'd whispered, feeling a tear leak from the corner of her eye.

"Always, Talwyn. We take it one day at a time," he'd replied, dipping down to take her mouth with his.

Then they'd claimed each other in other ways.

It had been later, when they'd been sharing a bath, that they had filled each other in on everything. What she had been doing. What he had been doing.

They'd hardly gotten any sleep when they finally went back to bed. A few hours at most. That didn't really matter for Az, but for her…

Azrael was up, dressing and donning leathers with the same lethal grace and proficiency he had for centuries. She took in a deep breath before she got up, doing the same, albeit much slower. He was handing her a leather band to tie off her braid as she made her way to the door, following him out.

Ermir and the Wind Court General, Sion, met them in the foyer, both dressed for battle.

"The Witches are at the stables," Ermir said to her.

"Their forces will cross the main wards within the hour," Sion was saying to Azrael. "We have all the mortals secured below in the cata-combs, along with several Fae to keep them comfortable."

"The forces are in the locations we discussed?" Azrael asked.

Sion nodded. "Some of our strongest are in the tallest towers, ready to work against the seraphs in the skies, as well as give the Witches any advantages they can."

"Anything I need to tell Jetta and the others?" Talwyn asked.

"If you can down them, we will make sure they stay down," Azrael said. "Just knock them out of the sky."

Talwyn nodded, holding his stare for a moment, before she turned away to prepare with the Witches. She should probably say something in case the worst happened, but they'd never been much for heartfelt confessions.

But Azrael was tugging her to a stop and spinning her back to face him. His hand cupped her cheek, tilting her head back to look up at him. "Meet me on the battlefield," he said softly, echoing words she'd said to him weeks ago.

She nodded, her eyes closing briefly when he brushed his lips across hers. Then he was turning back to Ermir and Sion, and she was rushing down to the stables.

Someone had already saddled Thorne for her, and he appeared to be as irritated by that as he was about everything else. He let out a loud, screeching cry when she stopped right beside him. The sound had her flinching back, and she glared at the beast.

"Glad to see you are in the mood to be a prick." He flared his wings wide, sending her stumbling back with the force of it. "Gods," she muttered.

"The next unit will not be here until late tonight," Jetta said, coming up to Talwyn and handing over a bow and a special quiver that arrows snapped into so they didn't spill out when in the air.

Talwyn had figured as much. That didn't bode well for them. The thirty of them against seraphs with unknown abilities? They were as good as carrion.

"We down as many of them as we can," Talwyn said, pushing aside the thoughts of imminent death. "Azrael said if we down them, they will keep them down. We just need to keep them out of the skies.

There are Wind Fae in the highest towers. If we can keep the seraphs within range, they will help us."

"Noted," Jetta said, moving over to her brown and tan griffin. She glanced at Thorne. "Trust your griffin, Talwyn. He'll know what to do."

She didn't say anything in return. Just hoisted herself into the saddle, strapping herself in. She was scarcely seated when Thorne was running and leaping into the sky, clearly ready to stretch his wings. When they were soaring high above the Citadel, Talwyn could see them. The ground forces and the ones in the sky.

At least two thousand troops on the ground, more than one hundred in the air. This wasn't an attack. It was an extermination. They didn't have an hour. They had ten minutes at most. There was no way they would withstand this with only the forces inside the Citadel. Five hundred ground troops would have likely been enough to secure their victory. Alaric had overtaken every other part of the Wind Court. When Mordecai had said the Maraan Prince had wanted to squash any perceived rebellion, she hadn't realized he had meant it quite this literally.

She yanked on Thorne's reins, forcing him to bank hard as she watched the Wind Court soldiers fall into formations and stations. She didn't even know where Azrael was stationed in this mess. If they lost this stronghold, Alaric would come for the Witch Kingdoms next; and if the Witches were forced to stay back and defend their own territory, the rest of the continent would fall. Alaric was putting pieces into place for a final move that would end the world as they knew it.

How had they gotten so many seraphs here? She knew they'd been bringing them over for decades, but hundreds of them? Possibly thousands? She'd been part of that. Had helped Alaric in that in some ways. Even fighting on the other side now wouldn't abate that guilt. It never would.

"We let them come to us," Jetta was yelling over the swirling winds that were picking up. The griffins were all back-flapping to hold their positions as the Wind Fae worked to shield their home. "They have the numbers, so we force them to make the first moves," the Witch continued. "Preserve your arrows."

The Witches said nothing, stoic and cold and ready to shed blood, so Talwyn joined them in that place. She drew an arrow, nocking it to her bow and waited.

Minutes later, she felt the air shudder when the airborne seraphs slammed into it. She could tell there were some with wind magic themselves based on the arrows that made it past the shield too easily. But the griffins were already moving. For their size, they were incredibly nimble and quick, swooping and dodging, somehow avoiding each other. She'd trained with the Witches some, but it had been nothing like this.

The griffins were in their element as much as the Witches who fired back arrows with deadly accuracy, the Fae wind helping them find their marks. But the seraphs didn't go down easily, even with arrows embedded in their wings.

Talwyn had no choice but to follow Jetta's advice of trusting Thorne. They developed their own communication system. Talwyn squeezing with her knees when she needed him to hold steady when she was ready to release an arrow. He'd clearly done this before, knowing the precise moment he could move again once the arrow was released. She suddenly found herself thankful for all the times he'd had her stomach in her throat from the free-falls and surprise dives. She was prepared for them now as he banked hard to avoid an arrow that would have struck her in the side.

Talwyn and the Witches managed to force a good number of the seraphs to the ground or face plummeting there if they took another hit. Perhaps a third of them were now on the ground, fighting with the mix of mortal and Fae troops.

But when they finally broke through the wind shields, that was when Talwyn truly saw the strength of the griffins. Cries of fury and wrath came from the beasts as they all flew straight towards seraphs. Talwyn's hand clamped onto her saddle horn as she hastily looped her bow across her back. She'd drawn her sword a moment before the seraph Thorne had set his sights on was bellowing in pain when talons tore into his torso, exposing bone. Thorne twisted, popping up behind the seraph and giving Talwyn the perfect angle to slice off wings. The seraph was plummeting to the ground, but Thorne was already honed in on his next target.

Maybe she had been wrong. Perhaps this unit of Witches and griffins would be able to do more damage than she'd thought.

She fell into the song of battle as Thorne took her from target to target. They took wounds of their own. Some seraphs got in their own shots before she or the griffin finished them off. She had a deep slice along her bicep, Thorne rolling a moment too late. The griffin had taken an arrow to one of his hind flanks.

Then he'd proceeded to shred the offending seraph entirely with his talons, leaving Talwyn to gape.

"Why haven't you been doing that this whole time?" she snapped as Thorne shot them into the sky for a brief recovery.

He twisted to look at her, his beak clicking in dismay a moment before he was dropping back down in a steep dive that had her cursing him soundly.

She thought they might actually have a chance, might be claiming a victory at the end of this if things were going as well on the ground as they were in the sky, but then more seraphs were flying up from the ranks below. Not a few dozen, but another hundred.

The griffins were tiring. The Witches were tiring. Talwyn's muscles ached, and the wound on her arm was still steadily dripping blood. Now their only hope was holding out until the next unit of Witches arrived, but they would be just as exhausted from flying all day.

To make matters worse, more than half of the new seraphs had fire and water magic. There were no more offensive attacks from the griffins. Now it was completely avoiding the whips of flames and waves of water that came for them. Griffins started to fall. Other Witches catching riders to save them as they screamed for their bonded mounts that wouldn't rise again.

Thorne rolled again, letting out a cry of rage as flames singed the feathers on his wings. They needed to land. Needed to regroup.

But there would be no resting. Not unless that rest was the eternal kind.

"Go high," she yelled to Thorne. "Go high and then bank."

He took off as Talwyn pulled her bow and unsnapped another arrow, aiming for the seraph that had thrown fire at them. She took a breath, readying to release the arrow, when she was jolted, Thorne's piercing cry ringing in her ears. She lost the bow as she grappled for the saddle, sliding as he rolled twice before managing to level out.

"Thorne!" she cried when they dropped faster than they should be.

She frantically searched him, twisting around. Nothing on the left side, but on the right, a flaming arrow was lodged in his front shoulder. The fire was small, just enough to slowly burn away at the wound, but it would burn away internally too. How he was still airborne, Talwyn didn't know.

Not until he flew closer to Jetta.

"Jump, Talwyn," Jetta demanded, her griffin swooping under them.

"Jump? No," Talwyn said, her fingers tightening around the reins. "He will be fine."

"Talwyn, jump!" Jetta ordered again. "It is their last act of honor to save their bonded rider. It's why he's fighting to keep in the air. He won't last much longer. Trust your griffin and jump!"

But she couldn't do it. Not after he had chosen her. Not now that they had formed this stupid bond. She couldn't—

She yanked hard on the reins, forcing him to bank again, and he let out another screech.

"Talwyn!" Jetta cried.

But she didn't listen. They were near enough to the Citadel. If they could just make it to one of the towers—

Thorne picked up on her idea a moment later, trying to level out, but fire was spreading. She could see the edges of the wound blackening as the magic of the flames devoured more and more.

"A little farther!" she urged.

They fell the last thirty feet, his talons scratching along the turret of the roof as they slid down the eaves. Thorne twisted once more at the last second so he landed on his left wing instead of on her. Talwyn heard the crunch of feathers and bone, the wing crushed beneath his massive weight when they finally came to a rest on a balcony.

She was already unstrapped and out of the saddle, wrenching the arrow from his wound. She didn't feel the burn on her hand as she patted out the embers still sparking along his feathers.

His chest was heaving, head on the ground, avian eyes full of pain.

"Don't you dare," she hissed at him. "Not after I've put up with all your shit. You don't get to choose me then leave me. I can't do that again."

Cries of alarm from below had her scrambling up and peering over the balcony railing. There was a wall below, Fae soldiers running along it and pointing. Her gaze flew to whatever it was they were seeing, and her mouth fell open.

Because there were warriors pouring out of the main gates.

But not Fae soldiers.

Avonleyan ones.

That was a dark queen moving among ashes with arrows of death-stone flying from her bow three at a time.

That was a mythical king, long thought dead, atop a horse as dark as the coming night.

That was an Ash Rider moving faster than the smoke he commanded.

Those were dragons flying up and out of the main gates.

One of shadows and one of flames.

A king and queen atop them.

Scarlett was finally here.

And she had brought an army.

# CHAPTER 41
# SCARLETT

They had run. Raced through the catacombs, past crying children and mortals praying to the gods. Sorin and Rayner were shouting at people to move out of the way as Scarlett ran faster than she ever had before.

They had still been in the Citadel foyer when her shadows had begun to swirl and form around her. Scales. Wings. A dragon of flame taking shape alongside it.

They had burst from the front gates to find chaos.

Then she'd added some chaos of her own.

Their plan had worked. Her newly acquired power had connected with that of the mirror gates, and she now controlled them to a certain extent. They could still be used by anyone to communicate with another realm, but she controlled when they could be used to move between lands and worlds. She had been able to make them all portals whenever she wished.

They had rested another day after she had assumed control of the mirror gates, spending the time planning with Eliza and Razik, who had finally ventured down from that cave in the Nightmist Mountains. Eliza and Razik would take a few more days to heal properly, then they would be going to the Fire Court. The rest of them were going to track down Cassius and Cyrus. The mirror gate in the Citadel had been the most logical one on the continent to use, especially since they couldn't cross the Wards with Cethin.

Razik had agreed with her that if Cethin left Avonleya by way of a mirror gate, he wasn't technically crossing any Wards. The mirrors operated on a different plane. Not a spiritual one or a physical one. A different plane all together. She was pretty sure that's what she'd gotten out of Razik's detailed explanation of why it would work. Scarlett thought she had read a lot, but she had nothing on the male who devoured any book he came across, not only reading it but remembering every detail.

She'd hugged Eliza tightly before they'd left, once again demanding chocolates and wine when they were done saving the world. No twin flames invited.

Scarlett had gone through the mirror gate first with Sorin and Rayner. Auberon, Hale, Neve, and Tybalt came next. Then she had held her breath, waiting for Kailia and Cethin.

With her new godlike status, she had been able to fill Cethin's reserves the way Saylah had been for decades. It had taken a toll, and she had understood why Saylah could only do so a few times a year in her weakened state. It wasn't something Scarlett could do often, but she could do it more than their mother had because she had a Source and Saylah did not. They'd also wanted him at full strength for going through the mirror gate, giving him every advantage possible in case there were repercussions for trying to alter his curse.

When Kailia and Cethin had stepped through, she still hadn't released her breath, waiting nearly a full minute for something to happen.

"You did it, Starfire," Cethin had said in awe.

"Partial freedom is better than none, I suppose," Scarlett had said, smiling softly at her brother, knowing he wouldn't truly be free of the binding Wards until they took them down.

But before they'd been able to say anything else, the very walls had shaken around them. Then the sounds of screaming and shouted orders had reached them, and they'd known then they had emerged in the middle of a battle. Or the end of a losing one, judging by the frantic clipped orders of the priestesses in the library.

Cethin had turned to Tybalt, commanding him to go and get

troops and to send the cadres immediately. Everyone was pulling weapons from pocket realms and tunneling down into their magic as quickly as possible. Within minutes, there were several warriors coming through the mirror gate, and Cethin was barking orders. The cadres had been mentioned a few times in meetings, but there had always been more pressing matters at hand. Apparently they were some kind of special forces in Avonleya, trained to be ready at a moment's notice. Something like the High Force maybe? She didn't really care at the moment. She only cared that they were here and that they reported Tybalt was sending more forces. Even as they spoke, another unit came through the mirror gate.

And then they'd run.

When she and Sorin had leapt atop their dragons, they'd left Cethin in charge of ground defenses, and now they were soaring up to aid the Witches and griffins who were being overrun by seraphs in the sky. She felt her lips tilt up as her shadow armor slid into place, but more than that, the Chaos inside of her seemed to thrum in excitement. That was new, but she didn't have time to evaluate it. Not as her shadow dragon reared back with a roar before releasing a stream of starfire on a small host of seraphs. Sorin was soaring through their ranks a moment later, his sword drawn and slicing through wings and flesh alike. The seraphs were plummeting to the ground moments later for the forces below to finish off.

They managed to surprise another unit before the seraphs shifted their focus, abandoning the Witches and coming for them. They would be shielding against flames now, the seraphs using their stolen magic to combat them. Her dragon roared orange flames this time. A sweeping arc of them that she froze and was leaping atop of in the next breath. They formed a semi-circular platform, and Sorin was landing beside her a moment later. Her shadow dragon had dissipated, but Sorin's fire dragon continued to fly around them, herding seraphs right to them.

She met his gaze. His golden eyes were molten flames, a grin of pure wickedness filling his face.

*Let's set the world on fire, Princess.*

*High Queen,* she sent back down the bond, pulling her sword and a long knife from a swirl of shadows. Starfire ignited down the spirit sword, and Sorin had drawn his short swords.

They turned back-to-back, and while his fire dragon herded more and more seraphs to them, they fell into the song and dance that had always been them. Wild and chaotic. Push and pull. Fire and shadows.

Flames of orange and white, blue and black, lit up feathered wings, forcing the seraphs to land on the platform or drop to the melee below. And when Sorin and Scarlett found their magic doused by wind or water, their blades did the rest.

Scarlett spun, landing a clean kick to a seraph's chest, sending him stumbling back. He slipped on the platform edge, nearly careening over it, his wings flapping to keep him balanced. His hand snapped out, a rope of vines exploding from his palm and wrapping around her throat, squeezing tight. She had starfire burning it away a second later, but the seraph was fast, already before her with a dagger aiming for her side. She whirled, but wasn't fast enough. The blade grazed her skin before her shadows latched onto the dagger, yanking the seraph forward.

The male's eyes flew wide when he couldn't yank his arm back, her shadows fusing him to his weapon. Scarlett smiled before she let her shadows have him fully. They wound around his chest, squeezing just as tight as his vines had, before they went down his throat, darkness invading his being. This time when she kicked at him, he went toppling over the edge of the platform.

Scarlett straightened, turning in time to see an arrow coming for her. Her hand shot up, catching it by the shaft less than an inch from a clean shot to her heart. She blinked once, not quite believing it. Then she turned to Sorin, whose blades were currently locked between two seraphs.

"I caught it!" she cried.

Sorin's gaze flicked to hers as he dropped a sword to wrap flaming fingers around one of the male's throat. "Caught what?" he called back.

She dropped low, sensing the seraph who was diving for her, her shadows coating his wings in black and snapping them clean off.

"An arrow!" she hollered, still clutching the thing in her hand while her sword went through the seraph's gut.

"Great, Love," he yelled back, the other seraph he'd been fighting dousing his flames with water before managing to get him into a compromising hold. "Care to send it my way?"

In the next blink, there was a swirl of shadows by his hand, and he pulled the arrow from it, stabbing up and back directly into the seraph's eye. The seraph howled, immediately releasing Sorin, who set the arrow tip flaring as he drew it across the seraph's throat before plunging it into the male's chest and pushing him off the platform.

They fought and killed. Blood sprayed and magic flared. And then Scarlett heard her name being screamed. She was looking around for the source of it when she spotted Talwyn on a balcony of one of the tallest towers of the Citadel. There was a griffin on the ground beside her, but she was pointing frantically down at the grounds below.

Scarlett dodged another blow, swiping out to deflect a blade as she made her way closer to Sorin. He saw her a second later, a knife of fire appearing and lodging into the seraph's shoulder to give her the reprieve she needed. Sorin grabbed for her, spinning them so he could continue combat with the seraph, clearly sensing she was trying to work something out.

The ground forces had rallied as more and more Avonleyan forces had joined them, but at the back of Alaric's soldiers was a group who appeared to just be…standing there. Until one peeled off. The figure was smaller than the others, but she would recognize how she moved even from hundreds of feet in the sky.

It was Nuri.

Her gaze jumped ahead to the direction she was traveling in, and it landed on a flash of silver hair that matched her own.

Cethin.

Nuri was going after Cethin.

How Talwyn had put together what was happening, Scarlett didn't care. She was only grateful, once again, that Sorin had convinced her not to kill the female.

But she couldn't leave Sorin and the Witches up here to keep fighting the seraphs alone.

Until two dragon roars ripped through the air. One belonging to a spirit animal and the other to the Legacy he was bonded to. Ranvir and Tybalt were soaring up, and the seraphs were scattering as dragon fire left those in its path in ashes.

That was all she needed.

She leapt from the platform, free-falling through the air at the same time she said to Sorin, *I need to go help Cethin. Cover me.*

Her shadows were forming beneath her, the dragon taking shape as she fell. She flipped in the air, seeing the seraphs diving after her, but Sorin was already there, already catching up to them.

Not on a fire dragon, though.

No. He had godsdamn wings of fire.

He tackled a seraph from behind, the two of them rolling in the air before blood was spraying, and the seraph's wings went one way while the male himself plummeted.

Gods. She could watch him like that all damn day. Fire and blood and—

Right.

Cethin. Nuri. Death to bestow.

She could swear she felt Sorin chuckling darkly down the bond as she flipped around, not even realizing she'd landed atop her shadow dragon.

Still not finding Nuri, she soared towards the place she'd last seen Cethin, catching a glimpse of Kailia when she appeared and disappeared before Scarlett could blink. She landed a hundred yards away from her brother, her dragon shifting to panthers as her feet hit the ground. She was running, the dark felines snarling and taking down soldiers as she moved, effectively clearing her path.

Scarlett broke through another group of fighting mortals and Fae at the same moment Nuri appeared, and Scarlett stepped through darkness, reappearing in front of Death's Shadow with her sword raised, meeting her blade in the air.

"Sister," Nuri crooned. "You made it. About damn time."

"You know I like a little flair with my entrances," Scarlett retorted, falling into movements she had done thousands of times with Nuri.

Only this time she was a High Queen.

Her shadows thickened, wrapping around the two of them and encasing them in a sphere of Chaos.

Because that's what they were.

Two daughters of the darkest part of the world.

They leapt back from each other. Nuri began to pace in a tight circle on her side of the sphere. Scarlett clutched a stitch in her side, breathing hard, the darkness blocking out the sound of battle around them. "Tell me the order," she said between gasping breaths.

"Kill the Avonleyan King before the battle is won or lost," Nuri said, sheathing her scimitar.

"So if the battle is ended before you kill him, you will not need to fulfill it?"

"Yes."

"Okay," Scarlett said, her mind whirling with options.

"Scarlett."

She glanced up at her sister to find her eyes filled with dread.

"There is a Maraan Lord here."

Scarlett straightened. That changed things, but it also didn't.

"Which one?"

"Roderick."

The last Maraan Lord. The only one Scarlett had not known.

"What is his stolen power?"

"He is like Veda, only much stronger. Veda could only manipulate one person at a time. Roderick can touch dozens at once," Nuri answered.

"Where has he been hiding?"

"He has been organizing the seraphs as they have arrived over the decades," Nuri answered, her pacing becoming frenetic. "This battle is far from over." She drew a blade, fisting it tightly. "I don't want to, Scarlett. Know that. I didn't want to kill Sawyer or any of the—"

"I know, Nuri," Scarlett interrupted. "Other than Mordecai, are there any others with Roderick that should be spared?"

Nuri stared at her. "You cannot take them all on, Scarlett. Even with your magic, starfire alone will not be enough to defeat him. He is too strong."

"Answer the question, Nuri."

"Only Cai."

Scarlett nodded before she said, "I apologize in advance for how much this is going to fucking hurt."

She lunged at Nuri, tackling her and sucking her darkness back in at the same moment. Yelling and screaming filled her ears, Cethin still there, eyes frantic when they appeared.

"Kailia!" Scarlett screamed. The queen was there in the next breath. "Bands to hold her."

Two deathstone bands appeared in her hand, and she slipped them onto Nuri's wrists, binding them together.

"How will these hurt?" Nuri asked.

"They won't," Scarlett said. "They'll keep you from fighting back when I do this."

A shirastone dagger appeared in Scarlett's hand, and she stabbed it deep into Nuri's shoulder, a scream sounding from the Night Child. Deathstone and shirastone would keep her down.

Scarlett hoped.

"Watch her," she said to Kailia. Then she looked to her brother. "You're with me."

She Traveled them to the trees where she'd first spotted Nuri. Mordecai was there, giving orders to seraphs who flew off to deliver them to various units.

"We need to take care of the dragons," Mordecai said to a male that Scarlett had to assume was Roderick.

"Godsdamn overgrown lizards," the male answered. "They were supposed to be taken care of centuries ago. How are they appearing in the various realms now?"

"I do not know, my Lord—" Mordecai answered. "But their dragon fire will decimate our ranks if they are not taken care of soon."

"How many bolts do we have?"

"Ten."

"Make it happen."

Mordecai's wings flared out, preparing to take to the sky. "And you, my Lord?"

"I am waiting for her. Now that she is here, she will come to me. I do not play the games Alaric does," Roderick answered.

"A word of caution, my Lord," Mordecai started.

"It is not needed. Go do your job," Roderick spat.

Mordecai nodded, taking to the sky.

"Can you begin draining that one subtly?" she whispered to Cethin. "He is a Maraan Lord."

If that was news to him, Cethin didn't show it. He'd likely felt out his reserves the moment they had appeared in the trees. "For him not to notice, it won't be much," Cethin replied. "But I will do what I can."

She nodded.

*Sorin?*

*What do you need, Love?*

She looked up, not surprised to find him fighting above her, easily within range. Fire flared from one palm while he swiped with one of his short swords with the other hand.

*Did you see Mordecai take off?*

*Yes.*

*I need him far, far away from me, along with all of our people. And as many seraphs pushed my way as possible.*

There was a pause before, *What are you going to do?*

*Unleash Chaos.*

She glanced up again, already seeing him shooting higher.

*How much time do I have?*

*Minutes.*

*Fuck.*

She choked on her laugh, but a few moments later, she started hearing the cry ring out.

"*Fall back! Fall back!*"

"You can start draining him fully now," she said to Cethin.

That made him start, his head whipping to her. "What? Then he will know we are here."

But she was already walking out from the trees, shadow panthers at her sides. "Roderick, right? I don't believe we've met."

The male turned to her, holding up a hand to still the warriors that had immediately drawn blades. They obeyed instantly, and Scarlett knew beyond a doubt that this male was Alaric's Second-in-Command. It was why she had never seen him. Alaric trusted him implicitly. He didn't feel the need to oversee his actions, leaving Roderick to prepare the armies he had slowly accumulated in these lands.

"Scarlett Monrhoe," Roderick said, a note of derision in his voice as he reached up and pulled back his hood. "Alaric's proverbial salvation." He jerked his chin at the few remaining warriors. "Search the surroundings. She won't be here alone."

He had the same nearly black eyes as Alaric and Mikale, but his dark hair was cropped so short, one could hardly see it. His angular features were twisted with contempt as he beheld her.

"I'm flattered you've heard of me," she said, bringing her hand dramatically to her chest. "One minor correction. It's Scarlett Sutara Aditya now."

"Yes, yes," Roderick mocked. "A Fae Queen who is not Fae."

His eyes went wide then, and she knew he was feeling Cethin. Suddenly, she was being yanked to him by invisible hands. He had her spun and against his chest with a dagger at her throat before she could process what was happening.

Well, then. Nuri hadn't been exaggerating about the strength of his power.

"Tell your brother to come out," Roderick snarled into her ear.

"Honestly, I'm much better company," she replied, feeling the Chaos inside her stirring more as it sensed Roderick's power.

His hand slid into her hair, yanking her head to the side. "Your smart mouth is not endearing to me. I am not your master," he sneered.

"No one is my master," she said darkly, the Chaos growing and growing. She felt Roderick stumble. The dagger dug into her throat, and she flinched when she realized it was deathstone.

"Ah, so you do know what this is? That it will not kill you, but will hold you in the in-between?"

"Yes," Scarlett gritted out, knowing he wasn't drained enough yet for her to do anything.

"Tell your brother to come out."

She ground her molars, but she called, "Cethin."

He stepped from the trees, violence dancing in his silver eyes. "Release her. Now."

"Get your claws off my power, and we can discuss it."

"No, Cethin!" Then she cried out as Roderick dug the dagger in a little more.

*Sorin! Is everyone safe?*

*A little longer, Love. Almost.*

Roderick began dragging the dagger down her flesh to her collarbone. She could feel her blood sliding down her skin, and she whimpered.

*Scarlett? What is happening?*

*You need to hurry.*

"All right, all right," Cethin said, and Scarlett felt Roderick instantly relax a little.

"Cethin, keep going," she demanded.

"That is deathstone, Scarlett," he retorted. "It was created specifically to contain the gods."

"Smart king," Roderick said, jostling her against him.

"Cethin, either keep draining him or Travel out," she said, the Chaos becoming turbulent within.

"Scarlett—"

"Go!"

Her voice was a dark order that had her brother glaring at her, but he was gone a moment later.

"Pitiful," Roderick spat. "Here I was, a touch worried when I heard the Avonleyan King had emerged at last."

"I know," she sighed. "You should have been worrying about the World Walker."

She felt the bark of laughter rumble against her back. "The World Walkers are not a worry to me. A nuisance trapped in their animal forms, yes, but nothing we are not prepared to handle."

"Oh, I meant their High Queen," Scarlett said, her shadows creeping out and beginning to coil around his wrist.

"There is no High Queen. Not any—"

Then he was hissing a curse, the dagger sinking in a little farther before her shadows wrenched it from his hand. Roderick dropped to his knees, Scarlett darting away as Cethin reappeared beside her, pulling every last bit of power from the Maraan Lord. She felt Roderick's power reach for her, but her brother's magic was holding it too tightly now.

Cethin's hand clamped around the male's throat, his darkness spilling out, an inky pool of black at his feet. Scarlett's Chaos strained at the sight of it. She gritted her teeth, trying to give Sorin a little longer.

Veins of black were spider-webbing across Roderick's skin. His face. Down his throat.

A strangled cough rattled from the Maraan's throat, and Cethin laughed. It was the same wicked laugh Scarlett had, and she found herself smiling when he said, "One would think your prince would have taught you to shield against this kind of power. Then again, I can feel you trying. *Pitiful.*"

*Now, Scarlett!* came Sorin's voice down the bond.

She pushed out a heavy breath of relief, shaking out her hands and rolling her shoulders. "Is he drained?"

"Almost," Cethin retorted. "Physical contact allows me to drain him much faster."

Roderick hissed out a curse as Scarlett sauntered forward. She bent down to speak directly into his face. Cethin still held him by the throat, the black veins seeping down beneath his tunic. "Correction. You should have been worried about the Avonleyan King *and* the World Walker." She looked up at Cethin. "When he is drained, you need to leave. Back inside the Citadel with the others."

There was no questioning her. Just a nod of understanding, and a few seconds later, he released Roderick, who slumped over onto his hands and knees, another rattling cough sounding from him.

Cethin gave her one last look, then he Traveled out. Scarlett slowly began circling the Maraan Lord, still keeping a tight hold on the Chaos within. Her panthers snapped and snarled at Roderick.

"Before I end you, I have a question," Scarlett said, stooping to pick up the deathstone dagger. She moved before him, crouching in front of the male. "See, a few years ago, my sisters and I killed one of you. But none of us had our gifts yet, and I cannot for the life of me figure out how we managed it so easily when the rest of you are so fucking hard to kill."

"Why would I tell you anything?" he rasped out.

She placed the tip of the dagger under his chin, tilting it up. His eyes were wholly black, and the black veins from whatever the hell Cethin had done were unnerving, even for her.

"Because I can make your death quick or last for days," she

replied, digging the tip of the dagger into the flesh of his jaw. "Even if I weren't a god, I would be your god in this moment."

"You are not a god," he coughed, the motion making him cut himself on the dagger, and he hissed another curse.

"True," she said. "I'm a High Queen."

Roderick went unnaturally still. "That is impossible."

Scarlett held up a palm, and Chaos erupted from her. It crashed into Roderick, hurling him across the small clearing and into a tree. He crumpled to the ground.

"The best I can come up with," she said conversationally, standing and making her way over to him, "is that he had to be completely drained somehow. But even then, he didn't seem as pathetic as you look right now."

"He did not have a descendant of Arius merge death with his blood by their touch," Roderick spat.

And *that* had Scarlett pausing.

That was an interesting talent.

"But he was drained?" she asked after a moment.

"My Lord, we are not sure what it is happening, but—"

The seraph stopped short when he saw Roderick on the ground, and his gaze swiveled to Scarlett. Before he had taken a single step towards her, she let the Chaos loose.

It exploded out of her with such force, she was lifted into the air where she stayed. The Chaos slammed into Roderick and the seraph, obliterating them into nothing. But it went beyond them. The Chaos radiated out and out and out. It swirled around her and into the air, pulling her starfire with it. White flames and darkness that took what it wanted. She could feel it, seeking more and more as it destroyed whatever life it found in its path, and she hoped Sorin had truly gotten all of their people inside the Citadel.

It took everything in her to stop the outpouring of that power, but she knew if she didn't, the Chaos would kill her. That's what her mother had said. If she'd have given up all her Chaos, she'd have died. And Scarlett had learned in her time between the stars that if she let it, the Chaos would take from her until it killed her.

That was the true cost of harnessing it. Finding the balance between the blessing and the curse that Chaos was and not letting it consume her.

Her feet landed on the earth as she dropped the few feet she'd been in the air, and she doubled over, her hands braced on her knees. She felt him appear beside her. He didn't need to say anything.

"Fire wings?" she panted, lifting her head to look at him.

"You told me to be more creative, Love," Sorin said with a wink as he scooped her into his arms.

He Traveled them back to the Citadel. Up to the balcony where Talwyn had screamed to her. The griffin was being tended to. Several Witches were gathered around it while Talwyn paced back and forth in front of Azrael. The Earth Prince had some scratches and bruises, but otherwise appeared fine.

Cethin and Kailia crowded around her when Sorin lowered her onto a sofa just inside the room off the balcony. A large suite of some sort. Rayner was off to one side with Auberon, Neve, and Hale, and as Sorin was doing his mother hen thing and checking her for injuries, the door opened. Tybalt entered with two others that Scarlett guessed were from the Avonleyan cadres. Between them were Nuri and Mordecai. There were deathstone bands on Mordecai's wrists. She had no doubt he had allowed them to bind him, but Nuri still had the dagger in her shoulder.

Scarlett shoved Sorin's hands aside, lurching to her feet. Her knees nearly gave out.

"Scarlett," he barked, snagging her around the waist and hauling her back to the sofa. "You need to sit."

"Someone take the dagger out of her. Now," she ordered.

"We wanted to wait until we all had a chance to speak with them," Cethin said.

"You can keep the deathstone bands on her, but take the fucking dagger out." When no one moved, she looked at Rayner. "Please."

He hesitated, but then strode forward, yanking it free. Nuri gave a shout, and the seraph let out a snarl that made Scarlett glad he was in deathstone.

"You don't need to keep your hands on them. Let them go," Scarlett said, again trying to stand.

Cethin jerked his chin, and the cadre warriors stepped away.

Mordecai was immediately pulling Nuri into his chest, his wings wrapping around her and shielding her from the rest of them.

"He will summon us back at any moment," Mordecai said, looking only at Scarlett.

"And you will be unable to follow that order because you are detained," she answered. "Will that be enough?"

She knew Mordecai understood what she was asking. Will that be enough for Nuri to defy what Alaric demanded of her?

"It should be," he answered. "She will require a Healer."

"I will make sure one is sent to her."

"Thank you. For helping her."

Scarlett nodded, finally letting herself settle back into Sorin on the sofa. Food and drinks were brought in, Azrael joining them after a time. Talwyn apparently refused to leave the griffin's side.

They did not speak of the battle that had just happened. They did not speak of future plans. They did not speak of the Maraans or the seraphs. They just...took the moment to appreciate that they had all managed to survive yet again.

Scarlett had swiped a third pear tart from the tray when a water portal appeared. Conversation ceased, and a moment later, Briar and Ashtine stepped through. The princess smiled widely, her hand clasped tightly in Briar's.

"The winds whispered of victory," she lilted, gaze sweeping the room. Then her sky-blue eyes met Scarlett's. "And they spoke of power being reborn."

"A story for another time," Scarlett replied with a soft smile from where she was nestled into Sorin's side. Her feet were tucked under her, her boots and weapons discarded on the floor.

"The entirety of the Wind Court is secured?" Briar asked, leading Ashtine over to the chair Rayner had vacated for her. She lowered into it, hands coming up to rub her swollen belly.

"We believe so," Sorin said. "Ermir and Sion were sending scouts. If any of Alaric's forces remain in the Court, they will be dealt with swiftly."

Briar nodded. "Do you plan to stay here for now?"

"If that is all right," Scarlett said. "We need to regroup and recharge. Figure out our next moves."

"There is plenty of room," Ashtine said.

"I have around three hundred soldiers here as well," Cethin said.

"I will speak with Sion," Ashtine said. "We will make sure they are given quarters."

"Thank you, your Highness."

Light conversation started up again, and before she knew it, she found herself being jostled awake as Sorin lifted her from the sofa. Apparently she'd nodded off.

She lifted her head as she murmured, "Nuri?"

"They took her to a room to be tended to," he answered. "Mordecai is keeping his bands on so he cannot Travel them. Nuri's were removed so the Healers could work."

"Not in cells, though, right?"

His eyes softened as he carried her down some stairs. "No, Love. Not in cells. They are being given a room near ours. There will be guards outside it, but no bars."

"Thank you," she whispered. She knew it was him that would have fought for that while she had slept.

"Let's get cleaned up, and then you can sleep."

He was lowering her to her feet so he could open their door when she said, "Sorin?"

He paused, glancing down at her. "Yeah, Love?"

"The fire wings were…"

Gods, she couldn't even say what that had done to her. To see him with godsdamn wings of flame? The blood and blades. She didn't want to know what kind of person that made her, but her blood heated just thinking about it.

A soft chuckle rumbled from him as he ushered her inside. "I know, Love. I felt exactly what you thought of those fire wings."

She felt her cheeks go red, and she turned away from him, hiding her smirk. His dark laugh followed her into the bathing room, where she shut the door behind her.

# CHAPTER 42
# ELIZA

They stood on the same ledge they'd been on a few weeks ago overlooking Solembra. She wasn't trying to figure out a stealthy way in this time. No, this time they would walk right through the front gate.

Niara had finally cleared both of them, and they'd ventured down from his cave. She'd never admit it to Razik, but the cave was growing on her. She was a particular fan of the hot springs, although when he had taken her down to the treasure room, she'd become a fan of that room too. Probably something to do with the promised fucking atop the gold.

He hadn't been exaggerating about the gold and treasure, and all she'd been able to do was laugh as she stared at it. He'd had shelves carved into one wall, and she'd run her fingers along the spines of the books lining them. She hadn't needed to ask if they were from other worlds. She already knew they were.

But she had asked, "Do you wish to go back someday? To Nordrir, I mean?"

"I was so young, I do not remember it," he'd answered, leaning against the wall and watching her. "Besides, it is no longer what it once was. I told you, it is not even called Nordrir anymore. It is known as The Requiem."

"Why?"

"I do not know the history, and Tybalt does not speak of it."

"Does Saylah know?"

"Saylah and I are not on the best of terms, but even if that were not the case, I don't think she knows either. She is young for a god."

That had been odd to think about. The idea of a god being considered young.

Razik shifted beside her, his arm brushing against hers. "I still think we should fly in."

"Not all of us have wings, Razik," she muttered.

"We already discussed this. I can—"

"No."

"It will be easier to evade any wards if—"

"No."

"Eliza," he rumbled. "Do you think I would ever drop you or let you fall?"

"Of course not. Because I will never be in the godsdamn air. Travel us like a normal Avonleyan," she retorted.

"As you wish, Milady," he said, extending his hand with an exaggerated flourish.

She resisted the urge to flip him off as she placed her fingers in his palm, but then he yanked her forward, his arm curling around her waist. "I will convince you to fly with me someday," he murmured into her ear.

"Absolutely not."

He made a low humming sound of contemplation, his lips brushing her temple. Then he asked, "Are you ready, *mai dragocen*?"

Eliza took in a deep breath, counting down from five before she exhaled. She met his gaze when she said, "I don't need you defending my honor or any of that shit in there."

His brows knitted together. "Why would I do that? You are more than capable of defending your own honor."

Gods. She could kiss him for that one statement.

Could, but she wouldn't. Not when they were about to unleash themselves in her own home.

"I simply want to remind you to check your possessive-dragon nature."

"Eliza, you threatened to cut off body parts, set them on fire, and shove them down a male's throat at the mere *thought* that he would touch me. I do not think I am the only possessive one here."

"Whatever," she grumbled. "Let's go."

They appeared right outside the Fiera Palace gates, and she immediately dropped Razik's hand. Palming a dagger, she threw it directly at one of the Fae on guard duty before he'd had a moment to comprehend they were here.

"What the fuck?" the guard cried when it grazed his cheek before embedding in the wall behind him. He whipped around, sword half-drawn when he saw her. His face visibly paled, and he took a step back.

"What the hell is going on?" asked the guard on the opposite side of the gate. "Who the fuck are you?"

Razik's large stature hid her smaller frame from the guard, and when Eliza glanced up at him, he was giving the guard the same bored once over he gave everyone else.

"General— Eliza. What are—" At the fiery glare she sent the guard, he audibly swallowed. "Is the, uh…prince expecting you?" He winced as he said 'prince.' Likely at the flames that burst to life at her fingertips.

"This is more of a surprise visit," Eliza said with a razor-sharp smile. "And it is going to stay that way."

"We, uh—" She turned slowly to the other guard, who was still eyeing Razik.

"Spit it out, Anton," she snapped.

His eyes widened. Anton had been one of the newest members of their forces before everything had gone to shit. He'd been good in the sparring rings—exceptionally skilled—which is likely how he'd already earned a position at the front gates. But even if that hadn't been the case, she would have remembered his name. She knew all of her warriors. Anton just hadn't been around long enough to know that. He also wasn't seasoned enough to have earned a position at the front gates yet.

The soldier scratched at the back of his neck, eyes dropping to the ground. "We aren't—"

"No. Try again," she interrupted.

His light brown eyes snapped back to hers. "What?"

*This* was why he shouldn't be a guard at the main gate yet.

"You do not let the people at the front gate know you are intimidated by them. You are the first line of defense for your prince. No one gets past these gates by intimidation tactics. Try again," she demanded.

Anton's perplexed gaze flicked to the other guard. The other guard, Conrade, had been with the Fire Court forces for a few decades, and he clearly recalled that interfering with her training resulted in unwanted consequences as he kept quiet.

Eliza snapped her still flaming fingers at Anton, sparks flying as she did so. "Let's go. I have a throne to take. If you plan to keep your position once I do, you damn well better show me I can trust you as my first line of defense."

Razik audibly sighed beside her. "If she sits on that throne, and you let someone in who hurts her, she will be the least of your worries. Shoulders back, chin up. Draw a weapon. Look her in the eye when you demand—not ask—what her business is here."

Anton looked back and forth between them before he did exactly what Razik had said. His back straightened, a hard look filling his face as he stared back at Eliza. "You aren't entering these gates until you state your business." It was a harsh tone, and she saw the flash of flame in his irises, a nice subtle touch.

"Better," she said. "Now get me the stand-in commander. He can escort me himself."

At that, the uncertainty flashed in Anton's eyes once more. "He is a seraph, General."

"Even better."

"He does not like to be—"

"Do not mistake my moment of teaching as negotiation. Summon him, Anton. Now."

"Yes, General." He reached up, drawing a fire message that immediately disappeared. He looked like he was about to fidget, then caught himself, straightening his posture once more. She nodded in approval before turning to Conrade.

"Why the fuck are you all blindly following Bastien?"

"It was that or death, General," Conrade answered, his gaze fixed on the ground.

"And where do your loyalties lie?"

"With Prince Aditya. With you, if you take the throne," he answered.

"Tell me, Conrade. Who should I spare when I enter these gates?"

"That is not my call to make, General."

"No, it is not," she agreed. "But I am asking you to tell me if there are any, aside from Bastian and the seraphs, that have turned against the Fire Prince of their own choosing."

"You will know them," he answered. "Bastien gave them new positions with special uniforms."

She didn't get a chance to ask another question because the front gates were opening and a seraph was walking towards them. He had pristine white wings, and his blonde hair brushed his brow. He paused when he saw her standing there, then his lip curled back when his gaze flicked to Razik.

"Keres and Varlis obviously failed," he said, fire winding down his arms.

"He's observant," Razik said dryly.

She almost let a laugh slip out. "You are the one leading my forces?" Eliza demanded.

"I am the one leading the Fire Court armies," the seraph replied, his fire flaring brighter.

It didn't matter.

Eliza released a wave of flame that rose up before crashing down on the seraph.

"Let's go," she said, walking past the still burning male.

*So excessively violent, mai dragocen,* Razik purred down the bond.

Her lips did twitch then.

As they stalked along the path to the main doors, guards rushed to meet them, and she saw what Conrade had been talking about. Most of the guards were in the usual Fire Court guard attire, but some had gold tunics with fine embroidery on it rather than the standard deep red and black. One of the guards in red skidded to a halt when he realized who she was.

"General? They told us Prince Sorin was dead, and that

everyone else had abandoned the Court," he said, a mixture of shock and relief in his eyes. Two of the three guards in gold appeared to be trying to slink into the back of the group, but the third had straightened and puffed out his chest. She knew him too. Bronn.

"Eliza," he said tightly.

"General," she corrected with a sharp glare. "Or, if you'd rather, your Highness, as I will occupy the throne of this Court very soon."

"You will never make it to him. We have seraphs with fire nearly as powerful as yours," he mocked, his companions in gold getting a little braver.

"And you?" she asked, flames beginning to creep up her legs, over her knees, up to her torso. "Will those same seraphs protect you?"

Bronn glanced up, but Eliza didn't need to. She'd already heard their rustling wings and shouted commands. Bronn looked back at her, a taunting smirk on his lips.

Until Eliza smirked back, her arms encompassed in flames now too. She looked at Razik. "You take the sky, I'll take the ground?"

"Do I actually get to do something now?" Razik asked, arching a brow.

"Do you not want to join me in excessive violence?"

A wicked grin of his own appeared. "Always, *mai dragocen.*"

There was a soft flash of black light, and he was flapping his newly healed wings, a roar of challenge sounding as he went to face the seraphs. She wished she could watch him wreak havoc in the sky, but she had her own carnage to make.

She turned back to Bronn as she let her flames wind up farther into her hair, nothing but a burning female of wrath now. "Shall we?" she asked, drawing her sword.

"General, we didn't know," one of the guards in red started.

"I'm aware, Tobias." He seemed relieved, until she added, "But I look forward to hearing your thoughts on this matter in a training ring when this is all over."

He nodded, his face paling a little. They all knew when *she* joined them in a training ring, there was a reason for it. Rarely was that reason a good one.

She didn't have time to think about any of that right now, though.

Not as Bronn advanced, choosing to fight rather than try to talk her out of ending him. Honorable, but pointless.

When sword met sword, her fire rushed down her blade, wrapping around his. She paused for the briefest of moments because that had never happened before. Bronn let out a yelp and dropped his sword as if it had burned him. Which was also odd because he had fire magic and shouldn't be able to feel the burn of flames.

Bronn's eyes went wide in shock a moment later when she sank the still burning spirit sword into his chest.

Then she lost herself to the dance of bloodshed, making her way to the main doors. Any guard in a gold tunic and any male with wings was left either bleeding or burning in her wake. She could hear Razik above her, ash floating down to the ground like fresh snow as he matched her song of death in the sky.

By the time she reached the main doors, two guards in the standard issued uniforms were opening them for her. Both of them avoided her gaze as she prowled past them and into her home.

She wished she could take it all in. The seven levels of fire glass bridges that connected the eastern and western sides of the Fiera Palace. The Tana River that flowed through the middle. The six-story library and the private training area beneath the glass palace roof.

As it was, staff and guards alike were darting out of her way as she made her way to the Great Hall. It was also the throne room, but Sorin rarely used it as such. In fact, she couldn't remember the last time he had actually sat on the throne. Granted, he was gone for three years, but even at the Samhain feast, it had been out on display but never sat on.

That was not the case when she threw open the double doors of the Great Hall, a trail of fire blazing behind her. There were two dozen guards in gold tunics between her and the Fae seated on the throne.

Bastien glared at her, his dark auburn hair tied back at the nape of his neck and flames sparking in his navy blue eyes. Eliza flipped the spirit sword in her hand, blue wildfire igniting down it. He knew if they fought, she would win. Just like she had every other time he'd tried to best her. She'd tried to conserve her magic, but while Bastien was a pain in her ass, he was smart. Hence the two dozen guards to wear her down.

That was fine.

She had her own backup.

*Raz? Are you done with the airborne acrobatics?*

*The grounds and the skies are clear.*

*Great. There is a terrace on the west side. I need you to make an appearance.*

*Are you asking me to come defend your honor?*

*What? No. I just want all my magic for this fucker.*

*When we are finished with this, we should go flying.*

*Razik,* she hissed.

But then a spiked tail was shattering the terrace doors before a black diamond-shaped head appeared, smoke furling up from his snout. Sapphire eyes went directly to her.

"All of them except the one sitting on his ass," she said.

*So excessively violent.*

She could hear his dark laugh down the bond as he opened his mouth. The guards began scrambling, but it didn't matter. Dragon fire erupted into the space between her and the throne. And when the guards were no more than fluttering ash, those black flames brushed against her own in a caress.

"This is the part where you get the fuck up," Eliza snarled, stalking across the hall towards the throne. Ashes were still drifting down around her as she moved.

"Or the dragon will step in?" Bastien sneered.

A whip of fire shot from her hand, wrapping around Bastien's throat, and she yanked on it hard. He fell off the throne onto his knees. She could feel his magic battling against hers, feel his flames trying to force hers back.

As she closed the space between them, she said, "I challenge you for the royal seat of the Fire Court, Bastien Eynon."

She pulled on her flames again, and he lurched forward to catch himself on his hands where tendrils of flame snaked from her and wrapped around his wrists, holding him in place. Then she yanked once more, forcing him to bow before her with his nose to the floor.

"I yield," he gasped. "I godsdamn yield. The throne and Court are yours."

She loosened her flames enough so that when she tipped his chin up with the tip of her sword, he could look into her eyes as she said with lethal softness, "The only surrender I will accept is your death."

"That is not the honorable way this is done," Bastien rasped, his eyes growing round as she raised her sword.

"While that is true, I've been told I am excessively violent," she replied, and then she brought her sword down, his head rolling a few feet away when his body collapsed onto the floor.

She sent her sword to a pocket realm. She'd clean it later. Then she yanked the tie from her braid that was already half out of its plait. The sound of footsteps had her turning, then she froze, her fingers still tangled in her mess of hair.

"You're naked."

"Violent *and* observant," Razik replied.

She sent him a bland look while she continued to unwind her hair. "Why are you naked?"

"I shifted."

"But when you shifted back in the mountains, you were clothed."

Razik shrugged.

"You *wanted* to be naked?"

"I always want to be without clothing around you."

"Oh my gods," she muttered. "What if there had been other people around, and you needed to shift back?"

He leaned in close, tucking her hair behind her ear. "I suppose someone would have gotten rather possessive."

She shoved him away, rolling her eyes. "Let's go find you some clothing."

"Are you not going to sit on your throne, your Highness?"

"First of all, don't call me that. Second, no. It is not my throne."

"But it is. You challenged the sitting royal and won...Princess."

She gestured dismissively at the throne. "It was never his to begin with."

"Maybe not, but that doesn't change anything I just said."

"Why are we even talking about this? Especially with you naked?"

"We can do something else if you wish."

"Yes. I do wish," she said. When his head tilted with interest, she smiled coyly and added, "I wish to go find you clothing."

"Violent, observant, and a liar."

The sound of frantic footfalls had them both turning to the Great Hall entrance where a number of warriors stopped short, looking from her to a very naked Razik to Bastien's headless body. She pointed to a male near the front, as she stepped in front of Raz.

"Find Quinn, Kenna, and Bridger. Send them here immediately. Tell Bridger I want to know where every single one of our forces is currently stationed, and tell Kenna I want to know the status of our weapons and supplies."

"Right away, Gen— Uh, your Highness," the male said, turning on his heel and rushing out of the room.

She sighed internally and started to turn away, but her gaze collided with naked flesh. "And for the love of Anala, someone find my twin flame some godsdamn clothes." Razik smirked at the very public statement of claiming, and she jabbed a finger at him. "Don't say a godsdamn word."

Of course he opened his mouth anyway. Or he did down their bond.

*Violent, observant, a liar, and possessive.*

*I swear to Anala, Razik.*

She dismissed everyone else, sending them scampering from the Great Hall, and when the doors shut behind them, she let out another long breath, dragging her fingers through her hair again. The hall was a godsdamn mess. The terrace doors were shattered. There was ash and blood everywhere. There was ash and blood everywhere on *her*.

Eliza opened her mouth to tell Razik that they should help with the cleanup, but before she could say a word, he was crushing her against him. Lips crashed onto hers, and she was kissing him back with all the leftover adrenaline of the fight.

He started walking her backwards, and she broke away to gasp, "We are *not* fucking on Sorin's throne."

"But it's yours," he countered.

"Gods, what is your obsession with—" Her eyes flew wide. "A throne is *not* godsdamn treasure, Raz."

"One could argue a throne is very valuable," he replied, mouth dragging down her neck as he tugged aside the collar of her tunic.

"Fuck me against a wall like a normal person," she gasped when his teeth sank into the soft place between her neck and shoulder.

"I will add eloquent to your list of endearing attributes," he murmured darkly.

A throat clearing had them both stilling. She peaked over Razik's shoulder to see a guard standing in the doorway. His eyes were averted, but he held clothing in his hand.

"I, uh, have these. For your consort, your Highness," he said.

"Your Highness," Razik murmured against her skin.

She growled, shoving him back, and he chuckled lightly as she strode across the room to collect the clothing. The guard quickly disappeared once more, and she made her way back to Razik. Throwing the clothing at him, she said, "Get dressed. We need to clean up in here, and I need to check in with the others."

"And the wall?" Razik asked with a grin, slipping the tunic over his head.

She sighed. "Will have to wait. I have no doubt we'll be interrupted again in a minute."

"And the throne?"

"Oh my gods, Razik," she chided. "Stop with the throne, and I'll get you some treasure from Sorin's vaults below."

He chuckled, pressing a kiss to her temple. "We'll circle back to this topic."

"We are not circling back to this, Raz," she retorted, leading him out of the Great Hall.

She felt his contemplative hum in her bones, and she sighed, trying to shake off the want still coursing through her.

They were nearing the bridges when he said, "You could wear a crown too."

With a hard shove, she had him tumbling into the Tana with a splash. His laughter followed her across the bridge, and she found herself smiling like a fool.

# CHAPTER 43
## SORIN

" I am sorry, Briar," Sorin said the moment he stepped into Ashtine's private rooms.

Briar shut the door behind him, and Sorin pulled the male into a quick, tight embrace.

They hadn't had a chance to talk much since the battle for the Wind Court two days ago, outside of updates and planning sessions. Ashtine had stayed out of sight for much of that time, but word had already spread that the Wind Princess was with child. As expected, there were varying degrees of reaction to the knowledge that Briar had sired them.

That wasn't why he was here, though. Sorin hadn't gotten a chance to check in with his friend since Briar had learned of Sawyer's death. He didn't know when he had been told or how, but he knew there hadn't been time to properly grieve in the middle of war.

"What do you need?" he asked, stepping back and following the Water Prince deeper into the sitting room.

Briar didn't say anything for a long moment, instead pouring Sorin a cup of tea and passing it over. "Ashtine is still sleeping."

"Good," Sorin answered with a nod of thanks. "She needs the rest." He paused before adding, "So do you. I can come back later."

"No," Briar said quickly. "I am fine."

"What do you need, Briar?" Sorin asked again.

Icy blue eyes met his. They were as turbulent as the waves he could command. "What do I not need at this point? I need to protect Ashtine from the archaic thinking of our people. I need to protect my children from the same, but first I need to make sure they have a safe world to be born into. I need to get my own fucking Court back, and I need to hold a proper Farewell for my brother who——"

Sorin was pulling him back into another embrace, swallowing thickly. He had grown up with Briar. They were nearly the same age, and when Sawyer had come along, he'd eventually fallen in with them without question. He'd known the Drayces longer than he'd known any of the other Fae, and while his Inner Court was his family, so were Briar and Sawyer. Only he and Briar were also both responsible for entire Courts. The weight of that responsibility was something understood by only a select few. It had created a different sort of bond.

So he'd known Briar would hold it together. He'd known his friend would do what needed to be done while keeping his own storm internal. He was glad he'd had Ashtine, but he would have hidden some of this from her. He would have flipped their roles, comforting her instead of letting her comfort him. Sorin could practically hear him murmuring words to her to assuage her feelings of guilt and ensure she knew Sawyer would make that same sacrifice over and over.

But inside, his heart would have been shattering.

"He will be honored, Briar," Sorin said after a time. "When we have reclaimed our lands, and when the realm is at peace, he will be honored. Sawyer. Nakoa. Finn and Sloan. All of those who gave their lives so that the realm might retain its freedom will be remembered."

They'd moved to a set of armchairs, and Sorin tossed some extra flames into the hearth. The temperature of the room had dropped noticeably while Briar had been speaking.

"You know that the Fire Court will stand with you and Ashtine regarding the babes, right? I would be willing to bet Luan will too, and Scarlett, of course," Sorin said.

"Even with the entirety of the realm's rulers behind us, there will still be politics at play. You know this, Sorin," Briar said, a finger steepled along his temple as he watched the flames.

"Be that as it may, we present as a united front. It will still make them act with caution knowing they will be going up against all of us."

"Perhaps," was all Briar said.

"Scarlett also has some ideas on how to handle this situation," Sorin continued.

Briar huffed a laugh. "Of course she does." He took a drink of his tea before he added, "Where is she?"

"With the High Witch," Sorin answered.

Hazel had arrived yesterday with another small unit of Witches. Too late to fight in the Wind Court battle, she said they had forces prepared and waiting for orders all along the western border of the Witch Kingdoms. From there, they could easily be in Toreall or the Earth Court territory at a moment's notice. Which was good, because they had also received word the Night Children were on the move, and Sorin could only assume they would be joining Tarek in the Earth Court. It was foolish, with the Witches and Shifters so close. It would be a fairly easy battle, but there would be large losses on both sides. Then again, maybe it was brilliant. It would lessen the Fae, Shifter, and Witch numbers, and all Alaric and the other Maraans would have to sacrifice is vampyre lives that he clearly deemed expendable.

They really needed to get aid to Earth Court.

Eliza had sent word this morning that she had successfully taken back control of the Fire Court. She had units throughout the territory removing any additional threats, and the Fire Court forces were back under her command. She was getting things organized to have them all start moving to the southern borders along the mortal lands. If they could gain control of the southern courts too, they could hammer from the north, south, and east.

So many moving parts in all of this, especially when he realized Scarlett had been moving pieces of her own into place this entire time. Her plans for what she was going to ask Briar and Ashtine were no exception.

They were discussing the merit of bringing a fight to the Earth Court before they had a chance to strengthen their hold with the additional Night Children when Ashtine appeared. Her long silver hair hung loose around her shoulders, and her pale blue dress matched her eyes.

Briar was immediately on his feet and closing the distance between them, pressing a soft kiss to her cheek as he murmured, "Good morning."

"There are new arrivals," she said, reaching up to run her fingers along Briar's jaw.

"Where?" he asked, one of his large hands resting on her rounded stomach, a thumb making sweeping motions back and forth.

"In the receiving foyer." Then her gaze flitted to Sorin's. With a soft smile, as she added, "Cyrus and Cassius."

Sorin shot to his feet as he reached out to Scarlett down their bond. *Cyrus and Cassius are here, Love. The receiving foyer.*

She didn't answer, but he felt her jolt of relief. He knew when he got to the foyer she would already be there.

"Do you wish to see them or stay here?" Briar was asking Ashtine.

"Ermir and Sion have cleared the foyer and are having a council room prepared for us. We should not meet anyone untowardly this morning," she answered.

Briar nodded, folding her hand into his a moment before a water portal appeared, and they all stepped into the entrance foyer where Scarlett was indeed wrapped around Cassius in a tight embrace. Then she was reaching for Cyrus to do the same.

"That was faster than expected," Sorin said as Scarlett fussed over the two of them. She was currently checking Cyrus for any type of injury, turning his head from side to side.

"Stop it," Cyrus grumbled, brushing her hands away. "Sorin's mother hen tendencies are wearing off on you."

"Fuck off. They are not," she admonished, instantly dropping her hands to her side.

"Darling, you were just fretting."

"Fret this," she retorted, flipping him her middle finger.

"We actually went to the Witch Kingdoms first," Cassius said loudly, cutting into the bickering. "We are looking for the High Witch. We were told she is here."

"She is," Scarlett said. "Why do you need to see her?"

"According to Nuri and Mordecai, she is the only one who can help us find what the Sorceress is after."

"Is that so?" Scarlett murmured darkly. "They haven't said anything about that."

"They are here?" Cyrus asked.

"They were here for the attack on the Citadel but were detained as prisoners of war," she answered.

"Clever, Seastar," Cassius said.

"They are being kept under surveillance in a room."

"Princess?"

They all turned to find Sion.

"The council room is prepared. There is also food and drink."

"Thank you, Sion. Would you fetch Nuri and Mordecai? It sounds as though they should be part of the upcoming discussion," Ashtine answered as she and Briar began leading the way to the council room.

They were filling breakfast plates when Scarlett asked Briar and Ashtine, "Have you two discussed where you will live with the babes at the end of this?"

Briar's hand halted in mid-air before he placed the cinnamon roll he held on Ashtine's plate. "We have had little time to discuss such matters yet."

"Hmm," was all Scarlett said in reply before she moved to the table, setting her plate aside and immediately forgetting about it.

Sorin lowered into the seat next to her, handing over a pear. "At least eat this, Scarlett."

She made a noise of acknowledgment, mindlessly taking a bite while lost in her thoughts, no doubt altering her plans to accommodate whatever news they were about to get.

Everyone else was getting settled with their own plates when Mordecai and Nuri were brought in, and behind them was Hazel. The High Witch's eyes went straight to her son, who stared back at her with a terse expression.

Azrael, Cethin, Kailia, Rayner, Hale, and Auberon had also been summoned for the meeting, and when Luan had appeared with Talwyn beside him, Sorin tensed for Scarlett's reaction. But she said nothing, looking over the dethroned queen with a quick assessing glance before turning away.

"There's something you neglected to share, Sister," Scarlett said, fingers drumming on the table beside her plate.

Nuri dropped unceremoniously into a chair that Mordecai pulled out for her. "Is there? It is hard to remember every little thing I have been doing for you, especially as I've been recovering from having godsdamn shirastone shoved into my shoulder."

Scarlett propped her chin in her palm. "You're welcome, by the way."

Nuri gave her a snarky sneer as she flipped her off.

"I am assuming since these two are here," Mordecai cut in, pushing Nuri's finger down and nodding at Cyrus and Cassius, "this is about the Semiria rings."

"Why would this be about those?" Scarlett asked, straightening in her seat.

Breakfasts were forgotten as Cassius and Cyrus told them what they had learned, with Mordecai offering clarification when needed. Nuri didn't say a word, and Sorin had to wonder if she didn't want to, or if she couldn't due to some order from the Blood Bond.

When they were done, Scarlett twisted to look at Hazel. "Can you do this? Help them find this missing Semiria ring?"

"Yes," Hazel answered. "There is a spell in my mother's spell book that will work."

"Then we need to get the other two. To destroy this portal key, correct?"

"Eventually, yes," Mordecai said.

"Not eventually," Scarlett replied. "I want all ways into this world closed. Anyone who wants in, will need to go through me. The mirror gates are taken care of. We find these rings and destroy this portal key." Her gaze went to Hale. "And we figure out what to do about the kings."

That particular detail Nuri and Mordecai *had* filled them in on. How Drake had learned of the unexpected cost of taking down the wards around the mortal lands. Scarlett had been quiet and lost to her own thoughts ever since.

"Tarek had one of the rings the last I knew," Talwyn suddenly offered.

"Why?" Rayner asked.

"He retained Eliné's ring after taking it from Sorin."

"Alaric would have surely taken it back by now if he wants all three," Briar argued.

"No," Scarlett and Cassius said together.

Scarlett nodded at Cass, and he said, "He would have kept them separated until he had all three. If he kept them together, they would be easier to steal."

"So we think one is in the Earth Court with Tarek. One is lost in the Fellowship remains. And the third?" Cethin asked.

"Would be kept close. Not on Alaric, but likely in Baylorin," Cassius said.

"Balam?" asked Cyrus.

"No," Scarlett said softly. "Mikale has one."

The name alone had Sorin stifling a growl, and Scarlett cast him a quick glance.

"When he trapped me in that dream the last time, it was on his finger. I didn't realize that's what it was because the stone is different. Emerald instead of the sapphire my ring was," she added.

"Which one should we go after first?" Cyrus asked, turning to Cassius.

Cass pushed out a harsh breath, rubbing at the back of his neck. "While Hazel is working on the missing one, we can go after one of the other two. I know Baylorin to get the one Mikale has, but the Earth Court—"

"We will get that one," Scarlett said. "We were planning on taking back that Court next. Those plans can be escalated. Are the Witches restored enough to fight?"

"The host that came with me is certainly ready, and we have units waiting at the borders. Jetta can lead them all in my absence," Hazel replied.

"Cass and I will go after the other one then," Cyrus said, gaze fixed on the table as he picked at a chip in the wood.

"I will go with you two," Sorin said, and Cyrus's head snapped up. "Why?"

"I need a reason to help my family?"

"No, but..." Cyrus stared back at him.

"It is not a reflection of you, Cyrus," Sorin said, knowing his friend too well. "I know you are capable of this, but you are facing a

Maraan Lord and possible other unknowns. Additional power would be wise."

"He has a point," Cassius said, but he looked at Scarlett. "Seastar?"

She waved him off, clearly already thinking about something else. "We'll have plenty of help with the rest of the Fae Royalty, the Witches, Shifters, and Avonleyans. If he wants to go—" She stopped abruptly, turning to face him fully. "You want to kill Mikale."

A slow, malicious grin tilted on Sorin's lips. "You can have Alaric, Love, but Mikale's death is mine."

"You cannot kill him, Sorin. Callan's life and his are bound together."

"I am aware," he said, settling back in his seat. "There are so many things worse than death."

The three of them stood on a rooftop across the street from the Tyndell manor in the dead of night. The same rooftop where Scarlett and Nuri had found him one night. The same night he had learned who Scarlett really was.

"He had the wards altered," Cassius said. "I can feel them from here. They are not the same ones I put up."

They had expected as much, which is why they were here, figuring out what additional measures and protections had been added since they had been here last. Whatever had been done to the Tyndell manor would surely have been done to the Lairwood estate and castle.

"Can you get past them?" Sorin asked.

"Yes, but it will take some time," Cass answered, brows furrowed as he tried to work through something he and Cyrus could not feel.

"Maybe we should figure out where Mikale actually is first," Cyrus said. "So we don't spend all our time finding our way into one place, only to learn he's at another."

"How do we figure that out?" Cassius said.

"He'll be at his estate if he's not required at the castle," Sorin answered.

Cyrus glanced at him. "The reason behind that assumption?"

"He likes power and to feel in control. With the Fellowship gone, Alaric has taken up residence in the castle. Mikale will only be there when needed. At his estate, he holds all the power and is the most important man in the place," Sorin said.

"That's...a really valid point," Cassius agreed.

"And even if he's not there right away," Sorin went on, "we can use the time to get in and wait for him. That might actually be better for us in the end."

Cyrus shrugged. "Works for me."

Sorin Traveled them so Cassius could maintain as much of his magic as possible to break through the wards. They were as close to the estate as they dared get, hidden in the shadows of a copse of trees near the east wall that ran the perimeter.

"It'll take a while," Cassius said again.

"Do your witchy thing," Cyrus said, plopping down onto the ground to wait. "Let us know if you need anything."

Sorin heard the muttered cursing beneath his breath as Cassius turned away from them. He lowered down next to his Second, leaning back against a tree while constantly listening for any sign that someone or something might be coming.

"How are you doing, Cyrus?" he asked in a hushed tone so as not to disturb Cassius.

"Great," Cyrus muttered, plucking at some blades of grass.

"You realize if you hadn't made that bargain with the Sorceress, we would have never learned of this portal key, right?"

Cyrus's fingers paused for half a second before he pulled out another piece of grass. "If you're trying to make me feel better about this mess, it is not necessary."

"I am not trying to do that," Sorin replied. "Just stating facts."

"These rings could have been dealt with later. Fuck, we could have destroyed them after the Maraans were dead. It would have been a lot easier to track them down, that's for sure."

"That's a fair point," Sorin conceded. After a long stint of silence, he said, "You know no one blames you for any of this."

"Yep. I know I am the only one doing that," Cyrus said. "But I can't… Or I couldn't. Not until—" He paused, struggling for the words.

"Not until Cass," Sorin said in understanding. "I get it, Cyrus."

"He doesn't fix me or whatever, but he grounds me. When I need it most."

"I am happy for you, my friend."

"I think…" He paused again, and Sorin knew if he could see him clearly, his features would be tight, lips rolled together as he gathered his thoughts. "I think I'm happy for me too, despite all the shit right now. I think I'm happy."

"Good, Cyrus. You deserve happiness."

"Yeah. Yeah, I do," he agreed, and the way he said it had this air of almost awe to it. As though he couldn't believe he'd voiced the words.

They fell silent after that, letting Cassius steadily work his way through the wards. It took hours, and dawn was breaking when he announced he was done. He looked utterly exhausted, and Cyrus shot to his feet.

"Are you all right?"

"I'll be fine," Cass said. "It took longer because I had to be careful not to set anything off while I worked, but we'll be fine to go in."

"Maybe you should wait out here," Cyrus said.

"No."

"Cass—"

"No, Cyrus," he repeated, and Cyrus sent Sorin a look as he got to his feet.

"He can Travel out if needed, right, Cassius? Your reserves are fine?" Sorin asked.

They should be. Witch gifts shouldn't drain his magic like his dragon gifts would. This was more mentally taxing.

Cass nodded, and Cyrus looked like he wanted to argue, but begrudgingly kept his mouth shut.

"The front foyer?" Sorin asked.

"No better place to start," Cassius replied with a shrug.

They both knew the house well. Cassius had been to the estate a handful of times, and Sorin had studied a makeshift map of the place for hours on end before he'd come here to rescue Scarlett.

Sorin Traveled them in. They were prepared to take out guards the moment they appeared, but the house was oddly empty.

"Shouldn't there be...people?" Cyrus asked, looking around the stately foyer.

"There used to be, but maybe with Veda and the true Lord Lairwood gone, he didn't need as much staff?" Cassius said, his eyes having shifted to see better.

"Let's just take the gift," Sorin said.

They searched the main floor fairly quickly, only seeing a few maids bustling about. They were quiet enough with their Fae abilities to move unseen, and they made their way to the second floor. This level would have the wing with Mikale's rooms as well as his study, so Sorin wasn't surprised to hear movement.

"Once we have the ring, you two can Travel out," Sorin said. "Mikale and I have business to discuss."

"Here? Wouldn't it be wiser to take him somewhere else for said discussion?" Cyrus asked.

"Eliza has a room prepared for me," Sorin answered darkly.

Cyrus slowly turned to look at him as he uttered a low, "Fuck."

Eventually, they would all be meeting up at either the Fire or Earth Courts, depending on how things fared for all of them. It was a nightmare trying to incorporate the Witches' and griffins' travel time with the ground forces that needed to march or be Traveled. Traveling that many drained any Traveler, but the Avonleyans could Travel, which helped.

"Ready?" Cassius asked.

Sorin and Cyrus nodded, and Cass led the way down the hall. They found Mikale in his study, seated behind a desk, going over some papers. He heard them sooner than Sorin would have liked, but seeing as Mikale was also immortal, it was to be expected, he supposed.

Mikale shot to his feet, reaching for a dagger, but Cyrus already had bands of flame shackled around his wrists, snapping them together.

"A lot of good that dream-walking nonsense will be now," Sorin said calmly, leaning against the doorjamb with his hands in his pockets. "For a *king*, you'd think you'd have better security in place."

"How did you get past my godsdamn wards?" Mikale demanded, his wings ripping free. Gold. Like his sister's had been. He snapped them away from the manacles that Cyrus made flare brighter, embers flying.

"Seriously," Cyrus said. "Why don't you have any guards?"

"Because my wards were supposed to be impassable. We got them from—"

Cyrus burst out laughing, and Cassius and Sorin exchanged a look of confusion.

"Are you saying you trusted wards that came from Gehenna?" Cyrus asked when he got himself under control.

"Alaric made a deal with her," Mikale gritted out, slamming his fists on his desk as the flames burned into his skin more.

"Oh, I know all about her *deals*," Cyrus said. "Actually, that's why I'm here. I have a deal of my own to fulfill with her."

Cyrus crossed the room, tilting his head to study Mikale's bound hands. "Scarlett was right. You do have Talwyn's ring."

"How could she possibly have known that?" Mikale spat, trying to lurch backwards when Cyrus reached for the ring.

Cyrus set the chair behind him on fire, and Sorin's smile grew as Mikale swore, twisting around to protect his wings. In the mayhem, Cyrus managed to rip the ring off his finger with a vicious yank that had Mikale howling.

Cyrus held it up to the window where the growing sunlight glistened off of it. "She saw it in the last dream you appeared in," he finally answered. Then he turned to Sorin and Cassius. "You are sure, Sorin?"

"I will meet you in Solembra," Sorin replied.

Cyrus and Cassius were gone in the next second, leaving him alone with Mikale.

Sorin put out the flaming chair and the manacles, leaving Mikale heaving with his hands braced on the desk.

"She sends you to exact her revenge?" Mikale spat.

"She does not need to waste another second on you," Sorin replied, pushing off the doorway and striding into the room. "But that aside, she is mine to defend. Mine to consume. Mine to avenge. And you touched what is mine."

"You cannot kill me," Mikale snarled, straightening as Sorin drew nearer. "We are not killed as easily as seraphs."

"I am aware," Sorin said. "That is why I have these." He pulled two bands of deathstone from his pocket and held them up.

Mikale's face paled. "How did you get those?"

"That is not important," Sorin replied, clinking the two bands together. "What is important is that they will accomplish two things. They will drain your magic, keeping you from healing and replenishing, but they will also keep you from dying, which keeps King Callan alive."

"How do you know about that?" Mikale spluttered while Sorin slipped a band around his wrist.

"Again, not important," Sorin answered, slipping on the other band. Before Mikale could speak, Sorin Traveled them to the Fiera Palace, specifically to the rooms beneath it. He hadn't needed to come down here in decades. When he did, the others were usually with him. It was why Cyrus had cursed when he'd told him where they were going. He knew what these rooms were used for. This time, though, it needed to be just him.

Mikale blinked, looking around the obsidian room. "You cannot Travel," he sneered, confusion on his sharp features.

But finally being here, in this place, with this male in his grip?

Sorin's control shattered.

Mikale was flying into a wall as Sorin hurled him back. He didn't know if the sound of bone crunching came from Mikale's body or his wings. He also didn't give a fuck.

"You took from her. Again and again," Sorin snarled, setting fire to one wing. But he didn't let it simply go up in flames. Oh no. He controlled the burn. Dragging it out. Making it slowly creep along, feather by excruciating feather.

Mikale screamed, fingers clawing at the stone floor where he still lay on the ground.

Until a gag of fire formed between his lips.

"Scream again and I will burn away your vocal chords," Sorin said simply.

Mikale nodded, hatred shining in his black eyes while Sorin burned the wing slowly to ash.

"The idea that you could ever have her?" Sorin growled, starting on the other wing. Mikale let out a strangled cry, and Sorin let the fire in his mouth singe his lips. Mikale slapped a hand against the stone in agony.

Sorin only smiled, taking even more time with the second wing.

When he was done, he let the gag of fire go out, and Mikale panted, tipping his head back against the wall.

"What now, Sorin?" Mikale rasped out. "You are just going to leave me down here to rot in pain?"

"Yes, but if you think we are done here, you never heard the rumors about why the Fire Court was the most feared," Sorin answered, lowering into a crouch before him. Mikale turned his head to look at him at the same moment Sorin's hand shot out, flaming fingers wrapping tightly around his throat and squeezing. "You touched her. You locked her up. You caged her. And then you trapped her in her head, in her dreams. You took and tortured and *broke* what is mine, and I am going to burn away every part of you that touched her."

Mikale's eyes went wide, his feet beginning to scramble against the floor as he tried to push away from Sorin.

When Sorin began with the little finger on Mikale's left hand, he didn't bother with the gag of fire. He let him scream. He relished the sound of his agony with each finger he burned to nothing. Then came hands before he moved on to far more sensitive areas.

And when he was done, when every part of the male that had touched Scarlett was either charred flesh or burned away to nothing, he shoved a deathstone dagger into Mikale's side to hold him in the space between life and death until he could come back and finish the job.

# CHAPTER 44
# TALWYN

T alwyn sat atop a brown mare next to Azrael, who was on a slightly larger black horse. She wished she could be in the sky with Jetta and the other Witches who had all left the day prior, along with Sorin, Cyrus, and Cassius, but Thorne was nowhere near ready to fly.

She'd stayed with him in the stables for the first two nights. Last night, Az had insisted she sleep in an actual bed and get a decent night's rest if she was planning to come with them to fight in the Earth Court.

The Witches were adept at healing all types of life it seemed, and the past centuries of tending to the griffins had made them experts on the beasts too. It had still taken three of them to get Thorne to a place of sure survival, and even then, once they got him moved down to the stables, one of them watched him for the next day to make sure that remained the case. Talwyn had paced in that stupid stable that smelled like shit and wet fur until Az had appeared with a stool and forced her to sit down so her still bleeding arm could be tended to.

She rotated her arm now as they sat waiting, Azrael glancing at her out of the corner of his eye.

"The Healers sent along some herbs and ointment for that," he said.

"It is fine."

"It is not, Talwyn. You need to—"

He stopped speaking abruptly, a muscle ticking in his jaw.

"Say it, Az," she said sharply.

Azrael looked around before moving his horse off to one side, and she followed. When they were far enough from the others, he said, "You do not heal as quickly, Talwyn."

She barked a humorless laugh. "I am very much aware of that fact, Prince."

"Are you?" he countered. "Because I am not so sure you are."

"What in the realm makes you say that?"

"Because if you truly understood that, I assume you would be smarter about your choices."

She glared at him, waiting for him to go on, because she knew him well enough to know he had more to say on this subject.

"You are at every disadvantage now. It is stupid to not take every advantage offered to you now," he continued. "The herbs will speed along your healing, while the ointment will make you more comfortable. I know you need to fight in the war, and you should. You are an asset with your sword and bow, but what happens when your arm is too stiff for you to lift that sword because you refused this?"

"I get it, Az," she grumbled. "The lecture can stop."

She reached down into a small saddle bag. She'd never needed to have one before. Always able to store items in a pocket realm. Azrael had needed to get all her things from there.

His hand clamped around her arm, causing her to lift her eyes back to his. He had moved his horse closer, their legs brushing against one another.

"You do not 'get it,' Talwyn," he said, his voice low. "I need you to take every advantage offered to you so that we can delay the eventual release of your Staying as long as possible. That means taking gods-damn care of yourself."

Oh.

*Oh.*

Her features softened some. "I get it, Az."

"I want every second the Fates will give us. If we can barter for more of that time by doing simple things like this, then we are damn well going to do them."

"Okay," she whispered, gently uncurling his fingers from her arm.

He helped her with the wound care before they steered their horses back into position. Not everyone had horses. It would be easier to stream bodies through the portals that were going to be created rather than having everyone on horseback. The Avonleyans, having never been there, couldn't simply Travel. Ashtine wouldn't be going with to fight, but she would be creating a portal here. Azrael would be going to create one for the Shifters, and Briar would be going to the Witches. Scarlett was just waiting on signals from the other territories that they were in position.

Their forces were tired. Many of them weren't able to go right into another battle a few days later. It wasn't ideal, but at least most of the Witches and all the Shifters would be in prime fighting condition.

She had to hand it to Scarlett. The female had taken her sweet time coming back from Avonleya, but she had returned not only with an army but also with plans. There was nothing slow about her tactics now. She moved from one plan to the next, one battle to the next, as if checking them off some sort of twisted list. The queen had so many plans and power moves, Talwyn truly wasn't sure how she managed it all.

Then again, she did know. Scarlett had figured out the one thing it had taken Talwyn far too long to realize.

Loyalty earned is far more valuable than loyalty demanded.

She looked over to where Scarlett was standing with her brother, the Avonleyan Queen, the Avonleyan Commander, and several other Avonleyan warriors. She appeared to be listening intently to something one of the warriors was saying, then she threw her head back, laughing while her brother shook his head with a half-grin.

Scarlett would Travel them when they received word from the others. Hazel and Arantxa wouldn't be there yet, but the Witches stationed along the borders were closer. By the time those leaving from the Wind Court arrived, they would be able to offer a reprieve to those in the sky if needed. It was a strategic move to keep the aerial host from tiring all at once. A small unit had also stayed behind to watch over the Citadel and Ashtine. That was the only reason Briar was coming to fight with them.

"You are sure you won't go through my portal?" Azrael asked, grip tightening on the reins he held in one hand.

"You know why that is a bad idea," she replied, eyes sweeping over the rest of the assembled forces. She knew Azrael was a seasoned enough fighter to maintain his focus, but she also knew if she were near him in her new *vulnerable* state, she would be a distraction to him. Sure he trusted her skills, but as he'd just proven with the herbs and ointment for her arm that her own wellbeing was a top concern. He didn't need that in the middle of a fight.

Azrael appeared as if he were going to say something else when a flourish of violet-tinged shadows appeared, followed almost immediately by the same of teal. The signals Scarlett had given to the Witches and Shifters.

Everything began happening at top speed after that. A Wind Portal was opened, forces streaming through. Scarlett checked in with the Fae Princes before she was gone with her small group of Avonleyans.

Talwyn steered her horse to the portal, but she looked back over her shoulder, meeting Azrael's gaze. "Meet me on the battlefield, Prince."

He held her stare a moment longer before he Traveled out. As she positioned her horse to go through the portal, she caught Ashtine's eye.

"Be brave, Talwyn," her friend said, a sad, tight smile tilting her lips.

Talwyn nodded, urging her horse forward and into the winds. Soldiers were forced out of the way of her horse, and she felt like an ass for it. But when she emerged on the other side, she forgot all about those feelings.

There were seraphs here, but not nearly as many as there had been in the Wind Court fight a few days ago. However, there were Night Children. Everywhere. They'd been hoping to beat the vampyres here. The Earth Court had been taken by surprise, though. Talwyn could see they were scrambling, trying to get people into positions. There were frantic orders being yelled, and soldiers not fully armed rushing out to meet them. But Scarlett and her Court had planned this well, having the portals appear on three different sides of the Alcazar. She had Traveled her small party in on the fourth side, effectively surrounding Tarek and his forces.

Talwyn joined the fray with her sword swinging, cutting into a vampyre and knocking him to the ground. Shirastone would be needed to keep him down, but someone else could get to him while wounded. She needed to stay atop her horse as long as possible. She didn't have the speed or strength anymore, and while she had fighting leathers on, they wouldn't be as effective without that Fae grace and fluidity she'd once possessed. Azrael had suggested heavier armor, but she didn't have time to train and learn how to move properly with it.

She managed to make her way to the outer walls of the Alcazar before a Night Child tackled her from her horse. The air was knocked from her lungs when she hit the ground hard, her back screaming at the impact, but instinct had kicked in. She had a shirastone dagger shoved into the vampyre's chest with her fangs inches from Talwyn's throat. Working to suck down air, she shoved the female off of her, getting to her feet. Her horse had run off, and she had lost one of her swords in the fall. Drawing her other from her back, she kept the dagger in hand and let decades of training take over.

All that training kept her going longer than a regular mortal would have been able to, but as the minutes of battle dragged on into hours, she knew she would need to find somewhere to take a reprieve. She knew the Alcazar as well as she knew the White Halls, so when she finally reached a side gate, she slipped in and raced for a stairwell that would take her to a parapet atop the wall. There would likely be an archer or two inside, but she could handle them and then breathe. For just a moment.

She stumbled as she climbed the steps, her boots slick with sand and blood. Somehow, she only met one soldier in the stairwell, and he was so surprised to see her, she easily sank her sword into his gut. He was falling down the stairs as she continued up. She had been right. There were two archers inside. The Fae archer she handled fairly easily, her smaller form still allowing her to dart around his more muscled body and strike from behind. The other, however, was a

Night Child, and while Talwyn was yanking her sword out of the Fae, the vampyre was sinking fangs into her throat.

She cried out, lurching backwards and slamming the Night Child into the wall behind her, but that just caused the fangs to sink in further. And holy gods, the *agony* in her being as the vampyre drank and drank. Her knees gave out first, hitting hard when they cracked against the stone floor. Her limbs were heavy, her vision going blurry. Which is why it took her so long to realize she still gripped her dagger. With the last of her strength, she struck, lodging it deep into the vampyre's skull.

He went limp against her. Talwyn didn't have the energy to push him off, slumping to the ground beneath his heavier body. Someone would find her. Azrael would find her. That's what she kept telling herself. It was the only way she kept herself sane as she lay there beneath a dead Night Child, unable to do anything.

The sounds of battle carried up to her. The clashing of swords. The pounding of feet and flapping of wings. The cries of wrath and the screams of the dying.

Then she heard Azrael's bellowed commands over it all. Yelling at *his* forces to turn their godsdamn weapons on the Night Children.

His forces. Not Tarek's.

If his warriors had recognized that he still held the royal seat and not Tarek, it would change everything. She just needed to wait for someone to find her.

She tried to free an arm to at least attempt to staunch the bleeding at her throat where the vampyre's fangs had left a jagged tear. Wiggling as much as she could, she finally worked a hand free just as the body was shoved off of her.

Thank the gods.

But it wasn't muddy brown eyes staring down at her.

They were pale green ones.

And that was dark golden skin and black hair hanging in a face she had spent countless days and nights with.

"Oh, Moonflower," Tarek sighed, his tone full of a disappointed remorse as he lowered to a crouch beside her. "This is not how things were supposed to go."

Talwyn was in too much shock to comprehend that he had

reached out and gripped her chin, tilting her head to the side to look at the wound. It wasn't until the flash of blue from the ring on his finger caught her eye that she realized he was touching her, but it wasn't as if she could do anything about it.

Tarek clucked his tongue. "You could have had everything, and now you are...this." The disdain was clear as his eyes dragged over her. "When I heard you had become as powerless as a mortal, I hadn't believed it. Then I saw you fighting from where I watched on a balcony. Still cutting down enemies with the same viciousness you always had, but there was no wind or earth magic. No bolts of energy or shifting to a wolf. So foolish. No heir left behind. Even if I left you alive, you couldn't produce one now anyway. Azrael cannot have you and leave his Court without an heir. Such an utter waste. The female I knew would have never sacrificed her power, her birthright. You were a *queen*, Talwyn. Now you will die as nothing."

And it made sense. That this was how she would ultimately die. That Tarek would be the one to do it after he was the one who had sufficiently blinded her to everything that should have mattered. That she would die alone and unable to fight back. She'd like to think she could take Tarek out with her, but she knew she couldn't.

"You have nothing to say before your death?" Tarek asked, drawing a dagger from a sheath at his belt.

"Did you know?" she rasped out, unsure why she needed to know the answer to this question so badly.

Tarek paused, his head tilting a little at the question. "Did I know what?"

"That Azrael was my twin flame?"

"Oh, that." He smiled softly, reaching out to brush hair from her face. "You feeling the stirrings of that bond with him is what helped me convince you it was me." She winced at his touch, and he gave her a pitying frown. "You did love me at one point, Talwyn. We did share that, even if it wasn't a twin flame bond."

"You stole it from me," she said in a harsh whisper. Tears welled in her eyes, because while she knew she should feel the most guilt over turning against her people or being so godsdamn foolish to believe she was owed some type of revenge, her greatest regret in this life was that she had failed Azrael so completely by choosing Tarek over him.

"I stole nothing. You gave it willingly," Tarek replied, turning the dagger idly in his hand. "Eager and focused on what you wanted, it wasn't all that difficult. It took time, of course. Decades of tenacity. But in the end..." He shrugged. "It would have been worth it if you hadn't lost sight of what was yours for the taking."

"You will not survive this war," she said, forcing the tears not to fall. She wouldn't give him that satisfaction. "Scarlett will win, and you will be in the After before the end of it."

"We shall see," he said, a half-grin tilting on his lips.

He raised the dagger, and Talwyn squeezed her eyes shut. Peaceful things are probably what she should have been filling her thoughts with, but all she could think about was failing Azrael yet again. Of failing the people once entrusted to her. Of abandoning a griffin after she'd demanded he didn't do the exact same thing to her.

But a strangled, gasping sound had her eyes snapping open before the blade touched her skin.

There were vines around Tarek's throat, thick and full of thorns. Blood was dripping down his neck where they dug into his skin. The ground was vibrating beneath her, and with the vampyre body off of her, she was able to push onto her elbows.

To find Azrael.

There was nothing but feral rage on the Earth Prince's face as he stalked into the small lookout room. Tarek scrambled for his magic, but Azrael was stronger, more powerful. Always had been. It was why the Ordos family had been overthrown by the Luans. It was why Tarek had come up with this elaborate scheme in the first place.

Two sharp wooden stakes appeared in Azrael's hands. He hadn't even looked at her yet, the entirety of his focus on the male who had fallen forward onto his knees. Tarek's hands were bloody and ripped to shreds as he clawed at the vines around his throat. There were slices on his face and neck where he'd tried to cut them away with the dagger in his hand. When he saw Azrael advancing, something flickered in his eyes. So much malice shone in them, and as if understanding he would not survive this, he spun.

And plunged the dagger deep into her torso, right below her ribs.

Azrael's roar of fury was muffled as she collapsed back down, a hand moving too slowly to her side.

Tarek was ripped away from her, and then he was hanging on the wall with two stakes shoved through his chest, his feet dangling off the ground. Azrael left him there, dropping down beside her, leaves swirling away nearby carrying a message off to someone. A hand slipped beneath her head, lifting it up.

"Talwyn," he said in a low command. "Keep your eyes open. Do you understand?"

But she'd lost too much blood between the fighting, the Night Child, and now the stab wound. She could feel his magic wrapping around her, trying to hold her together.

"Az," she whispered.

"No," he said sharply. No room for argument. Just like always. "You deserve to live, Talwyn. You *will* live."

She lifted a shaky hand, laying it atop the one pressed to her side. "I am sorry I did not love you better."

"You have decades to make it up to me," he said, his hand sliding around her head to smooth back her hair. "Help is coming."

She didn't want one of the last things she said to him to be how there was no helping her. Not anymore. So instead she said, "I'll meet you on a battlefield beyond the Veil, Az."

Darkness closed in around her as breathing became a little harder. There were these sharp stabbing pains in her chest with each inhale, and her exhales felt murky and stilted. Like the air couldn't get all the way out.

But then the darkness receded.

Not darkness.

Shadows.

Scarlett stood before her, a hand on Azrael's shoulder as she dropped down beside him.

That was good. That his queen had come to be with him when he faced this. That he wouldn't be alone.

Scarlett looked down at her. A queen with every right to hate her with all that she was. A descendant of the god of endings and a goddess of her own making.

She held up a hand, darkness crackling with embers of white. There was blood smeared across her face and hands. Her spirit sword was sheathed down her back. Her lips were moving, but Talwyn couldn't hear her. That was fine. She wanted the last voice she heard to be Azrael's.

Az was nodding, and then Scarlett's silvery, glowing gaze connected with Talwyn's. Her features were softer than Talwyn had ever seen them as she said, "You've given enough, Talwyn."

Darkness engulfed her, but it wasn't the darkness of the After. Or maybe it was. She really had no way of knowing in the chaos that danced around her. A sudden flare of bright white light had her slamming her eyes shut, and when she blinked them open, Azrael was hovering over her.

"Talwyn?" There was strained hope in his voice that she had never heard before. Fingertips brushed along her cheekbone. "Say something."

"If you followed me to the After, I am going to kill you," she croaked.

Azrael huffed a breath of laughter, bringing his brow to hers. His eyes fell closed, and this close, she realized there were tear tracks cutting through the grime on his face. She lifted a hand to cup his cheek, but froze when she saw the black Mark on the back of her hand.

Her right hand.

Directly in the center. No bigger than a coin.

"What is this?" she demanded, trying to push herself up.

"Go slow," Azrael ordered, helping her into a sitting position.

Scarlett was still here, standing back and giving them this moment.

"What is this?" Talwyn repeated, turning her head to look at Azrael's hand, where a matching Mark stood out against his brown skin.

"It is not a twin flame Mark," Scarlett said. "Not even a goddess can restore that. But it is a binding Mark of a sort. I didn't know if it would work. I sort of had to combine some elements from other Marks to make this one, but..." Her eyes darted to Azrael. "He wanted to risk it."

"What is the cost?" Talwyn demanded.

Scarlett gave her a small, soft smile. "It binds your lives together, Talwyn."

"No," she said, shaking her head. "Absolutely not. His life does not get cut short because of me. No."

"It was a cost I am willing to pay, Talwyn," Azrael said, trying to guide her face to his.

"No," she cried again. "No, no, no. This is not—"

"I may have taken some liberties with the creation of this particular Mark," Scarlett cut in, and they both turned back to her. She was studying Tarek's corpse as if it were a fine piece of art as she continued. "It binds *your* life to his, Talwyn. As long as Azrael lives, you cannot die."

"A mortal body cannot survive for decades longer than it should," Talwyn argued.

"Which is why your Staying will not fade. I ensured it," Scarlett answered.

"How?" Azrael demanded, his mouth slack in as much shock as Talwyn was feeling.

Scarlett simply shrugged, reaching up and slipping the ring from Tarek's finger before his body went up in white flames. "I have enough Chaos to share a spark. It will not give her magic, and it will not restore any of her other gifts. That sacrifice must remain for Sorin's sake, but it will allow her to maintain her Staying. A gift of thanks. To both of you. For what you sacrificed and lost in all of this."

Scarlett was gone in the next blink, and Talwyn found herself crushed in Azrael's embrace against his hard chest. She was numb with shock, nearly limp against him.

He tilted her chin up to look down into her eyes. "Say something, Talwyn."

"I love you, Az."

It was the first time she'd said those words to him. She wished that wasn't the case. She wished he'd heard them from her so many times, he could never doubt the truth behind them.

She'd make sure he knew now. For the rest of their years together.

His mouth crashed into hers, somehow intense and calming all at once. Just as he had always been for her.

And as she clung to him, she remembered how to dream.

# CHAPTER 45
# CYRUS

"This had better be the last time I am digging through piles of rock and body parts," Cyrus muttered, tossing aside another chunk of stone. He couldn't believe he actually wished Luan was here to take care of this for them.

"In theory, if this works, it should be," Cassius answered, chucking his own piece of debris to the side.

They had been beneath the Fellowship for an hour now, Hazel having used some enchantment to guide her to where this last ring supposedly was. At least the Sorceress had been right about that. It was here. If this worked anyway.

"So if we find it here, then what?" Cyrus asked.

"It is here," Hazel said from where she was hauling away as much rubble as they were. "Once found, it will be up to the queen what she desires to do with it."

"Destroy it," Cassius said, digging out another large piece of debris. He hadn't said much to his mother. He'd be cordial and polite because that's who Cassius was, but he only spoke to her when needed. And the High Witch was respectful of that, even if Cyrus did catch her eyes flicking to her son every so often.

"I will help her do so if that is her wish," Hazel answered.

"Is there a reason she wouldn't want to destroy it?" Cyrus asked.

"All options should be evaluated when dealing with something of such great power," Hazel replied. "The portal keys were made so that such magic would not be taken from existence."

"But there are more of them," Cassius interrupted. "Destroying one wouldn't be the end of the world."

"Perhaps not this one," Hazel said.

Cassius and Cyrus both paused to look at her.

"Would it?" Cass asked. "Affect other worlds?"

"Everything we do has an effect somewhere down the line," she answered. "A seemingly innocent action can change the course of history, for good or bad. I would imagine destroying something of great power will have a great impact."

Cassius had stopped working, staring at his mother. Cyrus continued to haul away rock, trying to do so unnoticed to give them… whatever this was turning into.

"If Scarlett does not destroy it, it leaves an opening for Achaz to come to this world," Cassius argued.

"Which is why it will be up to the queen to weigh the costs and make a choice," Hazel answered.

"But if you had knowledge of those potential costs, you would share them. Right?" Cassius pushed.

"I just did."

Cyrus rolled a large hunk of rock out of the way, finally creating an opening big enough for them to squeeze through. He hated to interrupt this sort-of bonding moment, but he also really wanted to get the fuck out of here. He had no doubt Alaric knew they were here. Nuri had known, which meant Alaric had. The Maraan Prince was likely waiting for them to find the ring for him, just like he'd waited for Scarlett to find the Avonleyan Keys.

"I think we can get in now," Cyrus said, not waiting for them as he squeezed through the gap. He made it. Hazel had no problem. Cassius was a little broader than he was, but he made it through, too. Barely. But once Cassius was inside and looking around the room, his face paled a little.

"What's wrong?" Cyrus asked. Hazel was already moving deeper into the room, but she paused and turned at the question.

Cassius cleared his throat, back straightening some. "Nothing.

This was one of the Fellowship's rooms for…extracting information. With everything in ruin, I didn't realize this was the room we were digging into."

"You spent a lot of time in here?" Hazel asked, studying her son intensely.

Cassius dragged a hand through his hair. "You could say that."

But Cyrus was putting two and two together, sifting through the one memory he had of navigating these passages and the few things Scarlett and Cass had shared about their upbringing. "You weren't always the one doing the extracting in this room, were you?"

"No," Cassius answered, seeming to shake off the memories that had surged.

"When was the last time you were in this room, Cassius?" Hazel asked.

"Does that really matter right now?" Cass retorted.

"It does," Hazel replied. "If this is the room where you received the injuries I healed, it would be why the ring is here. Likely where your blood was spilled."

"How is that possible?" Cassius asked.

"The enchantment used is drawn to its creator. Or, in this case, the ancestor of its creator."

"Then how did Alaric and his people miss it during their searching?" Cyrus asked.

Cassius still hadn't moved further into the room, and Cyrus wanted to tell him to go back out. That he didn't need to be in here, reliving memories. Some memories are better left buried deep. He knew that better than anyone.

"Descendants of the Witch Goddesses have more power," Hazel said. "Our wards are stronger. Our enchantments are more complex." She crouched down, waving a hand over a section of the floor. The dirt swirled away, revealing blood-stained stone. "We have a few enhanced abilities we can tap into from time-to-time."

She beckoned Cassius closer, and he moved to her side, lowering stiffly down beside her. Hazel held up her hand, nodding at him to follow her instruction, and Cyrus watched as the High Witch guided Cass through the same movement she had just used. She reached over, making subtle adjustments to his fingers, tilting his palm a little to the left. When he waved his hand over the ground, the dirt didn't swirl like it had for Hazel, but it did shift some, as if the floor vibrated beneath it.

"Good," Hazel said with a nod. "With your mixed bloodline, it will take more concentration, but in time, you will become proficient."

Cyrus silently came up behind them, studying the red stained floor they'd uncovered. "Was that little lesson supposed to do anything? Because I don't see a ring anywhere."

He'd become used to having Hazel around at times. He'd been in the same room with her for days when Cassius had been healing. They'd stayed at her home to kill time before they'd gone to collect Talwyn. The cool glare the High Witch leveled him with reminded him exactly who she was, and he quickly dipped his chin. "My apologies, my Lady."

"The enchantment that was done would have hidden the object if lost. The object would have tried to get back to the Witch who performed the spell. As such, it is here," Hazel said.

"Wait," Cassius cut in. "Scarlett always said the Avonleyan keys were always trying to find their way home."

Hazel nodded, an almost smile forming. "Yes. This is the same concept. Magic always has its own agenda, guided by Chaos and Fate. That is why you are trained to control it rather than letting it control you."

She pulled a vial from the pocket of her witchsuit. Uncorking it, she poured the clear potion inside atop the blood. Cyrus recognized the layout now. Knew this was where Cassius had been lying in a pool of his own blood. Where Scarlett had been chained just out of reach. Where Cyrus himself had said Cass wouldn't make it.

The blood appeared to fizz for a few seconds before a red bubble rose up. Cyrus's lip curled in disgust. He knew it was blood magic and all, but that was taking it too far. Hazel reached her fingers inside, and when she pulled them back, she indeed held a Semiria ring. Eline's sapphire ring had been a crest with a golden owl above a flame, and Talwyn's ring had been an emerald with a silver wolf howling to the moon. This ring, however, was a blood red ruby with an obsidian snake coiled around a sun.

Hazel held it out to Cassius, dropping it into his open palm when he extended it to her. Cass picked up the ring, pushing back to his feet while he studied it. "This is what the Sorceress wants so badly?" he murmured.

Cyrus took it from him and slipped it into his pocket. "I guess so. Scarlett and I are working on it."

Cassius sent him a dry look. "That never bodes well for anyone."

Cyrus flipped him off before turning to the High Witch. "Any chance Cass can Travel us out? It's not like we ever plan to come back here, so it doesn't matter if we set off some wards."

"I can hold them open long enough for Cassius to Travel us out," Hazel agreed.

"Great," Cyrus said, intertwining his fingers with Cass's. "Let's do that."

It took a moment for Hazel to signal there was a tear in the wards, but the moment she did, Cyrus blinked.

And he was home.

He was godsdamn *home*.

They'd come to Solembra after getting the ring from Mikale, but after being gone for so long? Not knowing if he'd even make it back? He breathed it in like he had the first time. The mountains. The river.

No fucking sea.

Eliza appeared a few moments later, no doubt alerted by the wards that newcomers had just appeared inside the Palace. They'd had their reunion. He was certain Eliza had even cried, though she would deny it until her last breath.

As she approached him now with Razik at her side, Cyrus dropped to a knee, bowing his head. "Princess," he intoned with dramatic reverence.

"For fuck's sake," she muttered. "I cannot believe I actually missed you."

"Where is the other royal pain in the ass?" Cyrus asked, getting back to his feet and stretching his arms over his head.

"They should be back soon. A group of them went to Avonleya. Rayner wanted to check in on Tula, and Cethin and Kailia needed to check on some matters of their own," Eliza answered, folding her arms across her chest. "Did you get it?"

"Yep," Cyrus answered, taking the ring from his pocket and

tossing it to her. She caught it with one hand, holding it up to look at it in the light.

"To think Eliné had a piece of a portal key all this time," she murmured.

"To think *Talwyn* had a piece of a portal key all this time," Cyrus said.

They'd been informed what Scarlett had done for the Earth Prince and Talwyn after the Earth Court battle two days ago. It was odd to look back and think about how much had changed in a year. That they were all on the same side. That Scarlett had *saved* Talwyn after everything.

Fuck, after everything Scarlett had been through in her short life, they were lucky she didn't just burn their world to nothing at this point. He didn't think he would blame her if she had.

Her ringing laughter pulled him from his thoughts as the main doors opened behind them and a group strolled in. Cethin, Kailia, and Tybalt. Rayner and Sorin. And there was Scarlett, hand-in-hand with Tula while the child chattered on about something or other.

"You brought Tula back?" Eliza asked, her brow arching.

"She will be just as safe here as she would be across the Edria," Rayner answered, tracking the child as she ran full speed to look at the Tana River. "Plus, I am pretty sure she would have found her own way back if I had left her behind again. This was the safer option."

"Did you bring any of the other children back?" Cyrus asked.

"No," Scarlett answered. "Only because it's something we could not oversee right now. We need to get to Callan and figure out this life-binding thing. That is it?"

She took the ring from Eliza, and the obsidian crest seemed to pulse.

"What was that?" Cassius asked.

"The portal key. Talwyn's ring did the same thing when I took it off Tarek's corpse," Scarlett answered. She looked at Hazel. "We can do this now?"

"Wait," Cassius interjected, and Scarlett tilted her head in question. He glanced at his mother. "Hazel said there are some things we need to consider before destroying the portal key."

Sorin had come to stand beside Scarlett, and he asked, "Such as?"

"Just that this could have repercussions we are unaware of. We might not know what they are right away," Cass answered.

"That can be said about every move we make," Scarlett argued. "The mortal kings are bound to Maraan Lords because we took down wards without knowing the full extent of those actions. We will face them like we do everything else."

"The High Witch makes a good argument," Tybalt said, and Hazel's violet eyes flicked to him, holding his stare for a moment.

Cyrus had not seen Hazel and Tybalt interact much. If they'd had any conversation or discussion of their past, he had not been around for it. The little he had seen them converse was simple, polite conversation. Then again, polite conversation was odd for a Witch, so maybe they had spoken at some point.

"You think we should leave a way into this world?" Scarlett asked.

"If you have the portal key, what difference would it make?" Cethin countered.

"Me," Cyrus said quietly. "I'm the difference. We have to give the ring to Gehenna, or my bargain isn't fulfilled."

Everyone turned to him, and Cassius was reaching for his hand.

"When the portal key is out of the ring though," Sorin said thoughtfully. "We can still give the Sorceress the ring. Would we need to destroy the portal key?"

"Portal keys are like the mirror gates," Razik said. "At least, that's what my research has led me to believe. They can be connected in a way. Drawn to each other."

"Someone could essentially use a portal key to activate another portal key?" Scarlett asked, her nose scrunching.

"It would stand to reason that items keyed to the same lock would call to each other," Razik answered with a shrug.

Scarlett made a disgusted noise. "Do not speak to me of locks."

"I do not know why we are debating this," Eliza said. "We destroy any foothold Achaz could have into the realm."

Spoken like a true war general.

"I agree," said Cethin. "We are doing all of this to keep Achaz out and protect the realm. Scarlett will be the guardian of the mirror gates. The only way in or out. Leaving a potential crack in that defense is foolish."

"So it is settled, then?" Scarlett asked, looking around at everyone. "Cass?"

Cassius nodded. "It just seemed like something that should be discussed."

"Then let's take care of it," Scarlett said. "What do we need to do?"

"We should be outside," Hazel said, speaking for the first time since they had arrived back at the Fiera Palace. "The power needed to destroy it will be great."

They all filed out to the back gardens, Rayner staying behind with Tula. Sorin led them to a large clearing. "Will this do?"

Hazel and Tybalt were at the back of the group, speaking so low Cyrus couldn't even hear them with his Fae hearing. But then there was a swirl of black flames, and Tybalt was pulling a book from a pocket realm. It was worn and weathered, the cover black and faded. Hazel took it from him, flipping it open to a page already marked, and Cyrus realized it was her spell book. She ran a finger down the page, eyes moving as she skimmed it before she snapped it shut once more.

"I can pull the fragments from the rings and reform the key," the High Witch said, moving forward. "But you should destroy it immediately. The realms will sense it has been reforged. If there is anything connected to it, it will seek it out."

"Understood," Scarlett answered, pulling the other two rings from a pocket realm of her own.

Hazel stopped in front of Cyrus and Cassius, her violet eyes seeming to search for something. Then she held out the spell book to Cass. "Hold this for me."

Cassius took it without a word, turning it over in his hands as Hazel made her way over to stand by Scarlett in the center of the clearing.

"You have enough control to keep the others safe?" Hazel demanded in her usual sharp tone as she pushed back the sleeves of her witchsuit.

"Yes," Scarlett answered. "But they are prepared to Travel out if necessary."

Hazel nodded, and Scarlett dropped the three keys into her palm.

Cyrus watched as the High Witch drew an upside-down triangle in the dirt, placing one ring at each point. Then she drew a small knife from her belt, slicing her palm and holding it out to drip into the center of the triangle. She began chanting a language Cyrus didn't know, but a moment later, the rings rose into the air until they hovered nearly eye level with the Witch before a light sprang from each one, meeting in the center.

Scarlett had started pacing back and forth, holding up her hand to stay Sorin, who had clearly expressed concern down their bond. Cethin and Kailia were watching with interest, while Eliza and Razik had guarded looks, as if waiting for something to go wrong. Tybalt, however, was watching Hazel.

A white object of some sort was taking form where the lights were merging. Cyrus couldn't make out the shape, and he'd never get the chance to as Hazel gritted out, "Now, Scarlett."

Darkness exploded out of her, but she managed to keep it contained. Cyrus suddenly realized why she'd been pacing. The Chaos in her was being drawn to the magic in the portal key, being drawn to its own kind. Shadows and white embers swirled so thickly that he couldn't see the portal key, the High Witch, or Scarlett, and Cassius was clutching at his arm, dragging him back from the storm of Chaos before them.

But Scarlett was right. She did have control over it. It did not spread or strike out at any of them, but that was because it was drawn to the portal key more. Either way, when the darkness finally dissipated after several minutes, there was no portal key in the center of the triangle. The rings were on the ground a few feet away, as if tossed to the side. The precious gems were cracked and dull. Scarlett was on her knees, chest heaving, and Sorin was rushing forward, dropping down beside her at the same time he was slicing across the Source Mark on his forearm.

And the High Witch was...gone.

"Hazel?" Cassius's voice was a confused rasp as he looked around.

Scarlett's head snapped up, eyes looking around frantically. "No," she said, shaking her head and trying to shove off Sorin. She tried to stand, but her legs buckled, sending her back to her knees. Sorin caught her, and she struggled against him some more. "I didn't... I had control over it. I kept it away from her." Her eyes went to Cassius, tears shining in them. "I didn't, Cass. I swear it."

Cassius wasn't saying anything. He was just staring at the spot the High Witch had been standing.

"You did not kill her, Scarlett," came Tybalt's voice as he strode forward. He stopped between Cassius and Scarlett, looking between them. "Hazel's mother was relatively young for a Witch when she Faded. Hazel assumed the role of High Witch when she was scarcely a few centuries old. Her mother Faded so young because that was the cost of separating the portal key. It took so much of her power, she did not have enough left to maintain her Staying. The cost to put the portal key back together took even more power."

"Are you…" Cassius took a step forward, his mother's spell book held limply at his side. "Are you saying she…"

Cyrus was reaching for him, but he shrugged him off, taking another step towards Tybalt.

With a sympathetic look, Tybalt said, "She Faded, Cassius. I am sorry."

"No," Cassius said, shaking his head. A hand came up, raking through his shaggy strands. "She can't just Fade away. Just be gone like that."

"That is how Fading happens," Sorin said gently from where he was holding Scarlett to his chest. She was silently crying, tears streaming down her face. "Beatrix Faded while I was embracing her."

"Cass—" Scarlett said, a sob escaping. "Cassius, I am sorry. I didn't know. We didn't know."

"She knew," Cassius exclaimed in a harsh whisper. "She knew, didn't she?"

His father looked like he wanted to reach for him, but he didn't. "The Witches are very cautious about how they interfere with fate. They understand that changing one thing can cause a ripple effect—"

Cyrus sensed it a moment before it happened, and he lurched forward, clamping onto Cassius's wrist as he Traveled from the gardens. He hadn't gone far. Only back to Cyrus's rooms inside the palace, likely because he didn't really know the place well enough yet to go anywhere else.

He stood there. Still in the center of the room. Staring at nothing.

"Cass," Cyrus said tentatively, still holding his wrist. He reached up, cupping his jaw and guiding his face to his own. Cassius seemed to look right through him. "Cassius, I need you to say something. Tell me what you need."

"Say something?" Cassius repeated, his voice a harsh hiss. "What is there to say? She abandoned me to the mortal lands. It should be no surprise that she abandoned me again."

Cyrus remained silent, letting him get this out. Nothing he said right now would change anything.

Cassius jerked his arm out of Cyrus's grip, but he didn't move, didn't go anywhere. "She could have said something."

"I know, Cass."

"But she didn't. She didn't say a fucking thing. She just..." He lifted his other hand to drag through his hair, but the spell book was still in it. "She just handed me this. *This.*"

He held it up before throwing it across the room, and Cyrus winced. That spell book was old. As old as Gehenna's, if he had to guess.

The book hit the floor with a thud, but something had fallen out during the turmoil, fluttering to Cassius's feet. An envelope with his name scrawled across it in tight, elegant handwriting.

Cassius saw it at the same time Cyrus did, bending to retrieve it. His hands were shaking as he stared at it.

"You do not have to read it now, Cass," Cyrus said after a moment. "You do not have to read it ever if you do not want to."

Cassius was silent for another long moment before he said, "Why do I care, Cyrus? I spent my entire life without a mother. A father. Why do I care that she is gone when she was never there to begin with?"

"Cass," Cyrus sighed. He reached out and clasped the back of his neck, pulling him into his chest and wrapping his other arm around him. "She was still your mother, even if you only knew her for a short time. Maybe that shouldn't matter, but it does. It's more than her. It's everything that might have been. It's unanswered questions. It's something you were still trying to decide if you wanted, but now the choice has been made for you."

Cyrus got him to move to the sofa where he kept an arm around him, Cass leaning into him and staring sightlessly out a nearby window. Cyrus let him be with his thoughts, knowing he'd speak when he was ready.

It didn't take as long as he'd thought it would before Cass said, "I want to read it."

"All right," Cyrus answered, reaching for the envelope he'd set on the side table. "Do you want me to go or—"

"I never want you to go," Cass murmured, taking the envelope from him and breaking the wax seal. To his credit, his fingers only shook a little as he unfolded the paper inside, and Cyrus read over his shoulder.

Cassius—

I do not know if you will ever read these words. I may have given you life, but I do not fault you for not bestowing me the honor of calling me 'mother.' I imagine my actions this day have only increased that disdain.

There is a Rite among the Witches. It is not known outside our bloodline. We are secretive and untrustworthy by nature. When a Witch has her first bleed, she is sent to see the Oracle in her land. The Oracles have always had the purest relationship with Fate, which is why she gifts them glimpses of what could be. But those glimpses are just that. What could be. The Oracle told me I would live to see the world burn and power reborn, and that I would have a hand in it all.

It is also a Rite to go see the Oracle when a Witch learns she is carrying a child. I learned that day that the child I carried had the potential to save the world or bring it to ruin, but if it stayed among our own, the child would only know death.

When you were born, Eliné took you. I went to the

Oracle within hours of bringing you into the world. You were gone, and my soul was empty. That is when she told me that one day one would come who would know you. On that day, you could return. I could see you again, but the time would be brief.

Tempting Fate is often a slippery slope. We hear one thing and assume, painting a picture with our limited knowledge. So many have lost hours, days, years trying to figure out Fate, but in the end, her secrets are never revealed. The smallest action can cause the largest shift, and everything changes. The world changes. Fate changes.

The choice to save you was easy. The choice to leave you behind was agony. The only way I survived was by letting Eliné hide you, by having no knowledge of where you called home. If I had known where you were, I would have come for you. I came so close so many nights. I could have done it. I could have found an enchantment to find you, so I forced Arantxa to charm my spell book. I could not retrieve it until the day of my Fading. To pass it on to you.

You cannot rule the Witch Kingdoms. Only a female can do so. The title will pass to my niece and your cousin. It is for the best. Our ways are cruel and unforgivable. Everything you are not. Although perhaps a young queen and her sisters will free more than just one kingdom.

I have seen the world set on fire. I have seen power reborn. And you, my son? You have saved the world. If I had not let you go, you would have never met Scarlett at such a young age to form the bond you have. You saved her, Cassius. Not her mother. Not her *brother. Not her twin flame. She would not have survived these years if you had not been there. You are everything I am not, and because of that, you saved the world. Because if I could have, I would have come for you. I would have tempted Fate and let the world fall to ruin.*

*I can Fade knowing you have found love and family. That you know more than heartache and abandonment. Live well, Cassius.*

*But know that I would have come for you.*

She did not sign it, and when Cass was ready, they climbed into bed.

Cyrus wrapped an arm around his waist, tugging him back against his chest, and whispered, "You break, and we clean it up together, Cass."

Cyrus held him close all through the night.

When he woke the next morning, Cassius was still sleeping, and Scarlett was there, curled against Cassius's chest. She wasn't sleeping, though. Her eyes were red-rimmed and swollen, but there was a hardness there. A glint that told him she needed to work out some aggression. Or stab something.

With his arm still curled around Cassius's waist from behind, he lifted his head looking for Sorin. He wasn't there, but the movement stirred Cassius awake.

"Seastar?" he murmured, bringing a hand up to rub at his face.

"I just...needed to be with you," she whispered. "I'm sorry, Cassius."

"Shh," Cass soothed, pulling her into his chest.

"I am supposed to be comforting you," she cried softly.

"We comfort each other, Scarlett. Nothing has changed."

Cyrus pressed a quick kiss into Cass's neck before he eased from the bed and headed to his bathing room. When he reemerged, the two were murmuring softly to each other. Cassius wiped at her tears before she hugged him tightly once more, and Cyrus realized the High Witch was right. Cassius had saved her.

But she had saved him too.

"You two want some breakfast?" he asked, leaning against the doorjamb and crossing his arms.

Scarlett pushed to a sitting position, settling her silver gaze on him. "Actually, there is breakfast waiting. Ashtine and Briar are here." She glanced down at Cassius. "We need to go see the Sorceress. If you're not up for going—"

"I'm going," Cass said, throwing back the blankets. Cyrus moved out of the way as Cass went into the bathing room, shutting the door behind him.

"How is he?" Scarlett asked, worrying her bottom lip.

Cyrus shrugged. "Like one would suspect, I suppose."

She nodded, climbing off the bed and stretching her back. "Are you ready for this?"

"More than ready. You think it will really work?"

She smiled that wicked thing that made him wonder just how much of Arius's traits had passed to her. "She will beg by the end."

Cyrus strolled down the stairs to the Sorceress's area of the prison. His hands were in his pockets, and he toyed with the Semiria ring, running a finger along the edges of the ruby. This was so godsdamn risky.

He took a deep breath as he neared the bottom of the stairs, sweat already beading on the back of his neck. She hadn't trapped him in a memory lately which meant she was likely low on his blood. She wouldn't let herself run out of it. It was too much leverage.

Forcing himself to keep his steps slow and casual, he sauntered into the passage outside her cell, meeting eyes of bright violet.

Her head tilted, that lank black hair shifting over a shoulder. "Fae of Fire."

"Gehenna."

She clucked her tongue. "I have missed your company, so I will let that be this time."

"How generous of you." He fidgeted with the items in his pocket as he said, "I have something for you."

Her hands curled around the bars in eagerness as she pressed her face to them. "What is it?"

He withdrew a piece of paper folded into fourths and held it up.

Her face screwed up in disgust. "What do I want with that?"

"It's something to remember me by."

"I will not forget you, Pretty Fire Fae. Your demons taste divine."

"That is disturbing," he muttered, slipping the folded paper back into his pocket. Then he shrugged, "All right."

"Did you bring me blood?"

"I think I will be keeping the rest of that."

Her eyes narrowed, irritation beginning to flicker there. "We have a bargain."

"Really, Gehenna, you should be more specific with your bargains," Cyrus said. "A sacrifice of betrayal?"

The Sorceress watched him, irritation shifting to amusement. "Do you think you can get out of this, pretty Fire Fae?"

"Wouldn't dream of it, Gehenna."

Her lips pursed. "You know better than to call me that. Do not do it again."

"Ah, but as of this moment, my bargain with you is fulfilled."

"Then where is my spell book?" she hissed. "Where is my ring?"

"Right here," Cyrus said, slipping it from his pocket and holding it up. "Sacrifices were made for this, you know. People died."

"But you did not," the Sorceress said, eyes fixed on the ring. Then they snapped back to his. "And my spell book?"

"Delivered to you as promised," purred a voice of darkness as Scarlett stepped into view, the spell book in her hand.

Gehenna straightened, her nostrils flaring. She took a step back from the bars. "You smell like...stars and deceit."

"You would know all about that, wouldn't you?" Scarlett said, beginning to slowly flip through the pages of the spell book.

"I do not deceive," the Sorceress said in outrage. "I make bargains. It is no folly of mine if one does not understand the terms when the bargain is made."

"Agreed," Scarlett said, snapping the book shut. "Now, since your business with Cyrus is completed—"

"It is not!" she sputtered, hands gripping the bars once more. "I do not have my spell book or my ring!"

Scarlett waved her off. "That is between you and Cyrus. I am here to make a bargain of my own."

That had the Sorceress shifting to face the queen fully. "Unless you can offer me a way out of this cell, I am not interested in a bargain with you or anyone else."

"But that is exactly what I can offer you."

Back to the bars, her face pressed against them, feet braced against the bottom. "You lie, Daughter of Saylah. You are not Fae. Only a Fae Queen can free me."

"I have one of those."

"*Lies*," she hissed.

Scarlett shrugged. "If you do not wish to step outside that cell, then I will take my leave and let you two finish up."

She took one step towards the stairs before Gehenna shouted, "Wait!" When Scarlett glanced back, she said, "If I were to believe you, what would be the cost?"

"I need to know how to free someone of a Blood Bond. According to this book, you know how to do so," Scarlett answered.

"A Blood Bond?" Gehenna repeated. "Is that all?"

"Would you like more terms?"

"No!" the Sorceress snapped, but Cyrus recognized that glint in her eyes. He'd spent enough time with her to know that the excitement in her was a twisted sort. The sort that said she believed she had won something. "State the bargain."

"I will let you out of that cell, and you will clarify how to free someone of a Blood Bond," Scarlett said. "Do we have an accord?"

"It is an accord," the Sorceress said in a quiet purr.

Scarlett lifted her tunic a moment later, and Cyrus glimpsed the red Mark in the shape of a raindrop above her hip. It was probably a good thing Sorin had stayed at the prison entrance with Briar and Cassius. He would likely go feral seeing that on her skin. It wouldn't stay there for long if things went according to plan.

"Let me out," the Sorceress demanded.

"Relax," Scarlett scoffed, lowering her tunic. "You've been in there for centuries. Another few minutes won't kill you. Tell me how to free someone of a Blood Bond."

"The order of the bargain stated you let me out first," the Sorceress sang, beginning to drag her fingers along the bars. "It is no folly of mine if you do not understand how these things work."

Sighing dramatically, Scarlett said, "Fine."

And a few moments later, Ashtine stepped into view.

The Sorceress's gaze immediately went to her rounded belly, a hunger shining there that had Cyrus shifting in front of the Fae Queen.

For that's what she was now. The Courts had come together and pledged loyalty to her and Briar, now Fae King of the Courts. It was temporary. Until the babes were in a position to take the thrones, because those babes would be the most powerful Fae in the realm. Some of the most powerful Fae in all the realms if what Saylah had said was true.

"Princess of Wind. Fae Queen of the Courts," Gehenna sang, fingers clinking against the bars once more. Then she stopped. "Temptress of the Fates and Breaker of Canons."

"She is here to let you out, nothing more," Scarlett said. "If you make a single move against her, it will be the last thing you do."

Gehenna tipped her head back and laughed. "You cannot kill me."

Scarlett only smiled at her.

"Yes, yes. I understand," the Sorceress finally said. "Let me out."

Scarlett nodded to Ashtine, and the Fae Queen extended her hand so Scarlett could slice a thin line along her palm. Scarlett forced the Sorceress to retreat to the back of her cell before Ashtine placed her bleeding palm on the door, the magic around it crackling and flaring before it slowly swung open with a high-pitched squeak.

Cyrus was already tucking Ashtine behind him, shielding her from where Scarlett stood a few feet in front of the door as the Sorceress stepped from the cell.

One step.

Two.

Three.

"That is far enough," Scarlett said. "Your end of the bargain."

The smile that filled the Sorceress's face was as wicked as Scarlett's when she said, "Only Fate can free someone of a Blood Bond."

"Yes, I read that in your little book." Scarlett held the spell book up as she spoke. But when the Sorceress reached for it, Scarlett held it from her reach. "The bargain was that you would *clarify* what I already know."

"That is simple enough," Gehenna answered, her head tilting. "You must speak Fate's name."

"The Fates have a name?" Scarlett asked.

"Of course the Fates have names," Gehenna said sharply. "But you must speak *her* name."

"Where do I find it?"

"It is lost among the stars."

Scarlett stilled before she said, "I am well acquainted with the stars."

"Our bargain is complete," Gehenna snapped, her violet eyes sliding to Ashtine as she stepped around Scarlett. "Tell me, Queen of the Fae, would you make a bargain to protect those in your womb?"

"Their protection is already ensured," Ashtine replied calmly, holding the Sorceress's stare.

"And when the balance must be corrected? Who will protect them then?" Gehenna countered, eyes dipping to Ashtine's belly. "I could keep them safe. All that power—"

"Speak one more word of my children, and you will know death at my hand instead of confinement, Gehenna," Ashtine interrupted.

The Sorceress laughed, lifting her arms and spinning in a slow circle. "You cannot kill me or confine me. I am a deity. Your blood might lock that cell, but only a god has the power to contain me." She turned to Cyrus. "Give me that ring."

"Sure thing, Gehenna," Cyrus said, pulling the ring from his pocket and tossing it to her.

She had surprisingly fast reflexes for being stuck in a cage for centuries, but she caught it in the air, clutching it to her chest. Then she jerked it back, studying it intensely.

"This is not the portal key," she hissed. "This does not fulfill our bargain."

Cyrus pulled up the sleeve of his tunic. The Bargain Mark on his arm was gone. "Apparently it does."

"This is not the portal key!" she shrieked, throwing the ring to the stone floor.

"It was in there," Cyrus shrugged. "I did retrieve the item Alaric was seeking. That ring. And your spell book was delivered to you here. Just as our bargain stated."

Gehenna whirled to Scarlett, pure malice and fury emanating off the deity. Scarlett was leaning against the wall, flipping through pages of the spell book.

"No!" Gehenna wailed. She spun back to Cyrus. "You will pay for this, Fire Fae!"

Cyrus's features went positively wicked. His voice was low and lethal when he said, "I have a new bargain to make with you, Gehenna."

"I want nothing else to do with you. I still have some of your blood. You will never be free of me. Death will be a mercy when I am done with you," Gehenna hissed, pulling the vial of his blood from her pocket. It was what they had been waiting for, needing her to confirm if she still had any of it.

She was thrown back by a wave of darkness. Coughing out a gasp as shadows wound around her throat, she gasped, "You are not a goddess."

Scarlett's smile was pure poison. "Think again."

"How?" the Sorceress rasped, clawing at the shadows. "How did I not know?"

"I guess it was hidden by deceit," Scarlett replied, another wave of darkness slamming into the Sorceress.

"You are a World Walker," Gehenna cried, eyes wide with understanding. "They deceived us all!"

"You came after one of mine, Gehenna. You tortured him. Tried to break him."

"No!" she screamed as the shadows began to drag her across the floor and back to the cell. Her fingers were cracking and bleeding as she tried to grab anything to slow her. "We had a bargain!"

"That I would let you out of that cell. It is no folly of mine if you do not understand how these things work," Scarlett replied. "About that new bargain with Cyrus though…"

Scarlett looked to him, twisted delight dancing in her eyes. His queen. His friend. His family. Who had given to save him. Who had never turned away from him despite his failures.

Loyalty he was deserving of.

Cyrus strolled forward, picking up the vial of blood from where it had rolled across the floor. "A sacrifice of blood."

"No!" Gehenna screamed.

"A sacrifice of betrayal."

Scarlett shoved her into the cell, Chaos surrounding the bars. He could feel her magic holding, caging, imprisoning.

Ashtine stepped forward, reopening the slice on her palm and smearing blood across the door, sealing it once more.

"A sacrifice of time. A long, long time. Eternity perhaps," Cyrus finished.

Gehenna was a panting heap curled on the floor, fingers pulling at her hair the same way Cyrus had done every time she'd trapped him in a memory.

He moved up close to the bars, just short of touching them. He knew Scarlett had done something to them. They weren't just shirastone any longer.

"I have one more thing for you," Cyrus said, pulling the folded paper from his pocket.

"I will kill you!" Gehenna snarled, lifting her head. It was feral madness that stared back at him. Wild violet eyes. Bared teeth.

"This is the last time you will ever see me, Gehenna," he replied casually, flicking the paper through the bars to her.

She crawled forward and snatched it up, unfolding it in such a haste it nearly tore. But it was enchanted to never be destroyed. Not by hand nor by fire. Not by any type of power.

It was a drawing.

Of him.

"What do I want with this?" she hissed.

"I told you. It was something to remember me by," he answered, lowering down to a crouch so he was on eye level with her. "I wish I could say you didn't break me, but you did. You tainted so many things in my life. Trapped me in a house of memories that we sadistically built together. But now, Gehenna?" He pushed back to his feet. "That picture is to ensure that I always have a place in your house of memories too. For you to always remember that *I* was the one who ultimately broke *you*."

She was screaming, high-pitched wails of agony as he turned away. Ashtine and Scarlett were waiting for him at the bottom of the steps. Ashtine went first, somehow still gracefully gliding up the stairs even with her rounded belly.

"You are all right?" Scarlett asked him with a soft smile as he tucked the vial of his blood into his pocket.

"Yeah, Darling," he said, dropping an arm around her shoulders as they followed Ashtine out. "I'm perfect."

They made their way through the prison to where Briar, Sorin, and Cassius were waiting for them. Cassius reached for Cyrus the same way Sorin and Briar reached for their females, all of them clinging to each other.

"It's over?" Cass rasped, his voice hoarse.

"It's over," Cyrus answered, taking a small step back and holding up the nearly empty vial of his blood.

Briar took them out of the prison, and they Traveled back to the Fire Court. Cyrus opened his mouth to say he was going to bathe, but Sorin spoke first.

"Scarlett."

"Wh—" she started before she inhaled sharply, causing everyone else to turn.

To where shadows were shimmering like mist.

"Callan," she breathed.

# CHAPTER 46

# CALLAN

"**M**ake sure all the herbs and tonics are brought with. We do not need to be wasteful with those," Callan said as he helped a woman struggling to fit all of her belongings in a pack.

"Yes, your Majesty," answered the man Callan had been addressing.

Callan gave him a warm smile. "Thank you."

The man bowed his head, hurrying off to carry out the task.

They were moving. Finally. Scarlett and the others were coming in the morning to move everyone to the Fire Court. There would be no slow meandering through the forest. They would make portals to quickly and efficiently move everyone in one clean sweep.

Callan had made sure the other kingdoms were taken care of first. When the Wind Court had been secured, Ashtine had moved Toreall refugees across her borders where Hale was there to greet his people. When the Earth Court had been secured, Azrael had taken in the Rydeon rebel camps.

Callan had had to go to the other kingdoms to convince the people that the Fae were allies. He'd had to introduce Hale to the Toreall people, their faces full of distrust and wariness. He'd only just returned from the Earth Court a few hours ago. The Rydeon people had been a little easier to convince. Somehow word had spread among their rebel camps of what he and Azrael had done at the Necropolis.

And now it was his own people's turn. Finally.

Then they could focus on getting Tava.

It had been a week. A torturously long week since they had moved her to the castle. Drake hadn't gone back. He'd stayed here, using all his contacts and connections he'd built over the years to learn as much as he could about happenings in the castle and trying to work out a way to get Tava out, but things had been silent.

Too silent.

If Callan had learned anything over the last year, it was the feeling before everything changed. It had taken him a while to figure out what it was. To recognize it when it came calling. As if the world had stilled and the stars were watching to see how things would play out. As if even fate had pulled her hand back, allowing the pieces to fall where they may.

He'd felt it when he'd followed Scarlett to the Fire Court.

He'd felt it when he'd come back and started the ruse with Tava.

He'd felt it when they'd gone to the Lairwood house to search for an Avonleyan Key.

He'd felt it on the ship to Avonleya. In the Necropolis when they'd taken down the wards. When he'd fought to come back to this continent.

And he felt it now.

Then he heard the screams.

Callan lurched to his feet, the pack he'd been trying to close spilling out everywhere. He glanced down at the woman he'd been helping, her eyes wide.

"Do you remember the evacuation plans you were told when you first arrived here, Eileen?"

The woman nodded, her voice trembling as she said, "Y-yes, your Majesty."

He smiled encouragingly, not letting her see his own dread rising up. "It will be all right," he said, as more screaming rent through the air. "Go to your assigned area and help where you can."

She nodded, and he watched as she hurried away, personal effects left forgotten on the ground. As soon as she was out of sight, Callan turned and ran towards the screaming. The further he went, the more mayhem he found. People were in utter panic. Men and women were yelling at one another. Children were crying. He ran past them all to the screams of terror. He hurtled over makeshift fire pits, grabbing weapons wherever he could find them as he ran. A knife left out here. A dagger near a guard post.

But when he finally cleared the trees at the edge of their camp, he came to a standstill.

It was a bloodbath.

There were soldiers and seraphs as far as he could see. It had to be the entirety of Windonelle's armies and hundreds of seraphs. Here. To crush any hope. Men and women Callan had been training these last weeks were fighting. Or trying to. They were nothing in the face of this. Seraphs with fire magic were setting tents ablaze, while those with earth magic were simply creating holes in the ground, swallowing people whole.

Juliette and Arantxa were in the sky on griffins, their beasts managing to evade attacks as the two Witches battled against a horde they would never defeat.

He saw Drake across the way, struggling against a group of seraphs keeping him separated from the fighting. They weren't trying to kill him. They were trying to detain him.

Which meant they were here for Callan too.

To keep their Maraan Lords alive.

The seraphs spotted Callan at the same moment he pulled the vial Scarlett had given him from his pocket. He tossed it onto the ground before him, crushing it beneath his boot and watching the shadows swirl up. Then he swiped up a sword from one of the fallen men nearby, tightening his grip on the dagger in his other hand. He did not have armor or leathers on. It made it easier to move as he let them come to him, forcing them to expend that energy to initiate the fights. He leaned into their attacks, causing them to jerk back to avoid fatally injuring him as he parried blades and dodged attempts to detain.

Scarlett should be here by now.

That's all he could think as he sliced at the whip of vines that had been wrapping around a wrist. He ripped the vines free at the same time he dropped to a knee to avoid the reach of yet another seraph while he thrust his blade up and into the seraph's gut. It hadn't taken her this long when he'd been facing Veda.

Maybe she couldn't come. Maybe she was stuck in her own battle. Maybe she was fighting for another kingdom right now. Maybe she couldn't come, and they were left to defend their own as they had been from the very beginning.

But he wouldn't let them take him. He would go down fighting beside his people, giving as many as he could time to get away. If he went down, he took Mikale with him. It would help. That in itself would be a victory for them. Scarlett would fight for his kingdom, even if he were no longer here to rule it when this was over. They had Tava. She would care for Eva, and she would rule as the queen she had been for years now.

The screams continued to echo around him as he drove his dagger into the chest of a seraph. It wouldn't kill him though. It wasn't shiras-tone, and there was no fire to keep the being down.

So Callan kept fighting beside his people as the sun sank lower in the sky, knowing he would not see it rise, and he hoped Tava would forgive him for breaking his promise to her.

# CHAPTER 47
## SCARLETT

**N**o.

That's all she could think when she saw Callan's shadows. The shadows that were her summoning from him because something had gone wrong. Very, very wrong.

Tomorrow. They were going there tomorrow. She just needed one more day. One more day, and everything would have played out perfectly. The game would have been over.

One more day and—

"Scarlett," Sorin repeated, drawing her from her spiral.

"We need to—"

"Sorin! Scarlett!"

They all turned at Eliza's voice as she came rushing towards them, Razik with her.

"Eliza? What has happened?" Sorin asked.

"We just received word. Alaric is attacking in Windonelle. The entirety of his forces. They are coming here. For us. For the Fire Court. Burning everything in their path as they move."

*Burning* it all. A message to the Fire Court. A message to her.

"The rebel camps are in that path," Cassius said, voicing the thought no one wanted to say. "That's why Callan is summoning you."

"Okay," Scarlett said, shoving aside her panic as her mind swirled

620

with possibilities. Wind and Earth Court armies couldn't leave. They'd risk losing their own territories. But Ashtine and Briar were already here. Cethin, Kailia, Tybalt. She was a goddess. Sorin was basically a god. And they had—

"Briar, you and Ashtine go get Azrael. He can Travel everyone to the rebel camp. Eliza, get everyone else ready for battle so you can go when they get back. He's the only one of us who has been there. Make portals for our forces to go and defend the mortals. Sorin, I need you with me," she said, turning and running before anyone could say another word.

She raced to the second floor where Mordecai and Nuri were being kept under surveillance. Bursting into the room, they both leapt to their feet, grabbing nearby weapons.

"What the fuck, Scarlett?" Nuri said with a glare.

"Alaric is coming," Scarlett said. She was still holding the Sorceress's spell book, and she flipped it open, frantically searching the pages.

She listened while Sorin quickly filled them in on everything that was happening, and when he finished, Nuri demanded, "What the hell are you doing here? Go help them, Scarlett!"

"We're going to," she muttered, finding the page she was looking for. She looked up, meeting Nuri's eyes. "And you're coming with us."

"I can't," Nuri balked, the little color she had in her skin leeching out. "He will make—"

"Not if you are no longer bound to him," Scarlett interrupted, turning the book so Nuri could see. "I know how."

"It is not possible to nullify a Blood Bond," Mordecai cut in, taking the spell book from Scarlett and studying the page. "Only the death of the one she is bound to can end it. It is fate."

"A goddess can end it when she can name Fate," Scarlett corrected.

Mordecai's brows knitted together. "The Fates' names are not known."

"Gehenna said *her* name," Scarlett said, turning to Sorin.

"That is not possible," Mordecai argued. "Her name has been lost since the time of the World Walkers."

"But I know it," Sorin said as understanding dawned. "Beatrix told me the name. Their family had been keeping it a secret for centuries."

"Quick," Scarlett said, reaching for a knife from her belt. "We do not have time to debate this."

"You are sure about this, Scarlett?" Nuri asked, extending a shaking hand to her. "If you are wrong…"

"This will free you, Nuri," Scarlett said, drawing blood and beginning to draw a Mark on Nuri's palm.

"That does not match the Mark here," Mordecai muttered, glancing between Nuri's palm and the spell book.

"Mine is better," Scarlett returned.

"Explain," Mordecai demanded.

"No time," Scarlett retorted, continuing to draw.

She was so focused she didn't see the rustling wings, but she heard Nuri scoff. "Relax, Cai. If this works…"

"Will you fight with us?" Sorin demanded.

"Of course I will fight with you," Nuri said, shooting Sorin an annoyed look.

"Not you," Sorin replied.

Scarlett glanced up at Nuri, who was looking at the seraph. "He can't," Nuri said softly.

"Then he will stay here," Scarlett said, the Mark on Nuri's palm beginning to glow brightly atop the red Blood Bond Mark. "Sorin."

"Just say the name?" Sorin asked, moving forward.

Scarlett shrugged. "That's what Gehenna said. A Mark spoken with the name of Fate."

"*Avana.*"

The name was scarcely past his lips when the Mark radiated with such force it shoved them all back. Sorin caught Scarlett before she hit the wall. When she turned back, Mordecai was already back at Nuri's side, holding her hand in his own and inspecting her palm.

"Did it work?" Scarlett asked, and when Nuri met her gaze, there were tears glimmering there. Scarlett gave her a wicked smile. "What shall we burn first, Sister?"

Nuri's features darkened, fangs snapping out. "We burn it all."

Turned out, they didn't need to start a fire.

Everything was already burning when they stepped from the shadowy mist that took the three of them to the spot Callan would have crushed the vial. Sorin was already in the sky, those magnificent fire wings of his flaming brightly as he worked to put out the fires Alaric's forces had set.

An arrow flew past their heads, and Scarlett and Nuri both whirled around to find Juliette.

"I was worried you would not make it," Juliette said, hurrying to their side. "Come."

They did not question their sister as she ran. Juliette let another arrow fly, and when Scarlett saw it hit its mark, she raced past them.

"Callan!" she cried, pulling a dagger and slicing away at vines.

The arrow had gone through a seraph's throat, and with scarcely a thought, the male was burning in starfire.

"Callan," Scarlett repeated, tearing away the vines that had been around his wrists and throat. "Are you all right?"

There was blood dripping down his temple, and he wasn't in any sort of leathers or armor.

"You came," he gasped, sucking down air.

"Of course I came, Callan. Can you stand?"

She tried to help him up, but he stumbled. "They have Drake," he murmured. "I was trying to get to him."

"Rayner!" Scarlett screamed. The Ash Rider was there a moment later.

"What do you need?"

"Find a Traveler to take Callan—"

"No," Callan grunted. "I'm staying. I can fight."

"You can barely stand," Scarlett argued.

"I am staying," he answered, straightening as Rayner helped him up. "I will fight with my people, Scarlett. Do not take that away from me."

She studied him for a heartbeat, a king staring back at her.

"Stick close to him," she said to Rayner.

He nodded, and Scarlett turned to find Nuri and Juliette both engaged with two seraphs. With a surge of power, the males went up in starfire. Her sisters both turned to her with scowls on their faces.

"Rude," Nuri griped. "They were our kills."

Scarlett rolled her eyes, stalking forward. "There are literally hundreds of other seraphs."

"*In the sky,*" Nuri retorted. "You couldn't let us have the ones on the ground?"

"We have more important things to worry about," Scarlett said. "Callan said they have Drake." That had her sisters straightening.

"I'll track him down, then come find you," Nuri said, pulling up her hood.

She was gone before Scarlett could say anything else. Turning to Juliette, she said, "Shall we?"

Juliette smiled, and together they charged into the fray. Between Juliette's glimpses of what could be and Scarlett's power, they cleared a way through the field like the Wraiths they were. Scarlett fought with flames and blades. Blood sprayed as she plunged her sword deep into a seraph, and her shadow panthers took down enemy soldiers one after another. Juliette released arrow after arrow, never missing a target, and when she ran out of arrows, she tossed the bow aside, drawing her sword.

She caught glimpses of the others. Sorin in the air with Razik, Cassius, and Tybalt. Flames of orange and black lit up the fading sky. Kailia was a blur as she appeared long enough to fire three arrows at once, already in another spot and firing again before the first set hit their marks. Cyrus, Eliza, and other Fire Fae were burning the seraphs everyone else fell, keeping them down. Cethin was clearly working to drain seraphs of their gifts, making them easier for the Fae to fight. His power was great enough he still had nearly full reserves after the Wind Court battle. The Avonleyan cadres were fighting with a precision and skill that Scarlett wished she had time to stop and marvel at, because fuck could they move and kill and decimate.

"Scarlett!" Juliette cried, and she didn't need to ask what. They'd done this so many times, Scarlett knew from the way her sister said her name to drop low as Juliette's sword swiped, going through an enemy Fae that had come up behind her.

Scarlett rolled, popping back to her feet with a dagger flying from her hand. Flames ignited down the blade a moment before it struck a seraph in the chest.

And then Nuri was there, her blades nothing but steel blurs as they moved through the air, taking down two soldiers at once.

"Did you find Drake?" Scarlett shouted over the screaming of the dying around them.

"Yes," Nuri answered, flipping backwards a second before an arrow pierced the air where she'd been standing. "But Scarlett, there are Night Children here. Just arrived. They are still loyal to Alaric, even if I am the Contessa. And Drake is so heavily guarded, even I cannot get near him."

A swirl of ashes appeared near her head, and she reached up, pulling a message from them. It was from Rayner, and all it said was:

*They are coming for him.*

"Fuck," Scarlett spat. She turned to her sisters. "Make your way to Drake. If you have a chance to take him, do it. I have help coming."

*Sorin?*

*What do you need, Love?*

*Find me.*

That was all she said as she raced back in the direction she had come. It didn't take long. Only a minute or two before Sorin was landing beside her, fire exploding out in a wave to give them a moment.

"They have Drake," Scarlett panted, bracing her hands on her knees. "But they are coming back for Callan. Rayner is with him, but this isn't enough, Sorin. None of it is enough. We are losing too many. Even if I use all my Chaos—"

"Not an option. This is the time to bring them over, Scarlett," Sorin interrupted.

"Now? We were saving them for the last battle."

"This could be that. If things do not turn in our favor very quickly, this could very well be the last battle in the war," Sorin said. "Call them."

"They are a one time weapon, Sorin!"

"And now is the time to use them, Scarlett. Look around you!" he retorted, pulling back his flames for her to survey the carnage. "Do it! Or the mortal kings are lost, and this was all for nothing."

He was right and that was terrifying. That this was their last card up their sleeve, and they had nothing else. No other power moves. No other secrets.

"I need some space," she said, looking up into amber eyes.

An arm wrapped around her waist, and Sorin was hauling her into the sky. She could feel the heat from his wings and the shield he was holding around them as she began tunneling into herself. Into the Chaos. Into a place where she could call to those she now shared a power with.

All of them.

A panther as dark as the night.

A dragon who had fought in the Wind Court.

A phoenix with flames like the one he was bonded to.

A silver hawk who could command the winds.

A red stag of the earth.

A horse of water.

An eagle of the wild and untamed.

A wolf of the moon.

"Holy gods," she heard Sorin murmur, and when she opened her eyes, she could only stare as the spirit animals entered the battle. She suddenly understood exactly why Saylah had gone to get them to fight in the war for this realm. She understood what Cethin had meant when he said they'd been preparing.

If bonded, they'd appeared next to those they were bonded to, amplifying their gifts. Azrael was astride Rinji, the two of them creating giant crevices in the earth while Maliq was herding and forcing soldiers into them before Azrael buried them alive. Briar and Abrax had a cyclone of water stretching to the sky where Nasima was forcing seraphs into it with mighty gusts from her wings. Ranvir was soaring with Tybalt and Razik in their dragon forms. Shirina mauled and tore apart soldier and seraph alike while Amaré flew close, setting them all on fire.

Scarlett twisted to look up at Sorin. "Our turn."

His mouth crushed to hers for the briefest of moments before he was diving back to the ground, clutching her close. Their feet hadn't even touched the ground yet when his flames flared out in a wide radius around them. Shadows poured out of her, merging with them to create shadowfire. They let it devour. Tendrils of it reached into the sky, snagging low-flying seraphs and pulling them down, never to rise again.

She and Sorin kept moving the entire time, trying to find Rayner and Callan. Until they finally spotted them. Callan was even bloodier, and Rayner—

Well, the Reaper had definitely come to fight as he moved around Callan faster than Scarlett could track. There were piles of ash around them. But now that they had found Callan, she needed to get to Drake and her sisters. She sent a message off amid a swirl of shadows.

"Stay with Rayner and Callan," she yelled to Sorin.

"How are your reserves?" Sorin demanded, yanking on the shadowfire to block a group of advancing soldiers.

"Fine. Once we have Drake, I think I can end this."

"Do you need them filled?"

She shook her head, stretching her hand into the air. "I've been conserving. Kind of."

It was partially true. There was a reason she hadn't been in the sky with her shadow dragon, and she'd been trying to make use of her blades more than her magic. Just like there was a reason she had sent a message to Cassius, who was currently swooping low and grabbing her arm to swing her up to him. She looped her arms around his neck as she was once again hauled into the sky.

"Do you know where they are?" she asked Cassius when he banked hard to avoid a torrent of water that had been sent their way. But the number of seraphs in the sky was greatly diminished. Between the dragons and the newly arrived spirit animals, they were making headway.

"Yes," Cassius answered, rolling to avoid a dagger of fire as he sent dragon fire at the seraph who had hurled it at them. "Shirina and Amaré were making their way to them."

She spotted them a moment later, and Scarlett couldn't help but smile, watching her sisters fight alongside the spirit animals.

Then she saw where they were trying to get to and realized the dragons weren't the only reason there weren't as many seraphs in the sky. Nuri hadn't been exaggerating. There were at least a hundred soldiers—seraph, Fae, and mortal—surrounding Drake, who was unconscious in the center of them. She knew he wasn't dead because of his connection to the Maraan Lords, and while Nuri and Juliette couldn't get to Drake, the opposing forces also couldn't get him out. Scarlett's own forces surrounded them.

"What's the plan, Scarlett?" Cassius asked, giving her a moment to survey everything from the sky.

"It's more of a theory," she answered as she watched the spirit animals each move with their own grace and speed.

"Can this theory be put into effect now? Even with the spirit animals, we're being overrun. We simply don't have enough forces here. Maybe we retreat while we can," Cassius said.

"No," Scarlett argued, pieces of a plan falling into place. An insanely risky plan, but they were out of safe options. "This is our only chance with the spirit animals. They will be too drained after this. We use every advantage they can give us. If the Fae and Avonleyans can help shield the mortals, and the spirit animals spread out to help me control the Chaos, I think I can end this."

"End this? The entire battle? There are still several hundred of Alaric's forces down there, Scarlett."

But the Chaos inside her was already vibrating at the thought, and whether from the Chaos or because she was their queen, the spirit animals were already following her plan. She could see them disappearing and reappearing in soft flashes of light in areas throughout the carnage below.

*Sorin! Tell the others to shield as many of our forces and the mortals as we can.*

*Scarlett—*

*No time.*

She slammed up her mental barriers to keep him from distracting her. Her focus needed to be solely on this. On controlling the tempest of power within her.

"Cassius, I need you to take me up and get us as centered above everything as possible, and then I need you to hold on. No matter what." She twisted to look up at him, glowing red eyes meeting hers. "You understand?"

"That's what we've always done, Seastar."

"Don't let go," she whispered.

Because she had no idea if this would work, and if it didn't and she couldn't control the Chaos...

"You can do this, Scarlett," Cassius said, his arms tightening around her and pulling her more securely against his chest.

"Don't let go," she whispered again.

And she let the Chaos out.

It spilled out of her. She felt it reaching for the spirit animals. Other World Walkers with the same gifts. She felt their own power rising up to meet it and guide it. More and more she gave, letting that power take and destroy, break and remake, and the more it took, the deeper she sank into it.

Until she wasn't there at all but among the stars.

No, not the stars.

She watched as another battle played out. There were seraphs and Fae, but also dragons. So many dragons. Gods and—

World Walkers.

There was a female around Eliza's size. Not small, but one could tell her body was honed from decades of training. Her sleek black hair hung down her back like a sheet of night, and she had several small gold hoops running up the curve of her rounded ear. But it was her silver eyes that Scarlett recognized.

Shirina.

This was her other form. No arched ears like the Fae. She looked human.

Before she could get a good look at the others, she was pulled from whatever this place was to another.

Here were two beings so ethereal, Scarlett knew instantly they were gods. One was a female with silver hair flowing past her navel. A crown of white flames as bright as starlight sat upon her head. Thick kohl lined her eyes, dark red on her lips. She wore a black, nearly sheer gown that stood out against her bronze skin.

Serafina.

Which meant that the male beside her was...

He was devastatingly beautiful in the same way that Cethin was. Angular features with a chiseled jawline. His black hair curled around his ears and a lock of it fell forward, brushing his cheekbone. Eyes as green as emeralds were fixed on Serafina, but they flicked in Scarlett's direction, as if he could see her. He wore all black— pants, tunic, jacket. All of fine make. There was a sword strapped down his back, but Scarlett couldn't imagine why the God of Endings would ever need such a thing. There was no crown atop his head. He did not need it. Not with the darkness that swirled in his eyes and drifted around him. There was no mistaking who he was.

Then he turned away from her, and she felt as if she were tumbling back through the stars to another place.

There was a female who appeared to be around her own age. Scarlett couldn't tell if she had gone through her Staying. Her golden hair was dull and limp as she appeared to be sneaking away from the large estate of buildings behind her. Scarlett watched as she took one last look behind her before darting off and disappearing into the night.

The Chaos took her again, and Arius was here once more, this time with another. The male beside him was the same height, but his hair was as golden as the sun and nearly reached his chin. His complexion was darker than Arius's, more golden and tan. His features weren't quite as sharp, but he was just as beautiful. His eyes were blue with brilliant flecks of gold, and he seemed to glow, as if light swirled around him the way darkness followed Arius.

With a start, she realized it was Achaz.

"Scarlett."

She could hear her name, and she tried to find the source of it.

"Scarlett."

She could feel the spirit animals, their power still guiding, directing.

*Scarlett. You did it, Love. Pull it back before you give it all.*

No panic. No worry in his voice. Just a soft command that grounded her.

That called her home.

When she finally managed to blink her eyes open, she was on the ground. Sound was muffled, but there was no screaming. No sounds of battle. No seraphs in the sky, just a black dragon circling above them. Cassius and Sorin were hovering over her, but a feline was also there.

Amaré was perched on Sorin's shoulder, and when she turned her head, she realized they were all there. All of the spirit animals were gathered around her. Some pacing. Some laying down.

"Did it work?" Her voice sounded weird.

"Did it…" Cassius glanced at Sorin before he looked back at her. "You don't remember?"

"Remember what?"

"Scarlett, you…" Cassius dragged a hand through his hair. "You dragged me all over the battlefield. We appeared next to each one of the spirit animals, and they… They shifted to their human forms, and the two of you decimated everyone within range that our people were not shielding."

"They shifted?" Scarlett asked, trying to push onto her elbows to see them.

"Briefly," Cassius said. "It was as if your power gave them the ability to hold the form long enough to help before they were forced back to their animal forms."

Sorin was dragging a blade down his forearm and reaching for her hand, and she yanked it back from him. "No. You have to be drained."

"Not as much as you would think," he replied, reaching for her hand again. "You need it more than I do."

She didn't like it, but she let him slice her palm, a shudder rolling up her spine when his flames melded into her own gifts. "Drake and Callan?"

"Safe," Sorin said with a soft smile, brushing back hair from her brow. "Being tended to."

"And the mortals?"

Sorin hesitated a moment. "There were losses. Mortal and Fae. You know that with war, but we saved as many as we could."

"It would have likely been worse if there had been Maraan Lords here," Cyrus chimed in, appearing over Cassius's shoulder.

Scarlett was fairly certain her heart stopped. "What did you just say?"

Cyrus gave her a quizzical look. "That if the Maraan Lords had been here, the losses would have likely been higher."

"None of the Maraans were here," Cassius repeated slowly, dread filling his eyes as they connected with Scarlett's.

And the obviousness of this now was like a slap to the face.

None of the Maraans were here.

This battle was the biggest one yet. There were more forces here than there had been at the Wind Court or the Earth Court, and more Night Children had been sent. Roderick had been present at the Wind Court when the only battle was over a Citadel. This had been a massive raid through Windonelle to attack the Fire Court, and none of the Maraans were here? Knowing they would be facing her and Sorin? The Avonleyans? The Fae Royalty?

And while Alaric's forces had certainly been killing innocents, they had seemed to be singularly focused on one thing. Getting to Callan and Drake and keeping them alive.

The most ironic thing was, Alaric had made this exact move before. She'd caught it then. When he had sent Night Children to distract them at the Fire Court border while he had been about to infiltrate the Night Child territory to search for the then-Contessa. She'd met Tarek there. This time, she might have realized it too late.

This entire battle had been a distraction to keep them busy and their focus elsewhere.

And it had worked.

# CHAPTER 48
# CALLAN

"The Eternal Necropolis is surrounded by seraphs," Rayner reported, slumping onto the ground. The Ash Rider's grey eyes were hardly moving, and even Callan knew his power was about tapped out.

"I should not have stayed away so long," Nuri said, arms crossed where she leaned against a tree. "I would have been able to warn you."

"No," Scarlett said. "This is not your fault. This is… Well, it is no one's fault. He's had us running and running, scrambling to stay ahead of him. We should have seen this coming."

Callan studied the Wraiths and the Fae scattered around him among the carnage of Scarlett and her power. She and the other World Walkers had left nothing of the enemy forces. He hadn't been surprised to learn the magic she now possessed was called Chaos. It encompassed everything the High Queen was.

But she had come.

She had come for him.

After all they had been through together. After all the love and the hate. The pain and grief. She had still come for him.

Just like she had always promised.

"He is trying to do something with the mirror gate," Scarlett said, chewing on some food someone had scrounged up for them. "I can feel him doing...something." Her brow pinched in confusion, and Juliette took the opportunity to reach over and snatch a piece of meat. Scarlett nearly upended her entire plate trying to grab it back.

"Gods," Azrael muttered. "There is plenty of food, and we can get more."

Someone had gone to get Talwyn, and she was sitting close to Azrael, leaning against him. The former Fae Queen looked exhausted yet content, her cool jade eyes surveying them all. Callan had been told so much information in the last two hours, he was still trying to sift through it all. But more than any of that he was waiting for—

"Ezra," Drake said, pushing to his feet when the guard appeared. He was as bloody as the rest of them, but he'd gone back to Baylorin to see what news he could find out about the state of the capital and Tava.

"The city itself is untouched," Ezra said. "There were a small number of forces left behind to guard the castle, but..." His pale blue eyes went to Callan. "They took her with them. Balam refused to leave her behind."

"Them?" Callan demanded.

"All the Maraans are with Alaric," Ezra answered. "And Tava is with them."

"Alaric just lost over half his forces," Eliza said from where she sat on the ground next to Razik.

"Half of his *known* forces," Cyrus said. "Where the hell has he been hiding all these flying fuckers?"

"Roderick had secret bases all over the mortal lands," Nuri said. "Deep in the Xylon and Dresden Forests. More than that, they have an entire network of bases underground. But from what I have been told by Mordecai, what was done here today was more than half his forces."

"Rydeon and Toreall are vulnerable right now if their Maraan Lord is at the Necropolis," Briar said. "So is my Court. We could easily go in and take them back with their forces spread so thin now."

"But none of that will matter if Alaric succeeds at whatever he's trying to do," Sorin countered. "None of that will matter if the

Maraans still remain. We need to figure out how to kill them without losing the mortal kings."

"What if that is the only way to stop them?" Nuri asked.

Everyone went silent.

"Shut up, Nuri," Scarlett muttered. "That is not happening."

"Someone had to say it," Nuri shot back. "This could all end at this very moment. Kill the kings, and that's three Maraans down in one clean sweep. Then there's just Balam and Alaric left, but it will weaken Alaric too much to lose all the other Maraans and so many seraphs."

"No," Scarlett repeated.

"All options need to be discussed," Nuri said. "Gods, I wish Cai were here. He understands that sometimes the only real option is sacrifice."

"Do not speak to me of sacrifice," Scarlett snarled.

"No, Sister," Nuri sniped back, taking a step towards the queen. "*You* do not speak to *me* of sacrifice after what I have been forced to do these last months while you have been learning fancy tricks across the sea."

Sorin was holding onto Scarlett, and Cassius had grabbed the back of Nuri's cloak as everyone held their breath to see if the two were going to continue this argument with fists and swords.

"For the love of Reselda," Juliette sighed. "If I have to break up a fight between you two, I'm using deathstone to do it."

"You don't have any deathstone," Scarlett said, turning to her.

Juliette gestured across the way to Cethin and Kailia. "I'm sure her Majesty would let me borrow some."

"I would," Kailia agreed simply, resting her chin on her palm while she observed.

"I thought the three of you were...close," Cethin said carefully.

"We are," the Wraiths all answered in unison.

"If you are wondering if they are always this ridiculous, the answer is yes," Azrael muttered, thumb and forefinger rubbing at his brow in annoyance.

"What if a sacrifice is the only way to end this?" Callan suddenly asked. He'd been half-listening to the conversation around him, mulling over something Nuri had said.

"No," Scarlett said firmly.

"Nuri is right," Callan insisted. "This could end far quicker if the Maraan numbers were taken down to two. Countless lives would be saved. Would a sacrifice to end this sooner rather than later not be wise?"

"No," Scarlett said again.

"It is not solely your decision to make, Scarlett," Callan said with a sad tilt of his lips.

"There is another way," she said, dread seeping into her tone.

"We are out of time," Callan countered.

"We're not," she insisted, her voice breaking. "We've all been making sacrifices. We've all given enough."

"You're right," Callan agreed. "But what if… What if only a few had to give a little more to end it all? So that this?" He made a wide sweeping gesture with his hand. "This can truly be the last time these people have to do this. Your people. My people. This world."

"Then it will be me," she said vehemently. "Not three mortal kings when their people need them most."

"The realm needs a guardian, Scarlett. That is you."

"This world needs *light*, Callan," she answered, two tears slipping free. "And that is *you*."

"What if the sacrifice was not three but one?" Razik suddenly interrupted.

"It is still one too many," Scarlett snarled.

"It's a valid argument that needs to be heard, Scarlett," Eliza said gently.

"No," she whispered, shaking her head. She turned pleading eyes to Sorin. "Tell me we can figure something else out. Tell them."

There was so much love and pity in Sorin's eyes as he looked at his wife, bringing up a hand to cradle her jaw. "Let's hear what Razik has to say, Love."

She shook her head, and Callan knew Sorin was saying more down their bond. He left him to handle the High Queen and turned back to Razik. "Tell us what you are thinking."

They turned down a passage of the Necropolis that would take them to the center where the mirror gate was. There were only a handful of them. Most of the Fae had been too drained to come with, their magic reserves depleted. The Wraiths were here. Drake and Hale. Cyrus and Cassius. Razik and Eliza.

They did not slow their steps, the Wraiths leading the way. They prowled straight down the passage and into the center of the Necropolis.

Ezra had been right. Tava was here. She was off to the side with Balam, her fingers twisted around the amulet at her throat. They'd told Balam Drake had picked it up for her as a gift. She was in a dress of deepest green, her golden hair unbound and flowing around her shoulders. Her turquoise eyes went wide when they appeared, a hand covering the small gasp that came from her.

The Maraans all turned as seraphs converged on their company, but they didn't make it very far. Cassius and Razik had a line of dragon fire drawn between them, causing the seraphs all to pause. Orvyn and Idris stepped to Alaric's side, but Balam stayed planted next to Tava, tucking her behind him.

"My Wraiths," Alaric said, a vindictive smirk filling his face. "All of you together again. Well done, Nuri."

"What is that supposed to mean?" Scarlett demanded.

But Nuri was leaving their ranks, leaping across the dragon fire to saunter to Alaric's side.

"After your stunt in the Southern Islands, I realized I would never be the one to convince you to come home," Alaric said, nodding in approval at Nuri as she fell into line beside the Maraan Lords.

"So you…sent Nuri?" Scarlett asked. "But she didn't… That's not why we're here."

"No, you came to stop me," Alaric said, his grin growing wider. "Am I correct, Death's Maiden?"

"I came to kill you," Scarlett sneered, starfire flaring in one hand while darkness pooled in the other.

Alaric clicked his tongue, turning away from them and back to the mirror. "Do not be foolish, Scarlett. You cannot kill any of us at the moment. Not me, and certainly not the kings." He had moved back to the mirror gate, running his fingers along the symbols around it, but he glanced over his shoulder as he said, "You do know about that new caveat? I assume that is why Mikale is still alive somewhere."

"I know all about the life bonds created when we took down the wards," Scarlett retorted.

"Then you know your threats are utterly pointless right now. I taught you better," he said coldly, turning back to the mirror. "I, however, have no such compunctions about killing the mortal kings."

"What?" Idris and Orvyn demanded, spinning to face their prince.

"Relax," Alaric sighed in obvious irritation. "Scarlett will not let her precious mortal king perish. Try as I might, I could not drive every last shred of compassion from her being."

"I do not understand what is happening right now," Callan heard Eliza mutter to Razik.

"Alaric is about to tell us," Cassius said grimly.

"Here is what is going to happen, Scarlett," Alaric said. "You are going to come over here and use that magnificent power you have acquired to unlock this mirror gate."

"Have you forgotten the part about Achaz wanting to kill Arius's entire bloodline?" Scarlett drawled. "That includes me. Why would I let him come here?"

"He will not kill you, Scarlett," Alaric admonished. "Not with World Walker power reborn in you."

"And when I refuse?"

"I kill the mortal kings. You so nicely delivered all three to me. Or rather, Nuri did."

"You want me to believe you orchestrated all of this?" Scarlett said, crossing her arms.

"Just like I orchestrated you bringing me the Avonleyan Keys."

Scarlett snorted. "Because that worked out so well for you."

"Watch it, Scarlett," Alaric said in a low tone, and Callan felt his power wrap around him for the briefest of moments. It was something he'd never wanted to experience again. He staggered, and some of the others obviously felt it too, everyone but Scarlett and Razik having some kind of reaction.

"Enough," Scarlett growled, her shadows breaking free and panthers forming at her sides.

"Then get on with this," Alaric said, stepping to the side and gesturing to the mirror gate. "I am done playing games, Scarlett. You had your fun. Now it is time to come home."

Scarlett glanced at Callan, and he could see it in her eyes. The hesitation to carry out the plan they'd devised mere hours ago. The plan that would truly end all of this. He gave her a soft smile before he subtly nodded his head.

They'd already said their goodbyes.

He watched her swallow, her throat bobbing, before shadows started winding up his torso.

Alaric eyed her warily. "What are you doing? Your shadows will not shield him from me."

"I know," Scarlett said, her voice nothing but venom. "Know that I will kill you for making me do this to yet another one of mine."

"What are you talking about?" Alaric sneered.

"Callan?" Tava said, her voice soft and hesitant. She tried to step around Balam, but he held an arm in front of her, keeping her back.

And this? This was the only part of the plan he'd regret in the After. Knowing that Tava would understand, but she didn't know it was coming. She wasn't prepared to watch him die again after watching him nearly do so in a throne room months ago. She'd have Drake though. At the end of this, she would have her brother.

But giving his life to save his people? To keep the mortal kingdoms from being used yet again in a war that had never been about them? That choice had been easy.

"Scarlett," Alaric said. "What are you doing?"

Her back had straightened, darkness beginning to seep from her. The seraphs standing between her and the Maraans took another step back. "What will you do when your Maraan Lords are dead, Alaric? When your seraphs are nothing but ash? Who will stand between us then?"

"You won't kill the Maraans," Alaric spat. "We have already established you will not kill the mortal kings."

"Mortal *king*," Scarlett replied. "Only one. King Callan Solgard of the Mortal Kingdoms."

He had been the obvious choice when it had come down to it. The Maraan Lords were bound to mortal kings, but what if there was only one? What if there was only one mortal king like there had been long ago? Wasn't that what Arianna had once said to him?

*The three mortal kingdoms were once ruled by one. I am merely suggesting that perhaps your destiny is another path, but it is not one that can be chosen for you. You must choose it yourself.*

Because destiny was a fickle thing.

When this was over, the kingdoms would be returned to their rightful rulers. Rydeon and Toreall were heirless, but Windonelle? His kingdom had Eva, and Eva had Tava to help her become a queen worthy of their people. Tava would rule as the queen she was always meant to be until it was Eva's time to take the throne.

But for now, he was the only mortal king. Hale and Drake had abdicated to him, signing formal documents an hour before they'd come to the Necropolis.

The only mortal king now tied to three Maraan Lords.

One sacrifice instead of three.

Alaric was gaping at her, speechless, but Tava—

"No!" she cried, pushing past Balam and trying to rush to him. Drake broke away from the group, snagging her around the waist, and this scene? Gods, it was a repeat of that throne room.

"No!" Tava screamed again and again as she bucked and thrashed against Drake's hold.

Swords were clashing, and magic was swirling around him as Alaric yelled at the seraphs to get to Callan, get to Scarlett. Anything to stop her and her shadows.

The shadows wouldn't be what ended him though. Scarlett appeared at his side, a dagger in her trembling hand. He was certain he'd never seen her so much as twitch when it came to taking life.

"Quick and painless," she whispered, stepping behind him while he lowered to his knees.

"Thank you, Scarlett," he said, raising his voice to be heard over the panic around them. To be heard over Tava's screams. "Tell her…"

"I will, Callan," Scarlett answered, a hand reaching around to cup his chin and hold him steady. He felt her position the blade, right where it would sever the spinal cord.

"Scarlett!"

Someone screamed her name before she was tackled to the ground, the dagger grazing the back of his neck. Callan twisted to find her struggling against Idris. He was on top of her, and while her shadows were coiling around him, he still didn't move from atop her.

"Scarlett!"

That time it was Cassius.

A surge of darkness came from Scarlett, flaring out and into the room and throwing everyone back. When it had receded, the mirror gate was glowing and Alaric was gone.

"What the fuck?" Razik demanded, moving closer to the mirror.

Orvyn was chuckling softly. "Foolish girl," he chided. "He had already Marked the mirror. All he needed was some of your Chaos. Achaz comes."

Scarlett scrambled to her feet, her face pale. "No."

"He is right, my dear," came Balam's solemn voice from across the chamber. "The only way to stop it is to kill Alaric. To kill all of us. You will never get to him in time."

"We go now," Nuri said, reaching her sister's side. "We go after Alaric and leave the others to finish things here."

"I can do it, Scarlett," Eliza said, bending to retrieve the dagger that had skittered along the floor. Callan could still see some of his blood glistening on the blade. Grey eyes met his. "I will do it."

"We are wasting time," Nuri urged. "I know where he went."

"You cannot betray your master," Orvyn snarled.

Nuri ignored him, clearly no longer interested in maintaining the illusion of loyalty she'd had to portray for Alaric when they got here. "Now, Scarlett," she snapped, Juliette appearing at her side.

With one last lingering glance at Callan, she grabbed her sisters' hands, and the Wraiths disappeared.

Drake released Tava, and she raced to him, throwing herself into his arms. He clutched her close, stroking her hair as she cried into his neck.

"We will give you as much time as we can," Eliza said, before orange and black flames sprang up around them, keeping back the seraphs and Maraans.

"Little Fox," he whispered.

"No, Callan!" she cried. "No."

"I love you."

"Stop! Please stop."

The cries became sobs.

"You taught me to see our people, Tava," he went on, wanting to get out everything he had not thought he would get to say to her. "You taught me what it means to be a king, and you are going to be a queen they are deserving of."

"Not without you, Cal." Her entire body was shaking with the intensity of her sobs.

"You are so strong, Tava Tyndell," he murmured, his own face wet as tears tracked down it. "Braver than I could ever hope to be."

She lifted her head, pressing her lips to his. It was all wrong, her wet and salty tears tarnishing the pure sunlight taste he'd never been able to accurately describe. There weren't words to describe her. There never had been, not in any language.

"Solgard," she murmured against his lips. "Tava Solgard."

He brought his hands up, cupping her face and thumbing away tears. It was pointless. More instantly replaced them. "They deserve rulers who care for them as mortals."

"So selfless," she whispered. She tried to smile, but it never formed, and the pain of knowing he was doing this to her was worse than any dagger to the head was going to be.

"Know that I thought I knew what love was, but I was wrong. I did not know what love was until I found it with you. You are my light, Tava."

The surrounding flames flickered before Eliza appeared behind Tava. "We are out of time, Callan. Something is happening with the mirror."

He nodded, eyes never leaving Tava's. Her hands came up to frame his face, and she forced a sad smile. "I love you, Callan. You are a king worthy of your crown. I would have followed you to the ends of the realm and beyond."

She held his face this time, and he held her stare. He didn't know what he'd done to deserve to stare into her eyes as he crossed the Veil, but he'd thank whatever gods he needed to when he got there.

He felt his hair stir as Eliza positioned the blade. Heard her suck in a sharp breath. Unlike Scarlett, the fire general's hand did not tremble. Sure and steady, he felt her pull the dagger back to make the blow, but then he was jerking Tava into him and rolling as Idris appeared behind her. A dagger raised to make the same blow against his wife. He knew he would have never been that fast without all the training he'd been doing these last months.

But it turned out his reflexes hadn't been necessary.

Energy burst around them, sending both Eliza and Idris flying. He heard Eliza bark a curse as he scrambled to his feet, trying to find where Idris had gone.

"What was that?" Tava asked, Callan pulling her up beside him.

"I don't know," he muttered.

Where had Idris gone?

He'd pulled a short sword from his side, but there was so much godsdamn fire everywhere he couldn't see anything but black and orange flames.

Until they all suddenly went out, pitching the chamber into darkness.

He clutched Tava closer to his side. The only sound was labored breathing before the cave was illuminated once more by soft glowing flames above them. Cyrus's doing Callan realized a moment later. But then—

"Drake?" Tava asked, her tone full of confusion.

Callan turned to find Drake kneeling on the ground beside Balam, a dagger protruding from the center of his chest. Eyes scanning the room, he found Idris and Orvyn unmoving on the stone floor as well.

"Are they…dead?" Tava asked.

"They cannot be," Callan answered. "I am still alive."

"They are dead," Drake said, lifting his gaze to Tava.

"I don't understand anything that is happening right now," Cyrus said, propping the flat of his sword on his shoulder.

Tava took a tentative step towards her brother, but stopped, still clinging to Callan.

"He said…" Drake's eyes dipped to Balam's body once before

meeting Tava's gaze again. "He said that he'd made a vow to our mother. That he'd vowed we would never know the pain and suffering she had. He was drawing something on his arm. I don't know—"

"Where?" Razik demanded, striding forward from where he'd found his way to Eliza's side. The general was clutching at her left side, and she gave Callan a tense look.

"I have never seen a Mark like that before," Razik said, crouched over Balam and examining his left arm. "This one, however," he added, pointing higher up to the inside of his bicep. Callan couldn't see anything. "This is a Blood Vow Mark."

"To who?" Drake asked.

"No way of knowing now, but from the sounds of it, I would say it was to your mother," he answered. "A Blood Vow demands fulfillment."

"He said he couldn't save her, but he'd promised to save us," Drake said hoarsely. "He finished drawing on his arm, and then he pulled this dagger from the air. It all happened so fast."

"That is a deathstone dagger," Razik said, eyeing the weapon. "Are you saying he stabbed himself in the chest?"

"He did," Drake said. "And then the other Lords just…dropped to the ground."

"He somehow transferred the life bond to himself," Razik muttered, back to studying the invisible Mark that was apparently on Balam's forearm. "That shouldn't be possible, but there is no other explanation."

"Are you saying Callan does not have to give up his life?" Tava asked, her voice trembling for an entirely different reason now. "Is that what you are telling me, Razik?"

"It would appear that way," Razik confirmed. "It would seem that the male who raised you cared for you both very deeply. More than he cared about what he was sent here to do."

Cyrus let out a low whistle. "If that's true, Sorin is going to be pissed he didn't get to finish off Mikale."

"He wasn't going to finish him anyway if we'd actually killed Callan," Eliza said, rolling her eyes. "Sorin got his vengeance and more. You know how he gets in the black rooms beneath the palace."

Callan had no desire to know what that meant. Ever.

He turned back to Tava, opening his mouth to say something, but paused when his gaze snagged on her amulet. The white sapphire itself was still there, but the swirling mist inside it no longer was. He picked it up between his fingers. "I guess it was not simply the Beta's flair."

She smiled, fresh unshed tears glimmering in her eyes as she let out a breath of laughter that Callan felt in the depths of his soul.

"Razik?" Hale asked, drawing all of their attention to him. He jerked his chin to the mirror gate. "Do you know what is happening here?"

The mirror gate was no longer a mirror, but instead it was a swirling mass of black with what appeared to be white lights among it. They were moving so fast, Callan couldn't make anything out. Just glowing blurs among the darkness.

"I do not know what is happening," Razik said, pushing slowly to his feet and reaching for Eliza. "I would suggest we not be here when whatever is going to come through arrives though."

"What if she's not fast enough?" Eliza said, stepping into Razik's side.

"Then we just lost the war," Razik answered grimly, Traveling Eliza, Hale, and Drake out while Cassius held out a hand to him.

As they reappeared in the Fiera Palace, Sorin met them in the foyer. He'd come here to make sure Mikale actually died when Callan did, wanting to witness the male's death himself.

"What happened?" Sorin demanded, taking in those who stood before him. "How is Mikale dead if Callan is still alive? And where is Scarlett?"

"We'll fill you in," Eliza said. "But as for Scarlett, she went after Alaric."

"Alone?" Sorin asked sharply.

"No," Cassius interjected. "The Wraiths went hunting."

# CHAPTER 49
# SCARLETT

"I still don't know why you think he came here," Scarlett muttered when they reappeared in the tunnels outside the Baylorin castle.

She knew these tunnels like the back of her hand. She'd used them almost nightly for a year to sneak into the castle and see Callan.

*Callan.*

Was he gone from this world already? Had Eliza already done it? Had the general's hand shaken with grief and regret like hers had?

"Were you not listening?" Nuri retorted, leading Scarlett and Juliette down a tunnel. "They have entire networks underground. Why do you think he is so well-versed in the underground?"

"We know these tunnels just as well," Scarlett argued.

"Because *he* made us learn them," Nuri shot back, taking a turn at speed. "He always thought we'd be at his side once you came into your power."

"Where does this tunnel lead to?" Scarlett asked, rubbing at her chest. She could feel whatever Alaric had done to the mirror gate. Something wasn't right.

"It eventually connects to the Fellowship, but there is another area," she answered. "Up ahead."

"Do we have a plan here?" Juliette asked, her hair flying out behind her as they ran.

"We'll probably run into some seraphs shortly," Nuri answered.

"Thanks for the head's up," Juliette retorted.

"One would think you'd see that coming."

"Fuck you," Juliette snapped. "How is Cai, by the way?"

"How is Arantxa?" Nuri shot back.

"Wait, what?" Scarlett cut in as Nuri rounded yet another corner.

"Our sister has adopted quite a few of the Witch's ways, and I do not mean bonding with a griffin," Nuri called back to her.

Scarlett's head whipped to Juliette to find a small smirk playing on her lips. "Really?"

"You should take Arianna up on her offers sometime," Juliette replied.

"Oh my gods! How do you know about that?" Scarlett demanded.

"Incoming!" Nuri shouted.

Juliette and Scarlett drew blades simultaneously. "Who puts beings that can fly beneath the ground?" Scarlett mused, sending shadow panthers ahead of them to take care of the first seraphs coming their way.

"Better question. Why aren't you leaving any for us?" Nuri groused. "I've had to kill them in secret for months now."

"Fine," Scarlett sighed, pulling her shadows back.

The tunnel was small. The three of them could hardly stand side-by-side let alone fight side-by-side. The seraphs could scarcely fit two of them side-by-side with their warrior builds and wings. It gave the Wraiths an advantage, even if the seraphs did have magic.

Nuri went straight for the throat, her fangs snapping out and tearing straight through flesh and muscle. Juliette took the other, rolling to avoid a torrent of water the male sent her way, before she was back on her feet and dragging her blade down a grey wing.

While her sisters had their fun, Scarlett stepped through her shadows and appeared behind them to find another group of seraphs coming their way. She planted her feet and smiled, letting starfire build and build around her before she released it to barrel down the tunnel. She stalked forward before the flames had cleared, sword already cleaving wings and heads.

All the while, the feeling in her chest kept growing. The Chaos was vibrating as it sensed what she did. Something powerful was coming. She knew. It wasn't something. It was someone.

Achaz.

She could keep him out for a time. She controlled the mirror gates after all, but whatever spell Alaric had put on that mirror would eventually let the god in.

Together the three of them made their way down that tunnel, killing as they went, just as they'd been trained to do. When Juliette dropped for Nuri to come down with her scimitar, Scarlett was there to slide a dagger home, while Juliette was already taking on the next target. They moved in tandem, knowing exactly how one would move to make room for the next. Scimitars sliced through wings while Juliette's sword went through throats and chests, and Scarlett's flames set fire to it all.

When they had finally cleared the passage, their hands, faces, and clothing covered in blood, they took a moment to catch their breath. Scarlett had a hand braced on her hips, and she rubbed at her chest again. Nuri was leaning against the wall, and Juliette was bouncing from foot-to-foot.

"For the love of Arius, please tell me we are close," Scarlett said between harsh breaths.

"Straight ahead," Nuri answered. "Are we ready to do this?"

Their gazes all connected at the question.

"It seems right. That it is us," Juliette said. "I saw so many ways this could play out, but I always hoped it was us. The three of us. Where it started."

"Where it will end," Scarlett said, smiling at her sisters.

"Is he in there for sure?" Juliette asked.

"We'll know in a minute," Scarlett answered, pulling a vial from her pocket. Cethin's blood. She had it in case she needed to get back into Avonleya, but that's not what she was going to use it for now.

Pulling out the cork, she tipped it back, wincing at the coppery taste. "Gods, Nuri. How can you like that?" she asked, tossing the vial aside. It was ashes before it hit the ground.

Nuri shrugged. "The more powerful, the more divine it tastes."

"Cethin is pretty fucking powerful, and it still just tastes like blood," Scarlett deadpanned.

"Are we ready?" Juliette cut in, always the peacekeeper. Half of the time anyway.

Scarlett tugged up the sleeve of her tunic, seeing the interlocking circles glowing faintly on her arm. A Melding Mark. It could only be used by those who shared blood, but for blooded siblings, it allowed them to share gifts for brief periods of time.

And she could feel Alaric.

"He's in there," Scarlett confirmed.

"Of course he is. That's why I brought us here," Nuri retorted.

They fell into step beside each other once more, and when they came to the end of the passage and turned left, it opened into a cavernous space. It reminded Scarlett of his dungeon study. Dank and cold. A desk. Liquor cart. Sofa. One small bookshelf.

Alaric was leaning against the desk, swirling a glass of amber liquid, his black eyes fixed on them.

"My Wraiths," he sighed. "What am I going to do with you?"

They prowled into the room, fanning out. Nuri to her left. Juliette on her right.

"I think the better question is what are we going to do with you," Scarlett mused, taking in more of the space. There was a small bed tucked against a far wall. A nightstand beside it. A chest of drawers was on another wall, and atop it was the only thing with color in the space. A vase of red roses. She sauntered over to it, feeling Alaric's eyes on her the entire time. She ran her fingers along various items as she moved before she plucked a rose from the vase, bringing it to her nose to smell it.

"It's rather anticlimactic, don't you think?" Scarlett prompted.

"What is?" Alaric asked, tilting his head in question as he took a sip of his drink.

"After all this, you are going to die in some underground hideout. I wish we could have made a more public spectacle of your death," she said with a wistful sigh. "I wish Cassius were here to see it."

Alaric's lip curled back at the name. "When Achaz gets here, the dragons will be the first to go."

"Achaz will not make it here, I'm afraid," Scarlett said with a pout, twisting the rose stem between her fingers.

Alaric's smile grew. "He is almost here already, Scarlett. I bet you can feel him. Pacing on the other side of the gateway. Eventually your new gifts will falter, and he will break through."

Juliette and Nuri had been wandering around the room too, picking up random objects and studying them. Alaric's gaze kept bouncing between the three of them.

"What are you two doing?" he snapped.

"Looking for something," Nuri replied, picking up what appeared to be a small wooden box of some sort.

"And you, my *daughter*," Alaric sneered, eyes narrowing on Nuri. "How many days will you spend in the sun for your insolence on this day?"

"I am going to make you scream," Nuri said casually, setting the box back down and turning to face him.

Alaric scoffed, knocking back the last of his drink before dropping the glass onto the desk behind him. "Your threats are becoming tedious, Nuri."

"Why aren't you lecturing Juliette?" she asked, slowly beginning to peel off her gloves.

Alaric's gaze flickered to Juliette, where she was lifting the lid of a teapot and peering inside. "I wrote her off long ago. The day she let herself die."

Juliette acted as though she had not heard him, moving on to the next item without a glance in his direction.

But Scarlett said, "*Let herself die?* As if you didn't know exactly what was going to happen that night."

Alaric shrugged. "I did not know how that night would play out, but… She did, didn't she?"

"Fuck all the way off, Alaric."

"Watch that mouth of yours, Scarlett," he snarled, pushing off the desk and taking a step towards her, but the sound of something crashing to the floor had him spinning back to Juliette.

"What are you looking for?" he gritted out.

"Nothing," Juliette answered sweetly, kicking the tin she had dropped off to the side. "When did you become so paranoid?"

He glared at her, making to turn back to Scarlett, but Nuri said, "Which side would you prefer?"

"Which side of what, Nuri?" he asked in exasperation.

"Which side of your throat should I rip out? Do you have a preference?"

"What is the purpose of this pointless conversation?"

Nuri shrugged. "I was trying to be courteous, but I can do either side. I'm not really picky. Although, I have this ache in my neck from earlier, so maybe the left side would be better. Not as much strain and all."

"Enough, Nuri," Alaric spat. "Stop talking. It's an order."

He turned back to Scarlett. Then he went eerily still when Nuri said, "But I have something to show you, *Father.*"

"How did you do that?" he asked in a soft tone that had once made Scarlett tremble.

Nuri held up a fist—her left one—and slowly lifted one finger at a time, revealing her bare palm. No red Blood Bond Mark adorning it.

"Now do you have a preference?" she asked, her fangs snapping out.

"How? That is not possible," Alaric barked, taking a step back.

"Oh, you know, Gehenna," Scarlett said, as if discussing some silly antics of a child. "She just *loves* to talk when given the right incentive."

"It is not—"

But another crash had him whirling around again. "What the fuck are you doing, Juliette?"

"Distracting you," she answered.

"From what exactly?"

"Scarlett draining your power."

"Scarlett, cannot—" But he paused then, and Scarlett knew he was feeling it. The steady pull at his stolen magic. Cethin had taught her how after the Wind Court. How to steadily use his gift to drain someone, but to make it subtle, she had to go slow. Her sisters knew. They'd discussed how this would need to go before they'd gone to the Necropolis. It was why it had to be them. They knew him best. How to get under his skin, keep him occupied.

She felt his magic try to fight back, but Cethin's magic was stronger. *She* was stronger.

Scarlett clucked her tongue, still twisting the rose between her fingers as she casually moved forward. "I discovered my brother has a very interesting talent. He can let his darkness seep into someone's blood just by touching them. Isn't that fascinating?"

"No," Alaric gritted out, taking another step back. He bumped into his desk, knocking his glass to the floor where it shattered.

Scarlett continued her advance, Nuri and Juliette closing in on the other sides with blades drawn.

Cethin had explained that power to her after the Wind Court battle too. When physically touching someone, he could send his darkness into them. She could do the same with her shadows, but his darkness stayed, mixing with blood and soul. Marking them with death. A marking of Arius himself. It poisoned, tortured, and rotted until death was a mercy.

Much like the Wraiths of Death themselves in a way.

She stopped in front of Alaric, her head tipping to the side. Alaric tried to scramble away from her, but her shadows were holding him in place now. His magic tried to claw at them, sink in, devour. Her ice and fire battled back.

Scarlett smiled. Lifting a hand, she reached for him and dragged a single finger along his jaw. Black lines flared out, spider-webbing across his cheek and down his neck. He let out a cry of pain, unable to move away from her touch.

She sent him a mocking pout. "Together we will keep this world safe. Is that not what you desire most, Alaric?"

The black lines were bleeding from his eyes now, and he let out another gasp of agony as she no longer slowly drained his power. She ripped it out of his being the way he had ripped the life forces from Sloan and Finn, tearing away every last shred of magic.

Alaric sank to his knees, a rattling cough sounding as Scarlett let her finger slide away from his flesh, severing their physical connection. She wished she could drag this out. She wished they could take their time with him. Spend hours showing him just how thoroughly the students had surpassed their once master. But he was right. She could feel Achaz getting closer, and the only way to keep him out now was to make sure the Maraans were dead.

She knew in her being the other Lords were gone. Her court and her family would not fail her in this. She wouldn't let Callan's sacrifice be a waste in her own need for vengeance.

Nuri and Juliette drew closer as Scarlett reached for a scrap of parchment on Alaric's desk.

"I do not think I will be ripping your throat out after all," Nuri commented while Scarlett dipped a quill into a jar of ink and scrawled a single word onto the parchment. "I do not want a single drop of your blood to pass my lips. It is not worth it when the blood is powerless."

Alaric made some noise of outrage, and Scarlett turned to find Juliette pushing him onto his back with the toe of her boot. Scarlett rolled the parchment around the stem of the rose before ripping a thin strip of fabric from her black tunic. It wasn't a ribbon, but it would do.

The three of them stood over him, staring down at their former master. His face was nothing but cracked lines of black that bled into his hair and down his neck into the collar of his tunic.

"I could have saved you," he rasped out. "I could have saved all three of you. My Wraiths. *Mine.*"

"We saved ourselves," Nuri spat. "We were never yours."

His black eyes went back to Scarlett. "He will keep coming for you. He will come for his entire bloodline. He will not stop until there is not a drop of Arius blood left in existence. The gods don't stop. They never stop," Alaric managed around a cough, blood spraying from his lips.

"Oh, Alaric," Scarlett simpered. Her shadows writhed behind her, a mist of darkness. She lowered down so she could speak directly into his ear. "*We* are your gods now."

Her shadows struck, winding around his ankles and wrists, holding him down as Juliette drew a dagger and Nuri bared her fangs.

"After all I did for you three," he spat, another cough rattling from his chest.

Scarlett's head tilted to the side as she studied him. Nothing but a powerless male before them now. "He is right," she said. "We should be thanking him." Her sisters met her gaze, darkness staring back at her. Her shadows wound up, tightening around his throat, and her lip curled as she peered down at him once more. "We are exactly as you trained us to be."

"Ruthless," Death Incarnate purred, her dagger coming down into his gut.

"Vindictive," Death's Shadow crooned, a scimitar slicing deeply across his chest.

"*A weapon*," Death's Maiden said, summoning starfire to her palm and bringing it to his mouth.

He thrashed beneath her shadows, his head jerking from side-to-side, trying to get away from the fire that would end his existence, leaving nothing for the After.

"You are the master of nothing anymore, Alaric," Scarlett whispered into his ear. "Not a fellowship of assassins. Not a land of mortals. Not an army of seraphs. Not my sisters. Not me. You are not even the master of your own death. You are nothing. A prince without a throne. A failure. The game is over." And as her hand slipped over his mouth, starfire seeping between his lips, down his throat, into every vein of his being, she said, "I won."

She burned him from the inside out, and the three of them didn't say a word as they watched white flames and pools of darkness devour. Scarlett knew the moment he was truly gone. She felt power slam against her soul. Felt a roar of rage and fury at being kept from this world yet again when whatever enchantment Alaric had put on the mirror gate failed.

Scarlett tunneled down into her Chaos, to the very core of it, to the essence that had created this world, and she locked the realm. No one in. No one out. Unless they came through her and her Prince of Fire.

When she opened her eyes, there was nothing but a pile of fine white ash on the floor. Scarlett lifted a hand, dropping the rose she still held atop it.

A rose with a black ribbon wrapped around a piece of paper containing a name.

The name of her final assignment as Death's Maiden.

None of them looked away when she held out her hands to her sisters, Traveling them out of that underground passage.

Where they left the Wraiths of Death to die with the one who had created them.

They reappeared in the foyer of the Fiera Palace, and Sorin was dragging her into him a second later. She'd had to shut him out to stay focused, and now she breathed him in. Ashes. Cloves. Cedar. Him.

It was over.

It was over.

It was over.

*Breathe, Love,* came down the bond, a hand taking hers and guiding it to his chest. She could feel it steadily rising and falling beneath her fingers.

In and out.

In and out.

In and out.

She tried to match their breathing, but it wasn't working. She hadn't realized she'd started crying. Great sobs that wracked her body. It was over, but so much had been lost. They had won. The realm was saved, but the cost…

She clung to him, his arms tight around her. At some point, he'd lowered them to the floor. She couldn't hear anything else around them. Sound was muffled, as though she were under water, and he was the only one who could pull her back to the surface.

Because they had won. It was over. But the world was not as bright as it once was. So many stars were gone from the sky. Lights she had known, and so many more she hadn't. Finn. Sloan. Nakoa. Sawyer. Hazel. Callan.

*Callan.*

"Love," Sorin said softly. "I need to show you."

"I can't, Sorin," she managed between a sob. "I can't right now. It is all too much."

He shifted some, and then she was being jostled, as if he were going to pass her off to someone. Odd, but she didn't fight him. Cassius would hold her just as tightly. Cyrus. Eliza. Rayner.

But there was no ash or smoke to fill her senses when new arms wrapped around her.

This was spring rain and pine.

This was—

She jerked her head up, looking into hazel eyes with flecks of green. Brown hair. High cheekbones and a soft smile.

"Callan?"

"You did it, Scarlett," he said, his voice gruff and hoarse.

"You're alive?" she managed, reaching up to cradle a cheek.

"Seems that way," he said with a huff of laughter.

"You're alive," she repeated, her own laugh of disbelief escaping. "You're alive."

She didn't care how, only that it was real.

She threw her arms around his neck, and he returned her embrace. He didn't belong in her darkness. That had always been truth. But he had always been a light for her. The first glimpse of the stars in a void of unending dark. Despite the mess they had become, despite the crowns they now bore, despite the new loves and partners, this would remain. A bond forged between two kindred souls.

A soulmate.

# CHAPTER 50
# TALWYN

I t was still jarring to wake up in the Fiera Palace.

She hadn't stayed here in decades, and now Talwyn was waking up in a guest suite.

Even more strange was having Azrael beside her. The strange part wasn't him in her bed, of course. But having him at the Fire Court after so much animosity between all of them was…

Well, it would take some getting used to.

She felt out of sorts these days anyway. She did not really have a place to call home anymore. The White Halls were reserved for the Fae Queen of the Eastern Courts. To be honest, Talwyn didn't think she could stomach living there anymore, even if it was an option. So many memories. So much guilt and grief and anger in those Halls.

She had just finished braiding back her hair when Azrael came into the room. He had been in some meeting or other. Something she was no longer invited to, and that was fine. She was more than happy to be here, resting and healing. She was, however, anxious to go see Thorne in the Wind Court.

"How are you feeling?"

She sighed in annoyance. "I am fine, Az. Just as I have been every other time you ask this."

Talwyn hadn't been able to fight in that final battle in Windonelle.

Briar and Ashtine had appeared, said Azrael was needed, and they were gone. Less than a minute. That's how long it had taken. She had still been sitting at the table with a fork halfway to her mouth when Azrael had met her gaze. He hadn't said anything. They rarely did. She saw it all in his eyes.

It was an hour later when a wind portal had appeared and Ashtine came through. She'd smiled softly, and together the two of them had sat and waited for two Fae Princes to come back alive.

She stood from the mirrored vanity table, flicking her braid over her shoulder. Comfortable pants and a tunic. That had become her daily attire as she slipped her stockinged feet into boots. "Can we go see Thorne now?"

"There are some things to be discussed first," Azrael said, watching her carefully.

"Can they not be discussed elsewhere?"

"They are waiting for us."

"Who is they?"

"The Fae Royalty and Scarlett."

She went completely still. "Why?"

The corner of his lips tipped up. "Relax, Talwyn," he said, gesturing for her to follow him.

They could have Traveled, she supposed, but instead they walked side-by-side through the Fiera Palace and down to the council rooms. Everything was the same as when she would stay here before she took a throne, and yet everything had changed.

She had stayed in the guest suite most of their time here, only venturing out when Azrael was around. She'd like to say she wasn't hiding, but she was. She simply didn't know where she fit into his world and with all the Fae now.

She could hear the arguing long before they reached the council room.

"It doesn't count if no one saw it happen," came Cyrus's voice.

"What?" Scarlett cried in outrage. "Sorin was there! He saw it happen."

"Did he?" Cyrus questioned. "Sounds to me like you had to tell him about it too."

"Tell him, Sorin," she demanded.

Talwyn gave Azrael a questioning look, but his face was full of irritation. "I cannot believe they are still arguing about this," he muttered.

Talwyn came to a stop in the doorway as she took in the scene in front of her. Scarlett was on her feet, hands planted on the table, leaning towards Cyrus who was across from her next to Cassius. Sorin sat casually next to his wife, a thumb hiding the smirk on his lips. Eliza had her nose in a book while Rayner was watching everything warily. Briar and Ashtine sat beside each other, both eating a tart of some sort at the head of the table.

"In all fairness, Scarlett, I did not actually witness it," Sorin said, and Talwyn could hear the laugh he was trying to keep from his voice.

"What?" Scarlett shrieked at the same time Cyrus said, "Ha! Didn't happen, Darling."

"You cannot be serious!"

"I do not understand what is happening right now," Talwyn murmured to Azrael. "Why do I need to be here for this?"

"No one needs to be here for this," he muttered. Then with an audible sigh, he added, "Apparently Scarlett caught an arrow in midair."

That didn't seem all that impressive. That was normal Fae training.

"And?" Talwyn asked, listening to the continued bickering between Scarlett and Cyrus.

"And I guess she has never done so," Azrael said. "I do not understand it either."

Cyrus held up two palms before him. "All I am saying is that there were hundreds of people there and *no one* saw you catch it? Seems a little far-fetched, Scarlett." He picked up a cheese cube from his plate, tossing it into his mouth.

"The witnesses are *dead*, Cyrus," she snapped. "Would you like to join them? Then you can ask them yourself."

"I have the perfect dagger for this," Eliza chimed in without glancing up from her book.

"No one is stabbing anyone," Sorin sighed.

"I don't need a blade," Scarlett snarled.

"I saw it," Talwyn said.

"Thank you!" Scarlett cried, gesturing towards the door. She turned, her eyes going wide when she realized who she was siding with.

The room went silent and still, a tenseness settling over everyone.

"I was on the balcony directly below them," Talwyn went on. "I saw her catch the arrow, then send it to Sorin in a swirl of shadows so he could shove it into a seraph's eye."

Sorin's golden gaze was fixed on her, his hand having slowly dropped to the arm of his chair. He smiled at her as he said, "That is exactly how it happened."

"Ow," Cyrus muttered, moving as if rubbing his leg beneath the table. Cassius was giving him a pointed look. "I guess if there was an actual witness, I can believe it," he grumbled.

"You are a jackass," Scarlett groused, dropping into her seat and crossing her arms.

"You are a whiny brat," Cyrus retorted.

"Can we get on with this?" Azrael cut in, a hand coming to Talwyn's lower back, ushering her in. "I have better things to be doing with my time."

"Got a sand castle to build in all that sand, Azzy?" Scarlett drawled, picking up a pear tart from her plate.

"For fuck's sake," he muttered, pulling out a chair for Talwyn next to Ashtine.

Talwyn glanced at him. She couldn't sit there. Ashtine was the Fae Queen now. Talwyn could not sit to her right.

"It is all right, Talwyn," Ashtine lilted. "Sit."

She slowly lowered into the chair, feeling everyone's gaze settle onto her.

Scarlett's entire demeanor had changed in a matter of moments as she said, "Where are you planning to live, Talwyn?"

Right to the point then.

"I…"

But she didn't have an answer because she didn't fit anywhere anymore.

"With me," Azrael cut in. "This much has already been discussed."

"And her role there?" Scarlett pressed, a hand coming to the table and fingers beginning to drum atop it.

"She will be my wife, Scarlett," Azrael said in that low tone that promised violence if she disagreed.

*Wife?*

But that would make her—

Scarlett's eyes slid to Talwyn. "And her role in your Court?"

"What business is it of yours?" Azrael retorted.

"Careful, Luan," came a low warning from Sorin. "She may not be the Fae Queen any longer, but she is the High Queen of this realm."

But Scarlett was still looking at Talwyn when she said, "I may have spared your life and extended your Staying, but that is the extent of the forgiveness I am able to offer."

"It is more than enough," Talwyn said.

"You cannot occupy a throne in a Fae Court. Not again," she went on.

"I do not wish for one."

"And what do you wish for, Talwyn?" came Ashtine's lilting question.

Talwyn turned to her, her friend's hands resting atop her rounded stomach. Briar's arm was settled along the back of her chair, and Talwyn couldn't help but think about how casual they all were. A year ago, this room would have been filled with tension and short tempers. The short tempers part was probably still true, but the rest?

When she just stared at her friend, Ashtine gave an encouraging nod. She wasn't used to this— speaking about her feelings aloud. But she took a deep breath and said, "I wish for a purpose that does not involve a throne, whether that is helping train new forces or scrubbing dishes in a kitchen. Somewhere beside people, not above them. I wish for someplace to find that purpose. I wish for somewhere I can be with Thorne, and we have room to fly. I wish for somewhere close to Azrael, but not on a throne beside him. I do not wish for nor deserve such a thing. If that is what you are asking of me, I will decline it."

"Do you feel you can find that purpose in the Earth Court?" Ashtine asked. "Or will you feel confined there?"

"I want to be with Azrael."

Ashtine's gaze moved to Scarlett. "A Consort then. In title only. No responsibilities. No say in political matters or policies, but she will retain the protection of a prince's Consort. Is that agreeable to you?"

Talwyn met Scarlett's silver gaze across the table and held it while the High Queen searched for whatever it was she was looking for. Finally Scarlett said, "Is that acceptable to the rest of the people at this table?"

When no one voiced a disagreement, her gaze slid to Azrael. "Is that acceptable to you, Prince Luan?"

"It is," Az answered.

"Then that is decided," Scarlett said, before fixing her attention on Briar and Ashtine. "What of you two?"

"What of us?" Briar asked, eyes narrowing on Scarlett.

"Where will you reside?"

Briar glanced at Ashtine, who only smiled up at him. Pure love and adoration.

Talwyn leaned forward and grabbed an apple as she listened to the conversation around her.

"If you are still offering, we would like to take up residence at the Black Halls," Briar answered. "We can both portal to our respective Courts as needed. Ashtine has Ermir, and I have Neve to oversee matters when we are not present. Until the babes are of age and ready to take their thrones."

"I made the offer when I asked you to be the Fae King and Queen. I am not rescinding it now. As long as I can visit during the dismally cold winter months," Scarlett answered with a bow of her head in their direction.

"And you, Sunshine?" Briar asked, his icy blue eyes bouncing between Scarlett and Sorin. "Where will you reside?"

"In the Fire Court, obviously," Eliza drawled, twisting to look down the table. "Right?"

"You are the Fire Princess," Sorin said, rolling his lips to keep his smile from forming.

"No, I am the Fire General," Eliza gritted out.

"We will remain at the Fiera Palace for now," Scarlett cut in. "The White Halls will remain empty until a new King or Queen of the Eastern Courts is ready to inhabit them."

"Is there anything else we are needed for?" Azrael asked.

"I believe we are done here," Scarlett answered, and Azrael immediately pushed back from the table. As he reached for Talwyn's hand though, she said, "Wait."

They both paused, Talwyn halfway out of her seat.

"Thank you. Both of you. For everything you gave. For fighting," the High Queen said. "Just...thank you."

Talwyn didn't say anything, and Azrael nodded in a bow to her before he Traveled them to the Wind Court. She was taking Thorne to the Earth Court today, and the griffin was standing outside the stables when they appeared.

His wing was still heavily bandaged. The Witches said he wouldn't be able to fly for at least another month, and even then, only small, short flights for a while. The griffin had been in a pissy mood about it since he'd been able to stand on his own again.

He made a disgruntled sound when they appeared, clawing at the dirt with his front talons.

"You are sure about this?" Azrael asked, eyeing the griffin. "He could go back to the Witch Kingdoms. Be with other griffins. I can make you a portal whenever you wish, Talwyn."

She walked forward, reaching up to run a hand down Thorne's beak. He huffed into her hand before lowering his head to nudge at her, right where she had been stabbed in the side. Talwyn smoothed a hand down his neck.

"He'll let me know when he needs to go spend time there," she replied, holding out the apple she still held in her hand. Thorne crunched it down with a few snaps of his beak, immediately lifting his head and looking for more.

"At home, you overgrown buzzard," she muttered when he nudged her harder than necessary. The griffin seemed to still at the words, and she ran a hand down his neck again, keeping it there when she looked up at Azrael. "Are *you* sure about this?"

"About a griffin at the Alcazar? Not in the slightest," he answered, moving forward and stretching out a hand towards Thorne. The griffin shifted, a warning growl rumbling, but he let Az run a hand along his feathers.

"No," Talwyn said. "About me being your Consort."

Azrael's hand fell to his side as he turned to face her fully. "Why are you asking me a question you already know the answer to?"

"Because you will need an heir, Azrael," she answered quietly, fixing her gaze on Thorne. She had thought about this far more than she would have liked. "I cannot give you that."

A thumb and forefinger gripped her chin, turning her face back to his. "I understand that if we ever had a child, they could not rule the Earth Court as a demi-Fae. Do you want a child, Talwyn?"

Gods. She couldn't even fathom that. The idea of motherhood had never been one she had ever truly contemplated. She wasn't sure it was something she ever wanted.

"I can scarcely manage myself right now, Az, let alone a child," she answered truthfully. "But what of your people? Your Court? You will leave them heirless?"

"No," he countered, stepping so close there was no space between them. "We will learn who the successor will be and train them to rule the Court properly. The Earth Court will have an heir worthy of them, and you, Talwyn Semiria, will have all my love."

This, she realized as she looked up into earthy brown eyes. This was all she had ever wanted. Not a throne or some vengeance she thought she was owed, but something she didn't need to fix. To never doubt someone who said those words to her. Someone who wanted her just because she was breathing.

All she'd ever wanted was this.

Talwyn pushed up onto her toes so her lips brushed across his. She reached out to touch Thorne as she murmured, "Let's go home."

# CHAPTER 51
# ELIZA

"I cannot believe you said that in that meeting," Eliza said, throwing a ball of flames at Sorin.

He laughed as he caught it, the flame going out in his fist. "But you wear a crown so well, Eliza, dear," he replied with a wink, a crown of flame appearing above her head.

"I swear to Anala, Sorin, if you do not take back your title," she grumbled, crossing her arms and glaring at him as she immediately put out the crown of fire.

The prick could have taken the title back days ago, before this war had even ended. But no. He kept coming up with reasons to wait, but now everything was over. Things were settling down. He could take it back right now, for fuck's sake. They were just standing around, waiting for Razik to come back and let them know Cethin was ready for the Wards to come down. He'd gone back to Avonleya with Cethin and Kailia two days ago.

"You don't enjoy having all that power even just a little bit?" Cyrus asked from where he sat on a sofa with Cassius.

"I am more powerful than you either way, Cyrus. I don't need a godsdamn crown for it."

Cyrus huffed a laugh. "Admit it though. You sat on the throne, even if only for a moment."

"No, I did not."

"Do you think something is wrong?" she heard Scarlett ask, and she shifted her attention to her friend.

Scarlett had been quiet since the meeting with the other royals. She'd rested for a few days like the rest of them. Sorin had said Scarlett had slept for nearly three days straight. The moment she had woken though, she'd thrown herself head first into rebuilding tasks. She was constantly Traveling to the mortal lands or the other Courts.

Quite simply, Scarlett needed a break, and worrying over her brother now was not helping matters.

Sorin reached out, tugging her into him. "Everything is fine, Love," he replied, guiding her head to his chest. "Are you sure you are up for taking down the Wards today? It will be draining on you."

"Yes," Scarlett sighed. "It needs to happen sooner than later. I'm sick of giving my blood to everyone and constantly traveling through mirror gates. Plus, the mortal coronations start tomorrow. Cethin should be here for those. Unity and all that."

Sorin dropped a kiss to the top of her head, and Eliza shifted impatiently.

"You appear restless, your Highness," Cyrus quipped.

Eliza was ready to lunge at him when Razik appeared in the den. Sapphire eyes instantly found her, and his brow furrowed. "Why do you look like that?"

She dragged incredulous eyes to him. "Look like what?"

"Like you are about to become excessively violent."

"The Fire Princess is agitated," Cyrus called out, stretching his long legs and interlocking his hands behind his head. "But since you're here… She sat on the throne, didn't she?"

The crease between Razik's brows deepened. "I don't think I would consider it sitting."

Instead of tackling Cyrus, she was launching herself at Razik, who let out a grunt as he caught her.

"I know you missed me, *mai dragocen*, but—"

"Is Cethin ready?" she asked, speaking over him.

His lips twitched. "Yes."

"Then let's get on with this."

"At the top of the hour," Razik answered, his thumb beginning to drag back and forth along her hip where his arm was still looped around her waist. "We have a few minutes."

She twisted out of his hold, ignoring the flash of heat at feeling his touch after two incredibly long days. Turning to Sorin, she said, "Perfect. Just enough time for you to take back the royal seat."

"Eliza, it can wait—" Sorin started.

"I do not want it, Sorin," she interrupted. "The only reason I challenged Bastien was to take the Court back until you could get here. I have only kept it this long because I knew you needed to focus on other tasks, but those are done now. The Fire Prince needs to be at those coronations. He is the one that will be working with the other leaders of the realm. I do not wish to be something Varlis wanted for me, even if it is fire instead of earth. I do not want it for one second longer."

Sorin's features had softened, and Scarlett had stepped away from him so he could move closer to her.

"I am sorry, Eliza," he said. "I did not realize—"

She held up a hand to stop him. "I do not regret it. If it was the only way, I would gladly keep the title and throne. But it is not the only way. It is yours by birthright and by power. You are the most powerful Fire Fae. A sword belongs in my hand more than a crown belongs on my head."

"That it does, General," Sorin answered with a small smile.

"I abdicate the royal seat of the Fire Court to you, Sorin Aditya. Do you accept?"

Cyrus and Rayner were already on their feet, having moved to her side so they stood before him.

"I do," Sorin answered, his smile widening.

The three of them bowed in unison, palms over the Marks on their chests that signified the loyalty to their Court and to Sorin. The Fire Prince and his Inner Court. The way it was almost meant to be.

Sorin reached out, pulling her into an embrace. "Thank you for stepping up when needed, Eliza. Your loyalty to this Court knows no bounds," he murmured into her ear.

"Thank you for saving me all those years ago and for giving me a chance."

He gave her an extra squeeze before releasing her.

"If you are all ready, we can go to the island," Razik said, eyes watching her intensely, despite speaking to everyone else in the room.

There were murmurs of agreement, and moments later, they were standing on an island just outside the Avonleyan Wards. It was the calmest the island had ever been. The winds and waves were always unbearable every time she'd been here. Now there was a light breeze, waves gently lapping at the shore.

"You are sure this is going to work?" Scarlett asked, beginning to push back her sleeves. "Cethin will survive?"

"Yes," Razik answered, sounding bored, but Eliza could feel his trepidation down their bond. He wasn't as confident in this as he was portraying.

She reached over and ran her fingers along his arm, and he instantly snagged her wrist, pulling her into his side.

*Raz?*

*This will be fine.*

But he was rigid beside her, and there was nothing she could really do about it.

Scarlett was drawing Marks in the sand, and each one had Razik's arm tensing more and more around her.

*So this cave…*

Razik slid his gaze to her. *What about it?*

*If we wanted to spend some nights there, I wouldn't be entirely opposed.*

She could swear his eyes darkened. *And the rest of the time?*

They hadn't really discussed this much. Where they would live at the end of this. She would need to be in the Fire Court, and he would need to be in Avonleya. Logistically, it made more sense for Razik to stay in the Fire Court with her. He was the one who could easily Travel, and with the Wards about to come down, it wouldn't be complicated anymore. But…

She hadn't been back to that cave since they'd accepted the twin flame bond, and she found herself missing the stupid place.

A godsdamn cave.

*I guess we split our time between the two. As long as we're together.*

*So you did miss me.*

She gave him a flat look, but before she could respond, Scarlett drew both their attention back to her as she began calling Chaos to her palms, darkness growing and pooling.

"So she just has to funnel Chaos into the Marks? That's it?" Eliza asked, head tilting as she watched.

"That's it?" Razik repeated. "Everything has been leading up to this moment, and you say 'that's it?'"

He had a point. If they hadn't found this lock, Scarlett wouldn't have this power, and the Wards wouldn't be coming down.

She sighed. "Will there be more required of the High Queen to take down these Wards, or will she finally catch a godsdamn break?"

"This will work. If anyone has to give anything more for this, it will be Cethin."

"This will work, Razik," she said quietly.

His lips just pressed into a thin line, and he gave a tight nod.

Scarlett was pouring Chaos into the Marks she'd drawn, and it was taking more power than Eliza had expected. These Wards were extraordinary. It wasn't hard to believe they came from gods and goddesses as Scarlett gave and gave.

Finally, minutes later, she dropped to her knees, the power flaring out. Sorin was instantly there, tilting her face up to his. She was pale, her silver eyes dull and more blue than silver. Eliza hadn't seen her this drained since she had become a World Walker.

"We should be able to see it," Razik muttered.

"See what?" Eliza asked, still distracted by her friend.

"There is always mist along the shores, but we should be able to see the Nightmist Mountains."

"Can you Travel in?"

"That was not the agreement. I was to wait here until Cethin and Kailia Traveled out and crossed where the Wards had been."

"But what if—"

She stopped speaking when the air shifted in front of them, ashes swirling and Kailia appearing.

Razik's eyes narrowed. "Where is Cethin?"

"He is coming," she said. "But I..."

Her amber gaze cut to Eliza, and she wasn't sure what was happening. She'd never seen the female so unsure. Razik clearly understood what was happening though. He brushed a light kiss to

Eliza's temple before he unwound his arm from her and reached for the Avonleyan Queen. "Come here, Lia."

Kailia was instantly in his arms. She was tiny and petite the way it was, but next to Razik, she appeared even smaller. This fierce female who could summon deathstone at will was clinging to Razik as she waited to see if her husband survived this.

His family. He had told her that he, Cethin, and Kailia were close, but she had never realized that they were a unit as much as the Fire Court Inner Court was. A small smile tilted on her lips as she watched Razik comfort Kailia while they both waited for their king to appear.

It took another few excruciatingly long minutes, but Eliza sucked in a breath when the mist began to lessen. The peaks of the Nightmist Mountains far off in the distance began to take shape, and then Cethin was standing there.

Razik was passing Kailia to him as quickly as Sorin had dropped to Scarlett's side.

"All is well, Tiny Fiend," the king murmured into Kailia's hair, and a small sob escaped from her. Razik clapped Cethin on the shoulder, the two of them exchanging looks of relief before Cethin turned to Scarlett, taking Kailia with him.

"You are free?" Scarlett asked, lifting her head from Sorin's chest to look at her brother. Her hand was pressed to Sorin's forearm, taking power from him to ease some of the strain of giving so much.

"We're all free, Scarlett," Cethin said, lowering to his knees before his sister. "Because of you, the Fae? Avonleya? The realm? We are all free."

She turned the page in her book as she sat snuggled on the sofa before the fire in the cave. They had Callan and Tava's coronations to attend tomorrow. Hale's and Drake's had already happened over the past week. One more day of celebration, and then they could all take a nice long break.

Razik was reading his own book beside her. One she couldn't read, of course. He promised to teach her more once things settled down, but it still bothered her she couldn't read most of the books here. Or in his study at the Greybane Estate. Or in his rooms at the Aimonway Castle.

"You are restless," Razik commented, turning the page of his book.

"I am not."

"You are."

She huffed a sigh, snapping her book closed. "What are you reading?"

"A book on runes and Marks."

She hummed something in response before she got to her feet and made her way to the small kitchen. Opening the icebox, she found some dried meat and grapes. When she turned back around, he was leaning against the counter. Shirtless. Obviously.

"What?" she demanded, setting the food on the counter.

"I have been searching for days trying to figure out how Balam transferred that life bond. It should not be possible."

She gave him an incredulous look. "You are still on this, Raz? Does it matter? It worked."

"But at what cost?"

"That seems pretty obvious," she answered, popping a grape into her mouth. "His life was the cost."

He made a noise of contemplation. "Maybe, but I came across something else."

"Okay...?"

"If there was a way to remove that Mark atop your heart, would you want to pursue it?"

The grape she was about to eat dropped from her fingers, rolling across the ground. "We had an agreement not to talk about this again. Ever."

"I never actually agreed to that."

"We are *not* discussing it, Raz."

"Eliza—"

"No."

Then he was sweeping her off her feet and setting her on the counter, caging her between his arms. He brought his brow to hers, his

671

voice low, as he said, "Hear me out, *mai dragocen*. After that, if you never wish to speak of this again, I will agree."

Her lips pursed. "Fine."

"There are other worlds out there. Worlds these books came from. Worlds more advanced than our own. There is a chance that someone out there knows how to remove this curse, Eliza."

Her mouth nearly fell open. "You want to go to other worlds for this? Absolutely not."

"No," he countered. "But Scarlett can now control the mirror gates. I am suggesting we not discount an obvious resource: those in other worlds. If I can find something in a book and figure out which world it came from, we could contact someone in that world."

"Do you even know how to do that?"

"No, but anything can be learned, *mai dragocen*. That is the joy of books."

"Is this that important to you?" she asked, trying to swallow down the tears welling in her eyes. They had talked about this. She thought he was fine with her not being able to have children.

A hand came up, cradling her cheek in his palm. "I would pursue this no matter what Curse Mark adorned your skin. It is not the type of curse, but the fact that it is a curse to begin with. But if this is not something you want, I will let it go, Eliza."

She stared into his sapphire eyes, getting lost in everything she found there. She moved first, closing the distance between their lips and kissing him slowly. He broke the kiss after a time, a finger tipping her chin up to look into her eyes.

"If we find a way, it does not mean we have to have children, Eliza, but I want you to have that choice. If we decide not to, then that is because we decided, not because of some Curse Mark from a dead Fae fucker. I cannot promise we will find an answer, but if this is something you want, I need you to tell me."

"It is something I never thought I could have," she whispered. "It is something I have taught myself not to want. But so were you."

His lips lifted into a small smile. "And now, *mai dragocen?*"

"And now you have ruined me."

"In the best way possible, if I remember correctly," he said, lips drawing closer to hers.

She huffed a small laugh. "It terrifies me to allow myself to hope," she admitted.

"I will say nothing else of it unless I have found an answer, but I want your permission to look into it."

She searched his eyes, his lips hovering above hers. "Maybe hope isn't such a bad thing."

# CHAPTER 52
# CALLAN

"Tava?"

She started, shooting to her feet. She had been sitting in a chair near the window, looking out over the city below. He'd been watching her for a good minute now, wondering how in the world they had made it here.

"Callan, I did not hear you enter," she said, smoothing her hands down her silk robe before clasping her hands in front of her. Habits that had been ingrained in her from childhood. Then, as if suddenly remembering such a thing was no longer required, her cheeks flushed.

His lips quirked to the side as he crossed the room, pulling her into him. A small sigh escaped her as she settled against his chest, and he ran a hand up her spine.

"What were you contemplating so deeply?" he asked.

"Nothing important," she murmured. "Is Eva awake yet?"

"She still sleeps," Callan answered, taking his wife's hand and leading her out to their small private dining room. Eva and the other children had returned from Avonleya when Scarlett took the Wards down a week ago. Most of the children had returned to Baylorin with it being the only home they knew. Nuri, Juliette, and Scarlett had been working closely with Callan and Tava to find them permanent homes, but there were so many of them, there were still a couple dozen to work through. Those children were currently being housed in a wing of the castle with constant caretakers. Tava spent most of her days there, and Eva was always excited to go see the other children the moment she woke.

But today would be different. At high noon, he and Tava would be officially crowned King and Queen of Windonelle. Soon there would be staff bustling around them. Tava would be rushed off to bathe and dress. They would send him off to do the same. But for the next hour, he had her all to himself.

There was a small breakfast spread laid out for them, and he pulled out a chair for her to sit before taking the seat across from her.

She was pouring them both tea as she asked, "When is everyone else arriving?"

The Lords of the various Windonelle territories had all been gathered since the war had officially ended, and Lords from Rydeon and Toreall had been making their way here after each coronation. It was why they had started in Toreall and worked their way west. Drake and Hale themselves would arrive with one of the Fae royalty using portals for Traveling.

"Throughout the morning," Callan answered.

"And the celebration afterwards?"

Callan smiled at her. "Everything is being handled, Little Fox. There is nothing for you to do but enjoy the day." She smiled, but it was tight as she turned her attention to fixing her plate. "Tava?"

"It is nothing, Cal."

He was up, around the table, and sliding into the chair beside her in the next breath. He took a serving spoon from her hand and set it aside before taking both her hands in his as she twisted to face him. His thumb swiped along her knuckles and across the ring she now never took off.

"Tell me, Tava, and do not tell me it is nothing."

"I am simply not used to so much attention," she answered with a soft smile. "I was always a spectator at such events."

"You are no longer in the background, Tava."

"I know. It takes some…getting used to."

"I will be beside you. All day. If you need a moment, I know the perfect small conservatory to get some air."

She huffed a soft laugh, pulling a hand free of his to cup his cheek. "I truly do love you, Callan."

He reached up and gently grasped her nape, pulling her to him. As her lips parted for him, he resented the fact the staff would be here soon to begin preparations when he'd much rather take her back to bed.

With willpower he did not know he possessed, he pulled back. Her turquoise eyes followed his lips and that willpower almost shattered. "Was this what you were thinking by the window?" he asked, swallowing down desire.

"What?" Her brows knitted together for the briefest moment. "Oh, that. No. I was thinking of Balam, as odd as that sounds."

"I do not think it is that odd," Callan replied, tucking golden hair behind her ear. "He did raise you."

"True. And I think…" Her gaze fell to her lap for a moment before she said, "I think he truly loved my mother, and perhaps by extension, Drake and I."

"I think he also loved you both," Callan said. "Everything he did was to keep you both out of harm's way, just as he vowed to your mother."

"I think that is why he did it," she said, fingers reaching for her amulet and dragging it back and forth along the chain. "He made the comment he vowed that Drake and I would not know pain and suffering as our mother had, but he had known it too. He rarely spoke of her. I think it hurt too much to do so, and if you had…"

Callan thumbed away the single tear that had slipped free. "If I had what?"

"If you were gone, I would have known the same pain and suffering he had lived with for the last two decades."

"Immortal beings do not seem to love the same way mortals do. I do not know if it is simply because they live for so many years or if it is something else, but I think you are right, Tava. I think Balam loved you both. If I have learned anything over the last year, it is that to love is to sacrifice."

"I wish I knew her story," Tava whispered, swiping at another tear. "I know this is silly. I have lived my entire life without my mother, but I wish I knew what happened."

"It is not silly, Tava. From the sounds of it, her story was not an entirely happy one," Callan said gently. "I think that was another way of keeping his vow to her. That you would not be burdened with the knowledge of her suffering."

"That is a beautiful way to think of it."

The door was thrown open, startling them both, and Callan turned to find Eva skipping into the room. She stopped suddenly, a frown appearing on her face.

"Why is Tava crying?" Then her eyes flew wide. "Are you leaving again, Cal?"

"No, Eva," he said quickly, getting to his feet and going to his sister. He crouched before her. There were still sleep lines on her cheek. "We already discussed this. No more traveling for quite some time. When the time does come again, you and Tava will come with me." She nodded a few times, worrying her bottom lip, and Callan reached up to tug it from her teeth. "Would you like some breakfast before it is time to get ready for today's festivities?"

Her face brightened at that. "Yes, please," she said, skirting around him and bouncing over to climb into the chair he had just vacated. She and Tava were already in a deep conversation about dresses when he lowered back into his chair. As he watched them, he found himself grateful for a Maraan Lord that had learned to truly love so that he could have these moments.

"Do I get to steal away a High Queen for a dance tonight?"

Scarlett looked up at him as she tried to hide her smile. "It would be foolish to refuse an invitation from a king, would it not? Although, I do prefer my invitations written on paper and left inside books."

Callan barked a laugh, taking the hand she extended to him. He nodded at Sorin before he led Scarlett to the dance floor.

"Here we are," Scarlett said while they moved seamlessly through the dance steps. "Back where it all began."

"A lifetime older and perhaps a little wiser," Callan agreed.

Scarlett scoffed. "A little? I have been told by many that I have become wise these last months. And you?" Her features softened as she looked up at him. "You have become a king worthy of his crown, your Majesty."

"Thank you, Scarlett."

"Are you happy?" she asked after a moment.

He scanned the room, finding Tava across the hall speaking with Drake and Ezra. Eva had been with Tula almost all evening, and he found them on the dance floor. Tula had apparently convinced Rayner to dance, and Eva had dragged Cassius to the dance floor with her.

Finally, he said, "Yes, Scarlett. I am very happy."

"The light suits you," she replied, releasing a hand to spin under his arm. Her black dress flared at her feet before he pulled her back to him.

"And you, Scarlett? Are you happy?"

"I am."

"Are you free?"

She studied him for a long moment, and he could see the tears shimmering in her eyes. There was a thickness to her voice when she said, "I am, Callan. I am free."

The song came to an end, and he bent to press a soft kiss to her cheek. "I am glad, Scarlett."

There was a swirl of shadows before she was pressing a vial into his hand. "Should you ever need me, I will always come."

He watched her make her way back to Sorin, but she never made it. Cyrus was intercepting her and swinging her back onto the dance floor as she tipped her head back in laughter.

Tava caught his eye, and she excused herself, making her way to him. Callan tucked the vial into a pocket before immediately pulling her in close.

"You were wonderful today," he said, dipping his head to murmur into her ear.

He watched her cheeks turn a light pink. "You have told me that multiple times now."

"You look beautiful."

Her blush deepened. "You have said that multiple times as well."

He hummed. "Did you go shopping for me for tonight, Little Fox? Something in blue and grey? Perhaps to celebrate the coronations?"

Her eyes went wide. "Callan!" she admonished in a whisper, that blush going even deeper.

He laughed. A real one that he felt in his soul as he bent to brush his lips across hers. "Do you need some air?" he murmured.

"Yes, please," she whispered.

They made their way through the side room, and Callan led her down the hall to the conservatory. It was different from the last time they had been here. It had been cold and the middle of winter. Now it was late spring, and several of the windows were open.

He was watching her run her fingers along some new buds when he said, "I have been meaning to ask you: do you wish for Ezra to continue being one of your personal guards?"

"This again?" she sighed, glancing over her shoulder.

"You are a queen, Tava," he answered. "A queen needs personal guards."

"Not following me everywhere every moment of the day."

He arched a brow. "I am going to assume there is no place to sneak off to anymore, and if there is, you will be taking me with you?"

She rolled her lips to hide her smile. "Of course. But since that is indeed the case, a personal guard seems silly."

"Tava…"

She sighed again. "It would probably be better if Ezra was one of your guards instead. He could follow in his father's footsteps, I suppose."

"Why is that? I did not get the impression I was his favorite person, despite my relationship with his father."

A faint blush appeared on her cheeks again. "Do you remember in the gardens in Avonleya when I told you I had only kissed one other?"

"What?" he demanded, taking a step towards her.

"We grew up together. He told you that when you learned of the rebel camps. We were friends. Balam was trying to arrange for something more before everything happened."

Well, that explained a lot.

A noble being betrothed to a guard, even a royal guard was not common, but it would have kept Tava in the background. She would have been safe, and any children they may have had would have not been considered noble. He could see it all now. How thoroughly Balam had been trying to make sure the Middell heirs stayed safe and hidden away.

"He is a good man, Cal," Tava continued, pulling him back to their conversation. "It would have been a fine match, but it would have never been this."

Callan slid his hands into pockets, mainly to hide his clenched fists. "Captain of the Guard. We can promote him to Captain of the Guard. We will find new personal guards for both of us."

Tava huffed a small laugh, making her way towards him. "As you wish, Callan."

"It was only one kiss, right?" he asked when she came to a stop in front of him.

"Only one," she answered, pushing up onto her toes. "The rest are yours."

He could live with that, he supposed, as he wrapped an arm around her waist and kissed her soundly.

## CHAPTER 53
# CYRUS

"**M**y feet hurt," Scarlett whined when they appeared in the foyer of the Fiera Palace.

Cassius had just Traveled them all home from the celebration of Callan and Tava's coronations, and Cyrus could understand why Scarlett's feet hurt. He rarely saw her off the dance floor.

"I have something for that," Cyrus said with a grin.

"Is it a bed and uninterrupted sleep for hours?" she grumbled. She'd already taken her shoes off before they'd left, and they currently dangled from Sorin's fingertips.

"Some would argue it's better than that."

Her nose scrunched. "What could be better than sleep?"

There was a burst of flames, and Cyrus held out a palm.

"Where did you get that?" Cassius asked, eyeing the five rolls of mugweed.

Cyrus shrugged. "From your stash."

"Godsdamnit, Cyrus," Cass sighed. "That is for potions and herbal remedies."

"And thank the gods we have a Witch in the family now. This will remedy her aching feet." Cassius shook his head, but he didn't argue further, which Cyrus took as a good sign. "There's enough for all of us," he urged. "Besides, Scarlett did say after this coronation we were all taking some time to relax."

"I do not think she meant literally the moment we returned home," Sorin said.

"I definitely did," Scarlett cut in, swiping a roll from Cyrus's palm. "We can share."

"See? One for Eliza and Razik. One for Cass. One for Rayner. One for me. Perfect," Cyrus said, tossing one to each person, respectively.

They all looked between each other as if debating this decision, and it was Rayner who finally shrugged and said, "Let me put Tula to bed, and I will meet you all in the den."

A fire portal appeared a moment later.

"So you do not have to carry her up several flights of stairs," Sorin said by way of explanation.

Rayner was holding Tula, who was sound asleep on his shoulder, and he nodded his thanks before he stepped through the portal.

"Is that ever going to be addressed?" Eliza asked when the portal snapped shut behind them.

"Yes, but not tonight," Sorin answered.

Scarlett was already halfway across the bridge, making her way to the den. They followed after her as they always seemed to, and a few minutes later, they were all in various states of undress from their finery and taking pulls from the mugweed.

"I cannot believe you did this without me last time," Scarlett said with a pout as she took the roll back from Sorin.

"Should I tell her how many times you and I have smoked this since I met you, Cass?" Cyrus asked.

"Why would you do that, Cyrus?" Cass muttered when Scarlett immediately made another sound of outrage. Cyrus let out a laugh. "Calm down, Darling. Soon enough, you're not going to give a fuck about it."

Sorin took the mugweed back, and she crossed her arms, looking disgruntled. It didn't last long. Sure enough, within minutes, she was melting back against Sorin and propping her feet in Rayner's lap, who sat at the other end of the sofa they occupied.

"Tell me about this cave, Eliza," she suddenly said, silver eyes sliding to the fire general.

Eliza's lip curled up. "What about it?"

"Why do you go there to sleep all the time?"

Cyrus huffed a laugh, taking a pull from his mugweed. "I assure you, Darling, she is not going there to sleep."

Eliza flipped him off from her spot on the opposite sofa, but the fact that she didn't spout something back to him told him she was feeling as relaxed as the rest of them.

"So you have a bed in that cave?" Scarlett asked, tilting her head as she studied Razik.

"He has an entire home in that cave," Eliza said, blowing out some smoke. "It's rather cute."

Razik looked down at her. "It is not *cute*."

"What would you call it then?"

He blinked at her before finally grumbling, "Not cute."

She smirked, passing him the mugweed.

"Is it like a lair where you hide all your stolen treasure?" Scarlett continued. She was even lower on the sofa now, her head in Sorin's lap. Sorin had been methodically removing all the pins from her hair, and now he was winding various strands around his finger.

"It is not stolen treasure," Razik deadpanned.

Scarlett's brow pinched. "But you were going to steal a bowl."

Eliza snorted a laugh as Razik growled, "I was not going to steal that bowl."

"What kind of treasure do you have there?" Cyrus asked, sinking lower in his chair.

That had Eliza perking up. "Books," she said.

"Of course," Cyrus muttered.

"Books?" Scarlett asked, lifting her head. "Can I come see them?"

"Yes," Eliza said, at the same time Razik said, "No."

"No spare beds?" Scarlett mused.

"No," Razik repeated.

"But it's a giant cave."

"No."

"Rude," Scarlett said with a frown. Then she was shoving at Rayner with her foot. "What about you?"

"What about me?"

The Ash Rider's elbow was propped on the arm of the sofa, his finger steepled along his temple as he took a drag from his mugweed.

"Do you have a secret treasure cave you take all your female friends to?" Scarlett pushed, and it took all of Cyrus not to burst out laughing when Rayner's lips twitched. It had Scarlett pushing onto her elbows to study him closer. "Do you have a secret treasure cave?"

"No, Scarlett," Rayner sighed. "I do not have a secret treasure cave."

"Do you have a secret female friend?" Then she frowned in contemplation. "Or male friend? Both? Like Arianna and Stellan?"

A dark grin curled on Rayner's lips, and he slowly began dragging a single finger along the top of her foot and up her calf. "Are you thinking about new *experiences* again, your Majesty? You did mention that after saving the realm, you'd be interested in some of them."

And fuck. The sensual purr of his voice had Cyrus immediately contemplating hauling Cassius back to their rooms...

Scarlett's face went bright red. "What? No! I mean— I don't—"

Cyrus couldn't contain his laughter this time, and Scarlett turned to him, flipping him her middle finger. She spun to Sorin, who had slipped down the sofa, his head tipped and resting along the back of it.

"Sorin."

"No experiences tonight, Love," he answered, not even bothering to open his eyes. "If you are still interested in the morning, I am sure Rayner and I can come to an agreement."

"That is *not* what I was going to say!" she cried, reaching out to smack him in the chest, but he caught her wrist, dragging her up and into his lap. She was laughing by the end of it, and they all fell into conversations about nothing, enjoying the stars they'd all fought so hard to keep.

"Cass," Cyrus whispered, nudging at Cassius's shoulder.

They were on the floor of the den where they had eventually slid to when sitting in a chair had become too much. Everyone else was asleep where they had been sitting the night before. Scarlett was curled against Sorin's chest. Razik had Eliza tucked into his side. Rayner—

Well, he wasn't here. Cyrus assumed he'd eventually gone to his rooms to be there when Tula woke.

He shoved lightly at Cassius's shoulder again, and Cass gave a low groan.

"Shh," Cyrus hissed. "Everyone else is still sleeping."

"Then why are we awake?" Cass grumbled, throwing an arm over his eyes.

"Come on," Cyrus said, nudging him harder. "Get up. We need to get dressed."

Cassius lifted his arm so he could peer up at Cyrus with narrowed eyes. "Why?"

"Get up," he repeated, getting to his feet, joints cracking that definitely shouldn't.

Gods, whose idea was it to sleep on the godsdamn floor?

Cassius managed to contain his grumbling until they were outside the den and trudging up to their rooms.

*Their* rooms. Because Cassius was staying here, obviously. Cyrus would remain the Fire Court Second, and Cassius would remain Hand-to-the-High Queen of the realm. Together. They would all be together.

"What are we doing, Cyrus?" Cass sighed, kicking the door shut behind him.

"Just get dressed," Cyrus answered, crossing to the bedchamber and into their dressing room. He quickly shucked off the formal attire he was still somehow wearing before pulling on far more comfortable pants and tunic. He was sliding on his boots when Cassius finally appeared in the dressing room, still looking ready to fall into bed and sleep instead.

"How are you this awake?" Cassius asked, changing at a much slower pace than Cyrus had.

But the truth was, if he didn't do this now, he'd probably lose his nerve.

"Get changed, then we have to wake Sorin," Cyrus said, pushing past him and back out to the bedchamber.

He was trying not to pace when Cass came back out dressed in similar pants and tunic. He Traveled them back down to the den without a word, clearly realizing that this was something important to Cyrus.

Cyrus crossed the room, managing to wake Sorin without disturbing Scarlett. The worry that had immediately appeared quickly vanished when Cyrus told him what he needed. Sorin nodded, a fire portal appearing near the door where Cassius stood waiting.

Cyrus clapped Sorin on the shoulder in thanks before making his way back to Cassius, who was looking at him with concern in his eyes. One brown. One milky white. No eye patch. Not anymore.

He followed Cyrus silently through the portal, and then he went completely still when he saw where they were.

The cry of gulls filled the air as the sun bathed the land with its morning rays. There were already people bustling around the town, unloading ships and calling to each other from the docks. The smell of the sea filled Cyrus's senses, but it wasn't as agonizing as it had once been. Not with Cassius standing beside him.

Cyrus slid his hands into his pockets, waiting as Cass took everything in before his eyes settled back on him.

"This is Aelyndee," Cass breathed.

"You once told me this was the last place I felt truly deserving of something, and you were right, Cass," Cyrus said, watching as two workers loaded a cart with various items. Items he would have tracked and stolen a lifetime ago. "I loved Merrick, and I loved Thia. Gods, did I love Thia with everything I was." He looked back at Cassius once more. "But everything I was... Pieces of who I was died with them, and while I had my family, I still never felt completely whole. I didn't think I ever would again. That brokenness was just part of my fate that I needed to learn to live with. That I thought I was deserving of. But you..." He swallowed thickly, Cassius quiet as he let him get this out. "Who I was then? That person was made for Merrick. Was made for Thia. But who I am now? That person was made for you, Cass."

Cassius smiled at him as he reached up and pulled something from a pocket realm. When he opened his hand, the vial of his blood the Sorceress had kept was lying there.

"To new memories, Cyrus" Cassius said, black flames flickering to life in his palm and devouring the symbol of the hell Cyrus had been living for the past weeks, years, decades.

"To deserving happiness," Cyrus replied, watching while Cassius burned even the ashes to nothing.

Then he was reaching up and hauling Cass's mouth to his, not caring that they were standing in the middle of bustling docks on the shores of the sea.

"Show me everything," Cassius murmured when they finally broke apart.

So Cyrus spent the day showing Cassius around Aelyndee. It was different. A lot had changed, but much had stayed the same too. He didn't know if the loft would be the same. If it would be vacant. Likely not centuries later, but he showed him where he and Merrick had lived for their short years together. He showed him where some of his best cons had gone off seamlessly, and he showed him where he'd hidden when his father had died trying to steal him some bread to eat.

He showed him everything, just like Cassius had asked.

Because while this place was where Cyrus had lost so much and so much of who he was had ended, it didn't have to stay that.

After all this time, it became a place where something new began.

Something he was deserving of.

# CHAPTER 54
## SORIN

"Hey, Tula Bug," Scarlett said, crouching down to the little girl's level. "Care to join me for a walk? I have a super secret garden to show you."

Tula's eyes went wide with excitement. "Really?"

Scarlett nodded, taking the child's hand and leading her to stairs that would take them up the levels. They could Travel, but Scarlett would walk, taking her time to reach the Princess's Gardens on the top level that Sorin's father had designed for his mother.

Rayner waited until they were out of sight before he turned to Sorin and said, "What is it?"

"We need to discuss something," Sorin replied.

"I figured as much when Scarlett took Tula off so she didn't overhear the discussion," Rayner answered. "Where do I need to go?"

"Nothing like that," Sorin said, shaking his head. Folding his arms along the bridge railing, he leaned on them. He stared out the floor-to-ceiling window, Solembra sprawled out in the distance.

"Then what?" Rayner asked, taking up a similar position next to him.

"We need to discuss Tula."

"She stays with me."

There was no room for discussion or negotiation in that statement.

Sorin had been expecting as much. But it still needed to be addressed, and he knew he needed to be the one to do it.

"I understand, Rayner. But the Shifters have Charters that need to be considered."

"Arianna and Stellan can fuck off," Rayner retorted darkly.

"You know Scarlett and I are on your side in this."

"Then why are we having this discussion?"

"Because we need to take care of this before it becomes an issue with the Alpha and Beta. They will argue that Tula should be raised among her own. They will see it as their duty to protect her because of how powerful she is and will become," Sorin said.

"No one will protect her better than I will."

"I know, Rayner, which is why Scarlett and I are proposing something else."

He slid his grey eyes to Sorin. They were swirling, but they were not as turbulent as usual. They had all been completely drained after the battle in Windonelle, and Rayner always took longer than the rest of them to refill reserves. He likely needed a Source with his Avonleyan roots, but that was a discussion for another time.

"Scarlett has created a Bonding Mark of sorts," Sorin went on. "It would connect the two of you. Similar to a Guardian and Ward relationship, but more of a..." He sighed. There was really no other way to say it. "It would create a parent-child relationship, Rayner. Until Tula was of age to decide her own fate. If at that time she wishes to pledge loyalty to the Fire Court, we will, of course, grant that, and this can remain her home. Until then, you would be responsible for her."

Rayner straightened. "You speak of me adopting her."

"Yes. But the Bond Mark would overrule any claims from the Shifters," Sorin answered. "Scarlett is speaking with Tula. To make sure this is something she wants as well. But if you are ready, Scarlett can give you both the Mark right now."

"Yes," Rayner said without a moment's hesitation.

Sorin smiled at his friend, creating a fire portal up to the gardens a moment later.

They stepped through to find Scarlett and Tula near the pond Sorin had asked Briar to alter to house the seastar that lived in there now. The moment they appeared, Tula was racing to Rayner, who was scooping her up.

"Scarlett said I can stay with you," she said.

"Of course you can stay with me, Tula," Rayner answered, smiling down at her as the child toyed with the collar of his tunic.

Her little nose wrinkled. "She said I just have to be brave one more time, but I don't have to be brave."

"Oh?"

"Because she said you will be there too. You never let anything bad happen to me. You are always brave for me," she chattered, head tilting as she studied some of the embroidery on his tunic. "When we are done, can we bake cookies? The ones with the extra chocolate in them?"

"You actually bake?" Scarlett asked from where she was waiting for them near the pond.

"No," Rayner said.

But Tula was giggling. "We make those one cookies, Rayner. The really yummy ones. We can make them after you're done being brave, right? You will let me help? Oh! Can we make that cake with the strawberries too?"

"You actually bake," Scarlett said, her eyes shining with amusement as Sorin and Rayner made their way to her.

"What do you need for this Mark?" Rayner asked, ignoring his High Queen.

"Just some blood from each of you," Scarlett said, pulling a dagger from her shadows.

Sorin stood back and watched as Scarlett drew the Mark that would bind Rayner and Tula, and he smiled as their family grew a little more.

"Discover anything interesting?" Sorin asked when he walked into the chamber that housed the mirror gate in the Runic Lands.

Scarlett stood before the mirror in a simple amethyst gown, her hair loose around her shoulders and shadows drifting around her.

She huffed a sigh as she crossed her arms. "No. I wish I did. I would love to meet the female who could actually speak to us through these things."

"She was interesting," Sorin agreed.

"So I hear," Scarlett murmured, still scrutinizing the mirror.

He had told her of the female with deep red hair who drank from a cup made of paper. The things she had said and how she had helped them call Scarlett back to this world. Scarlett had spent a few hours a day here whenever she could. The books she had hauled with her were scattered across the long table, scribbles and notes written on parchment.

"They are waiting for us," Sorin said before she could get too lost in her thoughts again.

Her brows shot up. "Already? I did not realize so much time had passed."

"You tend to lose track of time when you come here," he answered, dropping a hand to her lower back to usher her out of the chamber.

When the doors were securely closed behind her, Sorin Traveled them to Shira Forest where Cethin, Kailia, and Saylah were waiting for them. Eliza was in Avonleya the most out of all of them, but Scarlett and Sorin had a standing dinner arrangement with Cethin every week. Scarlett made it a point to Travel over more often though, and he knew a few of those times she and Cethin had spent time at the Elshira Castle with their mother.

However, the goddess had finally regained enough strength back to be able to leave.

They had only had two of those weekly dinners, but it had been discussed at great length over those meals whether or not Saylah could remain in this world. Halaya. That's what he'd learned their world was called in other realms. There was an argument to be made that she could stay. But in the end, the goddess had made the decision for them.

That didn't stop Cethin from asking one last time, "Are you sure about this, Mother?"

"This world has faced enough because of my presence," Saylah answered.

"Achaz will still come for us," Cethin argued.

Saylah gave him a tight smile. "Perhaps someday, but I believe Temural and I are a higher priority at the moment. As for you two." She turned, fixing her muted silver gaze on Scarlett. "He will not come for you until he is prepared to face an equal. He cannot fight both a World Walker and Arius. My leaving will draw his focus elsewhere for a time."

Still trying to protect her children, even after all this, Sorin realized.

A panther stalked from the trees, coming to sit at Scarlett's side, and she ran her fingers through his midnight coat. The spirit animals would be leaving as well. Saylah had explained she had bargained for their help to fight in the battle in Halaya. Now that it was over, they must return to the sides of the gods and goddesses they were bound to. But Sorin had seen Scarlett's notes. He knew that someday she would come for them as their High Queen. Someday she would find a way to free them of the curse that bound them to gods and to their animal forms.

With a final scratch behind the panther's ears, Scarlett moved forward, Chaos flowing from her and into the mirror gate, funneling into Temural's symbol. The glass of the mirror swirled with darkness, embers of white light blurred as they whirled past until a male stood in the mirror.

Taller than any of them, he had long black hair that was tied back at the nape of his neck. Twin swords were at his waist, and a crown of gilded leaves and feathers sat atop his head. Pine green eyes narrowed on all of them before the cry of an eagle sounded and Altaria appeared, diving to Cethin's shoulder. The male in the mirror tracked the eagle, before his gaze flicked to Saylah, and he gave a jerk of his chin.

Temural.

Saylah would be going to whatever world her brother currently inhabited.

"He and Altaria are very close," Saylah said, the eagle clicking his beak. "Both are anxious to be reunited."

"Are all the bonds with the spirit animals that way?" Scarlett asked. "With the gods and goddesses, I mean."

"Many of them are, but there are others. There are those bound to Achaz and those who fight on his side of the Everlasting War," Saylah answered, more of the spirit animals appearing. Scarlett started to ask something else, but Saylah held up her hand. "This was before my time, Scarlett. I do not have the answers you seek."

"How did Shirina and Altaria become bonded to you and Temural if that took place before you existed?" Scarlett asked.

"There are many bargains made in secret, High Queen," Saylah said. "And those secrets become currency used when it matters most."

"Great," Scarlett muttered.

"I must go," Saylah said, turning to her son. "I am proud of you, Cethin. You lead these people the same way your father did. You sacrificed much and would have given more if required of you. I am glad you found love when it was not meant for either one of you."

Cethin bowed his head, Kailia stepping into his side a little more.

Sorin didn't know their full story. It was one he would learn over time, he supposed.

And then Saylah was turning back to Scarlett. "And you, my daughter." She stepped forward, cupping Scarlett's cheek in her palm. "My wish for you is that you know no more of loss and sacrifice." She bent, pressing a kiss to Scarlett's brow. "Always remember, Starfire, hope is for the dreamers."

Sorin leaned against the doorjamb as he watched her play. Her eyes were closed, fingers gliding along the keys. This wasn't a song in minor chords. Not one of anger or loss. There was sadness to it, though. It was to be expected. Today was hard. Tomorrow would be harder.

He swirled his glass of amber liquid, the sound of clinking ice alerting her to his presence. She looked over at him, her fingers never missing a note as she smiled softly and slid down the bench a little bit.

Sorin crossed the distance, plunking his glass down atop the piano before lowering down beside her. She played a little longer, and when she finished her song, she rested her head on his shoulder.

"We face tomorrow together, Love," Sorin said quietly into the stillness of the room. The sun had long since set, and the only light was from a few flickering orbs Scarlett had glowing above them.

"It will be different. Without…"

"I know, Scarlett."

"Everything is different," she murmured.

"Nothing stays the same, Love. You will watch many things come and go in your immortal years."

She was running a finger along the keys. "But you and I?"

"Will only fall more in love."

She lifted her head and rolled her eyes as she muttered, "Shut up."

He laughed, pressing a kiss to her temple before he gently gripped her chin and tilted her face up to his. "We will face all the changes together, Scarlett Sutara Aditya. The ones that hurt and the ones we celebrate. We protect what is ours."

She shifted, climbing into his lap and straddling his waist. The gown she was still wearing bunched around her thighs. "Thank you. For always coming for me. For seeing all of me and still coming for me."

"Like the stars love the night, Scarlett," he replied, fingers sliding into her unbound hair and pulling her mouth to his.

"All the way through the darkness."

# CHAPTER 55

# SCARLETT

"**T**hose are my daggers," Scarlett groused, watching as Nuri shoved a set of blades into a pack.

"No, they're not," Nuri scoffed.

"Yes, they are," Scarlett said, stalking forward. "They have an 'S' on them."

"Yes. That stands for *Shadow*," Nuri drawled, pulling the pack away when Scarlett reached for it.

"It does not stand for Shadow, and even if it did…" Scarlett smirked as her shadows burst free.

Juliette was lying on her back sprawled across the bed. "I believe those are the daggers you lost to Nuri when she won a bet."

"What bet?" Scarlett demanded, hands going to her hips.

Juliette rolled onto her stomach. "I do not know which bet, Scarlett. We bet on everything."

"You cannot recall the bet, but you can recall the prize?"

"Surely you can part with them," Nuri said, shoving a cloak into the pack. "You have super special friends that can create you bright and shiny new daggers."

Scarlett rolled her eyes, but stopped arguing with her. She was right, of course, and she was just…in a mood. All three of them were.

Which was about to be quite a conundrum for the males and female in their lives.

Scarlett crossed the room and plopped down onto the bed beside Juliette. She pulled a small bag from her shadows, opening it and tossing a few nuts into her mouth. Juliette immediately snatched the bag, dumping some peanuts into her hand.

"Do they not have food in the Witch Kingdoms?" Scarlett asked with a scowl.

"I was in a hurry to leave this morning," Juliette said with a shrug, dumping out another handful.

"I literally came to get you." Juliette shrugged again, passing the bag back to Scarlett. "This is over half gone now," she cried in outrage.

"I think that is everything," Nuri said, and Scarlett and Juliette fell quiet, turning to her.

Silence settled over them as the three of them looked between each other. Scarlett was the first to look away as she said, "You do not have to go, Nuri."

"I do, Scarlett," Nuri answered. Her voice was softer than Scarlett had ever heard it. "I cannot stay here. Not with everything I was forced to do to the people on this continent and in this realm."

Scarlett understood. She truly did. They had discussed this for hours. First the three of them and then several more discussions with Sorin, Mordecai, and the others. Nuri had already stepped down as the Contessa of the Night Children, Auberon becoming Count of the territory. He had not called for Nuri's execution, but she had been banned from the territory. Scarlett understood that too. She had murdered their Contessa who had reigned for over five hundred years. Banishment was a mercy, really.

Juliette cleared her throat. "We really should get going. I have to be back at sundown for a meeting with various coven leaders."

Juliette. The new High Witch, taking the place her aunt had left vacant. There had been a question whether or not Juliette could be both the High Witch and the Oracle, but apparently bloodline was as important to the Witches as it was to the rest of the lands. It was really Juliette and Arantxa leading the Witch Kingdoms now. Arantxa's official title may be the High Witch's Second, but Juliette left many responsibilities in her hands. She had been Hazel's Second for decades and knew more of the customs than Juliette did. They would figure out a balance at some point. The fact that Juliette and Arantxa had developed a more intimate relationship certainly helped matters.

"Are you sure you have everything?" Scarlett asked, looking around the room Nuri and Mordecai had been staying in these past few weeks. Mordecai had been packed and gone before the sun rose, ever the efficient warrior. But he'd also known Juliette and Scarlett would be here at sunrise. Now it was nearly high noon. They'd had the morning together.

One last time.

Scarlett gave her sisters a weak smile as she held out her hands to them. Nuri shouldered the pack she had just finished filling and picked up another one that had been set off to the side. Juliette grabbed one hand, and Nuri's hand slipped into the other before Scarlett Traveled them to the Citadel.

Scarlett preferred the mirror gate in the Runic Lands. It was the most private of them all. Juliette couldn't leave the continent though, so this was the best mirror gate to use. The doors to the Citadel immediately opened, Ashtine and Briar there waiting for them. The Fae Queen smiled and Briar stepped aside to let them pass. Mordecai, Sorin, and Arantxa were already here, along with Cassius. Scarlett did not particularly want anyone else present for this.

Mordecai immediately took the packs from Nuri, adding them to his one pack he was holding before they made their way silently through the halls to the libraries beneath. Scarlett felt as if she had blinked and suddenly found herself here, before the mirror gate. Briar and Ashtine left them in peace, pulling the doors shut behind them, the thud of it echoing in the silent chamber.

No one spoke as the females silently stared at each other once more.

"Juliette?" Scarlett rasped, holding Nuri's stare. "I need you to tell me we will see each other again."

"There are many possibilities, Scarlett," she answered softly.

"But that is one of them, right?"

A tear slipped free.

She heard Juliette's voice crack when she said, "Yes. There are many that find our paths crossing again. Some in this life. Some beyond the Veil."

"You can stay," Scarlett said again. She glanced at Mordecai. "You can both stay. You will be safe here."

The seraph shook his head. He had only stayed this long to make sure that all the remaining seraphs had been dealt with. "Even you cannot stop this, your Majesty. You have just saved this realm. If I stay here, you will find more than Maraans in your lands."

"You will keep her safe?" Scarlett asked, more tears slipping free, and to her shock, two tears were sliding down Nuri's cheeks. Scarlett had never seen her cry. Not once. Tears in her eyes, yes, but never real tears. Not even when Juliette had died.

"With my life," Mordecai answered.

Scarlett nodded her head a few times, swallowing down the sob trying to crawl up her throat. "I guess this is it then."

"For now," Nuri agreed, as the three of them fell into each other's arms.

What would it be like to be missing one? It had been the three of them since they could walk. She would never feel whole with one of them gone.

"Scarlett," Sorin said quietly.

"I know," she rasped, but instead of stepping back, she only clung more tightly to Nuri and Juliette.

It was Cassius whose hand came to her back as he said softly into her ear, "They need to go, Seastar."

"I can't do it."

"You can, Scarlett," Nuri said, squeezing her one last time. "For me. I cannot stay here."

Scarlett pressed her lips together and sucked in a sharp breath before forcing herself to step back.

"Alaric forced us together, but we have always chosen to be sisters," Nuri said, looking between her and Juliette. "That will remain across the stars."

She tried to flash them her signature grin when Mordecai moved to her side, but it never quite made it to her face.

Scarlett silently summoned Chaos to her palms, letting it build. "You are sure about this?" she asked the seraph.

"Unlock the mirror gate long enough to let us pass. I will find our way to where we need to go," he answered.

Scarlett had questioned the seraph about this over and over, but the only answer he ever gave was that he had access to technologies and things not found in this world.

"I swear to you, Scarlett, she will be safe," he said, a wing curling around Nuri.

Scarlett nodded as Mordecai gently gripped Nuri's elbow and tugged her towards the mirror gate. She did not look at him. She kept those honey-colored eyes on her sisters. Scarlett lifted her palms, ready to open the gateway, waiting for Nuri's signal.

"I love you both. So very much," Nuri said.

And Scarlett knew if she did not do it now, she would not have the willpower to do it. She funneled the Chaos into the mirror gate and the moment she did so, Mordecai was pulling Nuri through it with him.

Scarlett immediately pulled the Chaos back, resealing the gate, and she dropped to the ground. Juliette went with her as they clung to each other and cried over a piece of them now gone.

Arantxa and Juliette were the first to leave, the Witch gently reminding Juliette they had to meet with coven leaders and that Juliette would probably want some time to compose herself. Cassius left with them to Travel them back to the Witch Kingdoms.

Scarlett found herself lying on the floor, her cheek pressed to the cool stone. Within moments of the others leaving, Sorin was lying down beside her, fingers brushing back her hair.

"I cannot get up right now. My heart hurts," she whispered. There were no more tears. Apparently she cried them all with Juliette.

"I know, Love," he answered. "I will sit with you in the dark until you are ready."

Seconds turned into minutes. They turned into an hour. Two. She lost count until she was ready to face a new world.

Sorin helped her to her feet, tucking her in close as they left the Citadel libraries and made their way back upstairs. Once outside, Sorin would Travel them home. At least that part of her world would be right. Her family would be there waiting for them.

The guards at the main doors were just pulling them open when her name was called causing her to pause and turn.

"Yes?" She managed to muster a tight smile as she beheld the Fae Queen.

Ashtine gave her a small, knowing smile. "The winds speak of new beginnings. They speak of beings and worlds awakening. They speak of a genesis because of this day. You were not the only one chosen."

"I do not understand," Scarlett said, Sorin tucking her tighter into this side.

"None of us do," Ashtine answered. "But we will. In time. As with all things."

Ashtine turned then, heading back into the depths of the Citadel, and Scarlett and Sorin stepped outside. He Traveled them straight to the den at the Fiera Palace where their family was waiting. They all looked up at their arrival, sad smiles filling their faces as they waited for her to say something.

"I've had a shitty day," she finally said. "I expect everyone to let me win at cards and billiards tonight."

Cyrus scoffed. "How will that be any different than every other night, Darling?"

"You do not *let* me win."

"And we're not going to start now," he retorted, raising his glass of alcohol in a cheers motion.

"That's fine, Darling," she sighed, sauntering over to the billiards table. "I'll kick your ass either way. I could use some new shoes."

Cyrus let out a chuckle as he pushed to his feet from the sofa, making his way to the table.

She caught Sorin's eye across the room and gave him a soft smile.

The world may look a little different, but she was finally home.

# THE BRIGHTEST STARS

***Two Months Later***

"You are fidgeting," Sorin said from where he sat beside her on a small sofa.

"I am not," Scarlett answered.

He reached over, placing a hand on her bouncing knee, and she sent him a bland look.

"Why are you nervous about this?" he asked.

"I am not nervous. I am excited."

"I am aware, Love. You have been flitting around the palace since Juliette sent word that the babes were coming."

"I have not been flitting anywhere."

"Mhmm," he hummed, resting his temple against his fist.

Truth was, she was nervous. She knew Fae pregnancies were harder and more complicated. They didn't last as long as mortal ones, but all that power growing along with a babe took its toll. The actual birth, though, was even more intense.

And Ashtine was doing it twice.

Scarlett had been fretting around the palace. Sorin had told her they did not need to go right away. That it would be hours, possibly a day or two before the babes would be here and Ashtine and Briar

701

would be ready for visitors. She'd tried to keep busy, but the day had dragged on. She hadn't slept, and it had indeed been the next morning before a flurry of snowflakes had appeared near Sorin. He'd plucked a message from it, a wide grin filling his face. Scarlett had Traveled them to the Black Halls before he'd even said a word.

She knew Sorin was just as excited. She could feel it down their twin flame bond. Briar was like a brother to him. The twins would not be presented to the rest of the Courts and the realm for another week, but these first days? They were just for those the Fae King and Queen wanted to visit. Family and close friends. The rest of the Fire Court would come another day. Briar and Ashtine's Inner Courts tomorrow or the following day perhaps.

The doors opened, and Sorin was on his feet before Scarlett.

*Now who's excited?* she quipped down the bond.

But Sorin was already striding forward to embrace Briar, before the Fae King was turning to her. She threw her arms around him as she whispered, "Congratulations, Briar."

"Thank you, Sunshine," he murmured, giving her an extra squeeze. "Are you ready to meet them?"

"Yes," she said, releasing him to follow him into the suite.

They moved through the sitting room and into a large bedchamber. Ashtine was propped up in the bed, and Talwyn was there. Scarlett was not surprised. She was one of the queen's closest friends, despite everything. Talwyn held a cup for Ashtine to drink from before setting it aside.

"I will give you all some time and fetch some food," Talwyn said, nodding at Scarlett and Sorin before she slipped out of the room.

Ashtine held a babe, and Arantxa was moving to Briar with another small bundle in her arms. The Witches were the only beings entrusted to deliver Fae babes. Juliette had been here to learn, but Arantxa would have delivered them.

Briar was taking the babe and moving to the bed, climbing atop it beside Ashtine before he beckoned them closer. Sorin's hand fell to the small of her back as they moved forward together, and when she was close enough to see them, Scarlett's breath caught.

"They are beautiful," she whispered.

"They are," Ashtine lilted with a soft smile. She looked utterly exhausted, and Arantxa was staying nearby to monitor her closely.

A mix of their mother's pale complexion and their father's dark skin, warm tawny faces peeked out from the blankets they were bundled in. They both had pale hair, although one was more silver like Ashtine's while the other was the pale blonde of Briar.

Briar nodded to the babe Ashtine held. "Prince Nakoa, Heir to the Water Court and the Western Courts."

Scarlett swallowed when Ashtine extended the babe to her. She took him, cradling him close as he slept soundly.

"Princess Sawyer, Heir to the Wind Court and the Eastern Courts," Briar said, passing the babe to Sorin.

Tears immediately sprang to Scarlett's eyes at seeing Sorin bring the babe close.

"Hello, Sawyer," Sorin murmured.

The babe Scarlett held shifted a little, a small sound coming from him as a tear slipped down her cheek. "Welcome to the world, Nakoa," she whispered.

Something in her chest loosened as she stared at the babe in wonder.

For them.

She had saved this world for them. For the future Fae babes and mortal children. The twins making it to the world safe and sound was like the final piece of the game finally settling into place. The final victory to claim.

"You made it," she murmured to the tiny prince as he managed to work a hand free of his blanket. "We made it."

Sorin had moved closer, and she looked up at him, his features so soft and adoring as he cradled the newborn princess. "We made it," he echoed. "What now, Love?"

She hummed. "A wise, ancient sage once told me it is important to take time to enjoy the stars."

"Did he now?" Sorin said with a soft huff of laughter.

She looked back down at the babe before meeting his golden gaze once more. "Now we live, Sorin. We live, and we make sure the stars never go out."

# SNEAK PEEK
## RAIN OF SHADOWS AND ENDINGS

I am so excited to announce the first book in The Legacy Series! Book one will be released August 31, 2023, and the ebook is available for preorder now. Turn the page for a sneak peek.

A world the gods forgot.
An heir of death.
A chosen that was never meant to be.
But he'll take it all anyway.

# THE BEGINNING

I n all things there must be balance.
      Beginnings and endings.
      Light and dark.
Fire and shadows.

The worlds are no different. Beings emerged from the Chaos to create such a thing.

Among those to emerge were six Firsts: Falein, goddess of wisdom and clever-ness; Celeste, goddess of the sky and moon; Anala, goddess of day, fire, and the sun; Serafina, goddess of the stars and dreams; Achaz, god of beginnings; and Arius, god of endings.

Achaz and Arius emerged first. They became the most powerful, working together to maintain the balance. Beginning created. Ending judged.

The First gods created the Lesser gods. They went to various parts of the stars, setting up their own kingdoms and maintaining balance; and from them, the worlds grew and prospered. Some grew faster than others. Some were favored more than others. Some were lost, and some were forgotten.

New beings were created and scattered among the realms. Other beings were created and kept close. But as more and more came into existence, tension bloomed among the gods. Power balances began to shift, and the gods began to create beings with mortals— Demigods, whose descendants became their Legacy. Fear took root *that one of those bloodlines would become more powerful than the rest, so an accord was struck:*

*There would be no more Demigods created, and the Legacy across the realms were to be brought to one world. A realm created solely for them to grow and prosper and thrive. The Legacy were gifted mortals in their world to do the mundane tasks required for survival. They were also gifted the technologies from the most advanced of the worlds.*

*And they were gifted the Fae.*

*Beings created to balance out the power of the gods that ran in the veins of the Legacy. Power that was too great to let go unchecked. The magic flowing in the blood of the Fae fed the power of the Legacy, forcing them to rely on the Fae. In exchange for being this source of power for the Legacy, the Fae were given their own gifts—one of four elements. They were granted enhanced senses and an extended lifespan. All of these were given by the gods so that the Fae could watch over their Legacy and keep their bloodlines safe.*

*And then the gods left that world, agreeing to never interfere there again.*

*Over time, Chaos descended among the stars. Wars raged and the balance tipped. Some worlds were ended. Some were abandoned. Some were reborn.*

*But gods are fickle beings, and things meant to be forgotten never remain so.*

# CHAPTER 1
# TESSA

"Are you hiding in an alcove eating chocolate?"

Tessa froze at the sound of the low voice, said chocolate halfway to her mouth. She thought she'd been hidden well enough. Obviously not.

Damnit.

She quickly turned, hiding the chocolate behind her back. Which was stupid. He'd already seen it.

"I, um…"

She trailed off when her gaze landed on who had spoken to her. She could swear darkness swirled faintly in the dark emerald green eyes that were studying her, a slight frown on his full lips. His ebony hair was messy for the formal occasion they were about to attend, and a couple strands fell forward, brushing dark brows. His hands slid into the black pants that were clearly tailored to fit him perfectly, along with the black shirt and black vest that clung to his torso. He didn't wear the formal suit jacket that many of the other males had been wearing as she'd watched them slowly filter in. The top two buttons of his shirt were undone, and there was no tie in sight.

This night definitely called for a tie.

His head tilted to the side, and Tessa swallowed thickly, her mouth suddenly too dry. The *thing* inside her lifted its head, and she shoved it back down. That was the last thing she needed right now.

"Are you unwell?" he asked. Not because he cared about her well-being in any way. Very few actually *cared* about her, and that was definitely a thread of annoyance in his tone.

He had a slight accent that she'd never heard before, and it snapped her out of whatever trance she was in. She quickly dropped to a knee before him. Gods. He was a Legacy, and she'd just been standing there staring at him. Fantastic. Corbin was going to laugh himself into tomorrow when she told him about this.

"My apologies," she murmured, making sure her tone sounded like she meant it with her eyes fixed on the male's black shoes.

"You may rise," the Legacy said impatiently.

Well, that was easier said than done. She was in a dress that clung to her figure as much as his own custom-tailored clothing. This was the only occasion she would likely ever wear something of such elegance. The gown flowed down one of her arms completely, while leaving the other bare from her shoulder to her fingertips. It pooled at her feet, and she'd already tripped on the damn thing multiple times tonight. Her shorter than average height didn't help matters, even with the four-inch heels she'd been forced to wear. The dress was black with a sheer emerald green coverlet adorned with black beads that glittered in the flickering flames of the sconces.

Sconces, not lights and electricity like every other building had in the six Kingdoms of Devram. Because... Honestly, Tessa had never really understood why the Pantheon was void of all modern advancements, save for cell phones. But even phones had to be placed on a special setting that only allowed for incoming calls. Nothing else. Something about wanting to honor the humble beginnings of the worlds. She'd always thought it rather silly. The gods didn't care about their world. Why would they care if there was basic lighting in the Pantheon?

A hand was suddenly in her face, and she glanced up at the Legacy in confusion.

"Well?" he demanded, wiggling his fingers. "I assume it will be difficult to get up in that dress, especially as you seem unwilling to put down your chocolate."

Tessa felt her cheeks flush, but she slowly slid her fingers into his palm. His hand wrapped around them, tugging her to her feet. When she went to pull her hand back, his grip tightened.

"Why are you out here by yourself, away from the other Fae?" he asked, his voice deceptively low and innocuous. It wasn't quite as entrancing as the compulsions the Legacy could use, but it wasn't that far off either.

She knew she shouldn't be out here. Dex was going to be livid. Not so much at the fact that she had sneaked off, but that she'd done so without telling him so he could join her.

"I was—"

"I would strongly suggest not lying to me," the Legacy said coldly.

"I wasn't going to lie to you," she retorted, and his brows rose at her address.

She sighed internally. This is why Dex never let her sneak off alone. She was remarkably good at moving about unseen and sneaking into places she wasn't supposed to be, but she was also rather impulsive at times.

Okay, a lot of the time.

"I was finding some place to eat this without having to share," she said, waving the chunk of chocolate before his face. Her other hand was still clasped in his.

He just stared at her like he wasn't quite sure what to say in response to that.

"Which is why I was hiding in an alcove," she added, beginning to fidget when he still didn't say anything. She hated enclosed spaces. The alcove hadn't been her first choice, but desperate times and all that. "I will just, um… Go back to the grand hall?" she said, trying to tug her fingers from his grasp. But his grip only tightened further.

"That would be the wise thing to do," he agreed.

"Okay, well, then I sort of need my hand back."

Instead of releasing her though, he stepped into her, crowding her back further into the alcove. "Are you slated to be Selected?"

"What?" she asked breathlessly. This was bad. So bad. Why in the world did she think she should come out here without Dex?

"It is the first time in a millennia that all six Kingdoms have heirs selecting their Sources at the same time," the Legacy said.

"I know that."

"It is a historic night."

"I know that," Tessa repeated.

"Everyone is incredibly apprehensive. The Lords and Ladies are on edge, and their heirs are full of anxious anticipation. The Fae are allowed to join in the celebrations, and you are out here." His other hand came up and plucked the chocolate from her fingers. "Hiding and eating chocolate."

"Hey!" she protested, reaching for the sugar, but he held it out of her reach. She was shorter than average, sure, but he was also taller than average. Taller than Dex and Brecken.

"And arguing with a Legacy," he added harshly.

Tessa snapped her mouth shut. She was hungry, and he'd just taken the one bit of sustenance she was likely to get for the next four hours. He gave her a smug look as he set the chocolate on a ledge that ran above them near the sconces.

It was definitely going to melt up there.

She sighed, and he frowned at the petulance. "Are you slated to be Selected?"

"What?" Her breath hitched at the fact that he'd asked this question again. If she had been slated for such a thing, that would mean she had already been claimed, and he would not be allowed to touch her without offending one of the heirs and their parents.

But she was not slated to be Selected.

"Do not make me ask that question again," he said in a soft warning, leaning in and twirling a loose golden curl around his finger. "I am not a fan of repeating myself."

"No," she whispered, her eyes falling closed as she waited for whatever he was going to do to her.

"You are upset by that?"

"No," she said truthfully. Because she wasn't. It might have afforded her some measure of protection at this very moment, but she'd never wanted the *honor* of being Selected to serve as the personal Source of one of the ruling family members in any of the six Kingdoms.

"No?"

She shook her head, opening her eyes to meet his curious stare.

"Really?"

"You told me not to lie to you," she bit out.

"That I did," he said, his lips almost lifting into a smile, but it didn't fully form. "Do you always obey orders so well... What is your name?"

"Tessalyn," she answered bitterly, knowing she couldn't deny a Legacy.

"Do you always obey commands so well, Tessalyn?" he asked, stepping into her even more. She could feel a hard chest brushing against her front.

"Rarely."

"Another truth," he said, that finger letting her curl go free and sliding along her jaw. She forced herself to remain still. "So you are either more obedient than you care to admit, or..." He trailed off, his fingers dropping to her bare shoulder and brushing down her arm.

"Or what?" she gritted out.

"Or it is just with me," he answered.

"It is neither of those things."

"Ah, now you are lying," he said, his lips finally turning up into a small smile.

She frowned. "I really should be getting back. I'm sure the Selection is about to start at any moment."

"It likely is."

"And I should be in there. So should you. To see your future Lord or Lady select their Source," she added, worrying her bottom lip. His eyes dipped to the movement.

"We definitely should be," he agreed, amusement seeming to flit across his features. "Be in there, that is."

"So..."

For a long moment, he didn't move, then finally he stepped back from her. She could have sagged with relief, but the surprise flooding through her was more overwhelming at the moment. As a Fae, she didn't really have the right to deny a Legacy. Fae were not allowed to deny a Legacy *anything* unless they were claimed and Marked. She could *say* no, but that didn't necessarily mean anything to them.

She slipped past the male and into the empty hall, pulling up the sides of her dress so she wouldn't trip on it. Her black heels clicked on the stone floor that was kept in immaculate condition, and she concentrated on not tripping yet again.

"It was a pleasure, Tessalyn," he called after her, and she knew she' should turn and acknowledge him. She knew it would be seen as incredibly disrespectful not to do so, but she didn't. She hurried down to the small side door she'd found to slip out here and rushed back into the grand hall where the Opening Selections would be held. Fae and Legacy alike filled the vast space, although none of them mingled together.

"Where have you been?"

Tessa jumped at the familiar voice in her ear, spinning to find a tall male with eyes such a dark shade of brown they were almost black glaring at her.

Dex.

She pushed out a breath when he slipped an arm around her waist, pulling her back against his chest, and she relaxed into him.

"After the Selection is done, we're still sneaking out, right?" Tessa asked, scanning the other Fae who were of age for Selection as they milled about the grand hall.

"As long as we're not Selected," Dex replied, resting his chin on the top of her head.

Tessa huffed a laugh. "We both know we're not going to be Selected. We can sneak off as soon as the Selection is done. The gods know it'll be hours before we're offered any food, and I'm starving."

"I told you to eat before we left."

"I tried," she protested with a pout, shoving him off of her. Moving him wasn't the easiest thing she'd ever done. He was a good eight inches taller than she was, and while his muscles weren't as defined as some of the other Fae, they were definitely there. "Some Legacy prick took my chocolate."

"Wait, what? When?" Dex demanded, spinning her to face him and gripping her shoulders. The sleeves of his suit jacket pulled up just enough that a Mark was visible on the inside of his right wrist. The Celeste Estate symbol declaring which estate he was raised at. It matched the one on the inside of her own wrist. Eventually two more Marks would join that one. One to declare their element and one to declare which Kingdom they were assigned to serve.

"Five minutes ago," Tessa groused. "I was out in the corridor with a piece of chocolate I snagged off a passing tray—"

"The trays of food for the *Legacy*," Dex clarified.

"Yes, those trays," she said, rolling her eyes. "Anyway, I was caught, and he took my chocolate."

"He?" His eyes widened. "Are you all right? Did he—"

"I'm fine," she said, cutting him off.

"You shouldn't have gone off without me," he said tightly.

She sighed. "I know."

There was a tense moment of silence between them before he released her shoulders. "Who's sneaking out with us? Oralia and Brecken?"

Tessa nodded, her eyes continuing to roam around the room and searching among all the gathered Fae. There were more than she had expected, and they'd all been split up as they'd been herded down the various halls to this space.

"I'm sure Brecken will convince Katya to come," Tessa said. "Lange and Corbin will obviously come too."

Dex nodded. "Assuming none of us get Selected, you mean."

Tessa tsked under her breath, continuing to scan for any of their friends. "None of us are getting Selected, Dex. The heirs picked their Sources long before tonight. The Legacy ruling families have been watching us all for years. We know the Celeste Heir is choosing Jasper, and the Falein Heir is selecting Dade—"

"And the Achaz Heir is selecting Sasha. I know what we all think we know, Tessa. It's just..." Dex sighed, raking his hand through hair as brown as his eyes. "Until it's a done deal, anything could happen. And the Arius Heir is still unaccounted for." An emotion crossed his features Tessa couldn't quite read. Unease? Frustration? She wasn't sure.

It was true. The Arius Kingdom was incredibly private, and they rarely ventured out of their borders. When they did, nothing good ever happened. The Arius Kingdom was the definition of cruel and wicked, which fit she supposed, since they were descendants of Arius, the god of death and endings. The Kingdom's ruling family embodied all of that and more with their mysterious gifts that were not well-known. Few outsiders were ever allowed into the Kingdom, and while it was known there was an heir of age there to Select a Source, he hadn't been visiting the various Fae estates the last several years to evaluate his options like the other heirs had.

Tessa reached over and grabbed Dex's hand, gently squeezing his fingers. "I know something crazy could happen, but we both know the odds are low at this point. So let's just believe that none of us will be getting Selected, and that we'll all be drinking and, more importantly, filling our stomachs within the next two hours."

Dex gave her a lop-sided grin, but it didn't meet his eyes. He reached over, tucking a curl of her honey-blonde hair behind her ear.

Tessa pushed up onto her tiptoes and pressed a soft kiss to his cheek. "We're going to be fine, Dex."

He held her gaze for another heartbeat, then pushed out a long breath. "I know, Tessie. I'm just ready for it to be over."

"I think we all are."

The Opening Selection Ceremony was just the beginning though. This was a year-long event that was just getting started. The Selection was held every five years. All the Fae who had come of age since the last Selection were brought to the Acropolis. The Fae would have their gifts awakened during the Emerging Ceremony, then they would be put through various tasks and trainings while being observed by the Kingdoms. Eventually, they would be assigned to whichever Kingdom they were to serve in. If an heir was of age to Select a Source, it was done during a Selection Year. Once the heirs all chose their Sources, there would be a brief break of a few weeks to allow the heirs and their new Sources to get acclimated. Then they would rejoin the rest of the Fae back at the Acropolis. With only six Kingdoms, that did not happen often with the extended lifespan of the Legacy. To have all six Kingdoms with heirs of Selection age at one time?

Historic night, indeed.

She finally spotted Oralia's pale blonde head of hair making her way towards them. Brecken was following close behind her, and sure enough, he had Katya in tow.

"Nervous?" Brecken taunted when they reached their side. He waggled his dark brows up and down.

Tessa rolled her eyes. "No. Like I was telling Dex, we all know how this is going to go. The heirs have had their Sources chosen for the last year, if not longer. This is all formality at this point."

Despite that knowledge, there was a general sense of unease in the grand hall. What the Legacy in the alcove had said was true. Nervous laughter rang out from around the room, and everyone was fidgety. Couples held hands a little tighter, and conversations were hushed and whispered.

They were taught that being Selected was an honor. It was ingrained in them from birth that being Selected was the greatest role in society a Fae could ever hope to achieve, and that to be the Source of a ruling Lord or Lady was as good as nobility. Only those who were already tapped to be a Source truly believed that, and Tessa was pretty sure that was out of necessity to come to terms with their fate. Once they were fully-bonded, they would believe it though. Their Masters' desires would become their desires.

The Legacy could fill their deep power wells naturally over time, but to fully refill them from a completely drained state would take weeks, if not months, to do so. They had the powers of gods in their veins after all. That took a while to recoup, and in the meantime, they'd be left vulnerable. But when they drew power from a Fae, their power wells were refilled instantly.

Which is why no other descendants of the gods were allowed a personal Source like the ruling families. It was a rite performed by a Priestess who bonded the Source and Master with four Marks that connected them as one. When all the Marks had been given, they could sense each other's presence, feel each other's emotions, and hear each other's thoughts.

Tessa hated the very idea of it. She didn't want to be in anyone's head, and she sure as shit didn't want anyone inside her head. She didn't even want to be inside her head most days.

She was excited for her gifts to emerge though. Unlike the Legacy, Fae gifts didn't emerge naturally. They had to be awakened by the Legacy, which would happen a few weeks from now for all the Fae in this room. Tessa was hoping for the fire element. But it was the rarest of the elements, and all of her aptitude tests were predicting air as the most likely element for her. Which was probably a good thing, she supposed. It had lessened her chances of being Selected. Because of its rarity, Fire Fae were coveted most among the kingdoms, especially the Achaz and Anala kingdoms.

"Poor Sasha looks terrified," Kat said quietly to Tessa, drawing her attention to the brown-haired beauty standing at the edge of the group of five Fae who had been slated to be Selected. For all intents and purposes, they were already claimed by their heirs. They knew they would soon be unwelcome by their own kind. Everyone was already treating them differently. They would soon be bonded to a Legacy, able to be found at a moment's notice, and no secrets withheld from their Masters.

Sasha was a few inches taller than Tessa, and her hair hung down her back in loose waves. She looked stunning in a gown of amethyst against her bronze skin. She was wringing her hands together and worrying her bottom lip.

"I would be too if I knew that the Achaz Heir would be Selecting me tonight," Tessa answered.

Oralia sighed. "This just needs to be over."

"I just need to eat an entire pizza. By myself," Tessa grumbled.

"I told you to eat," Dex taunted into her ear from behind her.

A grin tugged at Tessa's lips, but she didn't let it form. She took a small step back as she retorted, "And I told you I tried."

She felt Dex step into her, so close she could feel the small chuckle emanate from his chest. "Oh, Tessie," he murmured so that only she could hear. "What am I going to do with you?"

More of the Legacy were starting to arrive. They were dressed in their formal finery and gowns, just as the Fae were. Tessa watched as they interacted with one another. Family Guards, Fae chosen from their Kingdom's armies to guard the ruling families, were beginning to line the edges of the room. Some had bows and quivers full of arrows. Others had swords at their waists. The mortals of the realm had guns, but they didn't do anything against a Legacy or a Fae. Both races healed quickly, and unless those bullets were made of shirastone or nightstone—which were incredibly expensive and heavily regulated—they weren't going to do anything. Even then, they would have to hit the head or heart.

Servers were plentiful now, offering flutes of champagne to the Legacy, and Tessa pouted. Now she was hungry *and* thirsty.

"Have any of you seen Lange and Corbin?" she asked, continuing to watch the Legacy move about the room.

Brecken snorted a laugh. "I'm guessing they found a room for a quick fuck before the festivities."

"They wouldn't," Katya gasped, her amber eyes widening in shock. "Here?"

"Oh, they totally would. Those two go at it whenever they can, and they like the thrill of forbidden places," Brecken answered with a wink.

Kat's cheeks took on a slightly pink tinge at the implication of Brecken's words, and she averted her gaze from him. Brecken had had his eyes set on Kat for a few months, although Tessa didn't know why he bothered. The odds of any of them getting assigned to the same Kingdom were not great. She didn't understand why any of them formed relationships to be honest. If she got separated from her best friend, that was going to be hard enough. She couldn't imagine being separated from someone she loved so intimately.

But just as she thought that, she saw Corbin and Lange slip into the room, hand-in-hand. Corbin's shaggy brown hair was definitely disheveled, and Lange's shirt was mis-buttoned beneath his jacket and tie. The cocky grin on Lange's face said he'd definitely just gotten some.

"What's going on, guys?" Lange greeted when they reached the group.

"You tell me," Tessa replied, reaching to fix his buttons before straightening his tie. "Which room do I need to avoid the rest of the year we're here?"

Corbin and Lange exchanged mischievous grins before Corbin's hazel eyes met hers. "We'll never tell," he said with a wink.

"We're all getting drunk as soon as the Selection is done, right?" Lange asked, his sky-blue eyes wistfully following a server with yet another tray of champagne.

"Yes," Tessa agreed. "And doughnuts. The ones with chocolate on them. Not the powdered sugar ones. Then drinking."

"For the love of the gods, Tessa. You're acting like you haven't eaten in days," Dex said with an exasperated sigh.

Tessa merely shrugged, shifting from foot-to-foot. These heels were killing her feet. She was used to sneakers. And pants. Not dresses. "I'm bored. How much longer until this thing starts?"

"Sweetheart, you need to find someone to take you to a coatroom. It makes time go by so much faster," Lange taunted, and Corbin elbowed him in the ribs.

Tessa stuck her tongue out at them both. The Lords and Ladies and their heirs had to be arriving any minute, and then this thing could get going. Maybe she could sneak a glass of champagne somehow…

Her eyes fell on a couple of Legacy who were standing near the edge of the crowd. One had his back to the room, but the other seemed to be watching everyone intensely. He was slightly shorter than the one with his back turned but only by an inch, if that. He had dark brown hair that hung past his ears and piercing sapphire blue eyes that Tessa could see from across the room.

Then the other one turned to look out over the crowd, and Tessa sucked in a breath.

It was the Legacy from the corridor. The one who had cornered her in the alcove. He appeared to be watching everyone as intensely as the other male. Every once in a while, he would say something to the Legacy standing next to him, and he would be handed a folder of some sort after a moment. Where his companion got the folders from, Tessa had no idea. If they were outside the Pantheon, she was sure they'd be looking at tablets rather than paper documents. The two would look over the contents of the folder, heads close together, flipping a few pages, before the first would hand it back to the second and continue to observe the crowd. Tessa forgot about trying to steal the champagne as she studied the two Legacy, trying to figure out what they were doing.

"You're staring," Dex murmured into her ear.

"He's the one who took my chocolate from me," she answered, the Legacy again being handed a folder.

"What are you going to do, Tessie? March over there and ask for it back?" he chided.

"No," Tessa admonished. "But I can certainly fantasize about ways to hurt him for it."

"Is that all you're fantasizing over?" he teased.

"Fuck off, Dex. You know I would never fuck a Legacy. Not by choice anyway."

Before Dex could respond, a commotion at the main entrance drew everyone's attention, and a moment later, the first of the ruling families came through the door. Of course, it was the Achaz Lord, his wife on his arm and his Source a step behind him. On his other side was the Achaz Heir, Dagian Jove. He had golden blonde hair, sharp cheekbones, and golden eyes. He was in a black suit with a white shirt. A gold vest was visible beneath his black suit coat, gold thread running along the cuffs and lapels. A gold tie matched his vest. His eyes went straight to the Fae slated to be Selected, and Sasha gave him a weak smile.

As the ruling families began parading through to the front of the room, Tessa's mind and eyes began to wander. She found herself looking back to where the Legacy from the alcove had been standing before, but the two were gone. She scanned the crowd, searching and finding no sign of them.

Dex squeezed her waist where his arms were still wrapped around her. "You're fidgeting."

"Bored and hungry will do that to a person,"she muttered back. As the words left her lips, her gaze landed on the missing Legacy. They had slipped into the center of the crowd at the back of the room, almost as though they were trying to avoid being seen. The thing was, when Tessa had spotted them, she found herself looking straight into emerald green eyes. A roguish grin tilted up one side of his lips, and he nodded slightly at her.

Tessa quickly averted her eyes. She'd had a feeling he wasn't done with her. The male would likely try to seek her out at some point in the evening. Which was fine. She'd managed to avoid the untoward demands of Legacy for a few years now. Another skill she'd acquired. She would be long gone and stuffing her face with pizza by the time he was free to look for her.

As surreptitiously as she could, she glanced back at him. He and the other Legacy were bent over another folder, flipping papers and whispering back and forth. The other Legacy shook his head a few times, and the one from the alcove was pointing at various things on whatever it was they were looking at.

A resounding thud echoed throughout the room when the heavy main doors were thrown open, and a Legacy strode up the center of the room. He was tall with light-golden skin and thick black hair. He had hazel eyes, and everyone seemed to shrink back from him. A woman of exquisite beauty was on his arm, dressed in a black gown that dipped low in the front. Her dark red hair was piled in curls on her head, and ruby drops hung from her ears and around her throat. Behind the male, a Fae followed, her eyes cast down at the floor and her hands clasped in front of her.

The Lord of the Arius Kingdom— Valter St. Orcas.

Then Tessa's legs nearly gave out and an audible gasp passed her lips when the Legacy from the alcove peeled away from the other, finishing knotting a black tie at his throat. He slid his arms into the sleeves of a suit jacket that was as immaculate as the rest of his clothing, buttoning it as he fell into step beside the Arius Lord.

But that couldn't be. That wasn't possible.

Because if he was walking next to the Arius Lord and Lady...

Emerald eyes cut to her, and the corner of his lips ticked up in a cunning smile.

He was the Arius Heir here to claim a Source.

# A Note from the Author

I don't even know how to start this note this time. I am sitting here, staring at my computer screen with tears in my eyes. This moment is so incredibly bittersweet. I wrote a whole dang series! But saying goodbye to some of these characters is so dang hard.

There characters are my babies. We've been through so much together. They came into my life when I was drowning. In a way, they pulled me from the river. We've fought and cried and fought some more, and I know that sounds strange, but these characters… Sometimes they were just so dang loud with their need to be heard.

THANK YOU for loving on me and these characters so dang hard. My greatest hope is that you know the stars are always worth fighting for. That when you're drowning, it's okay to let someone pull you from the river. That you remember what it's like to be lost in the dark and give grace to someone who hasn't found the stars yet. That you remember while the dark can be haunting, it can also be beautiful if you know where to look.

While this part of Scarlett's story may be over, we are far from done, my friends! There are so many exciting things to come. First and foremost, a new series is coming this summer! *Rain of Shadows and Endings* is book one in The Legacy Series. While it takes place in another world, remember that I write in one universe so there is always a possibility you'll see a familiar face…

There is also a prequel series planned for Cethin, Kailia, and Razik! We'll learn more about them and what the heck was going on in Avonleya during the *Darkness* books. There may also be some novellas and other fun surprises in the works.

In addition, there are four other series on my marker board just waiting to be told. Like I said, we are just getting started.

I'll see you in Devram—

*XO- Melissa*

## ONE MORE THING

Your reviews on Amazon and Goodreads help other reader determine if a book is one they'd enjoy. I'd be forever grateful if you could go over to one (or both!) of them and leave a short review of *Lady of Starfire* to help Scarlett's story reach others who might love it. Word of mouth is an author's best friend and much appreciated. Shouts from rooftops are great, too.

My social links are below, but I'd also like to extend a special invitation to you to join my reader group on Facebook at Melissa's Dragon Cave. I drop teasers as I'm writing new books, share about my writing process, my life, and love interacting with all of you. I'd love it if you joined us.

To stay up-to-date on release dates, new series, and more, be sure and sign up for the newsletter, too!

## WHERE TO FIND ME!

- Website: www.melissakroehrich.com
- Signed Books & Merch: www.mkrtreasureshop.com
- Instagram: @melissa_k_roehrich
- TikTok: @authormelissakroehrich
- Facebook Page: Melissa K. Roehrich
- Facebook Reader Group: Melissa's Dragon Cave
- Pinterest: @melissa_k_roehrich

# ACKNOWLEDGMENTS

I would be remiss not to start this off with thanking you, the reader. Without you taking a chance on a new indie author when you picked up *Lady of Darkness*, this series would not be what it is today. On the hard days, you guys were there cheering me on. On the good days, you were there begging for more. You love these characters as much as I do, and you made the writing process so dang fun. Thank you for having fun with me in the Dragon Cave. Thank you for making the Monthly Wishlist Book Gifting so successful. Thank you for sharing the love of Scarlett and crew. Thank you for taking the time to send me messages of encouragement and what the books mean to you. Those things mean more than you can possibly know.

My Book Slut Besties… Once again, what is there to say? How did we get here? We made it through an entire fucking series! Thank you for being there through it all— the anxiety, the celebrating, the imposter syndrome, the tears of defeat, and the tears of happiness. I am humbled and honored to call you dear friends. Don't ever speak of leaving me. It's not an option. You're stuck with me forever and ever.

To my editing team: Megan Visger, Ashley Nolan, and Diane Dyk, thank you for making this book better. Thank you for putting up with my high functioning anxiety and my penchant for pushing deadlines. I appreciate you beyond words.

To my ARC/Street Team, you guys are simply amazing. Thank you for cheering me on, for shouting from the rooftops, and for loving on these books so dang hard.

To my boys— Thank you for understanding when mom needed to write and edit. Thank you for your patience when I needed to be in front of a computer screen extra hours. I hope you see that dreams take work, and no one will work harder for your dreams than you.

To my husband— I still choose you. Every damn day. All the way through the darkness.